My Journey to Lewaro

Paperback: ISBN 978-1-737-4087-0-3
Ebook: ISBN 978-1-7374087-1-0
Library of Congress Control Number: 2023904819

Printed by in the USA.

LEWARO ROAD

Adapted from the screenplay Journey to Lewaro

(later retitled)

White Shadows, Black Dreams

JUSTIN SWINGLE

Lost Beginnings

1

THE BURNEY PLANTATION was the entire world for me. I was born at Grandview two years after the Civil War, that bloody struggle the white folks blamed us for, and after which they sent us packing to nowhere.

As a child I was convinced the moon rolled over the big house cooling it on hot summer nights. I'd been told by the old 'croppers that the nightglow reflected off the big house was to keep out the heat and the field dust the 'croppers stirred. White folks readily assured us that this was the natural order. The Lord meant for the fields to hold the burning sun by day 'cause that's where the coloreds lovingly toiled alongside the farm animals. If that sun wasn't up there ready to blind, they reminded us, a colored might lift her eyes from the rows of cotton and get to wondering what could be out there that might replace the drudgery? I yet wander back to my lost beginnings looking for answers, even if the questions are yet tangled.

My folks' place was on the swampy side of the Burney plantation close to the river. We all knew the shadows down there were inhabited by the tortured souls of those who came before; their spirits never stopped wandering our memories. Were they yet searching for that part of their soul that had been wrenched? Well, the Burney place might have been a stone's throw out of Delta across the river from Vicksburg, yet it remained deeper in the heart of the South than you can imagine. So, early on I sent my imaginings to that beyond, even if I didn't know where that place was.

My daddy was born to Grandview, and never left till death provided an escort. He was still young and yet old when the day came when he could not rise from his stone sleep. Owen was tall and soft-spoken. He never got worked up 'cept maybe when Minerva was. Oddly, Daddy getting worked up is what seemed to soothe Momma. He could pull her back into his warmth just by turning down the corners of his mouth. It was a signal that he'd had enough of her fussing over things—things that she could never have fixed anyway. Caressed by his gentle words she'd finally let loose of the moment that had tormented her. It was the only serenity that Momma ever knew, the surrender to his powerful arms.

My daddy and Samuel, Ella's cousin, went fishing most Sundays and sometimes late summer nights. Alex trailed along when he was old enough. I remember once asking Brother if they talked to the fish down there. He claimed they only talked about not talking to me. Like my daddy, Brother didn't say much. Still, he heard every word I uttered. At times it seemed that he could even hear between my very thoughts. I remember Alex saying Daddy and Samuel talked about having an acre of their own one day, when the credits owed Burney were paid off. But, Lord, that date would never be found on no calendar printed in the South. It was only a borrowed dream. Still, I learned early that borrowed dreams get us to the next day.

Momma was a tiny woman. Granny said Minerva was the runt of her kids and that's what made her tough as pig's hide. Guess you got to be to hold your place at the table when you're barely five feet tall and got three brothers a foot taller. What food there was went to those who reached the quickest. Ain't that life anyway? Momma learned early to grab what she had to. Well, some claimed Minerva was known to keep a pinch of nightshade hidden back somewhere. Nightshade, the poison of the South, made some white folks jittery just at the thought. One that surely seeped through their nightmares. Yes, Momma could sure give folks the eye. She'd look at me, my brother Alex, or even Owen, and you knew real quick what was what. To stay clear of Minerva's temper you'd quickly take the path she meant for you. But it wasn't just my family. Nobody seemed to mess with Minerva, a person so small she could be put down with one blow, yet folks knew she was tough enough to somehow, someway strike back. Didn't ol' Isaac go running off mad to escape her? One day I'll tell you about that.

Up in the big house where my friend Jackson Burney lived and Ella, his nanny, worked and slept, it was always cool, wasn't it? Through Ella's eyes I could see through the vistas of her fantasies of life up there. She once told me that in the big house there was the purest of white clouds that drifted through a hundred rooms to cleanse them of the powdery field dust that sifted through our lives and seemed to settle at the bottom of our dry throats come sundown.

"Just like them snow-white clouds," Ella told me, "they comes with the summer rains and fills up the rooms in the big house and float gardenia petals all the way up them stairs to Miss Burney's bathin' tub like she tol' 'em to."

Ella's explanations came like the whispered hush of some sacred truth nobody ever understood. Or maybe it was the kind of untruth that bound our lives to the plantation class.

"You carry water up for Miss Burney's bath?" I asked.

"No, chil'e. This is the way it is; sweet summer rain pours into her bathing tub bigger than a pond. Comes straight from heaven through a secret window ain't no colored can see through. Then it lifts all them white petals till they near float over the top of her tub. But they never do, 'cause they ain't 'pose' to."

Ella knew that nothing happened at Grandview unless Melinda Burney decreed it was to be.

"I bring 'er white linen towels beaten soft as silk. That I do."

I believed everything Ella told me. Wasn't it a version of the truth, that Melinda Burney's world was a whole lot closer to heaven than to mine?

"Don't the rains down at the shacks come from the same clouds?" I wondered out loud.

Our conversation quickly drifted to another place just out of reach, one where silky clouds could never cleanse away the unpleasantness.

Most mornings Jackson's daddy sat out on his white veranda looking at his paper like there was nothing else to do. I was sure that man never truly saw us—he sure never looked us in the eyes. It seemed he only spoke to coloreds out of the sides of his mouth, us trailing a respectful distance behind. I was so scared of Master Burney, him with those pale blue eyes. I thought with them eyes he couldn't see us. Yet my friend Jackson could sure see me. He was my age. He had brown eyes. Maybe the color of coffee with cream. How many times did I look up at the big house and see Jackson climbing under the table and through his daddy's legs while Ella stood silently behind Burney fanning him with a turkey feather fan? Why'd she do that? Wasn't it already cool up there? I figured it had to be one of those things poor colored women did—fanned white folk that were so cool they looked to be drenched in whiteness. Up there was a world where warm white suds laundered the white linen shirts Master Burney favored and where he sat on that white veranda, ten times the size of my shack, waiting for a breakfast table to be set with glistening white china. You know that table was drenched in so much white linen it pooled at the bottom of the table legs. And up there close and yet so far from me was my friend, a white child with white hair playing in all that fragrant white gardenia scented coolness. From the shadows under the magnolias where I'd watch, I could see him, even if his white world chose not to see me. So, I figured that meant they couldn't see me inhaling the fragrance of their big gardenias. How I twisted my thoughts wondering how I might smell even more. Those softly scented blooms were bigger than my hand and grew in well-tended pots on that veranda. White flowers cut daily to float aimlessly in a crystal bowl as clear as tears, so much like their lives at Grandview had floated from day to day for a hundred years. Why? Why did I wonder if Jackson could smell them gardenias? He never acted like he could smell nothing. But what was there to smell in his world other than fragrant flowers? I never stopped asking myself why my world was so close to his yet still so far? Such thoughts have a hold on me and still tug me back to my beginnings.

But, Lord, the heat of them fields; didn't it feel white hot on our backs? Was out in that dry dirt our Promised Land? There the heat was sure guaranteed us, and the white folks promised it would never run out, even as everything else did by the end of the month. Even when the salt of my brows burned into my eyes, the old folks whispered their own sacred truths, which vowed we should never stop thanking the white folks that the burn in our sweat-filled eyes was different from the rock salt that burned in the wounds of those who'd prayed as the lash crossed over their backs. Well, maybe they were only recalling the voices of those who haunted the shacks begging for answers that would never come—like why were they denied a dream, that sweet smell of freedom, a taste of dignity? I guess it's all in the figures. Ain't it always?

After breakfast, Master Robert Burney never seemed to do much more than look at his horse as Isaac brushed it, while Miss Burney stood on her veranda like a porcelain doll wrapped in fragility. Melinda was that certain kind of plantation woman that evolves from the deepest secrets of the South. Her up there cooing at him as she tossed her fine honey-colored hair back, waiting for Ella to fetch the brushes to arrange her hair high to reveal her long neck. I heard Ella tell Momma that Miss Burney's gaze at her husband suggested she was truly longing for him to stop riding his horse and come ride her. It would be many years before I could read a woman's broken but carefully punctuated sighs to understand such things. But no matter how sugary Melinda's voice was standing in the shade of her veranda, she never seemed to capture the master's absolute attention. No, word down at the shacks was that Burney took to a different kind of fragility. Whereas Miss Burney could always deny the master what she teased with a toss of her hair, some of us could not, and had to surrender what he lusted after. You see, the kind of fragility he took to was pounding his dirty deeds from behind. Like I told you, he never looked us in the eyes.

One summer night, peering through the bottom of a glass of bourbon he was tipping, Burney swallowed an eyeful of my older sister Louvenia. She'd blossomed that spring, along with the peach trees on Orchard Hill. Lord, didn't we pay a high price to the same people who banked that our lives had no value? Seems that Miss Burney saw the twinkle in Burney's eye and told ol' Isaac to send that girl-child packing. It was all done quietly. Louvenia was sent off with nothing but her lost innocence to inoculate her for a life off the plantation she was born to. Like a stray dog, Isaac prodded Sister with a stick all the way down the oak-lined drive that led away from Grandview. She never saw Owen and Minerva again. Them acts tend to shadow you like the nigger dogs. Yes, they slip up on you to nip at your heart, gnaw at your hopes and tear at your soul a bit more.

We were all driven by the lash of his tongue to hate Isaac, a mean ol' man. Seemed like Burney's overseer always knew what Jackson was up to; it was his job to watch over this plantation prince. But then he knew what we were all up to because he had eyes all 'round his head. The white folks told us so, and snickered at our bowed faces when they did. Once I tried to look up under the back of his greasy ol' hat, but couldn't see no eyes up there. Nonetheless, I knew they were there. Down at the river's edge, ol' Clara preached that the devil's got eyes back 'a his head to see if Jesus is coming at him with a stick. We all waited for the Lord to beat the hell out of Isaac. Then Momma did it for Him.

Jackson didn't seem to care 'bout no eyes anywhere on Isaac's head. No, he didn't. He'd walk past that man paying him no mind, 'cause he was walking proud with a special task Ella had given him of toting down to my folks a tin of meat renderings she'd spirited out of her kitchen. Guess that freed him of her apron strings long enough to find some mischief. Like me, Jackson was only five or six, but unlike me he'd learned early that his world didn't require that he address servants in passing or explain his actions to nobody. Ol' Isaac was powerless against this white child, 'cause if he messed with Jackson, his daddy would put an end to Isaac being overseer. Had to be that way to prepare Jackson for the day he would be master of Grandview. He had to grow up knowing he answered to nobody. Those were the rules, and nobody dared to say otherwise. Well, I guess Jackson knew it from the beginning.

"Young Master Jackson, where you goin' with them burlap bags?" Isaac inquired in a tone of silky politeness that never tidied up his words to us.

"I takin' a walk, don't it look like? And it ain't none of your business, huh?"

"Why, no, but maybe yer daddy, he be wondering whereabouts you're headed, 'cause he tol' me to keep an eye on you. You know yer momma don't want you down with them dirty niggers! Heard her say so. Yes, Sir, I sure did."

Jackson looked him in the eyes, the front ones. It was surely a moment that gave Burney's overseer heartburn. "I reckon my daddy's wondering why his horsey didn't get brushed this mornin' like he tol' ya."

Isaac knew when Jackson was mimicking his daddy. He got a daily dose, and by his expression it was mighty bitter to swallow.

"Now, Jackson, you saw me down there brushing yer daddy's horses, 'cause you was talkin' real nice then."

"Maybe I did, but now I forget."

Jackson had one hand on his hip like Ella did when she was about to smack him for sassing.

"I'm tellin' my daddy you been talkin' strange like you been at the bottle again. That's gonna get my momma to work up a cry when she hears what I gots to say. You know what happens when Momma sets herself to bawlin' on things she don't want 'a hear 'bout. Daddy's sure gonna come after somebody!"

"Now, Master Jackson, you'd be lying then. You'll go to hell for it!"

"My daddy ain't gonna like you tellin' me to go to hell."

Jackson was disinclined to further discourse and walked off. He'd communicated his position often enough for Isaac to know when to capitulate and step aside. Ella also knew 'bout Isaac, 'cause if she'd done the pilfering from the kitchen, Isaac would'a ripped her back open. He must not have thought thrashing a woman would send him any deeper into the hell he was destined for. Jackson and Ella understood that unique place they held in those tangled shadows of the big house, shadows that sometimes drifted all the way to the shacks. Each, in their own way, made that knowledge work for them. Seemed at times they had ol' Isaac dancing to their convoluted tunes, as though he was being chased by wasps. Yes, they had their ways of dealing with his daddy's overseer, Jackson and his Ella. These two were united in their need for each other. It was a love that seared through those white shadows, sparked off his folks' Southern sensibilities, and left them all singed up at the big house.

JACKSON'S GRANDVIEW

2

WHEN I WAS five or six, I'd wander from the fields up to the big house—that place where no coloreds but the house servants ever ventured. I'd go to meet my friend, and in so doing stepped over an invisible barrier that the rest of them always seemed to see.

Jackson and I loved playing in the dirt in Miss Burney's garden. Dirt is where I lived anyway, but Jackson wallowed in it, maybe 'cause Melinda hated it so—him getting soiled and all. Jackson defied authority as a ritual. I was in awe of that defiance, knowing that at the bottom of the path where I lived nobody ever heard of authority being defied without a lash or lynching rope as witness. Jackson would break Southern rules, get dirty, get nigger dirty simply to defy the order he lived in. White princes break rules and live to tell. Colored kids learn early that a backhand could be settled on us without any justification. There were no such consequences for Jackson. Playing with me near the veranda, he'd cover himself in dirt and then crawl up on his daddy's lap, covering him with the fresh chicken manure that Isaac had spread over Miss Burney's rose garden that morning. Burney would holler for Ella to come take care of the problem. He never yelled at Jackson; he was never the problem—Ella's inattention was.

Jackson always got what he wanted or needed, because Ella was there to see to it. Yes, it was Ella who hauled Jackson in, stripped him of his soiled clothes and bathed him in the warm white suds and then wrapped him in white linen towels as she hugged him. Yes, hugged, 'cause Ella was the only one up there who really loved that child. He survived on that love, because for the Burneys, Jackson was only the heir. They didn't love each other; how could they love their child? But there are reasons for all things. I'm gonna tell you 'bout that one day.

Jackson and I started playing together nearly every day till I was sentenced to the cotton fields. Jackson also had tasks to perform. He was being groomed to be a Southern prince, for the day he'd be joining the others who reigned over plantation society in those postbellum river parishes. Most days, he had riding lessons. As a child, I always thought it was strange how white folk thought of riding horses as fun, and even dressed up for it. We knew it only as work. We never got dressed up to ride horses or mules—what would we get dressed up in? As I recall, it seemed like Melinda Burney always made Ella dress Jackson like a toy doll. When he wasn't riding, he'd come out in his white short pants and shirt and sit in the dirt to line up his toys, waiting for me to join him.

"Your daddy don't mind me playin' up here?" I asked, knowing that Master Burney couldn't really see me, but knew his ma sure could.

"My daddy's out ridin' his horses. Ella never tells."

"What 'bout mean ol' Isaac?"

"He's out huntin' nigger problems."

"What's a nigger problem?" I asked.

"Don't know, do I? Guess Isaac don't know, too, 'cause my daddy keeps tellin' 'im the same ol' thing. I heard 'im!" Jackson jumped up and put his hands on his waist, mimicking his daddy. "'Isaac! Get on up to the orchard and take care of that nigger problem!' Guess Isaac just don't never mind what my daddy tell 'im, do he? 'Cause my daddy's gotta keep telling 'im like he do my momma all the time."

Even as a child I had to stop in my tracks to sort what came out of of white folks' mouths. "Your momma's a nigger problem?"

"I guess, 'cause my daddy keeps sayin'." Hands akimbo, Jackson re-assumed his daddy's posture. "'Melinda, don't be comin' back from

Vicksburg with no more new dresses! Hear?' I know ol' Isaac hears my daddy, but my momma, she don't hear nothin' she don't aim to! That's what my daddy says. Then my momma says right back ain't nobody in Delta cares what my daddy say 'bout nothin'."

"She brings back lots of dresses? New dresses?" I asked, utterly perplexed.

Sometimes I'd go off wondering about our talks for the longest time. Like, where do dresses come from? What's out there beyond those fields that pretty dresses are waiting? Like all kids from the shacks, mine came from flour sackcloth sewn together by ol' Clara when Momma was in the fields.

"Nobody hear your daddy, even when he's callin' you?"

"Nope, and I don't hear Ella when I don't want to, do I?" he said with a mischievous grin. "But I can sure make Momma hear me good when I aim to, huh? Don't I? I put mud on my shoes and go walking on her fancy ol' rug ain't nobody 'pose' to look at."

"Don't Ella hear your daddy?" I wondered.

"Guess she hear ever'thing, even when she don't, and do what he tell 'er even when she say she ain't gonna."

Jackson continued: "When Momma gets home from Vicksburg, she kisses my daddy's face all over, then he don't see all them dresses up in the attic. But I do, and I don't believe a word Momma says 'bout no damned ghost gonna get me if I get into things up there." Jackson's voice dropped to a conspiratorial whisper. "I told my daddy my horse stunk like Isaac. Now Isaac gots to give my horsey a bath 'fore I go riding, don't he? You know what?" Jackson whispered in my ear. "Once my daddy—he kissed his horse! I seen 'im, too!"

We fell over laughing.

"I ain't never gonna let my daddy kiss me! Are you?"

Again, I had no answer. Back then, I didn't worry 'bout Master Burney wanting to kiss me, 'cause I was sure his pale eyes kept him from seeing me. But Lordy, Melinda Burney sure could! Later that morning she ventured out onto the veranda where her breakfast waited. She'd just bathed, and Ella went to weaving freshly cut jasmine through her mistress's golden hair. Miss Burney suddenly got an eyeful of her boy all covered in chicken shit. Seeing us playing together put her in an awful state. Numb with fear, I wondered if I ought to run and hide in the fields. Could she reach that far? Nobody ever seen her past the veranda 'cept in her rose garden.

Jackson, his white shorts covered in chicken shit, never looked up when his ma stormed off the veranda like she was gonna wring his neck. But then the words she hurled were really meant for me. She aimed herself at me like a tornado and stomped down them steps as hard as her delicate feet were able, only to freeze when she realized she'd soiled her shoes in all that chicken shit we'd scooped up. She looked at me as if I was filthier than her slippers, and stomped over to Jackson. He didn't seem to care 'bout Miss Burney's fit coming on. Still, I knew the way that woman was hissing that she was gonna backhand me for being in her garden with her child. Nobody had to tell me what was in her head. Coloreds cultivate a keen intuition on these matters.

"What are you doin', Jackson Burney, playin' down with that nigger girl?"

Jackson was squatting close to the nest ignoring her such as he always did. But then wasn't it quite apparent he was laying an egg? Jackson was quick to change tack when he was in trouble.

"Momma! Why you got flowers growin' out 'a your head like that?"

A wiry sprig of jasmine had loosened and bounced about her neck gone red from rage.

"You know very well Ella arranges these flowers for your daddy."

"Chicken shit is what makes roses grow, don't it? We want flowers growin' out 'a our heads, too, don't we Sarah?"

"What? Why you little… You're in big trouble now, mister!" she hollered unconvincingly.

Miss Burney yelled for Ella like the bed bugs was eating her alive and clutched her long skirt up off the soil. "Ella! Get down here!"

Jackson paid her no mind. As he squatted there waiting for the egg to drop, he took a handful of chicken shit and dumped it on his momma's white kidskin shoes. Then he went to grunting like we'd heard ol' Isaac do in the outhouse behind his shack. I ain't never heard no hen grunt when she was laying. Well, I wasn't gonna stand and run, not within smacking distance of that woman. Thought to hug the ground till the storm passed. But Lord he wasn't finished!

"Daddy say there's a nigger problem, Momma. Them niggers gots too many new dresses, and they's gone to hiding 'em in the attic so Daddy can't get into 'em. Bet he's gonna get ol' Isaac to go up there and clean up that mess, ain't he Momma?"

I never looked up at that woman so she couldn't see me. But then out 'a one half-closed eye I squinted a tiny peek. Miss Burney's face, that never been in the sun, had turned scarlet. It left me wondering if white folks catch on fire when they get worked up real bad.

"That's what I said, Jackson! You're down here all filthy from playing with one of our niggers again!"

Jackson put his dirty hands on his waist and, mimicking his momma's spun-sugar voice, echoed her. "Ain't it what I been sayin' first, Momma! Don't you ever listen none?"

"Well, actin' like that aren't you your daddy's little Burney through and through? Yes, you are!" She looked towards the veranda doors for Ella to finally appear. "Ella, if I call you one more time!" she squealed like a tethered piglet.

About then Jackson dumped his whole pail of fresh chicken shit on Miss Burney's shoes and then did one better by polishing them with it. I just hoped when the blood squirted out of her eyes it wouldn't get on me none, 'cause I could hear Ella's feet come thumping down the stairs of the mansion as ol' Isaac, hearing Miss Burney's commotion, came running from the orchard to protect the mistress with his pruning shears. But done no good. She already gots her shoes ruined, and her child was down in the rose garden making chicken-shit nests, playing with somebody not even 'pose' to be past the lawn of the big house, let alone in the mistress's presence. Ella was in trouble! The only thing left for Miss Burney to do was to kick the loose chicken shit off her shoes and onto me, where I 'magine she intended.

"Jackson Burney! You awful little monster!" Melinda squealed in defeat.

"Now you're a big nigger Momma!" he let out.

Oh, Lord, what could come out 'a that child's mouth? Guess Miss Burney got him thinking having dirty clothes was near to being a 'cropper. She gave one nasty look at Ella who stood moping her brow with her dish rag and stormed back into her white palace where things would always stand down to her temper. And Isaac, he could only stand there sweating fear till the ground at his feet stank.

"Isaac! After you scrub up my horsey, you best get Momma up on 'im and scrub 'er down, too. 'Cause she smells like chicken shit, don't she?"

Yes, the prince had directed Burney's speechless overseer to bathe his ma. But Jackson didn't scare Ella none. She slapped her hands together, signaling Jackson was getting smacked the same, and swept him up, swatting his hinny good as she did. Jackson wailed like bloody murder had caught up with him, but it was just an act, 'cause he turned and grinned as he was being hauled in, leaving Issac there mopping his brow in relief. That man was so relieved, he didn't scat me out of the garden, and wandered back to his pruning mopping his brow. Jackson's diversionary tantrums had again saved me from a slap.

I sat there shivering, praying that Jackson wouldn't be lynched come nightfall when nobody was looking. See, back then I thought people got in trouble for being bad. Didn't know people were lynched just for being colored. Of course, Jackson wasn't lynched. Pretty much everyone wanted to buy peace with this six year old who so easily defied the rules we all lived under. Didn't mean he wasn't severely disciplined, though. According to Ella, Jackson was put in a shiny white tub filled with white suds, a supreme torture for him, then shuffled off to spend the evening in bed. There he'd secretly work on teaching Ella the alphabet, them both eating the hard candy Jackson had stolen from the big jar on his daddy's desk. It was the form of punishment they both loved to inflict on each other.

Once again I'd learned that there are different kinds of justice in this life and different ways to get some for yourself. I would carry these lessons and memories of my friend with me forever.

STONE SLEEP

3

THE MOONLIGHT THAT cooled the big house on those summer nights seemed to cool nothing down at the shacks. Still, enough found its way through our only window to lighten the deep shadows on my folks' weary faces. Through the dim light I saw that anguished look, the look of their tortured sleep—the sleep the utterly exhausted are driven to. Never serene faces lost in slumber; just hard like stone. No, sleep was never a release from our reality, 'cause even in slumber the white shadows throbbed at our bodies always for more. Then, seemingly moments later, the sun seeped through the cracks in the boards that made up the door to our place, a shack not fit for chickens. Strange how white folks claimed we were luckier than the chickens. Maybe because we had a fireplace, but come winter there'd be little wood for a morning fire, and surely never enough to warm away our stone sleep.

Every morning I woke to the smell of cow manure that filtered in— fresh steaming manure deposited by the ol' cow that tended to wander up through the shacks come dawn. Yes, the door was shut, but never locked. We were denied locks because the shack didn't belong to us, even though we'd paid for it many generations over. Nothing at Grandview belonged to us but the misery. We could have our fill of that, and always come by more if it ran out. But, Lord, it never did.

Our days started in deep darkness when Daddy got to smelling that cow too. If he didn't, he'd soon feel Momma's elbow.

"Get up, Owen. Alex, mornin' time."

Daddy struggled to get his breeches on; his boot somehow got on first in the darkness his eyes had first opened to. Or did that really happen in the sheer fatigue that devoured him that night and he never got them off? How many times did my folks collapse from exhaustion only to fall asleep half-dressed? Folks learned young that sharecropping meant one thing: after sharing with the plantation class, there'd be little left for us. Not even the rest we'd earned from our labors.

Alex slept near the fireplace on planks elevated by wood crates. Seemed like Brother had a hard time believing it was truly morning. It was it too easy for his body to deny the truth. Time fits differently after wearing it on your back thirteen hours in the sweltering heat of them cotton fields, where the white shadows stalked everyone but shade was nowhere to be found. Hard-worked muscles beg for more rest even if none is gonna come your way. It was easy for Brother's young body to deceive him. Still, he'd try to swindle a few more moments of slumber out of the waking hour. Was it restitution to make up for the abuse the fields had imposed the day before? Maybe just enough that his wronged body wouldn't ache so when the fields laid another day's labor on his tortured young back. The pains slashed through our calendars that nobody was ever gonna see, and then our days were no more than watching ourselves grow old before your time. Who asks a mule if they've worked too hard that day? Need more rest mule? Never would we hear that tendered. No, not ever. Folks had to somehow survive the day if only to see another. Got to be easier by keeping our thoughts contained and never letting them venture beyond the fields transported by those dreams of a better life. But was there really a place where rest was granted as easily as the Lord's absolution? The dreamless realities we lived under were ever constant. The tale we kept telling ourselves was that if we could only see our way to a far-off place, maybe to that Promised Land, things were gonna be better. That's what Momma always prayed: "Lord, deliver us from 'em!" This daughter of slaves discovered mighty young that the dreams of 'croppers are like rotting meat. They only turn blacker as the days passed us by, taking our hopes along with the yesterdays. Our lives in their white shadows smelled no better.

Momma's first words in the morning seemed to push out like she'd slept with a throat filled of cotton fiber. "Owen, get me my apron, I tell you…"

Had she really said that, or were the words leftover from some past morning? For the chronically weary, mornings can easily blur into all the days before. You see, we all knew that ol' Isaac would soon be coming to drive the 'croppers to the fields. To this day I still hear that snarling nigger dog screeching.

"Up, up, you damned worthless…. Anyone not ready for workin' loses a month's food credit!" His garbled words spewed as easily from his half-drunken mouth as whiskey poured down a throat.

Daddy might be hopping 'round the shack when Isaac was coming, his boots still not cooperating enough to let him pull his pants up over them while he struggled to reach the window and untie the apron that made as a curtain—the apron that would serve as my daylong companion. Momma would tie one of them apron strings to my wrist and the other to the bedstead, all the while reciting Bible verses in the dialect of the half-asleep.

"The Lord is my Shepherd, I shall not want…"

If Jesus was listening could He hear our supplications through my wailing?

Alex pulled a dried apple out of the old burlap bag that kept off fruit flies and handed it to me—well, at least dropped it into my lap, him not having time to wait for me to clutch it. No, ol' Isaac would soon be there pounding on the boards of our cracked door just as he pounded on our splintered lives. What good were my sobs of terror? I was a colored baby, a nobody more troublesome than the farm animals, according to ol' Isaac's scriptures. While Momma's verses promised that the nobodies were somehow gonna be the somebodies in the Lord's Orchard if only we could cross over to where His bounty waited. But it always seemed to be Isaac's verses that ruled our days and then laid siege to those nights of stone sleep. One of Isaac's gospels was that 'croppers worked better in the fields with no kids to fret over, as young'ens couldn't be sold for profit ever since that Lincoln made a mess of things. You see, the time wasted on babies came right out of labor that could be better spent tending Burney's interests. No, that wouldn't do. If you wanted to get in good with the overseer to get a bit more credit to stave off starvation in a bad year, you'd do best to abandon your baby girl late one night along the river's edge so nature would take its course and sweep her under the muddy currents. It was a horror forced on many up and down that river. Let me tell you sometime 'bout the momma who carried her baby down to river's edge, thinking she could keep the rest of her chil'ren if she'd only surrendered that child, and then returned the next morning to weep but found her baby still there smiling. The currents of life can quickly change. Do you look into your child's eyes for another tearful farewell and then walk off again? Never underestimate the power of hunger when it's beating on your kids' bellies as they sit looking into an empty bowl.

As a baby, I spent the day alone in the shack tied to a bedpost. You ask if it was bad for me. Well, maybe 'croppers' kids don't feel time pass in the stale silence of our shacks. Still, you know it was bad for my folks. Like most 'croppers whose kids were born in this new kind of slavery, they knew they could return at night and find their child tied to the bedstead all but dead. Wading through the cotton all day wondering on what you might find back at your shack could bring you to your knees faster than the heat and humidity of them fields. As a 'cropper you prayed hard that this wouldn't be the day your rickety door came open and a pack of those feral dogs living at the edge of the shacks wandered in for a kill. You knew ol' Isaac's drift when he heard your squalling kid and reminded you which path led to the river. Didn't we all know Isaac fed them dogs to keep them around and drive his point harder? The nigger dog that fed the dogs was that man.

Momma's dark skin was still so very hot when she returned late with Daddy, him nearly holding up Alex by then. Her mahogany face had turned red-brown like only a day of Southern sun, dirt, sweat and hunger can render. The first thing she did was free me from the apron and hold me with tears streaming down the channels of her dusty face. We'd survived another day. But could we survive the night? Some nights were longer than others. Longer than most babies' lives. How many times did Momma return sick and puke all evening while Daddy held her head? He'd fix his arm 'round her stomach so's it wouldn't come out when she retched out the heat of the day that had thickened in her gut.

"Is Momma gonna die?"

"Alex, go fetch some water," he mumbled in reply.

Owen shook his head as he glanced about. His own exhaustion had pounded on his back and numbed his words into blurs that still remain crystal clear in the tissues of my memories.

"Momma sick?" I asked.

Motionless, she sat there as though she was waiting for something to come up. But what do you puke when you don't got nothing in your belly but dust?

Owen would ease her from the basin, where he'd tried to clean her up, and over to the bed. There she sprawled motionless and stared at the timbers above. What was she looking for? Blinking the dust away, yet still seeing nothing. Didn't she see me then? Can't she hear me crying for her? I can't count the tears because they're still rolling down my cheeks. We learned young that even our loudest cries only crash into the silence of our exhaustion.

"Ain't no cryin' gonna help yer ma, Sarah, so stop fussin'." Daddy's voice was quiet-like. "Go help your brother fetch water from the well. Go on now."

I still see him going about, picking up this or that only to set it aside with the other hand, all the while looking strangely lost in our one-room shack.

I followed Alex, wondering if white folks in the cool white world throw up when they're exhausted. Maybe they never get that way. Is that 'cause they got us? So they don't have to throw up when the heat and dust is thick in their gut? But who'd ever seen white folks out there in the fields? I never understood why misery was such a part of our lives.

Lord, didn't that misery shadow Owen's life to the bitter end? And yet never once was he so miserable that he seemed to smell the puke as he held Momma's heaving head. No, he couldn't, because she was his wife and the mother of his children.

But I still do.

⚬

Isaac's shack was at the bottom of Orchard Hill, which he was entrusted to keep us away from when the peaches were ripe or he'd soon find himself walking backwards down the road that lead to nowhere. Ella told Momma that Burney told Isaac to tear down the hog's house and build a new one for them fine hogs he'd just brought in, and then said for Isaac to take the scraps from the old one and build himself a shack. The message was clear enough: Isaac was no account to Burney and could be replaced as easy as building a hog pen. Well, Isaac's place was nothing but a pile of splintered wood, but it had a tin roof that probably didn't leak much unless it rained. Folks at the shacks said under that tin was where ol' Isaac hid from his nightmares. Momma was sure he was the first born of Satan himself. Said she knew 'cause he smelled like he had to be. I knew how bad ol' Isaac smelled and that made me think twice about taking any path that might lead me to hell.

You see, Isaac had the same pale blue eyes as Burney, and that silvery hair that made him metallic looking. Metallic, like that broken mirror that ol' Clara found tossed away with the scraps of the big house. Clara told us that the devil must 'a lost that very mirror and he'd steal your soul away if you looked at yourself in it and then flipped it upside down. There you'd see Satan grinning back. "Devil gots your soul for sure," she claimed. Isaac walked hunched under the weight of the hatred that fueled him. He walked stooped like he was hauling the devil himself on his back. Momma got me to think that all blue-eyed folks were the progeny of some devil. She didn't know any better. I still believed it till years later when Sally, with her kind blue eyes, saved me from more than a few devils and many a hell not printed on any map.

Sometimes I heard Momma shake Daddy Owen awake in the

middle of the night if she thought she'd heard ol' Isaac on the prowl between the shacks. Was he on the run from the demons that chased him? For that ol' man it all got lost somewhere between those bottles stacked behind his shack. So many he'd drained trying to reconcile his hatred for my people and his need to find pleasure with one of us, one who had to give it up, give Isaac his pleasure as payment to keep her children from starving. You see, ol' Isaac was more than a drunk, he was as rabid with hatred as any nigger dog. That's all he was to the plantation class, a dog to be beaten into biting; tearing the flesh off the coloreds for bigger profits. Some said Isaac's hatred induced him to take his pleasure while her man was forced to watch the quick copulation. It was a way to rape the body, mind, and soul—the desecrated trinity of the slave-owning classes. Colored folks knew what starvation was, and that if you got thrown off a plantation, you'd be branded a vagrant—the sentence for which was yet another slavery, the chain-gang. Think your life's in the lurch? You were good as dead when they came with the manacles. Then it didn't matter no more, nothing did, even if you thought it once had.

One summer evening when I stumbled back home from playing too late with Jackson and cut through passing by hog's house, Momma yanked my arm and yelled.

"Never, ever, are you hearin' me chil'e, go near ol' Isaac's shack!"

"But, why, Momma?"

"'Cause he works for the devil!"

"He don't work for Mas'er Burney?" I asked.

"Like I say, he work for the devil!"

"Stay vigilant," womenfolk in the shacks said under their breath. Late nights I could hear their murmuring as they sat on the porch mending the rags we wore; them looking out while the men were down at the river catching something to put on the table. You could drift into sleep when your man was gone and fall victim to ol' Isaac. His lust could drag you between the shacks where his nightmare awaited. Lord, let me tell you, vigilance is a crushing weight when piled on all the others.

One morning, when I was a child of just five summers, my daddy and Alex slipped outside to wait for ol' Isaac, but Momma had slipped down a different path that her exhaustion had dragged her to. She landed on that stool where she sank over the table asleep. Hers had been another long night of heat sickness but them things don't matter none to Isaac. Only thing that did was getting the cotton in before prices fell and he'd for sure lose his hog's house.

"Minerva, get on out here! Isaac's comin'," my daddy pleaded as Isaac's glare settled at Owen's doorstep looking to scorch his pride.

By the time Momma roused and got out the door ol' Isaac was standing there. No, he didn't work for the devil; Isaac was the devil. He glared with hatred at the sight of a colored woman who didn't tremble in fear of him. His was more than hatred of 'croppers who worked for him or had to bend over for him. He surely hated himself for not being part of the plantation class he serviced on his knees. Only one more hired hand the camellia class used up like the rest of their livestock. Yet Isaac had a special hatred for Minerva, a tiny woman who looked at him with the silent courage that only a man taking on a she-lion with cubs could know. In the back of his whiskey-drenched mind, he knew that Minerva Breedlove was the only 'cropper on Burney lands who would have the guts to show up at his shack in the middle of the night to cut his throat and then sit on his bed grinning as his last breath gurgled away. Momma had more guts than most men 'cause she believed the Lord was behind her. Or maybe it was 'cause she knew Isaac's secret., that he took to girl-chil'es, and that gave her the strength of a she-lion.

"Here I am!" She glared like she towered over him as her contempt cut him down.

"That so?" Isaac demanded and licked his lips. "Thought you'd sleep in again, huh?" he growled. "You not 'memberin' or is it a case of you not appreciating Master Burney's generosity lettin' you'uns stay on after the war?"

Minerva's steady demeanor crazed Isaac. Yes, he knew she wasn't afraid of him, and that the other 'croppers were witness to it.

"I'll tell you one last time—we still keep the laws of the South!" he barked. "You caught with no work, you a vagrant. We all know that. You a vagrant, you go to jail like that!" Starring at Minerva, Isaac snapped his fingers. But it was in Owen's face he did it.

"That's what them jails is for, ain't it? Then what 'bout you kids? Huh? You in jail, they get taken who knows where? Yeah? Who gonna get 'em then? There ain't gonna be no vagrants at Grandview. Owen, you'd best make sure this woman sees to cooperating with me. We gonna have it Isaac's way, me and your woman. Ain't we now?"

Looking proud, Isaac chuckled as if he'd just served an uppity nigger her just deserts. But it was a false grin. Still, Minerva wasn't gonna let it be. Not while the other women looked on. She nodded at my daddy, loosened her jaw like she was gonna lash Isaac with her tongue, and hurled spit at that ol' man's back. Yes, she did, too.

Isaac paused, but then pretended he never knew spit was dripping down his vest. No, he didn't want to turn back for more. His nights wandering hell were already too long for him to stay awake fearing a visit from a nigger woman in rage. So, he moved on with that plaster grin of his. Owen held his hand over Minerva's mouth so her words wouldn't chase after him. Isaac surely thought he'd wait for the right time to retaliate—for that sweet moment when Minerva would be vulnerable enough to give it up peacefully, if only to see another day with her family.

But my daddy, he saw things different, and like most men of the shacks feared what Isaac could do to his family. What does it take out of a man to suffer motionlessly while his wife is browbeaten, and his boy stands there drenched by the shame of it? He so well knew what Isaac had been preaching was true; if you were suspected of being without work, you were put on a chain-gang along the county roads. It was a fact to the camellia class; if you strayed from the plantation you were born to, you were inciting trouble. It 'a be like burning a Confederate flag in their faces! There'd be no putting a foot down on the road to your dreams in the new South. Slavery wasn't over; it had just found a new label, licked and pasted over the sins of the plantation class. One I reckon would be more palatable to the good Christians in the North. Lincoln had been dead two or three years before I was born and couldn't vouch for what he'd meant in that Emancipation Proclamation that had caused such a furor among plantation folk. Clarification for these issues would preoccupy generations in the South. Meanwhile, best take any work a white man offered and tell him he was mighty Christian, whatever the pay, if there was any. Yet at our shack, the vagrancy laws gave ol' Isaac no power over Momma, 'cause before she'd be branded a vagrant and lose her kids, ol' Isaac would be gurgling blood under her nose. He knew it. Minerva's eyes told him so, and his every nightmare surely reminded him that come one day, Momma would surely be paying a visit to hog's house. And ain't that what happened?

&

After the moon had long slipped from sight and the sharecroppers had gone to the field, Jackson's momma would descend through all the misty clouds of her white palace and drift down the grand stairs. Her pastel dressing gown looked to float from one step to the next. Melinda was a beautiful woman with pale brown eyes and honey-blonde hair like Jackson's. But her beauty was only a thin veneer and could wither as fast as the gardenias plucked to float in bowls next to her breakfast turned acid brown. In utter silence, without so much as a rustle of her dressing gown, Melinda would enter Jackson's nursery brushing her long hair. It was the only thing Ella remembered seeing her do for herself. Like a hunter, Ella said, she came down to the nursery looking for a kill. There, summer and winter, Ella slept nights on a rag rug at the foot of Jackson's bed. Do you know how it feels to awaken having slept on a cold floor with your arm twisted up for a pillow? Well, didn't we all know what stone sleep was? By stealth, Melinda entered, intent on catching Ella asleep. When she did, she'd deliver a kick to Ella's head to fix that problem clean. Yes, it was a cold hard floor, and a colder kick that started too many of Ella's days back then. Don't matter none if Ella was up all night with colicky Jackson. Nobody asked why Ella had them bruises. They only asked why we didn't have a smattering of black marks to demonstrate we were at heel. Life let up on you when nobody looking? So, then what was Isaac doing with his time? Somebody's had gots to pay, and that somebody was always dark-skinned in those white shadows we carried on our backs.

"Ella! Are you sleepin' again when my son's awake? I'm thinkin' I best carry a switch with me all the time! You know how that makes me feel?"

Melinda's voice was not like spun sugar when she spoke to Ella. No, it was sharp enough to cut blood.

"No, ma'am. Nobody ought not to put a switch to ya so's ya knows how it feels," Ella said, distancing herself from another jab of Melinda's pointed slippers. "Jackson kept me up with the colic. Couldn't get no sleep."

"You think you're here to sleep? Is that what? One more time and you'll be out in them fields again. A day with the sun and mosquitas and you'll see what a blessin' you got in my house!"

"Yes, ma'am. I start tomorrow countin' the blessin's when I see 'em," Ella said.

Well, Ella knew how to speak between the words, because Jackson had taught her how to talk back. And so much more.

Melinda Burney was young and inexperienced at keeping her household. A white house in plantation country had to be kept like everything else, in a thick tradition much of which was unspoken secrets—much like she kept herself a secret from the real world beyond her rose garden and from that other world down by the river where I lived. The house slaves were not white, but they were considered blessed by the blessed class to live in those cooler shadows of the white house, because it was a bit closer to the scraps they were tossed. Like Jackson, Ella bridged the world between the big house and the 'cropper's shacks. It was a jagged contradiction that bridled Miss Burney till the day she died. There came a day when Ella told me about what she done to ol' Miss Burney.

Truly, Melinda seemed only as real as the clouds that filtered through the many rooms of her mansion, wafting the fragrance of night blooming jasmine as easily as the field dust swallowed our shack and penetrated deeper into our lives than any fragrance from the Burneys' gardens. Real women get hot. But the rules of Melinda's world required the coolness of a Southern white woman. The maintenance of the appearance that life was effortless, even seamless. It was complicated balancing the contradictions, trying to look fresh and soft like the petal of a magnolia and smelling like jasmine cleansed by a summer rain. Yes, looking luscious enough to want to fornicate with, but too innocent to really know about all that not-white-woman stuff. Only farm animals and coloreds had unbridled passion—despite the bridles that yanked at our lives.

You see, Melinda's world was more complicated than Minerva's. Momma's life was bound by only two passions: making sure her children didn't starve, and that her man didn't get taken off in the dead of night to be lynched. Dealing with few concerns, day in and day out your entire life, makes things simple, don't it? Because that is your life. There ain't nothing more to be looking for when you're a 'cropper. Your best jab at hope is only day-to-day survival. The thought of jasmine woven through her hair surely never entered Momma's thoughts. But for Melinda Burney, deciding which three or four dresses she would wear on a particular day could be confounding enough to send her to bed with head throbs. Ella told Momma that sometimes she stayed up till dawn ironing Miss Burney's pastel linen dresses before she was able to fall on that rag rug at the end of Jackson's bed for a few moments of sleep. I wondered if Ella ever slept long enough to work up a dream that one day she'd have her own bed. If she did, it had to be a black dream, the kind you rub out 'fore it strangles your thoughts leaving you feeling mean 'cause you know it ain't never gonna be for real. "Oh, Miss Burney, please sleep in a bit when the sun come up," was her mantra. But prayers of the dark-skinned could not be heard in the heavens. Perhaps the Lord had pale blue eyes and could never see us to know who was calling. But then perhaps we were turning to stone from sleeping too rough on the hard realities of our lives.

ORCHARD NIGHT

4

WHEN I TURNED seven, I'd trail off from the fields and head back to the shacks, where I'd try to own a chore or two for Momma. Come dark, I'd be standing at the door impatiently watching for my folks to drag in. It was a mere pat on the head, nod, or touch of their eyes that greeted me.

Momma's words sounded dry, as though they were coated with the field dust she'd inhaled that day. "Sarah, you soak them beans like I tol' ya?"

Daddy sighed and looked about as if he saw nothing. Even young, his eyes were going bad. Said the glare of the sun had put a haze over them. Was there enough wood at hand to cook a pot of beans, he asked? Like so many other nights, his question went unanswered, as simple utterances were lost in our shuffling about. It had been another day that had fallen under the weight of the shadows, where it crumbled under our exhaustion. If we somehow got to it, the next day would bring only more of the same. Yet a small portion of that night awaited and would deliver sweet morsels of the Lord's bounty.

"Yeah, Momma. Picked ever' bit of rock out of them beans like you tol' me."

"Alex, go find some wood and get the fire goin'. Your daddy is tired sick tonight."

Her words had barely escaped her chapped lips before she collapsed against her intentions. She could only fall over their moss-stuffed bed motionless, her legs dangling over the edge stiff and frozen-like. My daddy reached for her worn shoes to ease them off without paining those swollen ankles and raw toes. He poured out jagged rocks the size of peas and cursed every one. The voice that came out quiet most times wasn't gentle that night. But I knew it was only anger that his wife ached so and he was helpless to gather the drops of salty blood that burned between her raw toes.

"Why you in such a hurry, woman? We ain't gonna be hungrier if you rest a bit."

Holding on to Owen, Momma struggled to her feet despite the weight her eyelids had taken on.

"Tonight…" her words stumbled. "Tonight…me and Sarah… We's going up to Orchard Hill. Gonna make this family some peach jam for Preachin' Day. We gonna…"

Minerva could have just whispered halleluiahs so only the Lord could hear and still I'd know. It was orchard night, and the summer fruit was waiting.

Still, there were no halleluiahs coming from Owen. He looked at things differently and knew that Momma being in the Burney orchard could provoke Isaac. The thought of Burney's overseer at his wife's throat got him worked up. His voice strained lower, maybe as though Isaac might hear should he be stalking the night. "Minerva, you know what Isaac'll do if he catches you in his orchard 'gain." It was as though his words emanated from his flaring nostrils.

Momma's voice was not strained to a dust-ridden hush no more. No, it came from her depths, like she meant for Isaac to hear should he be prowling between the shacks. "And he knows what I do back at 'im!" she said. "Isaac done seen me cut up a hog with a butcher knife before it even knowed I been followin' it! Sarah, go pull some of that salted pork out. Just size yer fist, chil'e—no more."

Later, as I lay on my pallet, Momma's words put me back to the times when I heard the door creak open and saw a shadow of Momma slip out into the darkness. Still, she'd be back in her bed when I awoke.

So, then had she really gone? Dreams can blur when they're layered over our exhaustion.

We were down at the river one day when Alex told me. He said late, when Momma's aches wouldn't let her be, she'd wander down to hog's house to pay Isaac back for prodding her family like mules that day. Through his broken window she'd glare at him till he looked up and saw a shattered glimpse of Minerva standing somewhere on the other side of his nightmare. Maybe one more swig and the apparition would leave him be. Brother said I was to never tell nobody. He'd promised Momma he'd not say something or else somebody might go put a word in Owen's ear. Well, I reckon the apparition of an abused 'cropper stalking his dreams gave ol' Isaac many sleepless nights. I heard Momma tell Ella that Isaac didn't deserve no peace even in his sleep; no merciful rest that would release him to the mind-numbing stupor he searched for at the end of a bottle. No, for our survival Momma had to be at his throat just to keep him off ours.

The summer of our last walk up Orchard Hill remains the most vivid of my childhood. I wasn't sure if it would happen, because as soon as I picked up my first spoonful of beans, Momma seemed to collide with her exhaustion all over again. Still later she stirred. I watched from my pallet till she stiffly pulled up from her bed. She looked to be waiting, too. Waiting for her thoughts to come alive again. When her head stopped weaving on her weary neck, she nodded and then gently touched my daddy's cheek to know if he was deep enough in his stone sleep that he wouldn't notice her pulling her old boots back on.

Used to be Alex came with us, but not that last time. Still, he heard us rustle about.

"I too tired, Momma," Alex moaned from his pallet and turned over to catch the tail of a dream that probably hadn't waited.

"Go back to sleep, Son. This be a time just for Sarah and me," Momma whispered and patted his dusty hair. "Like when you go with your pa and Samuel down to fish. Like that."

"Stay in the dream as long as you can," Momma's kiss to the back of his neck signaled. She was right, because a few moments of sleep was the only reprieve we had. I was glad Brother got to stay in bed. By then the ever longer days of cotton picking had started working his young body hard. His only compensation was nights that worked him all the harder to make up for the hours of abuse the fields put on his back.

In his half-sleep, Daddy heard Brother stir. "Isaac gonna cut the blood out 'a you, woman!" He turned over and his eyelids followed.

"Then I cut 'im's throat good! That's what!" she whispered. "Now don't be worryin' none. I gots to show my girl how to survive—survive a whole lot of Isaacs that 'a come her way one day!" she said. "Come Sunday this family's gonna have us some biscuits and jam from them ripe peaches the Lord saved from the pickers this morning."

The real moment began when Momma took down the apron that no longer tethered me to the bedstead, but now curtained our only window. It would carry our bounty from Orchard Hill. She gazed out the window up to the attic of the big house. Finally, Ella signaled she could see Isaac's candle had gone out at hog's house.

"We's goin' to the orchard now," Momma said like we were readying ourselves for the passage over Burney lands to the promised one. "We's goin'!"

On the way up the hill I could feel the soil clinging between my toes where Isaac been watering that morning. I reached for Momma's hand at the moment we were hidden under the canopy of the peach trees. Their branches arched up over us like angel wings that protected us from view of the big house. Momma smiled as she put her hand over my eyes and whispered for me to see where we were simply by inhaling the sweet smell of ripe peaches. Then she pulled one apart, held it to my nose. How I still love fruit fresh off the tree that holds on to the sun long after it lets go of the day. Those peaches were so ripe they 'bout melted in my hand. Momma squeezed one and told me to lick the peach sugar. I still see those moments, all caressed by her look of joy as we partook of this ritual, the sharing of the Lord's bounty. Come Preaching Day all of us down in the shacks would share that jam with hot buttermilk biscuits slathered in the fresh butter the neighbor made. This sacred place up on Orchard Hill may have belonged to the camellia class, but truly the moment belonged to us, and I would lay claim to it for the rest of my life.

Picking up them peaches as fast as I could, I asked Momma why her voice hushed even in the stillness of the night?

"Go on now and keep recitin' yer verses," she whispered.

But why whisper? Who but the Lord could hear?

I recited the verses Momma taught me as I gathered the peaches she was hitting to the ground with a stick.

"Though I walk through the shadows, Jesus will see me forever in His Orchard. Momma, what's forever?"

"Today, tomorrow and all the days come af'er."

"Will you be here, Momma?"

"Yes, chil'e, just like Jesus. Gonna be with ya deep in yer heart, I be there waitin' and listenin' for your call."

Then Momma swung 'round like the whisper of an angel had cautioned her Satan was on the prowl. She grabbed my hand and led me to the edge of the orchard. Up there at the big house Ella appeared on the veranda where she slowly waved a candle like a warning from the Underground Railroad. The angels tell 'er to do that? Or for Momma to be vigilant against the one who always stalked us? Minerva tugged me back to where the apron held our peaches and grabbed up as many as her small arms could hold.

I broke the silence. "But why the verses?" I struggled to hold on to as many soft peaches as she.

"Yer life's gonna be a long journey. Only the Lord knows how far he wants ya to go or where he wants ya to end. Along the way these verses gonna protect ya from evil." Soft peaches rolled out of her apron as she dropped to her knees and took my hands into hers. "The verses and my dreams for a better day for my chil'ren is all I gots to give ya. Ain't my dreams so big nobody can steal 'em? Maybe that be the only thing they can't haul away with 'em."

"Why you cryin', Momma?"

"Why, I ain't chil'e! No need for it, 'cause we got the best dreams in the world. No matter what comes at ya in life, folk's gots the freedom to dream on anything they can set their mind on. So, you gots to set it big."

"Where I get a dream then?" I asked.

"I tell ya what I knows. What my own mammy tol' me. Sometimes ya got to run and catch yourself a dream even if the currents is pullin' you under. 'Cause maybe they's all gonna float away. Them dreams will. Maybe like when you try to catch a fish in the stream with your bare hands. You gots to run hard and fast all your days to catch up with a dream. Then when you catched a big bunch you bundle 'em up to make 'em bigger. As many dreams as you can. Big as a bridge to get yourself to the better side. Sometimes, now hear me chil'e, the other side is the place they don't want folks like us, 'cause that's the good side and they's savin' it for their own. So, you got to be keepin' plenty of dreams bundled up tightly in yer soul."

"What's a soul, Momma?"

"Ain't it a place to hide your dreams from the white folks?"

The spell was shattered with Isaac's cursing. Likely he'd crawled out of a nightmare and awakened to a room with only an empty bottle staring back.

Momma looked up and saw Ella on the veranda, where she snuffed the candle out. That was her signal there was a reward on our throats. She knew the Burney overseer was sure determined to collect on it. She held her hands over her mouth so fearful was she that a yelp would escape and set the nigger dog to barking. Wasn't it true that howling dogs always heralded white Satan's entrance into the halls of our lives?

"I's dreamin', too, 'bout havin' an orchard so's we can make jam ever'day." I struggled to hold my skirt filled with peaches. "Momma, how come we only pick fruit at night?"

"I told ya. 'Cause it's better for us. The Lord protects us at night. And 'the Lord is my Shepherd…'"

"Where's Jesus waitin', Momma?"

"In the Lord's Orchard…"

Yes, I truly knew it was His bounty we were hauling down the slope, even if the price tag was stamped 'Burney'.

"He keeps me out 'a troubles and out 'a shadows, don't He Momma?"

About then Isaac stumbled over his rage. We could hear the nigger dog yapping.

Momma took us deeper into the darkness yet through his drunken agony, Isaac could still decipher our scrambled movements. It must have stirred his ugly imaginings as we could count on Isaac's rabid hatred to vanquish his inebriation long enough to put him stable on the path that could lead him to inflict the horror of his severed soul on to ours…if he caught us.

"Minerva! I know it's you up there in my orchard 'gain. Huh? Now ain't it you up there?"

Momma tugged me to the shacks down the slope the other way.

"Come, yer daddy's waitin'!"

Daddy might be there for us, but if Jesus had been waiting in the Lord's Orchard, I was sure ol' Isaac had surely scared Him off. Well, Momma told me the devil is ugly, mighty ugly; would scare anybody off. She knew I would face him disguised in many forms along the journey ahead. Some forms filled with running blood gone toxic with hatred and then, too, some devils as empty as a stack of whiskey bottles in an alley waiting to be shattered over my hopes and dreams. I would find that getting through those broken shards would let blood over and over again. But then didn't we all bleed in torrents looking for the bridge to that better life?

From the sounds of Isaac's boots crushing the twigs he'd pruned that morning I knew this nigger dog was as near as his rage.

"I finally caught you, woman!" he yelled. "Now what are you gonna give ol' Isaac to keep your shack?" His voice crackled and hissed like it was from the very depths of the sputtering hell he would pull us down to; down for his lusts to gorge on.

Momma grabbed my arm and dragged me down a path of weeds that scratched my legs and stuck to my thin dress. She looked behind for the nigger dog. I could hear his boots pound the hard dirt like he pounded on our door. Nearly there, a peach dropped from Momma's heavy apron. But as I pulled back to grab it, she yanked my arm and hauled me into the shack. That very door we'd fled behind had but one defense to the outside world and Momma went for it. She kept Granny's big scissors hidden under the bed.

"Now get to bed! Don't make a noise no matter what ya hear out there," she commanded. Her glance pierced my thoughts more than the severity of her whisper. "And don't get your pa up for nothin'!"

I retreated under my blanket where my thoughts quickly fogged over from fear. What do I do now? Why for? Don't know. Don't even know if Jesus can hear my fears.

Momma rustled about and then slipped out into the darkness. I crawled up on the table to peek out the naked window, but Minerva had disappeared into the shadows between the shacks. Up on the steps of the veranda I saw Ella wringing her hands in prayer. Our glances swam back and forth, hers enormous with fear. "Oh, Lord, no! They's gonna lynch ever' one of us now!" Ella's eyes seemed to yell.

But I wouldn't let her see mine and covered them with my hands. No, I'd keep my fears to myself, like Momma said. Still, I kept at the window and watched between my shaking fingers. I knew I would. If Momma fell from sight I would disobey and yell for my daddy.

And then there he was. Standing there licking his lips and growling in a dialect of obscenities that Satan had taught him good—words I did not know but felt the meaning of nonetheless. Momma came out of the gloaming to face down his intentions and then waited while this nigger dog sniffed at her shaking flesh and undid his breeches for the feast. She held Granny's rusty scissors open behind her like two jagged knives: one to stab, and the other to follow till the bloody deed was done.

"You been stealin' from the Burneys 'gain," Isaac slurred. "I caught ya this time!" His tongue was thick from whiskey. "You accustomed yourself to gettin' away with it, huh? Yeah, you been messin' with me a long time, ain't ya?" His lascivious toothless grin was followed by a wink and another lick of his lips with his brown tongue.

"I ain't stolen nothin'! It be our sweat that tends that orchard," she declared, her head raised high. "We got a right to some of the fruit."

Isaac's voice got hard so's to punctuate his slurs with the distinction of a man wielding a stick in a woman's face. "Woman, is you blind? Can't see the color of your own skin? Ain't it the color that say you don't got no rights? Now come out of them shadows so I can see you clear. Yeah, come over here and show ol' Isaac what you gonna give me to fix this between us. Come on now."

Minerva's hand trembled until her skirt fluttered at the tattered hem where the points of Granny's waiting scissors gnarled the broken threads. "No! You come get. That's what you been aimin' for, ain't ya? Now I's waitin' for ya, Satan!"

Isaac chuckled through his imaginings and headed for the gorging he'd so longed for.

But just as I turned for my daddy, Isaac stumbled and passed out at Momma's feet. This was the moment. Momma pulled out her rusty scissors to deliver her promise swift and hard. I would rely on the verses to clear the fog that came down on me like hot steaming gravy. The Lord is my Shepherd. He leadeth me to quiet pastures. But where are them quiet pastures, Lord? I knew not near the Burney orchard.

Momma took a pail of water from the mule trough and tossed it hard at Isaac's face, laughing at the nigger dog as she did. Then she did it again.

On the ground Isaac groaned and twisted his face in the mud till it oozed up his nose. When he came to, Momma was on him. Her open scissors jammed under his jawbone ready to penetrate that ol' brown tongue that had abused her family so many times. At his first flinch blood trickled down the scissors.

"Well, ain't it like I always tol' ya? Your big ol' mouth, it ain't got nothin' to say no more? You thinkin' you'd steal from me what you stole from my oldest girl Louvenia, huh? You fouled 'er and then you put her off with nothin'. You too drunk to 'member, but I ain't. I think on it ever'day."

With Isaac's every flinch, Minerva's scissors let out another bright red blotch of confession that trickled down his hoary throat.

"No! I don't know nothin' 'bout that! I never did nothin' to your girl that I 'member," he gurgled.

But the blood smeared over Minerva's hand said he'd lied again. Yes, he remembered every moment. Probably reused the memory again and again when he found himself with only an empty bottle as companion and relied on his past sins to pleasure himself.

"Maybe that's 'cause what you did to Louvenia ya thinkin' is nothin'. Is that yer meanin'? I told ya after what you did to my girl, if you ever messed with my family I'd cut yer throat, sit on top of yer stinkin' carcass and smile in yer face while ya choked on yer guts comin' up. Don't it look like I's smilin'?"

"Huh? No, no, it don't. She never meant nothin' to me. That's why I let her off the Burneys' like I did," he lied again.

Not wanting to see what was coming, I ran back to hide under my blanket. I was crying when Momma came in. She lit a candle and waved it back and forth at the window, indicating to Ella that Isaac's throat been slit, and then blew it out. I was so scared I shivered, wondering why being in the Lord's Orchard was so costly to my folks?

So ended another day for us in the flaming white shadows.

Jesus at My Door

5

D ON'T KNOW IF I ever fell asleep that night so fearful was I of what awaited the next morning. Would Jesus be waiting at our door where Momma had surely dropped ol' Isaac's head? The next morning did come, but was different from most: we all slept in. Well, I didn't, 'cause I always woke up first. I looked over to see Momma still in bed staring at the timbers above. There next to her Daddy's face had turned soft and serene like only hours of contented rest can bring the unaccustomed.

"We be gettin' up now," she said softly.

Daddy jolted up. He looked puzzled as the room was filled with light. You see, nobody ever slept till light filled the room 'cept on Preaching Day.

"It's Sunday?" he asked and rubbed his eyes from the light streaming through the window. "Huh?"

"No, it ain't. Knew you had to have some rest."

He jumped out of bed like they'd just put the roof ablaze and ran to the door to see if Isaac was coming. But only dead silence waited on the other side of our door. Not much more than rustling was heard inside during those long moments our glances crisscrossed.

How could I not wonder if my daddy had seen Isaac's head out there? Or maybe the Lord holding that head by the ears waiting for

Minerva Breedlove to come talk to Him 'bout the happenings of the night before. Owen's hope waxed high.

"Isaac, he drunk? Never got up, huh? That what?"

"Maybe he still up at hog's house. Him on his knees up there!" Momma declared with the self-righteousness of one thinking themselves in good with the Lord from their deeds against the wicked.

"Yeah, I reckon that man still talking to Jesus."

"Huh? What's you talkin' 'bout?"

He looked away from Momma's air of proud silence to see what my eyes might reveal. Again, the chaos of our glances darted back and forth as I didn't know what the truth was. Still, I was certain certain ol' Isaac was burning in hell by then and could only wonder what that was like.

"Ever'thin's fine," she said. "I done made it so."

I pulled the blanket back up over my head, wondering what my daddy would say to Jesus waiting outside the door to hear why Momma cut that mean ol' man's head off. Well, Minerva could always defend herself. I could see she might step forward to acknowledge that cutting throats is a sin, but is it a sin to cut Satan's? What would Jesus say 'bout that, himself always fighting with the devil? I reckoned she'd best chat with ol' Clara to work out the best angle. Yes, my thoughts were going in circles and yet still heading nowhere, least of all out the door where I was sure Jesus was waiting!

"Sarah, come out from under that blanket," Momma hollered as the grits came to a boil. "We gots to go up to the big house while your daddy and brother eat. I got somethin' to tell Ella."

"What's you been at that you need to go up to the big house? You know they don't want us up there," Daddy asked, gulping his food so he could get to the fields.

Well, if I couldn't figure out what happened, and I was mostly watching out the window, then how could he? But I didn't have time to figure nothing, as we was gonna pay Ella a hush visit. I jumped up with feelings of self-importance as Momma and I had something going on even if I had no idea what. Daddy shook his head like he was flicking off a fly. Or maybe like he didn't understand no woman-talk and didn't aim to bother.

Momma pointed me towards the door. "Come on now, Sarah."

We left with me wondering if I'd have to step over ol' Isaac's head. If I did, would he wink at me? So I closed my eyes as I always did when Miss Burney stared at me in her rose garden. I still half figured that Isaac would look up at me like that hog Momma butchered once did. The one that stared at me for the longest time till I went screaming to Alex who been in on it with that hog 'cause he was carrying its tail in his pocket and he was the one told me to go stare at it till it winked. And when it did, I screamed till my daddy dragged Alex over by his ear, smacking him even though it was that hog that done winked at me.

No, I sure didn't want ol' Isaac, the man that lived at hog's house, to wink at me none!

Momma jerked my hands from my eyes as we headed up to the big house. "Why you got your hands over your eyes and you're stompin' on my feet?"

Did that mean she didn't see ol' Isaac wink at her none? Or did she just kick his ol' head aside when he did?

❦

It had rained that night, so the path up to the big house was clean of the powdery dust that usually rolled over our feet on the way to the fields. Before Minerva could even knock Ella was at the door, aghast. Then she'd probably never opened it for 'croppers, 'cause none ever ventured up there before. I was antsy to hear from Momma why we were up there.

"Oh, Lord, no! You still here? They's gonna lynch us all now!" Ella whispered loud enough that Jackson stopped slurping his grits 'n' cream and came over to get in on things.

"Be still, woman," Momma commanded, pointing to the heavens like a plaster saint. Still, Ella looked a bit crazed and kept glancing about her kitchen like Miss Burney might sneak up on her.

"What's you doing up here? You knows Burney gonna see ya up on his veranda. You got to get yourselves down to the river quick. No, no! You take off, they knows you done it for sure! Ain't that right? Huh? Ain't it now?"

"Done what, Ella?" Jackson asked as he pulled her apron strings to tie on the doorknob like he told me he tied down them Indians the time they come to the door on the hunt for cookies.

"Isaac, he ain't dead yet, 'cause he gots no place to go what with no head!" Momma said to clarify the matter. But it hardly did.

All Ella could say was, "Huh?"

"I said, the debil, he wouldn't take him, and you know the Lord won't have 'im. Ain't that the truth? So, I reckon he best fall on a pair of scissors and cut himself good in the neck. Ain't that what happened? That what you're a thinkin', Sister Ella?" Momma dragged her finger across her neck to mark where Isaac got his throat cut and winked at Ella. "You know what I mean, don't ya now, Sister Ella?"

"Huh?" was all Ella could utter from her gaping mouth.

Only news of the Lord's Second Coming via Vicksburg could have impacted her more. She looked my way, but I had no idea who was coming and who was going, 'cept Isaac was sure to be stuck in the mud someplace I could only imagine.

All the same, we were still impressed with Minerva's bit of a sermon. As good as ol' Clara's preaching any Sunday. But not Jackson. He groaned from behind Ella's apron and rolled his eyes like a heathen who'd been hit upside the head by the preacher's words too early on a Sunday morning. Jackson went back to slurping his grits. That's because there's a language secret to us womenfolk and I was working hard to decipher it. I figured whatever was really going on I was on the righteous side of things and expected Ella would soon join in. After a long pause and penetrating gaze first at Momma, then at me, Ella did come 'round.

"He near dead down at hog's house? Huh? That what? You put them scissors to him's throat like we talked on that time?" She whispered so's Jackson couldn't hear over his slurping. That's the way heathens eat their grits, don't you know? At least that's what Ella said when she went over and smacked the back of his head.

Lordy, didn't we all have our chins high nodding with satisfaction like the preacher's wife every time the traveling preacher said Amen!

We'd vanquished Satan's truest disciple, ol' Isaac himself. When were the angels coming to thank us?

Well, Momma went on whispering in the voice of divine sacredness she kept for Preaching Day down by the river, or maybe just 'cause she didn't want Jackson hearing, so he went slurping all the louder so's she'd speak up. He already forgot Ella's smack upside his head?

"Isaac, he on his knees prayin'," Momma announced.

But how'd she know what Isaac was doing down at the hog's house? Then I got to thinking, how'd he get his head back to his shack anyway? Seemed like most days he could barely see where he was going with it bobbing on his shoulders.

"Prayin', huh? Well, he best not pray to Jesus," Ella announced. "'Cause the Lord don't want to hear nothin' from 'im 'cause he's no good."

"Maybe Issac's prayin'. Him prayin', 'Thank you, Lord, for saving me from that Minerva!'" Momma declared, still nodding up and down. Dear Lord Jesus! Ella had gotten better stories from Jackson on how the cookie jar got emptied by them Indians.

"Amen, Lord, Amen!" Ella added, declaring her allegiance to our side of things.

Still acting like a heathen, Jackson knocked over his milk. It spilled over the table and onto the floor. Heathens drink out of their hands down at the river, Ella once told me. Then he jumped up hooting and hollering like he was gonna gallop off.

"Stonewall Jackson, save us all from Isaac gots no teeth! Huh, Ella?" he yelped.

Ella and Momma looked at him like they was 'bout to smack his face. First time I'd ever seen Jackson shut up without the usual prolonged discourse of which mouth was likely to shut down first. Surely that was a thing the South had never witnessed. Guess Ella figured if anybody was gonna save us from a lynching, it would hardly be some dead Confederate general Jackson was named after.

Still, Ella panicked when Momma pulled the big scissors out for her to hide.

"Now white folk gonna know you're figuring on killin' that ol' man 'cause them scissors. They's knows ever'thing we're thinkin'." Ella grabbed the scissors and remarked to Jackson: "You ain't never seen these here scissors of Minerva's, hear me, chil'e!"

"I still seen 'em, Ella. But near forgot if you give me a cookie!"

Ella lifted her hand like she did when she had smacked him minutes before.

I stood there thinking on Ella's notion 'bout white folk getting in our minds and all. If they be in our minds, how comes they ain't in our hearts? They certainly didn't spend much time in our empty bellies where there was always plenty of room for strangers. I started to get lost again in my thoughts when Momma's words tugged me back on the trail that she was prodding us on.

"White folks lying when they say they knows what we thinkin'," she said. "No, they never knows what's comin' from our folk. That's what protect us from the lash. They's afraid we might up and get 'em in the night. Right in they's own bed! Ain't that right? Now take these here scissors and hide 'em."

"Hide 'em where?" Ella asked, looking to see if Jackson was still plundering the cookie jar. He was stuffing cookies in our pockets; one for me and one for him, two for him, two for me.

"Hide 'em where the menfolk won't never look," Momma whispered.

"Where's that, Sister Minerva?"

Ella looked about her kitchen for the best place before smacking Jackson's hands off the cookie jar again.

"Under Miss Burney's pillow!" Momma said. "You think that woman's gonna let them men traipse through her things with they's dirty hands? Tell ya what, hide these under her pilla. I bet she thinks twice 'bout opening her big mouth at you when she sees how close you come to her throat with these here scissors!"

Guess Momma was right. The men would hardly be climbing through Miss Burney's bedchamber searching for a rusty pair of scissors that had met Isaac's throat. He'd for sure go howling that a colored woman from the shacks near killed him with them and ought to be strung up for it.

"I gots to go to the fields and pretend nothin' happened last night, 'cause ain't nothin' did. Did it, Sister Ella?"

Ella nodded to the whole mixed-up recipe Momma expected Ella and me to keep stirring. "No, I ain't seen nothin' or heard nothin' 'bout Isaac's head been near cut off like it ought 'a be! Amen, Lord!" Ella bit her lip to keep from laughing.

"That's the truth. Ain't it?"

Then she nodded to confirm that our tales were all consistent. Jackson only groaned. Don't know if it was because he didn't believe us 'bout cutting Isaac's head off, or because he was too busy stuffing cookies in his mouth with both hands before Ella could grab them away. Heathens eat with both fists; that's why they're heathens, Ella reminded Jackson. So, I quickly put one of my hands behind my back to keep from turning heathen, but then nearly swallowed a cookie whole.

That was the proudest day of my life. I walked back to the 'croppers' shacks holding Momma's hand. She held her chin up high like a preacher's wife leading us to the Promised Land.

⁓

Daddy and Alex were long out in the fields by the time Momma and I got there. Seeing us come along, the 'croppers paused to gauge Isaac's disposition on somebody showing up late. They could remember all too well that before emancipation this brazen conduct would have been rewarded with a lashing. They wiped the salty sweat from their eyes at the sight like they'd just seen a vision.

Right away Momma went to rubbing a different kind of salt into Isaac's wounded ego. The rag he wore on his neck to cover his meeting with a certain pair of scissors was brown from dead blood. He wasn't up for no more. No, he sauntered over to the edge of the fields, pretending he never saw Minerva coming along like the Queen of Sheba herself.

The humidity in those fields along the river can near kill you, but you never paused your labors to take water while the overseer watched. To make sure desperate thirst didn't cut your time away from the rows of cotton the overseer kept a lid on the water till feeding time. Then we'd line up for a swallow or two from the same can everyone else struggled to get theirs from. On a good day, you could get enough good water down to eat that day-old cornbread they fed us; scraps from a table in a big white house. You see, pure water, like everything else it seemed, belonged to the white folk. Still, they told us we could have all the water we wanted, so long as it came from the swamps and not when the sun was up and working us; that time belonged to them. Fever could kill folks after one sip of swamp water, after two days and nights of the purest agony the fever generously provided. After that, you'd soon enough welcome hell if Jesus had yet to come for you. Best wait for the clean water when it was given out, 'cause hell had to be a bit worse than life in the overheated shadows of a plantation. Yet how many were left wondering?

Minerva walked up to the water barrel, took a pitchfork and knocked off the heavy lid and filled a big tin of water. She lifted it high to the sun like a sacrifice, drank from it slowly and then turned in a circle, gazing at the others over the top of that tin. First Alex wandered over to Momma. Looking agitated as hell, Isaac reluctantly followed. He was eager to subdue the confrontation Minerva had manipulated before the others caught her fever. Speechless as beasts of burden, the 'croppers gazed at each other and then slowly walked a *pavane* towards the barrel of clean water.

"Momma, can I have some water now?"

"Yes, Son. We can all have our fill, 'cause this here water, it don't belong to that ol' man. It belongs to the Lord."

Minerva filled the tin and handed it first to ol' Clara, who'd been working the fields since she was my age. Clara passed it to her son, Samuel, and he to Owen and on around.

Led by my daddy, Isaac found himself surrounded by sharecroppers who closed in 'round Minerva. They held their pitchforks and scythes like butchering tools. Fueled with Momma's courage, they glared at Isaac in a fashion nobody'd ever seen. His hand dabbed at that rag tied around his neck to see if he was bleeding again. He was, even if he wasn't.

"Why, Isaac, I'm thinkin' ya sleepwalked out 'a yer bad dream again.

Or did ya just cut yer throat shavin' cause you been in a hurry fer Mas'er knows ya been drunk all night?"

Isaac never been talked down to by no colored woman. Sure not in front of colored men, some bigger than him. He glared at her and tightened his fists as his rage sucked in his toothless mouth.

Their message didn't come in so many words. It couldn't; them kind of words are frozen in the toxic fears that inhibit the thoughts you been keeping down. You see, these folks had never experienced talking to white folks direct-like, so tied up in fear were they. No, their message was sent from the tines of their pitchforks aimed at the empty cavity where Isaac's heart had never been. Were they thinking they'd stick them pitchforks in his gut, bind his carcass in corn stalks and let him disappear under the currents of that muddy river? No, there were too many angry souls lost in the Mississippi for that. Lynched, cut down with only their last gasps left for the kin to claim, and only then to be swallowed by the muddy waters of the Mississippi. That river was a sacred burial ground for so many of my people.

"Now you come by my place come Saturday," Minerva said standing tall, "'Cause that's the day we're butcherin'. I give you another close shave then. Yeah, you just might disappear in what they grind up. Ain't it so?"

Momma got up close to Isaac's face. He backed up against them pitchforks that helped him hear just as good as Minerva's scissors had the night before.

"Look here," she said. "I smilin' 'gain."

The 'croppers all grinned at him. In all their years at Grandview, they'd probably never looked Isaac in his face. Those grins surely brought his icy blood to a rolling boil.

"You get your damned water—then get back to your hoes 'fore Burney come by." Isaac's eyes pleaded for peace even as his nostrils flared with rage.

The sharecroppers took their time finishing off the water before they slowly drifted back to their task of nourishing the white shadows with their labors. The water we'd taken would still be squeezed back out of our pores before the sun settled the accounts.

Minerva's position in shacks had risen that day. There was now a peace between Isaac's oppression and the oppressed. It was a bitter peace, yet it helped lighten the load that let us crawl over to another day where a borrowed dream might be waiting.

SILENT CRIES,
BROKEN WHISPERS

6

THE MORNING OF that last summer at Grandview was unlike any before. A stillness hovered over our shack that jarred my young thoughts from the moment my eyes opened. What was wrong? Why hadn't Daddy gotten up to head to the fields? Momma went about getting a pot of grits on like she was sleepwalking.

"Alex, you and Sarah go down by the river and pick your daddy some them wild grapes. That 'a make 'im feel better. Go on now."

"What's wrong with 'im, Momma?" Brother didn't seem to expect an answer.

Silently she shuffled about, shaking her head at nothing, till she finally pointed us to the door. That was always her signal she wanted us out of the way. There'd be no grits that morning.

I always loved to meander down to the riverbank with my brother where there'd be a thicket of wild muscadine grapes or berries waiting. I squatted for the low vines as Brother reached for the higher. I loved listening to his tales of when the river would one day carry him off on some adventure. At the water's edge I chattered on 'bout this or that. Alex barely grunted at my notions. Even so, we put a bit more grapes into the basket than our mouths. I remember asking how many basketfuls we could eat in a day. He said nothing and that silence spread like a ground hugging fog. You see, Alex had stopped picking and was gazing up the slope to where Samuel stood staring back. Why'd he come down to the river? He and Daddy only went fishing with Alex on Sunday and they never let me come.

"Alex, you and lil' Sarah come on back," Sam said. "Your ma be needin' you. Come on now."

Alex didn't move. It was as if he couldn't. Still, his eyes followed Samuel. Sam's boots snapped the vines that lay over the path as he headed back up.

"Why'd Samuel come? Daddy up there waitin'?"

Most times Alex would rather jab me with a pointy stick than hold my hand. Yet he said nothing as he gripped mine.

Up ahead Samuel turned to see if we were following. His expression never broke loose from the haunted look he'd come with. I looked up at my brother, but he only mirrored that fear. You see, nobody had ever come looking for us down by the river. Why would they? It wasn't near dark and the river wasn't swollen from the rains. Our eyes darted back and forth looking for the comfort that would not be found. In crashing moments, the reality of that morning would hit me like a belt across my tender face.

The door to our shack was wide open and 'croppers, most I knew, were staring in. What were they looking for? Their heavy silences were deeper than the one I awoke to. Jane, Samuel's wife, was working near where Momma fiddled with some old bent tins. She stared into their emptiness like she was hunting for something she'd lost. Jane worked at the fireplace and mumbled bits and pieces of her thoughts to Momma. I figured it was woman-talk as I didn't understand the half of it. Still, I searched their sorrowful glances for something their words hadn't revealed.

Momma dropped her tin cans yet did not reach for them. She looked down at her feet like she'd simply lost them forever. Lost what, I wondered? Lost forever is a frightening feeling. I felt that fear as Momma's eyes strayed from mine, looking lost.

Jane finished filling a poultice with smelly bits of roots and herbs, which she dipped in vinegar and squeezed over the fire. Our shack quickly filled with ashy steam. She took the poultice over to my daddy and dabbed it on his forehead and looked to be telling him a secret. He flinched, but still only gazed at the timbers above as if he was searching for something he'd lost. Or was he merely trying to hold on to what he was losing?

I went to show Daddy our basket of wild grapes, but Jane shooed me back with one flip of her wrist.

"Back away, chil'e," she said.

With her finger pointing at my face she looked hard into my eyes to make sure I minded. At that I knew for sure there was trouble even before Momma gasped and put her hands to her mouth like something was about to fall out. I guessed she didn't want nobody to hear if the sadness in her eyes drained through her lips that couldn't close because of all those heavy sobs about to fall out. Again, Momma's hands cupped her mouth when she heard Jane telling Daddy a secret about Jesus and that it 'a soon be over. I guess Jesus heard her prayer, as on her last word my daddy's eyes stopped blinking forever.

I knew what had arrived at our door that day had brought the silent cries of one who has nothing and nowhere to hide from the void of it all. Who might save us? Who even would? Still Momma reached out.

"Sarah, go up to the big house. When ya get to the lawn, yell for Mas'er Burney to come."

Walking about the shack like she was in the wrong place, Mama's voice faded to whispers like somebody done wrung her throat.

My broken thoughts pounded to whispers in my head. Why'd I need to go up to Jackson's? What was I gonna tell Burney? I ain't never said a word to Jackson's daddy.

Jane wanted me gone, too. "Go on chil'e."

Momma's chin trembled when she noticed Alex sitting in the corner with his arms twisted about his head as though hiding his eyes could push it all away. What was it he so feared?

More alone than I could have realized, I sifted my silent cries, wondering why I needed to stop at the lawn up there at the big house? Did Momma forget that I'd long been past the lawn that moated it to play with Jackson? Or did she know I didn't really count—that to the white folks up there I was just as invisible as the fever that had visited my shack? Only a nobody; one of those who ain't 'posed to go that far into the shadows of the big house, I recalled Ella saying, unless the white folks are tossing scraps on Christian day. Yet I don't remember them tossing much of anything our way but misery. Still when I came close to the lawn for some inexplicable reason I stopped. There I yelled over the invisible barrier that now pricked at my fears. My feet felt strangely anchored on the dirt side even as my shadow loomed over the soft green lawn that ended steps from the white veranda; that certain boundary that I'd never seen before now held me back. So, I yelled over it.

"Mas'er Burney come quick! Hurry, come quick!"

I yelled for my daddy so Jesus would come and pull him back from Momma's sorrow and deliver us from the silence he'd fallen under. I yelled till I thought my throat might come out. It didn't, but Jackson did. Maybe Jesus could hear me then.

Jackson looked deep into my eyes as he teetered over the banister. I said no more, as the words wouldn't come. Jackson said nothing back, and ran to his door, yelling even harder than he'd ever yelled at ol' Isaac. He knew something was wrong, too. You see, there was no distance between Jackson and me.

"Daddy! Come out! Sarah's here!" Jackson yelled through the open door that was always closed to us.

What could I do to get Burney's attention? If my voice gave out like Momma's, would he hear my fears?

Still I knew, knew that only Jackson could get his daddy to come out, 'cause never before had any 'cropper come to the big house yelling for a Burney's attendance.

"Daddy, I said come out! Your horses got loose again and they's eatin' up Momma's roses. Daddy!"

Jackson knew Burney didn't like dealing with nothing but his prize horses, and didn't take to his son's manipulations, against which he was as defenseless as his momma's daily brew of tales she'd long dunked him in about her shopping. Nevertheless, he had to keep an eye on his former property, even if it was only driven by his son's foot stomping for attention.

Burney stepped out reading his newspaper with scant intention of going beyond his fragrant world. Now as I look back, he never really did.

"Daddy, your horses got out again!" Jackson pointed down to the shacks but that didn't fool Burney none.

"Where's my horses, Son? I bet they're in the stables where they belong, ain't they?"

"No, they's down visitin' Sarah. Go see!"

Jackson glanced my way to convey that his strategy was working as usual. But Burney didn't look to me for confirmation of his son's tall tale. I doubt if he even knew my name, or to which of his former slaves I was kindred.

"Now, Son, how are they eatin' your ma's roses if they're down in the shacks? That where your ma does her gardenin'? With our niggers? If you interrupted my breakfast for nothin', I'm tellin' Ella to whoop your butt good!"

"She already done it. You forgot," Jackson said.

In their convoluted ways Jackson and his nanny always covered for each other.

"Between you and your ma my memory sure seems to fail some-where, don't it?"

Jackson always knew how to direct traffic at Grandview.

"Yeah, down by Sarah's," he replied.

Burney headed down the path to the shacks, all the while mumbling something mean about the 'croppers; the very ones whose backs pro-vided him with a life that floated ever so seamlessly on that cool veranda hanging with the scent of jasmine.

Burney walked past me like I didn't exist. I knew to him I didn't, 'cause his eyes, like ol' Issac's, were that cold shade of near colorless blue. About the color pond water reflects on a winter's day. He couldn't see me, so how could his heart feel the anguish of those crumbling moments? Burney yet had to follow me, as he had no idea where Owen and Minerva, born to his property, dwelled.

I glanced back to see if Burney followed, as he looked all so blind to everything but the inconvenience of it all. The corners of his mouth told me so. They'd turned down so hard his young face appeared crimped. Still, he followed me to my door. There the 'croppers swayed an open path for the master—their eyes respectfully downcast as he walked up nodding to nobody. But then he probably couldn't see us.

All was silent in that dark ashy shack 'cept for Momma's wailing at the foot of the moss-stuffed bed. Then, choking on her sobs, she struggled onto the bed and across my daddy's legs. She grabbed on to them as if she could pull him back from the other side; But she could only lay there wailing tattered pieces of her heart. I stood wondering why my daddy couldn't pick up those pieces like he had so many times when the heat of the fields had sunk her low. Hold her sobbing head? Wipe her tears away? Because only her silent cries were left and even those were all but spent.

My daddy still stared up at that small hole in the timbers that surrendered a glint of light over his brow. Alex yet sat in the corner where he'd pulled himself tighter into his arms. There was little to go.

"Why ain't you out in the fields?" Burney demanded. "This ain't Sunday. Isaac's knows to get them crops in before the first rains. I'll cut you off all food credits if you don't get out there, and I mean now!"

But we knew what he meant even before he spewed the words. His glaring eyes spoke louder than his voice. Burney's words were hard, mean and therefore true to his deepest heart—that part of his soul that could not follow Jesus to the doorsteps of the downtrodden. So why do I yet look back after all these years searching for a glint of tenderness in his eyes, a drop of humanity somewhere in his uttering? 'Cause there was so much from his seven-year-old son? The heat of his anger singed my thoughts for I quickly realized where the ugly words that ol' Isaac openly spewed at the 'croppers came from; they were born from the very depths of the soul of one Robert Burney, former slave owner. And I also knew why he didn't mouth them himself. For those deeds he had Isaac around so his Christian mouth remained unsullied by the coarseness that his wife would surely claim to be offended by. But then maybe a mouth roughened by coarse words can't savor a mint julep. How could I have known?

The 'croppers withdrew in silence. Minerva moaned and choked as Burney stared on. His mouth twitched and his words fumbled as they reloaded.

"Owen, he dead…" Momma whispered.

Now like Alex she cried with no tears.

"He gone to Jesus. Now you ain't got 'im no more. No, you ain't!"

Her words were tangled in her sobs but still hit the walls like an ax hits dry timber and landed, splinter by broken syllable. I stood there fearful of my heart bleeding me away till nobody could see me. Not my daddy for sure. His still open eyes could see me no longer, and I yet begged for him to.

Burney jolted the way Miss Burney always did at the sight of me in her rose garden.

"Fever! Damn you!" Burney yelled. "You brought me to a shack with the fever! Look at you, you got it too!"

He reared back from Owen's stare.

"Owen dead…" Momma repeated; her sinking eyes still pleaded. But Lord, it was all too late.

I always cried when Alex did—figured I could rely on his instincts. That day I would have cried all the same as I struggled to sort the whys. Why was my daddy sleeping with his eyes open? Why was Alex sobbing so pitifully? Why did Momma seem lost and so far away?

"Don't…don't separate my kids. Don't run 'em off like stray dogs. We been workin' all our days fer you. Jesus is watchin'!"

Momma lilted to her knees, like she always did when she prayed, but there was no prayer left. She crawled over to clutch at Burney's ankles and beg for something that was too broken to possess again. Her twisted body folded at his dusty boots, which brought the look of terror to Burney's ashen face. Still I wondered how he would comfort her? Wipe her tears on the sleeve of his white shirt like he did Jackson's nose? Was he gonna sit a spell to offer thanks for all the years of work he'd squeezed out of Owen Breedlove? No, that was not why he'd come to our shack. There were no flowers hidden in his clinched fists or tenderly arranged somewhere his bitter words.

"Ain't nobody in the world watchin' a nigger die!"

But, Lord, somebody was watching. With my own eyes I'd seen much, and no, there was nobody counting. Not the life of Owen Breedlove; nobody but Jesus that is. Tell me what dying is? Why is Burney mad at Momma? I could no longer cry as loud as my brother, yet I still tried.

Momma mumbled broken whispers to comfort Alex and me.

"The Lord is my Shepherd. Though I walk through the shadow of death…"

But I reckoned the words were too brittle for the Lord to hear, even if He wanted to.

Momma's face screamed, but her words only crumbled to the ground next to her mouth. "God is watchin' you!"

Minerva Breedlove died the next day.

Something was gone, but how could I have known that it was my childhood?

Dark Deals

7

Later the day Momma passed, Ella came down to bathe my folks for their final journey. She whispered something 'bout the cleansing was so the filth of the plantation wouldn't keep the Lord from recognizing them among the dusty faces gathered at the gates of His Orchard. My folks' faces would be wiped clean of the field dust their lives were hidden under. No, no one ever heard their silent cries of desperation or their broken whispers of fear. These were held in trust for the next life along with their souls.

The winding sheets that shrouded Owen and Minerva seemed so strange to me. My folks never wore anything but homespun and sackcloth, but now were wrapped for eternity in the finest sheets woven of imported Irish linen. Jackson had pulled them down from Melinda's oak linen press and hid them under the veranda for Ella like she'd told him.

With Granny's rusty old scissors, Ella hacked out the Burney monograms and tossed them off like they were dirt. They lay strewn at her feet, these large circles of roughly cut fine cloth with those beautifully monogrammed "B"s in royal blue silk thread needled by former slave women who'd probably never slept under a sheet. I gathered the cutouts, the size of large magnolia flower petals, and gazed at them transfixed, thinking that in my very own hand I possessed something of infinite beauty. I gathered up these scraps of sheets as Ella sang the spirituals. But

Ella's warm voice couldn't bring Alex to the same place. After listening to my sad sighs long enough, Brother fled our wake to go off and scream his anguish alone. Then there was pounding on the door.

I thought it was Jane and her Samuel come to help. But Ella seemed to know it wasn't. She reached for Granny's scissors and aimed them at the door, as if it couldn't be opened against the rusty points. Did she sense the evil that lurked out there? Isaac walked in all the same and looked about uneasily, as if death might still be lurking in our shack. Ella pulled the Burney sheets up over my folks' faces. Isaac stood there glowering. But the flotsam of grief his appearance could so easily have brought was soon to be fixed by Minerva. Yes, even in death she protected her family. I'm telling you the way it was; them dark deals that came with Isaac that night. Ella knew why'd he'd come, because she knew how black his soul was.

"Sarah, go on down to ol' Clara's and help 'er get her biscuits on. You and Alex gonna be there tonight—then at Jane's tomorrow. Go on now, chil'e."

She aimed Granny's scissors in Isaac's direction as she spoke to me, and never took her eyes off that man.

"What Burney say?" she asked.

Isaac eyed me as I lingered near the door. His glance was like the hot breath of a nigger dog against the cold sweat of my fear.

"Burney, he say the boy's gonna stay. He got to work off the food credit. Yeah, that Owen, he borrowed plenty. It's gonna take a mighty long time to get things paid up. Yep, he sure belongs to me now," Isaac declared like a slave owner.

"What about Sarah. Then she stay on too!" Ella declared.

"No, she ain't! Miss Burney want 'er gone! Told me to make sure it happen no matter what Burney say. She say that child just like her ma and she don't want 'er 'round Jackson no more."

"She a baby, not even seven summers," Ella said.

"Now why that matter to me?" Isaac replied. "I do what I told. She gone tomorrow, or the next night and I be taking her off myself!"

Isaac tossed a grin my direction, chuckled and wiped the drool from his toothless mouth.

"No, that ain't how it's gonna be!" Ella announced.

"Who say? Huh?"

"Minerva! That's who!" Ella replied.

Isaac howled with laughter. But then his face turned on him and he looked as though he'd been smacked good and hard. He had been, and it was soon to be a fatal blow. "She dead. Dead, right there in front of you." Yet he wondered, didn't he?

"Minerva, she tol' Burney not to scatter her chil'ren. She means for it not to be."

Isaac chuckled at the notion that the same woman, cold with death, could still face him down. "Boy's gonna stay. That's all there is to it," Isaac repeated.

"Then what's gonna happen to the girl?" Ella asked suspiciously.

"She come with me. That's all." Isaac winked at me the way that butchered hog once did.

"I tellin' ya, it ain't gonna be that way!" Ella reaffirmed.

"What's that Minerva gonna do?" he asked. "Wake up from her dead and put some ol' scissors to my neck and say it ain't gonna be that way?"

"No. Jackson gonna do it."

"Jackson?" The color in Isaac's face evaporated. "He a boy. I ain't 'fraid of no boy."

But Ella knew better.

"Huh?" Isaac grunted and waited for more bad news.

"Jackson. He gonna crawl up on his daddy's lap and fill Burney's ears with lots of things he heard his Ella say 'bout 'ol Isaac, him's daddy's overseer. He gonna do that." Ella grinned ear to ear. Maybe like Minerva was smiling in his face again. And wasn't she?

"So what?" Isaac sputtered. But he knew what the what was and how much more rotten it'd be for him once things finally sifted over to Melinda's ears.

"Minerva, when she come up to the big house to get 'er scissors back, she told me things you ain't never goonna want Miss Burney know. Is ya?"

"Huh? What things Minerva say 'bout me?"

"She say, Minerva do, that you got blue eyes like the devil himself. Cold and gray like stagnant water."

"Huh? What that woman say 'bout my eyes? It ain't none of her business 'bout my eyes!"

"Yeah? That so. My boy gonna say somthin' Miss Burney ain't never gonna want to hear."

"Ain't nobody gonna tell Miss Burney nothin' 'bout what happened back then!" Isaac growled.

"No? Then you go up to my kitchen door 'morrow and call for Burney. You do that. Then ask 'im what Jackson been sayin' 'bout you. Where you get them blue eyes. Then ask 'im what Miss Burney gonna do 'bout it now that she knows the truth. Yeah, you a big man. So, go ask 'im if you still got a place here come a day er two."

"Miss Burney'll cut the blood out 'a you for making mischief she don't wanna hear! You ain't nothin' to her!" Isaac said.

"Miss Burney do that? Ain't never 'cause I gonna wrap 'er in winding sheets when she dead just like I did Owen and Minerva here. No, I ain't 'fraid of that, 'cause Jackson gonna scream bloody till ever'body in Vicksburg comes if I whisper that his momma gonna put me off Grandview. But Burney, up in the big house, he call you his hog-man. You think he gonna let his hog-man be after what Jackson tell 'im? No, he gonna come for you!"

"What Jackson say 'bout me? Isaac demanded. "What he know then?"

"Jackson? What it matter? I know 'bout you. Minerva give it to me! Ever' bit of what you done back then! But Jackson, maybe he twist things. He a chil'e. Yeah. But maybe he wanna make sure it go deep into his daddy's ear. You don't gotta know no more. That 'a be the way it is."

"What's you want then, nigger?" Isaac blurted.

It wouldn't be the last time Isaac found himself capitulating. Yes, he must have known that Minerva, even dead, had folded his cards again.

"You see? Minerva, she still got you, ain't she? Yeah. And she gonna keep gettin' you for the rest of your days. And all along, I still be here with my boy watching when she do it!"

"I said, what do you want, nigger woman?"

"Heard Burney tell you to go into Delta in the mornin'. Pick up his seed come over by boat from Vicksburg. In Delta, you gonna send a message to Louvenia Powell. Say her younger brother and sister is comin' to her. Both 'em. Yeah, they's coming together, like Minerva meant for it. No, Burney ain't gonna turn 'em into mules. Not even a gruntin', boot-lickin' hog like who's standing in front of me! Then you gonna go buy some ferryboat tickets for these kids to get over the river to Vicksburg. You gonna do what I say."

"I ain't got no money!" Isaac whined. "Where I get money for tickets? Then what happen when Burney finds out I let that boy off 'fore he work off them debt his folks owe?"

Isaac's heart must have beat harder than it had in years.

"You go tell Burney you're wantin' to lick his boots. You get down there and lick 'em good and he give you a dollar. If he say no, 'cause maybe you stink too bad, Jackson go get into his daddy's desk and get one, then go tell his daddy you stole it. Anyway, why'd a boy steal a dollar he don't need? Him's daddy's gonna ask me 'bout that. I say 'a course Isaac steal it! Burney knows you gots to have yer bottle, don't he? You drunk up all your wages already, ain't ya? Gone to stealin' form Burney now, ain't ya? Yeah, right from the big house you done it 'cause you're hurtin' for the bottle, huh? But that ain't my problem. Now you go do what I tol' you. Kids be ready after they folks buried proper."

"Yeah, well, you better get 'im buried quick," Isaac said. "'Cause Burney say get rid of 'em."

"No, hog-man," Ella said. "You gonna do it!"

"Me? I ain't got nothin' to do with 'em," Isaac said. "Burney, he done told me to dump 'em in river. They ain't no more to him than dead dogs! So, the 'croppers best do it quick 'fore Miss Burney catches her sheets is gone."

"Owen and Minerva, they ain't gonna be hauled off like some cart of manure. I say it ain't gonna be," Ella said. "They kids gotta know where they folk is buried. It's right they do. They was born to Burney lands and they gonna stay here forever to remind Burney of it."

"What in hell are you talkin' 'bout, nigger?" Isaac demanded.

"You gonna go tonight. I be standing there with the candle. You gonna dig two graves up top Orchard Hill. That's where they gonna be."

"Burney would shoot me dead if I let them niggers be buried up there. That orchard was planted by Burney's granddaddy himself."

"You decide if you more worried' bout Burney, or Jackson comin' for you, hog-man!"

Ella knew the answer.

Through his hatred, Isaac snorted long and hard before conjuring a new lie. "I tell you what, nigger woman, we'll wait and see 'bout that lil' girl standing over there. But that boy, he gonna stay put. Burney ain't gonna put a bullet in my head. So, I help ya get them niggers buried, 'cause I don't want you 'croppers up there making noise that brings Burney down on me. I help you bury 'em, but you ain't puttin' no grave marker there! I'm tellin' you, you ain't! Then you send the girl to me! That 'a be the deal. Hear?"

"Okay, Isaac. You keep the boy and take the girl off on your own. Guess there ain't nothin' I can do 'bout it!" Ella said, but it wasn't what she meant.

"Now you're hearin' good, nigger woman!"

Still, she'd really heard another voice more clearly, and that was the direction Isaac was about to find himself tossed.

⁂

It came about the next night. Down at the shacks the 'croppers waited with candles lit. We were at Jane's and standing there next to Brother was Ella, holding Jackson's hand. They'd crept out of the big house to come join us. Attended by all, Owen and Minerva would be delivered to their final resting place up on Orchard Hill.

You see, it seemed that earlier Ella told Jackson, again and again, till he figured something was up, that he best not sass his momma none at the supper table. Being Jackson, he kept mouthing off till his pa sent him to bed. The Burneys had no sooner retired than Ella and Jackson went through the house collecting every candle they could get to, all of them 'cept the ones high up in Melinda's crystal chandeliers. At Jane's, these candles were cut into pieces and passed around. Then we all proceeded to the top of Orchard Hill where the view back over the river and way off to Vicksburg was clear as the night the three kings went looking for the Christ child, ol' Clara pointed out. Even now, as I look back at that night, the wonderment remains. The moon, that I was sure only shone above the big house, guided us. It was like a hundred flickering stars traveling up the hill to the knoll atop, that sacred resting place of the Burney family.

Way up under the peach trees, ol' Clara led the' croppers in prayer. Then I heard a whisper that moved like a quiet wave from those down the hill up to the top where Ella held on to Jackson and my hands. Ella cupped Jackson's ears to his mighty annoyance. I couldn't hear what they was whispering, but I knew that ol' Clara's nod to Ella was some kind of message. Ella smiled and nodded back. Then ol' Clara lifted her hands up to the heavens and we gave thanks to the Lord for taking Owen and Minerva's weary souls unto a final place of peace, and for protecting their children from evil.

But what kind of evil? Well, among we 'croppers, evil always meant ol' Isaac.

We started back down to the shacks as Samuel, Jane's husband, suddenly appeared in front of us with his shovel in hand and started shoveling the soil over my folks' graves. Jackson and I helped Jane gather up dry leaves to scatter over their place of rest till it disappeared from view. Standing there alone except for his dry tears, Alex reached for my hand as Ella and Jackson disappeared on down the other way toward the big house.

MOTHERLESS MORNING

8

THE NEXT DAY at Jane's I woke up early. Standing silently by the window was Alex looking as though he was waiting for someone. Didn't know why, but I wondered if it was for our folks.

"Who you waitin' for?" I asked.

"Who say I waitin'?"

"It's me here talkin'."

"Samuel, he ain't come back yet. Been gone all night. I waited up to see."

"See what?" I asked.

Jane stood at the open door gazing out towards where that old well was and then turned and smiled. She took a seat on the porch steps.

"You get yourself a biscuit then come sit with me."

"Where's Samuel?" I asked, wondering why Brother hadn't if he'd been looking for him.

"He comin' when he's finished."

I ate my biscuit waiting for Samuel's return sitting next to Jane. Alex only stood there at the door. Guess he didn't want to sit out on the porch with no jabbering women.

Later that morning I wondered up to the big house. I stood at the edge of the lawn to see even as I had no notion what I was looking for.

Up there Ella had Burney's breakfast laid out nicely. She stood fanning him on the veranda so the humidity wouldn't bother him as he ate. Up close I could hear them.

"Isaac, he gonna bring yer horses 'round?" she asked.

"Don't mess with me, Ella," Burney replied without taking his eyes off that fine plate of ham and eggs. "You best go see if Sam has that well filled in like I said. Water gone bad. You know my wife can smell somethin' unpleasant all the way from Vicksburg. You tell 'im Miss Burney wants it finished today!"

"Yes, Mas'er. I tell 'im what you say."

But Samuel already knew.

By the time Ella got Jackson dressed, Samuel was all but finished. That well, the one my daddy told me never to go near, had disappeared. Nor was there a trace of Isaac from then on. Nobody ever seen him again. Word was that he must 'a gotten drunk and fallen into the river. But that talk was followed by a snicker or two. Who knew for sure? The tales on ol' Isaac got to be as tangled as the growth along the river. But what we all figured, talked about in nods and whispers, was that it was surely Minerva who'd tripped Isaac into a grave of his own, wherever that lay. From then on Isaac was only one more of Grandview's many secrets.

The next day I felt so afraid for Momma and Daddy that they'd be alone up there on Orchard Hill that I promised myself I'd come ever'day to talk to them. Still, I felt utterly lost. I was sure I'd hear my folks' voices if I could only make my thoughts quiet down long enough. But who would hear me? Then I heard her: Momma's voice as crisp as the air up on Orchard Hill the night the two of us gathered peaches.

"These Bible verses and all yer dreams, that's all I can give ya, chil'e, my dreams for my chil'ren!"

A couple of days later, I guess after enough time to get things worked out, Ella slipped down to Jane's. She looked at Alex and then me, but as hard as she tried, the words wouldn't come for her. It was left for Jane to tell us that we'd be leaving Grandview forever and would do so quietly, like runaways, with only Samuel as witness. It was a blessing, Jane murmured as I cried. Still I didn't understand why the women standing about offered their own tears. Or why I was a motherless child. Could Daddy still be looking for me from someplace? Where then was that place? Alex had no answer. Where was my home if not near Jackson's? Ella went silent. I can't remember the verses… Can you hear me, Momma? Say them again then. Where do I hide my dreams from the fears chasing them down? It all got quiet, except for the voices in my head.

The next day Ella came to help Jane get our things together. We had nothing, and Alex put it all in one burlap bag. I heard that Samuel would be waiting out of sight under the oaks at the end of the drive to take us away. We were leaving the only world we'd ever known and going to one we had no conception of. One that would possess us, like the Burney plantation, but still not want us. We were told there'd be a cart ride over to Delta. From there a ferry would transport us over to the docks near Vicksburg, where a short train trip would take us to that part of Vicksburg where coloreds lived. There, somewhere, awaited a woman whom I was told was my older sister. But what was a train? Alex tried to describe it, but he'd never seen one either. I knew he was only reciting what Samuel had told him.

Shortly I was to take the first steps on the longest walk in my life; a gravel drive only traveled by white folks driven by a colored, to the gates of Grandview. There it hung close to my face as we walked under the oaks—the long hanging Spanish moss that Jackson and I loved to pull down for Momma to stuff her bed.

We were only a way down the drive when I heard the screen door slam and Jackson run out hollering for me to wait for him. I could see Samuel up ahead fidgeting nervously as if ol' Isaac might suddenly appear and curse at him. Jackson chased after us under the hanging moss, screaming his fears and kicking at the gravel when Ella tried to pull him back.

"How come you're going somewhere?" he asked.

He freed himself from Ella's clutch to chase after us. I couldn't look him in the eyes, but didn't know why.

"We're goin' to live with my sister Louvenia in a big white house," I said to comfort my only friend.

I kicked the dust up something awful, anything to slow us from the direction we were headed. Alex jerked my arm to stop. Did he, too, want to slow the avalanche we might face? We could never have known what was waiting for us, and perhaps that saved us from the moment.

"But why? I got a big house, don't I?" Jackson said.

Ella dabbed his face with her apron to catch his tears. "You and Alex gotta live here with me."

I plied Jackson with other notions I'd created from my fantasies. "We's gonna have jam ever' day." Don't even know why I said that, as I'd never had a notion that there were folks that had jam ever' day.

"I like jam, don't I?" Jackson escaped Ella's clutch again. "Can't I go, too?"

"But Ella'd miss you," I told him. Would Ella come to know how much I would miss him?

"Who's gonna play with me till you come back home?" he asked wiping tears.

Ella ran to stop him from following after us. Her tears were not of happiness. No, her eyes had that same look as the time she told me 'bout walking from one end of hell to the other. I could only wonder why she was scared, like we were. What did she know? She didn't say, but held Jackson close to keep him from escaping the cool shadows of that fragrant world he didn't know he owned, only to escape to the scorched one that awaited us.

Samuel was there at the end of the drive with his wagon. He waved for us to come quickly.

Alex lifted me onto the straw in the back and climbed up next to Samuel. They had things to say and things that needed to be heard. See, Samuel had been Daddy's best friend. They were both real quiet, 'cept when they were down by the river fishing with Brother. Then their quiet voices worked up a howl over tales about things the womenfolk got into. Then Samuel went quiet before talking about our daddy and what a good man he was and how much he loved his boy. For the first time,

Alex cried as Samuel went on to recount their times on the river and the stories those catfish had told them.

Samuel kept his arm around Brother's shoulder till we reached the docs at Delta. Alex climbed down. He averted his gaze, guess 'cause he didn't want me to see his eyes red and wet. After tipping his hat to the white men who passed, Samuel lifted me down and kissed my forehead. It was like my daddy did. Then he pointed to the ferry that blew steam and handed two pieces of paper to Alex: tickets to our exile. Samuel dabbed at a tear like it wasn't no tear and climbed back up on his wagon and left.

Alex seemed to know where the train was that Samuel had directed him to. Brother could not hold my hand, as he was clutching those train tickets like our lives depended on their safe conveyance to the ticket man. Then he gestured with his head. Over there waited the steaming monster that would take us somewhere, and to that someone named Louvenia.

For what seemed like forever we sat on those hard wooden seats on that monster train that terrified me beyond words. Even more so when that old white man came up to our window, his eyes glaring like ol' Isaac's, and spat at the window as if the glass would not shield my face from his brown tobacco spittle. As a child I wondered if his stare might cut through that very glass? He spat again to punctuate his hatred. But the window was closed and sealed despite the heat and humidity. See, coloreds could only buy seats behind the engine, which spewed smoke and cinders. Two orphan children in the South. The man stumbled off, tipping his hat like a gentleman to a passing white woman.

Despite the old man's greeting, I was stuck wondering if we would ever eat again. Didn't know. Neither did Brother, or he'd answer me when I asked again and again. Maybe his mind had taken him back to the river where he always went to figure things and he could no longer hear me that far off. Nobody else could either. I was sure of it. My empty stomach kept reminding me.

At the next stop, another old man came up to the window. I ducked down into my seat. These instincts develop early for young coloreds. Alex wouldn't budge, but I knew he was scared 'cause he held my hand like he was gonna break it. Then another old man ordered us to get off the train and pointed the direction where he probably thought hell was waiting for our arrival. We got off and stood there lost till she walked up, this woman who looked as frightened as us. And just like Daddy. I didn't know who she was, so I looked at Alex. He only looked off maybe to find our future, perhaps the sight of which caused his head to quickly turn so his eyes wouldn't reveal the nothing he saw in all that noise and confusion. She waved to Alex, that woman, and a faint smile came to his face. First one I'd seen in days. There were tears in those eyes of hers that were just like Daddy's. This was surely my older sister, Louvenia.

Lost in the Shadows of Jesse's Alley

9

I NEVER SAW SO many people out and about as when we stepped off the train in Vicksburg, just across that great Mississippi River but farther off a plantation than anyone in my family had ever disappeared to. As a child this city was terrifying. Who were these people bustling about the station? More people than I'd ever seen, and from Brother's darting glances, more than he had. How far from home are you when you're truly lost? How far even is far?

The noise pounding off those buildings, some taller than the Burneys' big house, where did it come from? I'd never heard such a roar, even when the river was pounding the banks and breaking off pieces. Why were people talking so loudly? Were they trying to say something over the roar of that river we'd crossed but could no longer see? And why did they walk along shoulder to shoulder talking yet still never look each other in the eyes? They seemed to gaze ahead like they knew where they were going yet still meandered along like maybe they didn't.

Louvenia broke the din of my chattering thoughts. "Ain't ever been at a train station before, huh?"

"We ain't been nowheres," Alex announced.

But I had. I'd been under the veranda playing with Jackson Burney.

"Now Sarah, you're a big girl now." Louvenia noticed what Brother seemed to deny.

"I almost eight," I said in case nobody ever told her. I learned later that when we tried to work out how old Louvenia was that she couldn't count.

"How'd you know? You're a girl. You can't count nothin'," Alex said. I had to think on that.

"I can count! My friend Jackson teached me."

"You ain't got no friends 'cept that corncob doll, and I cut her head clean off so's she won't be talking back to me no more!"

So, it was Alex that done it! Jackson and me with all the chickens we could corral along with a duck held a wake for my baby. The one with the hemp hair that daddy had carved from a corncob that wore a dress sewn by Jane from the pockets torn off Burney's old castoff shirts.

"Jackson and me buried my baby and told Jesus you did it!"

But that was a lie, because we really told Jesus the devil did it, 'cause that's what Ella told us to tell the Lord when we prayed so He'd be sure to notice my baby in heaven even if she didn't have a head. But then later I revised my prayer when I found my baby's head where it had likely fallen off.

"I'm going back to live with Jackson. Yes, I am."

When Jackson was 'round nothing bad ever happened to me and my pockets were near always filled with hard candy or broken cookies.

"Then you don't know nothin'! Jackson's ma eats nigger kids!" Alex informed me. "You'd be sittin' down with Jackson for suppa and Miss Burney's gonna come up and cut yer throat good like she done all them coloreds come up on her veranda and sassed 'er. Before you quit yer whinin', you'd be in that old pot where they boil hog's heads! And you know sissy Jackson; he's gotta eat ever'thing Ella puts on his plate! Jackson's gonna eat you for suppa! You still wanna go back there?"

I knew Alex spent lots of time down at the river figuring things out, him being near two years older. Still, that wasn't the picture I had, 'cept maybe 'bout Miss Burney slipping up behind me and cutting my throat. She always looked at me as if she was of a mind to do that, didn't she?

I was working out these thoughts with one hand holding my throat in case Miss Burney slipped up on me if she was shopping in Vicksburg. That's when Sister-woman boxed Alex's head. Why was Louvenia mad? Or was she only as frightened as Brother and me? She looked as if something was about to slip up on her, too. Did all that noise on that street pound her thoughts too thin, too? Well, I was soon to learn that the one who led by his fist was always slipping up on Sister.

"Ain't nobody eatin' up nobody! Now I want you to listen good," she said. "Mr. Jesse, he don't want ya livin' with us. Yeah, we been together just a few years now and it ain't been easy. No, it ain't been nothin' but a hell! Don't even think on what I had to do for him to take you in. And if he don't take to you, where you think you're going then? Huh?"

Not really moving and yet feeling bustled, my head started to spin from the fear I read in Sister's eyes. To anchor my thoughts, I looked at the ground. Down there my pinched toes hidden in my borrowed shoes seemed to stay put even as visions of what Louvenia had said jostled my thoughts. I stood there feeling torn between that white veranda where I knew Jackson was surely waiting for me to play and the dirty street where I stood feeling lost. I clutched Alex's sweaty hand. Got me to thinking: maybe I best hug the ground till the storm passed and I could hear through all the noise again.

"I go live with Jackson!" I mumbled, with one of my fingers trying to hide somewhere in my mouth. I mumbled to my feet telling them to run! All my toes could do was squirm, like the rest of me. Them not knowing if they should go back or forth, up or down.

"No, Sarah, you ain't never gonna see Grandview or Jackson Burney 'gain. Not never, hear?"

Why wouldn't I? Sister words hit me in bits and pieces that I couldn't hold together to make sense of. Along that river was my home. What about Momma and Daddy up there on Orchard Hill?

"I tell you where you're goin' if Jesse don't take a likin' to youse," Louvenia began. Then she looked as if she was about to tell us the most awful thing we'd heard since Owen and Minerva passed, and would rather have bitten off the tip of her tongue than say these words. "He say he take you where they take all colored kids gots no home. Jesse take you where they take ol' horses got no work lef' in 'em. Yes, he will, too. He say it all morning and then some!" Sister wiped away another tear. In the dark days ahead there would be times when she couldn't even do that for us.

I truly had no real idea where Sister was talking about, but I could rely on Alex to sort things. One glance from him told me we best not wander in the direction Sister-woman was talking about, 'cause I knew the fear in Brother's eyes was real as they never deceived. Still I was thinking: Why wouldn't Jesse want us? Back then I held that only Miss Burney never wanted us.

I never walked so far in my life as that first day in Vicksburg. How far could somebody walk in one day on the very same feet? Then how far could somebody walk and still nobody know you? I was sure we'd walked a thousand blocks to get to Louvenia's, but then I'd never walked a block before to know. What could be waiting that was so far off from where I'd come that we were not yet there? My thoughts mumbled on, but still couldn't keep pace. Like me, they only wanted to walk backwards.

After what seemed like hours of walking down one alley after another, most so narrow no sunlight touched the old black brick walls, we finally reached our destination. But I tell you plain, there was no white veranda with a table of refreshments waiting. There was no white anywhere to be seen. The door we were marched to looked to be down a long shadow that I would soon learn ended at Jesse's place. It had to have been one of hell's dead ends.

Louvenia tugged us on down this service alley stacked with trash, broken bottles and reeking of the stench of fermented urine, to a screened-in porch. There, she shoved the old door open with her shoulder. That kitchen door seemed reluctant to admit anyone. Or, I'd soon learn, let anybody escape. Sister bustled us into her world and its moldering darkness.

I'd never seen a kitchen before, and couldn't figure on the purpose of so many laundry tubs stacked on the porch we'd passed through. Turned out they were tubs that I'd soon be dipping my hands into and spending the rest of my childhood trying to avoid touching the bottoms where that greasy, gritty filth waited. It wouldn't be the only thing I'd avoid the touch of.

Sister hurried us further through her kitchen to another room smothered in darkness that hissed with the creaking sounds of the old floorboards that taunted our every step. It was a room surrendered to the dark so a man's sins would be harder to decipher. Cardboard was packed against the only window and the walls were a collage of stains in hues of filth that only desperate living can layer up. Yes, this room was dark enough to hide the wickedness it was witness to, and where I saw Louvenia's husband for the first time. A cold chill went down my sweaty young back at the sight of that ol' man.

There he sat sputtering grunts and scratching at himself like he was eaten by lice. This was Louvenia's husband, the man who might not find us acceptable. He slouched in a torn old chair strangely situated in the center of the room. Like a throne it was, with oddly placed doilies covering the chair's gutted upholstery—the spilled inners that had long turned dirty brown. Yes, there was Jesse, sitting like ever'thing revolved around him. I was soon to learn it did.

After a stammer or two, he looked up. He'd been so preoccupied with the whiskey bottle he was trying to conquer that he hadn't notice us standing there, me holding Sister's hand from fear. She looked at that old man as if he might have something to pull out at us. A stick? Yet her pause seemed to tell him to take another swig—like it 'a clear your head, ol' man so's your vision's less muddy. He tipped the bottle and emptied it to the bottom in one guzzle, then wiped the thick drool from his mouth. I could smell him, and he smelled like a rotting form of ol' Isaac. I thought he had to be the oldest man in the world. Him with those worn old pants with suspenders hanging at his sides and that filthy yellowed sleeveless undershirt. There he sat with his empty bottle standing court as it surely waited for the next one to arrive and relieve it from duty. He held it tightly like it was a golden scepter. His horny hands were stained ochre from nicotine—as though he'd kept 'em buried in the yellow clay back along the riverbanks at the Burneys'. I would soon find that Jesse kept 'em buried alright. Buried in the swamp of lies he conjured so they'd never be exposed to the truth of hard work.

I could never figure how this man could be as black as that alley at night and yet never spend a day under the sun in any field. But Jesse's life was the night. A life where the bars and bottles could so easily entice him to flee the shadows of his own scarred soul. He stared up and down at me. I stared back and then looked up to Louvenia, having no idea what he was. She heard my thoughts and answered to help situate us on this man's good side, like it might assure us of our survival.

"Go on in kids. Don't be afraid. This be my husband, Mr. Jesse."

Jesse didn't get up; I figured he couldn't. Surely, he'd been in that old chair for ages and like an invalid, it now held him prisoner. He looked hard at me as though he could see something right through me. And he could. I was too young to know my innocence was glowing, and Jesse was salivating for a lick.

"These them nobodies you went clear 'cross town for?" he demanded, tipping his bottle for the last drop he'd already swallowed. "Leavin' me with no meal on the table? I tol' you, they's nothin' to me but two empty stomachs wantin' my food!"

The rest of his greeting melted into slurs that still needed no translating. No, every snarled curse fell on my ears crystal clear.

"Alex, you go put your things in the kitchen," Sister said, her voice soft and gentle like Daddy's. "Then have a piece of that pie, Annie, the nice neighbor brung it by."

Alex had carried our valuables all day, his other shirt, my other blouse and a corncob doll, and took them to a place that offered no safekeeping in the corner of Louvenia's kitchen.

Jesse looked me over, not noticing Louvenia squirming at the sight of his tongue twisting to get out of his gaping toothless mouth to lick at his brown lips. Then, in a blink, he was at the edge of his chair, pulling me to his rancid body.

Louvenia lunged to wedge her arm between Jesse and me. He dropped me to grab that arm and twisted her to the floor so hard I figured he'd broken it. He'd rehearsed this dance before, hadn't he? Just like she'd rehearsed springing up from the floor to distance herself from his fist on the next round even before counting her cracked ribs.

"Why ain't you a sweet lil' thing?" he said. "Crawl up on Jesse's lap so I can get me some sugar, lil' girl. That's what you be good for now, ain't it? Ain't it all you's good for, too? I know you done showed up here to take Uncle Jesse's mind off things. I be needing takin' care of, little pleasure now and 'gain, 'cause Louvenia here, she ain't good for nothin' that could please a man. Is you, woman over there? You don't got no work to get to, Louvenia? Then go get me a bottle! I got me some business here gonna keep me busy, ain't you, lil' girl?"

Sister wrung her hands and shook her head at Jesse defenselessly as he slobbered grisly kisses on my cheek and then neck. But when he twisted my head to find my mouth, Sister somehow wedged her body between Jesse's and mine.

"Jesse, let her be now, she don't know you. Let her be, I tell ya."

Louvenia wormed and twisted between Jesse and me so's to lessen his grasp.

How easily he could hold me and reach to slap her down again, a *pas de deux* that would be encored many times in the years ahead. All I remember is flailing as hard as my small feet could to land a kick in a place a man don't wanna feel no heel. He moaned and dropped me to raise his fist just as Alex reappeared. Praise God, Alex had Momma's eye. He looked at Jesse with a glare that caused his nostrils to flare. I don't 'member much after Louvenia hit the floor again. Only that I cried, Jesse bellowed, and so I cried louder. Alex twisted his fist into a confused knot hearing Sister's pitiful sobs, which were thick enough to slice the fog that shrouded me in confusion. Tears came down her sad face like rock salt done been pelted in her eyes. The initiation into the shadows of Jesse's alley life was complete.

Yes, a tidal wave had rolled over me. One of wrecked emotions that so easily drowned my young senses into all the nothingness we'd arrived at that day. What could I grab on to? The floor was too far away to hug and, anyway, Louvenia had already staked claim to the spot under his feet. Even through the fog that blinded me that black night it was crystal clear that we'd sure not moved into a big white house as I'd proclaimed to Jackson, and there'd be no jam waiting on our table.

Such a long journey on that train to have gone nowhere and I would be staying there for years to come, and even afterwards pieces would follow me along my journey as tightly stitched to my spirit as a shadow is to my heels. Yet all through these times I could still hear my momma's voice.

Momma, why do you keep whispering if you know I can't hear no more?

What are the prayers and the prospects of a child lost at the dead-end of a dark alley? I was lost in Jesse's shadows, and it would be years before he would find me—the man that would take my hand and lead me away from it all.

LOUVENIA'S BLACK DREAMS

10

I DIDN'T KNOW MY sister as a child back at the shacks. I was a still a baby when the day came when Louvenia disappeared from our lives. But from time to time I'd hear Momma speak of her and cry to my daddy 'bout what had happened. "Where's my girl now?" she'd beg. He shook his head but never could offer nothing large enough to catch her tears. No, how could he have known where his oldest child had ended up? He'd never left Burney lands himself. I didn't understand much of the story back then, just felt Momma's tearful rage.

You see there came a day when Sister was old enough to catch Burney's eye, and this sighting bludgeoned her childhood innocence on the spot. Momma had been able to fend off ol' Isaac but she could do nothing about Burney's lust. That put Miss Burney in a quandary. Melinda Burney knew how to maintain her facade of delicious innocence but still not crack the hard lacquer shell hidden beneath. She spent her days leisurely cultivating that most Southern female talent yet could turn on a dime to deal with anything that might insinuate on her life in the shade of them magnolias. The sweet jasmine Ella wove in Miss Burney's hair was a signal for Burney to come and pleasure himself. But she was only pretending, and he knew it. Knew most times there'd be a roadblock to her bed, and he wouldn't have enough for the toll she demanded. The attic was already filled to the brim with bright-colored tea dresses. Still made Burney mad when he came up against one of Melinda's roadblocks, as he must have figured he'd already paid a high enough price razing them as fast as she'd re-erected them. There was only one way left for him; she forced the issue, hadn't she? Burney simply meandered around her roadblocks to fix his needs elsewhere. That meant trips down to the shacks.

We weren't good at the kind of negotiations Melinda Burney knew so well. Not that we didn't take to weaving jasmine in our hair, but the only thing we had to negotiate with was our lives. So much easier to fold them; then your kid gets to see another day. Burney's arousals, which had no place to drift to but the shacks, left Melinda with only one recourse. Yes, when Burney went riding, she summoned his overseer up to the big house. The message was always understood even before it was sent. Isaac had best be at the back door by the time Melinda got downstairs. She had a bitter peace to brew and would not hesitate to toss her frothy rage on any servant not heeding her wishes. Long before this day, Melinda had already worked out a few dark deals with Isaac. It was easy enough for them to partner up. He might have been worthless as an overseer, but so long as Burney took his pleasure in breeding his horses and no more than that, she'd make sure Isaac had a bunk down in the hog's house. Keep an eye cocked for Master Burney's doings down at the shacks, the mistress commanded—then come up to her back door for the nigger dog rewards.

Isaac was told by Melinda that Louvenia was to be put off the place before Burney got back for supper. Otherwise, Melinda would take a switch to Sister herself and drive her all the way to the end of the oak-lined alley. For sure Isaac knew he'd then be walking that gravel path next. We all knew that the end of that drive only led to nowhere an unescorted woman would want to be come nightfall. It was checkmate for Burney. Melinda didn't have time for her own kid; there were to be no mulattos coming to unsettle her rose garden and incite chatter up and down church pews on Sundays. The Burneys had their name carved on the first pew reserved for their use only. Sitting up there, she'd surely hear the tittering behind her back. I 'member Momma saying it was

Ella's job to run down to the shacks and see if any newborns were half-pale. If they was, she was to drag it from its momma's breast and sling it into the river. Sacrifice for the sins of the father? Or eternal freedom for the child? 'Course Ella never hurt no baby. But some said maybe Isaac did. The fear of finding a half-white baby in your rose garden was at the top of the list of secrets that ruled plantation folks up and down that river. Christian souls tend to be jarred when unpleasant details show unexpectedly, such as a pair of soulful eyes that wait at your backdoor for the scraps… or maybe asking to take your family name.

"Just fix it!" she'd exclaim when Isaac stood in her presence. That ended her instructions for the day. Her expression easily communicated the seriousness of the situation, with not a speck of sweat drawn to her delicate brow despite the furor that must have been stirring in her head. It was all that was needed. Ol' Isaac might 'a gotten around Master Burney, despite his messing up after he'd drifted to the bottom of a bottle and failed to get the 'croppers to the fields before the sun come up. But he knew there were two covenants to Robert Burney's faith he best not violate: invoking the displeasure of his wife, and allowing anyone to conjure a notion that Jackson would not be master of Grandview come one day. Isaac knew his own fate teetered precariously on how low he bowed and scraped when she appeared on her veranda in her Southern regalia. Hers was a carefully arranged crown of jasmine that she could so easily unwind and lash his face with, leaving more marks on his nightmares than Jackson's daily taunting. His was surely a miserable black dream of being lost out on some county road, passing a chain-gang or two looking for new recruits even as he stumbled from ditch to ditch along them back roads looking for a whiskey bottle with one or two drops left.

Isaac was clear on the things his mistress meant him to do: get rid of Minerva's girl Louvenia, and do it cool and seamlessly, like white-flowering jasmine should look when woven through a white woman's golden hair. But the thing is, this man had long survived on their scraps, and the scraps also meant the women Burney cast aside. It was how things worked for plantation menfolk. He knew how to obey his mistress and still get his rewards. Yes, Isaac, he finally got to Sister too, didn't he? Play some cards? Roll some dice? Spin the bottle and see who it aims at. It pointed to Louvenia's young face.

He made a bargain with Sister that Momma never found out about till it was too late. If Louvenia gave it to him, like she had Burney, without fuss or protestation, ol' Isaac would let her stay on with our folks so long as she kept out of sight but still at his disposal for conjugal visits. If she showed herself at the big house's back door to tell the secrets, Isaac promised he'd cut the blood out of her, starting with her face. The point was made by stretching her mouth open with a knife. What could Louvenia do?

Sister told me she laid down for that filthy old man with no teeth till his grunting was over. Said she let her mind fog over till the deed was done. The only other option was to lay down and starve to death somewhere off the Burney place, just hoping Jesus found her before somebody picked her up for vagrancy and initiated her into a chain-gang. And best make sure your near-dead body ain't close to the big house when you get used up. That'd be untidy to white Christian sensibilities and could get you hauled off for loitering to some dark basement jail at the county courthouse. Lynching ropes are tied at both ends to make sure ain't nobody ever gonna leave the place alive. No coloreds ever did.

Louvenia loved Momma and Daddy and didn't want to leave them, and she didn't want to die all alone along some county road after the laborers had finished with her, so she went to the hog's house when Isaac bid her to come put some flesh down on her bill. It was her secret, one wrapped in too many layers of shame to count. Surely, when you're starving not to be vagrant in the new South, your mind tends to drift into that fog quick when called upon to do so. That's what happened to young girls that got kicked off plantations with or without their kid.

Did she ever ponder if Isaac would keep his part of the bargain? Well, Louvenia was sent away, wasn't she? It was the very day Miss Burney noticed Louvenia was with child. You see, there came the hour when Isaac confessed in a drunken stupor that he'd had her. But the coda to his confession was that Burney had Sister first. Miss Burney sought blood for the betrayals. Yes, we all heard the shouting from the upstairs windows at the big house. Louvenia was barely fourteen and had lost the baby, a little girl. Nobody 'round the shacks talked about it. Anyway, how was Sister's story different from all the others dredged through our collective shame?

Louvenia wasn't a strong woman when her life away from the Burneys' put her on shaky footing that would head her straight for Jesse's alley. No, in most ways she was fragile, but she had a strong faith that kept her from selling her body like so many women were reduced to doing. But then she already knew what that was all about. One sale to ol' Isaac to stay with her folks had already netted her off the plantation with less than nothing. After somehow getting herself over the river to Vicksburg and days of wandering the alleys with nothing in her stomach, Jesse didn't look so old and ugly. Hunger makes you see things differently, because it all gets veiled in that thick fog stewing in your head that keeps your thoughts numbed.

Well, it had been a long time since Jesse Powell had been a young man, but my sister went with him anyway. She knew she was headed down her very last alley, and he was the only thing standing there with that "Come on over here and let's do some plain talking 'bout you and me" kind'a look. Turns out, he'd long been waiting for someone like Sister; spirit broken and head bowed only to see his dirty shoes staring up her dress at her marred innocence. A woman who was at the point where there'd be no turning back for something less frightening than what she saw standing in front of her. Men like Jesse can smell hopelessness before they even fork up a helping. To Jesse Powell, it didn't make no difference whom he picked; a woman had little value beyond what services she provided.

⁘

Soon after Brother and I arrived at Jesse's, Louvenia started washing down the kitchen walls. The scrubbing left them a bleached-out ochre color maybe like old shellac; yellowed from years of the nicotine left by Jesse, his older brother, their men friends, whores, gamblers and the hustlers that made up his sacred choir on gambling nights. They all knew Jesse's place was good for a laugh and to freeload whatever food Louvenia had somehow come by.

The kitchen was where Louvenia spent most of her time working the tubs to earn enough to pay our weekly rent to the landlord and the bribes to Jesse for the rent on our throats. I didn't do much back then but listen while Sister worked her tub. Sister's words could be razor sharp. They were meant to teach me 'bout surviving in the alleys. But then it was a sharp life out there that ate up those not already too lacerated by it all to be ready to survive.

Sister was a gentle soul, but I think she knew she wasn't surviving and was determined that somehow, I would. Over the years bent over tubs at Jesse's there were scattered times when we managed to sort our lives out from under the weight of our days—days made heavy as a coffin weighed down with the debris of his life.

Yes, time was worthless as most of our days poured into each other as quickly as we poured out that brown tub water in the alley. Late, soon after Jesse returned from the bars, Louvenia would scream and moan somewhere in the depths of her nights when he slapped her against the walls that jailed her. No, there was no one outside Louvenia's place who could hear it; there was too much screaming and moaning going on out there already. Another life broken? Can't fix nothing you can't see, so why open your eyes to some other woman's wailing? Everybody down that alley had her own wounds to decipher. "You still ain't seen my husband yet? He been gone for days now," a neighbor once asked with a shadow of terror hanging over her, knowing if his life was spent, hers would soon follow. It was always the same mantra we heard bouncing from those alley walls; dark thoughts penetrating deeper wounds aiming to break apart hopes. Uncountable were the nights Sister and I held our hands tightly over our ears to protect us from that familiar loop: one, two, three, four, smash, crash, collapse, plead and then the beg-again chorus. "No more, please no more!" she'd beg. "Please, no more!" How high can Jesus count the terrors ringing in my ears? Days follow each other in an ever-deepening haze when you don't count 'em. And no one did at the end of Jesse's alley. But then nobody had much to count period.

Deep in his sleepless nights Alex would lie on his pallet staring off somewhere deep in that corner of the room, his face hardened with rage. Him looking for that place I knew he wanted to go, needed to go, but like Louvenia and me, couldn't find a way out. How do you fix a soul? So much harder than the breaking of it was.

During these eternally long nights, Alex would pull his blanket over his head so he couldn't hear Jesse's gospels being taught Louvenia upside her head. Jesse, he figured he had to preach his gospels hard with his fist so's his meaning would more easily penetrate Sister's seeming reluctance to learn proper. Alex's chest could still hear what his ears denied. It heaved up and down just like somebody jumping on it—pushing all those scrambled dry tears out into the open. He had to hide these tears in the daylight where he knew a man couldn't admit to crying himself to sleep every night. That kind of admission puts a man face-to-face with his own impotence and the fear that those lurking in shadows of Jesse's alley would swallow him whole. What did Jesse fear? Who would get him his next bottle? Did that fear beat the life out of him long before Louvenia showed up, or would he have lost his soul somewhere at the bottom of a drop of bourbon all the same? My brother, he couldn't cry no more, not even in dry tears. Now he had to be a man, deal with Mr. Jesse. Yes, it seemed that his childhood had been hammered away along with his hopes and dreams.

Come mornings Louvenia would shuffle her bruises into the kitchen to get the water boiling for the tubs and then near mid-day we'd get Jesse's breakfast going before he headed out clinking his dice. What money we were able to collect from our tubs went to feed him first. Alex and I didn't mind missing meals. We'd gladly do anything to keep Jesse satiated so he'd stay away from our throats. Almost anything. Sister would never leave me alone if Jesse got up early and I was still sleeping in the corner of the kitchen. When he'd finally return from the bars, she'd sit on my cot as I slept till she heard Jesse snoring in the back room. Only then would she go back to her ironing. As I look back now, I truly don't remember my sister having slept in peace an entire night at Jesse's. From her labors bent over the tubs, to Jesse's stalking in from the bars at ungodly hours, where were the precious moments hidden that she could claim for herself?

Sometimes late, after Louvenia wrung out the last rag for hanging, she'd shuffle into the bedroom and collapse somewhere deep in her exhaustion. With Jesse gone, I'd go back there and fan Sister while she rested, just as Ella did Burney, or at least in my mind it was. Maybe not really. Why isn't Sister moving, I wondered? The very thought jolted me. No, she ain't dead, Lord. She moved her shoulder, I seen it. She's just breathing irregular again. Yet as my thoughts simmered in fear, I yet wondered as the distances between each breathe seemed to grow longer. My thoughts ran wild. I'll fan harder, then. I'm not that tired, am I? No more than the night before.

While I fanned, I seemed to always go back to wondering—what would Momma think of us now, so far from any dream she gave me on orchard nights? Would she find pride in us? But where would she see it? No, I best not try to see some for myself. Not now. Don't have time for pride anyway. I'll just let my thoughts drift somewhere better. What was Jackson doing now? No, I won't fall asleep across the bottom of Louvenia's bed. Hell couldn't be hotter than this here room and Sister needs a few moments' peace, so I'll keep fanning, yet I can't help but thinking there's no sight of a cool white veranda at the end of our long monotonous days. Just the same ol' humid steam from our tubs that sucks our breath and singes our thoughts when we dared to think about something else to make the day go easier. Things like how long will Jesse stay gone tonight, Lord? How long do I have to stay awake wondering, 'cause I sure need the rest? I could just shut my eyes here for a few moments, but if Jesse come back looking for more of our wash money on his way to another craps game and discovered Alex was up on the roof eating the food I'd fixed for him, there'd be no way down for Brother but a last jump. In those days, when we had a notion of jumping, we all knew there was only one direction. No, we didn't jump for joy. Not ever.

"I be gettin' up soon. Just some more to rest my eyes and I go finish my ironin'."

Sister's eyes never opened to see if I was nearby.

"You stay and rest, Sister; Jesse gone now," I said mopping her brow. Her thin worn blouse had turned to thick paste against her back.

"No, he not gone," she winced.

"He gone, Jesse gone. Left hours ago—won't be back till morning." I rubbed her rough hands gone cold even in that stifling heat.

"No… He not gone…"

The aches in her body told her he was still hovering over her life like a curse from Satan hunts down the vulnerable. She couldn't escape Jesse's shadow. No matter where he was, he could still menace the peace her soul hungered for.

Yes, Jesse was Louvenia's black dream, and he stalked her like a shadow forever.

LYE SOAP-BURNED DAYS

11

FROM THE FIRST days after I landed at Jesse's door, the clearest notion I owned was that my days would be spent over a washboard. Being only eight, I had no concept of what a decade was. That spared me from the horror of knowing that I'd be working the tubs for years to come.

I know you don't want to hear about washing no clothes. You done it, we all done it, so what? But with your raw hands did you do it for thirty years and then some? Because, Sister, that's where I been. Come, roll up your sleeves, wrap your forehead to keep the salty sweat out of your eyes and follow me to that place where the air gets mighty thin even as the sticky steam is thick enough to slice.

It's a complicated process, at least the part that helps you numb the drudgery. First, get yourself some strong lye soap, strong enough to eat a layer of skin off, got to get them clothes clean, but still not so strong your hands bleed and ruin your white woman's things. From the minute your hands touch that stinking water you learn to set your thoughts so you don't mind spending hours wearing out your washboard. But then you can challenge your mind on where the next meal may come from. I tell you, you can stand on your feet till it feels like you're standing on hot rocks just wondering on a plate of food alone. That's far enough away from the moment to keep your mind working alongside you. How do

I get there, that plate of food? What if my white woman don't pay me tonight? Well, there ain't gonna be no white veranda with a table set for me at the end of my day. But could there be a decent meal up ahead? So, if that table's a real place, why is it I can only get there through some conjured daydream? Why can't I just buy me a ticket and go stay a spell; that place where we could eat ever' day? What if it's just outside our part of town? But then what if it's far deeper into the white shadows than I will ever get to? Keep yourself wondering so the time passes. Got to, but then you ain't got no option, do you?

How many times did these trails of thoughts lead me to thinking I may have to jump to find it, find some peace of mind—the ultimate end to the drudgery. Is it possible I'd survive a jump from the roof? Does the Lord deliver cripples got nobody to care for them if only to free them from their misery? How many times did I ask myself over the years? Who would care if I jumped? It wasn't the person that just put his foot on my back stepping over me 'cause he was looking for that same place, a place of bounty free of the worries that we were both told was just up the road a block or two. Because, Sister, when you jumped out of your place in that alley you get yourself slapped back down. Those were the rules that weighed down my days. Never even thought of scrambling them to make them work better for me. But why not, for heaven's sake? I'll tell you why: 'cause when you're a child you don't ask yourself those questions, and then when your childhood's worn out of you, you're too hardened to care.

Back in those first years at Jesse's, I asked myself why I couldn't be out in that alley playing with the other little girls skipping and singing. Well, ain't got time for no playing, I'd remind myself. It became my mantra; such a strange tune for a child. Got to get the tub water hot no matter how hot this damned kitchen is. "Sister is waiting" was the chorus that rang loops in my head; "Sister is waiting, Sister is waiting… Lord, Sister is waiting." What will become of me if I ever get my hands on a stolen moment to reach for a borrowed dream or two? Well, today I won't think, on it and maybe then it will hurt less.

Back then hard-working folks wore their things for a week or more before they sent them out to one of us tub women. You don't figure a white woman with any money did laundry herself, do you? No, washing was for colored women, because we have strong leathery hands that don't bleed as bad from the lye soap burns. That's what one white woman told me, whose hands were so delicate they couldn't touch mine even with a stick. To pay me, she dropped her dime to the ground and stood there like it would give her pleasure to kick me if I didn't come up with a smile of thanks plastered on my face.

Some days, when Jesse was gone, Annie from across the alley would come by and drink sweet tea with Sister and me. She was married to the preacher and already had three little ones when I came to Louvenia's. Still Annie treated me like I was one of her brood and always greeted me with a hug. Sister so loved Annie's kids her eyes seemed to swallow them up when they came 'round.

While the laundry was drying on the porch, Sister and Annie would pull out a bag of rags and sit around the kitchen table making rag dolls for Annie's kids. Some days they'd only get an arm or leg double-stitched and stuffed before another tub load beckoned. I'd watch and listened to their woman-talk as I helped stuff. Other days little dresses or breeches were made from old shirts given to Sister by one of the white women she washed for. When the doll was finished, and a little mouth stitched on, there was a hunt in an old tin for two matching brown buttons for eyes. Buttons sewn on the doll would get a big kiss from Sister before handing it to one of Annie's kids. Their expressions of delight was all Sister sought for those hours of sewing. Few things delighted her more. Louvenia's gaze over Annie's kids told me so.

Days for my brother on Jesse's alley burned him badly, too. There'd be no more trips to the river's edge to fish with Daddy and Samuel. It was like Brother woke up one morning to find Jesse now hovering over him like another ol' Isaac there waving his fist in his young face. Jesse wasn't ol' Isaac, but he was a mean drunk with no room in his heart for a young boy brimming with vitality and eagerness for life. Surely not a boy soon needing to figure out how to be a man among white folks who would not countenance a colored standing up like one.

But then Jesse was no man. His pride and virility was long spent when I arrived even as his life lingered to feed off ours. I long figured Jesse had lost his soul by yanking ours down dead ends to keep us tethered to him. Belts to women defined his manhood and this dominance was the only thing on his mind 'cept whiskey and whores. Yes, it was an endless cycle of yanks his way to tend his daily needs. No, we never went far from that alley. Jesse's game was all diversionary, wasn't it? He had to have known that if he didn't drag us along on the skids of his life we might up and head in the opposite direction, leaving him with only an empty bottle to bitch at. Drowning folks cling to anybody to get to that next drink. Jesse held our heads under the currents till the bitter end. Even that young, Alex easily reminded Jesse he was a bit of a nothing. Surely that gnawed on the ol' man. From the first day he threatened to toss Brother out, till he did.

My Brother, he'd never be caught doing woman's work like laundry, but was always there to help us get the white folks' things back to their side of town. Sister couldn't get out much by then, as all those cracked ribs and sprained ankles from slipping on Jesse's wet rage kept her home like a prisoner. But Brother, he couldn't deliver by himself to the white woman's door, so we both had to go the distance. The holes in our shoes never lied that somehow, we had. Just Alex and me along those dark dirty streets with him carrying the folded things piled all the way to his chin. See, if a colored man walked across town and knocked on somebody's back door the wrong way, the door might 'a been answered with a shotgun blast for his proximity to the white woman's virtue. Seemed like so much violence for so little virtue, but guilty as charged nonetheless. Was there another verdict? No, but there was always another rope at hand. Alex would carry the heavy load of freshly washed clothes real careful so's not to wrinkle and give the woman an excuse not to pay me. Then he'd hide from sight when I walked up to her backdoor. There I'd be paid a few coins, pick up her dirty things she'd likely toss at my feet and we'd head back across the tracks. Even with Alex himself carrying her rags, I'd 'bout gag on the stench of the woman's dirty laundry. No wonder we couldn't eat some nights, even if we had food.

Don't ever 'member one of them white women offering a sip of water. Guess the charity her Christian Bible called for did not extend to coloreds. We were too primitive to understand charity, so why waste God's blessings on us? That what she thought? Best save it for the horses then. They value a sugar cube, don't they? Anyway, weren't there plenty of horse troughs for coloreds to drink from? Brother knew well enough even before I was old enough to understand, that colored women weren't safe walking at night. You could be robbed of your wash money, innocence, or life. Alex made sure I got home safely, or at least as safe as he could till I was delivered back to Jesse's porch, the trapdoor to his hell.

Deep in his sleepless nights, Brother would lay on his pallet in the corner of the kitchen trying to figure the ropes of his new life off the plantation. His face would go hard with anger as he stared off somewhere into the dead-end corners of them kitchen walls. Him looking for that place I knew he wanted to go, needed to go, but like Louvenia and me, couldn't find the path to get there. How do you fix a soul? Let me tell you, it's so much harder than the breaking was. I'm reminded by those long nights before Jesse threw him out, nights when Jesse wound Sister's head tight around his fist. Alex would pull his blanket over his head so he couldn't hear Jesse's preaching being taught Louvenia upside her head so's its meaning would penetrate her reluctance to learn proper. In anger, Alex's chest heard what his covered ears tried to muffle and would heave up and down like somebody jumping on it, pushing all those scrambled tears into the open. Tears he had to hide in the daylight where he knew a man could never admit to crying himself to sleep. Surely that kind of admission can put a man face-to-face with his impotence and the fear that he might soon lose his soul. Maybe the blackness of it all would crush his manhood into pool of drunken self-loathing like the kind Jesse was drowning in. So quickly came the day when Alex couldn't cry no more, not even dry tears. He had to be a man, deal with Mr. Jesse. The devil comes in many forms, Momma told me so. And Jesse knew the devil well enough to call in a favor or two.

No, it didn't take Jesse long 'fore he tossed Brother out and told him never to come back or he'd get the law on him by claiming he'd been stealing. Never could figure out what Jesse might say was missing. Our laundry money? Who stole that but Jesse himself? Sometimes, if Jesse was passed out in the backroom, Brother would sneak in to eat something Louvenia had set aside for him. Then he would snatch some sleep on my cot. Other times when Jesse was up, Alex would head off walking all night, hiding in the cold shadows where he was safer from being picked up for vagrancy, his crime being not having a job as a boy-man. Why'd it always seem Jesse slept fine 'cept on the nights that it froze hard out there, or rain pelted the tin roof over the porch so hard we couldn't sleep anyway? Those nights Jesse was guaranteed to get up and wander about the kitchen wanting us to fix him another meal. These nights there'd be no sleep for Alex over in the corner, even hidden behind our tubs. Still, we managed to get Alex out the back door many times before Jesse was sober enough to know Brother was sleeping on his kitchen floor again.

As the months bled into years, Louvenia and me came to feel no better off than a pair of mules. We dreamed, but our prayers were never heard. It was that old loop again: somebody wouldn't pay us for our ironing, or Jesse drunk us up, or one of his women needed a new dress and the money we dreamed might one day buy us a ticket out of Jesse's alley was gone again. Gone again! Gone again…gone again. I can still hear it ringing in my thoughts. These things don't never go away. Not ever.

Still, by the time I was a girl-women, I'd gotten sick of all that. So, I started taking the wash money and hiding it 'round the place where Jesse might not get to it. Made no difference; Jesse didn't need to hunt the money down himself. He knew where to find Louvenia easy enough. That's all it took to assure himself of another night at the bars. When he found her, I had to give it up—put our money in front of him and apologize for keeping him from his appointment with a bottle, or he'd beat the air out of Louvenia till she found the money herself. Sometimes I'd pull out ever' cent I'd hidden and throw it at his yellowed face. Louvenia, with her cracked ribs would scramble over the floor to retrieve every cent. Then Jesse, with a smirk pinned on his face, would disappear again. He'd head out to swaddle his women in the lies our money bought while I swaddled Louvenia's ribs in the same tattered cloth that barely held our lives together—I guess the kind rag dolls are made of. And you know, no matter how many times I wound that old cloth around our wounds, I never saw a beautiful blue silk monogram on it reminding me of the Burneys. Why are dreams so hard to build and yet so easy to wrench out of you?

They were different from mine, but still the rules weighed heavily on Alex's young back. He never took to learning to read or write; he just couldn't sit still long enough, and had the notion only silly women wanted to read and all. No, Brother had things he wanted to get done, places to go, his own special dreams brewing of how he was gonna save Louvenia and me. He shared this notion, 'bout saving us, to give me something to hope on. The thing is, he couldn't read the signs to know which doors he needed to knock on to open up a new way. Ever' day I learned from Louvenia and what she didn't know, I had to go find for myself. Even then Sister was there prodding me along and turning my face from the view behind to the one ahead of me. But Alex didn't have a man to protect him from the Jesses of the world. Nobody to tell him that what he saw in them alleys was seldom real, or even what a real life is built on. Yes, things were sure hard to decipher under the layers of ashes from the lives burnt out on that alley, 'cause there's a sleight-of-hand in life and if you don't know where or who it's coming from you lose over and over again. Then what nobody ever tells anybody is when you lose long and hard enough, before it's all over you've already given up. Yes, in all the dust stirred from folks slapping you on the back for being such a damned good sucker, you don't even know it's because you done lost it all and it's already deep in their pockets by then. Then all the folks that stood by the side feeding you lies have one more back to walk over, clawing their way to their dreams one way or another, one back to the next. It's nothing personal—that skin off your back, it's just one more dollar for nothing, a simple sleight-of-hand. Let me tell you, I would swerve from many such folks in the years ahead.

I go into a rage when I hear the hollow sound of a hand across the face of somebody not expecting it. No time to duck or run, that is if you're not already run out by then. Jesse beat Louvenia bad. He beat her 'cause he was hurting inside and needed whiskey to ease his agony. He beat her 'cause she had no respect for him, and he knew it. If you're a colored man and your woman don't respect you there ain't nobody else who will. But along that worn path to his own hell Jesse kept drinking and beating the life out of Louvenia. No, he didn't hit me much. Just now and then. Louvenia said it was 'cause I had Momma's eye, yet he beat my soul, didn't he? Just fixing Sister's wounds was enough to do that, let alone what I knew he'd try to do to me if he could. Bodies can heal; don't know if souls ever really do. Maybe they only go on bleeding till you're dead inside.

The days somehow, somewhere, became years for us marked in the ledgers of our memories by the hundreds 'a tubs we bent over. Too soon I was no longer a child and hadn't been for most my childhood. Our lives had quickly become a carousel of Jesse's abuses riding our souls up and down and then down to depths deeper than anybody could have imagined. No, you don't think about escaping much, 'cause you turn off all the thinking you can. It's part of survival. Right after thinking comes those feelings that plunge the knives deeper. Like: why me?

SEEING THE TINKER'S DEAL

12

WHEN I WAS near to being twelve Sister let me deliver the folded clothes by myself. But never more than five or six blocks on the other side of the tracks from where we lived. I loved the freedom I felt making those deliveries. I could loop around as many blocks as I wanted and gaze into windows of the stores where white women shopped. I always took as long as I could to get home to be away from that alley but also to be away from Louvenia and Annie, 'cause they'd both been at me. It seemed like Annie hardly ever looked my way that she didn't pause in her tracks and ask if I'd been reading the Bible. Even when she didn't ask her eyes followed me about. But she knew I couldn't read, barely knew my alphabet, that's why I was sure it was Louvenia who put her up to it 'cause I'd been sassing her. I knew it was coming; Annie telling me the Bible said I'd go to hell for sassing. But I wasn't too worried 'bout going to hell. No, I wasn't, as I figured Louvenia would never tattle to Jesus 'cause she knew I'd for sure tell the Lord right back that she'd been smacking me when I sassed. Ain't nobody gonna win on that, so we best keep it out of our prayers.

It was after I'd finished delivering when it all happened. I would have sold my soul for a jar of cool sweet tea it was so hot. I paused to wipe the sweat from my eyes and saw an old white man perched up on a cart wrestling with his merchandise. What was he fussing over like that?

I stood and watched the commotion. The barrels piled up on his cart were wobbling so they nearly fell over and all the while he was giving his horse the low-down. I could see that horse was having problems understanding the man's thick accent. No, nothing would stay up piled-up on that cart, and he looked too old to be climbing up and down to fetch things. That's what I heard him say to his horse, and the horse never uttered a word to disabuse him. Reckon that ol' swayback was thinking they'd get home quicker if he kept his mouth shut and didn't get into it with that ol' tinker.

But no sooner had he climbed back up in the seat than a big barrel tipped off the back of his overloaded cart and rolled near in front of me. Stuff spilled out all over and that old man, he didn't look like he was none too happy, no, and his horse just turned the other way.

"What's all this stuff?" I asked. "Any of it still good?" I always heard Louvenia ask the same question, wanting to know what the value is 'fore she pulled her purse out. She said she could read a person's eyes to know if they was lying or not.

"Them mostly books, Missy, nobody wants 'em. So, you get a good price, but only today," he said. "'Cause if I have to pick 'em up again, the price goes up."

"If nobody wants 'em, then why I want 'em? I can't read none."

"Why not, colored girl, you blind, or somethin'?" he asked, looking right into my eyes looking right back at his.

"Now if you ain't blind, then you can for sure see I ain't blind!" That's the way I told folks off. And no, that ain't sassing.

"I can see good enough," he said, "and what I see is you can't see nothin', Sister."

About then I got a feeling that this man had gots to be a crazy. Like them ones hanging 'round the corner from the alley. I wondered if that was why his horse was looking the other way. He was embarrassed at what come out of that ol' man's mouth.

"Sister, huh?"

I walked up closer so's he could see I sure enough had two good eyes and they was working him over good to see what he was up to and he best see I sure as hell wasn't no sister of his! Well, up there close I could sure see that his mouth worked better than his eyes. He squinted and furrowed his brow till his nose wrinkled to the top of his forehead, which seemed to trigger his mouth all over again.

"There's different kinds of blindness," he said looking at me like the sun was blinding him, 'cept the sun was near down by then. "And I reckon the kind you're afflicted with feels good, don't it, Sister?"

"Yeah, what kind you talkin' 'bout then?"

"Ignorance! You know it like a sweet friend, don't ya? Can't read no fine books like these here I'm offering at a special discount. That's why I brung 'em 'round for you today. Didn't ya see 'em comin'?"

"Yeah, I saw you deliver 'em to my feet. Heaven help us if I took the other way home! Then you gonna tell me that barrel been rollin' up and down these streets lookin' for me?"

"You ever seen books roll up to somebody ain't ignorant and then stop to help 'em fix that? Now that don't make sense, 'less you're ignorant, I reckon," he said.

I wondered to myself when was he gonna pass the collection plate for that sermon. I patted his poor ol' horse's head so he'd feel less humiliated.

Well, I had my own view of the situation. But I didn't want to get into it with no crazy ol' white man. So, after looking at him long and hard, I decided to tell him off like Louvenia did the butcher who sold her a pound of gristle that time. No, I wasn't gonna let this tinker take up more of my time and think he was gonna get away with it.

"I ain't ignorant and it ain't my best friend! How much them books, in case I ever wanna know?"

Ain't used books like day-old bread? They got bargains on stale bread, don't they? Anyway, that proved I wasn't no ignorant colored girl. Silly fool!

"A silver dollar and they's all yours, Sister!"

"What?" At that I got to thinking he ain't half as crazy as he been acting, that ol' man.

"A silver dollar! I ain't got no silver dollar, do I? Anyway, I can see they ain't worth half a nickel and you know it!"

"No? Well, there you have it. Them books down there, all for a nickel, and the rest on credit. Yep, you take 'em! Then if you don't read 'em up in a year, you can bring 'em back to get your money back. All five cents of it."

While I was thinking on the deal, I moved my head side to side to see if his eyes followed. I got to thinking he might be working the kind of deal like Louvenia told me some of her customers had. Them white women asked her for credit but then just paid with more of their filthy rags 'fore they hit and run out of town, not paying for weeks of ironing. Maybe this tinker's deal was different. Didn't know, but I knew I had to think on the terms and keep an eye on him eyeing me.

"You get slow to thinkin' when you're half blind, ain't ya Sister?"

"I ain't the one that's blind here!"

Still, I started thinking there had to be a reason that barrel near rolled down the street and right up to my poor tired feet. These books meant for me then? Would I be blind if I didn't recognize a good deal when it near rolled over me? A nickel down and the rest on credit like Louvenia worked out at the grocer's?

"Well, then take a good deal when it rolls your way."

He talked like he'd read my thoughts. Stupid man. After handing him a nickel, I picked those books up, dusted them off and started off. I'd never worked a deal on credit before, and was eager to tell Sister all about it, thinking myself quite the businesswoman!

Then I got to thinking and yelled back, "Hey, Mr. Tinker Man, how I know you're gonna be here in a year if I wanna return these here books and get my nickel back?"

"If I ain't here, my cousin sure will be. Get your nickel back from him. Anyway, I seen yer kind, you can't think ahead that far, Sister!"

Well, well, he was thinking he sees things better than me, but still thought I was his sister even after I told him off!

As he loaded up his stuff he yelled, "You drive a hard bargain, missy!"

And I knew I had, too.

I headed back and didn't stop for more wash soap like I 'pose' to, 'cause I was too eager to tell Louvenia 'bout the big deal I'd made.

Figured I'd leave them books on the table to prove to Louvenia and Annie I was the best deal maker 'round Jesse's alley. Sure, I thought, there stacked in front of them was proof.

Sister was finishing the last of the ironing as I walked in. I piled them books on the table and waited for Louvenia to figure out what I had going. Then, without a word I went to pour us a jar of sweet tea. Sister stopped her ironing, looked at me closely and sat down. I told her 'bout them books rolling off his cart and over to my feet where they near tripped me! Louvenia looked as though she'd never heard of such a stupid man in her life.

"He was the stupidest blind man I ever seen!" I continued.

But then I began to wonder if I shouldn't have just stepped over them books and ran, not walked home! Yes, ma'am. I could have skipped this meeting with Louvenia and gotten to bed without the grief that was waiting for me as Sister and I struggled over the damned deal I'd just made. You see, she kept on patting them books and saying "My, my," like they were gonna give her their side of the story, and that being different than mine!

"My, my, don't we got the deals goin' on 'round here?" she said again. "Sure looks like it," she replied to herself. "If you hadn't hauled his books away, then he'd have to get down off his cart, pick 'em up and then go back to sellin' 'em all over again the next day. Wouldn't he? That right? And he never got it right today, huh? So, don't know how it's gonna be any better tomorrow."

I could see Louvenia understood the situation, and expected her to ask me if I told that tinker off like she did the butcher who sold her the gristle.

"So, I gots the better deal than him? Did I? Huh?"

"Well, it would sure seem. But then only if you don't end up haulin' them books all the way back 'cross town a year from now to get your nickel back. That be the case, he's gonna say you're the stupidest colored girl 'round to keep haulin' stuff that's worthless back and forth and, well, who knows where it could all end? You followin' me, Sister?"

"Don't know, do I? That means they's worthless and he gots the best deal and my nickel?"

"Well, you don't know how to read is the thing. But that didn't keep you from haulin' these here books down the alley along with a bag of dirty laundry. What was he thinkin', I wonder? Now, let's see here. We gots to figure this out. Don't want any stupid ol' man getting the best of my sister. No, I won't have it!"

"That's right!" I replied, yet really had no idea to what.

Louvenia picked up one of my books and examined it carefully, like she was looking for the value of the deal. Like pears from a farmer's cart was the way she looked them over. Don't want pears with bruises gonna go bad on you the next day. She looked close at them books and then even closer at me. What's that all about? She can't read none herself. She expects that book to tell her something? That ain't no pear. You got to be able to read to know what that book's got to say, I was thinking.

Then it hit me why Sister seemed to be working over the terms a bit too hard, like there might be a bit of gristle hidden in there. So, I grabbed that book and tossed it back on the table, so she knew, too!

"Then I just learn to read and them books gonna be all used up, and I gots the best deal and don't need to do no haulin' cross town to get my nickel back 'cause they's useless, huh?" I blurted in one breath.

"Well, you see then, he ain't as clever as you, Sarah. When you see 'im down there again, you tell 'im you ain't gonna be bringin' no books back 'cause you used 'em up already. He shouldn't waste his time trying to work a better deal. Not with my sister, that's for sure. See what he thinks on that. That silly ol' man!"

"Yeah, that's what I'll say to him. See what he thinks on that for sure!"

"Don't even know how a man can stay in business who is so simple-minded."

Sister finished her sweet tea like the meeting was over. Still, I was left wondering if Louvenia and I were truly traveling on the same side of the road. You see, I always got suspicious when we agreed on anything without rolling in the dirt first. So, I looked at Louvenia long and hard to see if she'd figured something out I hadn't. She went back to her work shaking her head at how unbelievably stupid that old man was to try to cut himself a better deal off of me.

On the other hand, maybe she wanted me to think something like that. Well, what did she want me to think? So, I went to bed that night wondering. But the next day I knew for sure. Sure did! Sister come back from Annie's with an arm full of dirty clothes, walked onto the porch where I was hanging wet clothes like she was aiming to get into it with me.

"Annie gots a couple of loads of her kids' things we got to help her with."

She stood there holding them things as if she had something hidden in them. Like maybe a stick. What's she got going on, I wondered?

"Yeah, so put 'em down over there, Sister. I'll do 'em after I finish Miss Brown's uniforms."

"She wants to pay you."

Louvenia kept holding onto that pile and looking at me as though she knew something I didn't. Or maybe I'd sure enough not want to know and she knew it, too.

"Pay us? She ain't got no money with all them kids," I said. "Just put 'em down there, 'less you're gettin' attached to 'em the way you're huggin' 'em."

Sister looked at me like she always did when I sassed and was about to head my way with the flyswatter. She shifted the pile in her arm and glared at me as if I didn't hear her the first time. "Annie says she gots to pay you! But she gots no money—that's what."

Then she started looking down her nose at me like she was ready to roll in the dirt for sure. I knew that look! "Yeah, so Louvenia, I do up her things and she pays me with nothin'. That suit you?"

"Yeah, that'll be fine. But not for Annie. She gots to pay somehow. You know how she is, Sarah."

I gulped and jumped in quick. "Now, don't take one of her kidney pies, 'less you're gonna feed it to Jesse!"

"See, that's what I was thinkin', too. We always think alike, don't we?" Louvenia announced.

"Yeah? Since now? And why are you clutchin' them dirty clothes like that? They gonna get away from you, or you got something hidden in there? Like one of her kidney pies you can't stand the smell of?"

"Best let her do what she can and keep her kidney pies home, huh? You're right, I agree with you, Sarah. You know what's best then. So then Annie's comin' over some afternoon when Jesse's gone, to start you on your readin'. That's what we'll do 'bout this. Hear me now?"

And I sure enough had. "Readin'? I got no time for readin'!"

I tossed some dirty shirts I was sorting into my tub, churned and pounded them on that washboard to show her what I would do to her and Annie if they fussed at me while I was trying to get my work done.

Louvenia closed in like she wanted to see if I'd gone crazy on her or maybe deserved a smack. She looked down into my tub and shook her head, for having no water in that tub where I was wringing the necks on them shirts.

"I ain't never heard of washing with no water. Have you now, Sarah? Well, I guess you have now, huh? Nope, not a drop of water in that tub."

"Then what do you want me to do with her kids' things?" I asked.

"Well, you might as well haul 'em back over there," she said, "'bout like you're gonna do with them books in a year 'fore your credit run out and tell her, her kids best wash 'em them little selves, huh?"

Louvenia looked down into my tub again like I was sure missing the point, so I knew for sure she was getting in my face. That's how Louvenia always starts things with me; she comes from behind and then asks me why I's standing in her way.

"How's Annie know how to read anyway?" I thought if Annie didn't really know how to read, then I'd stop this nonsense cold! We'd just sit there at the table over our sweet tea like any other day and talk 'bout that tinker man that's just plain stupid as can be. Then we could all agree I gots the best deal and be finish with it.

"'Cause her husband's the preacher and he teached her and you know it, too! Now you're the big deal maker 'round here. You gots a better notion? You been pickin' them books up day after day and lookin' 'em over like they was gonna teach you to read just by handling them."

"No, I ain't been pickin' 'em up 'cept they was in my way. And you been puttin' 'em in my way. I seen you do it, too!"

As Louvenia glared I went over and grabbed Annie's kids' things, tossed them in a tub and commenced churning the hell out of them like the devil been in that pile hiding and I was the one gonna cleanse his black heart with lye soap. Amen, Lord. Never once did I take my eyes off Sister so's she'd know I was on to her good. But that damned water she poured in my tub was so hot I started thinking it would be easier on me if I just learn to read some. Yeah, you don't know my sister—hell of a lot easier!

So I figured I'd only go to pretending to read, thumb through them old books, just like I seen her doing ever' time I looked over at her, looking over at me with a book in her hand. That would fix the problem. I was sure gonna teach her to mess with me!

"Then I just learn to read. So, Annie be happy that her bill got paid and her kids got clean clothes and we don't got to choke on no kidney pies."

"I don't see any other way out of it," Louvenia declared as if I'd fallen to the bottom of that tinker's barrel and she was the one who'd saved me! Hallelujah!

"You do cut a mean deal for sure."

Still I had the feeling them books were gonna cause me nothing but grief, no matter how good the deal was. Sister stood there quite pleased with herself. But then she'd won again!

❧

It was 'bout two days later, before I'd even got the chance to burn them books out in the alley, that Annie showed up—should I say sneaked up? She was looking quite official like she was on a mission to save souls and I was next in line. She walked in while I was finishing ironing her kids' things and stood there without a word. She could not have pinned her eyes on me better if she had Louvenia's clothespins on her.

I turned to Sister and got some of that eyebrow of hers, the one that arches like it wants to fly off her face when she's mad. What's wrong with these here women today, I wondered? They was giving me the eye 'cause they suddenly can't talk no more? I heard their big mouths flapping like crows out in the alley just moments before. 'Cept Louvenia, I could read her a bit better. She was giving me the "I got a stick and I'm gonna put it to your head" look again.

"Annie, you got something to say standing there eyeing me, or you just come over to make snortin' noises?"

Annie stood there with her mouth wide open, acting as though she was so insulted she'd turned speechless.

"Now, you know better than talkin' like that," Annie said, but looked to Louvenia.

Sister was sure looking high and mighty while I burned my fingers on that iron, watching them act like they was aiming to get me to the ground to get the kinks out 'a my hair—that's the way they was looking at me. But I didn't care none, 'cause I knew how hot my iron was and could fight them both off if they ganged up to pull my hair for sassing.

"Louvenia, you got something goin' on here that you want me to figure out before the Second Comin'?"

Then I poured the last of the sweet tea and drunk it up in front of 'em so they'd know I was on to them good.

But I wasn't, was I? I was just acting foolish 'cause I had a feeling Annie come over to get me to the table and force-feed me printed words. Kink by kink, wouldn't bother Sister none. I could see that plain 'cause she had a notion I was embarrassed not knowing my alphabet. But you see, I did know some of it, 'cause Jackson Burney teached me. He ran out of hard candy bribes at the letter "U", so I refused to learn more till he stole more from his daddy's jar on his desk. But he said I'd never need the rest of the letters anyway, so we went to doing something else, like laying eggs in our chicken nests in Miss Burney's roses. But Annie here, I could tell she been talking to Louvenia behind my back. They knew how to get me to the ground even without a stick in their hands. Yes, Annie hit me right upside my head with her sermon about white folks getting better stuff than folks on our side of town.

"Now, Sister Sarah, you know white folks don't want us to read none. You drink up all that sweet tea, honey? 'Cause if we can read, we just might be expectin' the same stuff they gots on their side of town. Now, you know they ain't gonna take to that business, 'cause they like feelin' they gots all the good stuff comin' their way and we're only here to clean up, right, Sister Louvenia?"

Louvenia stuck her nose in the air to confirm that business 'bout white folks.

"If you want to stay on the good side of white folks," Annie continued, "don't learn to read none. Hear me? They like us simple and ignorant."

Annie never looked at my sister, but I was still watching her out the corner of my eye. I knew they'd rehearsed this out in the alley. But they surely had a stick upside my head just the same, one on each side. Like damned book ends, the two of them were squeezing my head in a vice 'cause they knew I wasn't gonna take to white folks thinking I was no better than to clean up after them.

"You learn that sermon from the preacher?" I asked Annie.

Sister didn't take to my disrespect none. So, she moved closer to Annie's side to make sure I could see her glaring at me better.

Thank goodness it wasn't pouring rain in our kitchen, 'cause Sister would have drowned her nose was up so high. So, I sat down across from Annie and picked up one of those damned books. Sister must not have believed my intent to learn, 'cause she moved the ironing board over there near the kitchen door like a stockade and then went to get the iron heating off the stove for reinforcements against my possible escape. Well, Annie opened a book and started pointing out the alphabet and we started writing it down.

That's how all that got started; me reading and all. I guess I'd been thinking reading was something for folks who planned on going some-place in life and that never included girls like me, so I best just get my hands down in my wash tub so we could eat that day and forget about tomorrow. Dreaming was for others who had the time to waste on it. And yet from then on, I never moved ahead on the journey without a book nearby to help me find my way to something I'd only wondered existed out there.

CLIMBING IN A BOX
TO GET OUT

13

LOUVENIA HAD BEEN imprisoned in Jesse's jail for nearly ten years by the time my brother and I came to her. She was convinced that what Jesse had told her could only be true: if she left him, he'd get the law on her the moment she squirmed out his door. He warned that she'd go no further than the chain-gang he'd convinced her had to be all but waiting just around any corner she might turn.

Sister must have heard an echo of ol' Isaac in Jesse's words. When you live in brutality long enough, the layers of scars blind you to your options. There were precious few at the end of that alley, so best stay at your ironing board with the curtains pulled tight so you don't look out and only see yourself slowly dying.

We seldom left that hell hole of a kitchen 'cept to deliver our ironing or go buy more soap to pour into more tubs. Sure, it was easy to blame Jesse—a poor soul also a slave, slave to his bottle—but we had to find a way out, Louvenia and me. Mind you, I knew the two options for our women: bent over the tubs or being a whore. Got nothing against whores, but my momma put the fear of the Lord into me, and if there's anything I feared more than the Lord, it was Minerva up there with Him. That's the only thing ol' Isaac and I had in common: Don't want to cross that Minerva.

I kept thinking and daydreaming on it but still not really knowing for what. Guess it was only pieces of thoughts I'd strung together in my imagination. Like maybe dreaming of where a life of dignity awaited. Where is that? Didn't matter what the place was called. Momma told me a soul is a place to hide your dreams from the white folks. What she never knew was that we had to hide our dreams from plenty of coloreds, too, like the folks who stalked them alleys as well as Jesse, the man who stalked us in his four walls not much bigger than a wooden box.

Mornings when Jesse was snoring in his backroom, Louvenia and I started whispering. What 'a we do? We had that laundry business going good—why did we take it from him day in and out? Him busting our hopes as easy as he busted our lips like we was nobodies—but still nobodies good enough for him to live off. I figured if Jesse was not there at least what pennies we made would be ours. But Louvenia told me she done seen chain gangs and was scared he could all but rise to shackle her—the only promise he ever made that he was sure as hell to keep. How many times had he suddenly risen from a drunken stupor and put her face on the floor? Strangely, she didn't seem to be as scared he might one day up and kill her to make room for one of his whores whose names he blurted in his drunken sleep. Hard to understand how terrifyingly deep that dry well a colored woman can fall into when she's face-to-face with her own door and knows the only thing truly waiting on the other side is her final prayer what with no money, place to go and nobody to turn to. And yet all the same, even when you're kicked to the ground, life can keep booting you ever closer to that dark bottomless well, the one filled with the stench of rotting desperation, a place where no prayers are ever uttered.

"Look at them whores outside Jesse's alley," Louvenia challenged. "They know what I's talkin' about!"

Whores getting beaten in them alleys is what she meant. Life had taught us that when you jumped, it wasn't for joy. No, best not chance it. Stay put. Hug the ground like Jesse admonished, so the next storm wouldn't put you into a pine box six feet under. But even the whores figured they was better than us 'cause they didn't have their hands down in no tub of stinking brown water.

Most of the time Sister and I knew where each other stood on things, and we seldom stood far apart. But she'd somehow survived those years with that ol' man before Alex and I fell into her life. From those dark times I would come to understand that there were things she couldn't put to words. Things still too scabbed to pick open again. Why is shame the wound that resists healing?

One morning while Sister was ironing, and I was twisting the water out of shirts to hang, my jabbering about going on without Jesse got Sister cross. I still recall a saddened look of frustration and anger that seemed to weave through her expressions. She put her iron down and pointed to the table for me to take a seat.

"What?" I asked.

"Sit down over there. I got things to tell you. Things I should 'a told you before," she said. "Ugly things I don't want to go back to but now I reckon it's time. You got to know now."

"Know what, Sister?"

"You're always goin' on like all we need to do is stuff a pillowcase with our things and step out that kitchen door ridin' on nothin' but a big smile. Maybe like we ain't never gonna have to beg Jesse to take us back. But I know better, and I'm gonna tell you what I know, too!"

Louvenia paced the kitchen shaking her head like she was cursing at the very recollections she didn't want to look at again. I sat down to hear what she had to say.

"Not long after I came to Jesse, he told me he was gonna rent a buggy and we was gonna get out of town. Go for a picnic."

"Jesse take you on a picnic? When did he ever rent a buggy?"

"You just hush and let me tell you 'bout Jesse's picnic," she said. "He told me to make up a basket of food. And I did. Baked fresh bread the night before; fried us some ham and Annie give me some mustard she'd made. Even baked a cake. Never since I met that man had we gone nowheres I recall. Then I carried the basket to the stables. Jesse say I carry it 'cause his back was hurtin'."

"Jesse's back hurt so bad he couldn't carry no basket of sandwiches?"

"He rented us a buggy. Went all the way out of town and then down some dusty county road."

"Where was that?" I asked.

"Don't know. Just figured he knew a place where we could eat under some trees or maybe near a pretty stream. But then I seen for sure where we was headed. Way up there, in a cloud of dust there was these folks workin' a ditch. They was all colored and Lord, there was women in with 'em. I asked Jesse why we was headed over there. He told me he had somebody he been wantin' me to meet. Jesse stopped where them folks was working their picks and shovels. Them poor folks looked up but couldn't hardly see 'cause they was so blinded by that hot sun and the dirt covering their faces wet with sweat."

"What were they doin'?" I asked.

"They was diggin' a drain ditch along the county road. I tell you, there'd not been a hotter day that summer! No, ma'am." Sister paused like she needed to catch her own breath. "Hard labor, I 'magine. I was watchin' when a man fell over on the side of the road. Don't think he ever got up. Nobody done nothin' for him. Nothin'. Not even give 'im a swallow of water."

"Lord, Louvenia, why'd Jesse go there for a picnic?"

"Then Jesse waved to a man standing there watchin' over 'em all. You know that man was like ol' Isaac that watched us in the fields at the Burneys'. Jesse nodded to 'im. That man, with a grin on his big ugly face headed over. Lord Jesus, I got to thinking that he had that same evil look that Jesse does."

"Were you scared?"

"Jesse, he say to me, 'I want you to listen to me and listen good 'cause I ain't gonna say it but once. There ain't but one reason I took you in, and it ain't 'cause I wanted to look at that face of yours. No, Ma'am, it sure enough ain't.' He say, 'I only married you 'cause I gettin' old and gonna need somebody to take care 'a me when I need it, and that's all you's good for. You got nothin' else that interests me. No, you sure as hell ain't. But if you ever figure on headin' out, you be right down there in that dirt with them other niggers. Look at 'em good, 'cause you'll be down there yourself digging your way back to me with a pick and shovel. And Lord, you know I mean it, woman! You be digging your way back to where I told you never to stray and then be on your knees thankin' me for what I done give you, marryin' you and all.'"

"My Lord, Sister!"

"Just as that man come up to the buggy, I asked Jesse who them folks were. Jesse, he grabbed the basket off my lap and handed it over to the man with the ugly grin. He yanked the rag off the top and tossed it to the ground and went to eatin' my sandwiches like he'a hog. Jesse say to 'im, 'You tell Louvenia here who them folks yonder are. She gots to know to keep 'er straight with me and doin' what I tell 'er.'"

"That man, with a mouth full of my food, he say, 'Sister, that there is a nigger chain-gang. They's worthless. Owe the man money. But they ain't got none, so they come work the roads or the county ditches. They earn a quarter a day, and ever' cent goes to pay off the boss. Yeah, done lost me one just now. Think he's dead over there from heatstroke, that one,' he gestured to the man covered with so much dust you couldn't no more make out his face."

I was speechless.

Sister continued, "Jesse, he say to that man, 'Tell Louvenia 'bout them women over there!' The man grinned, and with his dirty hand grabbed a fist full of my cake and shoved it in his mouth, nodding to Jesse as he swallowed it down. 'Them women, they's whores, ain't they Jesse? Yeah, look at 'em. Dirty whores is all they is. Sure they are. They don't work hard enough out here. Ain't that right? You can plainly see for yourself. So, they got to give me overtime. End of the day, they service the men here. Yeah, they sure as hell do! The man that works hardest and gives me no grief, he first at 'er while the others watch. Then they gets their turn on her. Don't make no difference, she a whore.' That's what that man said, then went to laughin' like it was at me. Jesse, he laughed with him and turned the buggy 'round and headed back. That was my picnic that day. So, you still think it's easy movin' on? I got nowheres to go. Got no money, and after living in this alley I got no name people gonna respect. You see, Jesse and me, we weren't never really married, and you know what that makes me! So, now where we go? Huh? Well, you ask Jesse. He'll tell you where we had that picnic, 'cause that's 'bout where we'd end up!"

"But where we headed if we just stay here?" I replied. "We're climbing into a box. A pine box Jesse gonna nail shut and put six feet under the dirt," I said. "Ain't that also a 'where' you can't find on no map?"

"Let me tell you something else. That man, that nigger watching the others like a white slaver, you know who that was?"

"You know 'im?" I asked.

"That man is Jesse's brother, Fred. That Fred Powell. After that day, he started comin' 'round here to eat my food till he and Jesse got into it over a whore. No, he ain't no better now. Workin' for the man and his chain-gang off the backs of folks like me, he was back then. No, he ain't no better, 'cause I know what he does now with them women at the bars! He works the alleys with 'em!"

∾

At times I wondered if maybe Jesse could read our thoughts; we were sure he could. At least there were days when he seemed to sense there was something stirring behind his back.

Sister was still ironing one night, and I'd just washed my hair in the kitchen sink when he come out from his sleeping room like he was on the prowl and maybe wondering where he could situate our next helping of bruises. Yes, he watched night and day like he watched over his bottles. We were his bottles. That night, just as I was headed off to deliver our ironing, Jesse stopped cold, looked about as though something was amiss. Angrily, he looked as though he was gonna belt us.

"What's that girl doin' gettin' dolled up 'round here?" he asked Louvenia, standing next to me with the brush. "That a new dress that girl's got on? Huh?"

"That ain't no new dress, Jesse. You know it ain't," Sister replied in barely a whisper, as she knew he was looking for a fight. "Just one the neighbors passed down." Then she jumped to defend against his next accusation. "Where would we get money to buy a piece of fabric? I only put a new collar on it cut from an old white shirt one of my ladies give me. That ol' shirt was too small for you to wear," she said. "Sarah, hadn't you best get on with deliverin' your ironin' 'fore it gets dark. Go on now."

"Yeah, then bring me back a bottle or don't come back through my door, lil' girl. That's all I got to say to you!" Jesse snorted.

"Now, Jesse, you knows Sarah can't go buy you a bottle. She only twelve. I go get it when she comes home with the money, 'less you want me to go and leave you alone with your supper burnin'."

"That girl gots too high opinion of herself. You seen that? Yeah, well I sure enough have!"

"I sure seen lots of things, Jesse," Sister responded.

"Huh? If that keeps up, she be out on the streets like that boy, Alex. You remind 'er what I done to him for not respectin' me!"

"Don't worry, Jesse. Sarah ain't never gonna forget what you did to Brother that winter."

And the hurts piled up like lash scars; layer upon layer crisscrossing the backside of her soul. Jesse easily reminded me there were nigger dogs of all colors.

"I ain't in the mood for you," Jesse announced for the third time. "I'm goin' over to my brother Fred's. Yeah. May not come back tonight. You think on that!"

And, Lord how long had we? We'd been thinking on him walking out the door with his stolen laundry money and borrowed pride and getting so damned tripped up on his own life that he never found his way back. Yes, we prayed hard that before it was too late for us there'd come a day we'd step out of the box we were in—the pine box that might soon be our coffin if we didn't move fast enough.

Daydreams in the Nightshade

14

WELL, THE CHANGES came even if slowly. Our days were like standing tiptoe on a wobbly stool as Jesse was once again in good with Brother Fred. They'd teamed to court bottles and the women that followed the good times. Sometimes Jesse never made it back from Fred's place after the bars closed. That meant a bit of peace here and there for us. Even hours without curses bouncing off the walls and reflected off our swollen lips. Sister and I celebrated these mornings when Jesse never come home by pretending he was really gone for good. Amen, Lord. Amen, he gone!

You see, by then Louvenia and I had worked things out; we left food on the table for Jesse so's he had something to do with his mouth when he got up, which quickly put him in the mood to find the door and head to the bar. At the table with his plate of food Jesse seldom spoke to us and, Lord, we never answered when he did. By then his days were so blurred he never knew what direction he was swerving to or from. Monday was a full bottle, after a few drinks and nap or two and he'd somehow landed himself on Friday night all over again. Or had he really just gotten through the last Friday? "Who said that?" he blurted from his many stupors. But he had yet to realize that there was no one there to answer his knock at the door.

The day came when my hours over an ironing table got me counting more than the piles I had to get through. Mind you, the numbers were never large, but I counted things that meant something to me: a bit more laundry money hidden away, or just a day not pulled down by utter exhaustion long before night came. Even a nice pie good Annie left us could bring one of those splintered laughs from Sister. Made me smile, too. I thought about these rare moments of happiness and wondered where I could find more of the same.

Back then Alex would come by from time to time when Jesse was most likely to be passed out or still lost somewhere in a jute joint hunting the furrows of his empty pockets for the money he'd stolen from us. The money he'd already spent. To signal Brother it was safe to stop for a meal, I'd put the saltshaker in the window. It was our code things were safe in Sister's kitchen. However, one day I'd forgotten to take that shaker down and here comes Brother up on the porch though Jesse was still back there and Louvenia was paying the price of him having emptied his last bottle the moment when he badly needed another drink. Who gots to pay for that? You see, Sister had scrapped together enough to pay off the grocer for six months food bills. That left nothing for whiskey to slosh on Jesse's daily drought. Them times you know it was Louvenia's head that had to make up the shortage. When he was without a drink, the blackness of Jesse's existence quickly reflected off Sister's blackened face. Brother had committed to killing Jesse the next time he sent his fist her way. Now the time had arrived.

Alex walked in with his usual big smile. But when he heard Louvenia's shriek from the backroom his smile turned upside down as his fists turned right side up. Lord, Lord…Jesse was for sure gonna die that night! Brother's grimace told it.

"Alex, Jesse gonna see you here!"

He rolled up his sleeve readying to kill the ol' man. Sister's howls of anguish were shaking the cardboard-patched walls.

"I'm gonna kill that ol' man!"

Alex' face hardened with rage and his shoulders heaved as if he was gonna pounce right through the door to Jesse's head.

"Stop and hear me now, Brother. You know there ain't nothin' we can do. He say he ain't never gonna let Sister out of this house alive. Don't let this be the night he makes good on his promise."

"You gotta get out of here!" he said.

"That was Sister's head you heard lookin' for the door. I leave, then who gonna bandage 'er? What'a he do to her then?" I knew I had to think fast to stop Brother from killing Jesse. "You go on now 'fore he knows you're here and comes at you," I whispered. "Go buy me some wash soap at the corner grocer. Maybe he be passed out by the time you get back."

"You talk like you're oldest. I's the oldest, now ain't that right?"

I knew Alex's talk was aimed to cut through his powerlessness. Course Louvenia was really the oldest, but she was gone from the Burneys', so Alex maintained this somehow made him oldest.

"Well, it sure enough was when you stepped into this kitchen. But if you don't go he gonna get the law on you. He gonna say things so they take you in. You know he will, too."

Young men put their lives on the line and then pause to think afterwards—after their broken egos have settled in the ruins they brought down on themselves.

Louvenia came into the kitchen. Her face was already blue—or was that still from the last beating?

"Lord, Sister, Jesse busted your lip open again! You're bleedin' down your blouse."

"Get me a chip of ice. Glass 'a water." Her trembling hand dabbed at the blood dripping from her mouth.

"You best go now, Alex. Jesse, he possessed by Satan himself tonight. He gettin' dressed to go out. He gonna walk right by us swinging any minute."

Alex yammered 'bout Jesse needing to be put down for good.

"I ain't runnin' like no woman!" he said.

"Oh, hell, Alex, he kill you worse than any woman! He know how. Ask 'im about Fred's chain gangs." Sister worked her yanked-out back onto a kitchen chair where I met her with a chip of ice for her lip.

"He gots to have a woman bring 'im the pot to pee in and fill one on the stove to eat from!" I reminded Sister.

As I wondered how many were the times I'd put ice to Sister's face, I felt a pall come over all three of us. In silence, we could do no more than look at each other and dab ice that quickly melted from all the rage at that table.

"You go on Brother; need that soap so's we can finish up this laundry and eat tomorrow," I pleaded.

Alex murmured something gruesome he wanted to do to Jesse, and left to hold his sanity together while I attempted to calm Louvenia's exposed nerves and fix her flayed flesh. It took a spell before she had enough breath to say much more. Don't that always happen with a punch to the stomach?

"It's not that bad, honey. Worse last time—I know it was. Yeah?"

I gasped, seeing her new collection of bruises as I traced the ice over her face. They turned bluer as we spoke.

"Jesse say I got to fix him some eggs 'fore he leaves."

"What?" I bit my tongue when I heard that. He near killed her, and then reminded her she was his maid. It was 'bout then that Brother's urge to put Jesse away for good seemed to come over me, too. I wondered how I could pay Jesse back? Was Alex so wrong to want him put down for good? Is it a sin to kill Satan? Or even stab at him?

I knew these thoughts were looking for something to ignite, and figured if Sister had to recover from Jesse, then maybe he should recover from me. In that other room was a man I wanted dead, and here I had to serve him one more meal so he could hit the road with a pocket full of our laundry money.

So, I got to wondering: why not then offer up a Last Supper to ol' Jesse—a few bites for him to gag on for eternity? What would do it? A thimbleful of nightshade, the killing herb of the South mushed into his food? I knew there was a reason why slave owners had their slaves taste the masters' food. It ain't a quick and easy death, not from nightshade poison. No, you agonize from hell and back before your last breath. I try to believe Jesus watches over us, but since He already knew that killing Jesse was in my heart, I thought maybe He'd look the other way if I made that mean ol' man real sick, 'cause I didn't have no nightshade anyway. But I could torture him enough he'd sure think I did! Sick enough he'd wish himself dead, but not so dead the law might come for me. Jesse and me, that's where the two of us were headed.

"I'll fix 'em," I told Sister, and lifted her hanging lip with another chip of ice. "You stay here with this cold rag to your face."

Yeah, I was gonna fix him good! Louvenia looked at me quizzically, yet her throbbing lip kept her from asking what I was up to even as her eyes followed after me.

"He say he want his eggs right now. I'll help you."

"Don't need no help," I said calm-like so she'd not know I was worked up. "You keep that ice to your lip. I'll take care of him! You know I will, too!"

And, Lord, I meant to do some business on Jesse! I know Minerva would have taken Granny's rusty pair of scissors in there and teached Jesse the fear of the Lord like she done ol' Isaac. No thinking 'round this and that like Louvenia and me always did.

Then from the bedroom came more bellows from Satan's angel. "Where's my God-damned eggs? Hey, I'm talkin' to you out there!"

But he wasn't really talking to me, 'cause I didn't listen to him no more!

"Hey, what I say just now?" Jesse conveyed with his usual sweetness as I dumped every bit of cayenne pepper and near a whole box of salt into a mess of eggs that I'd cooked in rancid bacon grease along with more than a few jagged broken eggshells. Then I reached under the counter, pulled the garbage tin out, stirred with the spoon till I pulled up them blackened tatas I'd tossed out the day before, and mashed them up good in that skillet. Jesse gonna pay this time with a plate of food poisoning. I was sure gonna make his belly feel worse than Louvenia's lip did!

But then I got to wondering. Had a strange thought of what if I should have left the salt out of that stirred up pan of rot I was scorching? Don't they use salt to preserve hogs? The salt and all that alcohol Jesse already done pickled himself with might keep him going forever.

About then Louvenia, holding her ribcage, came over to the stove to see why I was taking so long. Mostly when I had to fix that man's food, it was a toss in a skillet and a dump on a plate for him. He ain't gonna get more from me.

"Here, baby. You know Jesse likes plenty of salt 'n pepper. Go on now, put some in them eggs 'fore he curses me they ain't the way he like 'em."

Sister reached for the saltbox and poured even more into that man's skillet of fried garbage. I was thinking ain't nobody on earth can eat six eggs cooked in rancid bacon grease, cayenne, rotten tatas and that much salt and live one more day to belly ache; it ain't never happened. Still, I figured if Jesse died from salt poisoning, we might end up with him staring down from the wall where I was gonna mount his stuffed hog's head. But then maybe we'd go to pickling him into jars so the law could never find out whatever ever happened to Jesse Powell who once lived at the end of that alley. Yeah, I had the picture of us putting those jars up in Louvenia's kitchen window then when his friends come by, all his gamblers, drunks and wife beaters following along behind Brother Fred, they'd know we'd had it with Jesse and they best not come to our door no more. I could see Jesse lying over that table where I wrapped Louvenia's ribs and we'd be carving that hog up like Minerva was guiding our hands. Then we'd stuff the butchered pieces down into jars, an eye in one and the other in the jar with his big brown liver lips. What would the neighbors think? Annie across the alley, her looking through her kitchen window down to Louvenia's and seeing Jesse smiling back from a jar! Lordy, he never more than growled at Annie in the alley when she said hello.

After I handed Jesse's plate to Sister, I was so excited about canning him that I decided I'd refresh myself with some sweet tea. Sister looked me in one eye then the other like something was amiss. Don't know if she was expecting a confession, but she only got a tail end of my mischievous grin.

Well, all the same, Louvenia took the plate back. I could hear Jesse grab it with a curse for taking so long and wolf 'em down like some hog that sure needed his head mounted on a wall! For Jesse, six eggs was only two or three bites for his big mouth ain't got no teeth. He never chewed any plate of food, just swallowed it near whole. I was sitting back there at the table thinking Jesse gonna be dead 'fore I drink my sweet tea down and then our lives was gonna change for good! Lord, we's for sure crossing over from Jesse's alley to a sunny day without bruises! I wondered what folks would think if we celebrated by putting a Christmas tree up in the middle of July and then handed out jars of pickled Jesse to his whores. Got some big red ribbons to put on them?

Lord, it sure felt like an early Christmas on Jesse's alley!

THAT BOY'S EYES

15

Bᴜᴛ, Lᴏʀᴅ, ʟᴇᴛ me tell you what happened next!

I knew I'd just committed murder even if Jesse was yet dead. But Jesus had forgiven me; I was sure of it. Because it was about then that this boy walked through the kitchen door and could only have been a gift from the Lord Himself. Was this my reward for putting Satan's progeny to torture? Yes, there in front of me stood the boy that Alex been calling Riverman.

The haze inside my head cleared at the very sight of Alex's friend, Jeffrey McWilliams, the boy he worked with at the stables. Never seen shoulders like his. Never seen lips like his, and what's the twinkle in his eye for? That glint was aimed right for me, I knew it was. This stranger walked in with a smile as big as any bouquet of spring flowers.

Well, Brother was sure not standing there offering no flowers. No, he plopped a box on the table like it was the answer to all our prayers. Alex motioned Jeff to a chair. But this boy's glistening eyes never moved from mine. I took mine off his long enough to look at that box. I could see it wasn't no box of wash soap. You see, it had a picture of a big fat dead rat on it! It sure did. It was rat poison that Alex meant for Jesse! Oh, Lord! I got to thinking this whole family was headed for hell, and then we'd never be rid of Jesse 'cause he surely had property homesteaded there. No doubt just down the way from Satan's place! Lord, Lord, I was 'bout to put Jesse up in canning jars and now there was this boy smiling at my breasts!

Alex introduced me, but I tell you plain, something came over me and I done changed into somebody else! Somebody that sure sounded like Minerva echoing in my ears!

"Jeff, this here is my sister, Sarah Breedlove." Brother shook his head like I was sure something else. "She's real strange like she's lost her senses. But we pay 'er no mind 'cause she can cook some when she puts her mind to it. But then she don't got no mind, I mean a whole one."

"I ain't worried none 'bout what she's missing. It's what she gots that counts. Yep, Sister, you're sure lookin' fine for a woman that ain't got half 'er senses!"

Those were the first words to me coming out of those pretty lips. Still I knew what he really thought was looking fine was my peaches, 'cause he could hardly take his eyes off them! Then that voice took over again. "Yeah? Then Mister, you're missing both halves of your senses if you're thinkin' I'm your sister!" I told Jeff. "I'm Miss Breedlove to you. Hear?" But that wasn't really me saying that. No, it was my momma. I knew it was. What she was gonna say next, I wondered?

Alex rolled his eyes like maybe he was wondering too.

"Sure got a lively one here, Alex."

"You ain't seen the half of it!" Brother moaned like he had a sudden case of indigestion.

"Real lively! Like a cat in a burlap bag. I can near feel them cat claws up 'n' down my back. A saucy woman makes me shiver all over like that."

That so, I thought.

Meanwhile in the backroom my deeds had taken hold of Jesse's poor ol' stomach. Guess that salt was stomping his gut good and hard. From the table I could see Louvenia in there standing barely out of punching distance watching Jesse moan pitiful-like and then hurl more puke her way. I 'magine Sister's thoughts were surely romping 'round that dark room, too, as Jesse's stomach surely was trying to crawl out aiming to squeeze somebody's throat. She could only have been thinking that if she helped that ol' man, he might live on and on, just like the ol' devil himself. And yet if she didn't help him, she might not live long herself once he came for his revenge. To me, all Jesse's puking was sweet music I could listen to forever. With her foot, Louvenia pushed the basin across the floor to catch what Jesse's mouth was hurling.

Meanwhile, back in the kitchen I filled Alex's ear with what I'd done to that ol 'man. Well, he was hardly impressed. No, he sure wasn't.

"Well now, ain't you a hardened killer? No wonder God made you a girl! He couldn't know what else to do with ya! Ain't that right, Jeff? Sister, you think Jesse's a snail? Salt ain't gonna kill nothing but snails in the alley. Now you only done made 'im meaner! What's he gonna do to you and Louvenia tomorrow?" Alex wasn't whispering. "Jeff, forget about what I said on Sarah's cooking."

Then Alex shoved that box of rat poison my way. "Now go do it right and put a spoonful of this in some mush for the ol' man."

"So, then who's a sick hardened killer again?" Jeff seemed to ask my peaches which he couldn't take his eyes off. Yes, my breasts seemed to get the boy near cross-eyed, didn't they?

"Want me to fix up somethin' real good to eat now?" I said to be polite. Jeff sat at the table, him grinning ear to ear and those eyes beckoning me to come sit on his lap. And I know they were, too.

"Yeah, that 'a be fine, Sister! I'll taste anything you put out!" he said.

Then, almost like a light had gone on the moment I'd been waiting for had come. It was time to call the undertaker to haul Jesse off. Yet all I could think about was that fine boy wanting to taste something that I figured had nothing to do with food. Momma! Come quick and say something for me! And sure enough she did. Yes, Momma's spirit filled me and lifted my arm to grab at that box of rat poison and shove it right in front of Jeffrey like I was gonna feed it to him. Jeff looked at that dead rat on the box and winked.

"Yep, this woman sure gots spirit in 'er, Brother Alex! And don't I like it!"

Right to the very beautiful boy with those lovely liquid eyes that followed my breast around the room, Momma said through my wicked mouth: "Want a big spoon, or you want me to feed it to you with my fingers a pinch at a time?"

"Now how am I gonna know, Miss Breedlove, 'less I taste your fingers?"

That boy stuck his tongue out and wiggled it at me. Now ain't that just like a dog doing that?

Alex guessed well enough that this had to be Minerva's spirit working my big mouth, so he tugged on Jeff's collar and headed for the door.

"Reckon we best be gettin' on. Yeah, for sure something come over Sister here."

"Lookin' forward to eatin' with you soon," Jeff said, looking into my eyes. What else he said, I don't even 'member.

With Jesse moaning like he was desperately holding on to the last ounce of his borrowed life, Louvenia came out, kicked his door shut and sat down safe in knowing Jesse'd be in bed for days to come.

"Jesse, says he must 'a ate somethin' gone bad over at Fred's this afternoon," she commented. "You think?"

Sister's grin was bigger than I'd seen in days. Thank you, Jesus!

Knowing we had a few days reprieve while Jesse' stomach was on the run, I stopped worrying 'bout what we was gonna do next. It was the first time in the six years I'd been living at Louvenia's that I'd stopped looking over my shoulder to see if Jesse was sneaking up. There was a light in my life, and it warmed me like the sun that never appeared in that dark alley. I was sure that boy Jeff had brought it on the tips of his fingers as though he held it like a kite on a string.

"Why were you so nasty to that boy?" Sister asked. "I could hear you sassin' the men even with Jesse back there howlin' 'bout Fred poisonin' him.

"Me? You heard me offer to fix him a meal. Ain't' that nice enough for now?"

∾

Well, for five days and nights poor Jesse was at death's door and we sure hoped that it would be the last one to open for him! I ignored him when he moaned for a sip of water. He hungry, he cried like a baby and went back to snoring only to find a scraped-clean plate waiting when he awoke. I'd eaten every bite myself and prayed he'd never wake up.

"Jesse, you already eat up that big lunch I fixed for you a while ago?" I hollered. "Best not eat too much, gonna get sick all over again. Ain't that the truth if you ever seen any?"

It only took three or four days of this abuse before Jesse was rearing to regain his lost territory. Yes, he was back to waving his orders in my face again.

"Hey, get me some real food! Fred got me sick with his cooking last week. Huh?" Jesse moaned. "Fetch me some eggs scrambled the way I like 'em! I's real sick in here!"

"You hear that jabberin' I hear?" Louvenia asked as she walked in from hanging clothes on the porch.

"No, ma'am. I ain't heard nothin'," I replied as I took a big pan of buttermilk biscuits out of the oven.

"Well, then it must be the neighbor's dog wantin' kitchen scraps." She snickered. "This ham be ready by the time you get the grits to a boil. Annie give us some blueberry jam her momma put up. We gonna have it with our hot biscuits."

"Ain't she sweet?"

"There's too much food here for two people, but I know Jesse's too sick to eat nothin'," she said loud enough for him to hear. And for sure he grunted like he was 'bout to gnaw the table leg off but still couldn't fix his feet on the floor to get at us or the food.

"You come on in here Jesse and get yourself some hot biscuits and blueberry jam," Sister taunted. "That what you're back there gruntin' for?"

"No, Sister. Don't you know, he gonna get better quicker if we don't mess with his poor stomach and let 'im starve," I said.

"Starve to death?" Sister asked. "Ain't he there yet?"

We laughed.

"Hey, get in here; I ain't eaten in a week! Maybe a month!" Jesse's words spilled slowly like the last gasps of a life well overdrawn.

"Who that?" Louvenia looked about for a ghost.

"One of them crazies in the alley, Sister. Don't mind 'im and he'll go away like a bad smell after the winds come."

After breakfast, and while Sister was over at Annie's, I started hearing them voices again.

"Get in here," he said. "I need me something to eat!"

I looked in on Jesse's hellhole. No wonder that old man wasn't dead. The Lord wouldn't want to look over anything as pathetic as that man lying there in his stinking brown bed.

"I'll go fix you some eggs, just as soon as I buy another box of salt. Maybe next week if nobody steals my laundry money!" I could say that 'cause I knew Jesse wasn't gonna get out of bed any time soon to swing at me.

"What? You know I gots the fever, I's real sick here," Jesse whined like he could wring a bit of mercy out of me.

"Yeah, Jesse, you been real sick, but that ain't nothin' new."

"What's you talkin' 'bout like that? Where's Louvenia when I want 'er to tend to me?"

"You know how Louvenia is. Bet she's gone uptown again. She sure likes shopping in them big stores, don't she? Some man she met wants her to pick out a new fur coat to wear while she ironin'."

"Shut that crap up!" he snorted. "Louvenia don't want to take care of me and I gots the fever bad. Had the runs, too," he whined.

I could only wonder; is it a sin to taunt Satan? "Tell me Jesus and I'll stop," I asked. But the Lord kept silent on it, so I opened my mouth all the wider. "No, Jesse, you don't got the fever." I yelled back. "You know that comes from swamp water. The closest you ever been to a swamp was back when you took a bath. 'Member? The color of that water after you dunked your tail in it? Now that was some real stinkin' swamp water!"

"What? Huh? Then why I dyin'? You kill me when I ain't lookin' and I'll tell Louvenia to put the law on your back! That's what!" Jesse tried to snap his fingers, but that was broken, too.

"Now, Jesse, you'd be real mean gettin' Louvenia on my back for killin' you, even if she paid me to do it!"

"I don't want to hear 'bout it. Just go bring me a pot to pee."

"Yeah, I'll do that. You just put a knot in it till I get to it! And tie it tight, 'cause I ain't in no hurry!"

I'd had enough of Jesse and went over to shut the damned window on him. It was July and had to be hot as hell in there. I figured I was just getting him accustomed to his final resting place on Satan's lap. Returning a favor, like all the ones he'd handed me.

Soon as the window was closed as tight as a coffin, I headed out to join Louvenia who'd been in the alley talking to Annie, and we headed off with her kids to buy ices with Italian syrup.

HIDING BEHIND A CRACKED JAR

16

A T TIMES I was jarred by the strongest feelings, as when my thoughts were chasing an iron over an old shirt. Like what would happen if Sister stepped out one afternoon and never returned? Because why ever would she? What was waiting at Jesse's but another tub of brown water and more bruised grief? Headed out to the grocer's one day, why wouldn't she just keep going as far as her feet would carry her? Well, I had to become a mother before I had any answers. Yes, Louvenia always returned simply because I was there waiting. That weighed on her more than notions of her escaping to a better life. I knew from my first moments at Jesse's, Sister was the only thing that saved me from that ol' man, or any ol' man.

The screen door slammed behind her. "Where's Jesse?" she asked as she walked in wiping her brow of sweat. She put the wash soap she'd gone for on the table and sighed as she looked at the piles of stinking clothes that waited.

"He dead," I said. "Undertaker done dragged 'im off already!"

"Think Jesse make good fertilizer?" Sister tittered.

I couldn't say nothing. But Sister could always read me and patted my hand to let me know she saw through the fears I'd been brewing.

Maybe the way a mother looks at her child and knows where her baby's thoughts are taking her. Her smile quickly sent my fears packing even as Jesse was still very much in our midst.

"I ain't dead yet! You know I ain't for real," he whined from the backroom.

Sister yelled back: "Now don't worry yourself none, Jesse. We'll tell the undertaker to come 'gain in the mornin'. You be finished by then. Hear?"

Whiskey numbs the memory and quickly erases days off the calendar. Louvenia could tell we were safe from Jesse's fist by the way he was grunting back there sitting on his pot. While we were sure he'd not 'member any of our abuse afterwards, we kept asking him what he'd eaten at Brother Fred's that had caused all the agony.

⁓

Sister had been sleeping in the kitchen since Jesse threw Alex out and Jesse couldn't swing that far even when he was sober. At least that was the lie we told.

"Ain't you finished pounding that ironin' board over there?" Sister asked.

I could tell Louvenia was planning on us having a sister talk. She poured us jars of sweet tea and pointed to the chair I was to take for the duration of her sermon.

"Why don't you ever let Jeff in from the porch when he comes by with Alex for a meal? Now why is that?"

I knew then I'd done a miserable job of hiding my secret. Yes, I'd been thinking of that boy for days. Near as many days as the shirts I'd scorched that week. Was that what clued Sister in? Yes, Alex had been bringing his friend over for a meal and they'd been sitting out there on the stoop to eat 'cause I was too shy to let them in.

"You're gonna let him in to eat proper-like at the table. I'm tellin' you, you are."

"What for?"

I wasn't really trying to start something. All the same, Sister squinted at me like she thought otherwise. Yes, she gave me the eye, which meant that she'd be the one getting the upper hand in this little chat of ours, or else I'd be getting it upside the head.

"What for, huh?" Louvenia said real huffed-up-like. "Alex says Jeff is the finest friend he ever had. A real good man that works hard over there at the stables."

Louvenia and Alex been talking, huh? That why she was so long in getting back? She was down at the stables telling Brother how easy it was to read my mind?

But there was more to it, and Sister knew. How could I tell Louvenia, who struggled with assaults to her dignity ever'day, who wore the color blue wound around her eyes like a target, that I was just too ashamed to bring that pretty boy on in? She might think I was ashamed of her. What Jeff was gonna think of us? I seemed to sputter around that cracked jar working up my defenses, yet all I saw was me covered in sweat from hovering over the tubs all day and hands looking like 'gator skin. Don't even got any kind of pretty dress. No, I didn't want the boy close enough to see what I saw in myself: a weary, confused, frayed and shy girl-woman; one afraid of looking into my own heart, let alone that of a man's. I think I figured I'd stay hidden from it all behind the old cracked jar I held up to the light. I couldn't look at her, 'cause she knew well enough that my heart sang a different tune. "Don't know why I should talk to him, Louvenia," I mumbled.

So I could catch her eyeing me and read her mood, I fiddled with my jar of sweet tea; held it up to the light as if I was looking for a nat in there. Or maybe I figured being hidden behind that jar she couldn't look into my eyes and see into my bared soul.

My mouth went numb as I kept on the trail meandering in my head, wondering what Jeff thought seeing Sister all black and blue after one of her all-night chats with Jesse's fist. These fears had looped 'round my thoughts for days. But maybe I was afraid he might think all them beatings…well, maybe he thinks that's the way it is. Nothing shocking about a woman getting straightened out by a man in those dead alleys. Is that what he thought? Couldn't just like me. No, who could like somebody

so beaten down like this girl-woman? The one I saw reflected off an ol'
cracked mason jar. Yes, I knew her well even through the pieces of her
broken dreams.

I'd never known a man before and didn't understand that at times
our men were as beaten down as we were; sometimes beaten into just
being an ol' drunk like Jesse. Is that where Jeff was gonna end up? Poor
Jesse, where did he lose his way? The day he put a foot down at the
mouth of that alley? Was his own vision of what lay ahead for him clear,
or clearly muddled as he glanced through his empty whiskey bottles
looking for all them days he'd gone and tossed away?

I went back to hiding behind my jar of sweet tea.

"I know you can still hear me if you're not holdin' that jar up to
your nose!"

"What did you say, Louvenia?"

"I said, he keeps comin' 'round all the time, don't he?" She peered
'round my jar so's I'd know she knowed there'd be no hiding behind no
damned cracked mason jar. "Yeah, your cookin' been gettin' real good
lately, ain't it? You notice? Huh?" She moved that jar away from my face
again.

Still, I wasn't gonna capitulate. No, I didn't have to notice nothing I
didn't have a mind to, even if Louvenia knew my story all the same. Yes,
clearly, she knew that boy had captured my heart. "What's you mean by
that, Sister?" I asked. "You never pushed a plate of my food back before."

"Honey, I'm ain't tryin' to start somethin' with you. Only you been
settin' out there food for two hungry men and then runnin' back in 'fore
they step up on the porch. Yes, you have, too. Best cookin' ever, and then
you're not steppin' out there to see that fine boy lap it up. Huh? Why,
now? Well, I think I know."

At that I came out from behind my jar of sweet tea. Yes, if Sister
could read my thoughts even when I shielded them behind a cracked jar,
then I figured she could just as easily put a thought or two into Brother's
head! And I knew she had, too, because the very next evening Brother
showed up right after that ol' man disappeared down the alley. A bit like
clockwork. Both the men came like twins tied together at the waist with

a rope so's they could get into trouble together! Howling and laughing, they were. Yes, I knew for sure there was something going on. You see, that morning Louvenia had decided she was hungry for Jeff's favorite meal and sent me out to the grocer for a chicken, some fresh onions and tatas. That night Alex and Jeff ate near a whole fried chicken and all them buttered tatas in half the time it took me to peel them.

Then when I thought they was both out on the stoop eating, Brother sneaked into the kitchen. He shook his head at me and nodded to Louvenia like it was the right time to put a flyswatter to my head. I knew Alex was gonna cause me grief and Sister, she'd be right there telling where to lay it on!

"Riverman say he ain't gonna leave this time 'less you come out. Why he even wants to talk to you is beyond me. But that's what he's set his mind to."

I waved Alex off like he was a fly buzzing around my head, and went back to washing the dishes.

"So, what's your problem this time?" Alex looked to Louvenia for backing. I knew that Louvenia had put him up to this.

"That what the boy say, or what Sister say?"

"Now, you stop that being rude to our guest, Sarah!"

"Hell, she don't know no better!" Alex added. "You best keep her locked up in here."

"Why?" I asked, "So no dogs get me? Like the one you brung that stuck his ol' tongue out like he gone rabid?"

"Yeah? So who gots the big yappin' mouth 'round here?" he asked. "Yap, yap, yap, that girl sure know how to yap up a storm!"

"Now you go out there and talk, and I don't mean talkin' no nonsense about dogs!"

Sister's eyes clearly held a flyswatter that I knew she'd soon be putting to my head. She grabbed that big bowl out of my hand.

"I'll wash the dishes tonight, so you can find some time to be polite."

"You comin' out then?" Alex persisted, but not nearly as much as me!

"Why would I do that? Go out there with two men who talk too much and eat too much?" I whispered that part, not wanting Jeff to hear, and then peeked through the curtain to see him out in the alley pacing.

"Sister, there's good men and there's bad," Louvenia cautioned as she dried that bowl.

"And then there's rabid dogs, ain't they?" I replied, but looked at Brother. "With their tongues waggin' at you! Well, ain't they?"

"Like I said, he ain't gonna leave till you talk to 'im," Alex said, all huffed-up-like.

He never had much patience for women, and was getting Louvenia's squinty-eye signal to hold the line no matter what fuss I slung at them.

"Then you best call the dog catcher man! Unless you need a pet dog to talk to. He sure follows you like one, don't he?"

It was about then that Sister near came to slapping me. I could tell by the way she pursed her lips, which always preceded a sound smack.

"That so?" Brother said. "Hey Jeff, best bring your plate on in here now," Brother yelled, then turned—I could have killed him—and winked as he yelled again, "There's pie in here waitin'! Yeah, poison Sister here baked it up just for you. Maybe she's sweet on you!"

Alex is just as stubborn as Louvenia any ol' day. Never could figure who they took after acting like that, Momma or Daddy, 'cause I don't have a stubborn bone in me.

I stood there feeling defenseless with my hair kinked from all the steam and my blouse damp from standing over the iron while I got their supper on. Satisfied with his deed, Alex stood there grinning. He was, too! If Louvenia was gonna swat anybody, righteousness would have it that Brother got the first smack. At that I heard Jeff's big feet stomping up the porch steps, Feeling beaten at my own game, I jumped behind the hanging shirts strung across the kitchen so Jeff wouldn't see me so frazzled. Louvenia jumped to bustle him back out to the porch.

"No, not this time Jeff. You best go on for now, I guess. But you take a pie back to the stables for later," Sister said. "I think that's best for tonight. Yeah."

Louvenia couldn't set up roadblocks to save herself, but still she could come to my defense with one. As soon as Jeff was out in the alley, Sister turned to Alex to work up something else.

"Now I got a plan here," she announced. "You tell your friend that if he wants to thank Sarah for her good cookin'—ain't she just a good cook, too—then he best come to the square in front of the First Baptist come Sunday, where you always go strollin' with your sister. After church, don't you know?"

"Go strollin'?" Alex blurted. "With my sister?" I guess he'd had more than enough of us. "What I know is I ain't never gone strollin' with no two sisters I ever knowed, and don't go to no church and you know it!"

I peeked through a hole in an old tea towel I'd just hung to dry see what Sister was gonna do to Brother for starting something with me. I figured he deserved at least a swollen lip. Louvenia put her hands to her hips and delivered her terms.

"Oh, you been strollin' up the wrong side of the street with this here sister, I tell you plain!" she said. "If you don't have Jeff in front of the First Baptist on Sunday, I'll be feedin' you Sarah's recipe for blackened scrambled eggs. The recipe that near killed Jesse, bless his rotten-to-the-core heart!"

Oh, if Momma couldn't speak through me 'cause I was holding my hands over my mouth to stop her, it was plain she'd go to talking through Louvenia's all the same.

Well, Alex didn't take to arguing with a couple of women, so he stomped off with the Riverman and my pie. It was still warm, too.

Sister watched out the window as they headed off. We could hear the men howling to the end of the alley even with their mouths full of pie.

Sister bustled me to the kitchen table. Lordy, by then I was sure tired of landing in that ol' chair for one of her talks.

"Sit down. I got a plan here: tomorrow we're goin' downtown," Sister informed me in a tone I knew meant the conversation was to have only one speaker and one listener, me being the latter.

Still, I couldn't keep my mouth closed. "Downtown? Why would we go downtown? I got no ironin' to deliver downtown and there's three days of laundry piled on the porch."

"Oh, I see plainly what's you got piled. Nothin' but piles of nasty attitudes is what I'm callin' it!" she said with that nose of hers in the air again. "You're goin' downtown and you're gonna buy yourself some kind of new dress."

"You're talkin' like a crazy woman," I said, but didn't get smacked for it. "I gots no money for a dress." We'd worked all those years just getting by wearing near rags—mostly things people left off at the church.

Louvenia went over to the woodpile, as was her habit; she knew to look over her shoulder to see if Jesse had sneaked up on her. Then she knocked about that pile till she found a rag all knotted up and pulled it out jingling coins. She looked back at Jesse's door again before spilling those coins out across the table like a crapshoot had just started up.

"Here it is. Least enough for a dress and maybe a pair of shoes. Don't worry 'bout Jesse; I take care of 'im so he don't notice nothin'. You're gonna look pretty when you see that boy come Sunday. In front of the First Baptist. I mean for Alex to see to it, too."

"Yeah, where I go strollin' ever' Sunday with him, huh?"

"Never mind, you! I can see in your eyes that he's special to you."

Sister pushed the coins towards me with a wink. What she'd tied up in that ol' rag was months of back-breaking labor. Louvenia had so little hope in her own life, but still she'd just handed it all to me to buy a dress, a silly piece of fabric to swaddle a dream in.

"I don't know if he's fine, do I?" I said, feeling confused.

"Baby, don't start out thinkin' all men are like Jesse," she whispered. "You ain't gonna meet somebody if you never leave the tubs, especially not with that attitude. You got to be nice and talk to that boy. I'm tellin' you, you are so's you can see for yourself that no matter what you think he's lookin' at, your peaches already sittin' nice and high, he's already seen what's in your heart, 'cause he's a good man. Really don't matter much else, do it? So, I'm tellin' you, you got to take the first step away from these tubs yourself."

Standing in the Sun

17

A S SOON AS Jesse woke up the next day Louvenia had something going to divert his attention from our plans to escape shopping. She was fixing his favorite breakfast of bacon and eggs with biscuits and gravy. Same meal we'd feasted on pretending we were celebrating his wake when he was dying from my fried garbage pail scraps. I reckon the smell of that hickory bacon done brought Jesse to the table thinking he'd slept in from July to Christmas morning and maybe Sister had somehow finagled more credit from the grocer. Louvenia had something else for that ol' man. She'd slipped out early and bought Jesse a bottle. You see for the longest time Louvenia had refused to buy his whiskey. But she'd worked it out thinking by the time I got back from town, Jesse's head would be too numb to know I had something new. A new dress never figured in Jesse's mind, unless he could barter for a whore with it. No, self-pride had no place in Jesse's world; after pride comes thinking big of yourself. Hard to keep somebody bridled if they take that tone.

Well, I fussed about going downtown so long that Sister finally tossed her dishrag down and went to get Annie. Sister and Annie decided they'd go get the dress without me then. You see, I'd never gone shopping like that, and it scared me. I was wary that Jesse might suspect something was going on and come home unexpected-like, as was his habit. For days he'd been looking at us strangely as if we might be keeping back our laundry money.

I spent the morning anxiously wondering what they'd come up with. What color it would be, and would it have some fancy trim or something. What might Jeff think about all this? Maybe every girl Jeff ever looked at had a real pretty, even store-bought dress. But were these girls so pretty he didn't even notice what kind of dress they had on? All these thoughts got me to biting my nails. Yes, I was getting scared of Sunday coming and started wondering how I could conjure a way to skip over to Monday to save myself the grief the day would bring. I was suddenly feeling sick-like, I knew I was, and thought for sure I had a swollen lip from chewing on it all week from nerves.

So, I came up with a plan to save myself. I figured if I worked hard enough, come Sunday Sister and me would be so tired the day would roll by without anybody noticing. I figured then we'd never even make it to the church. Anyway, I was sure that Jeffrey would forget he knew Alex because I was his sister and that was sure enough all the reason he'd need. He'd probably have left town long before Sunday even came.

But as you'd 'spect, come Sunday, my sister got up extra early to press my new dress again—she not liking the way she'd done it the night before. I was already wide-awake on the cot but pulled the blanket up to my eyes so she couldn't hear me good.

"Huh?" she huffed again.

From that I knew she'd not take to the notion I'd worked up to face her with that morning.

"Huh? What did you say, Sarah?"

You see, I'd long figured sassing her was less objectionable if I scrambled my words under bated breath. Then I could more easily recant before the flyswatter headed my way. After all, Sister was apt to misunderstand me giving her lip when I mush-mouthed the words. At least it worked sometimes. Or maybe Sister just let things pass.

"I can't go to church. Just can't," I mumbled.

Blanket pulled up over my mouth or not, Sister heard me all the same, and never paused with that iron in her hand to ask me to repeat my whining. I could tell she wasn't gonna take anything off me that morning. Louvenia never even looked down at me wallowing on my cot deep in the throes of my conjured predicament to see what I'd worked up. Nope, she'd not give a damn no matter!

"You're goin'!" she blurted. "You look fine in that new dress, and them new shoes ain't nobody worn before. You're goin', honey. Best head down the road I say to, 'cause I'll be waiting with a stick on all them other paths you tend to wander when you're trying not to hear me good."

"What did you say, Sister?"

"I said, you be up 'fore I get the grits to a boil. Or you're gonna find a boil upside something you ain't gonna want to put down on no hard pew at church."

But I wasn't gonna surrender.

"I just can't though. Something's comin' over me that I never felt about before. You think I'm sick?"

Fever in my head or done gone deranged like Alex said, made no difference to her. Thank goodness I didn't cut my hand off the night before cutting up that chicken. No matter to her, I'd still have to go to church. She'd only tell me to carry my severed hand 'round in a bag or she might drag it behind us tied by a rope!

"Why do you think you can't go to church? You always go to church. Now get up like I done told you, and for the last time!"

She been takin' roll at the church or somethin'?

"My nerves got me to bitin' my lip so bad all week—just can't go out there with it all red and ain't it gettin' swollen, too? I know it is. Go get me a mirror from Annie's," I pleaded unconvincingly, thinking Sister would get caught up chatting with Annie and she'd let things pass. But nothing was gonna work to save me from facing the fact Jeff would not be there, and if he was, it was only to see my gangrened lip hanging near to the ground.

"Your lip don't look half as bad as your head's gonna look if I take a stick to it. And even after I do, you're still goin' to church. Then we'll see who looks at your lip when it's pinned to the back of your head!"

Sister was acting more like Minerva by the minute. Anyway, I wasn't worried 'cause I was pretty sure she didn't have a stick. Still, I looked 'round the kitchen in case there was something else she could get her hands on.

"Jesus hears everything, Sister!" I warned. I figured Sister wouldn't want to mess with the Lord, especially not on a Sunday, and reminded her that words on the Lord wasn't sassing, or so I hoped. But my hopes were dashed with Sister's response.

"Yes, He sure enough did hear me ask Him where the rollin' pin is. Bottom drawer over there is where Jesus reminded me I left it. Do I need to show you He was right and then put it to your head?"

So, I guessed I'd be going to church all right. To save my soul or my head from a prayer meeting with Louvenia's rolling pin. Anyway, I was convinced that on most issues the Lord was already on Sister's side.

Louvenia finished ironing my dress and stood there waiting for me to finally get out of bed and put it on. I got dressed special that morning. Even felt special 'cause Jesse hadn't come home that night. He'd probably slept over at his brother Fred's where he tended to pass out after the bars closed. Maybe Jesus did answer my prayers. Still, I was sure only when Sister asked Him to.

My dress was so beautiful. My favorite peach color and covered in tiny little green apples, little bitty ones, and the buttons were shiny like pearls and the white collar made my face look a deep mahogany. We didn't have no mirror; all them got broken when the whiskey bottles were in transit for our heads. So Louvenia escorted me down to Annie's to look in hers and show off the dress she'd helped pick. What would people think of me at church? Lordy! They all were gonna laugh at me for getting all dolled up? They knew I'd never had a new store-bought dress. Didn't they? Wouldn't they all gawk when I walked in the church house? Who was I trying to be?

"Don't even look like me, do it?" I whispered to Sister as we stood in front of Annie's dressing table mirror.

"Sure it do. Just the outside different," Louvenia kissed my cheek and whispered as Annie touched up my hair with her brush. "And you know what? Look down deep into that mirror, even past your pretty smile."

"Why?" I asked.

"All them rabid dogs you're always goin' on 'bout is gone, ain't they? Just your pretty smile I see, and that's all that matters."

∾

Well, we made it to church despite the fact I was sure my shoes were lead-filled or maybe aiming to head some other way. I knew folks were staring, 'cause I was dragging my feet so much I might scuff my new white shoes, or maybe I was hoping I'd make us late so we'd have to sit in the back where nobody would notice I'd dragged my lip in behind me. Was he gonna be there after all?

Sister shook her head and mumbled something about me always mumbling.

When we paused to buy some paper fans from the boy on the corner, Jeff walked up and handed me a fistful of pretty white daisies. I didn't know what to do. Nobody ever gave me flowers. Sister elbowed my side to pry open my mouth.

"Ain't that sweet, Sarah?" she said. "Jeff you comin' in with us?"

"No, ma'am. But if Sarah has nothin' to do after, she might want to sit a spell in the park. If it's alright with you, Louvenia."

Still nothing would come out of my mouth.

"Sure it is, Jeff. She'll be right here on the front steps," Sister replied on my behalf. "Just standing in the nice sun. Ain't this day a blessin' from the Lord?" Louvenia looked at me and nodded.

Well even if my mouth could work, Jeff couldn't have heard me plainly 'cause I was hiding behind my paper fan, just sure my lip had swollen to twice the size since I looked in Annie's mirror. You see, I never believed Annie when she said there was no such thing on my lip as a bad ugly lump! Maybe it had turned black even, 'cause I knew she was just being nice.

Sister and me went into the church fanning ourselves, but not like the big-hat women who acted like they was waving off a swarm of horse-flies. Sister dragged me and my lip up to the front row where I took a seat and went to praying. Praying hard, "Oh, Lord, Lord, Lord," I chanted till Louvenia jabbed her bony elbow in my side again.

"What are you doin' there snortin' like that?" she whispered loud enough so all them big-hat women spun their heads to see my condition. But I was not snorting! Them were coded prayers to Jesus 'bout Him getting Sister off my back!

"I'm tellin' you, you bite that lip one more time!"

I paid her no mind 'cause I knew she didn't have the rolling pin with her. You see, I pulled it out and hid it under my cot to teach her a lesson. Sometimes the Lord can be wrong about where He hides things. Anyway, if she had a stick hidden, I knew she wouldn't use it on me, not in front of the preacher. But just in case I rolled my eyes at her till I was near crossed-eyed. Everybody in the pew gawked at me, so I moved down a few inches where it had to be a bit safer from her reach.

Sitting in front of us, the big-hat women's heads spun again like they's tops to see what Louvenia was fussing over. Sister's eyebrow, the left one, almost flew off her head at them. But I guess Jesus did hear my prayer this time 'cause Sister kept her mouth shut and let me be.

The preacher finished preaching; don't know 'bout what, 'cause I wasn't listening much. Probably about the devil being in our midst again. I was in a sorrowful state. The devil was near, and I probably lured him with all my thoughts about Jeff—and in my thoughts, what Jeff and me was doing wasn't praying. I looked back at the church doors knowing that Alex brought him just to abuse me, and they were surely out there just waiting to complete the humiliation Sister had commenced that morning.

Church ended. I looked at Louvenia. She must have known my thoughts were muddled and looked behind us at the church doors as though Jeff war surely there smiling.

I thought at first to sit tight and pray till ever'body gone, and then Alex and Jeff would surely have wandered off, too. But Louvenia wouldn't have it. She kicked me in the ankle, smiled big to all the big-hat ladies like she'd not even done that, and bustled me from the pew.

"Is there a reason why you were just sittin' there?" she asked. "You weren't listenin' to a single word the preacher said. No, you was sittin' there snortin', and then you stay put when he's done. My, Lord, child, what's come over you?"

Well, I followed her out wondering how much bigger my lip had gotten. Folks looked at me for looking at them to see if they'd noticed. Does a black lip turn green when you're in church? I tried to pull my lip out to see. Louvenia smacked my hand down.

As we neared the back doors, I could see the sun peeking in. Reminded me there was truly something warm and good out there and perhaps he waited for me. Jeff *was* waiting, and walked right up to me in front of them big-hat women always congregating on the steps outside the church doors to see who sees them with their fancy hats on.

I will never forget his smile. That morning I thought Jeff was the handsomest man in Vicksburg. He had a nice clean shirt on, not ironed, but clean. Louvenia proudly glanced at all the womenfolk looking on at Jeff's good manners. Still, Sister heard not a word on Brother's manners!

"What's on your feet?" Alex asked. "You get them shoes off some dead white woman?"

"Oh, you like Sister's new shoes?" Louvenia squinted at Alex. "Ain't they beautiful? Sarah sure knows how to dress fine, don't she, Brother?" she asked Alex, but tossed a smile Jeff's way.

"That right, huh? You read that in the papers this morning?" Brother asked, but got no smack from Louvenia like he sure ought 'a had.

"Miss Breedlove, care to join me down at the square for some lemonade?" Moses Jeffrey McWilliam, the man Brother called the Riverman, offered his arm and led me away from the church step. Unbeknownst to me, they would be my first steps heading to a new life.

Over the hours that followed that bright day, Jeff made me feel ever more special. It truly seemed he never saw nobody but me. Don't know how many white folks passing saw I had white shoes on like them, 'cause ever'body seemed to vanish but him.

On that first stroll around the square, Jeff and I talked and talked. I found out that, like me, he was the child of sharecroppers, and that his grandparents were also slaves ripped from Africa, thinking they was being savaged away by the white slavers to be butchered for meat, only to be hauled up to the white shadows still somewhat alive albeit with severed souls.

It was near dark 'fore Jeff walked me back down Jesse's long alley. I kept telling him Jesse not gonna like him coming near his porch. But he kept holding my hand as though Jesse didn't mean nothing to him, 'cause maybe only I did. For the first time in my life, I felt like I'd stepped out of a deep dark shadow and was standing in the warmth of the sun, where I'd caught a glimpse of dignity dressed in a dream all my own. Still I wondered how long it could last?

RIVERMAN

18

YES, I WAS floating in that soaring place where you can only fall hard; I'd fallen in love with Jeffrey McWilliams—the Riverman, and not just because he'd been hanging on my gate all those weeks.

For days I'd been right there listening to Alex tell Louvenia 'bout the man at the stables. From the beginning Brother and Jeff's friendship knew no bounds. In our world where folks only looked to peel a layer off others' backs, I'd never heard of selfless giving like this man's. Through Jeff's serene eyes, I began to see beyond my world to the one Sister had been pointing towards yet didn't know how to get to herself. Her deep faith had told her it was out there somewhere and someday, and somehow we'd get there.

He said his daddy called him Riverman even when he was a boy. His ma claimed it was because Jeff was big for his age and there was nothing he enjoyed more than fishing with his daddy. During those days when Jeff and his folks lived off the land, there were no fields to be harnessed to, no begging for credit from the plantation masters and no overseer pounding on their door and backs for more. With nobody bothering them, they clung to their only dream, to live free, and that's what they did for three years or so. Time travels quickly when your life is ripe with happiness, and there ain't no dread 'bout what tomorrow might hit you with.

Jeff, he was near six years older than me. I was born two years after the Civil War, so I never knew what being a slave was as my folks had. Sure knew that sharecropping was. Near to being the same shackle even if it was called by a different name. As slaves my folks knew that if they walked off Burney lands there'd be some kind of nigger dog pursuing. After the war, it was the chain gangs that barked for free labor along the drain ditches in the rebuilding of the new South. Knowing this kept many folks from looking for something better, yet it didn't stop Jeff's folks.

When the war ended, Jeff's ma and pa left the plantation they were born to in the dark of night even though they were free. Didn't even take a pot; didn't want to give the master cause to come after them with a pack of nigger dogs. Laws still don't mean nothing in the South. They was gone for good. That was all they needed to take with them, his daddy declared, as they headed to a dream of their own for the first time in their worn lives.

Many plantations along the Mississippi were deserted during the war with the North when white folks moved to cities as the South was near burnt to the ground. Towards the end of those bleak times even some white folks barely escaped the Yanks that stormed the South hungry as wolves. During those days, late at night Jeff's daddy went foraging on abandoned plantations for things they needed to survive. He piled up the goods he found: a few bowls, a wooden stool, some tools, bedding, a chicken or two, and carried off what he could haul in a cart. Never so much that he'd need a horse 'cause they was all gone by then. Jeff's pa led his family down the trails that followed the river as far from the planta- tion houses as they could, farther and farther from any sign of white folks. They worked their way to where the land was wild and untamed and where it would be easier to hide in the thickets if it came to it. Out there they lived freely for the first time. Every day Jeff's ma got them on their knees to pray that the white folks would never come to haul 'em back the way they'd hauled back everything else they'd lost during that war that unchained us from the shackles that we'd soon be wearing again in the new South.

Where the growth was thick Jeff helped his daddy build a shelter of sorts. Way out there, yet close enough to hear that muddy river crash the banks after the rains. They got by on hunting, his ma's berry picking, and fishing for hours just like Alex did with our daddy and Samuel. At times I wondered if was possible they'd seen Jeff and his daddy with their poles over on the other side of that mile-wide river.

Jeff said his pa told stories on how that river turned mercilessly on folks 'cause the white folks owned it and they was mean and that made the river jump and twist like a snarling rope, the kind that runaway slaves jerked against to escape from being dragged back. Still, the river took its revenge and one bad winter the banks broke off till Jeff's shack lifted and was carried away with the mud, along with everything they'd collected over time: a hearth of their own, a pot of fish stew and a few hand tools. There'd been barely enough time to scramble for higher grounds.

Time was done, his pa mumbled to his ma. Time was done… You see, that last flood had broken Jeff's daddy's spirit for survival. It too was done. Nothing left for them to scratch out a living with and no strength to forage a new life again in this new South. All done.

Jeff was only 'bout thirteen or fourteen when he had to bury his daddy. Jeff said his ma sat there under a tarp pelted with rain still talking to his pa as though he wasn't truly gone. Jeff, he had no shovel to dig, and the strength for digging had gone missing, too. He buried his pa by winding him in his tears and the last worn sheet they had. After their farewells, Jeff let his daddy be swallowed by the muddy waters.

I got tears in my eyes when I heard about that sheet. Those sheets may not have been monogrammed with blue thread like the Burneys', but in the end, our lives weren't so different.

After a few days, Jeff's ma kept talking 'bout how she couldn't get no sleep what with the aches that had settled in her joints. She gonna get better, Jeff kept telling her. But his better was not the same she longed for, nor the one she was resolved to slip away to. His ma struggled for the words to tell her boy where she was aiming for, but they never came.

But do they ever come for any of us? Pain numbs the tongue to silence, the pain of love.

Jeff told me that one night he suddenly awoke to the sounds of an eerie silence. The woods, he said, had suddenly gone stone quiet. What is the sound of the cold quiet you see in your blackest dreams? Maybe it's the sound of death searching for someone in the depths of the moment. It was the sound of that silence that brought terror to river people 'cause the icy waters can rise in silence all the way up to your neck waiting for you to swallow.

He rose from his blanket only to see his ma standing there in the moonlight looking back at him—a smile on her silent lips as she stood there knee deep in water—that river unrolled behind her like a glassy comforter. When he yelled for her, she crossed her arms over her chest as if she was arranging herself in her coffin and lay back over the glassy surface and drifted to her final sleep. Yes, that great river had answered her prayers and carried her off to be with his pa. Jeff then understood what she couldn't say to her beloved only child. She couldn't take no more. She had to be with her husband and didn't know how to ask her son to forgive her for leaving him an orphan.

From then on Jeff made his own dreams, and one was to have land far away from the floods of the Mississippi and the plantation folks always pointing to their feet for coloreds to come kneel for the day's orders. Nobody was gonna break his soil off and carry it away like that river done. To own his own plot of ground was the promise he'd made to his folks after they'd slid under the water on their last journey. That dream of a boy of thirteen summers never went cold on him. With his tears hidden deep in his empty pockets, Jeff headed off the banks of the Mississippi for the last time. There were to be many miles trundled before our eyes met for the first time.

Days after his ma's passing, Jeff dragged himself along till he made it to the docks at Vicksburg. The colored stevedores told him he best make it into the city 'fore they picked him up to work the county roads, 'cause there'd be no dock work for a boy too young to lift ten tons a day. Jeff told me for any kind of wage, them dockers looked mean enough to kill. Somehow Jeff managed to make his way to the heart of Vicksburg where he worked when he could get it and, I guess, stole the horse's food to stay alive when he couldn't. You see, apples for horses were plentiful even if opportunities weren't. Stable work was the lowest and paid miserably, so there were always jobs to be had at places that smelled like horseshit. Jeff got him one that didn't pay enough to feed himself. That's the way it worked for a colored man. After working the stables for all those years, Jeff still didn't have enough money to buy a decent pair of overalls. And yet at the stable he brought Brother under his wing and gave him a portion of his meager wages, even if that delayed his own dream. And if Jeff and Alex couldn't save for an acre somewhere, someday, at least they could swap dreams of what it would be like to own a piece of dirt to farm one day. But one days don't always come. No, they're mostly just borrowed dreams.

Still, it didn't happen like a poem, Jeff and me. It took a lot of hearing 'bout him from Alex to finally see a vision of the Riverman's soul. You know I needed to filter what I saw of men through my day-to-day life with Jesse and the kind of men that hung 'round that alley.

Back in those first days after our arrival at Jesse's, Brother kept his mouth shut, but then when Jesse took out his anger on Sister, Alex came after Jesse with his fist, aiming to put him down for good. One time I thought he'd knock Jesse's jaw through the top of his head with a right-hand hook. But at the last splintered moment, Brother let his fist collide with the wall instead, leaving a gash. Jesse looked stunned like I'd never seen before. He was only accustomed to us taking his blows. When he realized his head was still on his shoulders, he yelled about getting the law on Brother and fled like he was. 'Course, we knew he was really headed to Fred's to lick the wounds he didn't own. Fred was always good at stirring the blues and helping Jesse find a new woman to bandage things. Got a bottle, Fred? What was that woman's name again? 'Member? Well, them kind don't need no name, was Fred's singular reply. "'Cause ain't nobody care 'bout 'em!"

Alex knew he had to hit the road quick. Jesse still had his head and Brother his fist, and he knew the next round it would be Sister and me who would lose. So, he packed his things and left us to the lonely wails of that alley. He had only a thin coat and even thinner hopes to take with him.

Before Alex left, Louvenia and I pleaded with him, begged for him to stay put. Just stay out of Jesse's sight a bit, we would cajole and set things right, as we'd learned that life under Jesse's rule could be fixed with a bottle. "Ever'thing gonna be okay," we cried. But we knew better. There never was an okay at Jesse's.

That night I helped Sister dig through Jesse's things till we found some coins he'd stolen from her that week. Louvenia handed them to Brother sobbing, 'cause she had nothing else to give him. Alex walked off into that night as terrified as we. Him, only a boy of fifteen. The door closed, Sister and I covered our mouths so our sobbing wouldn't tug at Brother's last steps away. We knew that most people driven into dark shadows of them alleys were never heard from again. The price of freedom is always dear, and sometimes you're reduced to eating your foot off to escape the many traps. Working till late after Brother left us, Sister stuffed strips of old rags she'd dipped in laundry starch into the hole in the wall that Alex's fist made, should the law come for Brother. Yes, at Jesse's even the walls had wounds and bandages.

Jesse returned the next morning still drunk. He'd forgotten about the swing he'd barely ducked from the night before and never noticed the patched wall. Probably never saw the wall.

Louvenia wouldn't speak to Jesse for weeks, but that hardly offended ol' Jesse. Don't think he even noticed. He never heard her anyway, particularly when she pleaded mercy from his fist. Jesse was accustomed to laying out his needs in monologue; Sister best know her place was to fill those needs. Breaking her back over tubs or that old stove making his meals was the order of the day. A big mouth deserved a big lip, and when your lip hangs low enough, you learn to travel the way Jesse intended before the last swing weighed things down to greater depths than any soul can bear.

❧

Then after days of silent sobs in our aprons, Alex appeared on the porch. The Lord had heard our prayers; Brother had not been devoured by the winter's cold. He'd survived by wandering between the shadows of that heartless city till one morning, even before the farmers' carts rolled in with their produce, Brother came upon the stable where he met the Riverman. That morning, when Jeff opened up, he saw Alex across the way hunched under the eaves of the grocer's—his life trickling away like the rain trickled down his young cheeks, one tear at a time. The hunger had long disappeared, like it does when your belly finally goes small from emptiness.

"Hey, you shivering over there. Come on near the fire. I get us some coffee 'fore the boss come." These were Jeff's first words to a Breedlove.

Alex, shivering from the morning rain, followed him in where Jeff got a fire going in an old stove. He tugged Brother over to the heat before disappearing. Alex said the place was full of horses and smelled as bad. Jeff returned and tossed a shirt to Brother along with that big smile of his.

"Put yours over that chair. Be dry 'fore the boss come 'round, if he do." Jeff went over to where the food was stashed and pulled out some bread, cheese and apples. "Boss buys these apples for the horses. Charges the customers a nickel for two but never gives 'em to no horses. So I eats 'em when he not 'round and tell 'im they gone bad."

Alex said Jeff had the whitest teeth of any grown man he'd ever seen.

"Why was you over there, wet and all?" he asked Brother. "You don't know the grocer gonna chase you off when he opens? He been sayin' coloreds outside his place bad for business."

"I know. Was thinkin' on it," Alex said.

"I tell you what. I need me some help here anyways. You help clean up but stay low when the boss 'round and I share my wages. Ain't much. Don't get my wages then 'least you got a dry place to sleep up in the hay loft. Boss don't look up there. See? Don't got to think on nothin' now. Just gotta get on with it."

A body can only spend so many rainy nights out in the cold before you stop worrying about somebody gonna grab you by the ear, call you a vagrant and yell in it that you ought 'a be in the chain-gang. It don't matter no more 'cause you've already got one foot in a pine box and death couldn't be any colder than standing in the rain night after night. It didn't take but a day of working together, mucking out stalls and all, for these two men to become fast friends. Jeff's boss already laid the work of two men on his back, though he paid wages for only one, but at least they had a roof over their heads and all the bruised apples they could eat.

Three or four days after Jesse escaped Brother's fist, he came back to tell us 'bout the Riverman. We were filled with joy at Brother's return. Every day we'd wondered if he was gone from our lives for good. We were happy he'd found work, some kind of roof and a friend who knew where he'd come from and offered a hand to share and not one more backhand.

Got to be that Brother could figure the hours when Jesse was likely to be at Fred's or the bars and started coming by to eat. Annie, whose kitchen window faced the mouth of that alley, kept watch in case Jesse lost track of time, or lost enough money at craps and headed home early. If Annie saw that ol' man coming down the alley, she'd tell the preacher to yell out the door with his loud voice for his kids to come in. We could hear the preacher and would quickly hide Brother behind the tubs or somewhere. With Jesse back to his brown bed snoring, Sister would soft-foot over to close his door, then brace a chair against the wobbly knob, which could hold Jesse back a few moments in case he heard us and got up to tell us to close our God-damned mouths and then go bring him a plate of food. His kicking at that bedroom door that was always 'stuck' would give us enough time to bustle Brother out the back door.

I recall that the three of us had many whispered suppers this way. It was during these meals that I came to know about Jeff long before Brother started bringing the boy around. Yes, during those hours of hearing Brother's experiences with this man and through his love for his friend, I saw this man Alex called Riverman.

"He a good man, that Jeff, bringin' you in out of that rain like that," Sister commented many times. Then she looked at me with the most serene eyes I'd seen for ages, like she'd heard some real good news. Nobody ever heard much good on folks in them alleys. A good man? She seemed to want me to hear over and over. A good man, ain't he, Sarah?

Yes, Lord, somebody had saved our brother and with him, my sister and me, because I knew that Jeff's spirit and kindness helped us all not to give up.

With that bag of apples Brother had brought over, I baked a big apple pie and sent some back to this Riverman. Guess through Alex, he was hearing 'bout me, too.

BROKEN SHARD OF HOPE

19

I T GOT TO be that Jesse stayed out most nights so he could sleep well on all the days he never remembered. Late afternoons he'd call out for a meal or to empty his pot, but we didn't hear no more.

"You hear that?"

"No, I ain't heard nothin' no more!" Sister said.

"Must be somebody out in the alley then."

These were our cautious whispers as we gathered our hushed thoughts and bundled them into the daydreams we'd share on those nights we worked our irons over miles of old shirts.

Then sometime in the evening, Jesse would crawl out of the bed, put on his old suit, grab any money he could get at and head for the good times. He was still having them good times 'cause our wash money was coming in good, real good, and he figured he was getting most of it. But he wasn't. We worked hard, pressed and folded things like no other tub women 'round them alleys. It made us proud when we could pay Annie's boy, Tom, to deliver the clothes for us. Tommy earned himself some money and gave some to his momma. We all helped each other get by. Yes, life let up on us a bit down at the end of Jesse's alley.

But the day came when Jesse started looking at things more closely. Him looking down into our laundry tubs to see how much work we had. He surely noticed how hard we worked, so he figured there had to be something going on. Then one day, without a word, he went to the cupboards to see if they were bare enough. In all those years, I never 'member him opening them before. What was Jesse's thinking, and what would it cost us? Them cupboards were still mostly bare. Where'd we put it then, all that money coming in? Had he missed something during his last three-day binge? So, what was this business going on in his own house? Were we really putting all the money out? He surely wondered, and that made the bile at the corners of his mouth drip all the more.

But we weren't. Not no more. We only put out enough to keep Jesse drunk enough to be numbed off our backs. Then the rest we were putting in a hidden place. Jesse, his life was getting ever so desperate back then, had to have it. But equally, our own survival depended on him not getting at our laundry money. You see, he could smell a dream, too, and I bet she cost all the more the worse he smelled. When you're an ugly ol' man who lives off bottles, you gots to have plenty of money or no woman gonna pay mind to your offer. It's all gonna be a waste of her time. Ain't enough money in the world for his ugly ol' business, Louvenia whispered to me one night when Jesse cursed us for having only a dime sitting out for him when he took off. We'd decided that the next night it would only be a nickel. And it was. Jesse threw it back in Louvenia's face and left for bigger change.

Guess it was about then that Jesse got himself into some trouble trying to get at the big-man money he was desperate for. You can't put down a half bottle of whiskey and keep your head on straight at the craps. No, your life starts rolling faster than the dice, till it hurls itself back at you. Jesse always surrounded himself with folks, like Fred, just waiting to walk on his back, any back, for any amount. They were kindred in their ugliness right to the bottom of their rotted-out souls. When his pockets went dry, these same folks started pounding on Jesse's back to see if anything would drop out of his empty life. When they figured nothing was left, they still knew which two backs to stomp next. Word gets 'round who's not so down and out and might be good for a quick take down. Therefore, I knew it wasn't Annie pounding on our door late that night. A courtesy call from Jesse's caroling choir of drunks?

"Who'd come down that alley to our door this late?" Sister whispered like a runaway slave.

She walked over to the door knowing only somebody delivering grief would be standing there. She peeked out.

"I from the city here." The man's voice was loud, like he wanted all the alley to hear. "Yes, ma'am, the city sent me to this here address. This Mr. Jesse Powell's place? Huh?" The city inspector looked past Sister into her kitchen like he needed to see what we had.

"Yeah, but Jesse gone," she told him. "He say he don't want to talk to nobody."

Louvenia wrung her hands as she did when frightened. I stopped ironing and put the iron back on the stove to heat in case I needed to press my own message to this caller's face if it came to it. Then I walked over to Louvenia standing at the door with her foot fixed to it, so he couldn't push it open wider.

"What's you want?" I asked. "You don't know what time it is to do the city's business?"

"It don't matter none. I from the city. City inspector, I is. Official business here. Seems like they's been lots of complaints 'bout all these here bottles stacked up outside your laundry porch," he warned, jabbing his finger at the direction of our faces.

"Ain't there ever'thing stacked up and down this here alley?" I told him. "Ain't nobody ever come from the city 'bout it before, have they, Sister?"

Sister shook her head and looked towards Jesse's bedroom. Probably hoping he'd jump up to see who was in his kitchen. But not a curse came from him. He was too deep in another nightmare and couldn't have known another was unfolding at the door.

"Well, you bet they is now," the man from the city said. "If Jesse don't show up with the money tonight, this very night, I'm tellin' you the city's gonna put 'im in jail till he pays up."

"What money be that?"

Sister put her hand over her mouth to cup any puke her fear might bring up. I held on to her arm to still her trembling.

"That's all I got to say on it." The man turned to walk off, but then hollered back, "He's got 'bout forty-seven dollars in bad gamblin' debts some ornery men at the city done paid off for him. Now they wants their money. He better come up with it tonight if he knows what's good for him, 'cause they's people out there with friends who sure knows where the jail is."

He walked off shaking his thick finger at Jesse's thicker stack of bottles piled along the walls near as high as his jagged lies.

Louvenia locked the door and fell into the kitchen chair to sift the implications. I could tell the fog had rolled in on her bad 'cause she held her head with both fists and stared at the kitchen tabletop like right there was the bottom of a well she was about to leap down—her trying hard to think straight in the confusion that man had dumped on her.

But there was no fog come down on me this time. No, I started seeing up ahead what might be a clearing of sorts. Yes, even looked like an oasis of calm if we could only make it there. And I meant for it to be.

Jesse was still asleep as I pulled his door closed and sat down next to Sister to talk it out. She was trembling all over by then. That word jail was the same word Jesse threw in her face all the time. Jail for her, that is, for not minding him, because jail for Jesse could never have been a notion that would fit into her battered thoughts.

"If they take Jesse to jail, then they gonna come after me for the money. That right? They gonna come for me?" I held Sister's hands so they'd stop shaking. "What am I gonna do? We only gots 'bout six dollars saved up. Took us months. Ain't that near to being two train tickets to somewhere far?"

Louvenia was sorting her fears aloud. We sat there motionless to look at our options one by one, 'cause we never had two anyway.

"We just gonna do nothin'!" I announced. "Jesse cut his deals with them at the bar. They knowed he don't got money but they still played the dice like big shots. Let 'em work it out between 'em. No, we ain't pullin' our money out to pay down Jesse's gamblin'. And nobody gonna come for you tonight, not never, 'cause you got nothin' to give 'em."

"We gots near six dollars, I think. Got it for now, anyway."

She looked over her shoulder at Jesse's door like he might spring out and find her throat and use it to get at the money; six dollars hidden somewhere behind our secrets.

"No, we don't got no money. They can search the place but we ain't go it 'cause I'm takin' it over to Annie's. I know she'll hide it for us."

"Best go now then, 'fore that man come back. Or comes back for me! He gonna do that?"

I patted Sister's hand without another word. How could I have known what might happen to us? But I was determined we'd be ready for it.

Later Jesse crawled out of bed to go out. We'd been biting our nails as we waited for his exit to a jail cell. Sister had cooked up his food and laid it out extra nice. Jesse came in, looked at that nice plate of food sitting there and then at me like I'd dusted it with pinch nightshade poison. But I hadn't. Just wanted him to sit down and fill his mouth so he'd not be talking at Louvenia, as I was scared her trembling would alert him that something was amiss. If he figured there was some kind of trouble brewing out in the alley, his instinct would be to head over to Fred's till things cooled down as he did when he got into it bad with the whores' pimps.

Jesse looked hard at Louvenia. She kept her head down at her ironing. Then he looked at me. But I couldn't help but give him a real big grin so's he'd know something was up for sure! He quickly figured as much and pushed his plate back after only two mouthfuls. Eyeing us hard, he hit the road without his usual curses on our worthlessness.

Louvenia fell into the kitchen chair and slumped back into her old familiar fears. "What's we gonna do now?" she asked the tabletop. "Come away from that window and lock that door good!"

I did, and sat down next to her. "Let Jesus figure out what's gonna happen to Jesse." I knew if Jesus was in on it Sister would rest easier, 'cause she didn't take to my notions on Jesse most times, saying I best not tell Jesus what I wanted to do to that man.

We didn't talk much the rest 'a the night. Just went to bed wondering what the Lord would come up with. Was He gonna answer our prayers?

He was.

§

It was the next morning when Jesse's brother Fred showed up. It had to have been the earliest I'd ever seen him.

"Listen to me good! Jesse, he done got picked up last night at the bar," Fred blurted anxiously, or maybe already desperate for a drink. "He got put in jail and couldn't sleep a wink 'cause the noise. I just been there. All them whores hollering across the hall and the like. And it stinks down there. Nobody to empty the crap pots."

Fred kept eyeing sister's scrambled eggs like he expected her to go fetch him some.

"What Jesse do?" Louvenia asked and glanced my way. "He in trouble?"

"Like I tol' you, cops say he been fined by the city for not cleanin' up your damned pile of bottles out there and they ain't gonna let 'im out till you get that mess cleaned up. Then he gots to pay a big fine and I tell you, that fine gettin' bigger ever' day!"

"That what the city man say?" Louvenia asked. "Jesse get out when his bottles get hauled off?"

"Him fine 'bout fifty-seven dollars. You got that kind of money? Let me see it then," Fred looked longingly 'round the kitchen. "How much you got for me to take to 'em this afternoon?"

Guess he expected to squeeze us for any money he could above Jesse's fine.

"Him fine not forty-seven dollars?" I asked the old liar.

"How'd you know? The city man already told you, ain't he? City man said he come by and warned you what'd happen if Jesse didn't take care of things," Fred said, sinking in his own swamp of lies.

"Louvenia, you ever heard a man say that?" I asked.

"No, nobody ever come 'round knockin' on our door and he never said nothin' 'bout no fine I can 'member," Sister said. "Now you say he owes 'em twenty-seven dollars."

"I said forty-seven. You messin' with me?" Fred asked.

"No, Fred, I ain't. But you know how noisy it is out there in the alley. Can't hear a word most the time," Louvenia told him. "But I sure heard you say Jesse gone. You hear that clear, Sarah? Lord, have mercy! If he ain't locked up somewhere, too! Nobody done gone and lost the key over there had they? Huh?"

I stood up to Brother Fred in a way that would have made Minerva proud.

"Maybe somebody did come by, Sister, but you couldn't hear 'cause your hearin' got cut off from being hit upside your head by Jesse's fist."

Then I turned to Fred and put Momma's eyes on him till he flinched.

"Fred, you gots a heap of concern for your brother; he ain't eatin' good down in the city jail and his whores is annoyin' 'im something awful with their snorin'. Or is Jesse locked up with the same whores he owes money to? That what this is all 'bout?"

Fred never did take to me.

"Huh? What's that? 'Course I got concerns. Jesse my only kin. He my blood," Fred snarled.

I was thinking I'd never tell nobody that Jesse was my blood. Anyway, how can you drink that much whiskey and still have blood in your veins? It made no sense to me, but I could smell an alley rat, and this one's name was Fred.

"But you got no concern 'bout Louvenia here gettin' her head knocked against these here walls?" I asked, real nice, too.

"Now don't start up with me, sister-girl. Ain't none of my business what Jesse does to any damned woman. It be his house, ain't it?"

'Bout then Fred and I were scrambling to opposite sides of the road and I aimed to set a few rat traps along his side. "And it ain't none of my business if Jesse in jail. And Louvenia here, she's broke! Ain't you, Sister?"

"Don't shit me!" Fred said. "Jesse say he sure Louvenia gots it comin' in good! He say there's got to be enough hidden someplace to get him out of jail. Then he pay 'em back the rest with interest when he gets his hands on it."

"No, Fred. Louvenia spent ever' penny we made on men, craps in the alley and whiskey. But ask me real nice-like if I gots it comin' in good. Yes, I do, Fred. Jesse wants to borrow some money from me? That be so, then he's gotta come 'round and talk terms face-to-face. Maybe we work out a good deal on credit, but only after he clears up some past debts. Like eight years of borrowed drinking money you and him pissed out in the alley."

"How's he gonna do that, sister-girl? Come by and talk 'bout your situation here? Ain't I just told you he's in jail? Maybe you don't know what that means 'cause you're plain stupid?"

"Fred, I ain't gonna take issue with you. So, you best head off now, 'cause fixin' your problems is too hard for me. We talk again one day when I get smarter."

"Then Louvenia, you gots to come up with that money so's we can work somethin' out with the city folks and get our Jesse out. He don't like it down there, I'm tellin' you plain, he sure enough don't!"

Sister stood up and pointed her finger at Fred. "I real worried 'bout Jesse. Sure I am. Who gonna bring that man the pot when he don't want to get out 'a bed? Or fan 'im all night when he gets hot?" Louvenia feigned sorrowful grief and wiped a tear with her apron. 'Cept I know Louvenia; she was really hiding a grin and gagging down a laugh by biting the corner of that rag. "But the thing is," she continued, "I gots no work 'cause Sarah here stole my customers out from under me. Didn't you Sarah? Sure you did!" Sister looked at me like I was pure wickedness.

"Yep, Fred. That time when Jesse hit Sister and she had a bandage over her eyes and couldn't see what I was up to, I cleaned her out. Guess a bit like your brother Jesse done to her. Ain't that right, Louvenia?"

Fred stood seething from our mockery. I could see his fist twitching to belt his reply.

"Guess Jesse gonna have to stay in jail till you get a job, Fred, and then you can go down to the city and pay off Jesse's problem, a few cents every week or so. That's what I'm thinkin'," Sister said, hiding her grin in her apron.

Fred was in no mood for us. He no doubt saw a picture of himself suddenly unwanted at the bar where they took no credit and Fred's only cash came from Jesse's theft of our money. "I don't know what you're up to, but when Jesse gets out, you best expect he'll be mad as hell and come lookin' to backhand you with some of it!" Fred announced, like giving us hell was some new torture we'd never come up against. "And we just see what your big mouth gets you then. Don't expect it 'a be right side up like them bottles out there. You think, sister-girl?"

"He ain't out and we ain't gonna worry 'bout nothin'," I said, but that was a lie.

We were worried plenty, but Momma taught us to hide our fears; we'd let Fred figure out what Sister and I had going. But then we didn't know ourselves. I was thinking Fred was just gonna head off to hunt down a borrowed drink and probably wouldn't fuss 'bout ol' Jesse till he needed more whiskey money. After a day or two of stupor, he wouldn't even 'member he had a brother in jail.

All the alleys 'round here end up at the same dead-end: The bottom of an empty bottle that gets tossed onto a pile nobody wants to admit exists.

"When I comes by again, you best have them bottles out there in Jesse's alley hauled off," Fred said to Louvenia, but looked at me.

"I know you gots to go, Fred. The whores are gonna be fussin' for you. You best take some good cookin' over to poor Jesse on your way."

I contorted my face to look sorrowful about Jesse's situation. Louvenia went back to hiding her grin behind her apron. She had to know I wasn't finished with Fred yet.

"Now, that's better, sister-girl," he said.

I went over to the garbage pail and, with my back to Fred, pulled out two dry-as-board biscuits that Sister had tossed out, wrapped them in newsprint and handed them to Fred.

"What's you thinkin', girl? Jesse don't like biscuits none," he snorted. "You go fix 'im some cornbread right quick. I want me some, too."

But I took them biscuits, dropped them to the floor and stomped them hard and handed them back to Fred. "But he loves crackers, don't he? Here's two. Fresh from under my bare feet."

Fred left in a huff without his brother's biscuits, but I reckon he did take my message. I smiled, thinking how hard Jesse would have to swallow on it.

Before Fred got too far, Louvenia stuck her head out the door and yelled, "Fred, you gots some money I can borrow? I's broke and don't like Sarah's cookin'! You seen her biscuits! Near killed Jesse the other day, her fried eggs did. Need some money to buy a meal. You know I'm good for it, don't you?" Then she slammed the door and started laughing like a crazy woman.

Yes, we laughed and laughed like we hadn't laughed in years. Just like two crazies that had just made it to the other side of freedom. But then we fell into each other's arms wailing in fear and panic. What would happen to us next? Sweat broke out on my face. Sister turned silent thinking on our prospects. It was not a prospect that Jesse would one day return to take his revenge. It was a certainty.

We didn't hear from Fred for a few days and never heard no more on Jesse's situation. We didn't want to know. As that haze of fear evaporated, the days then followed in calmness and we found serene sunny mornings where we sat lost in all the quiet, drinking our coffee with not a snort from the ol' man to break our thoughts. Strange what life sounds like when you're not listening through the crash of whiskey bottles over layers of thoughts you hope to ride out to that somewhere better.

Picking the shards out of your borrowed dreams, the shards from our shattered and broken lives, is what hope is born of.

Living on Horse Shit Lies

20

ALEX AND JEFF worked hard at the stables. Still, sometimes the owner, Mr. Harold, claimed he didn't make enough to pay them. He'd say maybe next week be better, but it never was and never would be 'cause it was all just a tale Harold used to rope their lives in. Brother said he knew it was a lie because he could see Harold had lots of customers handing him money; he just didn't want to pay their wages. When Jeffrey tried to talk to Mr. Harold 'bout getting paid up, he told them they could go get work elsewhere if they didn't take to the situation. But things are different for coloreds. If the men headed off for new work, they'd sure be asked for references from their last job. Got no references, maybe you're just out of jail; don't need nobody today. Best get yourself lost looking for work elsewhere. We all carried the weight of our days under such rules.

Truly it was no lie that if you didn't have references, you'd get no job. Sleeping in the hayloft was bad, yet you knew come winter you could freeze in them alleys or be picked up as a vagrant. That's a destination where you'd share a pallet to sleep on with a filthy stranger alongside a shared slop bucket to feed from. Yes, chain gangs always afforded employment. Harold knew letting the men sleep over the horses in the hayloft was the only thing Alex and Jeff had to keep them from being lost out there. Got to be the men had to swallow hard their pride so they wouldn't gag on Harold's horseshit lies.

❧

Annie and I got to be good friends during the hours Jesse was gone. She couldn't come 'round much when he was home 'cause her little ones followed her ever'where and she didn't want them seeing that ol' man spewing his gutter-talk at Sister and me.

At times I helped Annie stay on top of her laundry for those kids. When Jesse was gone, she enjoyed visiting with Sister and teaching me to read better while Sister ironed their things. Those times Louvenia would pour sweet tea and listen to us talk about things that were in the books. She always loved to hear how some folks had lives so very different from ours. How did that happen, she often wondered out loud.

"Now, Louvenia, Sarah here's gettin' good with learning new words. When are we gonna get you goin' readin'?" Annie asked.

But Louvenia didn't like to hear 'bout it. She jumped to finish ironing that shirt. Still, I knew she was afraid of how words could tangle her thoughts. Maybe like having the key to your jail slid right in front of the very bars that held you back. The key to your escape close enough you could reach down and grab it, but you also knew you still really couldn't. What waited for you outside your prison may only be another borrowed dream, one blacker than the one you still bled from. Sister put her iron on the stove to heat.

"When Sarah comes home from deliverin' the ironin' she reads the verses," Louvenia told Annie. "She reads the Psalms while I'm ironin'. It soothes my nerves, don't it Sarah?"

Sister looked at me with pride. Once, late at night when she figured I was sleeping, I heard her praying. Telling Jesus that I'd read to her that night. No one in our family had ever been able to read before.

❧

Louvenia had fixed up a nice dinner late that evening. Jeff was eating with us as he did whenever he could get away from the stables and

Alex would cover for him. Sometimes Alex would come over while Jeff covered and then he'd take back some home cooking. It was one of these nights when Fred walked into our kitchen like he owned the place.

"I gots some real bad news here," the old liar announced. "Jesse gots big problems. The folks down at the jail done decided he ain't gonna get out for thirty days, maybe more 'cause he can't put his hands on no money to put down on his fines."

I had to bite my tongue to keep from thanking the Lord for this truly delightful bad news. Jesse paying for his sins for once! Louvenia almost fell into her chair as tears of joy welled in her eyes. But I didn't want Fred to see how happy we were and then go tell the devil's captive! I jumped to pull Fred's attention my way.

"Sister, them onions you chopped still botherin' your eyes?" I asked knowing better. "Go back there and rinse 'em good. I take care of Fred here."

Fred wouldn't have cared if Sister was walking around with both eyes hanging from their sockets after having collided with Jesse's fists. He situated himself at our table as if he thought himself a guest waiting to be served. He probably wondered why I was smiling ear to ear. You see, I had that box of rat poison down there in case he got too comfortable.

"Yeah, and Jesse say bring 'im some decent food. Him not eatin' good down there and gots the runs."

Fred kept eyeing Jeff.

"Who's this here boy in Jesse's house? Huh?"

"I'm Jeff McWilliams."

Jeff glared at Fred like he recognized the demon for who he was. Fred went to acting like he was now Jesse's shadow.

"What's he doing here? Jesse, he don't want nobody in his place."

Nobody but gamblers and drunks, I guess.

"Then who gonna bring 'im the pot?" Louvenia snickered.

Maybe she didn't count even as a nobody to Jesse and Fred.

"Fred, you best take some food to Jesse. You know he must be real hungry. I sure know how that is 'cause I been hungry right here in this kitchen after his friends stopped by for a meal, or two."

I got up and put a tin of food on the table for Jesse. Nothing but garbage I was 'bout to throw to the cats in the alley. When Fred not looking, I poured most of a shaker of salt in it before covering the plate.

"You best take this down to Jesse. Don't let it get cold now. You know how mean Jesse gets when his meals stand too long."

Fred was about to run off at the mouth when I bustled him out.

From out on the porch, I could hear Louvenia break down at the table and cry like her dam broke—that dam of emotions she had pent up for years. Lord, it was an avalanche, too. Sister wailed so hard she choked on her tears because her throat, so wrung with Jesse's hands, was now even more constricted with fear. But this time there was no thumbprint on her flesh.

"Jesse be gone for a whole month?" she sobbed to confirm Fred's news. "That what, Sarah?"

Sister needed my help to sort the implications. It was like she'd finally awakened from a real black dream that was yet nipping at the corner of her lip like the bite of a nigger dog. The sight of Sister so suddenly broken-down scared Jeff. Guess he'd never seen a woman undone over something he couldn't see to protect her from.

"Jeff, Sister needs her rest; you best go back to the stables for now. She be alright."

I was sorry for Jeff. Louvenia's weeping throbbed at our hearts. Yet I knew well enough that through this surge of pain there was also joy cleansing her soul of the years of Jesse's dirty dealings on her. Jeff read my eyes, nodded and then got up without a word. He stood behind Sister's chair, put his arms around her and kissed her temple. His own eyes were filled with tears when, in silence, he walked out into the lonely night.

I went to get Sister a moist cloth to put to her throbbing head and prayed. Louvenia gonna be better in the morning, Lord? We're still here, I reminded myself of our blessings. Then I sat down to read the verses.

"Yea, though I walk through the valley of the shadow of death, I will fear no evil…" At least I'll try not to for now.

Yes, we had survived, and there awaited another day ahead, and we would sure as heaven own it.

STOLEN MOMENTS,
BORROWED DREAMS

21

O N THOSE SUMMER evenings when we headed home from delivering the ironing, we'd steal a few moments here and there to window shop. One night Louvenia paused in front of that hat shop a few blocks from our place. At first, I couldn't think why, as we'd passed it many times without lingering. I could see it was the kind of shop them fancy big-hat women from church likely shopped at. It was on our side of town, but undoubtedly the finest store 'round there, maybe finer than any I'd ever been in. I stood next to Sister and watched her gaze through the glass. All the weary lines on her face eased and there was even a slight smile on her lips where too often only bruises hung. Hers was the kind of soft smile one has while watching a child at play. Her furtive gaze through the shop window revealed that she had glimpsed something that took her away from her troubles if only for a few stolen moments. Was it all them beautiful hats displayed in there that had captivated her? More ribbons, bows and flowers gathered in more colors than I'd ever seen.

Then I noticed what had put a gleam in Sister's eyes; she was fixed on that one particular hat displayed on a fancy pedestal—the one with the feather bird that was prettier than all the rest. The little brilliant-colored bird seemed to peer back like it desperately wanted to fly away with Sister. I was sure it was a tiny glimpse of a dream she'd shared with me long before. A borrowed dream of being a fine lady for a moment or two. Like Sundays when the big-hat ladies tossed aside their cleaning rags, put aside their irons and got dolled up to sit up there in the front pews like royalty.

It seemed as we ventured along that street Louvenia always paused to gaze through the window yet never went in. Only stood there looking at that particular hat with the little feather bird nesting in some pretty gem-colored flower petals. I'd imagined it was like a secret between them, Sister and that little bird. Yes, she had a dream hidden where nobody could steal it away. She'd never had such a fine thing. Probably never thought she might one day. We had no time to borrow dreams like that—but this time was different, because I decided to do more than follow Sister follow her borrowed dream; I would capture that bird and pleasure her with a few gilded moments.

A week later, after delivering' our ironing, I headed over to the milliner's with coins jingling in the purse I kept hidden in my blouse. Couldn't spend all I took in that week, but figured I could put some down on that hat. Enough to hold it till I could pay the rest. I stepped into that shop, but quickly felt it was the last place in town that might be expecting me that afternoon.

"I want to put some money down on that hat over yonder with the feather bird," I told the shop woman. "Want you to hold it for me."

She was a lot lighter than Sister and me. Could even pass, and had airs accordingly. "What's that you want?" She looked me up and down like I had a smell and seemed plum annoyed with the notion of letting one of her hats go without a fight. "You can't wear a fine hat like I gots in my shop!"

"Yeah? Why not?"

"Cause they're meant for ladies, not tub girls!"

I wondered how she knew I worked the tubs. 'Cause I was darker than her?

"How you know I work the tubs?"

"I see a laundress's hands comin' from a block away and don't want none in my place wastin' my time and crushing my hats with they's rough hands like they actually gonna buy one. They ain't never gonna buy nothin' here. Just want to pretend they's fine ladies and ride it on my dime. Ain't it so? Huh! Like I don't know no better! Anyway, you a child. These here hats are for women!"

"I ain't no child!" I said right up in her face. "I'm near thirteen and got breasts!"

"That so? Glad you told me on both accounts."

She came 'round her counter to look at my feet like she could confirm I was a tub woman by seeing if I wore shoes.

"Chile," she said again like I didn't hear before, "I got breasts when I was ten and a boyfriend when I was eleven! And nobody ever took me for some chile like I just done you!"

"Why I care? Maybe you a granny when you're twelve!"

"Granny, huh?" she barked. "I don't want your money and ain't gonna waste my time just so you can go tell folks you're a customer of this here fine shop."

Well, I guess Louvenia and me weren't the only ones who borrowed dreams from time to time.

"Who your customers?" I asked, figuring she beat them and tossed them out 'fore they bought something, 'cause there was sure not a single soul in there, 'less they was in the back getting their wounds tended from this woman's tongue-lashing.

"My customers, in case one day you're gonna open yourself a shop," she barely got those words out 'fore she was laughing like an alley cat in heat, "are the whores on First Street, and the best of them women bending the pews down with their fat asses at the First Street Baptist Church."

"You a whore?" I asked.

Sister always told me to never look into the face of one of them whores that hung round the mouth of Jesse's alley. So I never seen one up good and close.

"Do I look like one?"

"How I know?" I asked.

"I give up being a whore. Took my money and bought me this shop ten long years ago. I pay dear for rent, but I'm close enough to the whitey part of town where I need to be. Them white women venture over here so long as I pretend I give 'em a hefty discount for their troubles crossing the tracks. And I do their bills so they sure think so, too. Yeah, I charge them double and then give 'em a ten percent discount. Them white women pay dear for my hats, and that's all there is to that!"

"How you start your own shop?" I asked. "You got the money?"

"Honey, I stole my money back from my pimp!"

"Yeah?"

I had a vision of that woman and Jesse getting into it one night in some dark alley. He could sure sniff out our laundry money like some pimp!

"He don't come after you?"

"How he gonna do that now?" she asked.

"How? How he got your money from you to steal back in the first place?"

"No, chile" she said. It took her longer to get the word 'chile' out each time she hurled it at my face. "He a heartless man and he still back there countin' how much money he done stole from how many women. And he doing his numbers with my knife buried deep in his heart. See, it don't pay to be a heartless man, 'cause then a woman comes along with a knife and she jab it in there real good just to see if you really don't got one. Well, he lied 'bout that, too. He did have a heart and I cut into it like a rhubarb pie. I sure enough did. Just like he done to me all them years. Anything else you need to know now, 'fore you go on your way, lil' girl?"

"I didn't come in here 'cause I needed to know nothin'. I come to put somethin' down on that hat over there. Go fetch it for me."

"What? Go fetch it, huh? No, I ain't wastin' my time with you or your breasts, chile, 'cause I knows the only thing big on you is that mouth of yours! If I let you put a nickel or two down on one of my fine hats, then I got to save it till you come 'round wanting your money back, and all the while I could have sold it to some whitey! So, now off with you. I gots to make a basket of bows for them whores and them women at the First Street Baptist. And let me tell you something else: the whores and the women at the First Baptist, they all pray to the same Lord, and they be praying to be saved from the very same men! Now get on out of here. I got things to do!"

What could I say? I walked out thinking that if she'd asked me to prove she had a heart I'd for sure have to stick a knife in to see for sure. But I was not gonna let that woman put an end to Sister's bit of a dream. No, I wasn't.

I headed on over to the stables to talk it out with Jeffrey. It was summer and the sun was up till late so I could walk over there and still get back to the alley 'fore dark when Louvenia would for sure be headed up to the mouth of the alley to watch for me. And if I was late, she'd tongue-lash me all the way back to our porch saying things 'bout whores gonna interfere with me if I was out too late and all. "Don't go over to them whores," she'd say, "'cause they's callin' you sayin' they gots something you're gonna want to hear! You just walk on by 'em with your own mouth closed!"

Well, over at the stables I told Jeff everything. He smiled as he brushed down a horse. He asked me about the color of hat Louvenia had taken such a fancy to. I told him. He said he'd figure something out. Jeff's smile always calmed me down.

Next day, while his boss was gone and Alex was looking after things, Jeff headed over to the hat shop.

"Well, now look at you!" that woman said to Jeff as he walked in. "Ain't you an eyeful?" He said she looked him up and down and then in a certain place I can't say, but it was near the middle. "I think I see some dimples," she told him.

Talking like that I wondered if she'd done forgot she'd left her last vocation behind.

"I ain't here 'cept for a hat. One gots a feather bird up on it some-where," Jeff told the milliner, who was still eyeing his manhood like she was armed with measuring tapes in each hand—and not to measure no damned head!

"You don't look like you'd fit one my hats. Ain't been a man in here for me to know how to measure a head that big," she told him. "I bet you got a big one, too!"

"Ain't for my head," Jeff told her.

"No?"

"I put some money down on it. You keep it till I get paid, then I come for it."

"Oh, I see. So, then you gots a lil' girl someplace that wants a big hat to look like a big woman? Huh?"

Jeff ignored her.

"Alright. Give me a dollar. Guess I put your hat with the damned bird in the back for keepin'."

"That's all I come for," Jeff said.

"Well, didn't I figure that out quick enough?"

Jeff probably let her see his dimples—always got a woman weak in the knees when he grinned—then nodded to her and then nodded again till she finally grunted and went to fetch that hat. That milliner probably felt a bit annoyed that Jeff's charm got her to do what she was sure not gonna do for a no-account tub girl.

For days I bit my nails to keep from telling Sister what we'd gone and done. Then one night my heart sank low. It sure did. We were coming home when Sister paused at the hat shop. But you see, the hat that shared her secret was no longer on the pedestal in the window and was nowhere to be seen. She stood frozen, as if one more dream had slipped her by to catch up with all the others long gone.

A look of sadness came over her as we headed off in silence. She didn't have much to say the rest of the evening. Sister said that she was tired and went to lie down on her cot. I pulled the cover up over her and she closed her eyes and rolled over to face the wall. She never asked me to read the verses she liked to drift to sleep with. Still, I knew she wasn't asleep for real.

Sister was quiet over the next few days as we worked our way through the piles of laundry stacked on the porch. At the end of the day, I'd try to work up a chat 'bout the church's big summer picnic where ever'body would meet in the square after the service. We'd all be getting dressed up and spend hours the night before, or early that morning preparing our best dishes to share with those sitting on blankets near ours. Jeff and Alex had been looking forward to the day for weeks, even though they'd come up with all sorts of excuses why they still couldn't sit through the sermon that morning.

The Friday before the picnic, Alex and me finally had enough put together to pay the milliner and Jeff planned to pick up Sister' hat. Could hardly contain my excitement as Louvenia had never had anything bought new just for her. No, she wore mostly castoff hats with an assortment of this and that sewed on by Lord knows how many prior wearers; a broken flower, a bent bow, they'd all been sewn and resewn.

The Sunday of the picnic Louvenia and I got up early to finish cooking and iron our dresses along with a shirt for Jeff. He was coming by to pick up the picnic basket with the chickens all fried up, peach cobbler all golden brown on top, collard and potata salads with crumbled hickory bacon all ready. Everything was packed carefully in a spare basket of Annie's with a big jar of sweet tea.

The morning of the picnic, Louvenia came out of the back room all dressed for church. Thank goodness Jesse was still behind bars 'cross town. He'd have given her a cursing if he'd seen that pretty dress Annie had given Sister. It was something one of the churchwomen had donated to the church clothes drive, and Annie knew it would be just right for Louvenia. Sister starched it to look like it just came out of a shop window. She was prancing about the kitchen in it when Jeff walked in. He set the fancy-wrapped package on the table where Sister tended to sit.

"Want your coffee now, Sister?"

"Mornin', Jeffrey. You had your breakfast yet?" Sister pirouetted so we could better see her special dress. "My goodness, what's in that package with such fancy paper?"

I handed her a mug of coffee with the extra cream her stomach needed.

"Miss Louvenia, this here was just delivered to your door by the delivery boy."

I went over the table pretending to examine the package.

"Yes, I can read the delivery label. Says it's for you. Best open it now, 'cause that might be chicken in there. You tell that butcher man to deliver an extra chicken for Sunday picnic, Sister?"

"Now, you know there ain't no chicken in that kind of fine paper with little pictures of blooming cherry trees. You ought not to be fibbin' like that on the Lord's Day! Anyway, He's got to be tired of hearin' your mouth all week and needs a day of rest from it, don't He, Jeff?"

"Amen, Lord, Amen, Miss Louvenia." Jeff nodded towards the ceiling like the Lord might be peeking through one of the cracks up there.

Sister looked at the big box suspiciously. Finally, she sat down and slowly peeled the paper away—just enough to see that little feather bird peeking back at her.

Not a sound came out of Sister for the longest time. Only a long sigh and a well-worn tear fell from the corner of her eye, one of joy as precious as a glistening jewel, as right there it looked as though her moments of happiness were no longer borrowed from someone else's dream. Sister stood there wringing her hands as she did when she was anxious and then slumped in that old kitchen chair and cautiously peeled the pretty wrapping paper back to reveal all of her prized hat.

She pulled her hand back and twisted it up in the other, and then sat there with her head shaking nervously as her foot tapped on the leg of the spindly chair. Tap, tap, tap, it went. Must 'a been to keep herself from grabbing at that beautiful hat like it couldn't really be hers, so she ought not to be touching it. Tap, tap, tap, little pulses beating out a drum roll saying what her soul couldn't fold into words. But I knew. There it was, that tiny little feather bird looking up at her—a tiny dream to feed her soul with joy.

Sister's obvious delight was greater than I'd ever seen—greater than any Christmas morning. None of us could say much, so we all went on to church in our quiet joy with Sister wearing her big hat just like the big-hat women. And they all smiled as we took a seat and couldn't seem to take their eyes off Sister's hat and nodded their appreciation. Still, Louvenia's shyness got the best of her and she could hardly look up to acknowledge their nods. She could only let a shy grin escape here and there.

After the preacher finally finished talking 'bout the devil—don't he know nothing else to preach 'bout? And don't Jesus always keep the devil locked up on beautiful days like that anyway?—we rose to leave. At the front steps the big-hat ladies were happy to see Sister and remarked how fine her hat was. I left Louvenia to chat while Jeff, Alex and I went over to the park to lay out our picnic.

What can weave a dream through a broken heart? Where could I borrow a few more for my sister? I remember asking Momma back on Orchard Hill what a dream was. For her it was a day she could fill her family's bellies. She was right; sometimes a dream smells like a hot peach cobbler. But then sometimes it's only borrowed, yet don't it still get us to the next day?

✍

That night Alex and Jeff sat at the kitchen table with big spoons finishing off the last of the cobbler like two big kids. While I washed up our picnic things, Louvenia sat talking about her hat and how it was as nice as any of the big-hat women's.

"Best in the world, don't you think?" she asked as her eyes caressed that feather bird.

"Yes, Miss Louvenia, everybody sure had their eyes on that new hat of yours. That's for sure, ain't it, Alex?" Jeff asked, not taking his eyes off that pan of cobbler 'cause Brother might get his spoon in there faster for the next bite. "You know, Miss Louvenia, I don't know nothin' 'bout women's things. No, I sure don't," Jeff said.

His gentleness always eased Sister into talking freely like she could with no other man.

"Like what color is that flower? That one right there. That blue?" he asked.

"No," Sister said as if she was the milliner speaking to a customer. "That there is called lavender. It ain't really pink and ain't really blue, that's how you know. I seen that color on a flower once. Yes, I did.

Annie, she brung over some sweet peas from her momma's garden once. Little round flowers they was and they smelled so sweet. Yes, sweet and spicy. Thought it was the most beautiful smell in the world. Late that summer, Annie she gave me seedpods from her ma's sweet pea vines. Told me when to plant 'em."

"That's a good idea, Sister," I said, not ever remembering any flowers at Jesse's. "When you gonna plant them seeds?"

"Oh, Jesse, he seen them seedpods dryin' in the window and throwed 'em out. He don't want no flowers 'round him. Said it reminded him of the dead," Sister said. "Don't make no difference. Ain't nothing ever gonna grow in that alley. Not enough sun, and the soil's fouled bad out there."

"What color is that there bird, Miss Louvenia?" Jeff continued as he finished off the cobbler.

"That feather bird?" Her eyes got big—like a beloved pet, that bird delighted her so. "That bird's the color of a sapphire like princesses wear. I know it is. Preacher said all the princesses in Pharaoh's court wear sapphire-colored gems in their hair. Guess it's the most beautiful color there is if princesses wear it. You think?"

"Yes, ma'am, I sure do," Jeff said. "And I know that color is red, ain't it?" He pointed to small roses tied into a posey with a pretty ribbon.

"Some folks call it magenta. I know that 'cause one time I was deliv-erin' some clothes to one of my women. Long ago it was. She was real nice to me. Always gave me some sweet tea to drink on her back stoop if she didn't have no company in her kitchen. Then one day when I started off, I seen a beautiful rose along the path to her gate. I bent over to smell it. Smelled like the finest soap that gots flowers in it like I smelled in the white folks' houses I used to clean. That woman, she came out and yelled for me to stop. I ain't pullin' up your roses, I tol' her. Then she come up with a knife. Said that rose was magenta-colored and it was her favorite, too. She cut it and tucked the bloom in the buttonhole of my blouse. Said she only wanted me to stop so's she could give it to me to smell all the way home. Don't even 'member anybody ever done something so nice. No white woman, I mean. I held that flower to my nose all the way home just to smell it. Always thought if I ever had me a baby girl, I'd call 'er Magenta. See that flower, just under the little bird?"

"I see it," Jeff said. "What color is that?"

"That's a special color. So special it don't have a name."

"You seen it on a flower then, Sister?" I asked.

"Maybe, but know for sure I seen it at church. See, there's a woman that has so many pretty dresses. She gots one that very color. Her husband takes her hand when they get up to leave and pats it as they walk all the way to the door. He looks so proud of her. Proud enough to give her all them fine things she wears, I 'magine. What color is that? Guess, I don't know. Oh, well. What difference does it make?"

Sister's voice had gotten so quiet we could hardly hear her. I never knew how much she so loved flowers. That night, around the table, her thoughts seemed to flow like torrents in a spring rain fixing to cleanse her soul of woes. Yes, there was a look of peace that came over Sister's face as she caressed her soft sapphire-colored feather bird with love.

Fred Comes Calling

22

WITH JESSE IN jail our days delivered a peace that we so easily scattered smiles over. Running irons over those miles of old shirts, we talked about not hearing from Fred for days. Still, there were too many of those black dreams closing in on us when we fell over our cots at night from exhaustion. Yes, had to keep on the run, a step ahead of the man behind bars. We knew that Fred would try anything on us to chain us tighter to Jesse. How Jesse loved to brag in our faces about Fred getting fired from the county 'cause he was too damned mean to the folks that worked the ditches. Yes, we got his point, and the years living on that alley had only sharpened it.

Then one morning Fred came 'round reeking of desperation. I'd never seen him shake so. I figured he had to have caught it from Jesse; I knew that smell. It was the rank odor of Jesse's desperation for a bottle. That morning Fred was dripping sweat with big rings under his arms on a shirt he'd surely worn for days. He was looking for mercy in the form of money or anything he could get his hands on. These two who offered nothing to nobody had now found themselves begging.

You see, Fred had finally come clean as to why Jesse was in jail. Talk was that Jesse had some gambling friends who knew folks in the city jail. The guards over there would look after him till he squeezed money from some woman, else they'd be pleased to take him on a long drive from which he was unlikely to return. Folks said the Klan was sure to be down that road to nowhere, and coloreds who got lost out there were frequently found spinning from hanging trees.

Them city people coming down on Jesse didn't care 'bout some stack of empty whiskey bottles in no alley. They were merely helping good ol' Jesse pay up his gambling debts, and if getting down to business on Jesse meant a kick-back here and there, who'd care? That was life in the alleys; always whittled sharp. We talked about it. About when Jesse got out how he'd blame us for all his troubles as it was our duty to make sure he had no woes on his easy street where Fred was not the only squatter. Maybe Jesse been pacing that crowded cell looking for an exit to squeeze through like we'd been from that alley. Through it all, Sister and I kept to our promise; we'd not buy Jesse a ticket back with what little money we had. No, it would be our own freedom that came next. Or so we prayed.

And yet things were changing 'round Jesse's alley. At least the part where we'd finally begun to sort things harder than we did those piles of stinking clothes that waited on the porch. Things that Fred and Jesse couldn't keep an eye on, like our fears of their fists, were getting tossed out along with yesterday's garbage. Of course, I knew all along Fred was spying on us; he was Jesse's very own nigger dog. So, we decided never to let him in again. I tacked a note on the porch door reading we was out delivering ironing. We kept our kitchen curtains closed tight 'cept for peeks. But nobody could be out delivering that much, or then where's the money? Fred surely thought it had to be hidden in Louvenia's kitchen someplace. His thinking went sharp on him when he got to feeling that dry desert at the bottom of his whiskey belly and knew his brother had a similar condition as he sweltered over there in a cell across the hall from the whores he had unfinished business with—them wanting Jesse's bills paid up, too. Between these men, desperation was going 'round like a contagion.

Then once, when we was out buying canned goods, Annie said she seen Fred through her kitchen window as she did her dishes. He was down there pounding at our door even with the note there. Guess he sensed that his existence had to be getting perilously close to that bottomless well he was dancing on the crumbling edges of. He had to know that when Jesse came to the end of his final bottle, Fred's would be just as empty. That had them desperate with fear. We knew that somehow Jesse was sure to pry them iron jail bars open and then come put one to our heads. An iron bar, that is.

"You got some money? Huh, yeah? Huh?" Fred was there dancing on the other side of that latched screen door, gyrating like he had to pee ever so bad.

"No, Fred. I got nothing for you. Nope. Not a thing."

But he could see Louvenia had just put a nice breakfast on the table across from the open cupboards full of tins of food and mason jars of fruit the neighbor had canned and sold us.

"I need me a dollar," Fred whined. "I go take it over in the jail so Jesse can buy a decent meal. Yeah, give me a dollar then. No, two, like I say."

"Fred, I 'magine two dollar's only gonna buy you a bottle. Maybe two if you go across town. But Jesse, he say it ain't safe to go over there. They know you and your brother over there and they's likely to roll you."

At that I shut the door to Fred's pleading just as Jesse always did to Louvenia's after her head hit the wall again.

Despite Fred's dropping his needs at our door like they were his dirty laundry to be done up, there was yet a grace in our lives—that glorious lull from Jesse's curses. We enjoyed sharing the bounty our laundry money brought with Brother and Jeffrey, who started eating over most nights. That made their lives a bit better too. Had nothing but a hot meal to give them, and yet they savored every bite like it was a Sunday supper. The four of us, and sometimes two or three of Annie's kids, crowded 'round that little table for simple meals heaped with laughter. Jeff loved kids. He could tickle them with a grin when he aimed a finger at their tickle spots. Sister delighted in all the laughter and her joy spilled over to me as well. In those moments, thoughts of Jesse and his brother were all but forgotten. Gone like yesterday's tossed garbage.

∾

Saturday nights when we didn't have much ironing to finish up, Annie would bring her young'uns over to play. She said the peace and quiet back at her place helped the preacher prepare his sermons. Louvenia loved them kids so much, didn't she? She'd sit at the table chattering with them while stitching rag dolls together. One evening Annie brought over a box of brown buttons for dolls' eyes along with patches of old cloth for dolls' clothes. I baked batches of sugar cookies and every pan was gone near as quickly as I pulled it out of the oven. Annie, her kids, Sister, and I sat all evening eating cookies and sewing dolls and doll clothes. No sounds from that ugly alley ever penetrated these precious moments; no old man in the other room cursing away the nightmares that stalked him; the nightmare of him drowning under a desert of hot sand with not one bottle to be had.

Every day had gotten a bit better for us, but at the same time, every day was a bit closer to the day we knew Jesse would connive a way through his bars to go to one. At times that started to nip at my thoughts like a pack of nigger dogs. I wanted to slow the avalanche of fear rolling towards Louvenia, too. She couldn't suspend her notion as to what Jesse was gonna do to us 'cause we never paid off his gambling debts. Fred had made it clear that he was none too happy and sure as hell didn't take to the food I sent to the jail. Once in the dead of night I awoke to find Sister pacing about in the dark wringing her hands from worry. She didn't seem to notice me sitting up on my cot.

"Jesse not here, Sister, but ain't you still livin' in his hell hole if you keep it in your head like he is?"

She returned to her cot breathing heavy-like as she did on those nights when he'd come home drunk and went to bashing his words over our shattered sleep.

"He gots no power on you 'cept in your mind," I said. "You're still thinkin' Jesse can fly out of them jail bars and come hit you upside your head. If that's the case, haven't you done put them bars on yourself and given the keys to Jesse for keepin'? He ain't gonna do nothin' 'cause he can't survive without us when he gets out."

"He didn't know that all them times he put my head through the wall?" Her voice was tight, like he was right there squeezing her throat.

In the days ahead, Louvenia's every moment of happiness was stymied, wondering if Jesse knew the secret of his survival, which was no secret because it was only by Sister that he made it to the next swig. She wondered if that secret was just another distorted dream we'd already worn out by jabbing it too hard with our hopes all them years. Was it gonna be okay for us down the road someplace? Where, then? How far along the journey before I get me some? Could I hold out that long? Or if I did, would I even care by then? How easily our prayers so often turned into diluted pleas for mercy. The hardest place to sit tall ain't the pews at church; it's in the face of the curses hurled at your dignity.

Sister looked intense, but then sat up on her cot as though she was gonna try on her new hat. But she never said nothing for the longest spell. Still, I knew she was gonna try to be brave and let Jesus work his end of it.

"What's Jesse sayin' over there 'bout us not comin' up with the money to get him out?" she asked as if I could hear across town any better. How many times had he boxed her ears by then? Lord, she even ducked from the thought of him.

Towards the end of the night Sister's fears wore her out and she finally drifted to sleep. But the next morning she didn't drag herself up before dawn to catch up on the ironing that was, God only knows, never caught up. Not bothered by should Fred come calling, I got up and pulled the curtains open wide for the first time in days. It was a beautiful Saturday morning when Sister shuffled up for her coffee. As I ironed, she sat down at the table with her mug, looked over the rag doll we'd worked on the night before and smiled as she went through Annie's box of brown buttons to sort a matched pair for eyes. She stitched them on as we chatted. I still remember the look of serenity on her face as she gazed into the two brown button eyes of that little rag doll. I imagined that rag doll could see into Sister's exposed soul more than Jesse ever tried to. Lord, have mercy on him. If you have to.

"I want us to go downtown this afternoon," she said in that quiet voice that always reminded me of Daddy. "Want to get some paint; maybe a real soft color that's gonna remind us of Annie's sweet peas. We gonna paint this here kitchen where we been workin' day in and day out for too long."

"We don't gots lots of ironin' to deliver," I replied. "I'll finish that pile later. On the way back from deliverin' we'll get some paint if that's what you're thinkin'. Is that what, Sister?"

She rose and took the iron to finish my piece. "I'll finish here; you fry some of that ham so we can take sandwiches to Alex and Jeffrey."

Soon we headed downtown for paint. Sister met Annie down there and went with her to do some errands as I visited the men at the stables. Mr. Harold had not shown up that day, so things were good for us to talk about Jesse. Jeff said he was too old and weak to come home swinging no more. He figured Jesse was only gonna go find his bed and then reach for the easiest bottle he could get his hands on. Then he'd lie back in his dark bedroom catching up on old times with his captive bourbon buddy.

That Monday Louvenia seemed to keep her fears to herself and didn't say much. Yet even in her long silences, I knew things were different for her. We both felt it, just in different ways. When Sister had her work done, she went to painting our kitchen. She painted it a beautiful pale blue and put some bright green curtains up in the window made from fabric she and Annie had pieced from old choir robes. Hung in the same window where I'd planned on putting jars of pickled Jesse. Later that evening I read the Psalms as Sister hummed while she ironed our dresses for church. We'd worked hard for days and again put back some money in a place Fred or Jesse could never find. Or so we hoped.

Lurking in the Shadows

23

I RECALL IT BEING a warm evening. After leaving Jeff and Alex at the park I seemed to wander aimlessly. Had lots to think on and couldn't make myself head back to the alley. When the sun started down and I had no more shop windows to spend my dreams in, I drifted back to Jesse's taking the long way. But it could not have been long enough. The moment I stepped into that alley I could feel it: the presence of Satan. I knew the stench well.

Momma told me up on Orchard Hill that if you listen carefully an angel's gonna tell you when there's danger lurking. But most times I could hardly hear much of anything through all the screams in my life. But this time the angel sent word through one of Annie's little ones. Annie had little Nettie standing on a stool in her kitchen window to watch for me. At the sight of me, Nettie slapped at the window and waved and yelled for her momma. Annie dashed out drying her hands in her apron followed by her kids tugging at her. She yelled to the kids like they were in danger.

"Get back in the house!"

Her eyes said more than words. Something was lurking in the shadows of that awful alley!

"He's down there!" Annie blurted. "Jesse got home earlier."

Her words hit me like a kick in the stomach. Jesse home! She glanced down at my kitchen window as though Jesse might be watching for my return.

"No!" I resisted. "He ain't 'pose' to get out till late next week. Fred said!"

"Sister Louvenia said Fred's a liar!" Annie reminded me. "I know she's in there, but she never answered when I came to see if she's okay."

At that I knew that my prayer had gone unanswered; the prayer that Jesse's sins would end up storing him behind bars forever. It was not to be. Once again he'd squeezed through them bars as he'd squeezed through the many scrapes in his life. I knew that he would surely be waiting to inflict the revenge that Fred had so long promised.

"Fred brought 'im 'round earlier. Him cursin' like the devil himself," Annie said. "Guess they come from the bar. Fred, he just left. That man's so drunk he could hardly walk."

My heart fell into a tumbled rhythm as I sorted Annie's words. Then I realized that Sister was in there and not answering Annie's knock. Lord, have mercy. Annie wiped a tear.

Shaking, I walked up on the porch feeling my palms go wet from fear. Guess Sister had been hanging clothes across the porch earlier as they were still dripping in the stale alley air. I opened the kitchen door, and, there in all his glory, was Satan restored to his throne eating his supper.

Jesse winked like he'd been waiting for that door to creak open. He fondled his bottle like a trophy he'd just won. Jesse was used to winning. We had his trophies to prove it. A scar here, one over there and so many more where the wounds never stopped bleeding enough to scare over.

"You been expectin' me, huh, lil' girl?" he growled like a nigger dog. "Even got the place all fixed up for my homecomin', ain't ya?" His thick words were weighted under half-bottle slurs.

But where was Louvenia?

I suddenly realized there was a dead stillness, like an undertaker's parlor long after the candles are blown out and the last sobs put away. As that man stared and sucked the whiskey off his brown lips, I heard a faint whisper tap at my fears. Perhaps it was Minerva imploring me to hide them as I stood in the face of Satan himself.

"Got the place painted up here, ain't ya?" he said. "Lot better than the jail I been in. And then you gots enough food for the neighborhood canned up and waitin' on them shelves, ain't ya? But seems you can't get your hands on no money to get your Jesse out 'a jail. That be the case? Sure, it do seem, don't it? Now, what are we gonna do to set that right? Huh, lil' girl?"

"You out 'a jail if you're sittin' there," I replied. "Ain't that 'bout as right as you're gonna get?" I stood back, out of swinging distance from his chair.

"Yep, I sure is. Sittin' right here at my own table where I belongs. Thanks to my brother Fred who been lookin' out after you for weeks now, ain't he? And what's he gotten for it? Huh? He ain't got nothin' from the two of youse but grief and a smart-mouths deserving bustin'. So, I tell you, they done let me out early thinkin' I could get my hands on the money quicker. Follow my drift, lil' girl? Seems like ever'body knows there's money comin' back to my place. Ever'body but Louvenia. She don't know nothin', do she? That's what her story is back there. So I put it to her again and again, I did. 'I don't believe you, woman,' I tol' 'er. 'You're lyin' to me! You're lyin' to your own husband.' That's what I said to that bitch."

"Where's Louvenia? Where's Sister now?"

"Seems like she done had a bad fall over the news I was gettin' out. Must 'a happened right when the word got put to her ears a few times! You know her, she don't hear like she ought 'a. Then again, maybe she tripped over my foot when she went lookin' for my money to put things right between us. Don't think she's dead, but maybe. I ain't inclined to go back to see for sure. You know where that money is, or you want Louvenia to keep thinkin' where she put it with what's left of her head?"

Jesse guzzled his bottle and wiped the yellow drool from his mouth, then pulled from his pocket a wad, which he threw in my face. What crumbled at my feet were the pieces of Louvenia's little feather bird. I could hardly look as I knew what those shreds meant. Something was for sure bleeding to death. I jumped, aiming for Jesse's bedroom, expecting him to go for my throat. He only sat there on his throne knowing it didn't matter what he did; in his dominion evil won, no matter how far the fearful scattered. Nobody escaped, so why run from his fist because sooner more than later, he would exact his revenge and Fred would be nearby sniffing through the carnage for scraps to gnaw on. I headed around the table for the backroom.

Sister was sitting in the dark. She jolted when the door creaked open, as if somebody had jabbed at her ribs with a poker. She turned her head to that blank wall only a dozen inches from her face. Sitting there she held what was left of her hat with one trembling hand. The other arm hung down. Why did it hang that way? Like it needed to pick up a shred of felt from the floor, palm facing out limp-like and her other hand swollen ever so bad.

I glanced around a broken room where pieces of Sister's hat were mixed into the ruins with pieces of her face. No, Louvenia wasn't expecting a reunion with Jesse's fist that night. I'd never seen her so bad; that lip hanging all black and swollen. So distorted were her features that had she been on the street, I'd not known it was her walking past. She sat there rocking like her swaying head had given the struggle to stay balanced on her shoulders. She nearly could have held it in her lap the way it teetered that direction. Was it fear that kept her from looking at me through the swelling around her blackened eyes? Or did she see the silhouette of Jesse's fist coming at her again? Horror can distort every fear it hands you.

She held the pieces of that hat cradled to her, now no more than a knot of torn felt, smashed bows, crushed flowers and broken feathers. It was a dream murdered but not one she was ready to bury. Just the same, her sighs echoed a dirge. Thought she was about die, but then through the side of her badly swollen mouth a few words fell.

"He gots his bottle out there," she said breathing heavy-like over the longest pause I ever endured in my life. "When he get to the bottom… maybe I come out. You best go down to Annie's till he passes out. Hear?"

A broken piece of tooth followed her last words to join a piece of her face at her feet. She wiped her chin of blood and flesh.

Jesse's words from the other room were crystal-clear though. Like the old times, he cursed for Louvenia's attendance. Yes, Jesse was home again. His bellows heralded the occasion. "Hey, I done told you I want more tatas. Now's when I want 'em," he yelled from the table. "Get 'em peeled and fried up if you knows what's good for ya. But then it don't seem like you do, do it?"

His hollering could have been heard up and down the blackened brick walls of that alley. As broken as she was, Sister still wrenched herself up to get that ol' man more food. How many meals had he wrenched from her by then? Her eyes and that long sigh, like after a blow to the stomach, told me it wasn't only the pain from the beating this time. It had become the kind of pain that can only be eased with the thought that the Lord will soon come for you to take you away from it all and on to His Orchard.

"I go get that man's tatas on… Yeah, I do it…"

I pushed the debris off the bed and lifted her feet up to keep the swelling down. I reached to take the pieces of that hat off her lap. Still she held on to it tightly, held on to something that was no longer there. Louvenia caressed a bit of feather like it was the hair of a child even as Jesse rattled his threats. Guess he wasn't nearly as close to the bottom of that bottle as I'd wished. He was on another gambler's roll, him and his bourbon buddy. Yes, Jesse's good times were back, and his alley would soon be quaking for it.

"If you make me get up from this here chair, you're gonna see my fist again!" he slurred. "Jesse done come home and we gots some book-keeping to deal with now." His fist hit the tabletop. He was drunk, but it was nearly an eternal hour of bellowing and cursing before Jesse finally teetered into his plate snoring.

As I went for a chip of ice on Louvenia's face I stood looking at that ugly ol' man and asked myself, "Where's that rusty pair of scissors, Momma?" 'Cause right there was his naked throat daring me to stab into it. I figured I'd leave his half-severed head in that plate till Sister walked back into her kitchen wondering why he wasn't yelling for her no more. He dead, I'd gladly inform her. He gone! Momma told me how to do it and do it quick-like. Got to have mercy on an ailing animal like Jesse. Yes, stone drunk he was lying in his own plate. He'd not had a drink for weeks, unless Fred somehow got him a bottle. Satan only knows they could pull a bottle out of nowhere.

Over the next few days all Jesse did was guzzle our lives down as we ran bottles in circles to Jesse's throat to keep him off ours. It was like running empty buckets to a raging fire.

❧

In the days ahead, Jesse was truly back in jail again, however this one he owned. His cell was that dingy backroom where he'd spent endless hours in bed during those warmest of autumn days while Sister spent the same hours fanning him so the flies and acrid air from the alley didn't trouble his slumber.

So Jesse'd leave her be, I did Sister's work. Then she could keep to the fanning and serving. He never came for my throat. But I knew his revenge would come soon enough. How I prayed that when Jesse finally fell he'd drag Brother Fred with him. You see Fred was still sniffing for scraps and hounding Jesse for some of Louvenia's money, payment for keeping an eye on us all them weeks. Jesse had once again pulled us under the currents of his filthy alley as easily as if he'd simply dozed off for another nap. I was convinced the undertow would swallow us all if I did not act soon enough. Yet, what?

Well, it turned out Louvenia's good ironing hand got broken when Jesse drug her 'round the room that night trying to squeeze her head for where our money was hidden. Or did the room really spin her head so hard her arm got pulled out of the socket from the velocity? Head spinning, or the room itself, Sister told me the whole time Jesse pounded his revenge, Fred was there looking on with satisfaction, calling her the ugly bitch getting what she deserved. Nigger dogs like Fred can bark curses like their masters even as they salivate for the scraps. Strangely, under all that torture, Louvenia never told them where we'd hid our bit of money.

Maybe somewhere deep in her addled soul there was still a bit of hope left. A seed or two perhaps. But even a tiny mustard seed can grow into something, someday, somehow, I kept telling myself and then asked the Lord if I was right. Yes, I prayed and hoped that if we lived through all this one more time, the money we'd hidden away might buy us a ticket out of there before it bought us a pauper's grave. Maybe even a ticket to a crumb of dignity. Likely somewhere we'd never heard of. But who knew where that life was? The next whistle stop? Right after the junction marked with our broken skulls; the spot staked by our splintered bones? Or a hundred years even beyond that?

Sister had long known she was living with her back against his slimy walls, but like she kept telling me, that alley opened to no place better for her. Like walnut shells, her hands were gnarled at the joints from the years of hard work that never let up. No laundry house was gonna hire her for a few pennies a week, as there were countless young women leaping onto them tubs to feed their kids. Even young, Sister was no longer young, and the scars Jesse had bestowed only made her older. Louvenia had no choice. She was his slave till she could figure a painless way out. In her darkest agony did she secretly look for a clean jump to the next life? How many miles up is the roof if our backs are broken first by that ol' man? Far enough away from Jesse? Close enough to the clouds? That do? Or make it all worse if I should survive the fall? Then, Lord will you finally hear our prayers?

Yes, as the days followed each other in an ever-deepening haze, Jesse kept drunk and we kept bringing him the chamber pot as we washed up his life to hold on to ours in this bitter peace between servants and master. Yet I figured somehow there was still enough of that brittle peace for me to renegotiate the terms of our surrender. I asked Jesus for help, even if I'd convinced myself that He'd gone deaf to our prayers. Evil spreads like swamp fever, and no waving of a stick will ever vanquish it. Yes, our lives were all getting lost again in Jesse's alley just as he and his brother had regained theirs!

DROWNING UNDER MY DAYS

24

THE GRIEF JESSE'S return brought to our lives rolled over our days like a crashing tide. I knew that it would soon drown us all. "Lord," I prayed, "help me to swallow the rush of my rage so the end comes quicker; another act or two of violence might be all it will take." We were sinking in an alley of hopelessness that we couldn't escape and Jesse was holding our heads under for all we were worth.

You see, it got to be that Alex and Jeff couldn't come by for meals. Jesse'd take it out on Sister if he even thought I'd been putting home-cooked food for the men on the porch while he slumbered back in his dark room where time was as stale as the air. Maybe he didn't want another man seeing him wallowing in his misery back there even if he relished rubbing our noses in it. Being hard-working men, Jeff and Alex ate what they could get their hands on. But they hardly got their wages, and what they got went for miserable food that should have been tossed out. At times I would think on that when I took Jesse's supper plate to him still in bed. He'd be too thirsty to eat any of it, so it would sit there long after he staggered off to the bars.

Through it all I worked hard to keep things going as best I could. Then one night, after Jesse had finally headed off, I went about preparing supper for Sister, Alex and Jeff. But Jesse was quick to make detours to see if I was holding food back for the men. I was taking a pan of biscuits out when he nearly knocked the door down to see what he may have missed.

"You forget somethin', Jesse?"

"Who them biscuits for?" he snarled as he scrutinized the room carefully like Alex and Jeff might have disappeared under the table. "You know I don't like biscuits!" He growled till bile seeped at the corners of his mouth. "Don't want nobody in my house!" he shouted from the porch as he left for the good times.

His house? Our money that paid the rent! The math on that was troubling.

I helped Annie get her kids' clothes washed up even as Jesse cursed that I'd better get paid for it. Annie couldn't let her kids come over no more. Sister knew Jesse was the reason, yet still it wounded and made her hate the ol' man all the more.

I knew that things were closing in on Sister and she was slowly surrendering to it all; the darkness of hopelessness. Once in the middle of the night I awoke to her yammering and found Sister over at the table sitting in the dark.

"What are you sewin' over there, Sister? I can barely see you in the dark."

"It ain't dark no more 'cause I'm sewin' a real pretty hat to wear to church for when my face heals. Yes, gonna be the prettiest hat ever. I know it is 'cause Jesus told me so. You think my face's gonna heal one day? You think?"

I was thinking maybe not no more. Maybe no more times left. Hadn't we used them all up by then?

But I tell you, that was no hat Sister was sewing. It was another rag doll for the kids. She held it up for me to see, but it had no big brown button eyes. She mumbled something 'bout rag dolls ain't 'pose' to see the ugly of our days. But I knew rag dolls with no eyes saw only as well as ones with button eyes sewn on. My tears that night didn't keep me from wondering how good we were seeing things ourselves. I lay on my cot watching her look over that doll like a mother looks at her newborn. Time was running out for us. I had to save Sister somehow, somewhere before it was too late. But who would save me?

⁓

The next morning I struggled up early so's I could get the piles of laundry going and Jesse's food made, so then Sister could sleep in. Every minute of rest Louvenia got made a difference. Sometimes she didn't fall asleep till nearly dawn, what with serving Jesse's needs and helping me with the ironing. She'd spend her sleeping hours fanning him when the air was thick and only the stench of that alley coming through the window was her constant companion. Or was that really Jesse we smelled?

He screeched at the sound of a peck at the door.

"Who's at the God-damned door?"

"It's just the boy bringin' my wash soap," I yelled back as Annie slipped in the door.

"How's Sister Louvenia?" she whispered. "We've been prayin' for her at church."

"She's comin' together slow this time. Don't know how many more times she's gonna heal up though. Don't even know if she wants to, no more."

Annie cried too.

"Who's out there? Hey? I'm talkin' to you," Jesse growled.

"I told you Jesse, it's the delivery boy with my laundry soap. He wants a tip; you got a coin for 'im?"

Jesse went back to sleep on that. He wasn't gonna get out of bed to give a poor boy a coin, that's for sure.

"This is all I got to share, Sister Sarah," Annie whispered. "You know my kids eat my cupboards bare."

Annie uncovered a golden crust apple pie still warm from her oven. With tears I took that pie over to the cupboard to hide it back 'fore Jesse smelled it. If he found it, he'd take it over to Fred's for their whores. I knew he would, too.

"Annie, Sister and me just can't cook nothin' decent these days. That pie is a bit of holiday for us. It is. Gonna cut it when Louvenia comes home from deliverin'. Later, I'll take some to the stables for the men, too. Thank you for this, Annie."

Annie hugged me like it might help heal my soul. Or maybe I was really hanging on to her to relieve my pain. Yes, I 'magine I stood there limp like a rag doll gots no big brown button eyes 'cause I don't remember her leaving. Fragments of our memories are carried with the smells of every day. For a few fleeting moments that morning life smelled like hot cinnamon apple pie that Annie's sweet friendship delivered to the door of my agony—a taste of hope that there's some goodness out there that knew us by name.

Annie was always good to us. We never felt as beaten down when she was near. And she always was, even when Jesse was on the rampage. She loved her husband—had five kids with him, didn't she? But he was gone long hours visiting his parishioners, and that left her alone to make do. See, the preacher was the only person 'round who would listen to or cared about our people. His work was dedicated to leading folk's minds away from the squalor and hopelessness of them alleys to something he had faith was on the other side of that alley, a Summerland kind of place. Had to be one, he kept preaching, which kept us on the lookout for something like hope. At times I guess we found a nibble of it and that fed our desperation enough that we could step over to the next day after all. The preacher would have smiled knowing that he had succeeded.

Yet I still wondered if the preacher's notions were challenged by all the wakes he'd done. My people died easy-like, but never easy. In the alleys most folks just fell over dead. Yes, those tubs could stack up on you when you weren't looking out for yourself and the fall could be fatal. Even though we didn't drag the chains of slavery, the vices of the alleys still chased and mauled us in more ways than any nigger dog overseer could have devised.

I always figured Annie gave to her people by taking care of the preacher so he could do Jesus' work up. Nobody knew at church what she did without so he could serve their needs. Just knew she was the preacher's wife and could read and write good. Seldom seen her at their home when somebody dying, getting married or being welcomed into Jesus' family at birth. But none of this would 'a happened if it hadn't been for this good Christian woman.

She made me want to be like her. I wanted to help my people. Maybe I couldn't help the preacher myself to lighten his load, but I could help Annie and that's what Louvenia and I talked on. We would put in extra time by doing her laundry. Till when Jesse got out of jail, Sister would bring the little ones over two or three at a time for Sister to bathe. Sometimes the kids sang along with her while she sewed dolls. Young Roy would stand on a stool and preach like his daddy while the others were getting soaped down. Louvenia was always filled with joy when them kids got out of the basin and wanted her to sing the church songs. They'd try to sing along, all mush-mouthed, clutching tightly the brown button-eyed rag dolls Sister made them. When their eyes grew heavy, we'd put them down on our cots till the preacher came for them. Then one by one he carried them back, him kissing their cheeks as if living depended on it.

There were too few days back then when Jeff and I could slip away to spend a few hours together. Since coming to live with Sister, I'd never really gotten out of town. Gone no place much further than a circle of blocks where we delivered. One bright Saturday morning Annie fried up some chicken livers with crumbled bacon and Louvenia made a sweet potata pie all for Jeff and me. He came by with one of the stable's buggies and we went off to the edge of Vicksburg, far enough away that the din of the city was muffled by the sound of a stream. The air was fresh out there. Happy was I to leave that dusty acrid air trapped between the ugly brick walls where they burned the garbage but only when it got piled high enough it could burn itself. It soon became a regular outing for us, as we both loved the countryside. Out there, we'd talk, laugh, eat, and then talk and laugh even more. Then sometimes we'd do nothing and Jeff simply held me. I had so much to think on, because the fog in my head could easily stir up the darkness back then. Didn't need any words with Jeff. His very touch or glance brought a calmness that claimed the moment and left it safely in my memories.

Sometimes, somewhere early in those bright moments of our love I got to counting again. Counting the days where I found new joys and the blessings they came from. How many times did Jeff bring this feeling to my heart? However, I guess it was 'bout then that things started coming down hard on Jeff and Brother. They barely got by at the stables in the best of times when there were plenty of customers coming in. Jeff told me his boss, Mr. Harold, lost himself to a bottle most days by noon, if he showed up at all.

"His wife mean-mouthed you, too?" I asked.

Jeff told me he'd seldom saw Mrs. Harold, but she was always nice and even baked a pan of cornbread for them from time to time. Things between Harold and his wife got so bad that at times she'd leave him and head for her sister's. There he'd go pleading for another chance. But when she was gone, Mr. Harold was overcome by his own demons and would get crazy on the men. When you're at war with your life there's seldom peace for anybody. Harold's rage set him against Alex and Jeff. Where else could he shovel it?

Jeff and Alex knew it was bad for Mr. Harold so they did the best they could to keep things going despite his abuse. When Harold was back in the storeroom sleeping it off, they kept the stable going and then took the money, even though Harold owed them weeks of wages, and handed it over to Mrs. Harold who had four or five kids. When Harold come up from his dead drunk again, he'd say the men stole his money even when Mrs. Harold told him she had it fine. He was so mean he couldn't believe anybody could be honest. Harold's kids ate because of Jeff and Alex more than 'cause of their own pa. Even ate when the men hadn't.

Back then I was getting worried about my brother, 'cause you know he just had no patience with mean white folk. I was troubled that he might do something that might bring his life crashing down. "Please, Lord, watch over Brother," Sister and I prayed. Still, I got to thinking that maybe with all the screams and pleas coming from that alley, Jesus simply couldn't make out what we're praying on. Most times, neither could we. Ain't hopes frayed at the ends when they're near to being worn out? Guess that 'bout happens when they're gone for good. Seemed like every day we wondered what would come of us if another day did, and that made our dreams shudder.

Yes, blessings were running thinner by the day; about as thin as my hopes. But then times were bad throughout the South as plantations struggled against the competition they'd always strangled out. Vicksburg and townships around had throngs of colored folks squeezed off the plantations from what white folks called sharecropping, where nothing was shared but still divided—profits to the plantation owners and the debts and misery to the 'croppers. Suddenly cotton prices got so low it wasn't worth picking. We paid for the crop failures first. It was the only line we could stand at the front of, the lines for the empty-handed. It was the same old oppression with the same ol' bookkeeping for this new South. No, it wasn't just the alleys 'round Jesse's place, but all Vicksburg was crawling with desperation. I tell you, times were bad, but were they ever different for my people?

Mr. Harold's bitterness had to find a head to bash somewhere, and did so in keeping with the methods and devices of the South, right on a colored man. Seemed as though all his anger fell on Jeff and Alex, who wouldn't cower to his meanness. Sometimes Harold threw their half-pay at their feet rather than give them any courtesy. Something had to give. The men started mumbling that there was no light at the end of their tunnel. "Lord, don't let violence come of it," I prayed, and for Jeff to calm his anger. I never told Louvenia 'bout nothing going on at the stables. Lord, she couldn't bear the weight of no more woes.

On the way back that afternoon, Jeff got quiet. When I asked him what bothered him, he said it was Alex. He'd been getting quiet of late and seemed to get lost in his own silence. That worried me, as Jeff and Alex always talked easily. During one of these late-night confessions about their hopes and fears, Brother told Jeff 'bout when he went off one night to the carnival that happened every year in Vicksburg. He'd never seen such a sight. Folks, white and coloreds, coming from all over and not bothering each other; just gawking at the lights and the swinging rides and games with pretty colored prizes that everyone seemed to win. Jeff said Alex's eyes lit up like a carnival just talking 'bout this adventure. I'd never been to such a thing and could hardly imagine it. Alex told Jeff he'd encountered some man moving crates and boxes. He offered to help him. He paid Brother a quarter when the task was done. Alex asked 'bout work. This man, he laughed in Brother's face, and told him nobody was gonna stop him from spending his money at the carnival, but not to bother looking for regular work. No, that was no more than a borrowed dream.

Still Alex saw carnival work as an adventure that might carry him to new parishes and counties. Maybe where a man was judged by the weight he could haul in life more than the weight of the white shadows that dragged on him.

Drifting to a Dream

25

LATE ONE AFTERNOON when I returned from my deliveries, Sister was there busy frying bacon. "This is near cooked. I'm makin' bacon sandwiches for the men." She moved about like a storm was headed our way. It was.

"What's you in a hurry for?"

She banged a fry pan on the stove like they'd had a bad quarrel.

"Don't give that fry pan no mercy!" I said. "It ain't Sunday and it's burned too many fried eggs anyway."

"Want the men to eat this before we go hungry."

I was puzzled. "But I ain't hungry."

"No?" was all she said as she wrapped the sandwiches in newsprint.

"You goin' hungry here fryin' bacon?" I swayed back and forth to stay out of her way. "What's the matter, Sister? Jesse ain't here is he?"

"No. He gone. Probably won't stumble in till I'm sound asleep. Him wondering where his bacon is and droppin' this here skillet on the stove for me to get up and get busy with it."

"That's all you're worried 'bout?" I asked. "Jesse wantin' more of somethin'?"

"Was at the grocer's this morning," she said. "Jesse, he been putting bottles for him and Fred on the bill over there. Seems like ever'body at the bar gots a bottle, too. Yeah, Jesse real popular these days. He done told the grocer I's good for the money."

"Lordy, so there ain't no more credit for food?" I asked. "How we gonna make it to the end of the month?"

"I don't know how we gonna make it to the end of the week! That bill's up higher than anybody gots money for. Oh, Lord we's in trouble now!"

She handed me a jar of sweet tea with no chip of ice. We were out of that too, which was why Sister decided to fry the bacon before it went bad.

"But don't start in on what you know I ain't gonna do."

"What do I already know, that I don't know, for all you know?" I asked.

"I'm not in the mood for sass," Sister said. "What you know is when our money's gone you always remind me there's a few coins put back. That money's gonna stay hidden. I ain't gonna use it for Jesse's bottle bills no more than we used it for his jail bail. That means even if we go hungry, and after this bacon gets eaten up, that's where we's at! You hearin' me now?"

I'd heard. I took the sandwiches, kissed Sister on the cheek for having the courage not to pull her escape money out, and headed over to the stables. There it seemed strangely quiet, like nobody was 'round. I stood there peeking in. The sun was hot against my back, but it was real dark in there and I couldn't see nobody, so I called out. Only the horses replied.

Then I noticed the longest shadow looming my way. It was the silhouette of a man I thought had to be ten feet tall. But it wasn't. It was Alex, looking pained and confused.

"Brother? That you? Why you over there in the dark?" I asked. "Didn't hear me call?"

"Don't know where I's 'pose' to be," he finally replied. "Ain't nobody called me. Nope. Been here all morning. Nobody called me for nothin'. Nobody."

"Why you hiding over there? Come on out."

"I got no place to go."

Alex didn't move. He stood there looking like a lost child struggling to hold back cries for his ma. I tugged at his hand and pulled him into the light near the doors.

"Here. Here's you a bacon sandwich Sister made. Annie baked the bread this morning."

Alex held that sandwich like he didn't know what to do next.

"Where's Jeff?"

"Riverman went to take Mrs. Harold the returns for the week. Reckon he be back soon," Alex replied. Then he looked me in the eyes.

"Mr. Harold, he say somethin' to you? Somethin' mean?" I asked.

"He say he don't want me here no more. Said he gonna do something to me if he sees me 'round."

"That why you're hidin'?" I asked. "You tell Jeff? He know 'bout this?"

"Riverman, he don't hear me no more. Anyway, I know what I gots to do. Got to move on."

"Move on?" I asked. "What's you mean? You gots no place to move on to."

"Get on out of Vicksburg, is what I mean. I got to."

"Where to?" I asked.

"Maybe go back over the river to Delta."

"The Burneys'?"

"It ain't that far, is it? Got to tell pa something."

"Brother, we ain't never goin' go back to the Burneys'. It's a ways on the train and then over the river to Delta. Don't you 'member?"

"Got to go home," he said. "Go fishin' with pa and Samuel."

"Daddy, he ain't there waitin' for you," I said.

"I been 'memberin' us out on the river bringin' in catfish. Got to see it again, don't I?"

"What did Jeff say 'bout you goin' off?" I asked again. "You and him, you got to talk it out. If you go looking for work, you go together like brothers."

"I got to move on."

Alex stuffed Louvenia's bacon sandwich in his mouth like it was his last meal.

We all knew what it was to fall lost under a shadow and it swallow you so quickly that even your grief would be invisible to the outside world if they ever came looking for you. You'd then be counted among the many who took off for something better but were never heard from again.

About then Jeff walked up. He kissed me and patted Brother on the shoulder like they were brothers. Jeff's look at Alex troubled me; their glances darted back and forth and then headed in opposite directions like they'd had a face down. Figured maybe they'd been talking again 'bout one day having some land and couldn't decide where it was gonna be, or what they was gonna plant. Whatever they'd talked on it didn't look like Alex was going along with it. I was sure he was feeling lost, and that frightened me.

"Hey, let's head over to the square," Jeff suggested. "Gots to be less horseshit to smell over there."

"Harold, he ain't gonna come back tonight," Alex said. His face at last creased with a slight smile. "I watch things till you get back. I will."

"Won't be long," Jeff replied and we started off.

It was early evening by then. I turned back and smiled at Alex. The smile he'd just given me had already slipped away as he was soon to do himself. Lord, how could I have known that I would never see my brother again?

Jeff and I walked over to the square. He seemed to want to get away from more than the smell of horseshit. Well, I knew Mr. Harold was getting meaner by the day.

"That Mr. Harold, he always had it in for Alex," Jeff blurted after a long silence.

"Why did Harold treat Alex bad like that? Alex not a man, too?"

"What's you mean?" I asked.

"Ah, he's a white man. Alex and me, we're just another pair of mules to hitch every day."

"Him and Brother get into it?" I asked.

"You know your brother; he's got that strong pride is all. Ain't nothin' wrong with that. But that Harold, he thinks colored men 'pose' to tip our hats comin' and goin'."

"You tip to that man?" I asked.

"Sure, I do. But I got my fingers crossed behind my back and that means he smell like horseshit and that's all he is! Yes, sir, boss man pile of steaming shit standing there with nothin' to do but wave the flies off!" Jeff mocked. "So, Alex, he got into it with Harold and got told off. He been hidin' up in the loft while we figured out what to do."

"He got fired? What's Brother gonna do then?" I asked.

"No need to get worked up," Jeff said. "You Breedloves get worked up 'bout near everything."

"I got reasons to get worked up," I told him. "Brother goes lookin' for a job, the man gonna ask him where he been workin'? What's the name of his boss? What street that on? Then what's Brother gonna say? 'Ah, white man, don't get all worked up just 'cause I got no answers to hand you'?"

"Like I said, you Breedloves get worked up 'bout stuff before it happens!"

"Yeah? Did it happen for you this whole year? A year you worked for near nothin' but rotten apples and a place to sleep? That really never happen?"

"Me and Alex gonna get us a farm and divide the work like we been doin' all along. We figuring on growing corn for hogs. Then we ain't workin' for no horseshit white man no more!"

"That's how it's gonna be?" I asked. "And the bank done already come by with a bag of money for a mortgage on that farm?"

"I told you, we workin' on it," Jeff said impatiently. "We ain't got that far to know yet. But I 'magine you be the one bringin' the mortgage 'round, 'cause the banker man done give up and give you one 'cause you near smarted 'im to the point he sees no other way 'round it!"

"Who cares how it comes, smartin' or talkin' straight, as long as you gets your acre and seed?"

"Ain't nobody could figure out what you mean!" Jeff replied.

"That so?"

Over at the square we held hands till the streets got quiet. Then we circled 'round the park in silence before heading back to the stables. Standing there was a white man waiting. Him bringing his horse in for the night.

"Wait here till I take care of that man." Jeff dashed over to serve him.

"Where you boys been? I been waitin'." The man handed the reins to Jeff. "Thought you were closed."

Jeff yelled for Brother. "Alex! Alex," he yelled.

There was a quiet that I still hear.

Bourbon Blue Eyes

26

IT WASN'T LONG before our days seemed to settle back into the same routines as before Jesse went to jail. Some days Louvenia would deliver the ironing and then when she could, she'd escape for an interlude at the park where she'd watch the little ones at play. Guess she needed to see the joy and happiness in their bright young faces to remember it still existed. Sister spent so much of her life wearing Jesse's bourbon blues that she no longer cared what anyone thought about her broken face. Most folks that knew her already seen it all anyway. Bruises on bruises; some you see, some too deep to ever talk about, and sure as hell can't explain a single one. No, they all knew the denouement of her story. Fist by fist, they only mirrored their own, so who wants to hear it again. She lived in that deafening silence of 'It ain't my problem…sister'.

One day she returned as I was finishing the ironing. It always seemed as if Jesse was drunk or asleep till the very second Louvenia came home hot and exhausted from walking the ironing 'round town.

"Louvenia? Where you been? Get yourself in here when I call! Hey!"

But Louvenia didn't attend. No, this time she sat down at the kitchen table like he was no account. You see, she'd become expert at calculating the odds Jesse could bounce up swinging his fist by the thickness of his tongue.

"Oh, Lord, he's awake again," she commented, her eyes closing like her lids could shut him out. "Jesse, what's you want now?" she yelled.

In the past these words would have settled an empty bottle across her temple.

"Jesse gonna kill you 'fore you get out of here!" I announced like it was news I'd just heard in the alley.

"I got no place to go he can't get me. Lord knows, I got no place period," she reminded me.

But Jesse didn't need reminding who was slave and who was master. "Louvenia, don't make me get up!"

Yeah, Jesse was awake all right. Even in all the darkness of the moment it still hit us as funny. Jesse couldn't hold his pot to pee, yet we were bending to his threats of getting out of bed to put a chamber pot upside our heads. We buried our faces in dishrags so he couldn't hear us howling with mocking laughter.

"I best go get him a bottle," Louvenia sighed. "He been mean, real mean all mornin'. Mouth like the devil's. You get his supper on and don't start nothin' by droppin' a salt shaker in his tatas, hear?"

I nodded as Louvenia stepped out into the world that never heard her pain and went to buy Jesse his reprieve for another day. Or was it really our reprieve she was extending on credit?

I started getting supper on. Figured to put the best part of that cut of meat away for Louvenia and feed Jesse the gristle; that's all he paid for. I went to peeling my tatas, humming to myself and thinking 'bout meeting Jeff after I had my chores done.

Jesse was accustomed to me handing him a plate in bed 'fore he went out. 'Cept this time Jesse had a change of menu. He waited till he'd heard the porch door slam after Sister. Guess he didn't want her to know he wasn't that drunk, or she'd probably not leave me alone with him. Moments after she was gone, Jesse, he crept up and clapped his horny hand over my mouth as I stood cutting up that chicken. His cold acrid tongue on my neck made me jerk away hard.

"Huh! Didn't hear me comin' this time, did ya, lil' girl?"

The moment felt like I'd been dropped by my heels down that very well of desperation only to find myself up-side-down and face-to-face with Satan licking his chops to get at me.

"I could smell you, Jesse, a mile away!"

The butcher knife shook no matter how hard I held on to it.

"Feelin' handy with that knife, ain't ya girl? Yeah, well, you ain't no kin of mine!"

"I done cut up a whole lot of dead meat in my life. One slip from you, Jesse Powell, and I'll cut your throat so good your guts come up through your big mouth!"

"Listen to you!" Jesse slurred. "I'm tellin' you somethin', one slip and I gonna catch you, give you what's you're deservin' for not gettin' your Jesse out 'a jail, lil' nigger girl livin' off my table. That's what you been doin', too! Good for nothin' like your sister."

"Off whose table you say? What would be on your plate but flies if Sister didn't put it there? Can't feed your own wife and need somebody to hold your fork when she's not holding your pot to pee in, you ol' drunk!"

"Ain't you 'bout as high and mighty as I seen? Bet you never thought I'd come looking for my payday. But here I is, ain't I? Right here and now is Jesse's payday and I's hungry for some."

You see, from the heat that day, I'd unbuttoned the top of my blouse. Undoing his pants he stared through my opened blouse as if the buttons were all falling off. I froze with terror even before they dropped to the floor. He pawed to bend me over. I swung around with the knife to slash his face open. He pawed at me as though that knife was invisible and grabbed me stronger than I'd imagined any old drunk could. And the knife, my salvation, fell to the floor, where he kicked it across the room. He twisted my arm behind my back like it was an apron tie and brought me to my knees and did this gig walking on his pant legs dragging me.

It was then that I heard Louvenia's return with his bottle. Oh, Lord how many times can a bottle save us? The door swung open and so did Louvenia's eyes.

"Lord, Jesse! Stop! Here, I gots your bottle like you tol' me! Now, stop! Leave Sarah be."

She went to waving that bottle in his face as diversion.

"Here, here it is Jesse, here on the table," Sister pleaded. "Leave 'er be and come over here for your whiskey!"

"I got what I need right here!" he said. "You get out 'a here. Don't come back tonight! I got things I mean to get at and I gonna take my sweet time, too!"

He backhanded me hard when I sunk my teeth into his ugly arm.

"Gonna give this here lil' girl what's comin' to 'er!" he said and lifted his fist high over my face. "That's right! I's takin' what's owed me! I sure enough am. Gonna be right now, too."

Like I'd never seen her do before, Louvenia picked up that bottle and hurled it at Jesse's head. It shattered on the wall but stopped nothing. Not even his heckling.

"You think I's drunk, can't move on a woman and a bottle, too? I show you, bitch!"

I escaped his clutch and went for Sister, but he grabbed me at the table again. That ol' man dragged me, dragging Sister pulling the other way, along with the table leg she clung to. We dragged to his bedroom where he planned to catch up on his bookkeeping; Jesse, me, and Sister with the kitchen table as witness.

But grabbing on to every table leg along that alley could not have slowed the avalanche headed my way. I wrapped myself around the doorjamb as Sister beat at Jesse's hands on my throat—her kicking at him with everything she could muster. Still, he knocked her to the floor and yanked me towards his bed to perform his long-awaited deed of violation.

Oh, Lord, the fog in my head all but swallowed me, yet still I heard heavy footsteps on the porch. In a flash, I knew it was Fred coming for his cut. But, it wasn't. It was Jeff standing at our backdoor. He'd never come at that time before. Why that day? Did Jesus hear the prayers I was too dead inside to pray? Jeff looked over the room. Louvenia gasped as if she was having a stroke.

"Sarah, been expectin' you down at the stables." Jeff glared at Jesse who had one hand fisted and the other on my throat. "Mr. Jesse, I'm gonna tell you this but once: let her be!" Jeff looked as if he was 'bout to bust that growling ol' man to pieces.

Jesse snarled and grabbed my arm again. "Ain't none of your business what I aim to do here!"

"It's my business alright, 'cause I done ask Sarah to marry me. She said yes and I think she best come with me now."

All the cold fog started to evaporate as the Riverman stood there stabbing at Jesse with his eyes. "You're an old drunk, Jesse. If I come at you, I'll put you down for good. Now, let her free."

Her face bleeding, Louvenia ran to pull me out of Jesse's clutch. I was drenched in hot sweat and yet frozen stiff. It was hard for my mouth to let the words escape. Words that I thought one day I'd be saying with the purest of joy. "Sister, get your things. Hurry, now," I muttered. "We's goin' with Jeff now. We're leavin' Jesse's hell hole for good."

But she only stood there drowning in her own silence. Still Jesse's words were loud and clear.

"Louvenia, she ain't goin' no place! She do, I turn her in to the law! She'll end up in a chain-gang gettin' what she deserves, and then gettin' it over and over 'gain from the men!" Jesse blurted. "I done tol' her what it's like working the county roads."

Sister stood there like a hopeless rag doll with its brown button eyes ripped off struggling to see her way to the next breath.

"Come, Sister. It's time! Can't you hear me?"

I grabbed her to jar her frozen senses. But she couldn't move. She was like stone, a grave marker standing there already looking all but forgotten.

"I said she ain't goin' no place, not ever, she ain't," Jesse yelled. "I'm the law in this here alley. She ain't goin' no place 'cause a worthless bitch like this ain't got no place to go. Now ain't that right, Louvenia?" That was Jesse's tender proclamation to the woman who'd kept him alive through so many whiskey-flooded droughts.

Louvenia smeared blood over her face, trying to wipe it clear of her eyes. Without looking at me, 'cause she couldn't without exposing her shame, she shook her head against me. "Best be gettin' on with Jeff,

Sarah. You know he can't take us both on and make it. Go 'fore it's too late for you, too."

All I could do was sob on Jeff's chest till I near swallowed my tongue. I wailed at the very thought of leaving my sister behind to Jesse's mercy.

"Mr. Jesse, you ever hit Miss Louvenia again, Sarah say she's gonna to cut out your gizzard, fry it up and feed it to you while I watch!" Jeff said. "You hearin' me?"

"I ain't heard nothin'!" Jesse said. That was the only truthful lie he ever told.

"Go Sister, got to get out now," were her last words as Jeff led me through the wreckage.

"I'll come back for you!"

"Get out 'a my house! I'll put the law on you, too," was Jesse's farewell and thanks for all the years of cleaning up his filthy life, one bottle after another—enough bottles to fill a distillery he'd brewed of undiluted hopelessness.

Jasmine in My Hair

27

THE TUESDAY AFTER I left Jesse's, Annie came by the stables with her little ones in tow. I had to ask the kids why they were so quiet that morning. They opened their mouth to reveal melting lemon drops. The treat for me was Annie's message from Sister that she was getting by and longed for word on me. Annie told me that late one night when the alley was quiet, she heard Sister yelling at Jesse. I don't remember Louvenia ever yelling at anybody, not even that ol' man. According to Annie, Louvenia's hollered from the porch as Jesse headed for the bars. Sister followed clutching her rolling pen howling that if he ever hit her again, even raised a fist to her face, she'd kill him on the spot and then herself. Annie heard Sister say ain't no chain-gang ever gonna know the difference, plain as that. The words shook me. For Jesse this could only mean the power of his threats of turning her over to work the county roads had no power over her, even less than nothing, as he must have known that on most days she only wanted to die anyway. Guess she'd be more than pleased to push him into the very hell he was running from. Yes, one more swing at her head and his would land on Satan's lap.

Had Jesse finally gotten Louvenia's message? Seemed like after all the years together the lives of Louvenia and Jesse Powell had evolved into a truly bitter peace, but one that gave Louvenia scattered moments to heal some. Still, I knew the day would come when he'd box her again, if only to see if she'd really stopped buying into his threats. But for time being he had, and that's what mattered.

❧

My first days at the stables with Jeff were spent mostly sleeping up in the hayloft as I was so weary of the hard work from near the day I landed in that alley. But after a day or two tossing and turning up there the straw had quickly become my jail. Mr. Harold seemed to be at the stables more after Alex had disappeared. Him not doing much but looking over Jeff's shoulder to see if the customers' money was going into his pockets and not Jeff's. While Harold was on the prowl, I stayed out of sight. Can't count how many times I thought it was clear to climb down when Jeff spotted Mr. Harold coming along. I longed for the late hours after Harold had stumbled off into his night. Then I'd make us a pot of stew on the little coal stove. We'd eat and talk about our days ahead.

Jeff and I finally got the day fixed for our wedding. It would be in mid-September, and the preacher would marry us. The whole church was invited to celebrate our union with a picnic under the shade of them magnolias on the square.

But it was the unknown of our days beyond that worried me most. My fears grew as the day of our wedding drew near. Perhaps knotted up in these concerns was my fear that I didn't want to wake up on this special day and find all my happiness had been a borrowed dream now claimed by someone better than me. I was thinking that unlike me this had to be a special girl who was really intended for Jeff. As those early days of September passed, I could tell that Jeff wasn't scared. Every time I looked frightened, he said he was too proud of me not to think ever'body should come and celebrate with us, so why wouldn't he be the one to celebrate the hardest. Sometimes when I couldn't figure if it was all real, that this man really loved me, I'd look around the stables till the beauty of his eyes found me once more looking lost. He could always read my fears, I never could hide them. But then wasn't my soul bared to him from our first kiss? He'd look back at me, no matter what he was doing, stop everything it seemed, and smile till my expression yielded to his love that I was so tightly wrapped in. I knew there'd never be safer place in the world for me than next to Jeff.

The week before the wedding, Annie came by the stables on her way to the farmers' market. With a huge smile, she handed me a knotted up old rag. I knew that familiar jingle. It was Louvenia's money; seed money for her own escape. These were the coins she'd hidden back even when Jesse and his fists were on the hunt for them. She wanted us to have it to get started on. Here I was worried as to how I could somehow save my sister from that ol' man, and Sister had handed me her only chance of escaping him. Lord, how long had she gone without to save that money?

It was a few days before the wedding when Annie appeared across from the stables waving a kerchief for Jeff's attention. Guess she'd seen Mr. Harold in there and didn't want him asking Jeff what his business was with a colored woman. Jeff nodded her way and then signaled me with the broken tune he always whistled when Mr. Harold was prowling. I peeked over to see Jeff gesture to Annie. She stood out of the rain under the grocer's awning waving a piece of paper. When Harold finally disappeared to the storeroom, Jeff dashed through the pelting rain to grab it. Annie's note read that she wanted me to come by her place the following evening and she'd for sure have Sister there, too.

The next night after making Jeff's supper—tatas, some fried fish I got for a good price from the fishmonger—I ventured back to Jesse's alley for the first time. Nettie met us at the door and Sister soon followed. Annie's kids tugged at her like she was Santa with hard candy hidden in her pockets. She'd bought a nickel's worth every week to make sure there was.

"I got something for us tonight," Annie smiled.

I hugged Sister. She'd gained a few pounds, which meant she was eating better. She never could eat when her nerves had knotted her stomach up.

"So, don't you look like a bride to be?" Sister remarked. "Look at the shining smile. Now tell Sarah what's you got, Annie, or can you smell it?"

Annie pulled out a big pan of cake, with her kids hooting and hollering to get at it.

"Now you know it's too hot!" she scolded. "The grocer man had some pears. They's a bit bruised, so he give me a sack for a nickel. You know this is Ma's recipe for upside down pear cake."

"Gots pecans and buttered brown sugar on the bottom between sweet ripe pears just like Granny told me," Nettie announced. She was learning to cook.

"We gonna have a piece when it cools. But first we gonna see what I gots for you, Sister Sarah."

What I remember most about that moment was the gleam in Louvenia's eye. Couldn't image what they were up to. Then Annie returned from the backroom with a large box to show me. She opened it as Nettie brought down a stack of plates for the cake. Annie unfolded the paper and slowly lifted out a white gown. It was a wedding dress. She smacked at the kids' hands for touching it.

"Now, I told you, you can't touch it no matter how pretty."

There was lace on it and little pearls the size of seeds sewn on the front. Never in my life had I ever seen something so beautiful. I was afraid to touch it myself.

"This here is from one of the women at church. I was tellin' her 'bout you and Jeff gettin' started, and she told me that while she thought she'd never give her weddin' dress away, its value would double in blessings returned if some other woman shared the joy she did when she walked down the aisle wearing it. So, here it is. She done give it to you with her best wishes."

I didn't know what to say. The only fine dress I'd ever worn was the one Sister got for me to meet Jeff at the square. Sister hugged me and laid the gown over my arms. My only thought was that this beautiful dress simply couldn't be mine. Nothing so beautiful could be. Nevertheless, Annie said it was mine for sure, for my own wedding, and so much finer than any dress I could have somehow stitched from my greatest imaginings. Didn't matter none it 'a been worn once. The bride done had her baby when Annie told her 'bout me. The woman, Annie's friend, knew the answer to a prayer I'd not even had the faith to pray. She never knew me yet understood my dream, 'cause we all have it somewhere even if it's only as tiny as a seed waiting to unfold and take root someplace.

After we shared Annie's pear cake, and while the children were reading to each other, Annie asked me to go back and try on the gown. It was only a tiny bit too big.

"Lordy, Lordy, ain't you just a princess?" Sister remarked when I returned. "Who's the lucky prince takin' my sister off to a new life? Ain't he the luckiest?"

But then I suddenly wondered how Sister could get away from Jesse long enough join us. "How you gonna get away for the weddin'?" I asked.

"Joseph got it fixed for me," she said with a smile. "I reckon fixed right good, too. You know he's good with his hands."

"Joseph the locksmith?" I asked.

"I been helpin' his wife catch up on her ironin' to pay 'im. She sent Joseph over with a little bitty gift, and I been keepin' it safe on a string 'round my neck."

Sister pulled out a door key tied to a string hidden down her blouse. I couldn't figure out how that little key was gonna help her get to the wedding. But then Jesus don't always consult me on how He's going about getting prayers answered, even though I was sure most times I have better ideas than His. I looked at Annie. She smiled. Seemed like she knew 'bout things.

The Saturday of my wedding finally came. Jeff took off early for the church with the preacher so I could get ready. I kept thinking if he knew what was best he'd jump a boxcar and head off without me. I went to fixing up a washbasin in the storeroom and got myself bathed and dressed in my regular dress, 'cause Annie was taking my wedding gown over to the church for me to change. She'd been working on that hem till late the night before. She had a notion to fix my hair there at church. How could I not wonder what Minerva would have thought as Annie wove white jasmine, the kind that grew at Grandview, through my hair like a halo of fragrance.

I couldn't eat that morning 'cause I knew I'd throw up. But I decided

I'd best eat anyway, 'cause I'd for sure throw up if I didn't. My nerves would see to it. What if Sister couldn't get away from Jesse's jailhouse? Or what if he came looking for her even at the church? My stomach churned at the notion. I couldn't think on these things and still manage to get something eaten, so I decided to let Jesus work on it from His side. But I later found out that Sister and Jesus already had something going. She said Jesse looked stunned when she walked into his backroom late that morning carrying a tray of food like the servant he thought her to be.

"What's that food for? I ain't hungry!" Jesse growled.

Louvenia set the tray next to his bed.

"You tryin' to poison me again? he barked. "Huh? I know you is! Look at you! You're lookin' too happy!"

"Now you gonna have a long day here, Jesse. So, don't get worked up and make it longer for yourself!"

"Huh? You got your hands on some of that nightshade to put me in a pine box? Put it in that there food, didn't you? Sure, you did. I can smell it!" Jesse barked again.

"You can't smell that stinkin' alley you lived in the last twenty years, but you say you can smell a teaspoon of dried nightshade poison ain't even in there?" Louvenia said, her damp hair still tied up in rag curls. "We out of salt and rat poison and I got no nightshade, so best eat it plain this time," Sister said.

"Huh? What'd you say's in that food gonna get me? You poison me and I'll tell Fred to get the law on your tail like that!" He snapped his fingers as he did when ordering his meals.

"Jesse, just how do you know I don't already got Fred poisoned up? Didn't I say the poison box was empty? And you ain't even seen your brother 'round for days, have you?"

"What? Huh? Why you crazy woman! What day is it? Where's Fred? Where you been all this mornin'? You been actin' strange for days, ain't ya? You gone crazy on me again?"

Jesse's brain was too bourbon-soaked by then to figure out much of anything. Night was day and day night and only the drops left in a bottle measured the good times. Yes, it seemed as though everything in Jesse's mind was starting to rhyme with poison.

"Why, Jesse, look here! See, your brother Fred been 'round, God bless his damned to hell soul, 'cause looks like he come by with your Christmas present. Sure he did! Two bottles of whiskey right here."

"My brother Fred come with them bottles?" Jesse drooled from shock. "But ain't it July, or August? I know it's September. Ain't it for real?"

"And if you think your brother would ever bring you a gift, then you're too sober! Here, let me pour some into your coffee then."

"Huh? Louvenia, what the hell do you have goin' on? I ain't goin' out till dark, and you already gots my supper. Ain't it just breakfast time anyway? Pull that curtain back so I can see what time of day it is. I ain't hungry. Why Fred bring me a Christmas present in the middle of July? Did I tell you to fix my supper? No, I never said nothin' like that. You see, you gone crazy on me when I wasn't lookin'. Fred always said you would, too! I got to get ready to go out. Yeah, gonna go find me some peace!"

"You ain't goin' no place."

"Why the hell not? I got folks waitin' for me over there at the bar where they's got a big Christmas party tonight!"

"'You ain't goin' to no party 'cause maybe that rusty lock on that door got broken and you ended up locked in here all day while I's out."

"Out? Where you think you're goin'?" Jesse demanded. "I'm tellin' you woman, you best not be spendin' my money on no God-damned Christmas presents for that sister of yours!"

"Now you sit back and take it easy. Shouldn't be hard, 'cause that's the only thing you know how to do, huh, Jesse? Yeah, ain't that the truth? You been practicin' sittin' back doin' nothin' since we been together."

"You listen to me, crazy bitch," Jesse snapped. "I know what you're up to! You're goin' shopping and wasting good money on Christmas things gonna get smashed under my foot as soon as I put an eye on 'em!"

"No, I ain't listenin' to you and there ain't a soul out in that alley that's gonna listen to you no more. They all had enough of Jesse Powell and even if they hadn't, they still ain't gonna pee on you if you catch yourself on fire. Now, I gots to finish gettin' ready. Or you want me to strike a match to see if your friends hear the crackle and run over here to dump their chamber pots on your head?"

"What's that again? Ready for what? Huh? Hear what?" Jesse moaned. "What's you got goin? I don't got to pee. Who you say gonna come dump my pot in the alley?"

Sister later told me Jesse looked scared to death as she walked out. He figured she had to have gone and poisoned up that food she set there so he kicked the little table across the room. Louvenia didn't care 'bout the food dripping down the walls none. She went about getting her things out of the drawers and pulled out her little door key. Yes, she locked that ol' man in that sweltering room so he'd not go hunting for her that day, and maybe even make his way to the wedding. He was locked in that hell hole all by himself with all his food scattered over the same walls where he'd scattered pieces of Sister's face over the years.

At the church Annie helped me get dressed. I could already hear the folks arriving. Even above the din of chatter, I could hear Jeff's beautiful laugh.

Annie buttoned up the back of my gown so I couldn't escape. No matter how scared I was she knew I couldn't run fast or far in that big dress. Then a knock; seemed like Annie knew who was there. She opened the door and Sister slipped in. Louvenia, that woman had gone out and bought herself a new hat! And I'd never seen that dress before. Don't know how she got that way, so lovely, just knew it was for me. Sister brushed my tears away and adjusted the wreath of jasmine that held my veil.

"Got some good news. Did Annie tell you?" Sister asked.

"No, I never said a word." Annie winked.

Louvenia pulled from her pocket a pretty postcard. There was a picture of a big carnival on the front. She handed it to me to read. "I here. Alex Breedlove."

"Brother sent this to you?"

Sister smiled.

"But Brother, he don't know to how to write."

"He gone to the post office, bought a stamp and ask the postman to write on it for 'im," Annie said. "I know that's what he done. Sure it is."

"Then the postman brought it to me last week," Sister added. "I keeps it pinned up on my kitchen curtain just in the fold so Jesse don't see it. When that man gone, I open the curtain and look at it while I washing dishes. Alex, he alive! It say so right here!"

Sister took the postcard and kissed it.

"He there in St. Louis, right?" she asked. "He maybe works there at the carnival, don't he?"

"Don't know, Sister," I responded. "He sure may!"

"Sure he do! That means he gots work."

Only Brother being there would have made me happier than knowing he was somewhere and alive.

"Now, don't cry, Sister Louvenia," Annie said. "It's hard enough to keep Sarah's' eyes dry! Think we're ready. You best go take a seat up front there with the women. They's holding a place for you so's you can watch Sarah come down the aisle to her Jeff."

Sister nodded, dabbed at a tear, and headed down the aisle. Yes, Lord, it was for once a tear of happiness. She walked down that aisle with her chin high to take her seat with the other big-hat women. They patted her on the shoulder. About then Annie nodded through the door and the march began. Dressed in white with jasmine in my hair, I slowly walked down the aisle almost feeling like I was in a dream-like haze. Up there Jeff was no longer laughing. No, tears streamed from his eyes, the eyes that never left mine. As soon as he took my hand in his, a new forever had begun for us.

Days after the wedding I met Sister at the farmers' market. She told me what had happened. Said that when she got home late after the wedding supper, she found Jesse had sobered up and forgotten their chat that morning. But then when he was ready to go out for the night, he'd found his door locked. Thank you, Joseph! He was still pounding at it with both fists when she returned. Louvenia said he acted as though he'd awakened just as the undertaker was sealing his coffin. As Jesse pounded away, Louvenia took her sweet time pulling off her special dress and hat and hid them under her cot. Said she went about getting the iron going as though she'd been working out on the porch, or perhaps if she needed it to put to Jesse's face. Anyway, what was time to Jesse, but something else to steal? I imagine it gave Sister pleasure stirring turmoil into that poor man's troubled bourbon-pickled head. Him back there pounding on the door and yelling out the window for the neighbors like his fate had finally caught up with him and he wanted to see if a bit of mercy could still be had.

While Jesse was back there yelling, Sister pulled out Joseph's key and unlocked the door to his purgatory.

"Jesse, that you makin' that noise, or that the neighbors again?" Louvenia yelled back through the unlocked door. "You want me to go tell 'em to shut up and stop botherin' you?"

He only pounded louder. His reality was too altered to know if he was coming in after a binge or maybe feeling Satan creeping up.

"What's you want now?"

Sister poured herself a jar of sweet tea. She no longer scrambled after or from Jesse's howls.

"Open this God-damned door! You tryin' to poison me again? I need the pot to pee bad!"

"I thought you said you didn't have to pee a while ago! Sure you did. Now I's busy finishin' up this here ironin' so you go pee in the alley."

Jesse slowly turned that old doorknob and opened the door.

"You locked me in there, ain't ya?" he said. "I know you did, too! Huh? Didn't you?"

"And you been sayin' I gone crazy! Lordy, Jesse. That was you hollering back there like a crazy man? Oh, Lord, they gonna come for you now! Well, I'll give them some sweet tea when they get here." It had been a beautiful day and she was now armed against Jesse's hot rage with a heated iron standing guard nearby. "Don't know what you're talkin' about, Jesse. You had a bad dream? You just opened the door, didn't ya? Still got the doorknob in your hand."

Jesse jumped as if that doorknob had chewed his hand.

"Anyway, you done lost the key to that door years ago. 'Member? After you locked me in there that summer for three days with no food and water while you were out runnin' with your whores on my wash money."

"Huh? What's that? Where you been? Where's Fred? He dead, too? You poison us both then?"

"Probably stiff by now. Wasn't he already half dead when I came here? You best go see if the other half's dead. And take the rest of that rat poison over to him. There's just a bit left. Tell the law it was the box you been feeding your brother from. Well, anyway Fred says he seen rats at his place, 'less he means you, Jesse."

Sister had a bit of power there what with that hot iron in her hand and Jesse not knowing if the earth had stopped spinning 'cause his head still was.

"It Christmas night?" Jesse asked.

"Yeah, it's Christmas alright. What did the Lord bring you?"

Sister said she tried so hard to keep from laughing at Jesse standing there speechless in all his coagulated misery. There he stood holding himself like he'd peed his pants before slamming the door shut again. For the life of him, he couldn't take a step ahead of himself for fear of getting there. Louvenia said he never came out till long after midnight, him still trying to figure if he'd had a rotten dream or Louvenia had really poisoned him and he'd joined the walking dead.

Well, that was the week I was married so very long ago.

Two days after the morning jasmine was woven through my hair, I turned fourteen.

UNDER HIS CHESTNUT TREE

28

WHERE IN LOVE are you when the rest of the world drifts by heedless to your colliding smiles? Wherever that is, it's not the same place you were before you met. The air is lighter, the colors brighter and everywhere you look there are more hues than the day before the sun broke through the clouds of your life at the end of an alley.

Some days back then, while Jeff worked with the horses, and when I was sure Jesse would be gone, I'd go pick up Sister's ironing and deliver it to her customers. Then on days I wasn't delivering, I met Louvenia and Annie down at the farmers' market where we chatted while buying our bread and produce. There were moments when it seemed that Sister's smile had almost returned. Later I'd head back to the stables with a basket of whatever was had that day for a good price and get a pot of stew or something cooking on that little iron stove. While eating supper, Jeff and I had long meandering talks about our times ahead and what those days might hold for us.

But sorting our ideas didn't come easy. There was much to sift and there weren't many folks who seemed to have the pieces of their own lives patched together well enough for us to follow. So where was the path to our dreams? In the back of my mind, I wondered if somebody ever made it that far before, to a dream of a better life? Or was it all just borrowed talk over borrowed dreams ain't nobody ever really owned?

Jeff groomed the horses while we talked. His thoughts seem to always drift like smoke from a candle and yet returned to this same passion: he had to have a piece of land one day to call his own. A place where the soil could keep a family growing. A man's dignity, he told me, was upheld by owning his own place. And yet as our days surrendered into weeks, seemed like any plan we worked out quickly fell to the same roadblock, the one at the end of our empty pockets. You see, we had no money to move on with even if we could work up a clear picture of where that might be. In fact, we didn't have much else in life but each other and a few things the church folks had given us at our wedding. These were special gifts of handmade kitchen towels, a soup pot and some well-used pans, a few mismatched and once silvered spoons and a precious small vase that belonged to someone's grandma. All these things I loved to pull out as Jeff reconfigured his ideas for our future. His vision was always large but he never had the opportunity to learn to read or get to understand the meaning behind some spoken words, so he was frustrated when he couldn't rightly express his passions. But let me tell you, when I needed a word to fill between his to understand his hopes, I easily found it in the song his eyes sang—eyes bright with passion and glowing with hope. His was a passion to make a family, and that family would be proud of him for his dedication to our happiness. Yes, he didn't have to search for hidden words; I'd read them in the poetry of his eyes.

It was a bright Saturday morning when Mrs. Harold came by the stables to speak to Jeff. I'd wondered why we'd not seen her for a spell. That morning she asked what his plans were, knowing we were just married. He decided it was time he told her about going off to make his way in the world and that he'd turn over the stable money whenever she wished. He'd kept this money safe in a tin box hidden high on a shelf till she came for it, as Mr. Harold might lose it at the tavern and his kids face hunger by it. Mrs. Harold knew how much the men had made her life possible by keeping the stable going. Mrs. Harold said she'd been thinking about her own situation and that of her children and that's why she'd come by to talk to Jeff. Don't let anybody tell you folks who speak in kindness can't come together and do it for the better of both. She explained that Mr. Harold had disappeared somewhere a few days before, and it would be for the last time for that as she was selling the stable—it had been her daddy's—and moving in with her ma in Charlotte. She thanked Jeff for his loyalty and told him to pick out a buggy and horse and he could keep them, as the rest were to be sold off.

I couldn't stop thanking the Lord for hearing our prayers. Two people, a black man and a white woman, came together one day at a place where there was no distance in their humanity.

Then, like she'd been saving it for just the perfect moment, she told Jeff about a place her neighbor had just outside of town: only a deserted two room cabin with a couple of cleared acres that he was looking to let. Out front, she added, was an old chestnut tree that would drop a pile of spiny nuts come autumn. Said that with a smile like she sure loved roasted chestnuts. Her neighbor had told her about the chestnut tree like it was the reason anybody would want to live out there. This neighbor would let the place for a fair price to somebody willing to fix it up. As this man was getting on in years, Mrs. Harold suggested that come a day, he just might work something out with Jeff on buying the place. Jeff's eyes revealed everything the moment she said this. The borrowed dream we'd been searching for a way to get to had been sighted just out of town. Mrs. Harold had pointed the direction, and waiting there would be a glorious old chestnut to mark the spot.

Well, the place was down a dusty lane off the county road leaving Vicksburg. Even at first sight, we truly thought it dream-like. No, it didn't have a white veranda with white-flowering jasmine cascading over the rail. Just a cabin barely visible from the road till the day Jeff cleared the overgrowth so folks coming from town could find us. Beyond the cabin was a tall row of cottonwoods along a stream. I easily convinced myself that the leaves of these trees turned silvery the moment I glimpsed them. No, I'd never seen leaves on a tree flutter and reflect the moonlight like pieces of tangling pewter.

And there, not more than fifty yards from the porch, was that great chestnut spreading its heavy branches outwardly as though it had been waiting to embrace us. At the first sight, I could already see our children playing in its shade while I hung laundry near the porch. Jeff said that chestnut had probably been there fifty years.

"See that tree?" Jeff asked.

"That's the chestnut Mrs. Harold told us 'bout?"

"That tree, come the first cold night in October, is gonna drop us a pile of chestnuts."

"Just a pile at our feet?" I asked. "Don't have to climb up and pick 'em?"

"Nope, just gotta roast 'em. My folks, when we was livin' along the river, they sent me down the road to one of the plantations to get us some so daddy could roast 'em all winter."

Jeff, he walked over to that big tree like it was a lost friend found again. He was at home under that tree already. Lord, I could never have known how much.

Even before we'd looked inside that old cabin Jeff had peeled off his shirt and led me down the slope towards those shimmering cottonwoods that always marked the line of a stream along their thirsty root—a stream that would rinse away the dust of our long day. There we let the cool crystal-clear water flush over us without words leaving our lips, just held hands down there. Cool and pure that water was. In only a few hours, it was as clear to me as the sky above how much that place meant to Jeff.

As the days passed and Jeff went to work taming the place, I reminded myself it wasn't ours. It was only a borrowed dream. We'd just rented it for next to nothing as nobody wanted to live that far from town. Yet for the moment it was easy enough to pretend. While watching Jeff as he paced about, I thought about my folks and their dreams of having an acre somewhere. And maybe one day a few fruit trees like the Burneys'—enough to make summer fruit jam for Sunday mornings.

Nobody had been living in that place for years, but it was better than it looked. Jeff said he'd spotted an old chestnut tree stump out back that somebody had probably felled to build the cabin. Wood from an old chestnut lasted forever, he said, and slapped the posts that supported the roof over the porch. So, after not doing much that first week but holding hands and splashing in the stream, we went about fixing the place up. Jeff set out to patch the holes between the timbers and scrape the fireplace flue. The raccoons were annoyed with the ruckus, but they'd be more annoyed come winter when we'd have a crackling fire going roasting chestnuts. I lugged pails of sand up from the stream bed and went to smoothing down those splintered old plank floors with it. A few days later, when I was back in town, Louvenia gave me some aprons she'd patched together from old shirts her customers had given her. One I saved to put up in the window to remind me of the curtain Momma put up every night so Isaac couldn't see in.

"What's ya got an apron up in the winda for?"

I couldn't really say. Later, when I dropped it down to keep the moon from peeking in, he asked again.

"Come on back to bed. Ain't nobody out here gonna bother us."

"I get to thinkin' 'bout Momma when I see that apron up there. She never had a piece of store-bought fabric to save her soul. Never even been in a store, I reckon. Made our things out 'a sackcloth like your ma. Even the curtain over the window was just an old apron—the same one she tied me to the bed with so's I couldn't wander outside and the dogs get me."

"You thinkin' 'bout your ma, huh?" he asked. "Ain't nothin' wrong with that. But don't get to thinkin' somebody's ever gonna get at you out here. I ain't gonna let that happen."

With the warmth of his words, I fell into a gentle sleep.

I still remember our first mornings out there near the chestnut tree. I seemed to always jump up early, wondering why it was so quiet. There was no din from the city that always awakened us past mornings; no farmers' carts rolling over the cobble and no tinkers barking their wares. It was only the birds chorusing in that big chestnut that I heard as I got the fire going in the stove for biscuits. Annie had given us three jars of wild berry jam her ma had put up, along with a couple of jars of peaches. I opened a jar of jam and put it on the table Jeff had resurrected from a pile of old furniture stacked out back. He'd placed it on the porch for us to eat as we watched the sun creep over the tree tops. That morning, as Jeff continued his survey of where he would break soil for a winter vegetable garden, I started a pie from the last of the dried stable apples I'd soaked overnight. Louvenia and I had gone out and spent her laundry money on flour, baking powder and a bit of sugar before we left town. I made comments to Jeff out the window as he wandered about, but he was too intent on his chores to pay much mind—that is, till he smelled the biscuits I'd placed in the window to cool. He quickly came to the table.

"This the jam Annie give us?"

"The same you were eatin' out of the jar last night with a spoon," I answered. "Her ma made it. Louvenia kept one jar and made me take the rest."

"You gonna feel all alone tomorrow when I'm gone?"

"No."

"No?" he asked with his mouth half stuffed with one of my biscuits.

"How can I get lonely with all this work I got here?"

"Men be comin' for me early," he said. "Down the road there's a man needin' some stumps cleared. I reckon 'bout four day's work for us."

"Then when are you gonna put up my clothes lines? Chop wood to keep hot water going for my laundry?" I asked. "I brought three piles of laundry tied up in white sheets still in the back of the wagon. I got to get 'em washed so Sister can iron 'em and we can get 'em delivered by Saturday."

"You watch out for that Jesse when you're visitin' your sister. I ain't lookin' to get into it with an old man already gots no teeth to punch out and nothin' worth listenin' to when his big mouth had 'em!"

"Louvenia told me to knock at Annie's door first when I come by.

She knows when Jesse's home. Sees him out her kitchen window when he heads to the end of that alley."

"You know I don't want my wife working the tubs." Jeff scrapped his plate of scrambled eggs and spooned himself more jam.

"No? Who gonna wash your clothes then? A maid?"

"You know what I mean. Doin' tubs for white folks," he said. "It ain't right."

"What ain't right? I spend the day over the tubs and nights over an ironin' board? Or for you then, that your white man gonna pay you next to nothin' for clearin' stumps and that fixes what I got to do to help us get by. Which is right?"

"Someday I have this place turned out so we won't be needin' to work for nobody clearin' stumps or washin' clothes. Then when we do, I build a room on for Louvenia. Your sister's gonna leave that alley and never goin' back to that ol' man. Serve 'im right, too."

"When that someday comes, we all gonna have jam Sunday mornings. Just like Momma promised."

A few weeks later we were able to buy a couple of new tubs and a new washboard with his earnings from clearing stumps, and soon Jeff had everything set up for me. His dream that I not have to wash clothes was something we put aside for the time being. I still washed clothes, had five tubs soaking near ever'day. Some days when I was in town delivering, I'd eat something at Louvenia's if Jesse was gone and then go to night school to learn reading. It's what I promised Momma. Our lives were hard, but we were headed to a place we'd pointed out ourselves and it was on our own map, a place where our dreams could be built with one hard day stacked on the last.

Well, I guess things in town with Jesse weren't much different for Sister after all. The thing with that is, they were therefore worse no matter if there were fists flying or not. When you live for years at the end of an alley, even when things don't get worse, those never-ending days of no better eat at your soul like a slow-growing cancer. Yes, hopelessness can eat at you till there's nothing left. I think that's the way it got for Sister. She was walking through her days like a dead woman. Don't really matter which is gonna be the final step 'cause it's gonna be sooner or later but still just 'round the corner all the same. Which one is all that greets you every damned day. Monday or Tuesday, will I make it to Friday? Do I even care no more? Without me handling the washing end of things out in the country, Sister couldn't survive. I couldn't help fearing what would happen to her life if mine gave out first. But I knew. Hers would follow. Yes, the air between our tubs was always too thin to find a breath of relief. The thought that there was none to be had only fed the cancer.

From the beginning, Sister and I tried to work it out so our lives stayed tied. I got into town even when I was real tired so she'd know I was never so far away. She'd told me once. Said she'd not want to go on if there came a time when the distance between us grew so loud it shook her daydreams. All over again them pains of asking, "Where are you today, Sister?," ringing in our ears. Why would she, she added. Well, it was good that Jesse was gone most the time by then—him sleeping over Fred's 'cause he couldn't make it back home after drinking on an empty stomach that Sister no longer fed. He knew the people he called friends would roll him if he ventured alone into them dark alleys. His vision had become no more than blurs of days he'd already passed by. Everything was leaving Jesse behind and he knew it, especially the good times. Everything gone except them black dreams when he begged his sleep to leave him be. I reckon Jesse had started feeling the sharpness of those empty bottles stacked around his shaky days. Surely it sent shivers down his rotted-out spine. And then maybe all them sleepless hours he spent looking up at the ceiling, he could only hear what Sister had told him; that if he hurt her again, even one more time, she'd kill him and then jump off herself. Jump off that roof where she'd spent so many hours of her life listening to the shirts dry in the blistering heat just so she didn't have to listen to Jesse's mouth blister her.

Don't Need Nothing Else

29

One night as I washed the dishes on the porch, Jeff came up from the stream carrying two canvas bags of water. I wondered if he was aiming to water the vegetable garden and save me the work on the morrow. But, you see, he was there pouring water over the hard soil where nothing grew. Made no sense to me. I dried my hands and went over to see what he was up to.

"What are you doin'?" I asked. "Toting water up the slope and then pouring it over that hard soil?"

Jeff looked sheepish. "Now how are we gonna get this hard-as-rock soil loosened up 'less I till it? How am I gonna turn it over 'less I get some water soakin' in it?"

"You done made the vegetable patch over yonder. You get lost looking for it?"

"Maybe I did and maybe I know where I's going and don't need you tellin' me where my feet is standing."

"Oh, no?"

"So, I'm gonna plant you a flower garden. Right here."

He pulled out of his pocket a twisted piece of paper he opened.

"Where'd you get them seeds?"

"Got 'em from Mrs. Harold." There was a twinkle in his eyes.

"Mrs. Harold been givin' my man flowers and even dried 'em for the seeds!" I teased like he been up to something with Mrs. Harold.

"Me? No, I ain't."

"Look me in the eye and tell the truth," I demanded, teasing-like.

"I am not growing flowers for no woman back in town!"

"No? Well, then I know who you're growing a flower garden for!"

"Go ahead," he said. "If you think you know everything."

"You, Mr. Jeffrey McWilliams! You like flowers and you're making a garden for yourself."

"Ain't no man makes a garden 'less he can't eat what comes from it."

"Do tell! Then what did you say you were totin' water up the hill for when it's near dark?"

He pointed me to the porch. "Don't them dishes need another dryin'?"

"Yeah, and I got a jar in there we could use for your cut flowers," I replied. "You want me to fill it with water, or you aim to plant them seeds first?"

Couple of days later Jeff started turning the moist soil for his flower garden. The following day one of his friends come 'round with a wagon of manure that they shoveled over the broken soil. Then soon afterwards a small fence of sorts found its way 'round his patch. Sure seemed like only a few days later those seeds started sprouting. Never had Jeff told me before that he would one day make himself a garden filled with flowers that would bring color and fragrance to our cabin.

"Now you know, when these flowers bloom we gots to have Louvenia out," he said. "Your sister, she knows the colors of every flower there is. Even knows the names of colors I ain't never heard before."

"She's gonna come out one day. I been askin' her every time I'm in town."

As the days followed Jeff worked to make the front porch into a better laundry. The well he and his men friends dug made it easier than going down to the stream. He even had so much firewood piled up I could keep my tub water hot all day. Because I heated the water outside, our place was never hot and sticky like Louvenia's kitchen had been and, praise the Lord, I didn't need to climb to the roof with my wet clothes to get to a clothesline. Jeff had lines strung from the porch where the hot sun and fresh air did its work. There were clotheslines everywhere. Made me laugh when he got tangled up in them as he made his way to the shed where he kept his tools. Never seen a man taken down by a clothesline before; ain't it a sight! Or least Jeffrey made it into one. I laughed at his antics tripping over my tubs and washboards like an ox learning to dance the polka in a web of clotheslines.

Whenever I was in town for night school I'd sneak into Louvenia's to pick up her ironing for delivery on my way to class. So that Jesse couldn't drink it up, Sister had me keep her ironing money except for the bit she kept back to eat on. She told him that since he near crippled her right arm she couldn't work the tubs and therefore couldn't keep him in bottles no more 'less he worked a tub and she do the ironing with her left hand. He didn't look on that deal favorably and so went to announcing that he just might go get himself a new woman. Sister said she didn't know where he went ever'night since he had no money. Guess he still went looking for at least a shot glass of peace down one of them alleys that curved and twisted 'bout like Sister's beaten spine. No, I couldn't think on what Jesse's life ran on back then, but I sure hoped it'd run out soon.

I stayed with her those evenings as long as I could and shared every detail of our new place. The last question she always asked before I departed was, "What colors did Jeff's flowers bloom in?"

Jeff understood my dreams even when I could barely sort them myself. Late one Saturday, when he'd returned from work, he came in shaking an old tin can which he emptied on the table. Out spilled dozens of peach pits along with a message clinging to his smile; one he'd memorized from the white woman who gave them to him. She had an orchard out back of her place. I made Jeff tell me over and over again how she said to get them pits growing into trees. Had to get it just right, didn't

I? Put lots of holes in the bottom of some old tin cans. Mix plenty of sand from the stream bed in there so's the water won't stand too long, then add a bit of manure. Not too much; don't want to burn them roots when they get started. Jeff got so tired of telling me, he threatened to dig up one of the woman's fruit trees and plant it out front if I didn't quiet up. Well maybe, but when the day came it was Jeff who got on his knees, like when he asked me to marry him, and told me our peach trees had started to come up in those old cans. Twenty little trees lined along the edge of the porch to catch the morning sun. A few weeks later we planted them together, Jeffrey and me, in rows like they was gonna one day be an orchard—a place we'd follow the laughter of our children playing in the cool shade.

What color is joy? I wouldn't be able to describe all the hues I celebrated with Jeff that autumn by the chestnut. He had made another dream come true. One worked from the calloused palms of his hands and sprinkled with the sweat of his brow.

Those bright days were followed by long sweaty nights that have endured in my secrets to this day. We never wanted to go inside our cabin for nothing and seemed to mostly live on the porch, sat along the stream where we bathed, or enjoyed being under the canopy of his chestnut tree. From there we'd look over our newly planted peach trees like we could all but watch them grow in the moonlight.

On Saturdays, come early evening, Jeff would sometimes stop what he was working on around the cabin, and look for me between lines of sheets I was taking down. Sometimes I'd peek over my hanging clothes and watch for his glance. Yes, I was his woman and knew what he wanted. His shirt would already be pulled over his head by the time he made it over to me; him not wanting to waste time with no buttons. He'd carry me to the shade of the chestnut, lift me high and I'd hold his sweaty head between my breasts till he was finished. The taste of salty sweat running down his neck I'd catch in my mouth opened to his passion. Then he'd slowly ease me down till my feet touched time again. Then afterwards that stream felt so good. Down there we'd let the cool water undulate over us. Just my hand in Jeff's to keep me from floating away in all the bliss. He was always quiet when he'd finished having his pleasure, as though he lingered in the moment.

Even during the week we'd eat supper out on the porch in the moonlight. I'd fry up some fish Jeff had caught or a chicken one of the white folks had given him for his labors. That autumn Jeff started a fire near the porch to light our evening. I still hear the crackling of the burning leaves against the crisp air. He'd roll apples in sugar and then toss them in a can he'd place near the fire till they baked soft as custard. After there was nothing left to eat, Jeff would take my hand and walk me through where our peach trees were planted. Each time it was as though we were going somewhere special; a journey to some secret place, one that was no borrowed dream.

"What are you expectin' from them spindly little twigs we got planted?" Jeff asked. Asked me all the time just so I could dwell in our dream of an orchard. He pretended he was never tired of hearing the same story, 'cause he didn't really care 'bout my words, just the joy that came with them.

"Gonna be our orchard one day," I told him again. "Our own Garden of Eden just like the one Momma promised was up ahead for her family come a day she never saw."

As I look back to these moments I always see Minerva and Owen out in the dust of the Burneys' fields. And then, late at night, the look of Momma's weary eyes as she pulled up the bottom of that old apron-curtain to look up at the big white house to see if Ella was signaling Isaac had capitulated to his bottle—the battle he never sought to win, so we could finally head up to Orchard Hill. I remember Minerva's gaze as sad but happy at the same time. Call it hope, or whatever, even deep in her exhaustion her faith for the future of her kids never dimmed.

"What's the matter, honey?" Jeff whispered.

"My momma, she'd take me up to the orchard late at night. I 'member lookin' up at them tall trees, branches touching over our heads like angels' wings. Cool, the ground so cool to our feet where they'd been waterin' that morning. Just me and Momma up there close to the bounty that waited at the edge of the moonlight. Up there where Isaac couldn't hear us talkin' 'bout how it was gonna be someday when we got away."

"Look 'round. You got away from the Burney place. All your dreams are right here with me now."

"No, Jeff. Nobody ever gets that far, 'cause there ain't that far to run to. Them plantation days are gonna follow us like a shadow sewn to our heels. No matter how many miles we run, no matter how many years we struggle to rid ourselves of the memories, they'll still be chasing us down like the nigger dogs did our folks and their folks before."

"Ain't nobody gonna be chasin' us! I see to it," he said.

But maybe he didn't understand my tangled thoughts. Still I knew he felt the pain I had buried deep. His eyes told me so.

"You know, my momma, she tried to get away. Oh, Lord how she tried. But every day things got fixed against my folks more than the day before. No matter how hard they toiled, they still owed Burney more and more, always more. You think that's why the Lord took Owen and Minerva so young? He knew they didn't have it in 'em to work them fields no more?"

"Don't know 'bout them things," Jeff said. "But I know you keep your momma's dreams in you," he whispered. "I reckon that's where the Lord sees your soul. Like our kids one day gonna keep our dreams with 'em."

"Momma would be proud I goin' to night school."

"When you get all the learnin' gathered up, you teach it back to me. Yeah?"

"When, Jeff? You're always workin' till late."

"Got to get my hands on some big money. See, I got plans, too. Yes, ma'am! Gonna buy this here acreage one day. That's what I been thinkin' on. A man's got to dream, too."

"Where you get that kind of money?" I asked.

"I got something going. Me and the men; it's all gonna work out fine. Sure it is."

"You're not talkin' 'bout no still, are you?" I asked.

Blood drained to my soles at the idea. You see, I knew that Jeff was real busy back then. He was out most days well into the night and then coming home exhausted. Yet I mostly didn't know what they were doing. Maybe a job here and there up and down the roads leading back to town. It scared me more when Jeff looked off as far as he could toss his thoughts. What was going on out there beyond his chestnut tree, I wondered.

"It's business," he announced in a tone that meant I was not a party to his schemes.

So many times he'd said it was a man's dream to care for his family and that could come to some messy dealings at times. Yes, I knew what that meant, didn't I? 'Cause I could read defiance in Jeff's eyes even if he was quick to avert his gaze to keep me off the trail.

"They don't care 'bout nobody's dreams when they come callin' with their lynchin' ropes," I hollered at his back as he headed to the cabin.

He turned sharply and walked back towards me. Our eyes were sparing. "I ain't afraid of no coward hidin' under his momma's bed sheets," he proclaimed.

But I was. Didn't matter where they hid, the lynching rope be in plain sight for ever'body to see but the law. Yes, that rope tied hard to one end of a tree branch and the other 'round your life and from then on every day tightening on the necks of your family.

"Well, you damned well better be scared, 'cause nobody'll save you if the Klan gets on your back! Then what 'bout your dreams for us? I mean me and the baby?"

"The what?" Jeff's eyes got huge. "What 'a you say, Sarah? A baby?"

"Just maybe you're gonna be a daddy now. Don't want this baby's daddy caught bootleggin' under the Klan's nose."

He caressed my belly like it was his child's head. "Ah, there ain't no Klan 'round these parts," he said. "You and me and now a baby! Don't need nothin' else. No, ma'am. We got our heaven right here under the chestnut tree."

And Then Annie

30

I TELL YOU PLAIN, summer is never a good time to be with child. Not in the thick humidity of the South and sure not when you got a porch covered with piles of somebody's laundry to get through, and you know as you sit there unable to move, that your husband's gonna come home hungry for his supper before you can even get up again. Yet the very thought of cooking makes you sicker than when he left at dawn.

One morning after Jeff had left, I'd barely gotten out to the porch before I collapsed from exhaustion. The best I could do was sit there looking at them piles staring me back. I was sure them rags were cursing me or maybe waiting for a word as to how they was gonna somehow get into my tub. I finally gave up on getting any loads done and figured I'd wander down to the stream to cool my feet. But then just the ordeal of standing up got me afraid of what might happen if I got sick down there. I'd sure never get back up that sandy slope before I rolled down into the mud along that stream. Lord, I was a sight!

That day I put my hand under my belly like I was lifting a load of laundry. Given how hard it had been for me to do absolutely nothing that morning got me thinking as to what in the world I would do when the baby came? I knew I needed Louvenia, and if it wasn't for Jesse, Sister would be right there pushing the heat back with a turkey feather fan and a bowl of her egg custard.

Besides worrying about my baby coming, it was thinking of my sister that twisted my thoughts into grisly knots. I worried 'bout what was happening in that alley if I couldn't keep up with the wash for her to iron in town. Even when I had a load or two done, Jeff had no time to be going into town to leave it off. No, some nights my man came home so tired he didn't know which way he was headed. Where did that leave Sister? Sick as I was, I couldn't help but worry myself sicker on how she'd eat without that bit of ironing money coming in.

Weeks later Annie told me that Louvenia could hardly sleep over worries about the baby coming. Sometimes, after Jesse gone off, Annie brought over a plate of whatever she had put on her table that night. They'd sit there in the quiet of the evening while Sister ate her beans and rice or pork and collards and drank a jar of sweet tea together. Annie was gifted in the way she could get talk going, which eased Sister's mind off the cycle of woes that had belted her that day.

"Now you know Sarah ain't the first woman to have a baby, Sister Louvenia. That's been goin' on for some time now. Just look at me and the preacher."

"I'm so 'fraid for her," Louvenia said, patting one of Annie's little ones on the head as the child eagerly tugged at the doll dress Sister had just finished. "What if she goes to have that baby when she's out there hanging the laundry?" Louvenia shook her head to rid herself of the thought. "Can't get that picture out of my head. That baby come and Jeff's not 'round. Lordy, what's gonna happen then?"

Annie said that Sister was biting her nails to the quick.

"Now, now. You know that child ain't gonna be born over no tub."

Annie said Sister went silent and looked ever so lost.

But I'm sure my baby being born while I was working my tub wasn't the worst thing Sister conjured; me, where the nearest candle is down some rutted pitch-black road. Annie said Sister's eyes bled with despair till she came up with an idea. She told Sister she'd get the preacher to hire a buggy and take her out to our place.

"I can't do that," Sister said, stifling tears.

"Poor thing, why not?"

"I leave here, I got no place to come back to," Louvenia whispered like Jesse was already at her throat. "Jesse see to it. You know he would, too. He'd bring the law down on me," she said. "Sure enough he'd tell 'em something bad on me and then Jesse, he'd stand there holding the door open till they come. Wave 'em on in to take me off, he would."

"What he say about you that could be bad?" Annie asked. "You ain't done nothing!"

"It don't matter none. Jesse tight with the men at the jail since he been paying 'em off with money his whores give 'im to keep the law off their backs."

"Lordy, that man don't know how lucky he is he gots you!"

"But he sure knows he gots me, don't he?" Sister replied. "Whore money he stealin' now," she said in disgust, knowing what it felt like all them years Jesse picked her own pockets. "The law, they come for me and put me in a work gang on the county roads. I'd be out there for a quarter a day. With my gout and cracked ribs, how could I make it through a day? So they'd drag me back till I give 'em a full day, then another one or two till I ain't got no days left." Sister sobbed. "Lord, I don't wanna go that way."

"I know, honey." Annie said. "That Jesse, devil gets his worst meanness from watching your ol' man. Don't matter 'bout him. I know what we gonna do! I'll get my sister-in-law to watch my kids. Then the preacher can take me out to Sarah and Jeff's place. She ain't gonna have that child alone. No, she's sure enough not, so you put your mind to ease on that."

Louvenia could only swallow back the tears by finishing the supper that had gone cold.

⚘

It must have been only a few days later when, sitting there on the porch, I seen Annie and the preacher with little Nettie. Didn't know they were coming. Annie told me that they'd be at our place sooner than a letter could arrive. I cried at the sight as their wagon turn off the road to our place with Nettie waving a bandanna.

"Sister Sarah," the preacher hollered as they rolled in, "brought you a visitor. Seems like she's figuring on gettin' away from the kids and me and come spend some time here in the country. How's that sound to you?"

I don't remember my reply; all I could think of was my house being a mess, the porch covered with piles of stale clothes and I was sure I was about to puke in front of them.

"Oh, look at that woman! Ain't she with child?" the preacher said. "You best work yourself into that chair over there on the porch, Sarah. Annie here knows a thing about birthing. Don't you, honey?"

"Now don't be worrying none," Annie said as the preacher brought their things in. "Nettie and me gonna get everything ready for you and the baby."

"Momma brought an apple pie," Nettie said grinning ear to ear. "I cut the apples."

"Yeah, but that's for the baby, ain't it?" the preacher added with a wink. "Annie wouldn't let Nettie and me have a crumb of that pie on the way out here."

Annie was a woman who could divide and conquer. No sooner had they unloaded than she had her apron on ready to get busy. "Nettie, go get wood from the pile and get the water heated for the tubs. Want to get these piles washed and hung," Annie said. "Maybe they be dry enough so your daddy can take 'em back into town for Sister Louvenia to iron."

"Momma, we can't wash all them piles in one afternoon!" Nettie declared.

"How you know? Think you're taking too much time making a list of the things you can't do. You got that water boilin' yet, Nettie?"

"Momma! Ain't got the fire started yet."

"Sarah, honey, where's your broom?" Anne asked. "While the water heats, I'm gonna get the cabin swept so we can get something on for Jeff's supper tonight. If he's like the preacher, he don't know how to fry an egg without half the shell left in there!"

As Annie and Nettie were getting things done, I got to wondering what Jeff would think when he returned. The thought made me chuckle. Most nights he'd came home with a face smudged with grime, him expecting to sit down to a supper of corn mush. But that night there waited a fine hot supper. I know that cooking was the best thing he'd smelled in a long time. He stepped in the door looking as if something was amiss. Not a word came out of his beautiful mouth as I filled bowls with potatoes and carrots and put my big platter with that pork roast in front of him.

"You too tired to say somethin' honey?"

Jeff stared in wonderment. You see, Annie had taken Sally down to the stream to bathe, so Jeff figured I'd cooked that supper. Given my condition when he left that morning it would have been a miracle from Jesus. Guess it was all the same!

"Yes, ma'am!" is all he could say as he looked over the table of plates and bowls of Annie's fine cooking.

"You best sit down and eat 'fore them black-eyed peas get cold. Go ahead now. You ain't dreamin'."

I put the cornbread on the table just as Jeff put himself in a chair. He'd no sooner lifted a spoon of black-eyed peas to his mouth than Annie and Nettie walked in, their moist clothes clinging and their hair still wet from the stream. Then he knew. Jeff grinned near as big as when I told him I was gonna give him a child. Annie cut the cornbread and we sat down to enjoy the Lord's bounty like we were all family.

"There's apple pie waiting for you, Jeff, 'less Sarah got to it already," Annie said as Jeff stuffed his mouth.

"No, I never ate Jeff's pie. Nettie went and hid it so I wouldn't."

"I brought some peaches I put up last week. Gonna make a peach cobbler for Jeff's breakfast," Annie announced.

Jeff could only sit there with a grin fixed on his dimpled face.

That night I felt better than I had in weeks. Nettie and I washed up the dishes while Annie rested with Jeff on the porch. He didn't light the kerosene lamp so the 'squeeters wouldn't bother us none. About then Jeff had gone to smoking a pipe. He struck a match to light his pipe which lit his beautiful face. Forever I will remember how contented he looked.

"You got it so good, Jeffrey McWilliams," I heard Annie say. "So quiet out here at your old chestnut tree. Not like that alley where there ain't one tree."

Jeff pulled down a jug of corn whiskey from the ledge over the porch posts where he kept his tobacco tin and sloshed some into their crock mugs.

"It's a fine life out here. Ain't none better," Jeff said. "Ain't never gonna leave this place. Not ever. Got my woman at my side. Got a kid comin'. Even got us an orchard out there. Ain't them trees a bit taller than when you were here last?"

"Them trees is comin' along fine," Annie confirmed. "They sure enough is!"

"Sarah keeps promisin' them trees gonna give us a peach cobbler soon. But I forgot how many soons from now that'll be!" he said. "I reckon 'bout the time we're too old to pick 'em. But I'll still be here me tellin' my kids how hard their momma worked to have all the peach cobbler they could eat."

"Ain't nothing prettier in spring than when the ground under a peach tree is covered with blossoms," Annie remarked. "It's sure something to behold and then your kids out in that orchard playin' hide-n-seek."

"Annie, you and the preacher best bring them kids out and join us country folks. Get out of town where you can breathe the good air."

"Jeff, you know we would, but the preacher, he's got folks depending on him back in town. Most can't read or write you know. So, my husband's the only one that can help 'em with their needs. But Lord, he's promised me when our kids are married and settled, we gonna do just that. Leave that city. Lord, bring that day 'round soon. Yes, I can hear my creaking bones remind me all the time."

"You know I can't read or write none like the preacher," Jeff said. "But Sarah and me, we got a bit of our dream right here. Gonna buy this place one day, and then our children are gonna get schoolin'. Don't know how I's gonna do it, but I aim to no matter. Sarah, she always figures a way to get things done so I know it'll happen. Puts my mind at peace knowing it. Just like I know that ol' sun is gonna rise tomorrow and smile on them peach trees again. Yes, ma'am. Come a day somebody ask me where my kids is I'll tell 'em, they ain't in no cotton field workin' for the white man. Nope, they's all be in school workin' for a chance at their own dreams."

I went out onto the porch just as Annie was coming back in.

"I done worked for my daily bread today," she said. "Gonna get some sleep now."

"Just made up the trundle bed for you and Nettie," I said. "Don't know how to thank you for comin' all the way out here to lift my burdens."

"Ah, I just come 'cause I needed rest from the preacher," she whispered so Jeff couldn't hear. "That man, it don't matter how hot the night is, he figures on making it hotter for me near every night of the week he can get some," Annie winked.

"You gonna take a walk with me, Sarah?"

With a glint in his eyes Jeff reached for a bar of soap off the shelf, pulled a rag off a hook and offered me his hand. He eased me down that sandy slope and into a cool stream of water where I knew we'd be followed by a chorus of chirping crickets and giggling toads. We kept an ol' bent tin for bathing down there. I'd barely stepped out of my dress when Jeff poured cool water down my back and over my breasts. He poured that stream water like it had turned into May wine flavored with sweet woodruff and every drop he had to sample with his tongue. Then he filled the tin and handed it to me to pour over him. We sat there as the water churned over our ankles and talked about how our hard work had brought us to that moment.

"Been thinking, in a couple more months or so, just maybe I have the money to put down on this acreage," Jeff whispered in my ear and caressed my swollen belly.

"Are we near to buying this place?" I asked.

"Don't hardly make sense to plant an orchard, water it ever'day, then head down the road 'fore we taste the jam from them peaches you been preachin' 'bout."

"No, that don't make sense," I said. "But can't think how'd we get the money to buy much of anything."

"It'll come. Just like a peach from your trees up there."

Jeff pulled me close to him.

"You know, I sure thought we'd put them peach pits in some manure and get us a big peach tree 'bout the next week or so. You never tol' me I had to wait near a hundred years to get some of that jam you always promisin'."

"Well, you must not have planted them pits like I tol' you or we'd be havin' cobblers by now. Yes, we would. We'd be pickin' them right off the branches. Anyway, even a hundred years ain't that long to wait for something good, 'cause holding on to a dream is like holding on to somebody you love. Ain't it?"

"You don't gotta be holding on to me like I'm gonna disappear one day," Jeff whispered. "It don't matter none how many years in front of us, I still be right here in our orchard waitin' to find you looking for me under that ol' chestnut."

HER DADDY'S EYES

31

For the next few days, Annie and me, with little Nettie's help, got my work caught up and still found a few moments here and there to sit a spell on the porch and talk.

I told Annie I was eager to get Louvenia out with us, as Jeff and I were getting by and there was plenty to eat most days, and on leaner ones we still had a bag of cornmeal put back for mush. It was far more than our momma ever knew. I was sure that having Sister near to help raise our child would be a blessing. I figured that Jesse couldn't last much longer, him having dived headfirst into too many empty whiskey bottles by then.

Louvenia and me, we never knew anything about giving birth. Nettie and I were hanging laundry to dry while Annie was down at the stream when the baby decided to come. I didn't know how long it would be 'fore the baby showed, so I leaned on Nettie, praying I'd get to the cabin first. Inside, I fell over the bed moaning. Nettie yelled for her ma to come quick.

"Well, guess it's time you start on a long walk," Annie announced.

"A walk you say? I ain't goin' no place till this baby comes! And you know it!"

"Yes, you are, honey. You can count on it!" Anne replied. "Now get up and get to walkin', Sister."

Then it dawned on me. There was no movement in my belly. I'd felt none all morning. I held my ample middle feeling for life that was not there. That baby had been kicking at me for weeks and suddenly I realized I'd not felt a kick since the night before. Oh, Lord, I prayed my baby wasn't dead 'cause I'd spent too much time bending over them tubs!

"Get up now, Sarah, and start walkin' like I say."

But I didn't want to move. I was certain I'd lost my baby and only wanted to wail myself away.

"Momma, Sarah looks like she's lost," Nettie yelped.

"No, she's not lost. Just doesn't know where she's goin' is all. What's the matter, Sarah?"

"My baby, he's dead. I can't feel 'im move no more."

"No, that baby's fine. Just bashful about showing his face."

"Oh, Lord," was all that would come out of my mouth.

"You stand up now and let's see you walk about the cabin," Annie said.

"No, I ain't gonna take no damned walk. My baby's gone!" I cried. "I ain't never gonna walk no place again!"

"That so? A baby only stops fidgeting before it comes. Just a little rest before what comes next is all. Now get up and grab on to my arm. Want you to waddle around so that baby knows you're getting ready for 'im or he may decide not to come till next summer!"

"What?" Nettie asked her momma. Having witnessed the birth of her siblings, she knew more about birthing than me.

"Sarah's got to move around till it's really time. She's just worked up, is all," Annie told Nettie. "You fetch some water from the well."

Nettie scrambled out the door.

"Annie, if I die, tell Jeff I love 'im."

I cried hard as Annie shuffled me 'round the table in a circle. But that only made me want to puke all the more.

"If you die, honey, I'll tell Jeff you took off 'cause what he put in your belly and you're waiting in heaven with a stick to put to his head for all his orneriness," Annie said.

At first I laughed, but then started crying. No, I howled. "I got to lay down," I begged.

"No, you got to walk about like I said. You been 'round the table this way, let's turn and head the other way to see if the view's any different."

"Oh, Lord… I'm gonna die!"

"No, you're not gonna die. Just gonna wish you were dead before the day's out."

I think Annie had me walk a mile in circles 'round that table.

"Now, I guess it's time you best lay down on the bed. You're beginning to walk like you can't get your feet far enough apart. That means the baby's head is working its way down."

Nettie helped me get my feet up off the floor. Guess it was hours I rested, but seemed like only moments when Annie started tugging at me to get up and squat near the bed.

"Now I want you to push that baby on out now, honey."

But why was she yelling in my ear? I know she was, or was it only the pain howling. "What? Right on this here floor?"

"You're thinkin' this baby's gonna march right out of you?" she replied.

Well, I had no idea. I'd seen piglets born on the Burney place but nobody ever told that sow to push. That hog just lay there till them piglets came then she went for her supper. I guess that was my notion. I'd have that baby, get up and get Jeff's supper goin' and then maybe wash a few loads of clothes while the baby teethed.

After an hour or so of Annie yelling in one ear and then the other for me to push, she stopped. What was wrong? She felt my belly again and whispered that the baby was twisted up in there. Maybe it couldn't get out. I could tell by her expression that things were going badly. I knew I was gonna die when Jeff walked in.

"Sarah, ain't never seen a face as red as yours!" he said.

Nettie reached over and blotted my face again.

"My wife gonna be okay?" Jeff looked frightened like I'd never seen.

"Jeff, you best go out on the porch. It's a hell of a lot cooler out there," Annie said. "You got to push, honey. Push, I say! You can't stay this way for days thinkin' on it. You got to do it now like I say. I been where you are and know what it means if this child don't come soon!"

But I had no push left. My body couldn't seem to do nothing more than writhe in agony.

Annie got up. "Nettie, keep her forehead moist and keep fannin', child."

There was a lamp on the porch so I could see Jeff way out there under his chestnut, that big tree where I figure we made our baby that hot summer night. He always drifted over there when he had things brewing in his head. Annie called him back.

"Your woman, you know she's really just a girl, Jeff. She's not yet fifteen. That baby she's carryin' don't seem to want to come," Annie said.

"I go get the doctor."

"Ain't no doctor gonna come way out here before it's too late," Annie said.

"What?"

"I tell you, this girl's worn out, Jeff. All them tubs of laundry back on that alley. Getting your place goin' here. She's weary like I never seen no woman deliver baby alive."

"She's gonna have that baby just fine," Jeff said. "It's our dream to have lots of kids. I ain't gonna lose one."

"You got to go talk to her then. Show her where she can find something deep inside herself to keep it comin'," Annie said.

"Find what?"

"Find the will to fight till she pushes that baby out. 'Cause we're gettin' close to a bad place where she's gonna give up. Then we're gonna lose that baby." Annie bent over to whisper. "Could even lose your wife!"

Jeff returned to the bed looking determined to get some business done. Yes, I knew that expression, as he'd had it the time he was pulling stumps out.

He looked into my eyes like he was searching for something he'd lost. Don't know if I was awake the whole time 'cause it seemed like hours he held my hand. I still remember them calluses on his. A ridge across his palms.

"Sarah, you 'member when I first came up to your porch at Louvenia's?" he asked.

I think I just moaned. Wasn't in no damned mood to chat.

"And you were sitting there at that kitchen table. Your hair all up in the air like…"

"My what?" I groaned.

"Sure it was. Your hair stickin' up like a scarecrow gonna scare buzzards away," he said.

"What?"

"Now shut up, honey. I'm talkin'. Before I got in the door, you'd stuck your tongue out and wagged it at me like a damned ol' dog! Didn't you?"

Jeff drew up close and then winked.

"Yeah, like a bitch in heat."

"Like a what? What'd you just say to me?"

"Yeah. That tongue of yours. Lick, lick, lickin' at me. Huh? That's all you could think 'bout when you set your eyes on me. Ain't it so? Yes, ma'am, you sure fancied me. Lick, lick, lick…is what your eyes told me."

"I'm gonna belt you for saying that!"

With everything I could muster, I sent my fist to Jeff's mug. Hit the palm of his big hand and he smacked me right back with those dimples.

"See, that's the thing. You're lazy as an ol' sow. You'll probably be there for days. I just hope you don't spend all day stickin' that tongue out like you's hungry for me. Don't want Annie and Nettie here seein' you at it, do we? Huh?"

At that I could only think of killing Jeff. I struggled to go after my skillet and put it to his head. I kicked as hard as I could, what with having a baby goat in me—kicked at that man while he held both my hands with one of his.

"When I get up from here!" I screamed.

"Honey, that's what we been talkin' about. You don't seem to have a notion to get up any time soon, you ol' sow! Lick, lick, lick. Yeah, you sure 'nough said it."

Well, Lord. That did it. I squirmed and twisted to smack that man, but something inside of me freed the baby, or the baby figured it best come out and help her momma, because out she came. A baby girl.

Through all the joy of that moment I hoped she didn't 'member her folks cussing at each other.

"Yeah, you did it, Jeff. Got her all worked up. You best go back outside for now," Annie told him as our baby squalled at her daddy for talking to her momma like that.

Jeff went outside as Annie scurried around doing this and that. All I remembered was hearing them cry—out on the porch was my baby girl and my husband choking on his sobs. Yes, we had gotten through the birth of our first child because of Annie.

Annie and Nettie were with me for a few days after our baby came. Don't 'member now how many. When I was able to get up and walk a bit, I picked up our girl we named Lelia, and took her to see her daddy. He was out there next to the porch chopping kindling.

"This baby girl gots the best daddy in the world," I told my husband.

He reached for his tobacco tin sitting nearby and shook it hard. It rattled up a storm.

"What's you got in there? Peach pits?"

"Coins in here. Gonna be the education tin. Gonna save to buy our girl books and things she's gonna need for school," he said.

"That your dream?"

"A man's dream gots to be only what will bring happiness to his family."

Jeff took Lelia in his arms and held her up to kiss her forehead. I could see plainly that she had her daddy's eyes; two big brown button eyes that were already sewed tightly to our hearts.

Just for My Honey

32

SISTER COULD ONLY iron the things I left off in fits and starts. As she couldn't sleep well, she'd stay up late ironing in the still of the night when the alley was quieter. But that awful night it wasn't. It was long after dark when she heard Jesse howling his entrance to the alley between snorted laughs. Sister said some loud-mouthed woman echoed his howling. A trash-woman is what Sister called a whore. Yes, this time Jesse's whore was coming home with him. I wondered what kind of a woman could be persuaded to follow a man like Jesse down a dirty ol' alley? Lord have mercy on her and the likes!

Louvenia had taken ever'thing Jesse rubbed her face in, but in her mind, she didn't have to take having his whores in her home on top of it. Didn't Jesse love to flaunt his sins in Sister's battered face? He was always there to remind her he could do as he pleased, even as she put the money on the table to pay for it.

He walked in from the porch with this woman as though Sister wasn't standing witness to his transgression. But then to Jesse she was mostly invisible anyway.

"What? Who that? No, you ain't bringin' no whore in here!" She moved to block the woman from coming into her kitchen. "Not never. Get 'er off this porch."

To impress this woman of the streets, Jesse laughed in Sister's face

and graciously led the woman into Louvenia's kitchen where he paused
to begin his unbuttoning. She said he stank like he'd just bathed in alley
water soaked with cigarette butts and whiskey vomit. Sister told me this
woman looked about like she needed to know if that kitchen pleased her
good enough. Her looking 'round with Louvenia standing there with a
hot iron in her hand. Was this woman crazy, stupid or just drunk? Well,
she was all of these, wasn't she?

"You best get to thinkin' on painting this here kitchen 'fore you
move my things in. Hear, ol' man?"

Jesse was eager to please. "Hear that, Louvenia? You get to it tomorrow. Just for my honey, here," he said. "Paint it up the way she tell
you to!"

"And I'm tellin' you, you ain't bringin' no whore in here!"

"Watch your God-damned mouth, tub woman!" the whore said,
and then turned to Jesse. "Jesse, honey, this here do for now since I don't
got a place of my own just now. But what 'bout her? You ain't keepin'
her 'round if I move my things in, that's for damned sure, 'cause I don't
like the mouth she gots on 'er."

"Honey, I got no need for 'er now I got you, so I put her out on
the street if you don't want her takin' care of you. Is that what you're a
wantin'?"

Guess Jesse had been thinking on the terms for a spell. Him figuring
there'd be more pleasure for himself if he sweetened the deal by tossing
in a maid for this woman who spent most of her time on her back. A
live-in whore with no other place to call home all for an ugly old man
not gonna get none elsewhere no more. No, Jesse's life was all poured
down his throat and pissed back out in that alley by then. Yet for this
woman seemed to harbor a notion she was moving up in the world by
stepping down into Jesse's hell hole.

"You a whore!" Louvenia reminded her. "I seen you out there hangin'
on the corner of this here alley!" Sister reiterated as though the woman
didn't know her place in Louvenia's hierarchy of sins. "You ain't comin'
in my house, except one time. Then you're gonna be carrying your head

right back out that door." Sister pointed the direction of the door as her iron heated on that old stove.

But the woman knew who she was. Still, to her, Louvenia was even less. My sister was an unpaid whore and a colored man's slave too. Maybe most days this woman was better off than us 'cause ever'body knew 'round them streets, you mess with a whore, get rough on her or try to steal her money, she'd break a bottle and twist the jagged end in your face till you looked like ground meat. Then you'd know not to mess with her again!

"You a whore! And you ain't comin' in my house! Hear what I say?"

But the woman hadn't. No, she was busy looking over the kitchen like she was figuring what color she wanted it painted.

Sister then told Jesse off. "Get this whore out 'a here, and I mean now!"

Don't know why Louvenia thought her husband would turn and apologize for profaning her home and then usher the woman on out to the streets where she belonged. No, that wasn't Jesse. "Now, huh? That's when you want it? Then I give you what you deserve!"

With his fist Jesse spun the room 'round Sister's head in that old familiar orbit. Leaving Louvenia on the floor, he fondled the woman back to his bedroom.

Louvenia said at first she didn't feel the blood dripping down her forehead where she'd collided with the corner of that table. Her head had been cracked open so often the nerves in her face were mostly dead by then. She lay on the floor bleeding, wiping the blood out of her eyes, unable to get up even as her head spun. But the sounds of Jesse fixing to copulate the whore started to jab at Sister's old wounds. She told me she could hear them as good as if they were doing it right over the table she lay beneath.

"No honey, like I tol' you, she ain't good for nothin'," Jesse told the woman. "But I tell her to fix your meals like you want 'em and take care of your clothes real good," Jesse affirmed. "Sure, I will. I make her iron 'em up real pretty the way I like youse to look." Jesse coaxed the woman out of her blouse. "That woman out there gots no choice but do what

you tell 'er or she be out on the street cold," he snapped his finger. "Just
for my honey here, I'll do it for you, sweetie. You know I will, too."

"I don't give a God-damned what you'd like me to wear, Jesse Powell.
And I ain't your honey, you ugly ol' man! So, stop pantin' over me like
some stinkin' dog runnin' between the legs!"

Guess the whore was not entirely disposed to the deal Jesse planned
to squeeze wholesale out my sister. She slapped Jesse's pawing off and
wandered back out to the kitchen again. Maybe she had second thoughts
about the situation as she stepped over Sister like she was a bag of rancid
flour fixed to be tossed. Then Jesse must have figured he could woo
her into thinking he could get his hands on a bit of money to sweeten
the habitation deal he was brewing with the whore. Louvenia would
come through for his honey, wouldn't she? Cover his overcharges for
the night's pleasures? Didn't she always have some money hidden back
somewhere? Louvenia didn't need money to eat that week. Where was
it this time? A fist or two would produce the reserve funds to complete
Jesse's transaction and get the ball rolling in the backroom.

"I got some money comin' in," Jesse declared to the woman. "Got
a bit here and there, enough for my honey, if you know what I mean."

Well, Sister sure knew what he meant. Hadn't her iron put out every
coin that bought what she put on his plate and even them old used suits
on his back?

The whore, who knew he was a wasted ol' man, had to buy into it
because she'd run out of credit herself. You know she had if she wandered
down to the end of Jesse's alley. She had nothing else going for her and
no options, so she went on back to open her legs for him.

For Louvenia the moment had come. Living on the edge of hell for
so long, she might as well head there and call it home. The only decision
left was figuring what would deliver that fact to Jesse's head the quickest
and split it open the widest. Well, I guess just knowing that man had
lived his last day gave her the strength to crawl back up. She hoisted her
skirt to wipe the blood out of her eyes and reached for a chair to climb
to her feet. Jesse was already busy back there trying to mount the whore,
but the woman kept coming up with deal breakers that frustrated his

gyrations. Guess Jesse's working the whore's trade while abusing Sister added a bit of entertainment, so he left the door open for Sister to hear. But it wasn't to be the spectacle the ol' man had figured on. No, there was a tragedy unfolding on Jesse's very own dark stage, and there'd be little more light if he could open his coffin lid for another round.

Louvenia, propelled to her feet by Jesse's grunts and the whore's slapping at his back to get it over with, worked her way over to the counter where the other meat was cut up. Down under, behind some old mason jars, she kept the big knife. The one I'd pointed at Jesse when he came at me that time. Same ol' butcher knife, 'cept she'd been keeping it down there in a rusty tin filled with foul water so that even a prick, just a tiny one ain't nobody ever gonna see, would be lethal unless he was immune to blood poisoning. Yes, Sister knew the day had come; she'd been saving for it in that rusty tin.

Sister resurrected the knife and carried it back there dripping brown rust with one aim: to slit open Jesse's notion he'd have his whore in her home. How many past due bills of retainer were about to be settled? There'd be no trial. Satan was surely waiting for Jesse, and wasn't gonna fuss over the details of his final fall.

Despite her broken rib, Sister shuffled 'cross the kitchen he'd just bartered to the whore. Jesse was back there grunting like a mating hog and saw only pleasure coming his way. But there was to be more than he'd bargained for. You see, Jesse was panting so heavily he didn't see Sister also panting to get at his throat. She crawled 'round to the side of his bed and aimed the knife for the middle of his spineless back. Momma must 'a been there steadying her hand for the gut severing plunge that would put an end to Jesse. The woman, who'd been keeping her eyes shut to Jesse's ugly business, opened them only to see her own end coming down faster than dice hits a wall in an alley. In that flash, she could not have known if it was Jesse's mole-cursed back that would take the hit or if she'd end up with her thigh gouged. Not a good place for a whore to have battle wounds. And you know this time the woman finally realized she best jump to a respectful attention in Sister's presence. With the butcher knife in transit, she bounced so hard to rid herself of Jesse that he rolled over to the floor.

That knife missed Jesse's back but creased the whore's inner leg where it let blood. The woman now truly understood what the terms of Jesse's deal were, and that it was a slim chance she'd ever see any maid service from my sister in her future, which was now entirely uncertain. The whore got crazy at the sight of all that blood. Real crazy. Guess enough to clear up her whiskey head lickety-split. Suddenly she didn't seem to care no more 'bout how handy Sister might be in doing up her laundry and fixing her meals. No, getting butchered like a piece of meat was probably not as pretty as the picture of life on easy street that Jesse had smeared over her desperation to get the woman to stroll down his stinking alley with him. Sister told me the woman kept screaming and panting, but not the way Jesse wanted. No, she was panting gusts of terror. She had to have known that one-legged whores don't get much business. Those women only perform in alleys for enough raw cash to get to the next day, where things ain't never gonna be better. Wasn't she only a few steps ahead of them kind of women when she followed Jesse that night?

But Jesse's head was so bourbon-soaked and his eyes so amber-jaundiced, he couldn't sort the real commotion till he realized that somehow the whore was up there on the bed and he was now on the floor. But as Sister went to pull the woman out of her house by the hair, he sobered up quickly. Yes, he could still pull his fist back to deliver it to Sister's splintered face. He sent her reeling across the room and up against that dented doorknob that had clashed with her head before. Even so, the whore was smart enough to know when a sister had turned the craps table over.

Yes, it was painfully clear that Louvenia had flipped the deal even if she was all but indisposed—her gasping and gagging on the blood filling her throat. But the woman must have figured that if there was yet another round, they might all end up dead, and sure enough there'd be no freshly ironed frock hanging over a chair waiting for the undertaker to fold her into. The blood running down the whore's leg was surely a reminder of how fragile life was. One minute you're the reigning mistress arranging the new home you relieved a tub woman of, and the next you're waiting for the undertaker to situate what's left of you in a pine box. Hadn't Sister told her that when she put a foot in her kitchen? Well, maybe not clear enough.

Jesse finally gave up on his next round of pawing on the poor woman because her screaming was distracting him from working his rhythm back. He went cursing over to the door to get Louvenia out of the woman's sight so the whore might stop howling. He yanked Sister 'round to drag her out by her feet so's he could get back to his honey again. He dragged her like a bag of garbage to be hauled off. Sister said she felt them uneven floorboards as her head dragged across the room. When Louvenia came to, she thought she'd been buried alive as her skirt was twisted over her head like a winding sheet.

Jesse, he left her in a pile at the backdoor. But she wasn't dead enough, was she? Somewhere inside, Sister found enough left to finish the deed. Surely it was a surge of Minerva's spirit that brought her back from the edge once again.

Louvenia didn't 'member what happened later 'cept she'd crawled over to the laundry pile for a rag to stop the bleeding. Said the whore stayed back there in Jesse's bed screaming ever' time he went to mount her again. She cowered and bawled her eyes out till Jesse had managed to pour enough whiskey down her throat to fortify her for more. Then when she got her bourbon guts back, she aimed herself for the road. 'Cept the only escape route was through Louvenia's kitchen and the very door Sister had warned her not to profane. Well, the whore should have thought on that when she was sweet-talking Sister 'bout her plans to redecorate the kitchen. Maybe this time she'd for sure listen to a God-fearing woman like my sister.

Yes, it was a mighty serious problem the whore had gotten herself into, 'cause the power had shifted and the lowly and badly bruised were raised and armed with a rusty knife and an iron was heating on the stove as backup. All Sister had to do was sit at her kitchen table and wait for the woman to muster enough courage to risk getting past her and it wouldn't be the same manner as her grand entrance.

Louvenia pointed her finger at the whore's face as soon as she dared to peek out. "Woman, did I not tell your sorry ass that you weren't comin' into my home? Next time I see your face it best not be anywheres on this alley. Else you're gonna get my iron upside your head and you're gonna keep gettin' it till your hearin' gets fixed!"

Well, the whore must have been good and soused 'cause her damned mouth got the best of her all over again. "You tub woman! You near cut my leg off. I got to go find me a doctor. He gonna sew me."

At that Sister got up to fix her mouth for good. "Honey, ain't no doctor gonna sew your head back on!"

With that Louvenia picked up her heated iron. Using her stronger left arm, she slung it at the woman's head.

It only grazed the woman's face but that was enough to slap some sense into her vacant head. At that she fought her way through the screen door to get herself out of Sister's kitchen alive.

Sister said she never saw the woman again.

END OF AN ALLEY

33

JEFF AND I had long talked about getting Louvenia out to the cabin for a visit. Still Sister could never see past that ol' man's threats as to how she might leave for even a day. I got to wondering if she could work something out with Annie's help, thinking that one night, when Jesse was out at the bars, she would head down to her place. Then Annie would go tell Jesse that Louvenia was real sick, needed tending and he best stay away or he'd catch it, too. I knew Jesse was scared of getting sick as he'd already been feeling the rough edges of his own coffin by then. Hating Annie's kids, I knew he'd never bother checking up on Louvenia even to see how long before she'd be back to cooking his meals and cleaning up his life. Then while Jesse was thinking that Sister was just down the alley, she'd be on her way to us. At Jeff's cabin we'd hug the ground till the fears faded as I knew Jeff could protect us from Jesse if he and Brother Fred ever showed to drag their meal ticket back.

It was dark early and seemed colder than usual when Jeff got back with the wagon and I took off for town. All the way I wondered if Jesse would be there and what he might do when the day came he found Sister was gone for good. Perhaps that's why I shivered on the way. Seemed like there was a cold chill licking at my every thought. Maybe only a premonition, one that I was about to walk into a black dream. It was the night of the whore's visit.

Since I'd been with Jeff, Sister and I worked it so that Jesse was gone by the time I arrived or she'd be on her porch to warn me away. But that night was long brewed in tragedy before I got to the alley. I quietly stepped up on the porch, paused to see if I could hear Jesse, then went in. Louvenia sat there at the table frozen. I could hardly keep from crying out at the sight. Sister didn't cry. No tears, no sounds, it was all gone. Jesse had surely killed her, she just wasn't dead yet.

"Oh, Lord Sister, what happened?"

Louvenia was so head-battered she was delusional. Even her vision was scrambled from the blood welling in her blackened eyes. "Jesse, his whore come into my kitchen, didn't she? He brung 'er. That's what he done. She held me down while he did it. Killed her with my iron. Crushed her head open so's I could spoon her brains to Jesse. See, he was thinkin' on keepin' her on here. A whore, he was!"

"Where Jesse now?" I whispered, half expecting him to come at me from the darkness of his backroom.

"Where he mostly been. Back there passed out. Just maybe he ain't never gonna wake up again. Huh?"

She braced her head to slow the teetering.

"This time you gots to come with me. Jeff protect you from Jesse."

"Yeah, I go with you, but you best come for me after he gone. You know he won't let me out the door alive."

"I go tell Annie what we're gonna do," I said. "Down there I'll watch for Jesse. When he gone, we gonna walk to the end of this alley for the last time!"

I reached to hug my sister. In agony, she flinched at my very touch.

"Yes, you come back, Sarah. I be alright till then. Sure, I will."

Louvenia folded her arms on the table, turned her head away from me and laid it over them. Crying, I headed to Annie's.

But on the way I got to thinking that maybe Sister didn't really want me to read her eyes. Was that why she buried them in her folded arms? Maybe she was really determined to escape somewhere else. How many times had Louvenia told me she was praying for the Lord to take her? She was tired, she'd say, and in all her exhaustion she often called on

Jesus to carry her over to Summerland, that place where there'd never be a wound that never healed. Hadn't Jesse cleaned her out of everything but her soul? Even that Sister thought he and the whore would sacrifice if she let them profane her home. And they would. Realizing what was in her head, to go looking for Jesus, I dashed back to Louvenia's. I was jolted at the thought that perhaps my sister would already be gone, that she'd cut her wrists or worse.

Truly, I'd never heard such dead silence. Not ever. My heart only stopped pounding when I walked back in to see Louvenia struggling to pull her things together. I took a deep breath of relief that she was still there, and, at least, half alive. I went to peek into Jesse's backroom. There he lay half slung over his bed, still gripping the whore's underwear.

Back in that dark bedroom, Louvenia went to filling a pillowcase with her things. I'm telling you, probably everything she owned wouldn't fill one. She paused to look about as she crept around his bed, like she was gathering up memories of the years those walls had been her prison. Jesse moaned but never opened an eye. If he knew she was headed out, he'd kill her before she got to the door. He'd little to lose, as death was already on the hunt for him. Yes, surely throbbing at his nightmare was a deafening chorus of crashing whiskey bottles. All empty. The very ones that Sister's rusty knife was surely hammering a hollow dirge on. Did she aim to break his head open on the downbeat? All the same, his would be a slow and painful death by whiskey starvation if she ever got out the door, leaving him to his own means.

When Jesse growled in his sleep, Sister ducked and bit the corner of the pillowcase like her broken rib was gonna come out her side. He groaned again and reached for his whore's thigh, but his hand only rubbed his old pillow. "Lily," he called out. He called them all Lily 'cause he never knew their names. To him they needed no name. Then, in his sleep, he cursed Sister again from somewhere that surely had to be too close to hell.

"Hey, I gots to pee, bitch," he mumbled to his dead bed and then passed out again.

His Lily was gone and now only Louvenia stood there. But it seemed as though the years of beatings had taken over. Her rage surged as she found more of his rainy-day half-empties hidden about. Bottles she'd paid for. Her staying up till dawn ironing to buy herself a moment of peace. One by one she toted them bottles to the kitchen and emptied every drop of whiskey into her washtub and then lined them in precise rows over her table, straight—one bottle after another like on a grocer's shelf. They soon covered the entire table as they'd long mapped out her life. Then she fell into a chair looking over her deed. I bit my lip to keep from crying.

Jesse wasn't tearful. "Hey, where's Lily? Huh? She take off? Go out in the alley and see. I got somethin' for 'er! Go on now, I said… Huh?"

He crawled out of his brown bed and stumbled into the kitchen like he had no memory of what he'd done, or it simply made no difference. His life was one long blur that didn't require apologies to punctuate his assaults. I stood in the shadows of the porch shivering at the sight of him staggering about like he was waiting for his thoughts to catch up with him. He snorted and choked on his own congested filth. Then he noticed the bottles lined up. Sister sat there with a faint smile on her busted lip. Her eyes fixed on Jesse's sacrificial altar in front of her, dozens of glistening whiskey bottles with every last drop of hope for his final binge drained away. You see, Sister had determined that Jesse would be going to hell sober.

"Why you're a God-damned bitch! You done drunk up the last of my whiskey, ain't you?"

He lifted his fist to punctuate his message on her face but stopped cold when he saw Sister's hand swing out. She'd been holding that knife on her lap. No, this time she didn't duck from his swing. She aimed it at his face and twisted it like she was daring him to swallow it whole. From her honey, Jesse, it was time to exact her own justice. The bottle had truly spun and now pointed to Jesse's throat. His luck had poured out.

Sister held tightly to the knife like she was fighting the Lord Himself for control. But then plunged it into the tabletop so hard the bottles tumbled and crashed to the floor. Her eyes glared back, and still she kept that grin fixed on her broken face. The grin of contempt. Jagged pieces of whiskey bottles covered the floor between them.

"You crazy bitch! I get you good for this!"

But not just now; he was still too drunk to do the deed proper. Later, for sure, when Sister wasn't expecting a blow, he'd come from behind like the man he wasn't. Just for another piece of his honey's head. With his mouth finally shut down, he looked over the broken glass. But all he could do was disappear back into his hell hole where the walls soon shook from his snoring.

Sister looked frozen in the moment; her hand still knotted to that butcher knife. I stepped back into the kitchen and whispered. "It's time now, Sister. I help you get the rest of your things and we get out 'fore he come after us."

She sat silently but then nodded. I pulled some clothes off a clothesline and shoved them into a pillowcase. Think they were hers, but don't know; maybe her customer's. Made no difference at that point. We were too close to some place not hell and surely not heaven to care. Sister worked her way up from her chair but froze like all the rest of her blood done drained to her feet. Her face was so ashen it looked as though a layer of poster paste had brushed over it.

"Sister, you sit. I finish gettin' your things," I said.

"Just one thing I left back there. I can hear 'im snoring so I go tend to it now. It 'a all be over then."

Her voice was hoarse, constricted like Jesse had just taken his hands off her throat. Lord, I prayed, she ain't got nothing left for him to take; it's all wrung out of her. I knew I had to get us on the road. Had to be on the run before things ran over. Maybe like a cauldron of boiling lye soap.

"Hurry now, Sister. Sooner we gets on the road the quicker we be safe with Jeff. Jesse ain't never gonna bother us at the cabin."

I went back to filling the pillowcase and looked over that room, knowing it was the last time my eyes would swallow the throbbing memories those walls had long served up. So many years' worth I could have gagged. Sleeping on the cot in that corner; washing heaven knows how many tubs of stinking rags. Living most of my life in a space not much larger than a shed and then begging Jesse to leave me be one more day.

Then, as I looked over that room for the final time it hit me cold: why had the snoring gone dead back there? And what could Sister possibly have left in Jesse's room that she'd risk waking him? My soul vibrated with her words from not long before" "Jesse, you ever hit me again, I'll kill you and then put the knife to my throat."

I scrambled over the broken glass and through the silence of what was surely Jesse's black dream in progress. Back there was my sister sitting on the edge of his bed with that rusty knife at his throat. His eyes bulged. Yet it was not like all the times when he was about to punch her broken face.

"I owe you Jesse Powell and there ain't enough pain for what you done to us. Ain't I only payin' you back?"

"Huh?" was all Jesse could utter. But she'd heard that lie before, hadn't she?

She was nose-to-nose with that ol' man, just like Momma had been that time with ol' Isaac.

She looked about for a ghost.

"Can you hear him?"

"I can't hear nothin' with that knife," he stammered. But that was only one more of his lies.

"Sure you can. That's why I put it there. Make sure you heard me good and clear this time. That's Satan callin' you. He wants what's left of you after I finish the butcherin'! 'Cause you're gonna die tonight. Satan…he been waitin' for you too long. Now I'm gonna deliver you to 'im myself!"

Her torture drew blood that trickled down his neck. One budge and she'd cut that bulging artery under his jaw. Then with a hard thrust she'd plunge the knife through his tongue till the tip lodged in his palette. From that bloody moment on she'd not hear his curses no more. Jesse lay frozen with terror as he surely felt Satan squirming for his take. Sweat poured down his cold face.

There are different kinds of justice in this world, and I reckon we'll all be pleading for one or two in the next life. That night I pled for my sister's soul. I grabbed her wrist to pull the knife back from Jesse's bleeding throat. But, Lord, she wasn't gonna let him live. I held on to her hand with all the strength I could muster and whispered against her yammering about killing that ol' man.

"You will, Sister. You be payin' Jesse back when you go, 'cause when you leave this alley there ain't nobody 'round that's gonna do nothin' for Jesse Powell. Don't let him walk your soul to hell with 'im! Leave the rest to Jesus."

Her chin quivered with rage. For what seemed an eternity, I struggled to loosen her grip on the knife. The moments chased after my beating heart. For the only time ever, Jesse's eyes pleaded with mine for mercy. I knew if I let her, she'd plunge it deep and his life would be relinquished to Sister's rage. But her soul would then pay for eternity for taking a life.

Then finally I got the knife back from Jesse's throat. I raised her off the bed still aiming that knife to his throat. Holding her shaking arm, I guided Sister into the kitchen and over to the sink where I shook her wrist over the dishpan. Her eyes were glued to the knife like she couldn't let it drop; the rage was yet spent. How many years had that been the dream that kept her barely alive, to rid her life of Jesse? I held her wrist over that sink to the sounds of cold silence coming from Jesse back there. He never moved to come at us. Even his curses had run their course. Sister's hand shook fiercely, the knife rattled against the side of the tin dishpan. Finally, she turned to me, tears streaming down her bloodied face and said: "I ready now. It's time." At that moment the knife fell into the dishpan.

Jesus had heard my prayer. Sister had relinquished her desire to send Jesse to hell. Yes, she had returned to God's grace and would not break His commandment not to kill. I took a deep breath. It was over and Sister was safe. She hadn't murdered Jesse; she would not spend eternity in hell with him. No, Jesse was doomed to go there without his honey and there he'd be left to stoke the flames waiting for Fred's arrival. We'd walked out his door for the last time. Truly, he must have known that his would only be an aimless stroll to his own end. Only a few more swigs left to count if he could find a bottle hidden somewhere, and then what? Wash and iron clothes for folks? Call in favors from the many he'd abused? No, it was over. That night, the night of the whore's visit, his world had become as dark as the inside of the coffin he'd soon be visiting. It was the place he'd bought on overdrawn credit and buried himself in.

Weeks later Annie told me that from time to time she noticed Jesse stealing a peek out of the kitchen curtains late at night. Him there watching to see if Sister was headed back to him. Yet he really knew he'd not see her again, as he never put a light on out there.

Now I faced my own black dream.

White Sheets and the Beyond

34

THE STREET WAS wet. Louvenia waited in cold silence as I wrapped her ribs in a sheet I'd torn into lengths. Sister, who was always rail thin, shivered yet there was still a glimpse of a smile on her lip. She knew we were about to escape Jesse and his alley forever.

I couldn't get us away fast enough. Still, in all the fog of those tragic moments back at Sister's I saw visions of my husband waiting at our cabin door, him gazing down the dark road for my return. Louvenia was tired, not just weary from all she'd experienced that awful night with Jesse and his whore, but a bone deep weariness that had long dragged on her. On the road out of town she stared ahead but still at nothing. I chatted about everything I could think of to keep her from drifting to sleep and falling off the wagon. But my own weariness and the night's chill made it hard. Don't know how cold it is when somebody freezes.

"Sister…Sister, you say somethin' now," I demanded, or thought I had. "We got to stay awake on the road here."

"Jesse, he gonna come after me this far out?" she asked again, or had I only been reading her thoughts? Hers or mine, that is.

"No, he ain't," I assured her even as I searched for reasons to support my notion. "Where he gonna get somebody with a wagon to come this far? You ain't gonna see that man ever again 'cept in your thoughts till you wash 'em away. Every time you think of Jesse you gotta dump that brown water out of your tub on his head! He gone. You done handed 'im his ticket to hell an hour ago. He back there packin' for the fall!"

"What…What I gonna do…all day?" she wondered aloud.

Her voice sounded much like Daddy's most times, yet when she was tired her words cracked as Momma's did when she was exhausted. My sister, she never awakened to a day in her life that wasn't already breaking under the weight of the work piled on.

"Well, in the mornin', when you're ready to get up, you're gonna give Lelia her bath while I finish hangin' the loads I done washed."

"That all? Wash my baby?"

"Well, some mornings you might want to put a pan of biscuits in the oven. 'Course we don't have much jam comin' our way, but we sure will when our trees are growed! Yes, ma'am, we gonna!"

"You ever think about the Burney place?" she asked. "I mean, where our folks is buried and all."

"I do. I think about Grandview. I think 'bout Jackson and Ella. Wonder what they's doin' and if they ever think of us. And that always takes me to Orchard Hill. Our folks is up there. Ain't nobody but us cares, but we know they up there hidden under the weeds where nobody can trouble them."

"Ever' day…I pray for Alex." Sister said. "I wait for the day he comes back. Then we all be close again. Like our folks wanted it. We stay together from then on. I know we will."

We shivered as frost dusted the trees. Sister's eyelids grew heavier from the night air riding them down. But Lord, God, guess it was about then that she let out a holler that I figured my shifting on the seat had caused. She gripped her side like it was coming out, that cracked rib was. It was so foggy, couldn't really see where we were, but felt like we'd been bumping along the road for miles. I was frightened we'd taken the wrong road. I knew, with that broken rib, that every rut might put Sister closer to death. Her yelps at every bump grew more anguished. I knew she couldn't stand the agony much longer. I slapped at her to stay awake as my own weariness took command. I could hardly hold the reins no more.

"Hold on to me Sister. Don't fall out on the road. Back at the cabin, Jeff gots a warm fire going for us. You know he does."

Sister clung to me when she wasn't weaving in and out of agony. I kept thinking, was it our bitter peace to have salvaged our lives from Jesse only to perish from the cold? Where are you, Lord, when I'm on a road of darkness too thick to think on? Have the miles shifted out from under me? Am I headed in the wrong direction? A jagged corner of an abyss I've never been before? How far are we from Jesse's alley now? Not far enough…I wondered if my lips were turning blue. Sister's were, or was that only Jesse's fist following?

Time seemed to pause during the fleeting moments my dry eyes closed to escape the cold air. Thankfully, the horses did not drift from the road following my exhausted thoughts. Then I saw it. Way up ahead there was a light beckoning us. As we drew closer it got brighter and even whiter, like maybe Jeff seen us coming and hung lanterns along the porch, lots of white floating up yonder. I struggled to keep my eyes open. Then I remembered leaving them sheets out to dry that morning. Had to be them reflecting the light from the lantern that Jeff always set for my return. There was a heavenly look as them sheets danced through my blurred vision.

It was at that moment when Sister fell onto my lap moaning. Lord, I prayed, don't let her fall over onto the road—she don't really want to die. I knew the wagon's wheels would grind her before I got the horses stopped. Up there, almost in reach, hidden behind all them white sheets was the door that would welcome my baby's aunt for the first time. "Jeff is waiting," I whispered. In moments Sister could sleep in peace for the first time in her life.

It was then, and as I'd never heard before, even from the darkest corners of Jesse's backroom, when Louvenia let out an agonizing wail that snapped me from my daze like a bolt of lightning had penetrated my lip. I knew it had happened. Sister's broken rib had penetrated her heart. No words from Sister could follow that shriek of what she saw. You see, those weren't my white sheets fluttering on the clothes lines up there; somebody else's sheets, and somebody else wearing them. What my sister saw was Jeff. Him under his chestnut tree where we made our daughter. There, with arms bound like a slave and his beautiful face bloodied, he hung with a noose around his neck.

Jeff's eyes gazed back through all that fog. I know they did. It was as though to warn me that the horror of the white shadows had been visited upon us. It had come calling at the very place where we thought its horrors had been vanquished. Yes, the men who hide under white sheets had come calling: Knights of the White Camellia. Cackling like hyenas, they were dancing 'round Jeff with their whips. These men twisted their sin-worn ropes 'round and 'round Jeff like he was a maypole. Louvenia dropped over into my lap. She was dead.

I rode them tired horses like a demon to get to my husband. For fleeting moments, somewhere at the very drains of my hope, I conjured a notion them cowards were only scaring Jeff, playing like lynching 'cause they did nothing but laugh and hoot. I would kill them all the same! But it wasn't like that, was it? They stopped laughing and their faces bulged, so loaded with hatred were they. I galloped to strike back. Just as the wagon drew close, at the very last moment, they kicked the stool out from under my husband. Jeff looked at me to convey something beyond his love. What were these words, Lord? I leapt from the wagon——Sister fell to the ground. I ran to grab Jeff's legs to save him. I would hold him up so that rope could not squeeze his life away. I would do it. I would save my husband.

"Come on boys, still problem is broken in two now."

But it was too late. I could do nothing. The white men on their horses circled as I held my husband's ankles. Jeff's eyes looked down from his bent neck, but could not see me trying to catch his life before it escaped on the end of his last breath. Still his eyes, that would never see me again, stared back like they still longed to. The song they always sang for me was silent. There was no life to hold on to. Jeff had passed to the beyond.

Even as my husband's last breath evaporated, one of them came from behind and kicked me. First in the back, and then in the head. Don't know where else. I lay on the ground under my husband's dead feet. My last moments as I faced my own death was hearing the cries of my terrified baby girl screaming up on the porch and knowing they were surely gonna kill her too and I could do nothing. Nothing. It was beyond that, along with my husband's soul.

And yet strangely a moment of peace came over me. Somewhere in my last thoughts that night, I knew there'd be only a few moments of agony to endure. Then the slaughter would be over and we'd all be together in the Lord's Orchard.

Just before I fell to the fluttering white shadows, I heard their words echoing in the empty blackness that had swallowed me. "You find our money?"

It was all about money. Ain't it always?

"Yeah, enough to buy this here place," was the reply.

After stealing my husband's life and the savings he planned to buy that acreage with, the three men drifted away like a white cloud destined for nowhere. A cloud of pestilence.

Yes, white sheets had fluttered for me. Now I only want to be wound and buried in them.

A Bitter Place

35

I DON'T REMEMBER MUCH of the next few days, or was it really weeks that I'd surrendered to the clouds that rattled in my dreams? Truly, the days follow each other in an ever-deepening haze when you don't count them; can't find a reason to want to.

Like when my folks passed, the fog returned and steeped my thoughts till they blanketed my days like a shroud. Yet everywhere I turned in my despair Louvenia's dulcet voice pursued. Only her humming penetrated the numbness of those mornings fled, chased down by dead afternoons to be delivered to avoided evenings and finally the ever-dreaded lonely nights that only rolled me deeper in my misery.

In broken sighs I stammered back. "No! I won't come out! Stop!" Stop that chanting at my bedside, I thought as I covered my head with the pillow that he'd slept on moments before in my dreams. Yet her melodies seemed just as determined to break into my thoughts and weave them into new directions as I lay there under sheets gone sour from stale sweat. Let me find some peace in my sleep, Lord. Got nowhere else to go looking for some.

I still do not know how Louvenia got me inside on the night of the fluttering white sheets. Was it Lelia's crying, or the bitter cold of that night? For the longest time I could only imagine things in drips. How did Sister get Jeff cut down from his chestnut? Where did he wait to comfort me from my sorrows? Even now, I can barely glimpse back on those bitter days when I could only moan something about my husband to Louvenia ever at my bedside. "Where is he?" I asked the blank wall that stared back pitilessly. For days she sat fanning on the edge of my nothingness, softly admonishing me to let the pain bleed the wounds clean. Her words bled easily into the spirituals she hummed as she rocked Lelia. "Let it be for now," she said, and promised the pain would run thinner and thinner over the miles ahead. But I had no intention of going that far without him. She preached that I had to take the next step, yet I would not move in any direction. Where was my husband now? Where was Jeff? Where is that bitter beyond where he waits?

How I bless Louvenia that I did not have to face the sight of Jeff's crumpled body on the night of the fluttering sheets. Surely, my daughter would be one more orphan if it weren't for Louvenia, a frail woman who yet found the strength to save me as she'd done so many times.

Then late one morning Sister picked up the fan and flung it down and walked around the bed to see if I'd noticed. I turned my face deeper into my pillow only to see the same emptiness staring back.

"I ain't gonna fan you no more," she said. "So, when you get hot enough, you're gonna get up. That's what I think," she announced with words and eyes.

"Where is he, Sister?" I mumbled.

Moments passed in the thick silence before she picked up the fan again.

"I know I been askin'. But you been sayin' nothin'."

She went back to fanning, but her eyes darted about like they always did when there were things she didn't want to talk about. I knew she was hunting for those doors of escape. But I met her at every one. Even as I'd been hiding under my pillow, I yet knew Sister had been hiding from me because she couldn't reply for the longest spell. But then she finally told me and Lord, how I understood why it was so hard for her.

"You know how hard that soil is out there." Her words came like they'd torn her throat. "You know it is," she whispered and swallowed hard.

I waited and waited for more. "You got to tell me," I begged. "Where Jeff is won't let me be. Where is that place?"

"You don't 'member that night. Even after your head is healed from their boot kicks. I prayed for it to be that way."

I searched Sister's sorrowful eyes for her secret. "What, Louvenia?" I asked. "What's you need to tell me?"

"The soil was so hard where you said bury Jeff. Out near his chestnut, you told me. You know I just couldn't get the shovel in the dirt. Just couldn't." Tears streamed down her face like she'd forsaken me. "There was too much rock, Sarah."

"Rock? I don't understand."

Her dry mouth twitched like her words were filled with splinters. "Only place I could bury Jeff was…out there." She pointed out the window to some vague place beyond. Could I have seen where he was all along if I'd only looked through my misery far enough? Still I noticed that Louvenia couldn't look out that way.

"Sister…?

"Had to dig where the soil would take the shovel," she said.

"Yes. Where?"

"His garden. 'Neath the flowers he growed for you. That's where Jeff rests."

I reached for Sister's hand. She held mine tightly. We both choked on our tears as our thoughts ran wild looking for refuge from the calamities in our hearts. But our prayers were not granted.

"I understand, Sister. I know I do."

I fell back on the pillow begging for the fog to come quick and dangle my thoughts till the weight of them finally dropped off and released me too another long sleep. Still, all I could see was Jeff's smile on the day when he handed me that last fist of flowers he'd cut for me. When was that, Lord? What life did it still hang from?

"Don't matter that you turned his garden under. He be glad of it. To rest under the flowers he loved. I know he would," I remember mumbling to Louvenia as I stumbled off searching for the sleep that might release me from the pain of that moment. But it had revoked its promise and left me laying there more awake than I'd ever been. "Don't matter, Sister. Don't matter no more… Nothin' does…"

Days later we talked about the day she buried my husband. Sister finally told me that I came out that morning looking dazed. Like them men had kicked me in the head all over again. Or maybe like a dream had kicked me out of bed and I'd gone off to look for a hole to swallow the pain; my own grave near Jeff's. She told me that as she battled the hard soil to fill Jeff's grave, I could only gaze down at the shrouded body of my husband and sob.

"Pull down the shroud, Sister. Need to see my husband's face one more time."

But Sister shook her head. She wouldn't reveal Jeff's forever lost smile.

"No, he don't want you to see how sad he is for leaving you," she mumbled. "'Cause if you do, you'll carry the picture with you forever. No, Sarah. Got to bury the anger right here with 'im. I pray to God, you will come to, 'cause it will kill you if you don't. Then what about our baby?"

Louvenia went back to pushing the soil she'd dug into the hole. There was nothing left in me to fight with. No, I could barely get myself back into the cabin where I prayed for my bed to once more drown me and then deliver me to a bitter place next to my husband.

❧

Because of my sister I arrived at a peace over Jeff's passing. It was a bitter peace, but not so for Sister having buried my husband in the garden he so loved. I no longer resisted Sister's admonitions that I not trip backwards to that cold night when I lost him. She pushed me to keep looking onwards, even if that was a vague empty place I did not want to step into. Truly for us, like all children of 'croppers, it was etched on my soul that I was a child born to slaves so at least I was certain that what may be out there for my child and me would be no more inhospitable than where I'd come from; that Klan-cursed soil I stood on. It steeped in my thoughts that there could be little ahead for us no matter what direction

I drifted. Wasn't it all a profane lie that the mighty would fall and the downtrodden would rise and take a place at the banquet? All damned lies and nothing more. The mighty are not brought down and the weak raised. No, the nobodies do not become somebodies under the feet of those who hide under white hoods. Still, from somewhere in my heart, I knew that I'd spend the rest of my days and lonely nights spreading flower seeds over my beloved husband's place of rest.

One morning Sister carried my daughter over to my bed with a little rag doll she'd made from one of Jeff's old shirts. There were two mismatched brown buttons she'd sewn on for eyes, one little button eye and a big one. Who did she ever see with eyes like that? I looked at that doll and couldn't stop laughing.

"You think it's so funny? Then you get up and make a better one. That's what I think!" Sister's hands were on her hips, so I'd know she meant business on me.

"Is that what you think, Louvenia? You got a notion any child gots big brown eyes like that rag doll's?"

She handed my daughter to me so I could see for myself. The sparkle in my baby's eyes nearly blinded me.

"You think Jeff would be pleased if this child's Ma's in bed all day and then some?"

"Don't start in on me, Louvenia. If I'm in bed all day, that's 'cause there ain't *some* left to get up for. Just leave me be and go make us some biscuits. I ain't in no mood to roll in the dirt with you no matter how many times you stand there pointing to the ground you think it's time I stand on. Lord, don't I know it's time?"

Sister wasn't going to give in only to see me fade back into my pillow again. "Now don't rush none. No, if you're needin' some more sleep you can always take a bath next week or come another week…if you got a mind to."

"I said…don't start in on me!"

"Now ain't you feelin' sassy?" Sister remarked with a smile like she'd just won a bet and me getting out of bed was the prize.

So I got up determined to escape her. I took Lelia and her new rag doll and went looking for Jeff. Sister watched through the window as she rolled her biscuits.

"Yes, Jeff. Think you been sendin' Sister into me every morning. I know you have! The two of you been carpin' at me for days now. Well, you win! I'm gonna get up and take care of your baby girl."

Sister waited for us on the porch with a smile and a plate of eggs. On that bright sunny morning of yet another resurrection of my soul, even Lelia's rag doll had more faith than I had the day before that biscuit. I ate everything Louvenia put in front of me and fed Lelia the same time. When I couldn't eat another bite, Sister started cleaning up, and that meant me as well.

"You take the baby out to there where I got that tub of water warming in the sun and give her a bath."

I carried the basin over to the shade of the chestnut. It was under this same tree that I made love to Jeff—the very tree he was lynched from that I'd finally come to face.

What do I tell my daughter? I wondered looking up at branches Jeff had once climbed to shake down chestnuts. How do I explain to our child that men that never knew her daddy took him from us? Tell me, Jeff. "What 'a we gonna do now? I got to get on with it. Ever' day I just keep thinkin' 'bout you. God knows I miss you. If it wasn't for our child here, you know I'd come to you."

Just as Jeff did the day we arrived, I kissed the bark of that old chestnut. Then from afar I saw the preacher coming down the road with Annie. Over the weeks they'd been stopping by to visit and leave off food. Annie hugged me and kissed my forehead before walking inside carrying a basket of food. She knew the preacher wanted to speak to me. He looked deep into my sad eyes and nodded like he could read my fears.

"Where's a poor woman with a baby to go?" I asked. "Got nowhere to go and no man to wait for at night."

The preacher put his hand on my shoulder and bowed his head. But I had no mind to pray. Still he brought me along just the same.

"'Whether you turn to the right or the left, your ears will hear a voice saying, 'This is the way; walk in it.' Isaiah, chapter thirty, verse twenty-one."

I told the preacher that over the days I'd known spells when I saw little reason to go on and no strength to take me there even if I had. He kissed Lelia and nodded his understanding. Yes, the reason was in my arms kicking to get at life.

"'A man's heart plans his way, but the Lord directs his steps.' Proverbs 16:9."

"But what does the Lord do for a woman?" I asked. "I'm a tub woman. At the end of my day there ain't no air left between me and my days bent over one."

"I got no answer for that, Sister. Maybe nobody does. Still, keep seeking, and you will find it. That path that takes you to a better place. Amen, Sister. Keep knocking and the door will be opened to you.' Matthew, chapter seven, verse seven. Sister Sarah, you will take Jeff with you like you carry your folks' dreams for a life with dignity. He will always be right there with you, I promise."

During the ever-shorter autumn days that followed I cared for my daughter and tried to lose myself in my work so Sister could slow down from the weeks of doing my share. Yet in scattered moments, I started to think on things. I came to know that I had to move on. Yes, I had to resist the desire to stay even a few months, even as the place Jeff and I had built up, along with our small orchard, had such a pull on me. But I knew if I remained long I could too easily postpone my farewells forever. Where would that leave me? Would there be decades of drifting along till the time came when I finally rested next to my husband? Would our daughter pick the flowers over our graves and be asking herself why her ma did nothing to make her life better while I was young?

For days Louvenia's eyes followed as I paced the cabin sorting my thoughts. For the longest time I never said a word 'bout moving on. Couldn't, 'cause I knew what her response would be. I thought on how I'd tell her, but still couldn't bring myself to that moment.

For the first time in her life she had some peace there in the country where nobody was crashing a whiskey bottle over her head looking to cut out a piece of her life to go after the next swig. I was so torn. Torn about us separating, yet didn't want Sister's peace to evaporate. I had to accept that she couldn't make it in a city again just as I knew Lelia could never have a life out there in the country where Southern hatred easily tethered lives with lynching ropes.

"Don't know why you got to leave," Sister replied when I told her. "Don't we have it good out here?" Her eyes filled with tears as she rocked Lelia.

"You know, like I know, that it's got to be," I said. "Lelia ain't gonna get an education livin' out here. White folks won't have it. I been thinkin' we gonna move on to St. Louis where there's got to be work." But was I only convincing myself? "Why can't you come with us? Maybe we can find Alex up there."

"I can't go nowheres. You know I don't have it in me." Her eyes were heavy with weariness. "I'm too tired for change. You know I don't got Momma's strength like you, and that's why you gots to go on. Don't you see? You been blessed bein' strong like her; you gots to use it to make a life for you and Lelia. 'Cause you're right; it ain't gonna be near this old porch and them tubs waiting out there."

Sister's words gave me the answer I'd longed for when she handed Lelia to me with a smile.

"Life's gonna let up on us! Don't die on me thinkin' it won't," I told her. "We ain't gonna die like our folks did thinkin' there's gonna be a day when white folks is gonna share the fruit of the orchard, 'cause that come one day ain't on no calendar." I broke down, leaving Sister in a gulch of tears.

"I ain't gonna die," she cried. With her worn hand, Sister lifted my chin and situated her nose in the air like she didn't approve of my weepy-woman stuff. "Anyway, who's gonna water them peach trees? I been out there ever' morning waterin' Jeff's orchard and getting right good at it. Them trees are near a foot taller than when I come. Sure they are! You think?"

I did. "Someday I'll come for you! I promise!" Still, I knew such promises can never be kept.

Sister averted her eyes as she knew as well. "I be prayin' for that day," she said.

For days we hid our fears separately in that small cabin where we shared everything else. I spent the next several days thinking on what I would do in St. Louis, 'cept I really had nothing to think on 'cause I had no idea what kind of life I could find for myself and my daughter beyond that chestnut tree. What could possibly be out there for a father-less child and her tub ma—still not much more than a child myself? I wondered if the dangers of big cities could be greater than living on Jesse's alley. I was haunted with fear wondering if my notion of leaving for something better might carve up our lives.

To ease these fears, I lost myself in my work as we readied the place for my departure. I wanted to leave knowing Louvenia would be fine till I could get work and send money. We planted up the kitchen garden with winter vegetables and I prayed Annie and the churchwomen might come to visit and take some cabbages back with them.

Annie, always a blessing in our lives, knew a porter in her church that could get free train tickets for his family. She bartered ironing up his working shirts, dozens of them, and got a ticket for me to St. Louis. Sister didn't need Jeff's tools, so we sold them. Lord, I didn't want to, my husband wore his hands out on them wooden handles, but I had to. Sister met the man who came for them so I didn't have to watch Jeff's things being carted off. That same day, mostly in silence, as we knew our days together were few, we filled the emptied tool shed with chopped wood. When winter came, Sister could spend her evenings near a warm fireplace doing some mending for the churchwomen for a few coins. There near the fire her joints might not ache so bad.

Even with all the fussing dragging on the hours left to me at Jeff's cabin, the minutes still added up and the day I dreaded arrived. I had to stop preparing and face the very moment I'd step ahead on a new journey where there'd be no road maps and yet there was certain to be countless ruts along the way. I could only pray that I'd somehow make it over them.

"You know when spring comes and all the flowers bloom," I said on our last morning together.

"Yes, I'll cut the flowers 'round his grave and dry them seeds so's I can send 'em to you. I promise you. Then you're gonna know I'm here waitin' for your return."

I broke down. Sister held me briefly and then gently pushed me away from her bosom. She knew it was time for me to go.

Again, I was leaving my home feeling like an orphan. I packed Lelia's things and sat there at the kitchen table looking at Sister's biscuits. We seldom had biscuits except on Sunday. She knew the morning I'd for sure be leaving was upon us. I saw her out in the garden hanging clothes, her back to the window. She hid behind the clothesline so only the soil at her feet collected her tears among the drops from her wet rags. Lord, Lord, would I ever set eyes on my sister again? The silence of those thoughts was deafening.

I had our things at the door when Louvenia stepped back in, her eyes red but now dry again. She would be strong for us.

"I forgot something!"

"What could you forget? You been fussin' with your things for days now."

I dragged the chair over to the post that held up the beam under the porch. Up there, next to where Jeff kept his jug of whiskey was his tobacco tin.

"Lelia's education tin." I rattled it hard.

"That ol' tobacco tin?" she asked.

"Soon after the baby came, Jeff stopped smokin' and put aside this here tin to save money in for her schoolin'. Klansmen stole ever' cent Jeff saved up to buy this cabin. But they won't stop us. Yes, as I bend over the tubs, this child goin' to college!"

"College? You hear that, Lelia? Your momma sure can keep big dreams when she sets her mind to it!"

Lelia's brown button eyes smiled back.

"Our folks lived like animals. You know they did, Sister. I may be a poor widow and got no chance at happiness without my husband, but our child's gonna carry Momma's dream. She's gonna go to school and not be a slave to no tub. Even if it takes all that's left in me, I mean for it to be."

"Chile, can't you see? You already got the dream; it's in you like them peach pits you and Jeff planted out there. These coins in Jeff's tobacco tin means you never let a dream die with Jeff. And you gonna find that good soil to plant 'em in up there in St. Louis and grow a good life for you and your girl."

I kissed Sister. For the very last time she handed Lelia back.

"I got me a dream, too!" she confessed.

"What's your dream?" I asked.

"Well, I dream that you gonna keep up your learning to write and when you're real good, you're gonna write the president a long letter and tell 'im what these white folks been doin' to us. That's my dream. You're gonna write to the president one day and then thing's gonna get better for our folks when he knows. Just like when President Lincoln knew 'bout our troubles and broke our chains."

My eyes filled with tears. I couldn't hold them back no more so I bundled my daughter, picked up our things and walked out the door. From that first step I could feel my fears nipping at my ankles like nigger dogs on the chase of a runaway, yet I could not turn to say one more good-bye. But there never can be a last one.

On foot, Lelia and I disappeared over the horizon headed for Vicksburg and the Anchor Line that would take us to St. Louis. It was the start of a long journey away from Jeff's beloved chestnut, his garden of flowers and Louvenia.

END OF PART I

PART II

THE LONG YEARS AND LITTLE

NOWHERE TO SOMEWHERE

36

MY DAUGHTER AND I made it into St. Louis early the next morning. Don't know how long I sat there on the train holding Lelia so she wouldn't touch that filthy seat. Would I have set out had I known how far it truly was? No matter, we'd already journeyed too far to look back.

On those first nights away from my sister Louvenia all my dreams had the same ending: I saw her standing there on the porch of Jeff's cabin gazing over the horizon looking for our return. In the lonely nights ahead, I sometimes awakened with visions of Sister waving her gone forevers as we disappeared over the horizon and out of her life. Her standing there all alone was anchored in my dreams as I prayed this new place might hold new ones that were not borrowed. But for the next few days there were scant few glimpses of any such thing as a dream.

I was not yet sixteen-years-old and hadn't thought past somehow getting to the city and had no idea what we'd do after we arrived. But would a day be any different for me in St. Louis than anywhere else? I wondered and reminded myself that I had two hands to make a living at the tubs and that was good enough for any woman to make her way. What I hadn't figured on was so many other women folk chasing after that same dream; none of us knowing much of anything beyond the air between our tubs. I tell you, somewhere can be a lonely destination even if there are plenty of women heading there with you.

Lelia and I, along with dozens of other young women, got off the train like a herd of heifers stampeding for that same dime that waited at the bottom of a tub of stinking brown water. I looked about thinking I should go that way, or this way, or maybe around the corner some. So I only stood there. You see, the churchwomen back in Vicksburg had given me the name of somebody who might take us in till I got situated. I still wondered how I'd find that street. With Lelia strapped on my back, I walked a thousand blocks looking and not knowing where to turn next but still afraid to stop till my feet finally made me.

I stopped a woman who didn't look away as she passed us.

"Where be a boardin' house for us?" I asked.

"'Round the corner they's two for coloreds—but you know they don't want no kids 'round."

She may have walked on but her words snapped back. She say didn't want no kids?

My feet were bleeding; I could feel the moisture between my toes from the broken blisters. Lelia was asleep and weighed more than a winter's supply of flour hanging there on my sweaty arm while my other hand clung to ever'thing we owned, including Jeff's tobacco tin with my bit of money knotted in the old cloth I'd kept since our folks' passing.

Then I saw a boarding house with a vacancy sign. Glad and relieved we'd found something, I went up to knock knowing my feet wouldn't take us to one more door. A woman, a colored woman, peeked through the window. Why'd she look at me strange-like? That woman never opened the door. Just shook her head my direction and pulled the vacancy sign out of her window.

Well, maybe she rented the room that very morning and forgot to go pull the sign out. That's what I hoped. You see I knew to expect white men and white women and sometimes colored men to be down on us, but not other womenfolk. Then she peeked from behind her shades. Her sharp glance flashed that she had not one jar of sweet tea to share should I have worked up a notion of asking. How far would the two of us need to journey on the path where I stood for that woman to remember that at one time we all been on the same rutted road or sure gonna be come one day. I guess her putting some distance between us comforted her that her cupboard was safe from any tarnish my hunger might bring.

Then, when I finally took my eyes off my dragging feet and looked up the next dirty street, I saw a hotel. I'd never been in a hotel and Louvenia told me that good women never go near them. Could catch something awful especially if there was drinking going on.

I stayed on this side of the street and watched to see what kind of folks were coming and going. Sure didn't see no mommas with kids. But there were no more hotels up the street and none down the other way at least none that my feet could be persuaded to head to. Lordy, it was getting chilly and my daughter was tired of reminding her momma of this. Her eyes followed mine wondering if they would lead us to a decent plate of supper that night. I hoped that under my tight clutch she couldn't feel my heart pounding with fear.

I started across that filthy street when suddenly the streetcar came 'round from some place surely close enough to hell-on-fire and near ran us over. Don't they know to stop for folks? A weary woman with a child dragging her things can't jump out of the way that fast!

I walked into the hotel where a man at the desk looked up at me like I should 'a had a big hat with lots of big feathers 'fore I so much as thought of walking through that wide-open door that I guess was still not open to some folks.

"You lookin' for work?" he asked as soon as my foot hit the threshold.

Then how'd he know?

"Yes, I's a laundress and I …" but he never let me finish.

"Don't you know nothin'? We don't hire up front here. Get yourself to the backdoor and see what they got. But get rid of that baby. We don't want no mammies 'round this place. We got a reputation, hear?"

I heard yet had no idea what he was truly saying.

"How much a room then?" I asked.

"A room? Why, sixty-five cents. Seventy-five if you want a bath."

Guess not expecting me to buy, he went back to his task. But then he was right. I had only a few coins in Jeff's tin to keep us till I got work and a roof over our heads. Lordy, didn't my sweat run cold as it trickled down my hot neck. What do I do now? I got a child. Can't sleep in the park I'd passed where the drunks were already congregating. And the street had plenty of bars to supply the park. I know 'bout streets with bars. The preacher told us they only closed 'bout the time the frost visits the ground. He said drink dusts away the sorrows of some folks. Folks lost but hoping to dredge their woes for a cleansing that might lift some of the weight dragging on their souls. I knew what he meant, 'cause a bottle for Jesse only dredged up a living nightmare for Sister and me. Preacher told us when the drunks' bellies are full of whiskey, it don't tell their heads, so they're still hurting from the same ol' reason why they went to the bars in the first place. No, bourbon never fills the soul's emptiness and the numbness you buy with those drops melts faster than the frost.

I didn't want my daughter's young eyes to see all that business going on in the park. I stood there frozen-like trying to figure things out till Mister looked up like he finally found a way to rid himself of something bothering him, which appeared to be me.

"Listen now, down 'round the corner there's a place best for you. I hear they charge twenty-five cents a room and that's all they're worth, too!"

Pushing my feet ahead of me where they were still determined not to head, I left thinking he was real nice, that man back there, to give me a tip. Now as I look back, it's the only thing anybody gave me that day 'cause all else handed me was a smirk or a jagged glance. It was though the very sight of me caused their stomachs to go empty as mine.

Couldn't see no hotel at first, so I walked on and then on still further wondering how far till I was altogether out of town? Hoped it wasn't 'fore my arm snapped off and I could no longer carry my baby. How long can I carry my girl with no blood circulating in that arm? I shifted Lelia to the other and shook the stiff one till the blood ran again. I could only wonder how far from home I was? Knew Louvenia had cooked up something real good. Stew with sweet carrots and some of those red potatoes from our garden. At least that's what my empty stomach told me was on the table back home. Yeah, there waiting, wasn't it?

Then I seen what might 'a been a hotel. Guess the sign had fallen and nobody noticed as it sat propped against the building. That don't mean nothing, do it? Or that the paint's near faded off the front of the building? I decided I best go see 'bout this place 'cause this had to be the one Mister was telling me about. Unless all along he was merely pointing me back to Vicksburg!

I walked up close to peek in the window and was happy to see all the women in there were dressed up with feathers and ribbons and they looked nice and clean and liked lots of perfume. I could smell them through the open door. I peeked in every window to see what they was up to. They all giggled and pointed at me. Don't know why, 'less they heard my feet bitching 'bout wearing shoes got too small a few miles behind.

I walked up to the woman at the counter and whispered like I was in church. All them women stopped chattering and seemed to need to hear. I figured 'cause they had so much perfume on they was wondering if it bothered me and I'd come in to complain.

"You got a room? Best price…." I asked real nice.

She whispered so ever'body in that room could hear loud and clear.

"Honey, there sure ain't nothin' to hide 'round here. We seen it all and done even more than I bet you ever seen! How old are you child?"

That set them women sitting around the big table towards the back howling.

"I'm near sixteen!" I said. "And this is my baby girl, Lelia."

"A baby? Then I guess that makes her a bit younger than you, don't it?"

The women went to howling all over again.

"Well, who cares anyway? Down by the kitchen. Bed's still not made but I guess it won't be after you sleep in it. Thirty-five cents, that room."

Then one of the women, the one with the biggest feathers in her hair, spoke up with her nose in the air just like Louvenia when she was gonna start something with me.

"Millie, damn you! Don't be shakin' down that poor lil' momma-girl! It's three days 'fore Sunday and you'll go to hell for it come Monday!"

The woman's voice was sharp like she was pointing her finger at that front desk lady but really wasn't pointing nothing but her big mouth. Maybe she knowed that was all it took.

"Damn you back, Betsy!" that counter lady replied. "Nobody told you? We's already in hell, honey. Anyways, you ain't been to church since your last husband's funeral!"

"What? You say my husband's dead? Who told you that? Anyway, which one of my last husbands? The one that took off with a woman gots more names than I gots hats? 'Cause I know I showed up for some ol' man's funeral awhile back or sure enough meant to and that counts just as good!"

"Oh, shut up, Betsy!" the counter woman said. "Your mouth gets to goin' and we get exhausted just listenin' to you say nothin'! No wonder all them husbands of yours don't last," Millie said with a sour look. "They go off lookin' for a woman knows to keep her mouth shut!"

Millie didn't even look up from shuffling her papers as she told this Betsy off. She kept to her work but went to waving off that big-mouthed woman like she was a swarm of flies.

"Alright then, twenty cents. You crack a hard deal there, darlin'," Millie said, and I knew I had, too.

Betsy, that woman beating the air with her fan, winked at me as I pulled my money out. Millie grabbed at it and pointed the way back to my room. Betsy and the others smiled and nodded as we passed. They was nice, these women. I figured they sure had to be nice dressed so fine and all.

You know, I couldn't sleep that first night in town. Just couldn't. All that noise going on in the alley outside our window and folks stomping on the landing outside our door that didn't have no key.

I guess it was after I bathed Lelia and turned in that I got to thinking maybe I didn't make such a good deal after all. All night it kept tumbling over my rocky thoughts; like what if I'd gotten lost on that very day that was slipping away from me. Was this where it's at? Or what if I'm so lost I don't even know it yet? That happen? Do you only find out after it's a done deal and you're never gonna show up at the door you'd once called home? Because where's my brother Alex then? Or truly is it only when folks give up and stop looking for you that you're really lost? Is it then? What if Louvenia and Alex never heard from me again? Would their thoughts still keep hunting for me? Along what paths? Maybe not even the ones I'd taken! So, I laid in that bed wondering if I was already there. Lost!

I was too exhausted to sleep so I got up and walked around to think things through some. I kept telling myself my head hears lies when I'm tired, so I best stop answering my thoughts. What was all that noise was outside my window so late? Still I never pulled the curtains back to get a peek because I had the strongest notion that out there in the shadows of that alley was surely the bottomless well I so feared was waiting to swallow us. I could feel its edges crumbling into every thought I had that night.

WAY DOWN ON MAGNOLIA

37

THE NEXT MORNING, I woke up early. Or had I ever really fallen asleep? While Lelia slept, I wandered downstairs figuring nobody would be down there and I'd get into the kitchen to grab us something to eat. But watching my feet as they soft-footed down the stairs was Millie at the front desk. So, I figured it was a good time to chat with this boss-woman and then she'd think that's the real reason I'd come down. She had no one to talk to so I didn't think she'd mind.

"I need to get work," I began. "I a laundress and ..."

She cut me off quicker than I could take the next breath. I got to wondering if folks 'round there thought they could read minds or that their tongues can't help but chase after folks? Ever'body in such a hurry to catch the trolley to run over somebody the way they cut folks off after five words!

"Go way down on Magnolia. Ever'body knows that," Millie said shaking her head like it was most peculiar that I somehow didn't. "There's plenty of wash houses down there at the bottom of town where the whores live. Or, should I say the bottom of hell? Hell, after it finally burned to ash."

She laughed like a cawing blackbird.

"They do the women's things who service the men and overhauls for the same men that work the factories and buy the whores. Oh, pfewee them men stink! I can smell 'em headin' to my place 'fore they crowd my door come Friday nights. Did somebody tell 'em there's a shortage of soap so then they don't bother to pour a bucket of water over their heads once in a while?" She pointed her bony finger towards the door. "Just go on down Magnolia. They're always hiring downwind!"

"Magnolia Street you say? That's sure a pretty-soundin' place," I commented to be pleasant.

The very thought took me back to the sweet-smelling magnolias at Grandview. I still 'member Melinda Burney yelling out her upstairs window for Ella to tell Samuel to run cut a bunch of magnolia buds for her bedroom. Samuel soon appeared with an armful of branches for Ella to pick over and cut the nicest flowers for the big house. But the single nicest she'd set aside for Momma. Minerva would put that cream-colored bud, larger than my hand, in a jar of water on our table and tell me to watch it till it opened and we could smell its perfume but warned that it would never open if I said a word. I kept quiet at the table watching that flower for what seemed like hours. Momma just smiled.

Millie dashed these thoughts when she cleared her throat as though she'd just swallowed a chicken bone.

"What in tarnation are you standing there dreamin' 'bout, child? Honey, sweetie pie, wake up and listen to me. There ain't no magnolias down on Magnolia Street," she declared. "Whatever got you thinkin' that? In fact, there ain't no trees nowheres down that way as I recall. So, you best wear a big-brimmed hat to keep the blazing sun out of your eyes, but then there ain't no sun to be mindful of, is there now?"

"There ain't no sun? No sun down on Magnolia Street that ain't got no magnolias?"

I looked out the window as the glare of the morning sun peeked over the building across the street. That got me to wondering if that meant there was nothing but stinky men prowling for whores down that way.

"Didn't I say the factories is down there? Nobody tell you nothing 'round here yet?"

She chuckled like there'd sure be a few things I'd be finding out that day.

Millie went back to her task adding figures but then paused to shoot a glare my way like I was stopping her. But it was really her who was sure enough stopping me; stopping me from getting my hands on some of that bread I could smell baking in her kitchen.

As I got back upstairs I could hear somebody in the next room pounding on the wall 'cause of my baby's fussing. My Lelia knows when good folks get up even if they didn't! She was mad, too, for me not having some freshly baked bread with melted butter and maybe a boiled egg for her.

That morning Lelia was tired and cranky from the trip and went to fussing and trying to fly off my arm as I headed down the way Millie had pointed me to. I know she needed her Aunt Louvenia to rock her but then I needed Sister to rock both of us and we both needed one of her rag dolls with the big brown button eyes and a mustard seed of faith hidden in their rag stuffing to face the day down on Magnolia where hell was burning under. Save us Lord! But first tell me from what.

As we got to the bottom of the hill them rag dolls would surely not have seen any more magnolias than me, 'cause it was just as Millie had said. I'd never seen so many blocks of streets drenched in grayness. The sky looked like a black veil hovering over the top of them even blacker buildings. Even the sky was near to being black and sticky; a mixture of dirty air and fog that we were breathing in.

Yes, Millie was right. There were plenty of laundry houses down that way. I could 'a counted them but it was nearly too dark on them narrow streets to see where one ended and the next began. I headed down one alley looking at the different places hoping to find a sign posted for help. But once again I felt invisible; don't think anyone I passed or anyone who saw me peeking in windows saw me back. After walking near ten blocks I'd seen more shades of desperation walking those streets than ever found itself lost on Jesse's alley. Couldn't figure there'd be a darker or more drab place anywhere.

I tell you, I don't recall even one smile that day till I seen this old woman sitting between the buildings there. I paused because the sight of her looking right at us brought a calm to me. It was as though she'd been waiting all morning for me to come by and chat a spell. I headed over her way like a child knows to wander to her ma's apron strings. Strange, almost like it was meant to be. Maybe I was hungry for a smile or for somebody to say something kind. Her gentle eyes followed me as I approached. Beyond her were lots of women working between those two rows of old laundry houses but most seemed too old to be washing clothes. I didn't think women who got old as these women could even work. Some of them were talking over clotheslines strung from the walls of those blackened brick buildings to old black poles stuck in the ground that were leaning to and fro from the weight of wet clothes. I stood in front of this old woman; her smile followed as I looked about. Or did I simply look lost?

"You a laundress?"

I asked even as I couldn't imagine she could hold up heavy wet sheets to hang. I noticed that them clotheslines were especially high for some reason. Who could lift that high to pin?

"Used to work the tubs," she said. "Now I only watch 'em. Don't even do that like I used to. Near blind, ain't I? But I still seen you and your pretty baby." This old tub woman's eyes were gentle and kind. "I'm Hannah," she said." Hannah Mather Crocker is my name."

"Miss Hannah, what's you mean, 'watchin'? What's you 'watchin' for?"

"For them kids that comes and snatches the clothes the women done pinned up," she said.

"Why they do that?"

"The chil'ren grabs 'em down and runs off to sell 'em to the rag man. Then he gonna sell 'em for rag rugs. That's what he do. Ain't nobody gonna unravel a rug lookin' for they's missing shirt, is they?"

Her eyes twinkled as she gazed at Lelia.

"Then I 'magine they take their pennies the rag man pay 'em to their ma and she goes to buy some cornmeal. You know she does. Got to get by best ya can. You think? You get 'bout three pounds of meal down there for a dime. That'll last a ma with four kids 'bout two days if she handles it good."

"Somebody burnin' trash down one of these alleys?" I asked. "It stinks 'round here and it's already near black as night."

She laughed. Didn't look to have one tooth left.

"It ain't night, chil'e. The factory stacks do it, don't they? They bellow black lung turns the days into night. Ain't seen a clear evening for a fortnight. No, I ain't."

"What's black lung?"

"Coal dust like what kills the miners. They breathe it in till they lungs get filled. Then they go to wheezin' like me."

"What they do when their lungs get filled up like that?"

"Chil'e, when that happens the factory don't need 'em no more. No, they done for good. Boss-man tell 'em to get on back home since they can't put in a good day's work like a healthy man. After that the wives tend 'em till Jesus gots time to come for 'em. No more than a few weeks left to say their goodbyes. That's all there is to that."

She paused, and with a gentle smile, looked me up and down.

"So why you here? You ain't no more than a chil'e, is you? A chil'e with a chil'e. See it all the time 'round these laundry houses."

"I need me some work. I got strong hands."

Hannah reached for my hand.

"Yes, young woman, you sure do," she said. "You knows how to wash a rag good; these hands say so. I tell you what you best do then. Wander on down that way. Ask 'em where Minnie's place is. She down at the yella buildin'. But it ain't yella no more, is it? Down Magnolia they gonna know where Minnie's is. She loses her help ever' week. Picks 'em clean, she do, just like the factories. She be lookin' for somebody strong like you 'cause that woman is always lookin'! It'a do till you get something better. And you gonna, 'cause I can tell. You're a chil'e lookin' for it—that somethin' better to come one day.

"Don't know what you see, but thank you, Ma'am."

I had one hand in my pocket and felt a dime down there I brought with us. Was gonna use if for the trolley back. The rest of my money was safe in Jeff's tin back at the hotel. But I thought if I gave that dime to Hannah, maybe she could buy a meal or some day-old bread, or maybe a sack of cornmeal to get her through to the next day. Then I thought 'bout getting myself back up to the hotel at the top of the hill. My feet weren't figuring on footing back up, not after I promised 'em I'd take the trolley.

Hannah looked at me with eyes that had surely seen a hundred years and crossed over many horizons along her own journey where no trolley probably ever stopped for her.

"You got a precious chil'e there on your arm. I pray for you tonight," she said tugging on Lelia's chubby hand.

With that I knew what. Just knew. Her eyes got big when I pulled out that dime and handed it to her. She nodded her thanks and kissed Lelia's little hand.

As we walked off each of them tub women waved or smiled as though they knew me even if they never knew my name. I was sister and daughter to them all. We survived in that thin air together, kept our kids by us and made our way on bags of cornmeal and kept our lives pieced together working the tubs.

All the way down Magnolia that day, Lelia was squalling and kicking at me like she do when she hungry. She'd nothing to eat since dawn and hadn't planned to spend another day strapped to my sweaty back. Then I seen a building up ahead. It wasn't as dark as the others which left me wondering if that was the yellow Hannah meant. Didn't see no laundry 'round the corner yet it had to be the only place near to being yellow.

I knew she was Minnie the moment I walked into the café where white working folks were eating. Just felt it like somebody tapping me on the shoulder and pointing her out. Maybe 'cause her voice carried over everyone else's.

"You Minnie?" I asked.

"Still am. But the day ain't half over so I'm hoping I won't be by tomorrow," she said like she was ending a sermon she'd given before.

She had this one eye that looked me up and down while the other drifted over to her customers. Louvenia always said that was sure the sign of the greedy keeping a twisted eye out for their money.

"And you best hope you don't become Minnie after I'm finished with what's left of 'er."

She picked up a stack of dirty dishes and shoved them into the hands of her kitchen boy as he passed. Most of her customers were finishing lunch. She was serving black-eyed peas and pork that day. Lelia started kicking at me when the boy passed us with a plate of steaming cornbread.

"Well, what's you want comin' in the front like this?"

"I lookin' for work," I told Minnie. "Lookin' for tub work."

Minnie grabbed at my arm and felt up my hand like a fortuneteller. She don't think to ask me what I know 'bout the tubs pawing over me like that?

"I need me a woman today," she said. "Fired two lazy good-for-nothings this morning. You bet I did! Gonna fire the rest when I find the time. Laundry's out back of the café. Get on back there and tell that kitchen girl that Minnie say so and that I'm firing her tomorrow."

"Yes, Ma'am."

I started back there but Lelia was fixed on staying up front near that that plate of hot cornbread the boy set on the table next to where we stood. The customers stopped chomping probably 'cause they couldn't figure out what Lelia was calling them to their faces for not sharing their black-eyed peas.

I went through to the kitchen where a skinny man was chopping sweet red onions. Back there, a kitchen girl come up and stood in my face.

"Minnie sent me back."

"You should'a said then," that girl replied.

"I just did…"

"There's a table out back where the women eat across from the tubs. They 'bout finished so get on out there 'fore it's all gone. Izzy'll bring out a plate of food. That kid hangin' on your arm like buttermilk?"

"I gots no money."

"Well now, do folks take you for a rich nigger that gets to eat up front with them damned whities? Go find a chair out back. If there ain't none, tell that LouLou to get her fat ass up 'fore she eats herself under the table and sleeps there all afternoon like she done last week. I see what them women are up to! I sure enought do! I just don't open my mouth to Minnie."

Her voice dropped to a low grind as she pointed her finger to my throat like it was a knife.

"Don't ever open your damned mouth to Minnie 'bout nothin' you see goin' on 'round here! Hear?"

"Yes, Ma'am," I said, wondering what a bunch of tub women could get into. Well, I'd find out soon enough as lots of things come out in the wash, don't they now?

The tubs out back of Minnie's cafe had steam rising. In front of them was a long table across from the kitchen door where they's eating. It was covered with an oiled blue checkered cloth. That table had a broken off leg and was propped with a stack of wood crates. Thank the Lord there was an empty chair 'cause I didn't know which one was LouLou as none looked bigger than the next. So, as hungry as Lelia and me was, and me being the new woman, I figured I'd just sit down to see what would happen next.

As soon as I settled in my seat, Izzy, the skinny man who'd been chopping onions, brung out a plate dripping with black-eyed peas and big piece of pork. Real big one.

He placed it in front of me and winked.

"Izzy, go bring me another piece of pork like you done brung the new woman. You seen my piece?" this big woman whined. "I seen it once. I sure think I did but you reckon it's lost somewhere under one of my black-eyed peas? Come help me look, honey."

"Now LouLou, ain't you always wantin' another piece of my meat!"

Izzy looked at me to see what I might have to say about the size of his meat.

"But I ain't got time for it today, do I?"

Still this man sure had the time to go looking 'round that table to see what the other women thought 'bout it. They all turned their eyes down to their empty plates like they was looking for something they didn't expect to find.

"But I'll think on it for tomorra or maybe the next day if I get time to think."

Izzy set Lelia's cup of buttermilk on the table. Then the big woman, LouLou, went to looking at my food. Her tasting it with her eyes and smacking her lips. But hadn't she just eaten?

That woman kept after Izzy with a bit of a shrill whine. I decided I'd never mind trying to figure out what they had going on as my thoughts were already situated on that plate of black-eyed peas.

LouLou grabbed herself another piece of cornbread and dropped one on my plate, too.

I ate fast 'cause most them women were near to being finished. They were breaking off pieces of cornbread to sop up their plates just as the kitchen boy went around grabbing them up. I was soaking the cornbread in the buttermilk for Lelia when Minnie come out shaking her head and looking like she didn't know what to do with me. That was with her good eye. The other one looked to be pushing the glances of the other women back down into their plates. That woman looked sour-faced like somebody just told 'er café food was no damned good. Finally, she caught up with me with that good eye of hers.

"Now what are you expectin' to get done at my tubs with that baby 'round your hips? Huh? You bend over and that baby's gonna fall into the scaldin' water. Then I gots another mess to clean up."

"No! I'd never let her out of my hands."

"But honey, you can't wash no pile without your hands, now can you? 'Less you got something goin' with your feet I ain't never seen! No, it won't do. You come back tomorra and I'll put you on a tub to see what you can do with it. But you can't have that kid 'round. No! Gets too crazy 'round here at lunchtime and I don't need no damned baby cryin' and crazin' my good payin' customers in the café."

She looked down her nose at me.

"Yes, Ma'am."

I didn't know what else to say.

That one good eye of Minnie's never let loose of me. But she didn't know how good I was with a tub. I always have to prove myself; got no problem with that. When she heard the kitchen-boy drop a stack of plates she stormed back into the kitchen shaking her fist in the air like she was blaming the Lord for starting something with her.

Them tub women went to looking me up and down as they drifted back to their tubs. Maybe measuring me up to see if I could stand up to that Minnie. While they was working their washboards, they sang like a church choir of sorts. But maybe only the kind that opened their hymnals after the bars closed. But I didn't care what they was looking at. I got up to leave but first grabbed the last two pieces of that cornbread for our supper that night. Then as I passed the kitchen door, Izzy jumped out like he wasn't gonna let me pass.

"New woman, where you think you're goin'?"

"Goin' back up the hill," I said before I had a notion that it was none of his business.

"You ain't goin' nowheres. Not yet, you ain't. Come on in here," he said.

It dawned on me that maybe Minnie wanted that leftover cornbread for her own supper and he saw me snatch it. Lord, Lord, I thought. I get me a job and get fired all in one day and I gots only a bit of money left hidden in my tin.

I followed Izzy into the kitchen 'cause I knew I was guilty. I also wanted to see what else I could put my hands on for our supper. Guess he was kitchen boss when Minnie not around. In there he went about his business taking care of this and that. He looked through me like he knew I for sure had that cornbread hidden someplace. Yeah, he'd been putting the proof in a pail for me!

"Here's some fresh butter in this tin pail for that cornbread you got hidden on you and some leftovers from lunch. Yes, Ma'am. Got some jerked pork in there, too. Nobody eats cornbread 'round here without some butter and a bit of roast pork. Unless they gots a problem with my cookin'. That the case with you, new woman?"

He shoved the pail into my hand and smiled.

I was tired as could be leaving Minnie's and my little girl, who'd been tugged along all day on my sweaty arm was even more so and we still faced getting back up Magnolia with that pail of food.

I stood there on the street where there was no shade, just as Millie had said, and looked up the hill. As I was about to head up on foot, a girl standing over to the side walked up. She looked real nervous.

"You goin' up Magnolia, huh?"

"Yes, we're headed up there. Got to get back 'fore it gets dark," I replied.

Her clothes were nicely pressed, so I knew she was well cared for. She put her hand on my arm and tugged me aside like she didn't want others to hear.

"I'm 'fraid of the trolley. You go with me up to the top Magnolia then we sit together."

"What's you 'fraid of?"

"Just am. Don't never go up by myself. Mostly just with my brother."

"I don't got the fare. I gots to walk," I told her.

"No, no. I got me two dimes. My momma give 'em to me. See? Here, you take one and one for me."

"I can't take your money," I told her.

"But your baby gonna get up there faster. You walk all that way up the hill and it's gonna be near dark 'fore you get to the top."

Well, I nodded to this young woman and we stepped on the next trolley. She paid the man two dimes and we took our seats at the rear.

She talked and talked all the way up that hill which after all them stops must have taken near an hour.

"My name is Etta."

Etta put on a little smile to conceal her obvious distress.

"I'm Sarah. This here is my baby, Lelia. You go up Magnolia all the time?"

"I goes twice a week," she said.

She sat there so straight and tall.

"I goes to my piano lesson."

"You takin' lessons?"

Her hands were beautiful and didn't show the kind of wounds tub women get.

"I love the sound of organ music. Louvenia, that's my sister, we used to go down to the church some Saturdays if we got our ironin' caught up and sit in the back to listen to organ practice. Your momma sends you up that hill?"

"She do. She say folks is never gonna get tired of music and if I can play the piano or the organ, I can pay my way anywheres I can take my hands."

She held up her lovely hands and looked 'round like she expected somebody to jump out and bother her.

"My momma, she a laundress and when she saw me talkin' to the whores down at the bottom of the hill last week, she run out of the laundry house and yanked my ear. It's still sore."

"Why'd she do that? Just for talkin' to the whores?"

"She say she not workin' the tubs for her girl to be no whore."

Etta seemed to jump in her seat every time the trolley stopped to pick up passengers.

"You ain't gonna be no whore," I assured her.

"I know why my momma says things like that," she whispered with pained eyes. "That man say he's my daddy, I heard 'im. He say my momma, when she my age, she a whore. That's what I heard 'im say one night when they's fightin'."

"Ain't nothin' you can do 'bout what nobody, even on what your momma done a long time ago."

"My brother works for a barber cleanin' up. He couldn't go with me or his boss say he gonna fire 'im if he takes off early."

"But you're a big girl, near to being a woman, why you 'fraid of the trolley?" I asked.

"I ain't 'fraid of the trolley. Last week I read about it. I know what they's do to us."

Etta gripped my hand tightly.

"What's you hear that gets you so worked up?"

"Few days ago, it happened here in St. Louis," she said still looking for something to jump out at her.

"What?"

"This colored man, him named Homer Plessy, was headed to Memphis on the train. White folks say he sittin' in the wrong seat. They beat 'im and beat 'im bad till he couldn't hardly move. Then when the train was goin' through the white part of town, they throwed him off. Homer, he dead."

I know this young woman thought I was thinking about Homer Plessy when my eyes got teary. But I was also thinking of Jeffrey McWilliams; hung by a white man hiding under a white sheet only inches from his own door.

"Ain't nobody gonna throw you off no train." I told her.

At least my words eased her grip on my hand. But the thing is how could I know for sure? Many colored women were raped and abused by white men routinely.

At that moment Etta noticed a young white man up front who kept staring at her till she shrank in her seat. But at the next stop he winked at Etta and stepped off.

"Ain't nobody gonna hurt you, Etta!" I said like it couldn't possibly be any different.A few blocks further up the hill, Etta got off, looked around for those who would toss her off the train or even a trolley and disappeared down a street for her lesson.

I never forgot meeting Etta that day way down on Magnolia.

Minnie Looking Down At Me

38

I HARDLY SLEPT THAT second night in St. Louis. The fears I'd hoped to postpone for the next day couldn't read the clock and kept rattling in my head. You see, it was no more certain to me if I'd made a dangerous mistake leaving home the moment I'd headed to that somewhere. What was gonna happen to us in this big city?

It was so stuffy in that tiny room at the end of the hall where I tossed and Lelia turned for hours. The air was stagnant; worse than being trapped under hot blankets. It was cold outside but even late folks seemed to be meeting in the alley where their yelping jolted me. I feared they might crawl in on us if I opened the window for some fresh air, but I was also afraid Lelia would wake up from the stale air. So, I climbed over her and went for a piece of paper I folded into a fan. About the time it finally got quiet in the alley the sun was peeking over the tops of them black buildings. I'd seen it through a little tear at the top of the curtain that I'd stared at wondering if anybody was looking in.

An hour or so later I washed my face and gathered Lelia's things to take off. My baby was fussy as she missed her quiet mornings on her daddy's porch with her Aunt Louvenia. Out there Sister would hum the church songs while Lelia ate her biscuit dipped in milk.

Didn't want to eat that morning but knew I had to and wondered how I'd feed my baby that day as I figured it would be a long one for both of us. Even longer for Lelia 'cause she'd be spending it tied over my hot wet back while I leaned over them steaming tubs. I'd brought a large kerchief to cover her head from the sun. But I knew wrapping it on her head made her fuss and pull at her hair. What would I do with her at Minnie's? The very thought of facing that woman made my empty stomach knot.

Half way down to Magnolia, I stopped at a bakery. Had a signed posted in the window for day-old-bread. They had a shelf of it just inside the door so I bought a paper bag of rolls and some milk. That bread only a day old? Which day was that? I tore off pieces that I dipped in milk and we chewed it on our way. Got to thinking how I'd not mind if Minnie wasn't there so I could ease my way into my work without her looking over my shoulder all day. I'd convinced myself she was Isaac the overseer in a skirt reincarnated with the juice of the devil brewed in with those chips of ice that floated down her veins from her cold heart. Amen, Lord, that's all I gots to say.

As I came 'round to the back of her building I saw some boys pulling tubs out of a shed and stoking a fire to get the water boiling. The women were chatting as they sorted their piles. Each nodded and smiled so I didn't feel so much like the new woman.

"Minnie here?"

I asked LouLou as she tied her bandana 'round her forehead. The kitchen curtains were open, but I didn't see Minnie in there sharpening her whip—just a young girl peeling potatoes.

"'Course she is," LouLou said. "You don't know it—it's s'pose to be a secret but she live up there on top the café. The windows with dark curtains is her room. She keeps 'em pulled 'cept when she's lookin' to see who's slowin' down on her tub."

I glanced up to the rooms above the kitchen. All the windows were open, but the drapes were closed tight.

"Don't be lookin' up there now," LouLou cautioned. "'Cause she'll be looking down at you and her good eye's gonna catch you. Best get to your tub, but first get rid of that baby."

LouLou never took her own eyes off Minnie's window. Guess Minnie's good eye only saw the new women looking up there for her to be looking down!

"Hide my baby girl?"

"That Minnie, you know she won't like it none!" LouLou remarked. "No, Sister, and she done told you already. I heard her. But you reckoned you'd get in her face just to see if she mean it or not? Is that what? You best learn to hear Minnie good if you know what's good for you 'cause when she fire you, she gonna go tell the other laundry houses you're no good. Then you get work nowheres and you get there quick, too.

"I got nobody to take care of my baby," I whispered.

I was yet over them steaming tubs when my face broke out in a sweat from worry and then Lelia went to fussing at me.

"You don't know a granny?" LouLou asked.

"I just got in to town. Don't know nobody, do I?"

"We got to do somethin' then 'cause Minnie, she's an ol' bitch. She sure as hell is." LouLou's voice dropped to a whisper. "She's half white and that's why, ain't it?"

Violet, the other tub woman, heard LouLou. She looked up at Minnie's window and whispered over to LouLou.

"Tell Sarah 'bout that Minnie! Go on and tell 'er!"

"Here's what: see, her man beat her way back when and kept at it till one day Minnie up and knifed him for it," LouLou started. "Ever'body knows she done it, too. Even before they found his guts hanging on the clothesline right there between his clean shirts! His guts hangin' there like ol' knotted up neckties! That's what folks say happened."

"Lordy!" was all I could get out.

"Then after she done it, Minnie gone 'round smilin' for days like it be Christmas. She did! Even smilin' big at the law that come pokin' 'round when word got out she done 'im in. She sure happy her man gone and for good, too! He up and lef' her for his ma's, she tol' ever'body even if they's runnin' the other way 'cause they knows the truth. Minnie kept to her tale just the same. 'He gone and there ain't no address to forward his mail to!' she'd say. 'He won't be coming back, not never!' Said it laughing like a hyena till even the law was scared of her and never looked 'round her place for no missin' husband. Nope, the law, they don't come for her no more. No, Ma'am. They knows not to."

"Why? Why don't the law come for 'er?" I asked.

"'Cause she gots more on them than they gots on her," LouLou said and all the women at the tubs nodded confirmation. "From what I hears, Minnie been sayin' she just might head over to city hall one day and tell the mayor the cops been on her back if they come 'round again. She knows 'bout them cops and the whores. Yes, Ma'am, she sure do. Or maybe she heads over to the paper and tells ever'body ever'thing she knows 'bout them cops… and the mayor, too! Holy cow, and you know she would, that bitch! I tol' you she's half-white! She don't say much, but when she do she means to see some blood out of it for herself!"

My head was spinning with all this talk on Minnie.

"What's she know on them that's worth that much?" I asked.

"Let's just say she do the laundry for the whores and the whores, they pay 'er with tidbits on them men that come by the whore houses and then Minnie deposits it in her bank. Ain't no real bank; I heard 'er say so. She keeps it all written down in her account books till she needs to fix something. Like when somebody messes with her, gets in her face. Yeah, she sure do. The mayor, he takes to getting his ass switched 'cause he knows he's been a bad doggie sniffin' down where he ain't 'pose to 'cause he can't do no more than sniff it! Then he goes sniffin' 'round like a doggie looking for a pat on the head and a smack on his butt. And Minnie, when she see the mayor down on Magnolia, she yells clear 'cross the street, "arf-arf" and smacks her butt right in front of folks. 'Arf-arf-arf, you smelly ol' dog!' she say. Don't he turn beet purple and head the other way 'cause she sure knows why the mayor way down on Magnolia all right! And it ain't 'cause he gots something he's lookin' to talk to Minnie 'bout! Not that man. Minnie ain't foolin' none with him and she ain't fooling 'bout your kid."

"The way I see it, if ever'body heard it already then ain't nobody got nothin' on nobody," I said shaking my head as I adjusted my bandana to see if Minnie was up there looking down at me.

About then Lelia decided she'd caught up on her sleep while on my back and went to carrying on a conversation with the tub woman next to me. She pointed her little fingers at them jabbering so they'd know how to fix everything pretty as you please.

It didn't take us long before LouLou and me were wringing our rags hard as hell like we was squeezing the bile out of Minnie's heart. All the while I had Lelia tied to my back and didn't she gain another pound near ever' hour. Then that child went to kicking at me; one kidney then the other as LouLou tickled the bottoms of her feet.

"Don't you think it's gettin' too hot for your girl out here, honey?" LouLou glanced up at Minnie's window again. "You go put 'er in the shed."

"What?"

That woman thinks I'm gonna put my child in a tool shed?

"Here! It'a be more comfortable for 'er." LouLou said. "Them sheets on the line over there is dry. I'll go pull one down and we'll fold it to make a pallet for your little one. Let her take a nap while you're gettin' through your piles. Be cooler for 'er than your hot wet back."

LouLou tugged me towards the shed eyeing Minnie's window like a mouse looking for a hawk to descend. I never looked up at Minnie's window when I went back to conquer my pile of stinking rags. I know some of them overhauls hadn't been washed in a fortnight 'cause they no sooner touched the water than it turned black and stunk worse than the rot at the bottom of a garbage can on Jesse's alley. Still I was determined to show Minnie I was her best woman.

Come late morning I could hear banging in the kitchen where Izzy was setting up for lunch. Minnie fed us for a dime a day out of our pay. One woman told me it was the only reason she stayed on. Minnie did have good food. Izzy said he cooked it from his ma's recipes that he kept in his head but I'd already figured that there wasn't much else stored up there. I heard one of the women remark that this man loved to come out to grill so he could eye the women when they was bent over their tubs—their boobs swaying as their hands rubbed up and down their washboards. Sure enough that day he had a big grill going across from the tubs with blackened catfish. Later he brought out a big crock bowl of coleslaw with a bit of horseradish sauce and we had us some breaded tomatas cooked in sweet onions and yesterday's bread cubed with some fresh dill on top. There were four big pitchers of lemonade on the table with thin slices of lemons floating like yellow water lilies. That's what they looked like to me. The last thing Izzy brought out was a big bowl of banana pudding which he set over a basin of ice.

Sure seemed like that man been making lots of trips back and forth so's he could get himself eyefuls of the women. Yes, and every time he came out he winked my way. Then every time he headed back in he winked again. At first, I thought he only wanted me to feel particularly welcome. Then I got to thinking that he had some eye ailment that caused his eye to bat. But when he winked one too many times, I knew he was starting to think I was the welcome mat to the door him and me were never gonna be crossing together.

We were pulling off our kerchiefs about the time Izzy had taken the fish off the grill. I mopped my face and headed to the table where he had everything set up nicely. LouLou glanced at the shed and nodded. Lelia was still asleep back there. I was glad to let her enjoy her nap knowing she'd make up for lost time as soon as she smelled Izzy's good cooking. He never asked me where my baby was.

"You gonna bring out the whipped cream for that puddin'?" LouLou blurted after her first bite. "Now I knows you got some in there, don't you Mister? You ain't savin' it for your sweetie, is you? Who's your sweetie this week? The new peeler girl?"

Turned out that the whipped cream was only for the customers in the café, but LouLou figured she was just as good even if she was eating out in the sun with the help. I got to thinking LouLou best not have too much whipped cream, not if she fancies Izzy. She was already twice his girth. I decided after I'd eaten I'd slip some of that chilled pudding to Lelia and wake her up with a spoonful so she wouldn't sleep too much and then not let me sleep that night.

"Minnie always have good food out like this?" I asked Violet.

"She puts out what they got on special in the café. We just can't eat in there out of the heat or go in the kitchen for nothin'."

Violet mostly kept to herself. She was the quietest of all the women but then LouLou's mouth never shutdown long enough for the others to get a word in anyway.

"Nobody wants go in that kitchen," one woman said under her breath, but not before she looked up to see if Minnie was looking down on us. "Not when Minnie in there wonderin' if her knives are sharp enough to do some business on somebody!"

"Don't mind her," LouLou said. "You give Izzy somethin', he'll give you somethin' to take home with you, huh Violet?" she said batting an eye like Izzy.

"Sure will! And they calls it the clap," Violet said.

"Then how you know that?" LouLou asked indignantly. "Violet, she think ever'body gonna fry in hell!"

Guess Lelia heard that comment, Izzy having the clap, and didn't like that kind of talk 'round her momma. So, she went to babbling like she was giving a sermon.

"Oh, Lordy, me. That your kid?" Violet asked looking purely amazed as if there were more kids running 'round and she couldn't figure which was mine.

"I don't know nothin' and none of us done heard nothin' comin' from the shed just now, did we?" LouLou said.

LouLou shook her hands next to her head like she turned dumb with the last bite of banana pudding; her mouth was smeared with whipped cream as her whining every time Izzy walked by got him to pass a big bowl out the backdoor.

"You got your kid here again! Minnie find out?" One of the tub women asked.

I noticed the others stopped talking but still pretended they weren't listening.

"I don't know nothin', do I?" LouLou affirmed again.

"Oh, shut your mouth, LouLou. We all knows you got nothin' up in your head and what you had up there you done lost and forgot you did!" Violet said. I hadn't heard her blurt so much that entire morning and she wasn't finished. "'Cause we hear it all damned-day long!"

"You finished with that, honey?" she seemed to ask us all. "Pass it on over if you is."

LouLou paid no mind to what Violet had to say; she just went on enjoying the last bites of that fine plate of food Izzy had put on that wobbly table. Even after her pudding she still wanted a little bit more of that, bit more of this and some of that over there, too.

Well, working the tubs was hard work and if you did it on only one meal you best fill up or you ain't gonna make it through your day and then the long night ahead. You see, most of these women had rooms in boarding houses where no cooking was allowed else you might burn the place down.

Lelia must have heard us jabbering 'cause I could hear her fussing growing louder. So, the women, they all looked at me like my plate was on fire and them wondering why I just sat there and didn't go to put it out. My baby's fussing, that is.

"Minnie find out you got your kid back there, she'll run tell the orphanage," Violet whispered. "And they come take that baby away! They gonna put that child somewheres she gonna be washin' and moppin' floors 'fore she turn ten."

Her eyes were earnest like she knew something for sure 'cause what she said was no tub tale. I wondered if Violet had been down that way herself; an orphan-girl turned over to a family for domestic chores only for a place to sleep in the attic where Mister would come pay a visit when nobody looking. I started shaking in my worn shoes.

"My girl ain't no orphan and nobody comin' to take 'er away! Not never!" I said. Don't know what was in the mind of these here women. "My baby's not botherin' nobody and I don't want no more to eat!"

LouLou patted me on the back. "Yeah, that's right, honey. We all know what you mean," she said. "You finished with them breaded tomatas?"

I took my plate to the shed to feed my baby. Lelia was contented back there trying to catch her toes and greeted her ma with a big smile.

"Don't worry none, child. Your Momma gots a job and you gots some cool banana pudding here."

I was sitting on the pallet rocking my daughter and enjoying a few moments from that blistering sun when it suddenly sounded as if the entire choir of the African Methodist Episcopal Church had arrived to work the tubs alongside us. The howling out there rattled the tin washboards in the shed like hail rattled the tin overhang on our laundry porch back at Jesse's. Lordy! What could be going on out there? I knew it had to happen sometime and was glad it was the day I so dreaded facing Minnie. You see, I was sure it was the Lord's Second Coming being heralded by choirs of angels. That's what all the thundering noise sounded like. Praise the Lord, somebody seen Jesus coming down Magnolia Street. I been waitin'!

I stepped out leaving Lelia fingering the whipped cream and shut the shed door behind me only to find that what come up Magnolia was not Jesus, it was somebody more like the devil himself. You see, standing there nose to nose was Minnie herself. One of them eyes of hers was looking behind her at the howling over her tubs but her good one kept on me.

Yes, that Minnie looked at us like we were deranged. The howling quickly petered down to a deep-throated dirge of sorts. This be the woman who knifed her husband and then hung him to dry giggling all the while. For the life of me, I couldn't conjure a picture of this woman giggling over nothing!

"What are you doin' back here under the shade tree? You don't get no breaks from the tubs. No, not at Minnie's you don't! I don't give a damn how hot it is out there!"

She stood there shaking with anger.

"Just goin' for some soap, Ma'am," I said but stood there empty-handed. Gratefully, LouLou jumped in for me.

"Here it be! I found it. Already out here," she waddled over and plopped a tin of lye soap into Minnie's hand who shoved it into mine like it was a hot potata. "I should a' looked 'fore I sent you to the shed. Sorry honey."

LouLou and the others went back to work while Minnie went to looking over ever'body like one of us could be the kind that might steal a piece of her cornbread. The women went back to singing like a chorus of howling she-dogs in heat so nobody could hear if Lelia was fussing.

"Get these damned tubs filled. I done paid to boil enough water for it and I mean to see somethin' for my money!"

Minnie screeched as she looked over the shoulders of the woman to see how full their tubs were.

"I got my lunch crowd still comin' in and Izzy didn't make enough apple fritters again."

I saw Izzy watching through the window like it was the first time he'd seen a witch. Did I say bitch?

"And my customers are askin' for more. Now I gots to go back in there and deep fry 'em myself and I don't have time to be comin' back here to see if you women are gettin' through them piles. Them whores is gonna be mad if their things ain't ironed up by tonight when they land on the mattresses with their ruffles good and starched!"

Minnie looked at me as though I not only had her cornbread in my pocket but might have put down a platter of fritters as well.

Well, she went back in and pushed her kitchen curtains back to keep an eye on us while we stood in the hot sun feeling cold sweat drip down our spines thinking of her poor husband, wherever he rested in pieces. Like LouLou said, that woman could squeeze a nickel from every drop of sweat she could run down.

"We got the singin' worked up so the ol' woman wouldn't hear your girl back there," Violet said. "I tol' you, she hears that child she gonna call the Colored Orphanage and tell 'em you ain't a fit ma else that baby wouldn't be cryin' none! She will, too!"

"You got to keep that chil'e quiet," LouLou chimed. "We can only sing so loud else Minnie get on her high-horse and ride us all."

"What she care if I have my baby here? I get my work done, don't I?" I responded.

"'Cause she's mean and she's goin' to hell for it!" LouLou promised.

Well, I went back to my tub wondering how I was going to work ever'day over a tub and watch for Minnie to be looking down on me? I decided I could do no more than keep my own eyes on my tub and get through each day as it came.

Adding Things Up

39

T HE SUN FINALLY drifted down over the buildings—not that anybody noticed except in their throbbing arms 'cause the sky was never blue enough that day to see much sun.

I went to draining my tub for stowing when I got to wondering what I'd feed Lelia that night. The light was on in the kitchen and I could see Izzy in there chopping chunks of apples for fritters for the next day's lunch.

LouLou noticed me looking over there.

"Izzy give me some milk and butter 'n bread if I give him a nickel?"

"Sure he will, honey. I go see to it," she said. "I sneak by the window and see if Minnie's in there eatin' her supper. She watches over Izzy washin' up while she stuffs her mouth."

LouLou sashayed over towards the window snapping wrinkles out of the sheet and glanced through the window.

"She ain't in there," LouLou yelled back. "Probably out in the dining room countin' her money from lunch." She put her head in the door. "Izzy, get over here! The new woman wants somethin'."

Izzy came to the door with his hands dripping fritter batter. He gave me a big smile again. And I mean real big, too.

"You wantin' something from Izzy here, new woman?" he asked.

"Izzy, go put together some bread and milk for me. Boil me an egg for my girl tonight. I give you a nickel."

I then reached down in my pocket to find a nickel and handed it to him.

"Honey, I don't need no nickel. I gots me a nickel," he said. "And you need a boiled egg for your girl ain't 'pose to be here."

And I tell you, while his big mouth flapped he was eyeing my peaches!

"Here's my nickel. Now go get my food."

"Look here, my hands is drippin' batter. So you best put that nickel I don't need down in my pocket. Yeah, shove it in deep so's I can feel it down there."

No, he'd not be feeling my hands down in his breeches! I shook my head and put the nickel on the counter.

I waited and waited for my egg to boil. Lelia woke up from all the banging as the women started putting away their tubs over her head in the shed. Then it started up all over again. Their horse voices bellowing about Jesus coming. Come quick, Lord, they pleaded just as Minnie stormed out huffing like a Confederate general wearing an ironclad apron.

"My god, what did I just hear out here?" she screeched. "I know I did, too! Lord, if that's a damned baby!"

All the women went silent. But the moment they did, Lelia burst out louder than Minnie.

Minnie's roving eyes near tied a knot as she marched towards the shed. I followed rapid pace not knowing if this husband-stabber would harm my baby.

She flung the shed door open to find Lelia looking up with them two big brown eyes. But my baby wasn't afraid of no "arf—arf" husband-stabber. No! Not Minerva's granddaughter!

"New woman, didn't I tell you not to bring that kid 'round again? Ain't that what I said to you standing there like you're somebody special who don't got to listen to Minnie! How the hell did you keep her here all day and I not find out till now?"

Minnie looked around for my accomplices all gone silent standing between their tubs.

"The only reason I don't fire you is 'cause you're a good worker!"

"Then I a good worker just the same with my girl nearby, ain't I?"

"Sister, are you talking back? You bring that kid one more time and Izzy'll chase you off with his rollin' pin!"

Well, I never seen a man running down the street waving no rolling pin and sure didn't want Minnie to work up a show for me, so I let it be and went back to gathering my things for the night. Minnie snorted a bit but after a few grunts stomped back into her kitchen muttering all the way.

The women and I finished folding the last loads off the lines and headed off 'cause Magnolia Street was not a place a woman went strolling after dark, 'less she was selling sin from hoisted starched ruffles.

Before we left, LouLou, Violet and I sat down at the lunch table to catch our breath while I waited for Izzy to come out with food. They told me he usually brung out some sweet tea 'bout that time and talked a bit. That is if he heard Minnie creaking over the floorboards up in her room. He didn't appear with jars of tea that evening but still we could sure hear him banging 'round in there with his big pots.

"I know why that skinny man don't come out!" LouLou announced. "Izzy's sure 'fraid of the new woman, ain't he Violet? I bet he whispered something to Minnie 'bout your girl. I know he did, too, 'cause he always wants to get in good with 'er. Now he don't know what you're gonna do to him, do he?"

"Yeah, he in there to save his ass!" Violet added.

"What's you gonna do to that man?" LouLou asked. "We'll help. Then nobody can prove who done what the worst!"

I hadn't made up my mind what I'd do to Izzy but knew if I didn't take care of him real good then he'd for sure think he had the upper hand and might figure he could get anything he wanted from me by running his mouth off to that woman with eyes that don't want to head the same way at the same time.

"Don't know what I'm gonna do. That Minnie's on my back. I got no granny to take care of my girl and no money to pay if I did."

"Then sounds like what you gots is no choice!" LouLou declared.

"Why? I got to give something to Izzy to shut his big mouth down?"

"You'll be givin' up a lot more to some man if you don't got work," Violet said, "And he'll use you like a dish rag so you can feed that baby."

Was she talking about whoring for a meal?

"Now listen, LouLou. We gots to take Sarah over there," Violet said.

LouLou nodded and seemed to know where *there* was.

"Take me where, you say?"

"St. Louis Colored Orphanage. It ain't more than about four or five blocks from here," LouLou said grimly.

"No, it ain't but three blocks," Violet corrected.

"What's the matter with you women? I ain't never givin' up my child. Not never!"

"Now, hush and listen," LouLou admonished.

"You don't got to give her up none."

"Don't get her worked up," LouLou said. "Me and Violet gonna walk you back up Magnolia, Sarah. 'Cause you don't know your way 'round here real good."

"Lord, that ain't the half of it," Violet mumbled.

"I don't need no help gettin' back to the hotel," I told them.

"No, 'course not, honey," LouLou assured. "But you come our way; it's shorter and there's things along the way you ought to know 'bout, ain't they, Violet?"

"Like what then? What I got to know?" I asked.

"Where to buy the best soap at the best price," LouLou said.

"And where to get your girl shoes when she's old enough to wear 'em," Violet said. "Things like that, huh, LouLou?"

'Bout then Izzy stuck his head out the door like he was looking for a friendly face from these women. They smiled and that made his face light up like LouLou's did around a bowl of whipped cream.

"Izzy, you come on out now, honey-man!" LouLou said real pretty like.

"Why? What's you got goin' on out there? Huh?"

That man was grinning ear to ear.

"Come on out of the kitchen for a peek, honey," LouLou said batting her eyes.

About then she rewarded him by flipping one of her boobs out of her blouse. Just one, but one was big enough for Izzy 'cause he near tripped on his big feet to get at it.

No sooner had Izzy wandered beyond the safety of his kitchen than LouLou and Violet grabbed him by the ears and went to smacking on his head good. Real good! One side and then the other. LouLou's breast bouncing against his head as it swam between their fists.

"What's the matter, Izzy? You done forgot something you need to go tell Minnie 'bout, honey?"

Then LouLou punched him good in the stomach.

"You tell me honey and I'll stick it down in your pocket so deep you ain't never gonna Minnie on us again!"

"No! No, I ain't got nothin' to tell Minnie no more! No, Ma'am!"

Izzy was down on his knees trying to hang on to them ears getting yanked and twisted.

"No, honey? Nothin'? You got somethin' to say to Sarah then?"

"Yeah, I knows to keep my mouth shut 'bout things I ain't never gonna see no more. Sure do, Sarah!"

"Now what else you got to say?"

"Huh? Nothin'," Izzy said just as LouLou kicked his flat ass.

"Sure you do, honey. It's 'bout tomorrow's lunch. That's a hint and here's another smack to make sure it go down the right pipe!"

LouLou gave him another kick.

"Yeah, sure it is, and I thank you kindly for providing it. Yes, Ma'am, I's gonna put half a roast on your plate tomorrow. Sure, I am!"

These women shoved him into the shed and flipped the latch on the outside.

Izzy pounded on the door

"Said half a roast on your plate swimmin' in my brown gravy!"

"You hear somethin', Violet?" LouLou asked.

"No, I ain't heard no skinny man howlin' he gonna keep his big mouth shut to Minnie!" Violet replied. "Arf-arf!"

"When you gonna let him out of there?" I wondered.

"When I see that piece of roast up close!" she answered. "Like right in the middle of my plate!"

Violet headed to the kitchen and soon came out with her arms full of goodies. Although we weren't 'pose to even go near the backdoor, I quickly got the feeling she knew her way 'round Minnie's kitchen just fine!

"LouLou, now come let me out'a here." Izzy's whining could be heard down the side of Minnie's laundry. "You know how mad my wife gets if I'm late gettin' home," he squealed.

"We goin' on a picnic?" I asked as Violet passed around the plunder.

Those fritters were still warm and smelled of cinnamon. LouLou grabbed one and dropped it down her throat. She figured it was open house in the kitchen so she went for more fritters along with this and that and tied it up in big napkins. No wonder Minnie never had enough apple fritters for her customers!

Then I wondered how Izzy was gonna get that piece of roast to LouLou the next day if he was locked up. Well, Louvenia always said some knots only get worked out in the wash.

We packed our grub and headed off to face our nights. For blocks our mouths were busy chatting and nibbling on our spoils. Lelia went quiet eating her cinnamon-rolled fritters. I could feel the sticky on the back of my neck from her fingers.

I never could figure if anyone really lived down at Minnie's end, or just worked there. Guess some folks lived above their shops like Minnie. While we walked, I gave myself a little dream that come one day I'd have my very own laundry and live above it like Minnie. Wouldn't that be fine? Watch my daughter down there talking to the tub women I'd hire. And I'd sure have a boy deliver the clean pressed clothes in a cart. Maybe even get my name painted on the side of it. Yes, ma'am, every day I would walk down those ugly streets wearing a nice big hat with feathers to make the place look a bit finer. With a hat like that, Minnie'd sure know I got rich taking her customers 'cause I was the best laundress around.

Every step of the way LouLou pointed out different places she knew about and gossiped about folks we passed. Some nice, some not and more than a few just plain crazy. I guess life beats the senses out of us when the struggle's too long and hard. Once Annie told me that white folks built as many places to put crazy white folks in as they built jails to put us in. Yes, I saw plenty of ugliness up and down Magnolia but not one place built for a tub woman to hide from it.

Then as my thoughts were drifting along, I got to wondering where in hell was LouLou and Violet leading me to anyway? From what I could tell we were no longer on Magnolia and my baby was getting tired and cranky.

"This ain't a shorter way to the hotel," I said. "This is way out of my way—I know it is. The sun should be on this side of my face heading back."

I stopped in my tracks. Violet didn't say nothing and went to looking at the ground maybe like she had something to hide.

"Now, Sarah. I ain't no good at arithmetic," LouLou said real serious. Serious enough to give me the jitters. "Don't know how to read or write but you start addin' things up, and, well Sister, it just don't!"

"Add up what?"

LouLou knew I could read, write and add sums pretty good.

"Like how much money you got left?" Violet asked.

"Got a few nickels left in my tin. I count what's left ever'night. You know I's waitin' on Minnie to pay me this Saturday."

"Well, see, that's the problem we gots to add up," LouLou announced in a tone like Louvenia's when she meant for us to have one of her meetings at the kitchen table. "We'll help you, Violet and me. That ol' woman with one sick eye ain't gonna pay you if you ain't workin' for her," she said.

At that point I could only wonder what these two had going. Didn't understand her stopping us to add some things up when she just said she couldn't add nothing!

"You got to find a way to keep your job, honey," Violet said.

"That's all there is to it," LouLou added real quiet like it was a secret I didn't know and she didn't want the passers-by to hear. "Or you as good as dead on these here streets. Where you think that's gonna leave your baby then?"

"But I haven't lost my job. I do, I get another one."

"But they's all the same 'round here. Nobody's gonna put you on a tub with a kid on your arm. And you know it's true! It ain't gonna happen!"

Violet nodded confirmation.

I got to wondering where all this talk was meant to go. Then I saw for sure. Yes, Ma'am. Up ahead was a sign that answered what these women thought I best do. "St. Louis Colored Orphanage," it read.

All along they'd been heading me that way thinking I was gonna give up my baby girl. I drown us both in the river 'fore I'd do that. Yes, I would but first I'd tie a heavy rope 'round Minnie's neck to weigh us down. Heavier rope than what she had on my neck right then.

"Now don't get worked up 'bout what you don't know about. I gots a friend that works there and she's a good Christian woman and maybe knows something you best hear."

LouLou couldn't look me in the eyes.

"She may know of some granny can help you, huh, Violet?"

"Well, quit flappin', LouLou, and let's go see if she does."

Violet poked LouLou's side to move us on the direction they'd intended all along.

I was thinking a granny that had a clean place to watch over Lelia would sure save me from the misery I was certain to face the next day at Minnie's with my baby still with me. We walked up to the door to peek in. I held Lelia tight as she could bear 'less somebody tried to grab her away from me. No, I truly didn't want to go all the way inside for fear they'd think I was there to turn my girl in.

Looking in the door, I could see it was filled with little ones. A young woman smiled at LouLou and walked over to us.

"This here is Sarah," LouLou announced. "The new woman at Minnie's. She be needin' a place for her kid while she workin'."

"Sarah, you bring your girl here in the mornin', we work somethin' out," the woman said.

She wore a clean white smock and the kids all smiled up to her.

"No! I ain't here to give up my child!" I announced. "And I ain't gonna come back tomorrow or some other day!"

The woman put her hand on my shoulder and looked into my eyes. Then's when I knew she wasn't hiding behind no lie.

"You don't have to give up your daughter, Sister," she said in a kind voice. "You bring your baby by and then come back for her when you're off the tubs. That's all there is to that."

"All these kids leave this place at night then?" I asked.

"No. Some stay. They don't have a ma to pick 'em up at night. Then there's some that gots folks, but they can't work 'less somebody cares for their kids. County pays then."

I shook my head in fear like this woman had just pointed me down some bottomless well she aimed for me to toss my baby down and headed to the door in terror of the thought of leaving my girl with strangers.

"Somebody might come grab my kid in there," I yelled.

Then it rang in my ears again. Ol' Isaac yelling at momma that the law was gonna come for Alex and me to take us off who knows where. In the South lots of kids were taken away and never seen again.

"Ain't nobody gonna take your girl," LouLou blurted to my backside as I trotted off. "You think on it. Bring Lelia by in the mornin' and then come get her later. Or don't show up at Minnie's, 'cause she'll show you grief like you ain't never seen, that Minnie will!"

I clutched Lelia tightly even though she was bawling her eyes out from all the yelling.

As I walked off it seemed as though there were lots of folks out but they were all strangers. When you're tired, the shadows from your past can jump out to play mean tricks on you. Ever' time I looked up and saw a pair of broad shoulders I knew my prayers had been answered. You see, I was sure it was Jeff coming to save us. But it wasn't. It was only the loneliness hunting me down again.

Well, I knew I had to fix this problem with Minnie. Yet my head got to pounding a rhythm that only meant it was plum tired of fixing things for one day. I'll just get another job, I kept telling my baby. But I knew what they been telling me was true; it'a be no different anywhere else.

I walked into the hotel exhausted and eager to get Lelia bathed and under a blanket as the autumn night air had given us both a chill. I went up to the front desk for my key but Millie wasn't there. It was a different woman and she had a bad scowl like somebody'd just squirted lemon juice in her face.

"Where's that woman that works the desk?" I asked.

"Ain't ya lookin' right at me?"

"I need my key," I said. "I pay you now for my room. Here's my quarter."

"What's that? We ain't got no rooms for a quarter now do we? Fifty cents and you gots to pay every morning if you want to keep a room that night. And no credit, hear?"

She looked me over like I had to be too dirty to even have a nickel.

"I ain't got no fifty cents!"

"Yeah? That so? And I ain't got no room at no price. All rented out tonight! It's the first of the month, payday for the men. They come in early on payday, don't they? Lookin' for their monthly dunk in one of my zinc bathing tubs."

"What? That's my room back there. I got my things in there already set up," I said.

"Oh, stop your frettin'. Your things probably weren't worth taking up space in a rubbish heap. Kitchen boy gots 'em back there. Go back there and then get off with you."

I stood there trying to get my thoughts untangled.

"Go on now, I got work here," she said.

"I got a child. Where can I get a room this late?"

"Honey, do I look like your ma?" she said and went about her business as though I'd already disappeared.

I went back to the kitchen for my things trying to shake my fears like they were nothing but sweat dripping down my forehead. I told myself I'd just go find a place for us and everything would be all right.

Won't it? Yeah, like who said it would be all right, echoed right back all the louder.

I walked into the kitchen but there was only a girl washing up back there.

"Where's the kitchen boy? He gots my things."

She looked at me as though my question confused her. But she was only mad.

"That boy gone. Looky there! He left 'fore he got them pots from supper scrubbed up. Left leaving me to mop these here floors, too. I gonna beat 'im good if he comes back, 'cause he's 'pose to do the moppin' up, ain't he? But he ain't comin' back 'cause he knows I mean it!"

"Where my things then? From my room?"

"I don't know nothin' 'bout your things," she said.

Then right by the door I saw our bags waiting next to the garbage pail. I was so happy 'cause it had ever'thing we owned, even Lelia's education tin. The girl was still mouthing off 'bout what she was gonna do to the kitchen boy as I walked out the back door into that chilly night.

It had been a long hard day, but it would be an even harder night ahead 'cause I was soon to be dancing so close to that bottomless well that I could have seen the devil down there grinning back at me. Yes, he was down there waiting for the fall.

Mothers, Daughters and Our Mush

40

IT WAS LIKE a black dream hanging over me. I headed off from the hotel with my feet aching and my baby's tummy ached for her supper and her momma's heart ached because I had none to give her as I'd dropped Izzy's food somewhere in the darkness.

I figured I'd sit a spell and so headed over to the park to stitch together my thoughts. I figured on the way over I might see a place that would take us in for the night and then afterwards I'd figure out what I'd do about food. All the shops that sold bread were closed. I kept telling myself not to fret even as I had only a few coins left. Payday would come soon enough.

I headed for a bench knowing a few moments off my feet would relieve the blisters on my thoughts as well. I decided to pull out Lelia's clothes and put them all on her as we had no coats. I opened my bag to sift for her things. I felt all the way to the bottom and pulled out Jeff's tobacco tin. I shook it but there was no rattle. So, I shook it harder. The sound of that hollow emptiness was deafening. I can still hear it. You see, Jeff's tobacco tin was empty. Where's my money? Lord, Lord, where did it go? Did it just fall out in my bag? I thought surely, it's only at the bottom down there. But it wasn't. People back at the hotel must have stolen it. Maybe the kitchen boy that couldn't get off fast enough.

I felt a jolt of hot fear even as I sat there frozen. My daughter held on to me tightly from the cold. I folded up a small blanket; nothing more than two sackcloth dish towels Louvenia had stitched together for Leila, and pulled it tightly around her.

Stunned, it seemed like I could hardly move or even think as my thoughts were getting tangled. What did I face? Only that I had no money, no food, place to sleep or friends to beg mercy from. It started spinning in my head that I was as lost as it gets. What a silly woman I was to leave the cabin where I had a roof even if little more. Here, all along I'd been thinking I could make things better for us but what if I'd only walked my own child to her last day? Where did I get the notion things could be better up the road for us? And whoever heard of a colored woman getting along in life with no man? How do I even survive till I find some way to get us back to Vicksburg? Lord, what price will I pay for that train ticket back to nowhere?

I sat there in the cold feeling the very end closing in on me. It was too dark for me to contemplate. Yes, I could hear the voice of Satan laughing for my surrender. This night would swallow me whole in a rising tide that would wash away all my dreams and perhaps our lives. I could only pray. Lord, can't you hear my despair? How deep is the nothing I'm falling into and how bad will it hurt when we finally reach the bottom? Will you find mercy for my baby even? I cried with my hand over my mouth so Lelia wouldn't hear my sobs.

Then in the glooming at the edge of the path near the trees I heard a gentle voice.

"I know you over there! You're that girl, ain't ya?"

It was an old woman with her grown daughter. It was too dark over there in the shadows to see her face at first. They walked towards me almost as though they knew I'd be there waiting.

"Don't you 'member me? I'm Hanna Mather Crocker. You gave me a dime the other day, didn't you?"

"This the girl with the beautiful baby, Ma?"

"You get a job workin' for Minnie?" she asked.

Didn't know how to answer as my thoughts were too scrambled up in a mess of jagged fears.

"She gave me work, but don't want my baby 'round," I said trying to hold down my sobs. However, there was no holding back my tears.

"Why are you out here in the park this late?" Hannah asked.

"It's dangerous," her daughter affirmed. "Them drunks get to brawlin' out here some nights. We can hear 'em clear across the park at our place. Cops shoo 'em off the streets near the bars so they come over here, don't they Ma?"

Why was I out there all alone with a baby? My pride was too wounded to say much.

"You're new to town, ain't ya?" Hannah's daughter asked.

She bent down to look at that tiny corner of Lelia's face poking out of her cover. It was only one brown-button eye that following this woman's smile.

"We'd love to have you and your baby over to our room," Hannah said. "Would you be our guest for a cup of hot tea?"

My eyes filled with tears as Hannah's daughter reached for Lelia. Suddenly I could feel the blood circulating in my heart again as those throbs of hopelessness were driven off. I went with Hannah and her daughter, Rebecca, to their place on the other side of the park.

This mother and daughter shared a tiny room in the back of an old boarding house. Rebecca was a maid and always came for her ma so they could walk home together when it got dark and the tubs were put away. Hannah needed heat in the winter; her bones were old and most places had no heat at all. Rebecca told me how she was delighted with their room because it still had a working fireplace. She said their place had once been the dining room when it was a home for a white family.

There were two cots with worn but beautiful hand-stitched quilts long sun-bleached to soft pale-colors. On the table between the beds there was an old kerosene lamp and an old Bible which looked like the cracked leather binding was nearly off from years of devotions. There close to the door was a bureau where they kept their things. I 'magine everything they owned was in there, three drawers for each to hold the meager possessions of a lifetime of hard work. Their lives were like most of us who worked the tubs—a day to day struggle with little hope for anything more but maybe an easy passing when the time came.

I could tell by the way Rebecca put out the kerosene lamp as soon as the fire lit that they were watching every penny. Hannah dragged the last chair over with the other two and slowly worked her tired body into the hard seat. Rebecca and I sat near the fire with her. Think the wood she burned was the cheaper green 'cause it crackled and sputtered. The shadows caused by the flickering light played over our faces as we chatted in soft voices that barely sifted through our fatigue. Through the thin walls I could hear the woman in the next room barking at her husband. Seems he best not forget to bring that something home the next night, or he'd sure hear about it 'gain. Lelia fell asleep as Rebecca rocked her—seldom taking her eyes off Lelia's contented face. The rain pattered on the little window behind Hannah's head. I prayed thanks it was not pattering on my baby girl.

"I got a pot here," Hannah said. "Fix us mush with butter most nights. Then on Sundays, after church meetin', we goes for supper 'cross the street at that little café. You see, the landlady here, she don't want us cookin' none. She say might burn the place down. We do it anyway, don't we? Gots to eat. Grocer, he sell me four eggs yesterday and I boiled 'em. Most grocers won't sell only four, they say only six, but more won't keep."

Rebecca smiled. "Ma took care of the landlady when she was sick last winter. It was colder then. Took care of her for a fortnight, didn't you Ma? Up all night with her 'fore you headed over to where they hang the clothes." Rebecca looked down at Lelia before continuing. "She would'a been dead if not for ma here."

"No such thing!" Hannah said.

I could tell this woman had been fiery in her time.

"No, ain't me that saved her. Lord saved me so I could help 'er till she was back on her feet. Only the Lord decides when He's callin' us home."

"How long you lived in this place?" I asked.

"Think 'bout nine years come October," Hannah said as Rebecca handed me Lelia and went to get the kettle for tea. "You got family? Go lay the baby on the bed. I sleep with Rebecca. You and the baby gonna sleep on mine. That's best."

Lelia never moved as I lifted her over to Hannah's bed and pulled the comforter over her.

"I got an older sister, Louvenia," I whispered. "She's back in Vicksburg. Lives on the road out-of-town there. When I get something saved back, I'm gonna send for her. I know she misses Lelia somethin' awful."

"Got any other folks?" Hannah asked.

I gazed into the sputtering fire trying to conjure a picture of where my brother might be. But all I saw was Louvenia's postcard with the carnival picture. They last she received from Brother.

"Also got a brother. He took off lookin' for work but we ain't heard nothin' from him in a long time. I know he's alright, he just don't take the time to send postcards."

Rebecca spooned tea into an old cracked teapot she'd filled with hot water and placed near the fire to steep. There close to the fire Hannah wrung her hands that were gnarled from gout.

"You workin' down at the tubs?" Rebecca asked.

"Just got hired. Don't see how it's gonna work out though. That woman, Minnie, she don't like babies. I got no one to care for Lelia," I said. "And I ain't gonna hand 'er over to no orphanage."

"It ain't bad as you're thinkin', Daughter," Hannah said. "Lots of kids go there just while their ma's workin'. They couldn't keep no job if they didn't and then nobody eats. Ain't that the way it is for us tub women?"

"I been lost out there, too. Yes, Ma'am, I knows how it is havin' no place to go. We been there, ain't we, Rebecca? It ain't right. The Lord put down plenty for ever'body but some folks think they need to have their share and ours, too."

"Yeah, some folks tryin' to figure a way to wear two pairs of shoes at once just so they can say they gots a right to them four shoes, huh,

Ma? Even if other folks only got the bareness of their feet to claim all their own."

Rebecca looked deep into Hannah's eyes as her ma drifted on into her past. I could tell her memories still burned hot as that crackling fire—maybe somewhere still too near her singed heart.

Hannah got so quiet that Rebecca seemed to speak for her. She knew the story well.

"Momma, when she was a kid, her ma took her to the woods and left her," Rebecca said.

Hannah nodded and squirmed with these words as though her own ma was holding the hand that led her into that uncertain darkness.

"Why'd she do that?" I asked but then wondered if I was causing Hannah grief.

"My granny, I never knowed 'er, but ma told me 'bout 'er. She had five kids, didn't she Ma?" Rebecca said. "Ma was the youngest. Couple of days after they's all born, Mas'er come for 'em all. Year after year, he always grab 'em away soon as they's born. Gonna take 'em off and sell 'em. My granny begged 'im not to take no more of 'er kids. They's too young, she squalled. So, when ma was born, my granny told one of the old women they was gonna sell off the plantation with the infants born that spring to go hide. Yes, that woman was too old for fieldwork, so Granny told her to take my ma deep into the woods and hide 'er from the Mas'er. Just an ol' woman and Ma, a newborn, out there alone in the dark. Both gonna be sold off like animals if they didn't."

"How long they out there? In the woods?" I asked. "Where'd they get food and things?"

"Don't know. But sure know the Mas'er come and he weared her out with his belt. But she don't tell 'im which direction they headed. Then when they thought my granny was gonna die from her beatings, he say to hell with you! You go on and keep your damned baby then. Got no use for a dead nigger, he cursed. Even with her back blistered, my granny made her way into the woods lookin' for her baby. Lookin' for ma here. She found her starvin'. Ol' woman dead right there next to her there. Just my momma left cryin' till the wild dogs come for 'er, I guess."

At times Hannah's mouth moved and she fidgeted like that might help her recollections escape her tied down tongue. But nothing more would come. Sometimes bodies heal but don't know if wounded souls ever do. Seems like they don't.

The fire died out and so we went to bed. In the darkness I overheard Hannah pray thanks to the Lord for us and Rebecca. She reminded me of Louvenia's prayers in the depths of those black nights on that alley. I think I prayed most of the night myself. Prayed for poor Hannah and Rebecca, asking a blessing on them for bringing us in from the rain. Then I prayed I'd find the strength to face Minnie the next day. That's all I could ask for; one more day, Lord, one more day to be my child's mother. I knew that day was only hours away and yet I had no answers to the questions I knew the morning would pose. Truly if only to ease the weight on my thoughts I would have hid my fears. But by then I'd simply run out of places.

I must have gone off to sleep finally, 'cause Rebecca had to shake me awake at dawn. We didn't talk much. Rebecca and Hannah knew what I faced. How could I go again to Minnie's with my daughter in tow? What would happen if she got the law on me? Told 'em I was a bad mother and ought not to have a kid? Did she know how things worked in this city more than LouLou and Violet? Like the very things that might sweep my daughter from me that I never knew could happen?

Later, even before the sun rose to meet the sky, I'd finished some tea and Lelia had some mush with cream that Rebecca had made. She got the cream from the neighbor who had an icebox. Hannah's eyes were filled with tears as we packed to leave. She tugged at my sleeve but I could feel it all the way to my heart.

"You know I'd take care of that chil'e, but Daughter, look at my hands here. Couldn't even pick 'er up if she needed me."

I left for Minnie's only knowing that I had to take the next step to somewhere that day and hoped the Lord would point the direction and hold my hand when I tripped over my hopelessness. My daughter always greeted the day with joy. Like her Daddy's, her eyes swallowed her first glimpses of the morning with eagerness. Nevertheless, anticipation was pounding on my heart. If I didn't go back to Minnie's, I'd never get my pay at the end of the week and I had no money. Lelia looked up at me with all the trust in the world and patted at my face.

Never in my life, I tell you plain, did I ever think I would let go of my child for even a moment. However, as my feet headed me in the direction I needed go, I came to realize that I had to risk losing my child, if only to keep her.

I walked into the St. Louis Colored Orphanage and froze in a hot sweat. There sitting in small circles on a cloth were little ones; so many big brown-button eyes looking up to greet me. Did they want me to take them away? Save them? Would my child's eyes look up at strangers pleading to be taken away?

You came back?"

The woman in the white smock reached for Lelia and that startled me. Why's this woman reaching for my child? I ain't said nothing.

"Only if you want to."

She put her hand on my shoulder as she did the first time. Her eyes were gentle and kind.

"You stay and watch if it comforts you. We're getting the children's breakfast now."

Tears came to my eyes. I wiped them away as fast as I could.

"You can put your mind at peace and leave off your little girl. Then you come back like I said."

"But what if she needs somethin'?" I asked.

"That's why we're here."

"What if she gets hungry?"

"You see these kids eatin', don't you? They get mornin' meal and then lunch."

She took Lelia in her arms and kissed her forehead. Lelia grinned big.

"I know how to ease your mind," she added. "You come back when you take your noon meal."

I couldn't hold back my tears but the woman caught them with her next words.

"I got a baby, too. That one over there with the pile of wood toys is my boy, Alfie."

She understood my anguish. Didn't want Lelia to see her ma crying. My momma never cried; she knew to hide her fears. Thankfully, Lelia never saw her own momma's tears as she was so fixed on that sweet little boy down there playing with the pile of toys.

The woman sat her next to Alfie.

I left without another word.

THE AIR BETWEEN OUR TUBS

41

AT MINNIE'S, THE women were already hard at work at the tubs. LouLou smiled but didn't say a word. She could see I didn't have my baby. I caught an eyeful of Minnie looking down at us from her room up there like somebody might take an extra breath on her time. Profits are sacred and Minnie could smell them in every drop of our sweat.

Violet glanced to see how I was doing, but she didn't look right at me 'cause she surely knew I was near to breaking down. I kept reminding myself that I'd work that tub till I got through so many piles of clothes I wouldn't have to take my child to strangers for keeping. But my head was reeling from the voices still asking me; how can I tell folks I put my own in an orphanage? Truly, what kind of ma am I?

Well, this time Minnie watching me didn't make no difference to Sister LouLou; in her own way she knew how to handle this woman. She slipped over to the tub next to mine where another woman was pounding her washboard.

"Move over to my tub, Mary Jane." she told 'er. "Them overhauls need a real woman to get 'em clean!"

"What'd you say, heifer?" The woman barked like she'd been cursed at.

"That ol' bitch is watchin' us up there like a hawk. Sarah just started here. I gots to make sure she do it right to keep Minnie off our damned backs," LouLou said.

Mary Jane nodded and switched to LouLou's tub.

"Your girl over there?" LouLou asked.

"She there. She there…" was all I could get out.

"She gonna be fine. I tol' you, didn't I?"

"The woman says I can come by at lunch and I mean to."

"Why sure, honey! Now don't say nothin' but Izzy told me Minnie goin' out at noon to the bank where she keeps all her money and then to her hair parlor. That mean we all gonna sit and have a real nice meal while she gone! I'll tell 'im you're gonna slip down the back way. It ain't that far over there. Minnie ain't gonna know you took off, will she? Especially if one of them trolleys near the bank up and runs her over! Maybe she looking with her bad eye and can't tell which way that trolley coming till it get her! Huh?"

Violet saw LouLou chatting with me and winked. I sure felt LouLou and Violet's sisterly love that morning. They were good women, had no reason to waste time on me. They had enough just to get to the end of their own long days without navigating mine.

After it seemed 'bout eighty hours over a tub, Izzy come to the kitchen window and motioned to LouLou that Minnie slipped out on the sly. She was always afraid somebody would get her lunch box money or some customer might get by without paying if they knew she was gone.

"Sarah, go down the alley so you don't run into Minnie on Magnolia!" Violet warned.

"Yeah, she'll think you're off shoppin' with her money!" LouLou giggled. Then she turned and yelled at the kitchen door, "Izzy, I'm lookin' for a big piece of roast pork come lunch, honey!"

I took off down that alley. It took me only minutes to run over to the orphanage. There, I peeked in the window. Right in the center of the room was Lelia sitting with the others. She'd not looked so happy since she left her Aunt Louvenia.

The grannies had a tray of biscuits and were slathering them with what looked like strawberry jam. My heart melted. These little ones couldn't feed themselves but were trying to feed each other fistfuls of biscuits. The grannies were laughing; they were so delighted in all these little strawberry-faced babies. Lighter than I'd felt since I arrived in St. Louis, I ran back to Minnie's starving, but at peace. My daughter and I would survive another day and maybe a few more down the road if Minnie didn't bear down on me too hard, too often.

The women were just finishing their meal as I returned.

"Izzy brought your plate out." LouLou handed it to me. "Minnie in there eatin' now so go back in the shed and eat while we get back to our tubs. We gonna move back and forth so she don't know somebody not at her tub. Izzy tell us if Minnie comin' out. Sure, he will. He'll drop a big pot near the door if she is."

I disappeared into the shed and pulled off my shoes. Running had put blisters on my poor feet despite them being calloused like boot leather. But seeing my girl with strawberry jam all over her face put a grin on my heart worth all the blisters in the world.

Izzy had put back a plate of beef stew with red potatoes and carrots. The meat was tender. A big piece of hot buttered bread was on the plate, too. Lord, Lord, last night I thought you never heard my prayers and was sending me down the path to my final misery just to prove I wasn't worthy of your grace. You should have tol' me you're 'round watching over me. You startle me when you sneak up with a blessing or two! Yes, in that thin air between our tubs there were many blessings even if we didn't always count them.

The day went fast after that. There were lots of laughs over the tubs, which made it easier not to mind the lye eating into my cracked hands. I eagerly awaited the sun to go down so I could head off. Wasn't gonna wait for Minnie to signal from her window she'd wrung the last bit of work out of us and we could finally go home. Hannah and Rebecca were letting us stay with them, so I wanted to get Lelia and head over to their room before it got too chilly. Since they didn't have nothing but cornmeal mush to eat, I pecked at the kitchen door for Izzy's help.

"You got something in there? I got to take some food back to where
I'm stayin'; they got nothin'. I pay you when Minnie pays me."

"I see what I can rustle up," Izzy said. "You go fiddle 'round like
you're still workin'. Don't let Minnie see you waitin' at the door here.
She'll be on my tail for handing food out the back door again."

Some of the others had already drifted off for the night. I went back
to refolding some clothes we stacked to iron while Izzy put together
something. Never saw Minnie. Soon he returned with two tin lunch pails.

"Now get goin'. Bring these here lunch buckets back in the mornin',
'cause Minnie counts 'em," he said.

I took off down the alley and into the night. I wondered how I'd ever
get them pails back to Hannah's and still carry my girl. She don't like it
if she can't leap from arm to arm.

Turned out not to be so bad; my arms were strong from wringing wet clothes since I was seven. It was near dark when I got to the
orphanage. Lelia was delighted to see me, yet not so glad she didn't want
to stay with her new friends and toys. That child, she started bawling
when I carried her off. Well, thankfully we only had a short distance to
Hannah's, right through the very park I thought would be our home the
night before.

"We been worried 'bout you," Hannah said as I walked in.

They'd been holding off getting the fire lit till Lelia and I returned.

"I told you not to worry yourself, Ma. Sarah knows her way 'round
good now. Sarah, I'll get the water boilin' for the mush. You hungry?"

I put the pails on the little table and opened one of the jars from
inside. The stew was still warm and smelled good.

"What's you got there, Daughter?" Hannah asked.

Her bones were aching and she could hardly get up from her chair
next to the fire.

"Stew leftover from lunch and don't know what else. But Izzy made
it and he's a good cook."

I opened the rest of the lids and pulled out a jar of butter and some
rolls. There was macaroni and cheese and a large piece of chocolate cake
in the other. Their eyes lit up like it was a Christmas feast. Macaroni was

Hannah's favorite. Izzy had tossed in big pieces of cheddar to make it extra good. The four of us ate till we put the spoons to our mouths but they wouldn't open no more.

Thanks to Izzy, and a few of my sisters, I slept well for the first time in days. By the grace of God and these women we'd made it a bit further along our journey.

THEM BOARDING HOUSE BLUES

42

I WORKED HARD FOR Minnie. You know I did. Those weeks wore on my hands like years but we made it to the next day and along the way there were many smiles between the tubs we were bent over.

I arrived early at Minnie's and only left after the ol' woman nodded her blessing for us to leave her clutches. Still our days were good, even if Minnie seemed to have ever new devices to squeeze us for more. To survive we made up for it as most nights I went back to Hannah and Rebecca's with something Izzy had tied up in a napkin or a pail filled with food. If Minnie was down in her kitchen on the hunt for those stolen fritters and I had nothing to take back, there was always cornmeal mush to be had. We got by. Rebecca didn't make much money, so she appreciated the help I could offer and Lelia and I felt like we were staying with family; the four of us there at night eating Izzy's cooking next to the fire. During the long nights, Rebecca and I took turns reading the Bible while Lelia cooed along on Hannah's lap.

Over the weeks I saved a bit of money that I kept tied in my old cloth dropped in Jeff's tobacco tin. Rebecca hid it for us under the chest between their beds. Hidden 'cause folks were stolen from 'round there all the time. It seemed like it was those with nothing who got robbed the most. Ain't that always the case?

One Saturday after Minnie begrudgingly paid us, I grabbed my money, bid farewell to LouLou, Violet and Izzy and all the other good women and told them I'd not be returning. I needed to find something better for us even if I didn't know how far we'd have to go to find it. I expected it would be another bumpy journey if only a few blocks away. Still I was determined to find something as far away from the torrid shadows cast over Magnolia , the street where I was sure trolleys ran down folks' dreams faster than we could go chasing after new ones.

That Saturday I had our things pulled for our departure.

"You know you can always come back here with us," Hannah said.

Hannah's eyes were filled with tears. I know she loved the baby so.

"And you know we'll always come visit when we're in this part of town."

I kissed Hannah knowing I'd probably not see her warm smile again or Rebecca's. She was just getting on her feet after being sick for days and had lost time from work so I slipped some of my last pay under a doily on her chest. With that Lelia and I bid farewell and headed off into the unknown. Walking down Magnolia, feeling alone again I took myself back to that old worn-down dream; one of how good it would be if I could someday get a place like Minnie's. That was a dream almost too big to cling to. Life for most tub women was walking a tightrope even on good days. But still there were those other days. At times merely getting through another day with my daughter was an answered prayer. Yes, I prayed: where are you taking us, Lord and how deep will the ruts be along the road this time?

The women at the tubs had long been telling me I best try to find a boarding house for women on the other side of town. Lots of maids lived over there as it was a bit closer to where white folks lived. LouLou told me to head as close to the white part of town as they'd allow as the air was guaranteed to be sweeter. I never knew where this guarantee came from but found it to be consistently true.

I learned that even though folks had plenty of notions on how things were sure to be better up the street it seemed as though there were scarce few who put a foot down in that direction. The journey was lonely where I was headed so how could I not ask myself what did they know that I didn't? It echoed in my thoughts for days. Don't we all wake up hoping the Promised Land is only a trolley ride away from our real lives? Yet what would happen to our fragile hopes if we truly knew how far off it really was? Lord, help me get there, even for a moment or two.

On foot Lelia and I headed to that part of town they said was better, cleaner, safer, even if no trolley seemed to want to go that way. I headed up the steep hill in more ways than one and therefore as far away from Magnolia Street as I could. Yet I sensed folks walking around were hoping for the same betterment as they had airs like they wanted me to know they were first in the lines staking ownership of what dreams were left on that better side of town. No, these folks sure didn't look kindly my way, me wearing my old dress lugging our things with a baby on my arm. Sure, ever'body could tell I was a tub woman. Their sharp glances strongly suggested that they thought I best move on. Once more I found that folks who were already eating were closing their doors to folks like me showing up on their doorsteps empty handed.

Truly it again seemed like nobody wanted a ma with a kid even in low-rent boarding houses. Lord, I tell you, I went from door to door only to see vacancy signs fall out of the windows and doors bolted before I even reached to knock. The few that opened were slammed in my face by a kick of their foot. So, I kept on telling myself not to count the doors shut in my face, but to keep moving faster and harder to find the one that would finally open. But, Lord, what direction is it this time?

I went 'round the corner and saw way up there another place that looked like it might be a boarding house but had no sign saying so. That big old house looked to be near the last on the street as there was nothing much past it that wasn't abandoned or boarded up. I stood there feeling as though there were only a few more steps ahead and I'd surely fall off the world, my world at least. But where else was there for me to head? Walking backwards ain't no easier on aching feet, or ones hopes.

The steps creaked as I walked up to the porch and knocked. In the strangest quiet of that day, I stood at that door waiting but nobody answered. At first, I reckoned they just peeked out the curtain, saw my baby and went to hide. I'd been to them doors before, hadn't I?

Then, just as I'd turned to walk off a white woman with big red hair heavily flecked with gray opened the door. She looked down her little pinched nose at us. I wondered how white folks could breathe out'a them little nostrils? I also wondered why that woman stood there looking at me like that? You see her expression was 'bout the way Louvenia looked at the whores at the end of Jesse's alley.

"Yeah, what do ya want?" she asked then looked up and down the street as if somebody might see me at her front door and cause her house paint to peel even more.

"I lookin' for a place," I told that red-haired woman who probably couldn't breathe good enough to see clearly.

Don't know if your eyes need a good breath to see but recalled Jackson's ma had that same delicate little nose and hardly saw me 'cause her eyes near crossed with anger at the very sight of me in her garden with Jackson. This woman didn't look much different.

"What kind of work you do, huh?" the red-haired woman asked as she yanked her apron off to dry her hands or maybe snap me away.

"I'm a laundress and I iron and can read and write and …"

But that woman never let me finish. I was gonna add that I knew how to put up jars of jam if she thought I looked as strange as her expression suggested. And further, that I never killed Jesse even though we thought on it. Satan even told us to do the deed and even promised he'd not to tell Jesus we had. But what Satan promises don't count 'cause he never keeps his word. That's why he's Satan, is what the preacher told us. I was thinking all that when that woman finally stopped looking me over and blurted out like I'd insulted her.

"Laundress, huh?" she said. "Lordy, if that ain't all the women 'round here do! Ain't it then a wonder there's so many filthy clothes walking these streets given the number of tubs lined up out back of these old houses."

I held Lelia tightly, thinking this white woman could go ahead and blame filthy breeches on tub women but leave me be. I'd for sure already cleaned up enough white woman laundry to know what-was-what.

"That your girl?"

She asked as if maybe I stole my baby from the St. Louis Colored Orphanage or something. That what she thinks? Should I tell her Lelia looks just like her daddy?

"Know who the daddy is?"

Well, at that my thoughts span thinking I was 'bout to spin this here white woman's head off her red shoulders. Couldn't do it though, as I knew how white folks think backwards after a hundred years of them looking over their shoulders to see if we're working hard enough. But then I thought maybe she don't mean no offense 'cause she finally stop looking up and down the street like she was hoping somebody might drop by to deliver 'er something better to do than chat with me. Yes, for the tiniest moment she looked at me with those pale blue eyes as if she could see all the way to the bottom of my empty stomach.

Suddenly her expression softened. It was like she was a different woman. Maybe one who had met me once along her own journey and could remember the moment we'd shared a crust of bread and in so doing we made it to the next day.

"Oh hell, come on in here! It's not like anybody else is gonna take you in, don't you know that? Not with a screamin' kid, they won't. Guess we might as well work something out. And ain't that the story of my life at the end of this street?"

I followed her in trying to work my mouth against hers.

"I can iron and I can…."

"Yeah, yeah. Ain't I heard it all, Sister?" she said. "And from a dozen just like you who show up on my stoop 'cause the only place left is the undertaker's next door and his guests tend to only leave gift wrapped in a pine box. Don't they now?"

My thoughts were swimming different directions as I followed her down the long hall to the back of her place. This blue-eyed red-headed woman called me sister. Yes, I was then certain she had to be a crazy—crazy as that half blind ol' tinker that took me for his sister so he could get me to buy all his old books. Lord, I thought, I've followed this strange woman into a house of crazies. Ain't that where they put all the crazy houses; down at the edge of town so they don't bother nobody? That's what I was thinking but my feet signaled my head to stop spinning my thoughts so hard 'till they had me acting like *I* was really the crazy one talking nonsense.

Well, I was far too tired to think on either end, the top of my head, or the bottom of my soles. Just knew one of us standing there was crazy, but I wouldn't admit it could be me even with my feet screaming they ain't walking down no more streets and to take what this woman served up with my mouth closed!

This red-haired woman led me past her big kitchen and shoved open a creaking door to a small room that she gestured for me to go in. I was hesitant. She gonna bolt that door after me? I didn't budge and held Lelia tightly. She shook her head like she'd heard my feet talking crazy nonsense and then went in first.

The room had a window, which she pushed open some. Don't know why 'cause it only opened to a brick wall a few inches over.

"This'll be your room, so now get to unpackin'. From the looks of it, won't take you long."

She walked out like that was the end of it. I opened the curtain that fell over the window and reached out to see if I could touch those old bricks on the next building. It was an undertaker's place all right; I'd seen the sign out there. Then it dawned on me as I looked up and down the darkness between them two buildings that there was no way out 'cept the door I just came through. Lordy! Guess that meant if she were a crazy, there'd be no escaping through that window if she got worked up and started doing what crazies do on folks. Might have to fight my way out. But anyway, she was a skinny woman. No, I wasn't expecting to see no orchard out my window with spring blossoms blowing in. But, Lord, maybe a bit of sunlight at high noon would sure be good. Enough sun to keep the moss on them brick walls from turning into a hedge. My first glimpse at my new view looked like the mossy green-colored velvet jacket Jackson's ma wore when she went riding. Guess I figured that mossy green wall was gonna be my own Grandview.

I pulled open empty drawers in an old chifforobe thinking our things wouldn't fill one of them. As I did my belly felt just as empty and

I hoped Lelia was so tired she wouldn't worry if her ma had no supper for her that night. I went to chatting with myself, a word here and there as I always do when I got things on my mind to work out. But then I got to thinking, what if that woman was listening outside my door to see if she could hear me talking to my tired feet, or maybe them talking back telling me not to be acting stranger than some damned white woman. Maybe I said something about planning an escape route 'cause 'bout then she barged in looking like she expected to catch me climbing out her window. Didn't surprise me as white folks never knock on doors 'cause they're too primitive, got no manners. But then she couldn't have knocked. She was carrying a tray of food. No, I had no idea what she was up to but had to be evil; white folks can't do nothing that ain't half full of meanness. All the same, sure smelled good!

"I'm Sally, or did I tell you? Sally the boarding house lady," she said.

And Lordy, if she didn't start looking me up and down all over again. Well, maybe it was me looking her up and down.

"What?" she asked. "This? Irish stew. I wagered you and that baby hadn't eaten since mornin'."

Did I hear her right? At that my mouth shut down. She's thinking about my baby's empty stomach?

"What's that look all about?" she asked, looking at me like I was the peculiar one thinking strange things right back at her. "It's for you, Sister. You thought I was carrying a plate of stew around just to see if you liked the smell of it? Everybody in this boardinghouse loves Sally's stew. Of course, they do!"

She put the tray down on the little table near the bed.

"Why in Tara are you standing there lookin' at me like I'm gonna poison you? Huh? Now why would I do that 'fore I collected my rent ? Talkin' 'bout rent money, let's have it."

"Rent money? I ain't got that much now. Got to get work, then I get paid, then I pay you."

"What? You moved in here with no money? Honey, where on God's green earth did they send you packing from? You pay the rent money 'fore you live it out," she said. "How old are you anyway?"

"Gonna be sixteen soon. Real soon!"

I straightened my posture to look older.

Didn't know what else to say but sure hoped she wouldn't take her tray of food back if she didn't like what I come up with. You see, I always got paid, if I did get paid, after I did the work, not before. Do your ironing, get paid for it. So, why was she looking for her rent money now? I ain't lived it out yet. That's the way I looked at the deal.

"Well, the story you got sure has a new twist, dearie, but the I gots no money right now ending sounds familiar all the same!" She looked thoughtful. "In fact, it's the same tale I hear at the beginning of every damned month, right on the first like it's a holiday from payin' rent! Well, anyway, you and me, we're stuck in one hell of a door jamb here. You're already livin' here, so to get my rent, I'd best let you stay on! There's plenty of milk for the baby in the kitchen you passed down the hall. Be out there early for breakfast so you can meet the others. They'll help you get started up, hear?"

"Yes, Ma'am."

"And don't be yes Ma'amin' me, 'less I'm wearin' my diamonds and rubies," she said.

"You got them? Diamonds and rubies?"

"Trust me, I only wear 'em when I'm mopping the kitchen floor. Lordy, child. Where did you come from again?"

Yes, Sally sure looked at me strangely that day and I looked right back at her the same 'cause I was certain it was really her that had the best of the deal as she couldn't get nobody to live in that crazy house of hers. Sure, it had no bars on the windows like most crazy houses, but that's only 'cause the window is near bricked up and then this here boarding house lady wears diamonds and rubies when she's mopping the kitchen floor. No, don't think I'll ever figure out how white folks' minds work, or even if they really do. I kept to my notion that since they let coloreds do all their work their minds up and got soft on them like their backs. Still I liked this red-haired woman from the start and could only wonder what momma would have thought if she'd known Sally 'cause they sure have the same spirit.

Lelia looked up at me with Jeff's smile as I filled her mouth with a bit of soft carrot covered in gravy. Well, we all hear our own yammering crazy talk when our hopes have worn thin.

Jesus, when Sister prays tonight, pass along that I think I'll be all right here because her prayer was answered; this blue-eyed woman had saved us.

Brighter Days and
Bigger Tables

43

I T WAS OUR first day at Sally's and not like any I'd ever awakened to. Lordy! As I bathed Lelia that morning I could hear all sorts of commotion down the hall from us in the kitchen. Some of the other boarders had congregated for breakfast and were sounding like they's having an after-prayer-meeting social of sorts. But from what I could hear, I sure hoped the Lord didn't take those for prayers. He might a' called off Sundays till the air cleared of all the cackles and shrill giggles.

There was a big round table in Sally's kitchen covered with a starched white tablecloth and many pretty if mismatched plates. Some had beautiful flowers painted on them; more colors than Sister probably even knew the names of. There were big platters of food waiting; a platter of smoked ham and one of bacon and another of fried chicken livers with a heap of crumbled bacon on top. There was a big bowl of scramble eggs and a basket of hot biscuits next to a big bowl of chicken gravy. Sally was over at the stove stirring a pot of grits and one of the women was fetching jars of jam. Berry, spiced apple butter, don't know what else they had on that big table.

At first I stood in the door with Lelia not knowing what I was 'posed to do. Sally told me to show up early, but I didn't know for sure why.

They all watched as Lelia tried to break from my clutch to get at that plate of biscuits. They's not family, I got to thinking, but they all sat down 'round that big table like they was.

Sally was over there whipping a pot of grits like she wasn't gonna let one lump get away.

"Sit down, Sarah. We been waitin' for you," she said. "This here is Sarah and her baby. Go on now and take a seat. The women are hungry."

But I wondered if she wanted me to eat too, or sit till it was time to clean up?

"I'm Lucille Wilson."

Lucille was a tiny woman with the longest neck I'd ever seen. She wound it 'round the table that morning catching every word, moan or sigh that rippled across the table.

I sat down with Lelia trying to crawl off my lap and on to the table to get at them hot biscuits. I wouldn't let her grab at 'em so Lucille reached over, handed her one and rolled her eyes at me for annoying Lelia so.

"I'm Becky Lou Morgan. Been here at Sally's near five years."

"I'm Eula Mae, honey and Becky really been here eight years and still don't got a man. But she keeps sayin' she's the same age when she moved in! Now I'm wondering how can that be? Guess I'm not as good in math as Sister. Or just maybe she's savin' herself some time to get a young one! What's your baby's name again?"

"Lelia. My girl's name is Lelia."

Lucille looked at Lelia like she'd never seen a baby before. Guess she didn't know whether Lelia was gonna eat that second biscuit or rub it into her face or mine.

"That a pretty name," Becky said. "My girl's name was Janie."

"Where's your girl then?" I asked.

"Fever took her. Fever. Where you from?"

She gazed at Lelia like she so wanted to hold her.

"Was born at Grandview, the Burney Plantation just over the river from Vicksburg, 'less it's flooding. Then it's a whole lot further off."

"You come a long way up to St. Louis then."

She couldn't know how far. But I could tell that Becky did.

"Once my sister, she went all the way to Atlanta by herself," she said. "Ain't nobody heard from her again." Her eyes got real dark; I think she didn't want to look that far to things that could happen when somebody goes missing. "No, not never."

"Why you come all the way to St. Louis for?" Eula Mae wanted to know. "You got family 'round here?"

"I got a brother I hopin' to find. He's been lookin' for work. Might 'a come up this way. I lookin' for work, too."

"Get a job workin' in a white folk's house," Eula Mae said.

"House work pay better, don't you know?" Lucille added.

Just the thought of getting my hands out of the tubs lifted my spirits.

"Where do I get a house job?"

Then, as platters were being passed around, I noticed there was an empty place setting.

"Somebody not come down yet?"

I motioned to the waiting plate. These women grinned 'cross the table like they were in on a little secret just as she walked through the door. But that big woman was no little secret!

"I tol' you all not to wait for me none," she said. "Go on now and start in."

Her voice was whiskey-stained deep. She walked across the kitchen in a big silk gown with red Chinese lanterns all over it. I figured it must a' come from China or even downtown St. Louis. The woman didn't sit down at the empty place waiting; she sashayed right over to where Sally was banging pots and kissed her on the cheek. Guess Sally didn't know it was coming.

"I never drink coffee in the mornin'. No, just tea," this woman announced, but I wasn't sure to whom. "I drink coffee this early and all I can think on is finding a man to kill; gets me all worked up like that, coffee do."

"Ma Mere, what are you talkin' 'bout? You never get up till noon," Becky remarked.

"She ain't awake now is you, Ma Mere? She walks in her sleep like that!" Lucille said. "Boo, Ma! You awake?"

"And you don't know no man to kill anyway," Eula Mae added.

"No, but you do, honey. Could borrow one of yours," Ma said. "You gots so many scattered 'round town. This man, that one, too, and another over on that side of town and from what I hears, a few still waitin' back in New Orleans. Anyways, it don't matter none which one I kills; they's all the same to me. Come, bring that baby over here," this woman said holding out her arms. "I'm Ma Mere, honey."

"Ma's from New Orleans," Eula Mae commented. "Ain't ya, Ma? Claims she's part Creole. Guess that means she's got French blood in her somewheres. Huh? Do ya, Ma?"

Eula Mae took Lelia over to Ma and held up this big woman's wrist. With her finger, Eula Mae traced a big vein right up her arm till Ma smacked her for pawing on her like that.

"Creoles never let nobody see their French blood they got in them veins, do they?" Eula Mae quipped. "But they think we're all gonna keep believing they got some even if we don't get to see it! Now that just don't make sense to me."

"What makes sense to you couldn't have a bit of sense to it!" Ma Mere replied.

"Go on, Ma, show 'em your purple veins," Sally suggested. "Creoles, they claim to have purple blood like they's royalty. Sure they do, huh Ma?"

Becky reached over and whispered in my ear loud enough even the undertaker next door could hear.

"Couple drops French blood don't make her no better than us, do it? Huh, Sarah?"

Ma wasn't deaf and swished her hand Becky's way like she was waving angry wasps off her ample bosoms. Still, Louvenia once told me she'd heard that some of them Creoles down in New Orleans were sisters of princesses. I didn't know for sure, but Ma seemed to know the inside on that.

"I met Miss Eula Mae down in the French quarter. I sure did and she's been followin' me ever since, ain't you honey?"

Ma said cooing over Lelia who went to patting down Ma's face with her biscuit.

"Ma Mere, ain't nobody followin' you but the law!" Eula Mae declared to a table quickly congested with giggles.

Sally broke in to give instructions.

"Sarah, you eat while Ma holds the baby."

Lelia sure looked content on Ma's jugs and I was just as content enjoying that fine breakfast using both hands to eat.

"Now Sarah, you know you got to let us hold this little one," Sally said tugging on Lelia's hand smacking at Ma's butterfly kisses.

"You gonna stand over a wash tub all day long?" Ma asked.

Sally went back to beating that pot of grits but paused for my reply. "Sarah?"

"You gonna get a house job, huh, Sarah?" Eula Mae asked.

"She's already a laundress, that right Sarah? Even knows how to iron and count up what she done ironed?"

Sally smacked Becky's hand as she reached for the last biscuit and grabbed it for herself.

Well, all this bantering only confirmed what I'd thought from the beginning; I'd for sure moved into a crazy place. Yes, and they say the worst ones are nearest the undertaker's!

Later that first morning at Sally's, Lucille invited me to come along as she did her errands. She said she was headed in the direction I might find housework; close to downtown where white folks lived.

As we walked along that afternoon, the thought of not being bent over a washtub all day filled me with delight. I seemed to dance in my thoughts as Lucille jabbered enough for the both of us. But then her mouth all but gave out at the corner when she suddenly halted and claimed an urgent matter had come up that required her attention. She paused to look at her reflection in a store window and patted her hair down. But with all that fussing I had a feeling what she figured on tending was a man. She did the final tightening of all those silly bows in her hair and sashayed back off the same direction we'd come. So, I just kept on to where she said I'd find some big houses that might need help.

I soon found myself on a street with lots of houses painted white, most with pretty fences. The only way to know if somebody needed help was to start knocking and that's what I did. I knocked and knocked and then walked down another street and knocked on more not really knowing what I'd say if somebody came to the door as I had no experience being a housemaid.

Most doors I knocked on a white woman looked through the window and only shook her head back at me. Finally, I knocked on a back door and a woman answered, a colored woman.

"I lookin' for house work," I told her, but then wondered if she thought I might be after her job. Well, at least she spoke to me.

"My lady used to bring a girl in to help me once in a while but she don't want no babies in here." Her head kept shaking like she'd opened the door to a tub woman once too often. "No, she sure don't. No, Ma'am!"

At that she shut the door.

So, I went on down the street knocking on more doors till my knuckles were sore. Then, I guess it was the last place on the street that a white woman answered.

"I don't need a girl today!" she hollered as if I'd been at her door too many times already that day.

"A girl?"

Did she think I was leaving off my child to clean her floors and do her laundry? Or was she addressing me?

"I said, I don't need nobody!"

She slammed the door in my face. So, I stood there and gave myself a bit of courtesy she'd misplaced somewhere. Yes, Ma'am. My child is thirsty, but don't fret none 'cause we got plenty of water 'cross town not more than thirty blocks from here. But I was only talking to that woman's back door. Had a notion of knocking again to see what she thought of us coming in to take a cool bath while she made herself busy fixing us some fresh lemonade with a big chip of ice floating in the jar. But no, her words felt like a rusty file over my teeth. Well, I expect her lemonade probably tasted a bit metallic, too, so I headed on back.

I lost my way for a few blocks, but finally got back to the boarding house sometime after supper. They'd already cleaned up but Ma Mere brought in a bowl of soup and some warm cornbread that I ate while my feet soaked in the basin of cool water I'd just bathed Lelia in.

"You want some buttermilk with this cornbread?" Ma Mere asked.

"No, Ma. Buttermilk ain't gonna do my feet any good and the rest of me don't care much tonight."

She picked up sleepy Lelia who draped over her arm like a bag of flour and rocked my little girl while we chatted.

"They should a tol' you, them silly women. Ain't nobody gonna hire a colored with a chil'e. They all knowed that, too. Well, it don't matter. Sally and I talked it over after supper. You best work in the laundry down in the basement. We hang the clothes out back by the pear tree. It'a work so long as we got enough customers. Then you can keep an eye on your baby and we'll help you."

And so settled in one short afternoon what I'd being doing for the next dozen years!

CHURCHWOMEN AND OUR SINNERS

44

ONLY MOMENTS AFTER I'd closed my eyes that Saturday night it seemed as though morning was there shaking the bed to get me up. Don't think Lelia budged all night but she sure made up for it as soon as her momma's eyes opened. She went to kicking like it would propel us both to the smell of hot cinnamon rolls wafting from the kitchen. I could already hear the magpies in there banging pots and pans but it was the smell of coffee I heard the loudest!

I carried Lelia in to find the big table covered with plates like it was a holiday. They eat like this every day? Sally was directing traffic in her kitchen. She had Becky over there frying ham and Lucille handing out mugs of coffee as she fussed with the ruffles on her apron that I noticed strangely matched the bows in her hair.

There were many things to adjust to those during first days in St. Louis and that included the strange way city folks spoke to each other, or was it at each other? It was at Sally's big table that I seemed to have difficulty figuring out what the women were talking about. Strangest of all, no matter what their words were they tended to have the same tone as any white woman on her high-horse. At times I wondered if these women even understood each other yet all the same that never stopped their jabbering. Yes, their mouths were in constant motion as heads bobbed to see whether anybody was listening.

Well, I sure had a hard time deciphering all the talk pelted across the table that was punctuated with titters. I eased into a chair to listen and learn their ways in case I ever found a lull to stick a word or two in. But my baby girl found no such barrier at that table and went to jabbering alongside them and if they got louder, her little mouth soon caught up.

Sally slid a plate of hot cinnamon rolls in front of my baby.

"How are you and the baby doin' this mornin', dearie?"

Lelia poked her fingers into the melting icing her eyes seemed to have already tasted.

"Big storm didn't wake her last night?" Becky asked as she set plates around the big table.

"Storm? What storm? Never heard no storm."

I wondered how I could have been so tired I'd slept through a big storm?

"That was no damned storm! That a' be Eula Mae bouncin' the bed springs again!"

Lucille said this with her nose up in the air like Louvenia did when she passed a whore. Lucille then whispered loud enough the next room could a' heard.

"Did it roar down there like Freddie's in town! Huh?"

Sally shook her head at Lucille and put a bowl of mush on the table with a big dollop of butter melting in the middle.

"Ladies! This is the Sabbath," Sally admonished like she was ma to us all.

I sat there silently wondering where all this talk was headed. But it didn't take me long to catch the tail of these howling cats as 'bout then Eula Mae walked in looking weary-eyed, fighting to get a brush through that hair of hers. Lord, what had she been doing that got her hair stand-ing up like a she'd been baptized with lightening? But I knew. I sure enough did! That look on Eula Mae's face was the kind you get when you've spent the night pushing your man off of you but with ever' shove he thinks you're grabbing on for more. That's what I saw as she shuffled to the table looking too tired to pull her chair out.

But Lucille! That woman never stopped looking down her nose at poor Eula Mae so I knew she was aiming to start something.

"Eula Mae, you sleep through that mighty storm last night, honey?"

Lucille licked the cinnamon off her lips and then smack, smack, smack went that mouth of hers till it was ready to shoot again.

"Lordy! I thought your floorboards sounded like lightening they creaked so bad. They gonna fall through on top of me?" she said like supplication to the Lord for safe deliverance. "Sure kept me up all night prayin' for my life. Oh, I prayin' hard, too."

I would soon learn that the only thing Lucille truly worked hard at was sticking her nose in other folks' business.

Sally was soon standing next to Lucille waving a wood spoon as if she was gonna smack the daylights out of her.

"You ever heard of somebody dying 'cause some damned mattress fell through a boarding house ceiling, Lucille?"

I got the feeling she'd heard this kind of talk too many times to want to swallow another stale gulp.

"Well, maybe not. But then it's 'cause Lucille's prayers come in good. Lord, have mercy!" Becky mused. "Lucille ain't dead with her neck broken under some collapsed mattress, is she?"

"What in hell are you going on about, woman?" Sally asked real annoyed like she couldn't understand this talk herself.

"Then we all be witness to a miracle right here at Sally's boardin' house. Ain't that right, Lucille?" Becky said. "Yes, Ma'am. The Lord answered Lucille's prayer and kept that mattress from crushing her head wide open from Eula Mae's bouncin' on that man. I mean, if that's what she was doin' up there. It wasn't, was it, Eula Mae? But, come to think of it, if it was, I don't know if Sally best go 'round telling everybody. Might hurt this here boardin' house's reputation if they found out Eula Mae lets men in the backdoor like she prone to doin', huh?"

"Oh, my Lord," Sally said throwing her arms up and speaking to the ceiling like Jesus was watching her travails through that big crack in the plaster up there. "What did I ever do to deserve this cross I got to bear?"

"Amen, Lord," Lucille added. "We gonna all bear it together, Sally. Pound, pound, pound, he was up there poundin' good and hard while I was all but on my knees praying just as hard my ceiling wouldn't crash down on me. Ain't there all kinds of plaster on my bed this mornin'? I'm gonna go look after breakfast!"

Then Eula Mae, who'd been ignoring their flapping mouths, rose like she was gonna slap the grits out of these women with one swing of her big-boned arm. Sometimes I know when to keep my mouth shut; this was one of them. So, I grabbed another cinnamon roll and pushed my chair back to avoid being in the middle of the ruckus brewing.

"I'm gonna knock the craps out of you, you skinny…!" Eula Mae shouted.

Lucille only pulled her bows tighter and shook her head in disapproval at Eula Mae's hair standing on end. But I for one was sorely convinced Eula Mae meant business on somebody's head!

"Sit back down, Eula Mae," Sally commanded, shaking her head at the other two like she couldn't decide which was her worst brat. "Ain't none of their business what you were doing all blessed night long and then 'gain this mornin'!"

For reasons unknown to me, this comment seemed to calm Eula Mae back into her seat where Sally met her mouth with a forked piece of smoked ham. Me, I wouldn't have handed Eula Mae a big fork like that in the state she was in. Might a' ended up in somebody's eyeball! Well, anyway, Lucille didn't have to say more; her nose was still up in the air and that said plenty enough.

Still Eula Mae glared over the table as she chomped her ham, looking as if she was all but ready to cut the blood out of that woman across the table from her… sitting there a bit too close to me!

In the lull of the hostilities, Sally sat down with a big bowl of scrambled eggs and spooned a portion onto my plate.

"Sarah, you goin' to church with us today?" Becky asked as if nothing had just occurred.

"Don't think I could walk another mile today," I replied after Lelia and I had walked a hundred blocks looking for housework the day before.

"You go on, Sarah. I'll take care of little Lelia," Sally said. "She can jabber at me while I knead my bread dough."

"Yeah, you come and meet some folks," Eula Mae suggested with a big smile like she'd not heard a word these women had slung at her.

"Folks you say? Like women folks? Lordy, don't we all know Eula Mae only thinks on meetin' a man," Becky announced.

Lucille was a skinny thing but her mouth thought there was a big woman backing it and couldn't leave it be.

"And the man Eula Mae's looking for ain't Jesus! How is Freddie, Eula Mae?" Lucille asked.

Yes, she was working up a second round just as Ma Mere showed at the table looking half asleep herself.

"He a groaner, ain't he, honey?" Becky asked Eula Mae.

"How would you know what a groaner is? You already dried up!" Ma Mere said picking up the talk like she'd been there all along. "Dried up-prunes. That's all these women are. Everything dried up but their mouths."

Ma Mere headed for the last cinnamon roll left on the counter.

"Who? Who's a dried up ol' prune?" they all asked waiting for Ma to confirm.

"Where's my tea?" Ma asked as Sally took her plate back to the sink.

At that, the women 'round the big table went silent for the first time that morning. Not a word out of their mouths which lead me to wonder if there was gonna be another row, only this time between Ma Mere and Sally!

"I always get your tea, don't I?"

Sally grabbed the big wood spoon she'd scrambled the eggs with and aimed it at Ma's round baby-doll face. Even unarmed Ma Mere was still bigger and that wood spoon of Sally's didn't cut her down none.

"Well honey, like how am I gonna know you ain't gettin' my tea no more?" Ma Mere asked and then turned to see why the table had gone silent.

Ma shot a scowl our way 'cause we was listening in on her business with Sally. The women at the table went back to chomping but kept looking to see who was really boss between Sally and Ma Mere over there; seemed like both them hissing cats aimed to control the alley.

"My answer is the same as twelve years ago when we got this boardin' house and you still look for me to remind you who fixes your tea every Lord help us mornin'? Like I got to remind those women when it's the Sabbath every damned week!"

Sally slammed a tea tray together for Ma.

"Now don't be sayin' damned on the Sabbath, except on them damned women over there!"

Ma Mere gave Sally a big smooch.

"Damn it to hell, why not? Huh? You started goin' to church now, too?"

Thought for sure Sally was gonna break that teapot when she slammed on that tin tray.

"I'd hail Mother Mary on that one, but she'd smack me down for claiming such a lie! Ma goin' to church! Lordy, that'a be the day. Yeah, about the same day the devil gets down on his knees and says the Lord's Prayer!"

Again, Ma silenced the round of giggles with one searing glance. But Sally paid us no mind as she headed back to their room with her tea tray. Ma grinned and shuffled after Sally like a little kid following a lolly pop held out of reach.

"Is Ma Mere mad at Sally or she at Ma?"

I was trying to work out what I'd just witnessed. A couple growling in each other's faces, waving wooden spoons and then a peck on the cheek to top it off. I couldn't do that math on that one.

"Mad?" Eula Mae laughed. "You just fall out of the rain, woman? No, they ain't mad."

Well, I didn't think I'd fallen from the rain, but then I never heard the storm that night either. Eula Mae leaned over my way while the other two went to giggling again. She whispered in my ear what they was snickering about; that Ma and Sally was still fighting over who was the husband and giving the orders and who was to keep her mouth shut and take 'em like a wife ought'a.

Lordy, but wasn't I more confused!

"Sarah, you don't know nothin'," Becky commented, "'cause you come from the country. Here in the city folks don't do things the like the pigs and the cows."

Well that hardly enlightened me. Guess I still looked confused 'cause Eula Mae whispered in my ear 'bout what we were really talking about.

Maybe I figure things out slowly, but I did figure it this time with Jeff's help. Yes, I suddenly heard Jeff's giggles. Like the kind he ran up my neck with his tongue when he was acting like a dirty boy on those hot sweaty nights. Giggle, giggle, these women were, too. Just like a dirty-minded man. I tell you plain!

Their mouths were still flapping as they picked over the plates on that table, enough to feed a church social and nobody seemed to be worked up over the words said only moments before. Lucille even told Eula Mae she was gonna help fix her hair for church and Becky offered to iron her blouse so we wouldn't be late. All of which made me I assume a truce was in the making. But I tell you, if it was, it was short lived.

A bit after I downed my last sip of coffee, Sally took Lelia for her morning bath as Becky, Lucille and a haggard Sister Eula Mae and I headed off to church. But the hissing, elbowing, and arguing—this time talk on who gots whose best bracelet on and who stole whose blouse—did not let up. I wondered if we'd walk into church with bruises as these women were smacking and jabbing at each other with their elbows so. Lord, mercy on my sisters!

But that all stopped the moment the church came into view. Yes, it did! As we approached the doors the mouths of these women shut down like traps. Like perfumed man-traps that is. You see there at the steps was a tall, good-looking man in a suit. He sure looked like he was waiting for these women and accordingly they grinned like it was Easter morning and somebody done told them they'd for sure been saved despite their sins at the breakfast table. Hallelujah, Lord! There's a handsome man standing there waiting for something that rhymes with female.

"Why, Mr. Davis, you always holdin' the door for the women folks, ain't you now?" Lucille batted her eyes till they nearly dropped off.

"Why, no Miss Lucille. Just for you, honey. Well, and Becky and Eula Mae here and who might you be?" he asked me.

Typical of that morning, I couldn't get a word out.

"We don't got time to socialize, Mr. Davis. Can't you see the choir's up there already?" Becky announced.

Lucille quickly dragged us down the aisle and then to the center of the pew. I can tell you those seated hardly appreciated her motioning them out of the way to make room for the four of us on a pew that offered up not one empty place.

This Mr. Davis squeezed into a seat right behind Eula Mae and tapped her on the shoulder.

"Why, Miss Eula Mae, that a new ribbon you got your hair tied with?"

Before Eula Mae could respond, Lucille's head swung 'round.

"No, it ain't new. It's mine and I tied 'er hair 'cause the mess it was from all she been doin' all night!"

Mr. Davis' face seemed to light up when he heard this tidbit.

Lucille got Eula Mae's elbow in her kidney even as the rest of us faced the choir up there begging Jesus to be in our midst. That choir begged the Lord so pitifully hard that I reckoned they didn't really expect Him to show. Maybe Jesus knowed better not to, so I decided I'd be a bit cautious. When the choir's moans for Jesus to come among us petered to a drone, the preacher cleared his throat and started up on the sermon. But as soon as he did Lucille started on her own Sermon From the Pews.

Oh, Lord, all I could think was if I hadn't eaten that last cinnamon roll I could have squeezed myself back off that pew and be saved from any taint of having arrived with these churchwomen!

"As a people we have been denied the ownership of our bodies!" the preacher said and still got an eyeful of us with one swooping glance. Yes, I could tell he was on to us good, but noticed that Lucille didn't appear to care 'bout no preacher looking down his nose from the pulpit. From the way she was squirming in her seat it seemed she had something just as important to get out. But then I'd find over time that her mouth always had a mind of its own even without a decipherable position on anything. Yes, most of her notions seemed to weigh on her only 'bout as much as last week's weather. Lucille boomed as the preacher struggled to get his sermon to a pitch.

"Never knowed of Eula Mae denying herself to no man! Have you Becky?"

The congregation gasped, then fell silent with not one "amen" as we waited to see what the preacher was gonna do about this Lucille.

Grinding his teeth, the preacher looked down at her, but Lucille simply went on and turned to Becky for confirmation of poor Eula Mae's predilections. Then Lucille nodded to the Preacher affirming that he may continue. But as the menfolk had clearly heard Lucille's comment, they turned to see what Eula Mae had to add about her giving herself 'round town. Maybe that kind of giving wasn't as Christian as she thought. No. Then up and down the pews, women glared at Eula Mae and then at their husbands, them casting an ornery eye Eula Mae's way. The men smiled to themselves like they sure enough knew what Lucille was talking about and didn't that get the women to rustle in their seats! In unison, their eyes glared at the ceiling so they wouldn't see Miss Eula Mae sitting there looking quite contented with all the attention, the nature of which she'd yet to catch on to. The preacher glowered at Lucille who merely adjusted her head to the side so everybody would think the preacher was really giving the eye to sinner Sister Eula Mae.

But this woman remained oblivious and simply grinned at folks like she thought they were plum delighted to see her that morning. Especially the churchwomen. Yes, Eula Mae caught it on the rebound. These women, Lucille, Becky, and Eula Mae sure knew how to work a number on each other.

Finally, the preacher started up again but Lucille wasn't finished either.

"The colored man must vindicate his manhood and command respect from our families if we are to achieve respect. Our women must stand next to their men and support them," he preached with great solemnity.

At that Lucille sat up the way she did when she had a shattering pronouncement to make at the big table at Sally's. She put her finger in the air, guess so the preacher would know to pause while she spoke her gospel.

"Especially when he dead drunk and fallin' down at the door comin' home late again!"

Her words bounced off the walls like the preacher hit 'em there with a stick—one I'm sure he'd sooner put to Lucille's head.

Well, I guess that preacher got tired of Lucille's echo 'cause the sermon seemed to sputter off leaving the poor man standing there with his mouth wide open. Yes, the man stood there breathing heavy-like as he waited for us to fold our hands in prayer. I was sure it could only be a prayer for the wicked and the damned.

That moment of silence was a welcome relief from Lucille's mouth, 'cause I never seen a congregation fold and shut 'em quicker. I prayed for Lucille, too. Prayed hard 'cause it sure seemed like she was gonna need a bucketful of the Lord's grace slopped on her to escape the preacher's wrath that morning. The poor man was up there with his eyes closed like he wanted to work up a real good closing prayer, but for the longest time not a word came. No, he could only purse his mouth in anger and wring his hands like you would a chicken's neck. Don't you reckon that scrawny chicken's name was Lucille? With one eye closed, he commenced his prayer but still squinted through the other eye at congregation. Probably to see if he'd wrested control of the service back from Lucille. Ever'body seemed to look back at him with just one squinted eye so I closed one of mine and looked around wondering why we were all looking at each other with one eye closed. Didn't I tell you these city folk do things real strange like?

Well, I knew by then that Jesus had not answered the choir's pleas that morning. No, His Spirit was not around to be part of us, that's for sure. Pretty soon I realized everybody was looking at Lucille who wasn't the least bit concerned. Guess she knew what she wanted to work up when she shoved her performance center stage. I sat still with my own hands folded hoping Jesus was a patient man.

The preacher finally gave up wringing his hands and stood there looking stunned at having lost his flock to this skinny woman sitting between Becky and me. The congregation, not eager to prolong the Preacher's humiliation started to quietly slip out the side doors. Becky, Eula Mae and me eventually got up and followed Lucille with her nose in the air. She needed a sweeping exit in direct proportion to her performance that morning. The preacher was left standing up there snorting steam, but Lucille paid him no mind. Nor did she mind doing what she wouldn't let the preacher do—that is finish her own sermon on the church's front steps as the congregants fled. The women were pulling their hats over their eyes surely so Jesus wouldn't take note of who was fleeing His house; them tinged with thoughts of sin for wondering 'bout their men and my new friend, Sister Eula Mae.

Eula Mae wondered off as soon as we got outside, perhaps to avoid the sharp glares of the churchwomen, so the three of us waited near the front steps talking.

"That preacher don't know nothin' 'bout being married to no man!" said Lucille, who'd never been married herself.

Becky agreed. "That's true. Jesus come from God and the Virgin Mary! Ain't no man had any part in it 'cause God never could trust a man to get it right. That's where my ma said I come from 'cause I knows she never trusted no man!"

Lucille smirked.

"Yes, Ma'am, your momma was right not to. God couldn't even get Adam to keep his breeches on so he told Eve to go make 'im keep 'em on or she best force 'im to eat something awful way out in the woods when nobody lookin'. Probably like Sally's hard ol' grits, you reckon?"

I had to get in on this before my head swam away. I turned to Becky.

"Your momma got you like the Virgin Mary?" I asked.

"Well, of course she did. My momma say only followers of the devil come from that nasty stuff men like."

Lucille had an alternate view.

"Yes, it was the devil that made up all dirty stuff men folk love. That's why the Virgin Mary had to get her baby in a manger. I know it is! 'Cause if it'a be a man that did it to her, that baby be born in the gutter."

"So, where did your momma come from?" I asked.

"Alabama," she answered.

I never stopped to think on what state the Virgin Mary came from. Made no difference, as I was sure near every state in the South had claimed her birthplace. I stood there wondering if these women had taken as much time working out their version of the creation as the Lord did getting it done in the first place. I learned the verses from Momma but seemed like it was from a different Bible than these women in St. Louis read from.

Long about then Sister Eula Mae strolled up arm-in-arm with in Mr. Davis.

"Miss Becky, Miss Lucy, don't you ladies look fine today?" He commented. "Real fine, if I do say!"

Then he turned to me.

"I'm John Davis."

"I'm Missus McWilliams," I told him.

"Missus, huh? Why I thought you were Lucille's younger sister. The one she's been saying is gonna come visit her from Joplin," he said. "I guess you're no more than fifteen, sixteen. Where you live anyway? 'Round here?"

"Yeah, 'round here."

I answered this smooth-talking man with my nose up to signal I wasn't buying what he was surely offering free samples of anyway.

"I best be gettin' back to my little girl now."

"I be seein' you," he said tipping his hat and winking.

"If you're a church-goin' man you might."

I figured with this remark I'd see no more of Mr. Davis. Well, I got a lot of things wrong back then, didn't I?

"Ever' Sunday," John Davis replied.

But by the way Lucille and Becky giggled into their silly little hankies, I somehow figured John Davis had probably missed more sermons than the devil himself.

I left John so Lucille could catch him up on some of her own past sermons. I could still hear her jabbering at top spead when I walked off.

"Mister Davis, Sarah gots no time for you!" Lucille announced from her pulpit.

"No? Then how's 'bout us all takin' a real long ride then?"

"You ain't got no buggy big enough for three," Becky said.

"But I got something you can ride on, all you ladies one at a time! Sure, I do!"

Well, we churchwomen and our sinners! Lord, I only hope you're a patient man!

LONG DAYS AND
MY DAUGHTER

45

CITY LIFE WAS hard during those first months in St. Louis. During my early years at the Burneys' I never went further than the gates at the end of that long oak alee. Even during the years at Jesse's, I walked only a few blocks delivering ironing. Then living with Jeff near the chestnut, I ventured only weekly trips into Vicksburg to Louvenia's. Out there with my husband at the cabin was the only world I ever desired. This city was truly another one much greater than all my imaginings.

Looking to augment my tub wages, I continued looking for a day of housework 'cross town, but white folks preferred to hire the young German and Irish girls coming off the boats. In droves, they came all the way from New York landing on the stoops of St. Louis with no children and no family ties and desperately hungry to be maids if only for room and a bowl of potato soup.

Sally never asked me for rent back then. Never once. I'd go into the kitchen early and helped her get the bread baked or a soup started for lunch. She always treated me as if I was doing her a favor and not merely helping to pay my rent. It was her gift of grace and I knew I'd never have made it without this woman as there simply was nothing else to move on to let alone fall back on.

Over the long months which became years, Sally, Ma and I became fast friends. Sally was a white woman, but not from the cool white world of any camellia class. She was from a world like ours where life was a struggle just to make it to the next day. Along with Ma Mere, the three of us spent hours chatting over jars of sweet tea or nibbling on something Sally had baked that morning. We talked about the journeys that brought our lives together at that old boarding house on the edge of town.

Over these interludes around the big table, Sally shared what her life had been back in Ireland during the potato famine and I'd tell her about life as a daughter of folks born in slavery where famine was not an incident in our history, but our daily lives. As slaves we ate like animals and the English ruling classes didn't even offer animal feed during the Irish famine. Different worlds, Sally and me, but many of the rules we struggled under were yet the same. Yes, I knew the three of us chatting were poor with scant chance of ever seeing a glimpse of something better. The paths of the poor dragging their bones behind the shadows of ostrich feathers tucked in the hats of the rich who tendered the false promises of some Promised Land they knew only really promised them greater profits.

"What's your girl gonna do when she gets big?" Ma asked one evening as I rocked Lelia. "You reckon she's gonna work the tubs?"

Ma had no idea how determined I was that Lelia would not spend her life knuckles to a washboard even if I did to make sure of it.

"Lelia, she's going to school as soon as she's old enough," I replied.

"Look right into this child's bright eyes, Ma. She's gonna be a teacher one day. I know she is!" Sally announced. "Always gonna be a job for teachers. That's for sure."

Ma had told me that it was the greatest sadness of Sally's life that she was unable to get past two grades in school and could barely read or write. Ma shared that Sally's folks back in the old country counted on her to somehow get enough schooling to become a teacher one day.

That would mean a respectable job, no matter how meager the wages and then also one day afford a hearth for her folks in their old ages. But when famine crept over Ireland like a blight to all hearths of the poor, survival meant somehow finding passage to America. Sally never saw her folks again. Didn't even know how they ended their days.

"My husband, he wanted our girl to go to school," I told them. "Don't even 'member us talkin' about what she might do to get by, just knew she'd be able to read the signs to get where she aimed to go."

For tub women, our lives quickly turned gray and then only grayer as the decades passed over our leathery hands till our lives were just as black as that stinking water in the tubs that we bowed our heads over where the thin air always smelled like an open sewer. Many were the times after our late-night talks, when I was left wondering what Momma meant when she told me that the nobodies gonna be the somebodies come one day. Lord, when is that gonna be? It was sure never to be had in Minerva and Owen's lives. But I tell you, I wasn't gonna wait for that precious day to be announced in the papers. My daughter would not be a laundress even if I died bent over a tub reaching for that dignity which they said wasn't to be ours at any price.

Every morning, after helping in the kitchen, I'd bathe Lelia and head down to the laundry to heat water for the tubs. Sally and Ma made a bare living off the boarding house and that little laundry in the basement. Soon I helped bring in more business and the laundry was going better than ever. I felt that as a blessing even if it meant ungodly hours over those steaming tubs or with an iron in my hand. It meant my toils could repay Sally, fill my daughter's education tin and send a bit of money Louvenia's way.

It seemed as though we'd barely got to feeling like Sally's was home than Lelia was walking so Ma Mere kept an eye on 'er as she scampered up and down the hall and kitchen playing. Ma kept her from getting hurt down with me near the boiling pots. Yes, my days were long, but we were content as most meals there was enough food and never an unhappy moment for my daughter as Lelia visited back and forth between the women of her little world… and the one I was dreaming up for her.

Longingly I looked for letters from Louvenia. When Annie wrote, it was frequently that she, along with the churchwomen, or with the preacher and their kids in tow had made it out Sister's way. This eased my mind on her being alone out there. It was good for all, her notes consistently confirmed. Annie's kids needed to get out of that filthy alley and smell the fresh country air and Sister needed visitors.

Louvenia never learned to read, not because she wasn't smart or didn't value it. I think she was truly afraid of what pictures the printed words might settle in her dreams after reading the colored-owned weeklies.

"Who wants to read 'bout a man 'cross town got lynched leaving a shack full of orphans?" she asked once when I told her there were weeklies for coloreds.

We all had our devices to keep the ugliness at bay and for some, like Sister, this could be no more than simply closing her eyes to the horrors of it. I reckon that Annie must have known what happened to Jesse at the end of her alley but never said a word on it to Sister. Much later when I asked Annie about him she shook her head but wouldn't say. That was a blessing. Louvenia had enough of her own black dreams to keep at bay even before life put her on Jesse's doorstep. Yes, I understood why she never wanted to read the papers. We all got to live through our memories as best we can so they don't get lose only and crush our struggling hopes.

One letter of Louvenia's wrote that some Saturdays the Preacher brought Annie and their kids out to country for the day. Seems he looked forward to some quiet time for himself sitting out on the porch in Jeff's rocker, working on his sermon while the women gathered vegetables from Louvenia's patch for their supper as the kids dug for potatoes or played down at the stream. The Sundays that followed were always long and draining for this man. What with his two sermons, then prayer meeting, there was tending his flock by unknotting their tangled woes. No one else did, as there was no one in their lives but him to hear their grief or help sort their troubles. It was his promise to his people that he'd pass along their troubles in his prayers. Annie told me that it was truly a sorrow for the preacher that praying was about all he could do for his people. As always in life, when we jumped, it was hardly for joy. No, our lives were an ever-predictable cycle of jumping out of the way of white folks and then once again crawling up off the ground after they'd left us in the dust they'd stirred. We seldom risked the jeopardy of jabbing at a dream even to see if it could still alive. The preacher was ever there with a hand to lift folks up after they hit the ground one too many times. Tomorrow gonna be better, was the central theme of his sermons. But most of us failed to ever find that particular tomorrow on any calendar no matter how long and hard we searched. Yet, mercifully, most of us kept looking for it, that someday—the day when the nobodies gonna be the somebodies that would fulfill the promise that was the spilled blood of Jesus.

Then long after supper at Jeff's cabin,, when the sun was down and the women had worked over a rag quilt, the preacher sat down next to Sister and wrote out her letters to me by kerosene lamp. Through these words on paper we strove to honor momma's prayer that we somehow stay connected even if there were long distances and mighty barriers that separated us.

It was about that time when Louvenia wrote she'd finally gotten word on Alex—again a postcard with a carnival picture. He'd had someone write that he'd found himself a wife. Mary was her name and they'd drifted back near Vicksburg where they settled a few miles from Sister. She could see Alex again, but not often, as he worked so hard during the week there wasn't enough left in him to get out to Louvenia's and no horse anyway. No, there was once again a depression in the South. With crop failures the price of cotton was less than the cost of seed and so colored folks got squeezed for the difference. A depression in the South was calculated, counted and noted in newspapers in the cool white world, but for us a depression was merely the cycle of everyday life we walked the sharp edges of. No, we hardly needed announcements in newspapers on the price of cotton to keep us informed. Just a glance into our empty cupboards was all that was needed. It was all the same to us. When your shelves are empty, the count is the same no matter where you start at. Yes, nothing and nothing still add up to mean an empty belly when you put a pot of it on the table in front of your kids sitting there waiting for your magic to not happen again.

One of the Preacher's people lived outside of town and knew Annie. Somehow, they got word back to her that Alex had been trudging from parish to parish looking for work. He even swallowed his pride and offered to put in an entire day, dawn to dusk, for a bag of potatoes, but there was none to be had. Sure not for coloreds anyway. But then another postcard arrived from Brother, 'Gone lookin fer werk…' Maybe that was the last one Sister got from him as her following letters all wrote still "he gone… he gone…." And yet she never stopped praying. In her dreams, Brother was always walking through a shady orchard on his way back to us. Or perhaps like the one our folks' rested in at Grandview.

Louvenia worked hard keeping up her kitchen garden and Jeff's peach trees as well as earn a few pennies from the sewing the women brought her way. She used those pennies to buy a few of the things she couldn't grow or barter from her garden. And what she grew disappeared as quickly as she got it harvested; there was always another hungry stomach out there who might make it to the next day if somebody would only give them that proverbial glass of water—or a bag of potatoes. Hand somebody a peach pit and a tin can with holes in the bottom, and you've handed them the dream of having an orchard one day. Just anything left on the ground might keep a family till the next day. Anybody got some chestnuts to roast? Sister said she filled burlap bags with as much as she could from her kitchen garden, or the chestnuts she'd gathered so when Annie came out she could take some back. Nothing was ever wasted especially the love that abounded on these rutted back roads that kept us connected however tenuously.

Then came the day when Annie stopped by Alex's as she headed back from Louvenia's but there was nobody living there. He gone, as Sister's heart had foretold. This time the postcard with the carnival picture was tacked to the door without a message. Maybe his wife knew he would understand what it meant should he return. Good Annie took the long way back to town so to stop at folks who might know of Alex and Mary's whereabouts. She found some good people down the way—they told her that one night Mary showed up at their door near starving. She told them Alex had gone off looking for work but had never returned. They took her in and fed her. A few days later they brought her into town. They told Annie that Mary was still throwing up from being with child and not having eaten. She had a sister somewhere in town they hoped to find. He gone was all Mary could say in town. Where her fears a mirror of Louvenia's blackest dreams?

❧

I worked long days in Sally's laundry along with helping in the kitchen. Sally ended up putting me in charge of the tubs as the other women got lost somewhere in their own long days and seldom seemed to find the basement. Lucille, Becky and Eula Mae always had other things on their mind than getting new customers or keeping our regulars satisfied. I didn't blame or judge them for not putting much effort into it. Sometimes I wondered how long I could stay bent over a tub myself. But I was blessed with Jeff's daughter and for her came that dream she would not be spending her life over the tubs like Louvenia and me.

The women at the boarding house seemed to float along their own journeys believing that one day there'd be a man who'd come along in a fancy buggy and carry them away to a new life. For them it seemed as if the path to this dream was merely to get their bows fixed just right for so he'd come calling more than once. No, I wasn't waiting for no man to come rescue me. I prayed only for the Lord to help me through all the long days and dead tired nights it would take to fill Jeff's tobacco tin. Maybe I was too suspicious thinking that the men I'd seen 'round Sally's and at church all needed rescuing themselves and were likely only looking for a woman to be a lifeboat to keep them afloat till they could grab onto something better floating by.

Over the years, boarders came and went. Some I got to know others not so much. No matter as Lelia and I had a family going with Lucille, Becky, Eula Mae, Sally and Ma Mere. Got to be we could nearly read each other's thoughts—or at least we proclaimed we could. Yes, we knew when to placate and when we could get away with the provoking that mostly got settled around the big table after a round or two of hissing. We got by with each other's love, friendship and loyalty. Whatever you want to call it, we were family.

Ma Mere loved kids. Guess in most ways she was still one herself and seemed to remake her own childhood with a playmate like Lelia. She delighted in caring for my baby as she grew, pining pretty things in her hair or teaching her the names of colors, along with a hundred nursery rhymes Ma had memorized from some past place where she listened to nannies sing in the nurseries while she was on her knees scrubbing their floors. These two spent hours together dressing dolls while I worked the tubs or was out buying wash soap or doing the marketing for Sally who spent her long hours in the kitchen putting together our meals.

Before she started school, I had taught my daughter the alphabet and she was already starting to read. Her going to school got me hankering for a better education of my own, so I started back to night school. The school was for coloreds, held twice a week down the hill. I read everything I could soak my thoughts into as I never lost the notion that there were things I needed to figure out and held that the answers might be revealed on the pages of some book, if only I could get to it. Maybe I could learn by reading about someone's life, a better life that I could share with my daughter so she'd know it happened, at least for some folks, somewhere. Reading these books weighed on me as I wondered why things had to be the way they were. Yes, as of my days at Grandview I yet wondered why the white world was so different from mine. I was determined to give my daughter the answers to this and other things she was already asking.

One night late when Sally and I finished scrubbing pots, I returned to our room to find Lelia, her elbows on the chest holding her head up gazing into the mirror.

"What are you lookin' at?" I asked.

"Just lookin' I guess…."

"Your hair's a mess," I said with my face next to hers looking into the mirror for what she saw looking back.

"Lucille fixed it up with bows but then Eula Mae came and brushed it down. Then Becky brought her basket of ribbons and tied it back up. Then Ma came and told them she'd take a brush to their tails if they didn't let me go to bed."

"And then you got lost heading to bed like Ma told you?" I asked.

"Momma, what did Daddy look like," Lelia asked as she gazed at herself in the mirror.

"Well, we don't got any kind of picture, but one," I replied.

"One? Where is it?" Lelia asked surprised.

"You're lookin' at it. You look like your daddy all over again."

Lelia smiled and for the moment was satisfied with this tiny glimpse of her daddy looking back at us.

My little girl turned thirteen the week after this moment, the age I was when I met Jeff so many miles before.

Burning Rope

46

YOU CAN'T LOVE a husband as I lost and not forever hunger for him to weave through your dreams even as you walk your nights alone.

This man never stopped holding my heart as tightly as he held my hand as we walked through those tiny trees we dreamed would one day be our orchard. Yet we would not journey through life together watching our baby's life unfold. The daily sight of my daughter so easily reminded me of this.

For Lelia, I had daydreams of the horrors I knew could easily beset our people yet resisted talking to her about this for fear I'd only be painting these images in brighter colors that could turn into hate. Yet I knew my people could never be so innocent of any crime that we couldn't be easily brought down with a rope, raped or burned alive. How do you explain that to a child? How do you tell your little girl when she asked about her daddy and not be filed with fear or hatred? These shadows never stop following you and only grow darker as the weariness drags you down.

&

Other than for a bit of marketing, I seldom got away from Sally's for much of anything so I looked forward to my walk downtown for night school twice a week. Toward the end of each class we'd share things we'd read in books or in the colored weeklies. There were few places where we could speak with ease. Even in class our words were spoken with caution. Weren't we all convinced that even shadows of white hatred could penetrate the thin walls where coloreds congregated?

I remember it was a fine summer evening when I kissed my daughter and left for class a bit early. I always enjoyed watching people strolling up and down the streets to avoid the heat of their rooms and flats. There was an Italian man who sold ices on the corner. He told me that his sweet fruit syrups came from his brother all the way from Italy. Said the bottles were packed in sawdust-filled wooden crates he'd used to make his pushcart. I asked for the one most people liked and he poured thick berry-red syrup over ice he crushed and spooned into a paper cone. On that warm, clear-sky night this sweet cold treat was delicious and tasted like the berries and wild muscadine grapes my brother and I once picked along the river.

As I walked along, I made a list in my head of all the things I wanted to share with my friend LaLa at class. She'd always saved tidbits to share with me. In fact, we talked one another's ears off about what we'd heard, read, or seen that week. The women at Sally's hardly talked about much other than clothes and men. There were times when I was sure I could have pulled bows out of my ears and was certain that the stew for that night surely smelled like five-and-dime perfume.

LaLa had become a good friend. She was not from plantation country. She'd come from St. Louis. Her ma worked as a maid for some white folks. LaLa told me they were good to her and gave her things for totting. Good enough, I guess, for LaLa's ma to hunger for a better life that would provide such things for her baby. You know, LaLa got her name 'cause her ma hummed nursery rhythms she never knew the words to, humming to her la la la la… Oh, my sweet baby, la, la, la. It stuck, of course. But it was as good a name as any and LaLa was as good a friend as I'd ever had. Quiet and intense most times 'cept when she was sharing with me something funny and then her eyes glistened from excitement.

From an early age, LaLa's ma worked hard to get her child into reading and writing. You gonna be a teacher one day, her ma told 'er, and read everything them white folks is up to. Guess there was nothing her mother wouldn't do so that LaLa could become the teacher of her dreams. LaLa was real smart and always impressed me with all the words she knew. She shared things she'd read in the papers about our people as well as what a man named Booker T. Washington was doing to help us. She also read articles on lynchings, roof burnings and other horrifying acts—things that seemed to happen every week in St. Louis.

Then one dark night when I got there late only LaLa was there. Most class nights we arrived a bit early for our chats. However, her eyes didn't smile this evening when I entered.

"Where's ever'body?"

My friend sat there with her hands folded tightly under the desk.

"You didn't come last week, Sarah."

She looked about at the empty seats and wrung her hands tighter.

"No, my girl, she got a bad cold."

"Most left early 'fore it got too late."

She flinched when the door opened. A fellow student peeked in but seeing only two of us, left without a word.

"Why they leave early?" I asked.

"You don't read the papers over there where you live? There's been more burnings."

LaLa fidgeted anxiously.

"Burnings? Where?"

"The Klan! They's goin' 'round puttin' roofs on fire. Colored schools and even churches, they's sayin'."

"Why'd they do that?" I asked.

"There's gonna be an election soon. They say, the Klan do, that there ain't gonna be no coloreds comin' out to vote for nothin'!"

I could only wonder what that nothing was as that's all we ever ended up when we *could* vote. Still I declared: "They can't do nothin' to us!"

LaLa's eyes searched mine for supporting facts but she was the one who'd read the papers that week. I was insistent.

"It's true, LaLa. We's downtown. Lots of folks 'round. They ain't gonna let nothin' happen to us."

I looked around the room and tried to convince myself that the teacher had been sick that night and unable to teach but secretly I wondered if he'd also read the papers. My wet palms suggested that this might be closer to the truth.

Usually there were about a dozen of us learning at night school. But many of those who started gave up after three or four classes. Most folks worked so pitifully hard that our days easily drifted into the night—so there wasn't enough left in 'em to get downtown for school come sundown.

"Ain't it warm tonight?"

"Sure enough is," LaLa replied.

Her mouth remained open after those words slipped off her tongue but nothing else came. In fact, it wasn't so warm that her underarms should have been sopping like that.

Then there was a crackle noise that jolted LaLa. She looked up at the ceiling expecting a shower of red-hot embers to fall over us.

"Let's move back closer to the window; maybe a breeze gonna come up," I remarked.

We pushed our chairs towards the tall window.

"See them clouds?" LaLa looked up at the sky. "Clouds don't get that black this time of year, do they?"

"What's you mean?"

"The Klan, they's burnin' somebody out, ain't they? That's what them black clouds is.

Fire!"

I didn't think so and tried to distract her.

"You read the lesson for tonight?" I asked.

"Ain't gonna be no lesson. Teacher ain't comin'. You know it's so."

LaLa's eyes guarded the door against those that might barge in and discover her drenched wet with fear.

"How's your momma?" I asked.

"She didn't want me to come tonight."

"It's gonna be okay. Teacher's just late. He catches the trolley from the other side of town is all."

"Why nobody else come then? They all missed the trolley, too?"

I tried to ease my friend's tension by pulling pictures out of the book I'd brought. They didn't divert her attention but only stared into the stale air of the room waiting for something awful to befall us. We both knew that it had long been a crime in the South to teach coloreds to read. The only thing I could do was keep smiling and reassure her that the evening would be like any other and we would later walk off laughing for being silly over that ever-blackening sky out there.

I opened my book and pretended to read. But it was no use; I couldn't concentrate enough. So, to ease our tensions I went to describing the dresses of every woman I'd passed that night. Mostly I made things up. That's when it came; LaLa's terrorizing scream. She jumped so hard her desk toppled. She'd seen the man leering through the window—a grisly Klansman; the devil's own drooling nigger dog. Lord, have mercy, but LaLa's scream, that emptied her breath and left her gasping, sounded like the deathly howl my sister let out when she saw Jeff twisting under a rope. You see, just behind our backs at that window was a nigger dog gesturing with his fist to grab at my neck. He brandished a noose, or at least a rope to knot one.

I was frozen—partly from fear but also from the determination he would not jolt my dignity. I sat up tall as this drunken Klansman worked his way up into the window aiming to climb into the room—his whiskey-pickled eyes as yellow as ol' Isaac's. I could smell him all the way from my seat. This drunken coward came fortified with a bottle and an escort; his own pack of nigger dogs; their tongues a loll with hatred. He hollered so hard his spittle hit my face. Still, I would not budge from my seat and satisfy him that I was terrified.

LaLa's hysteria was a source of amusement to this man. She was so utterly shaken she could do nothing but stand against the wall scream-ing as if she was on fire and helpless to move away from the very flames consuming her.

"Nigger woman, I got somethin' fer ya to read! Hot off the press!"

He threw a lighted noose through the window aimed at my face.

"Yer roof's on fire, ain't it now? Ya best climb out the window here so's you can get home to tend it. Maybe me and the boys gonna stop by yer place with some kerosene to put it out!"

He slobbered his words between swigs. Then this pathetic man took another rope from his rabid-dog friend and set it aflame before flinging it at me. Nigger dogs do their tricks for bottles…and our bones.

I would not move away even as his noose blackened the floor at my feet. Like momma taught me, I would hide my fear even as my head swam from LaLa's deafening shrieks. The rope smoldered into the varnish of the floor. I breathed in as much air as I could so I wouldn't faint and held the desktop so I'd not jump to flee.

Finally, I slowly stood up with my posture strong and erect. As the men howled with laughter at LaLa's obvious terror, I went to the washstand for a pitcher of water and carried it over to the smoking noose to drown his gesture of Christian love. Then things got foggy for me as it always does when I'm scared. Afraid of fainting on the spot, I sat back down determined to ignore these drunks. With my head up, I prayed with my eyes open. But, Lord as I tell you, at that very moment all I could see was Jeff's eyes looking back at me as his life was being strangled from him.

About then this poor dog and his brethren mumbled a chorus of the usual obscenities they'd undoubtedly known since the cradle and fell back out of the window howling with laughter. I never thought the pathetic was amusing. The room stank something awful from the smell of the kerosene-soaked rope smoldering at my feet. Through these moments I could hear momma whispering in my ear, her voice so much more powerful over me than theirs. She reminded me of the verses she'd taught me on orchard nights. "The Lord is my Shepherd…. though I walk through the valley of the shadow of death, no evil gonna trouble me…. for the Lord walks with me."

Outside the window, the men crawled over each other like rats escaping a box and finally wandered off into the night.

Shaking, I went over to LaLa to try and calm her.

"They's just stupid drunks," I attempted to assure her. "They gone now."

"No, they ain't gone. They goin' up to the roof now", she said. "Gonna burn us out, ain't they? They gonna! Then they's gonna wait till we run out and do what they want to me."

"No, they ain't. I seen 'em walk down the alley. They ain't gonna do nothin' but fall down in the gutter drunk as dogs."

Her tears finished wetting her blouse. She'd peed on the floor as well. I squatted next to her while she held my hand so tightly my bones felt crushed. All the time she looked up at the ceiling as if expecting it to collapse quicker than she could say a prayer for a quick end.

We sat there shaking in silence for nearly half an hour.

"You walk with me home?" she finally asked.

"Yes, I will. We go in a few minutes when you're calmed down." I assured her.

I went back to the window to make sure there would be no escorts out there waiting for us. It was now strangely quiet and the sky was crystal-clear; the bit of breeze had blown that eerie smokiness away.

"Come here, LaLa. Come look at the sky."

"They's burnin' down our part of town now?"

LaLa grabbed my arm at the window and peeked out cautiously.

"No, see. The sky's crystal clear now," I said. "Ain't nobody even burnin' trash in the alleys tonight!"

LaLa nodded, took a deep breath and smiled.

"You're the best friend I ever had," she said. "We best go now."

We headed down to the street, looking up and down and behind ourselves for stray dogs. There was nobody to bother us, so LaLa headed her own way back to her ma's.

I never saw LaLa again. She never returned to class and I was sad of it. But strangely, when I think of her my thoughts often drift to the face of a woman I'd never met; over and over again along the journey, I still see LaLa's ma. In these daydreams she's still struggling to crawl off that wet floor she's scrubbing. She can't abandon her tasks, because to do so would be admitting that her dream for her sweet LaLa was worth no more than a smoke-blackened night. Maybe LaLa ain't never gonna be a teacher. Still, there ain't nothing left for any ma when there ain't no dream left for our babies.

I looked back at the mirror the following morning after I crawled out of bed to face another pile of clothes and what I saw was LaLa's ma's face, one I'd never even seen, looking back at me. Maybe she's wondering if I was to be the ma that gave up on my dreams for my child. Please, Lord, don't let it come to that. No, don't let my dreams for my daughter drain away from my weary hands like stinking tub water. I still hope LaLa is out there somewhere teaching and her ma looks down on her sweet baby girl from her orchard with gladness.

And you yet ask how I got through thirty and a few years at the tubs? LaLa's ma, Minerva, Louvenia, Annie, Rebecca and her ma Hannah, and all the other women I passed along my journey that tugged me to the next day or sometimes just to the next moment.

Lord, save us, even as the air between our tubs gets too thin to take another breath.

BOARDERS AND OUR CHURCHMAN

47

A T SALLY'S, LELIA and I treasured many joys along our days that quickly melted into years. Every day and even more as she grew tall, I saw in my daughter her daddy—and so often I know that this softened my anger. Jeff, he was never angry with white folks. Not ever. I wanted my girl to someday say the same 'bout me. Yet sometimes I found it hard to look into those beautiful trusting eyes for fear Lelia would see through me like Louvenia always did and know that I was hurting—hurting from the loneliness. Never told her that my biggest fear was that someday, after my daughter was off and gone, I'd not see her daddy's eyes smiling back and simply wouldn't want to look at nothing else no more. Well, one day I'll tell you the story about Marbella.

I think she was nearing sixteen when Lelia came to me with a big grin. What's that all about, I wondered? She was skittering about like Eula Mae did when she was trying to get some man's attention. Yes, my daughter was growing up fast.

"Have you seen Eula Mae's new man? He's mighty good lookin'," she announced. I think she was even wearing a bit of Eula Mae's perfume that morning.

"You're too young to be noticin' good-lookin' men," I said sternly knowing how much time these women spent talking about men.

"And you're too young not to. You're not yet thirty years old, Momma. How old are Aunt Lucille, Becky and Eula Mae?"

"Never mind how old they are. Anyway, even the Lord's probably heard so many tales on that, He don't even 'member!"

"What are you going to do when I'm off to college?" Lelia asked? "Don't you need some companionship? A man to keep you company?"

Lelia was too young to know her daddy. How could she have understood that no man could ever fill his place in my life.

"Maybe someday I'll see about gettin' a house job. Been thinkin' on that for a long time. Right now, all I care 'bout is gettin' my hands on ever' bit of laundry I can squeeze a penny from to fill your daddy's old tobacco tin."

"But what about you? Don't you have dreams for yourself?"

"I prefer the comfort of dreams of when your Daddy was here."

"Jam! Is that your dream?" Lelia asked. "When was the last time you had somethin' special for yourself? You can't get comfort from dreamin' about an orchard, Momma."

Lelia was right. But I had set aside a secret little dream. One of getting a small place in the country with a few fruit trees—somewhere Louvenia and I could grow old together with no washtubs staring back at us when we opened our eyes at dawn. Don't even know why I kept the dream to myself like it was a secret in my soul. "What is a soul?" I recall asking Momma so long ago. "A place you hide your dreams from the white folks," she replied. Well, only my daughter's schooling mattered and not my silly notion of getting' myself out of the tubs and into a house job. It eventually occurred to me that I couldn't expect my daughter to grab her own dreams if I didn't show her how. Lelia helped me to realize I had to start thinking about my life as something more than a day strung on a calendar like an eternally long clothesline stretched under that merciless sun.

As we returned to Sally's from church one bright spring morning, Eula Mae and I were chatting while Lucille and Becky followed behind giggling and snickering. Eula Mae's head was cocked to catch the comments tossed at the back of our heads, which she tacked her own comments to faster than she could pin wet clothes to a line!

"Lucille say she seen you lookin' around at all the men in church," Eula Mae whispered, then turned to join in on the snickering behind us. "They's all married. Good ones always is, ain't they now?"

"You tell them fools marching behind us," I replied, "that they don't know what my eyes see and it ain't none of their business anyways!"

"Hear that, fools?" Eula Mae barked and then joined their chorus of giggles.

"There's sure some fine men a church, ain't they?" Eula Mae sighed.

Yet I had the notion that what I saw in these men and their finely dressed wives was a shade or two different than what Eula Mae, Lucille and Becky tended to see as they never seemed to notice the wives with the men. Their vision was easily blurred by their batting eyes when a tall, good looking man happened by. But when I looked down the pews I was noticed something else: the fine, well-dressed women who didn't look haggard from a week bent over the tubs. Sometimes I thought about these nice folks, the men who tipped their hats to me and the women who smiled as we passed. What did their lives look like on the other side of that other block? They all have nice shops, dry goods places or some special trade going? There sure weren't many coloreds who did, but the weeklies seemed to know of the ones that prospered and printed their pictures next to ads selling nice things. There were nearly always newspapers on Sally's big table so I looked at the pretty advertisements wondering about all that. These smartly dressed colored folks gave us a feeling of pride; yes, perhaps even a glimpse of what hope looked like when it went further than only a day dream. Yet those feelings lasted only about as long as the morning papers because by the end of most days I was again feeling like a worn-out dishrag.

Well, I guess loneliness is never a good friend. No, it's a companion that lingers to tell you stories where the characters change like your moods. I never really thought 'bout men too much. While no man could ever replace Jeff in my dreams, I did at times wonder what it would be like if there was a nice, clean, hard-working man whom I could talk to once-in-a-while.

$$\backsim$$

Sally and Ma Mere worked hard to keep the boarding house up and the rooms filled, but things were hard down in our part of town where wages for all were slim. Slim, and if you even put in a thin word on it to your boss, you'd be on the street with nothing but a pocketful of empty days to carry around as you looked for work. Then the first thing they'd ask was what about your last job? Maybe you gave your boss grief. Huh? Did you? Sure you did or you wouldn't be looking for work! So, you learn quick to keep your mouth shut in hopes you'd be able to open it for a fork at least once a day.

Becky and Lucille found it hard to keep jobs for long and when they had one the wages were miserable and their bosses abusive. Neither of them had strong hands and arms like me and were afraid of walking the finished ironing 'round to our customers in the evenings. Past dark, the streets weren't safe for these tiny women who were apt to flirt even if they didn't mean nothing by it. Sally and Ma didn't get much rent from these two. In fact, Lucille and Becky went to sharing a room to make ends meet and while there wasn't much meeting of budgets their heads sure met often enough. I yet wonder if they're still fighting over who would get the bed closest to the window.

One morning at breakfast Sally looked real worried and yammered on about the need to find more boarders soon. Ma quipped that she didn't want no men 'cause they was sure messy and got into things. I wondered how that was any different from Lucille, Becky, Eula Mae, and me making a mess of things. But it was their house, they made the rules and these rules helped us all make it to the next day. We got by even if our soup got mighty thin some nights.

"I don't care none if it's a man or a woman boarder!" Sally snarled as she pulled that pan of biscuits out and dropped it on the counter like she'd just as soon put a hard knock to our heads. "We got to make the mortgage on this place or we're all gonna be out on the streets."

"You can be a maid again, Sally!" Ma quipped to resolve our crisis.

"At my age?" Sally replied. "There's a boatload of young women landing from Ireland every day. They come here to be maids. And then what would you do, Ma?"

Ma Mere's eyes looked frightened at the prospect.

"Me? I'll learn to make you tea every mornin' 'fore you go to work and wait outside 'till you come home at night."

"Ma, maids don't go home, dearie," Sally said. "They live up in the garret, roasting in the summer and freezing in winter. And they live there with no one else or they get fired. So, where in tarnation are you gonna be waitin' for me?"

Ma Mere's dark face went ashen.

"Now I want you women to ask 'round at church come Sunday," Sally instructed, "and I'm gonna put the word out at St. John's. Ask folks if they know somebody that needs a room. Now don't forget."

"Yeah, don't forget none or we're all gonna be livin' on the street and waving up to Sally in her attic window where she's gonna be all alone!" Ma added.

"Alone, but dry! That's more than you'll be Ma down there wavin' from the icy street come winter!" Sally enlightened.

Sunday came 'round and I awakened to the cackling of these hens down in the kitchen. I turned over to find Lelia already out of bed and out there with them. Although I hoped she was helping Sally with breakfast, I soon found she was helping Lucille, Becky and Eula Mae borrow and steal clothes from each other so to get real dolled up for church that morning.

"Where are you going dressed up like that?" I asked finding them all in their finest. "It ain't carnival night."

"We're goin' to church for a special errand for Sally and Ma Mere," Preacher Lucille declared as she adjusted that big silly bow drooping over her ear. The one she'd won at the last carnival for failing to get the ball in the box after fifty consecutive tosses.

"It's like a pilgrimage, so we best take food," Becky added.

"What are you taking?" I asked, hoping Lelia would chime in to offer a straight answer. She smiled at me, then at the others. It was hopeless. So, I posed a question to Lucille: "Who's the one gonna get all your mercy heaped on 'im this early? Somebody you don't like?"

I could tell these women had passed between 'em every bottle of perfume they owned and had tried them all on to see which was best to wear on their mercy killing. Their special crusade was to hunt down a new boarder, and apparently from the smell of perfume steeping 'round the big table, he best be male! Lelia and the women made it clear they were impatient to head off and in no mood to wait for me to work a brush through my hair, so, I gave up with my hair and waved them on and decided I'd just stay home and have a quiet cup of coffee with Ma Mere and Sally. The smell of cinnamon rolls coming out of the oven made it ever so easy for me to stay put that morning.

While these miscreants headed to church, undoubtedly perfuming the streets all the way, I enjoyed my coffee and caught up on a letter to Louvenia. Then I helped Sally write a letter to the old country. She still had brothers and sisters back there she'd just received a letter from through her church. She felt so guilty for not being able to send a few pennies home that she'd held off having me finish the letter for weeks hoping things would change for the better. While I jotted down Sally's thoughts, Ma interrupted to remind her of things that I should include. Ma couldn't write, but she had a memory of everything that happened to them since the last letter I wrote.

It was late that day before my daughter and her "aunts" made it back again. We'd gotten tired of waiting so we'd had our midday meal. But as the mission they'd undertaken was so taxing, going up to every man who had a glint in his eyes at the sight of all them bows and asking him if he needed a place, they had already filled up on cakes and cookies at the church social. Lelia later shared that these characters seemed only to ask the real good-looking men if they just happened to know any man who needed a room at a boarding house filled to the rafters with women and bows and steeped in dime store perfume.

Over the next couple of weeks, the laundry was going good and we got a few more customers by word of mouth so somehow we made it to the end of the month. Sure got tired of cornmeal mush every morning and then fried grits at night, but up and down our street there were folks who went off to work with empty stomachs and came home at night to only thin gruel. It was getting hard for me to squeeze many pennies out of my piles of laundry to send to Louvenia and still put some away for Lelia's schooling. The only thing I think I did other than the tubs was read whatever books I could borrow. Back then don't think Lelia and I even visited the Italian man for ices.

But then I started hearing weighted whispers of this and that on a new boarder. At first, I only let their talk drift by me. Finally, Sally announced that for sure she'd found a new boarder and he'd even paid the rent three months in advance. We were saved! We celebrated at supper by having a small piece of steak with our potato for the first time in weeks. That night at the big table Lucille, Becky and Eula Mae kept eyeing me, as they always did when they wanted me to guess what they were up to sure that I had to be thirsty to have the gossipy details served up by dessert.

"Why are you three lookin' at me like I'm the next bite of meat on your fork?" I asked.

"Some talk, Momma," Lelia said with a particularly big grin, "that the new boarder has recollections of having met you."

They all giggled.

"Sarah knows that man. Sure, she do!" Becky confirmed. "He used to be outside of church ever' Sunday 'fore he moved 'cross town. Ain't that right Lucille?"

"And now he's back our way." Lucille confirmed, sounding as if they'd covered all the more salient details at an earlier rehearsal of this performance.

"What?" I asked, not entirely happy that my daughter was in league with these miscreants who never got into anything that didn't turn upside down on their heads and often enough, the rest of ours, too!

"Ain't he tall?" Eula Mae added and then stood waiting for me to confirm his height.

But Eula Mae answered her own question just the same.

"He sure is, Sarah."

She waved her fork at my face with a wink as if she was forking over some of her latest fantasy for me to nibble on.

"Somebody say he rich," she added but her sheepish expression suggested she'd added up his money and had already figured to the cent how much he had in each pocket.

"Why don't you keep your malarkey to yourselves and tell 'er what you mean for her to know?" Sally demanded.

"It ain't no malarkey!" Lucille snapped. "We gonna have a man 'round and he been askin' if that nice Miss Sarah is still livin' at Sally's.

"Mrs. McWilliams, if you recall," I reminded them.

"See? She don't care 'bout no man movin' in and don't want to hear how good lookin' he is every blessed time you open your mouths that ain't never closed anyway!" Ma Mere somehow got out in one breath.

Sally came to his defense.

"Like I said, Ma, the man paid me three month's rent in advance. Now you don't got to be standin' on the sidewalk on cold nights waving up to me in somebody's garret wavin' back down to you as I pull my comforter around me tighter!"

I knew these women's bows were near to bursting waiting for me to ask about this new churchman. But I decided to make them squirm till the pain overcame them and their big mouths burst open to spill everything. Or I might get lucky enough to escape their flapping tongues by heading back to my work. So, I ate quickly knowing there'd always be a pile of drama waiting for me iron out of at Sally's.

Mr Davis' White Picket Fence

48

OVER THE NEXT few days tales about the new boarder sprouted like weeds in Ma's vegetable patch. The women halted when they passed, me headed to my chores, them escaping theirs to water more gossip in this garden they'd seeded and collectively tended.

But didn't they'd stand there speechless when they found me? Them surely having placed their bets on how long before I'd demand all the vivid details on the new man, a churchman no less, they endlessly reminded me. When I only nodded and walked off with a smile they'd huff and yank at their bows till their hair nearly fell out in ribboned clumps. Sure sign of extreme exasperation, if ever I'd seen one and then, I'd seen it all!

Then one night when I'd finished taking my laundry down, I came into the kitchen to find that Sally had started up a big supper and the women, including my daughter, were all particularly dolled up. Sally was wearing her special linen blouse her sister had sent her from Ireland with the beautiful handmade lace down the front. She put one of her big candles in the center of the table. The one with painted images of saints who waved as the light flickered. You see, this was to be the welcome supper for the new boarder man.

The welcoming breakfast for me years before was nothing compared to this spread. Back then these women were still half-asleep when they were introduced to me; now they were wide-eyed and ready for new adventures at Sally's. What kind, I preferred not to contemplate.

I was last to get my hair combed and arrived at the table where everyone was waiting.

"Mr. Davis, you know our Sarah, don't you now?" Eula Mae inquired as I took my seat.

"Sure he do!" Lucille reminded all.

But I really had only a faint recollection of meeting Mr. John Davis.

"Met you at church, didn't I, Miss Sarah?" he asked.

"He don't go to church."

Becky's quip was tailed with the giggle of a sinner if I'd ever heard one!

"No, he don't go to church. But he stops by when he can to see if any women be needin' a ride home," Lucille added. "Ain't that a good Christian deed, Sarah?"

"Miss Sarah, I do recall, you had your baby with you and now look! She's near growed," John Davis said.

"Mr. Davis, what have you been doin' all these years?" I asked.

"He's a business man and he gots some partners, and…"

Eula Mae was going down the list she and the other women had likely memorized like the order of hymns at church. All the while she looked at the others who nodded if she got something right or tendered a subtle flick of their heads if it wasn't shaded just right. Eula Mae had memorized her lines well. But for all of them this list seemed to chant the same hymn: John Powell was quite a catch. For whom seemed yet up for grabs and for the grabbing it looked like all nails were sure polished up. Yes, these women were tossing their nets to see what they could catch.

"I was asking John, honey. Appears he can talk, at least when he can find an opening."

I nodded to Mr. Davis to continue.

"Eula Mae's right. I'm a businessman. Me and partners gots our fingers in all sorts of things 'round town. Sure, we do. That's right."

As I look back now what I remembered most 'bout that first supper was John's fine table manners. It was as if he'd been eating in all the finest kitchens 'round town with real silver forks and not a spot on his sleeves from wiping his mouth.

Over the next few weeks I came to realize how good it was having a man around, if you can call John being 'round. I mostly heard of his great deeds through the busy-mouths as these women seemed to always know what he was up to. But over time, even Sally warmed to the idea of John helping in the kitchen. She said John lifted and fixed things and one day I saw him out there replacing the poles that held up our clothes-lines. While I hardly expected these women to ease up on their flirting, it was the spice of their days, John appeared to take it all in stride. Yes, we noticed John was a gentleman and, except when he was dressed to help Sally, he always wore a fine suit like the men at church.

Over time, I got to enjoy chatting with John as we passed now and again in the kitchen. His talk was refreshing after the babble of these women which frequently continued during the the night through the walls. But come to think of it, all they talked about back then was John! Still he and I would on occasion find ourselves late at night down in the kitchen hunting for a snack and we'd sit and talk a spell about things we'd been doing and the places we'd like to see one day.

John had traveled quite a bit and had even seen Niagara Falls and New Orleans. He had many stories to share about these trips, most of which he claimed were for business. After a time, I realized that I enjoyed talking to John and he appeared to enjoy listening to me. That wasn't something I was accustomed to. Chatting with the women at Sally's was not much more than sliding a word or two in. John must have sensed my enjoyment with our conversations as he asked, with great reserve, if we could have a conversation other than down in the kitchen.

"What do you mean, John?"

"I was thinkin' it would be nice, you know, to have a conversation over a bit of supper and not with a circle of ears listening," he said with a wink.

"What kind of supper?" I asked truly having no idea. Folks in our part of town didn't dine out. There were only a few places up the way that offered supper for coloreds and John had apparently frequented them.

"I'm thinkin' about a little supper where we can talk, sip some wine, but only if you don't think I was too familiar for asking."

And I didn't. I guess I didn't really know what to think as nobody asked me out except to run errands for them. I thanked John Davis and told him I'd think about it and I did for the next few days. Couldn't think why I wouldn't go out with this man. Figured it don't mean nothing having supper with a man in a public place. However, I couldn't ask anyone at Sally's if I was right, as John's invitation would have been broadcast by these women long before I'd even had a chance to say yes. So, I did.

The following week, all the boarding house women, including Lelia, got themselves ready for an evening at the summer carnival they eagerly awaited every year. They were to meet Ma Mere and Sally at catfish stand near the carnival. I told John I'd join him for a simple meal, and we agreed we'd not mention it to keep tongues from wagging off.

That Saturday evening, after the others had left, I ironed my Sunday dress and we strolled uptown for supper. The man who greeted us knew John and seated us at a nice table that had fresh flowers. It was a nice place with pretty curtains in the windows. A man dressed like a gypsy was sitting in the corner; his deep melodic voice danced along with his weeping guitar. Even the candles seemed to sway to his gentle music. I'd never ordered food from a menu handed to me, and not just marked on a board up front; seemed like there was everything there to eat. I couldn't make up my mind, so I ordered what John did, some sirloin roast and salad. The thing I remember most about this meal was John's ease with the fine surroundings while I felt like my hair surely had to be mussed or my collar was turned under wrong. I was certain I didn't quite fit in these fine surroundings. Our dinner started with consommé, which I was sure somebody had been in such a hurry cooking they forgot to put in the meat and vegetables. At the end of supper, the waiter brought us cherries that were flamed and poured over vanilla ice-cream he said was made that night. We enjoyed the evening so much we took the long way back to Sally's to continue our conversation.

I truly don't think anybody in that house realized for weeks that John and I had really started to court—that is, in between him being off to one of his business meetings and my long hours over the tubs or ironing board. Sometimes it was just to talk late at night after Sally and Ma had retired. I realized that John listened to me and even seemed to want to hear what I planned for my daughter's schooling. He always smiled big when I told him how long I'd been saving for it.

"A tobacco tin, you say?"

"It was Jeff's tin. Since I got settled here, I been tucking in as many rolled up dollars as I can."

He told me he knew the bankers round town where I should put my money and he would speak to them about it.

"I never even heard of nobody sayin' they's gonna do something and then never let go of the dream no matter what," John commented and took my hand. "Like you been doing savin' that money for your beautiful girl."

"I owe it to Jeff. It was his dream as much as mine that our girl has schooling. He'd be proud of her the way she's near growed up. What 'bout you, John? You keep quiet 'bout your own dreams."

"Ah, men, you know we don't talk on them things much," he said a bit embarrassed that he might have a dream of his own tucked away. "But I got things going. Guess that's as good 'a dream as any."

"Why, sure it is, John. What's you got goin'?" I asked.

"Well, I been savin', too. Got me a few dimes put away."

"What's you gonna do with it all?" I asked, remembering that the women were convinced John was rich as could be.

"Plan to buy a little house one day. Maybe like the one my ma worked at as a maid. Guess she worked there till near the day she passed. It was always after dark 'fore they let 'er off. As a boy, I'd go by late to walk Ma home. Was a little white house with green shutters and the porch boards painted gray. Right there under the porch were lots of white-flowered geraniums. Once ma, she snapped off a piece of one and stuck it in the dirt by the porch at home. I bet that geranium's still flowering there. There was a little white fence all 'round the place ma worked and the white woman had the palest pink roses growin' all through it like she wrapped a wreath of flowers 'round her place. You know, from a way them roses looked white but up close they were the palest pink. Maybe like they was shy 'bout me smelling 'em and blushed for it. My ma, she laughed at me when I asked 'er to never tell nobody she seen me smellin' roses like a girl."

I smiled at John and laughed to myself 'bout men being silly 'bout loving flowers. What's a woman but a flower? I guess I never said nothing 'bout Jeff's garden to John.

"You gonna have that house one day," I assured John. "You pray to Jesus to tell your ma you're gonna think of her when you do; her spirit will be there and her white geraniums are still smiling to remind you."

Tears came to John's eyes. He reached over and gently kissed me.

Over the last of the crisp days of autumn I kept to my work and didn't pay mind to what was going on with the others. It was just Lelia and me and now John too.

Darkness had come early that fall evening when I returned late from walking the laundry 'round to my customers. John was yet at one of his meetings. Being tired I went up to bed and as I'd done so many times, I sat on the edge of Lelia's bed savoring the quiet as she slept. That night Lelia awoke.

"Momma, you been down talkin' to John?"

"I been taking the ironing 'round. Just got in."

"Why do you do it so late? Isn't it getting cold out there?"

"I do it 'cause it means someday my girl ain't goin' to be workin' the tubs," I brushed her hair back to see more of her daddy's face. "I got something I been thinking 'bout for some weeks now. I want you to tell me what you think."

"Is it about John?"

"He asked me to marry 'im. I said only if you agreed that was best for us, you, me and John."

"But why not, Momma? He's a nice man. Everybody likes 'im and he's always good to me."

"John, he says if I marry 'im, he's got enough put back to buy a house. Maybe a small one but still on a good street."

"Why, Momma! You always wanted your own home. You could have a garden and grow your fruit trees then."

"I know, sweetie. And I told John, if we get us a place, we gots to have a spare room for your Aunt Louvenia."

"What did he say?"

"John said we ain't gonna get a place 'less it's big enough for all four of us and the spirit of his ma, too."

"You think Aunt Louvenia would come out this far?"

"Don't know. Annie wrote that Sister comes into town with her now and again but won't stay but a day or two 'fore she longs to head back to the quiet and her flowers."

"She'll come up here, I'm sure she will," Lelia said.

"I figured I'd fix up her room real pretty, paint it her favorite peach color and right in the corner we can put a pretty table with a nice cloth hanging over it. And you know what? Waiting on that table there's gonna be a real pretty hat."

"She's gonna come." Lelia hugged me. "You know she will!"

I had worked very hard for so long that the thought of John and me together brought a kind of happiness I'd rarely experienced back then. I know it did; even held hope that maybe things could be a bit easier up the road for Lelia and me. No, I didn't expect to be headed to a life like the women who sat next to nicely dressed men in church, but then I guess someplace I still yearned for that. It was a tiny splinter of a dream that had erupted and pierced my sunken hopes many times: me having it a bit easier and even a little house with a fruit tree or two. It was a good feeling. I was ready to let it happen and knew Jeff, waiting in his Orchard, would not be angry with me for marrying. The glint in his daughter's eyes promised me.

Yes, I could see us planting those flower seeds Louvenia sent every spring inside window boxes that John would carpenter with the white picket fence.

THE SLEIGHT-OF-HAND MAN

49

LELIA AND I spent the next few days secretly planning my trip to Denver where I'd be marrying John Davis. We discussed buying a nice dress to wear, but despite Lelia's urging I wouldn't dip into the education tin for something merely fabric. I thought about putting some new trim on my old Sunday dress, but figured it wouldn't improve it much. I wondered aloud if John minded my old church dress and he pulled out a roll of bills, peeled off several and told me to go buy a nice store dress. Said he had plenty of money on hand for us to enjoy our few days in Denver and wanted to start our married life just right.

Even with all the whispering back and forth between Lelia and me I was fairly certain that the others had no idea something was brewing. The following Thursday we slipped off to take a train down to Denver and left it to Lelia to work up something explaining my disappearance. I knew we'd all have a laugh when I returned.

It was a nice trip down to Denver. On the train, John mingled with the men passing newspapers between themselves while I chatted with the woman sitting across from me. I shared with her that we'd planned to buy a little house soon. She had all sorts of ideas on how I could get it fixed up nicely from when she got her own place. The thought of having a real home and my family around me put a smile on my face. My face was fatigued from smiling so by the time we stood in front of the justice of the peace. Afterwards, I so enjoyed walking up and down the streets of Denver as a visitor and not as a laundress lugging a pile of laundry. I could easily see why folks thought this city was a place where coloreds had an easier time of it. We saw nicely dressed people going about their lives and not just in the colored parts of town. Then before heading back to Sally's, I bought gifts for my daughter and all the women. There was a store-bought blouse for Lelia; perfume and hair bows for Lucille, Becky and Eula Mae; a porcelain wall plate with a painted picture of Ireland for Sally and a small oriental chest for Ma Mere. John paid for them all.

It was quiet the afternoon we arrived back. John stopped at the front door, left his bag there for me to carry up and went off to a meeting where he said they'd be waiting.

I slipped in so I could quickly arrange the gifts around the big table and found Sally there in her kitchen mopping.

"Where is everyone?"

I must have looked funny 'cause Sally's jaw dropped at the sight of me.

"They all walked down to get some buttered toffee from the vendor."

Sally stood frozen with a mop in her hand. Still grinning, I went over to the big table and laid out the gifts and then went over to give her a hand with those potatoes waiting on the counter to be peeled.

"Where have you been? Lelia said she knew you were all right. But I wonder, look at that table. You think it's Christmas, dearie?"

I wanted Sally to guess what I'd been up to, so without a word; I started peeling those potatoes as I waited for her to notice her lovely plate with the picture of Ireland.

But Sally only stared at me like she expected a confession. I looked her straight in the eyes and shaved a potato peel at her. Then flung a few more her way like I was tossing firecrackers at her feet. She never budged. I was getting ready to tell her where I'd been when a potato peel hit her face. She just stared at the crazy woman who was standing there in my shoes. Guess that was when my senses started trickling back.

"Till now, I'd seen every condition known. But woman, what are you sufferin' from over there with the flyin' potato peels?"

I held the potato I was peeling up to the light so she could see the wedding band on my finger.

"Well then I guess I know where you've been and don't it got something to do with John? Hey?"

"Did you get it out of Lelia?" I asked.

"No, Lelia never said a word."

"Who told you then?"

Sally stared down at the potato peelings at her feet.

"Ruthie, honey. Ruthie!"

"Ruthie? Who's she?"

"You know, I figure John's got an idea!" Sally replied.

"John and me, we got married in Denver."

I announced with a smile still frozen on my face.

"Did you, now?" Sally hardly looked pleased. "Then it's worse than I imagined. I best be the one to tell you then. Even standing here in this kitchen, you are as lost as a child can be."

"Child?"

Sally took the mop over to the back door and tossed it out. Shaking her head, she seemed to struggle for the words she would use to belt me back to reality.

"What do you mean, lost? Lost my senses?"

I had a notion that to hide my condition I'd best gather up them peels and quickly did.

"Come here child, 'cause the party is over for you. Yes, it's time to look at things real close. So, you best take a chair. Go on now. Take one before you fall to that wet floor I just mopped 'cause I got some bad news. Sit still while I get us a whiskey to ease what we gotta face here."

Sally's head shook as she combed the cupboard for a bottle.

I tossed the peeler in the sink and sank into the nearest chair waiting to hear what I knew by Sally's expression was sure to be awful news.

"Ruthie, she's a nice young woman. Gots big dark eyes and her nappy hair's pulled back under that crocheted hat. Little cap that's got holes all over it but guess it keeps the cold out better than nothin'. But maybe not then, hey, dearie?

"Sally, who's Ruthie?"

"She come here 'cause her landlady wants her out of her place down by the tracks," Sally said. "Seems like Ruthie's rent money got stolen."

"Stolen?" I asked.

"And she had a baby on her arm," Sally added. "That one is only a child herself, but she gots one."

"Who stole her rent money, Sally?"

"Who, dearie? Her baby, his name is John and he looks just like his daddy. I know, 'cause they sat right here at my table while I fed their empty bellies. Got a good look at that pretty little boy."

"Lord, what are you tellin' me? It's about my John then?"

I knew by the way Sally fed me this bad news that she was trying to bring me down easy-like.

"John, he ain't what he appears to be," Sally said cautiously like she'd just delivered the worst news of her life.

I gulped on them words and tried to push the platter of bad tidings away by reiterating what the women had told me over and over.

"He's a business man. A successful man, ain't he? Sure he is. He's good to me, Sally."

Sally looked at me with all the sympathy she could muster and then tried to tell me plain, like a good friend would have. Yes, I knew I was in trouble. Think I'd rather have been certified crazy than to hear what that woman had to say because I had too much respect for Sally not to know she was right.

"Ruthie told me that John, he cleaned her out of her rent money just before you took off on your little escapade."

We both looked at the ring I was anxiously twisting on my finger. Along with it, I wondered if that woman's money went to pay for all the gifts I'd just put in front of us that suddenly no longer seemed special.

"Honey, I don't like talkin' about my boarder's business, but that man owes me six months' rent," she said.

"Six months? You said he paid you three months in advance when he moved in," I replied.

"That was nine months ago. He ain't paid a nickel since. And sure, he's good to you, honey. He's good to all the women, which appears to be his business—if you get my drift. The women here, Becky, Eula Mae and Lucille, you've seen the way they flirt. But why haven't you seen 'em toss that man back and forth like a lapdog gots fleas? Yes, Ma'am, and then hightail it out the door clutching their pocketbooks tight. These women are as silly as magpies, but they still saw through the man. So, what day did you wake up blind to that man?

I sank deeper into my chair like I'd fallen over the edge of that bottomless well I thought, with John I'd scooted further away from. Yes, further and further, down, down, down my heart sank. My tongue was as numb as my thoughts so there was no more big talk to come out of my mouth.

For the longest time, Sally sat there patting my hand gone cold with the ring Ruthie's money bought still on my finger.

"Well, I bet there's a pile of ironin' down there waitin'. Sally, tell Lelia I'm home when she gets back."

Sally nodded.

I stood up feeling as if all the blood had drained out of me and headed down to the laundry to sort my thoughts. And sob. How could a man steal the rent money of his own child's ma? Did somebody get it all wrong? I mean somebody other than me? I cried in a rag down in that dark basement where by then I felt like I'd spent half my life. Don't let it be true, Lord, I kept repeating till I was only biting my lip with anger.

Down there were several piles of clean folded clothes waiting for the iron. So, all cried out, I heated a couple of irons and pounded my ironing board the same way my thoughts were pounding my throbbing head. What could I possibly do now? Why did I jump onboard with this man or had I only blindly followed him down the very path he led me? Was it 'cause I was too hungry to have a home of my own? Lord, Lord, what about that poor woman, Ruthie and her baby? Well, I'd gotten through hell at high tide before; I'd get through this bout.

First, I figured I couldn't take on anything but making sure my girl got into college. I wouldn't let anyone take that dream down. I hoped, even if just a little, that John was not really up to nothing with another woman. You know how everyone calls a color differently as they see it through their own eyes. So, I determined I'd stay quiet 'bout things for a few days while I kept my eye on John. But the image of Ruthie and her hungry baby at Sally's table, where I'd come hungry myself years before, only got me worked up more. I guess it was a day or two later when I decided to confront John and kept at him to see how his tales would meet the truth when introduced.

"I been tellin' you, I ain't her baby's daddy!" he said again. "She don't know who the daddy is, so she give 'im my name is all. The way I see it, there ain't no harm in that!"

I put it to him again.

"She says you stole her rent money."

"She says, or Sally say? Huh?"

"Only you and me here talking now, John. Did you?"

"I been givin' her a hand for some time, else she'd be out on the streets," he claimed. "She just paid me back 'fore we left for Denver is all."

"Where's she now, John, or don't you know?"

"I said, she told me she gots some money to pay me back. Now, how's that stealin'?"

"Her landlady don't care what deal the two of you had; she gots to have 'er rent money. You hear me?"

"Sure. I'll head over 'er place tonight and fix things. But I ain't her baby's daddy."

I was determined that John did exactly as he said, except it wouldn't be a late-night visit. No, I headed with him to the woman's place the following morning. I had to see myself what I could now that my eyes were wide open.

John knocked at her rickety door and Lord help me; I knew right when this young woman opened her door and looked at John with that smile that he'd been lying. Could see it in her eyes. He was her man and that baby, just as Sally said, was his all right. I saw to it that Ruthie had the money John brought. Some he'd borrowed from his business partners and some he borrowed from me, so she could get the landlady off her back and put some food on her table.

John, usually quiet, went to rattling off about this and that all the way back to Sally's, but I had no mind to listen to more of his crap. All I could think on was getting my girl in school and then I'd fix John clean for what he'd done. I'd do it in on my own accord only when Lelia was not around to see any blood-letting that I knew was likely to be. In figuring what I would do to rid myself of John, guess what drove me hardest, was that feeling of having been taken down by the shame of it all. Like Sally said, these women with carnivals of bows in their hair only snickered in the face of the man I then turned 'round and married! How did it all happen? Was I the one that wanted to keep our wedding a secret? Or was it really John's insistence to protect himself from the intrusion of these women's common sense? What did ever'body think of me now? Did I shame my daughter for being so stupid? Well, I had to put that all aside to sort later. I had to work extra hard to make up for the money I loaned John to give to Ruthie and that meant even longer days down there ironing.

It was the following week when I returned to our room to find John all stretched out on the bed with his suspenders hanging and half bottle of whiskey next to him.

It was the same picture Jesse had composed so many times before.

"What's the matter, honey?"

He asked and then shut his eyes to me to drift back to his snooze. Maybe, maybe not, but I thought there was a slur in his voice. John never drank much in front of me before; just a sip now and again. And so I was now counting the secrets to see how they'd match up with all the lies.

"Sometimes I think I got me something to hold on to and then, you know, then I wake up and find it's all a bad dream. Well, John, you look all tired out tonight. That business meetin' you headed off to this afternoon plum wear you out?"

"What? Huh? Ah, honey, you know it did. I gots to slow down some. You got my supper ready?" he said as he buried his face in the pillow with one more utterance. "Yeah and get me a clean shirt. I got to go see some business associates tonight. Might not be back till late so don't wait up for me."

I'm telling you, it was all I could do not to grab his belt off the headboard and lay it to him. I nearly bit my tongue so determined was I not to vent my rage; I would deal with this man only after my girl was safely off. But the time would come, and I was winding the clock for it.

From that day on began what was for John a long nap but for me many sleepless nights. In the weeks ahead, he would be waiting there for my attendance even as my helping hand no longer showed palm up. He had nothing to put on our table but leftover lies and it didn't take long before I found myself gagging on them.

Somewhere in my long days over the tubs I paused in my burdens to write Sister a letter. Annie wrote me that Louvenia held these notes in her pocket till she could stop by and read them to her. A letter became her lifeline to family and hope, even if it was just hope for Lelia and me and not so much for herself.

"Dear Sister," I wrote, "We got your letter the other day. Lelia read it to me while I ironed a shirts. She looks like her daddy and acts like him too, doing just as she fancies these days. Soon she'll be finishing high school and then, God willing college. Her daddy's tobacco tin is near full with tightly rolled bills."

"I still get up at dawn to get the water boiling. You know I never eat nothing mornings 'cause the smell of sorting clothes a working man's worn all week puts me off eating that early. I don't mind the hours; least what I make goes into Lelia's education tin but sometimes that lye soap eats into my hands so bad they bleed. I wrap them up and start in on the ironing till the bleeding stops and then I go back to my tub. But then I guess you know what my day looks like. You walked the same miles yourself. Them miles between our tubs where the air gets thin, don't it? But I can still breathe. I remember you saying once that a woman's day is reflected right back at her from her tub of stinking washtub water. Then you drain it and fill it again. Well, ain't it so? The worst pain is my heart is knowing you haven't seen our Lelia growing up. Every day I still look and pray for word from you on Brother. It's real hard to make it these days. Sometimes it seems the Lord don't remember us. Guess there's too many poor folk for Him to fool with us, too. When He does think on us again, I hope it's to bring us together once more. I pray on it every night and know our prayers meet along the way to the Lord's ears!"

About then Eula Mae had wandered down to the basement to work the tubs but only for a few minutes. You see her skills were more that of a consummate performer than a laundress. Yes, she'd put on the act of being a tub woman for a few moments waiting for the water to heat and then slip off stage again to tell ever'body how exhausted she was and would likely need a day of rest to recover.

But that morning I wasn't in no mood for it. Since my water was already hot, I poured some into her tub where she'd dumped some shirts so she'd know I meant for her to get busy.

"Ouchy! Why you got that water so damned hot?" Eula Mae whined. "We's washin' clothes, not scaldin' feathers off a turkey bird, woman! What's wrong? You look sad."

"My sister writes that Alex, somebody told Annie they think they seen 'im. It's got Louvenia worked up hoping for the best."

"How long he been gone?" Eula Mae asked.

"Long, long time now. Use to be that Sister got a postcard but not for a long spell." I told her. "I got this feelin', bad feelin' somethin' happened to him."

"No, nothin' happened if they seen 'im 'gain. He gone off for work—when he makes lots of money, he gonna head home like any man. They's all alike," she said pretending to wash some shirts with barely her pinkie finger swishing them rags in her tub.

"Where have you ever heard of a colored man goin' off somewhere to find his riches? Where in hell would that be?"

"Now, don't get all worked up. You just been worryin' 'bout Lelia going off to school, so you see bad things all 'round that ain't really-really."

"Really-really, is it? Do tell."

Eula Mae hadn't been there five minutes before she was planning her escape.

"What I'm tellin' you is that I can't work this here tub if the water's so damned hot! Guess I gots to wait till it cools."

"You goin' to the big meetin'?" I asked. "The National Association for the Advancement of Colored People, they's callin' it. They say Mrs. Booker T. Washington'll be there in person. She been in the papers," I informed Eula Mae as she couldn't read.

"Lucille tol' me she's half Booker's age. Anyway, he gots to be rich if he's in the papers all the time. That's what Becky say even if you say there ain't no such thing as rich colored folks."

"Don't know nothin' 'bout Booker," I said.

"Well, I expect all they's really advancin' is the collection plate. Guess then I'll head 'cross-town to visit my momma that night. You know how she's been ailin'. When you say you're going again?"

"Sunday night."

"How long you gonna be there?" she asked.

"How should I know? I ain't never been to no big meetin' like that what with Mrs. Booker T. Washington in person. Think of that! She's as famous as some white folks, ain't she?"

I was only jabbering to myself as Eula wasn't much interested in anything wearing a skirt.

Shortly after Eula Mae escaped for the evening, I went back up to my room to find John also gone. But had he ever truly been there?

Tears That Stain So Blue

50

Lord, how the weeks folded into months that seemed as long gone as the pages of a calendar I'd long tossed away. What is this month? This June? No, it's July! And tomorrow is August already… The only thing that truly mattered was my daughter and getting her ready for college.

John and I came to an accord of sorts. He'd be paying rent and putting money in the pot or find his things tossed out onto street. I knew that once Lelia was away, I'd see how a woman divorced her husband. John had made it amply clear he'd be going no place soon, including to work. So, I clearly knew that it wasn't gonna end easy for us. John had it too good at Sally's to leave like any man with self-respect. I talked this out with Sally and Ma Mere. They didn't like John, but understood I was chained to him till I could cut my foot off and somehow escape. I knew there'd be bloodletting that I didn't want my girl to be witness to. They understood.

Over the months that followed there were scant few things that kept me going. But I still possessed a mule's determination that I'd get Jeff's tobacco tin filled for Lelia's education and the need to keep Louvenia going with the small bits of money I could send her way. I tried hard, very hard, to set aside the thoughts that I might never see my sister again and wept when that voice in my head reminded me it had already been years since I'd walked off Jeff's porch leaving her behind. Seeing Sister ain't gonna happen in my life, the voice in my head drummed. So, beat down was Louvenia, I couldn't help wonder if she was gonna die before our smiles found a way to each other.

One day I was sitting down in the laundry at my little table where I always escaped to read my letters and pulled out a letter Sally had handed me that morning. There was something in that envelope that sounded like grains of sand. I didn't recognize the writing on the envelope, but it was addressed to me. I opened it and there was nothing inside but scads of flower seeds. No written words. Just flower seeds. Yet didn't that say it all? Yes, I knew who'd sent that letter. Maybe Annie wasn't around to write for Sister, but still I knew them seeds were from Jeff's gravesite. They missed me: Sister and Jeff. I thanked the Lord that the postman, who only went by Sisters 'bout every other month, was kind enough to copy my address on that envelope for Sister.

How I wondered during those moments if those seeds were only the last of our dying dreams; of no more value than last spring's dead flowers. Or were they going to be new hopes? Perhaps come the day the nobodies gonna become the somebodies and we will see them bloom.

No, it had not been a good week for any of us. We shared our troubles at breakfast that Sunday before heading to church. Lucille had been looking for work again. She was a tiny woman and most places she looked were wanting women who could work like mules and knew to keep her mouth shut like one. She finally landed a job at the tubs off Magnolia, not far from Minnie's. So scared was she that she'd be late that she went extra early every day.

The woman who headed the tubs was mean, maybe even meaner than Minnie. She hired her mules to labor over her filthy tubs and barely let them look up from that stinking water, let alone jabber up and down the rows. No, at her place, there'd be no chatting, no singing between the tubs to make the hours go faster.

Lucille never had much control over her mouth; even less when she was nervous or frightened. That head tub woman, a big colored woman with hands and arms like a man's, didn't touch nothing filthy herself. She just walked up and down the rows of tubs glaring at the women. Lucille tried to make nice with her. Everybody knew how charming and funny Lucille was. But the boss-woman didn't take to it. Lucille said this woman scared her so that one time she peed herself and stood there soiled all day. Then after only a couple of weeks, over which Lucille cried herself to sleep most nights, she got fired. Lord, doesn't that sound easy? Firing somebody that gots nothing but her friends at Sally's to count on. But it wasn't easy-like. That head tub woman thought Lucille was disrespecting her when she slipped and went jabbering her mouth off 'bout this or that. After a couple of warnings, the woman backhanded her. Sister Lucille landed against the wall. The swing put her out cold on the wet stone floor with one of her teeth lying next to her bleeding lip. Later one of the other women told Lucille that the boss woman glared at them if they thought to go over and help her; she lying there on that cold-damp floor till she finally awoke not knowing what had happened.

Breakfast that Sunday was the quietest I'd ever sat through. We were all waiting for her. Lucille was last to come down that morning.

"You goin' to church, honey?" Eula Mae asked.

Lucille's face was badly bruised and swollen. But her hair was fixed with her favorite carnival bow. She was going!

"It don't matter none what people think," she said. "I ain't ashamed of my face. I didn't knock myself down."

"You go on to church, Lucille!" Sally prompted.

Sally had been the one to ice Lucille's face the night before.

"You go on; sit tall in the pew so the Lord can see what that woman did to you!" Eula Mae said.

"Yeah, but that woman's goin' to hell so she don't care if Jesus knows she's mean!" Becky added. "No, she sure don't or she'd not hit Lucille, would she?"

"We best put the fear of the Lord into that bitch with one of Sally's carvin' knives!" Eula Mae suggested.

"Oh, hush, Eula Mae," Sally responded. "You couldn't carve a roasted chicken waiting on a platter in front of you with a knife stuck in it!"

"You gonna run down there and tell that big ol' tub woman that? Huh?" Eula Mae asked. "We all gonna head down there right now with big knives in each hand to see what we gonna see! Yeah! See what the big woman thinks when she sees us comin' for 'er! She gonna belt all three of us to the wall?"

"I bring a broom and knock 'er in the head with it," Becky added. "Broom, so I don't got to get too close to 'er!"

"Lord, would you listen to the three of you!" Sally said. "Are you marching for tub women, jail or the center pew in hell?"

"We just gonna march, that's all there is to it!" Eula Mae replied. "Guess wherever that big boss woman's hidin', we're gonna head that way!"

Bravado aside, it was plainly clear that we'd all stand up for Lucille but so many other tub women faced even worse assaults and nobody marched a single step for them. Nobody came to their rescue. to bandage their wounds or feed their kids while they healed.

We would hear about one of these later that morning at church.

Becky, Eula Mae and Lucille with her bruises and me headed to church. Don't know if I'd ever spent that many moments with these women in such howling silence. It was truly a blue day. What a sorry sight we were. I didn't bother ironing my dress for church that morning. I'd been arguing with that damned iron all week and couldn't face no more of its lip. Anyway, there was a warm rain that morning that delivered a thick humidity. Never seen so many straw hats go limp. My crinkled dress—along with my hair the rain caused to kink—made me look like a crazy woman on the march and I didn't feel much better on the inside.

In more ways than one, the Preacher looked drenched, too. He wiped the rain off his brow and neck or was that sweat? then looked at the floorboards for the longest time. There was something astir. One by one the fans up and down the pews stopped fluttering and dropped to our laps. Even our tongues stalled somewhere in all that brewing silence. The choir, not knowing what to do, started the opening hymn but the Preacher waved them to silence. Something was out of order. Something was terribly wrong. The Preacher's words jarred us against the fragility of our lives. Another life had been taken; a piece of humanity ripped to shreds and then tossed back in the faces of the family that mourned empty handed and from then on, empty bellied.

"Yesterday Henry Smith was accused of raping a five-year-old white girl child. But this man was known to be in another county when the crime happened. Made no difference. Not to the law. With knives drawn, they waited in the shadows for him to return home. They hauled him into town like an animal to the slaughter. There at the jail Henry Smith was tortured with red hot pokers. Such is the staggering depths of white hatred; a hatred that could only burn hotter in hell itself."

Your body can die by a hot poker, yet you will not die 'cause your heart is bleeding to death from the words only. Hearing those stabbing syllables that ends in… 'hot poker' and you feel death lurking. The kind that always lurked in the souls of some white folks.

"Henry Smith was then burned to death," the Preacher continued. "Lord, Jesus Christ, save us—that was not all. White schoolchildren were given a holiday so they could come to town and watch this poor man being burned alive. Trains, special trains were scheduled for the convenience of spectators. Despite the torture he endured, it took Henry Smith a horridly long time to die as the white folks wanted to deprive him of the mercy of death for as long as their hatred could prolong the agony. He pled for mercy as his arms and legs burned black from the fire. But these white folks, they savored the spectacle too much for it to end mercifully. It took a long time before the flames finally lifted Henry Smith's soul to where Jesus waited."

We sat there in stony silence like rows of gravestones expecting to be kicked over. Kicked over by the Klan. Even if the doors had been nailed shut and the roof put on fire, as was the pleasure of the Knights of the White Camellia all over the South, no one could budge. I don't think we could have run for our lives so frozen in our seats were we.

The preacher wiped his eyes and continued his words. He choked. Through our sobs his words were barely audible.

"After Henry's life was finally released to the Lord the crowds fought over his charred bones as souvenirs."

Becky held my shaking hand. I didn't know the face of Henry Smith, but I did the face of Jeffrey McWilliams, a young father; the father of my daughter and the keeper of the orchard of my heart.

"So, I ask you, where was the law?" the Preacher continued. "Was the law hiding from justice again? No! The law was there directing the mob to watch a human being burned alive! What must we do to break the silence of our leaders when our people are murdered?"

The sermon ended on the word that had shadowed me ever so long. Lynched!

In silence we walked out. What was there to say? Still hadn't we all heard the Preacher's announcement nearly daily from each other, or read it in the weeklies? The Preacher's question, "where is justice?" echoed in our churches, our schools and then tossed unrelentingly in our dreams, the place I'd always find Jeffrey still waiting for me to answer him… Why me?

It was still a very long time before I could share with the women at Sally's what happened to Jeffery that night now a half a lifetime ago and yet nearly that morning once again. Some black dreams shadow you to the very end.

Sally had put some ham and freshly baked bread out for sandwiches, but no one could eat. We couldn't do much of anything and disappeared into our rooms.

Ever since John and I were married Lelia was in a little room down the hall from ours that Sally could never find a boarder for. She and Ma Mere had fixed it up nicely. Eula Mae remarked it was something right out of New Orleans. Even had a Japanese scarf Lelia and Ma got at the carnival which was draped fancy-like over her bed. Sometimes I visited her room to enjoy her magic and get away from John, the tubs, or whatever my thoughts were tripping over.

It was late one day in the laundry when I looked down into that tub of water but simply could not move. The face that stared back tightly held me in her grip. I stood there watching my sweat pouring down my forehead and into that tub filled with indigo-colored overhauls. The reflection of my weary face down in that water was a gauzy blue-gray. I wondered who that tired old woman was looking back? For a moment, I even had a notion my tears were blue as they got lost in that water. I told myself, there ain't no such thing as blue tears even if everything in me felt blue as that tub water. Don't even know how long I stood there weeping.

Late that night I decided to visit Lelia in her room to see how her homework was doing. I hoped listening to my daughter's reading would soothe my mind as I often heard Jeff's voice weaving through hers. As I lay across her bed I felt something dark chasing my peace of mind. For days I'd had this nervous feeling like the nigger dogs had to be closing in on me again. I sighed deeply.

My daughter paused and looked at me intently, then went on read- ing. Maybe I'd been on run too long to escape my fears. I wondered if this was the time when them dogs were gonna take me down 'cause welling up in me was a pounding gush. There'd be no bitter truce, no postponement of the pain and, sure as hell, no hiding from it.

"Momma, I just read that same sentence four times to see if you were really listening. But you didn't notice, did you?"

Hadn't I? At that moment, all I saw was the wife of that man burned alive; this poor woman, maybe a tub woman like me. I could see Henry Smiths wife running as hard as she could just to feed her kids and them only dipping up a ladle of nothing to put on their plates. I wondered how she slept nights without him. I know how it is to sleep without your man; wondering in those wakeful hours where he waited and then him slipping through that blue haze to crossover and caress your dreams again.

I took a deep breath as I felt my heart seem to pound out of my chest. What I'd heard, but did not know I'd heard, was that my daughter needed my attention. I had to ease my gyrating thoughts somehow. Yes, again I had to kick the nigger dogs far enough from my weariness to deal with the moment at hand.

"Yes, I did hear," I said. "And the second time was best! I know it was."

"Momma, you've been so sad lately. What's wrong? Is it John?"

"Nothing, dear. You don't need to take on my burdens."

"Then I guess you don't need to take on mine then."

"What?"

Lelia was like Jeff the way her words could make me come out of myself.

"Momma, I only read that sentence once."

She laid her book down next to us on the bed.

"Are you worried about me going away to school?"

I took a deep breath but still felt myself suffocating. I was simply too empty inside for anything but a gasp. All I wanted to do was fall into a tub and drown myself in my blue tears.

Then it happened. At first I couldn't even breathe. When were the waters rising? Where were the warning signs that the undercurrents of my days were pulling me under? And for how long had I not been hearing my daughter's voice calling? I'd been slipping down a cliff and right in front of me I faced that avalanche of emotions that I'd refused to acknowledge for ever so long. Swallow me, Lord! I can't find a bottomless well deep enough to hold all my despair!

I started sobbing. Sobbed so hard I thought my stomach was gonna wretch out in front of my terrorized child; a gruesome pool of despair at her feet. I didn't just cry, I wailed and wailed. Lelia was duly terrified. She screamed and went for Sally and Ma while I buried myself deeper in her pillow to stop the hemorrhage of sobs that soon rolled me to the floor.

Sally ran in followed by Ma Mere. They eased me back up on the bed.

"Been workin' too hard again, Sarah? Don't you know yet—folks still gonna get by even if their clothes aren't ironed up just perfect?" Sally said.

Ma stood blubbering and fanned her little hankie over my face.

"Sure they is, honey!"

"Ma, for god's sake. Sarah ain't havin' a heat stroke. Put that damned hanky away and go get her a whiskey to calm her nerves."

"I'm going to get ya a whiskey, Sarah."

Sally mopped my sobs with her dish towel as Eula Mae and Lucille appeared with Becky just behind. They huddled at the door to see the commotion. Sally reached over with her foot and slammed the door closed in their faces.

"Sometimes I just get so weary and lonely," I sobbed. "Don't see how I can take another day at the tubs. I'm gonna die, then what about Lelia? What about my sister? Them wash tubs done killed better women than me. Just like the fields killed my momma and daddy. They weren't even my age."

Lelia wept and tried to comfort me.

"Don't know how to hold on to Momma's dreams," I wept. "I failed your grandparents. I took the only thing they could give me, their dreams and someplace I lost 'em. Lost their precious dreams. I know I have!"

"No, dearie, you ain't lost nothin' but a few nights of sleep. That's all it is." Sally patted my back as though I was a child. "Go on and let it all out for a good cleansing," she said. "The blues will be ten shades lighter once you've had some rest. Lelia, open the door and tell them women to go to back to their rooms. Then you best go stir the stew. Your Momma's gonna be fine after some rest. That's all it is."

"Momma…" was all Lelia could say.

From shame, I couldn't look her in the eyes. Lelia went downstairs as Ma returned with a whiskey. Ma was crying louder than me by then and waving her chubby hands in the air over my head like she could wave away all the pain.

"There ain't nothin' a few days of rest won't fix for you, honey. And I'm gonna do all your ironin', too!" Ma announced.

"Ain't that just what she needs now?" Sally said. "For you to go down there to the laundry and ruin her business by putting an iron to it. You go get the full bottle of whiskey in the bottom drawer under the towels and two more glasses. And leave the damned ironin' to us, Ma!" Sally's bark was followed by a wink.

Ma was hardly chagrined. "Now, don't start up with me, Sally. Just 'cause Sarah's in bad shape don't mean I won't give you the same."

"You're gonna stay right here, Sarah. Ma and I will bring up a cot for Lelia to sleep on bit later."

Well, I couldn't move from bed for days. Don't know how long as the time only floated by me. But, thanks to my sisters, so did the floodwaters of my soul.

Don't know if John ever wondered what was going on, where or why. Didn't matter no more.

⁓

Winter crept up on us that year as fast as the frost covered the ground where we hung clothes. I knew I was getting better when I worried about Sally feeding me so much. I mostly just stayed in bed and read or talked to Lelia. While I was in that room, all the women spent long hours in the basement to keep things going. Becky told me that Sally even set up an iron in her kitchen to work piecemeal as she cooked our meals. We got by. Yet I had to get back down there and get to work myself. John told Sally he had so many things going he couldn't come down the hall to see how I was doing. She said he'd asked after me but then only walked off before she got a word out.

With me still staying in Lelia's room, it turned into weeks before I saw John again. But this time I could really see him for what he was.

I was back down at the tubs wrapping my hands in gauze; the lye soap had burned them bad after being away when he walked in.

"That lye soap eat into your hands? Here, drink some of this and watch your pains go away."

John offered a bottle in a paper bag.

"Yeah? You watch your pains go away and I end up seein' 'em headed my way! What's the matter, John, you got pains somewhere nobody heard of?"

"I ain't down here to get into it with you," he said. "We're over that now, ain't we?"

"Yeah, well, I know what whiskey can do. I seen it. I lived it. We don't have no money for bottles."

John took particularly long swig and then looked me like he dared me to do something about it.

"You know I been laid up, got to catch up on my pennies for Lelia's college. She's going off in less than a month and you still owe me for the money I gave Ruthie."

"Savin'! Is that all you ever think 'bout? Sick of this savin' for Lelia's schoolin'. What's a colored girl need college for? To be a tub woman? Huh? There are plenty better things to put that money on and that's for damned sure! They're called investments!"

Lord, how these words echoed those I'd heard so many times before. His words sifted with the same tone that came out of white folks' mouths. His notion that women were destined only to be tub women; to serve a man's needs while still doing the work that truly put the food on the table he somehow thought he was head of.

"No, we ain't gonna have that talk again," I said as I squeezed the suds out of them old overhauls like I was wringing a fat pig's neck. Or was it John's?

"We'll talk on anything I got a mind to." His remark was followed by a belch in my face. "You do what you want with your money; she's your girl, not mine. Right now, I'm goin' huntin' for some sweet companionship. Somebody not living just to save up for some dream that don't add up!"

"From what I know, sweet companionship cost money. Where's it comin' from?"

John stood erect as was his custom when he had some new pronouncement on his big-man money schemes.

"I been workin' on something with my partners. Yeah, we figure we're gonna come out just fine on this deal. And it ain't gonna come soon enough to my thinkin'."

John walked out with half a bottle of manly pride poured down his throat. But I didn't care about his secret deals because I knew I could look into any garbage pail and see his pile of discarded rotting schemes waiting for the next big man to come along and harvest.

Comes Grace

51

For weeks we longed for the night when we'd go see Mrs. Booker T. Washington in person. From the weeklies Lucille had cut every picture of the woman and pinned them all over the kitchen so we could talk about Mrs. Washington's clothes. That special night we couldn't eat fast enough at supper, which was good as that evening Sally was screaming her head off at Ma Mere. Seems that Ma got tired of Sally's carping on the housework she never got done, and in particular the ironing, and decided she'd had enough and was going to do something about it.

It all started as we were finishing supper. Nobody knew why Ma Mere wasn't at the table till she walked in holding Sally's best blouse, her favorite one with the Irish lace down the front. She held it high in one hand and brandishing an iron like a weapon in the other.

Sally was about to put a fork in her mouth when she glimpsed Ma standing there waving her blouse like a war trophy. That thing was scorched so badly nobody knew what she was waving as some of them brown holes were burned through the once fine cream-colored linen. The fork headed for Sally's mouth never made as she realized the kill Ma was waving was once her best blouse. Sitting there aghast, only her face turning strawberry-red proved she'd not turned to stone. Ma Mere got in the first word.

"You women want me to press your dresses to go see Mrs. Booker tonight? I got the iron heated up good n' hot now, don't I, Sally? See, looky here!"

Ma dabbed a finger of spit on it. Lordy, that iron hissed like a feral cat.

"Don't come near me crazy woman!" Becky blurted and jumped from the supper table waving the stench of Sally's scorched blouse away with her napkin.

"Look what Ma Mere has up and done!" Lucille exclaimed. "I always knew she had a bit of the devil in 'er!"

"Yeah, well now it's my turn to do some meaness!" Sally informed us.

Sally eyes were glued to Ma's like two cats in the alley. She went over to the counter to select her weapon. Oh, Lord, I was glad the knives had been put away! The only thing lying on the counter was the potato peeler but there was a big bowl of them potatoes next to it. And if Sally didn't hurl them at Ma's head throwing with both fists as hard as she could. Ma squealed like a suckling pig as the rest of us fled to our rooms.

While the carnage continued in the kitchen, we all got dolled up for the meeting downtown. Except Lelia, who was finishing her homework and Eula Mae who got dressed up real nice, and wearing lots of Becky's nickel-and-dime store perfume and headed off to visit her ailing ma.

Lucille, Becky and I could still hear the potatoes bouncing off the walls and ceiling in the kitchen when we slipped out the front door.

❧

I looked forward to this meeting of the National Association of Colored Woman at St. Paul's American Methodist Episcopal Church. Becky had informed us dozens of times that just for coming they'd have a table of free refreshments laid out. According to Preacher Lucille, that's how they'd get us there to pick our pockets.

"I ain't never ate a piece of free cake that didn't cost me ever' penny I had in my pockets!" she said. "While you're feedin' your mouth with one hand, they's holding the other to see what's in it for them."

We got to the hall a bit late and I was glad of it 'cause by then we had to stand in the rear where I could more easily see over the big-hat ladies. I 'magine lots of folks came early to get up close to the front. Never seen such a grand place before. Must have been the biggest hall in the city with huge incandescent lights overhead. The place was filled with coloreds looking like they'd all been shopping for their outfits at the white folks' stores.

I'd never seen a famous colored woman. Maybe Mrs. Washington was the only one. She'd been in all the colored weeklies and was married to one of the most famous men I'd ever heard of, which I figured meant she was mighty formidable herself. I'd read that like me, she was the daughter of sharecroppers—come from a family of ten kids. That woman surely knew what a meal from a pot of mush was. Then a man, who looked too young to own such a fine suit, walked out on the platform and stood there till ever'body finally shut their mouths. And ever'body did except Lucille, but you know 'bout her. If she could preach alongside the preacher, no telling what she'd do alongside Mrs. Washington, whom she held to be her very best friend by the way she talked about the woman. Yes, Mrs. Booker and Lucille went way, way back… at least to some missing page from of one of Lucille's many tales.

"You know her," the finely dressed man said. "You've heard of what she's done for our people. She's president of the National Federation of Afro-American Women and President of the National Association of Colored Women; I give you, Margaret Murray Washington."

The applause came like a rolling thunder on a hot summer night. 'Cept from Lucille. She was gonna hold off till she saw for sure if Mrs. Washington would really show. After all, if she didn't they'd likely cancel the cake and punch. But then the great woman glided onto the stage looking every bit like her pictures in the weeklies. I can still remember the hush that came over the hall as she took center stage like a majestic queen with her chin high with dignity. Lord, I wondered if she got all that grace because her work called her to be that way? On the other hand, did she get to be up there because she started out real special to begin with? I could see how much impact this woman had before she even opened her mouth. I figured if she spoke even a bit better than

Lucille, which wasn't hard, Becky and I could go home after our free cake and would one day tell our grand kids about this night.

Mrs. Washington commenced speaking when she was sure the folks were done looking her over. And, no, her voice was not all nasal-squeaky like Lucille's. Mrs. Washington's was calm like she knew she possessed the power to command the seas if she had a mind to, or, in the least, a hall of antsy folks like us.

When Mrs. Washington spoke, she looked right at me. Right in my eyes, I know she did, too.

"We live in difficult times," Mrs. Washington commenced. "Times when our people struggle against enormous odds to participate in a society that has always denied us equal rights."

I imagine people's thoughts were frozen to her words as they lilted from her mouth because it all stayed quiet.

I whispered to Lucille: "You ever seen so much grace? Even right in front of all them folks lookin' her over and all."

But Lucille tended to see different shades to most everything.

"With that corset on, how'd you stand up there, honey?"

Lucille was loud enough folks in front of us shushed her.

"That woman couldn't bend over if Booker told 'er to."

I paid Lucille no mind as I came for the other performance. Mrs. Washington also ignored Lucile and continued speaking.

"For Negro women, there is another kind of prejudice we bear beyond that from white folks and it comes from our own men who also deny us equality."

"You mean I have something in common with Mrs. Washington," I whispered for my own benefit.

Lucille couldn't contradict Mrs. Washington but she could me. Lucille grunted at my preposterous notion.

"What? You honey? Huh!"

"A preacher told me once that women folk that pursued higher education risk losing their babies in childbirth."

Mrs. Washington continued but I couldn't hear the rest because Lucille figured she'd add her own views.

"I know that's true," Lucille announced for everyone's benefit. "I ain't ever gonna read nothin' no more!"

There were no "Amens" to my friend's vow of mental poverty.

I turned my attention back to Mrs. Washington.

"Negro women must pursue what they desire for themselves without consideration of the limitations imposed upon us by Negro men and white folks. We don't stand alone; we have each other as colored women and must fight the struggle against ignorance with and for each other. Let our motto be… Lift as we climb."

"Booker teached her that one, 'lift as we climb', 'cause he's a good climber, ain't he?"

Lucille said with a wink. But I don't think Mrs. Washington meant climbing on as she'd conjured.

"Shut your mouth up 'fore I stuff your shoes in it" Becky said, "And I won't be takin' off your damned feet first!"

She jabbed poor Lucille with her elbow. I'd never heard Becky talk that way before. Still, I was thinking just as ugly on our sister.

"I wonder what John Davis would think if he saw a woman like Mrs. Washington?" I whispered. "She's filled with such uncommon grace, ain't she?"

My words were directed to Becky, not Lucille as I didn't want to be responsible for inciting another one of Lucille's sermon's that might get us throwed out.

"I knows what he do if he saw that one up there," Becky said. "But I can't say 'cause I'm a Christian woman."

"Huh!" Is all Lucille could add.

I had no comment. Thank goodness for Mrs. Washington that Lucille ended up in the back of the room that night. Otherwise, Lucille would have climbed up there with her if nothing more than to poke at Mrs. Washington's ribs to prove she wore a whale bone corset.

Well, Becky and I were so mesmerized by Mrs. Washington that we headed home in silence after getting our free cake and punch that Lucille was never gonna leave without.

We proudly walked back like the three of us were Mrs. Washington's best friends now and forever. We knew she was ours, that's for sure. I kept wondering how'd she gotten her hair up so beautiful? And men folk listened to her and not just gawked because she was a woman. I'd never seen such a sight. But I knew I wanted to see more before my days were over if for no other reason than to identify a great woman of color to my daughter. Yes, the sight of that majestic woman filled with grace got a hunger in me that only grew. One to be just like her.

Trying to prolong the evening as long as possible, we paused here and there to glance into shop windows to see if there were any big hats or outfits Mrs. Washington would likely fancy. As late as it was, I was eager to tell Eula Mae about Mrs. Washington.

Becky poked her nose in the back door to see if the potatoes were still bouncing off the kitchen walls. I wasn't worried about Ma, because I knew Sally was really a better shot than the mess of dimples on our plaster walls from all the past flying potatoes suggested. The kitchen was dark, but we could hear Sally and Ma back in their room laughing up a storm as if they hadn't seen each other in ages. Looking back, I seem to remember I peeled an awful lot of bruised potatoes!

Well, knowing John would be sound asleep, I figured I'd go to bed and ponder the entire evening. I left the women in the kitchen and headed down the hall to my room. However, it turned out that the show had only begun!

Sister Eula Mae and Me

52

Poor Eula Mae. There she was naked in my bed with her boobs bouncing and they kept bouncing even after her riding of my husband slowed to take a turn I'd just hit them with.

As I stood in the doorway, she looked puzzled as though she couldn't quite decide if she was gonna dismount or keep John happy going another round. But it was certain that John was still in motion. Yes, he slapped her ass good and getty-up hard so's to get to the end of the track faster. Even with me eyeing her like Minerva would have, I decided I'd help Eula Mae save her herself.

"Well, honey. You waiting till I get the water boilin' to clean up the mess I'm lookin' at?"

I asked Sister in my new Mrs. Washington voice; serene, calm but surely turning red with rage. No, I wasn't clutching momma's ol' rusty scissors but Eula Mae fled the room as though I was. Nearly broke John's stick off. That woman galloped to her own room stomping the floorboards loud enough that I'm sure ever'body knew what she'd been up to!

"I told you I'd find me some companionship," John said like he'd proved me all wrong again. "Guess you must'a figured that didn't mean my men friends!"

Real calmly I asked him.

"Did you take care of Eula Mae, John?"

"What? Did it look like that woman was needin' more?"

He howled laughing.

"Oh, she's gonna get more! I'll deal with that a bit later. What I want to know is did you pay the woman for her time?"

"Pay 'er? Me? For what?"

John asked with all the incredulity he could muster.

I held my chin up with dignity like I had an audience looking up at me between the floodlights waiting for my next words. Got John looking at me like I was in some strange trance or something. But then he was truly seeing me in a new light and he sure didn't like the cast of it.

"You still thinkin' women owe you a free ride?" I demanded. "You get your sorry ass out of that bed and go pay 'er for her time. Now!"

With that I surely sounded more like myself than Margaret Washington.

"Ain't no woman ever told me to get out of bed!" John said looking like he had no intention of doing much of anything.

It was my turn to break out in laughter.

"John Davis, ain't no woman ever seen you out of bed!"

With that I picked up his whiskey bottle and broke the top off on the tabletop next to his head and aimed it at his manhood.

This time John seen his way to getting out of bed with not even a titter coming from his big mouth.

"You go pay 'er or your manhood's gonna be deep fried and fed to you at your next meal."

"I ain't got no money for a place yet," he said under his breath like he didn't want the rest to hear what they all knew anyway. And you know, I think it was the only truthful thing he ever said to me.

"Then you best get down there and earn it by washin' Eula Mae's panties. You don't have any problem gettin' them off 'er, do you?"

John pulled up his suspenders nice and slow to show me he wasn't the man to be pushed around by a woman.

"No, I don't have a problem gettin' panties off no woman," he smirked. "To prove it, I left Eula Mae's right there under your pillow. Go on now and see if they smell as good as when I peeled 'em off 'er!"

At that, the broken whiskey bottle went hurling to John's smug grin. Nearly took his ear off.

He hit the road with what was left of his head still attached. I slammed and locked the door behind him. That night I slept better than I had since meeting the man. I wondered if the others got some sleep because it was so quiet outside my door that I had a feeling they'd all been hanging on my doorknob while John and me were chatting about Sister Eula Mae's little visit.

❦

The next morning Lucille and Becky came back early from church and headed straight to Eula Mae's room since she hadn't voluntarily given herself up. I could hear them from the laundry below; pound, pound, pound, they did on that poor sister's door. They said Eula Mae thought she could peek out, a little hissing would ensue and once concluded, she'd crawl back into bed before it got cold. More than a thousand little tussles were settled up and down the hall that way with a knock, a hiss and then followed by a slammed door or two.

"What's you want this early?" Eula Mae demanded like a Creole princess.

The other Creole princess, Her Righteousness Sister Lucille started in on Eula Mae on the spot.

"You thinkin' 'bout not showin' up for work down in Sarah's laundry? No, Missy, that ain't the way it's gonna be!"

"Seems like you're headed for some hot water, Eula Mae!" Becky said. "That what you heard, Lucille?"

"She was walkin' that direction last night!" Lucille said. "When she took off for her ma's and went and found John's jackpot along the way! That what, honey?"

Guess Lucille and Becky figured they were missionaries for the Lord by catching themselves, in the flesh, a genuine real bad sinner! And since it wasn't one of their sins on the table for the picking over, they clearly aimed to bring Eula Mae to swift judgment.

"What? What's Sarah gonna do to me?" Eula Mae pleaded.

I can't imagine what that poor woman must a' been thinking.

"You're sure in hot water, girl!" Becky announced.

"No, Becky, Sarah's got it boilin' down there'," Lucille chimed. "That water could skin a hog!"

Eula Mae's lip quivered something awful as she was dragged by her ears to the gallows.

"I didn't start nothin'," Eula Mae said expecting these women to cut her some mercy.

"Huh!" was all she got from Lucille. "Didn't start nothin'? Honey, when you strike a match you aim to see fire!"

"John, he got me drunk," Eula Mae whined. "Thought you were over at that meetin'."

Eula Mae was working out her alibis on two seriously skeptical sisters. Yes, Eula Mae was running on empty.

"All while you were at your ailing ma's 'cross town," Becky said. "That what you said? Or did your momma up and die and get buried before John got you drunk last night? How long your ma been dead now, Sister? Four years, as I recall."

Eula Mae was sweating blood. Yes, those two scrawny women pushed Eula Mae all the way down to the basement and into my face. On every step I could hear Sister pleading for mercy but these women only shoved her along like the axman been kept waiting too long.

"He been after me, Sarah," she said when she landed in my face and I believed her but still wasn't interested in the details. No, I had my face rubbed in them the night before.

"You got Miss Wilson's uniforms ironed for her work tomorrow?" I asked.

"What? No, I been busy and….."

I never let the poor woman finish. It came out louder than I expected. That half of the church that had somehow missed Lucille and Becky's account of Eula Mae's fall from grace surely heard it from my mouth this time!

"I know you been busy, busy climbing on my husband! Are you hearin' me good and clear, Sister?"

"Yes, Ma'am. Guess ever'body on this street can hear ya. But I never meant…."

For sure Eula wasn't getting a lifesaver from me!

"You never meant to go to my room and ride my husband?"

"Well, no! But John Davis sure did though. You seen him!"

"Did John pay for last night?" I asked using my Mrs. Washington voice.

"Why, he sure did!" Eula Mae said gleefully. "Gave me an I.O.U. Even signed it!"

"He signed it? Well, now if that doesn't make it good as gold."

"Don't you know only whores take money for that business?" Lucille's big mouth blurted.

"Sarah made 'im pay me!"

"Every woman's been some man's whore some time," I told Eula Mae. "And honey, if there's anything you deserve for last night's bit of business, it's gotta be one of John's I.O.U.s!"

Becky and Lucille quickly slipped out to avoid any work themselves but Lucille returned minutes later to torture Eula Mae with some hot coffee.

Eula Mae was there at her tub sniveling like a baby—her wanting to get to the forgiveness stage of the morning's theatrics as soon as possible and figured her tears and snorts in a rag would speed her on her way to the rites of absolution.

"Here, Eula Mae, here's your coffee, honey."

Eula Mae took the mug and started slurping.

"How comes you put so much cream in it?" Eula Mae whined. "You know I just like a big spoon of sugar!"

Lordy, if that didn't get up Lucille's nose and jump start the second round.

"I would'a figured you'd had all the sugar you could stomach last night, honey," Lucille said. "Anyway, the cream's so's you can't taste that bitter rat poison Becky spooned into that mug!"

Eula spit that coffee out with most of it landing on Lucille. I threw Lucille a rag to mop her face.

"Where's Becky?" I asked.

We all looked up at the ceiling for sounds of footsteps—couldn't hear a creak from up there.

"Oh, I reckon she's dead." Lucille said and went back to slurping her coffee. "You see, for once Becky done what I told 'er. Yep, I told 'er to put a big heapin' spoonful of rat poison in the yella mug for Eula Mae and she have the blue mug for herself, then Eula Mae'd never suspect nothin'. 'Cause I told 'er to put that poison in the yella mug, I knew for sure she'd go and put it in the blue mug just the same, so I poured some poison in the yellow one. Or was it the blue one? 'Bout enough to kill a damned horse! Then that Becky went and drank the blue mug of poison I really, really meant for Sister here. Well, it ain't my fault Becky done what I told 'er this time!" Lucille said dabbing at crocodile tears.

"Becky's up in Sally's kitchen dead?" Eula Mae screeched.

"I reckon 'bout like a doorknob now 'cause she was sure in real agony when I came back down!" Lucille slurped her coffee again. "She was up there jerking somethin' awful on that old cold floor. Ain't nothing I could do after she swallowed her tongue."

"Lord, Lord," Eula Mae said bursting into sobs. "Lord save Becky!"

"Poor Becky, she's up there on Sally's floor tryin' to pull that tongue out'a her throat. Don't know why it was so hard 'cause she had herself a big mouth. Least she won't be sayin' mean things 'bout me no more. She always had a mighty ugly tongue, too. From stickin' it out at folks, huh? Well, she wouldn't want nobody to see her that way. Nope, so, I shoved an apple in 'er mouth."

"You done poisoned Becky?" Eula Mae howled. "And you was really aimin' to poison me 'cause I stole your gold chain," Eula Mae finally confessed. "I know you was!"

"That gold chain? The one that turned green? No, honey," Lucille said between slurps of coffee. "I stole that chain back along with your red glass beads and that little bracelet you been looking for all week!"

"Sit down, Eula Mae, ain't nobody gonna poison you," I told her unconvincingly.

"Then where's Becky? Eula Mae demanded.

With what these women put Eula Mae through, I reckoned she was never gonna speak to a man and probably not another woman for days.

But hallelujah! Moments later Becky rose from the dead, came down to the laundry and God save us, her big mouth was chomping on an apple. Eula Mae's eyes almost popped out like she'd seen Lazarus rise from the dead.

"Eula Mae, I never seen such a sight," I said. "Mrs. Washington, so dignified—standin' up there with a whole lot of people waitin' for her ever' word. What got her to be that way?"

Lucille had her own explanation for the mystery of Mrs. Washington's grace. "Booker made her that way! He trained her good, huh?"

Well, maybe, but I decided I wanted to be just like her myself; filled to the brim with dignity.

EULA MAE'S PAYBACK

53

J OHN SEEMED LOST after that night but wasn't that how I found him from the day we'd met years before on the steps of the church. Over the next few weeks our paths crossed now and again, but mostly when he was heading out for the evening and tripped on his misplaced hope that I might iron a shirt for him.

Don't think John grew as a man during the time we were together; he could only connive a semblance of manhood from day to day. You see, Sally told John to get out since he never paid rent. I was too busy getting Lelia ready to leave for college to worry about his problems. I finally put away enough in the education tin to get her started and the women had bought or sewn some real pretty blouses and things for Lelia to take to college with her.

Lelia had moved in with me so John could have her tiny room till the end of the month when he had to be out or else. The Saturday evening of his departure, John set his suitcase in the hall and came into my room for the last time. I felt a sense of satisfaction knowing he was departing my life for good and was determined to be gracious.

"So, where're you headed, John?"

"New York. They say there's plenty happenin' in Harlem," he replied.

John was all dressed up in what looked like a new suit and a fine new hat.

"Well, Jesus watch over you then."

He leaned over to give me the last hug. It was stiff as we were frozen with anger.

John walked out without another word and I shut the door thinking how good it felt seeing his backside for the last time. Yes, John Davis was gone for good and it was payday, too.

Every Sunday morning I counted how much from my pay I needed to send to Louvenia and how much I could put in Jeff's tin. This time was special, as I'd be counting money to send with Lelia for her school tuition. That very moment was one of the greatest joys of all my days. I decided to celebrate and take it easy that evening and went into the kitchen for a whiskey with Sally and Ma Mere. In the kitchen, Sally pulled out of the oven a chicken potpie as Ma set the plates on the table. There we sat eating near that entire potpie with the golden crust before I realized how late it was. Didn't matter, the three of us were celebrating Lelia's send off. I even figured a bit of whiskey would help me sleep that night. I did sleep but would never wish more that I hadn't.

⁂

The next morning I figured I'd get up early to press my dress and pack some of Lelia's new blouses for college before I counted out how much money I'd need to send with her the following day. So, as the iron heated, I pulled out her daddy's tobacco tin along with her college papers to see how much they required. I sat at the little table in my room and pushed the tin to the side. But that tin jingled like it was near empty except for coins. I opened it and Lord, the blood drained from my head to my toes at what I saw. There was nothing in Jeff's tin but some old key. John Davis' old key to Sally's door! Not a penny left.

When my heart stopped pounding enough, I howled as loudly as it would come out. The others heard and came running.

Sally screamed warnings to the boarders.

"Fire! You got fire down there?"

"Somebody been murdered? Who? Who been murdered?" Becky screamed.

They fell into my room looking about for the source of the commotion.

"Who's dead? Is it John, Sarah?" Sally asked.

"Did you kill 'im?" Ma asked.

I showed them Jeff's empty tobacco tin. The tin that held my life savings and our dreams was now empty; bone dry except for John's rusty ol' key.

At that moment it seemed much worse than any crime I could have imagined as it marked the end of all my hopes for a better life for my baby girl. All evaporated by the sleight-of-hand of the man wearing a new suit.

"Oh, Lord! Ain't you been robbed good?" Lucille announced.

"Lordy, Lucille!" Sally barked. "How in hell does somebody get robbed good, dearie? You go on and tell us."

"Momma, what happened? What's all the yellin' about?"

I couldn't speak I was so distraught. Ma braced me.

"It's John. He took all your college money!"

"Oh, God, did he get it all? Becky asked.

"Just like the Klan robbed my husband. Ever' penny's gone."

"John,you think? He's still down there at Eula Mae's. I could hear 'em goin' at it all night long," Sally said.

We tripped over each other heading to Eula Mae's room next to the kitchen where she always said she was sure lonely back there. Huh! Well, didn't we all know about the window she kept open on those lonely nights!

"I know they're still in there, too."

Ma pounded her chubby fist on the door.

We knocked and knocked till Eula Mae unlatched her door and we poured into her room. The first thing that caught my eye was John's new hat over there on the bureau. But no John.

"Where's John?" Sally demanded. I could tell she hadn't had much sleep. In fact, by the way she looked John had just departed after one last ride 'round the track.

"Caught the five A.M. train to California. Oh looky, he done forgot his new hat."

Eula Mae caressed that damned hat on her cheek like it was a kitten. I fell to my knees wanting to die. How could I have been so stupid as to not hide my money while John was still 'round? But then I realized I did keep it hidden, never really trusting John. He would have had to look high and dry, everywhere in our room to have found it hidden under a lose floorboard, just like Louvenia and I hid money back from Jesse.

"He got all Lelia's college money, Eula Mae," Becky said, crying as loud as me.

"Then Sister, you got nothin' to worry 'bout now." Eula Mae said. "'Cause ain't he gone? He sure is and I don't expect he's gonna be comin' back to visit and that's fine with me."

Sally shook her head at Eula Mae like she deserved a smack upside her head.

Eula Mae settled back on her bed and went to adjusting her fancy pillows as though she was expecting John's return any moment.

"Didn't you hear Eula Mae? Becky said he got every penny of Sarah's," Sally said.

"I heard!" Eula Mae replied. "Ain't you even heard me? You got nothin' to worry 'bout! Nope! 'Cause I gots your girl's money safe right over there!"

Eula Mae shook her finger at the plant in the big pot over in the corner of her room.

"What? What did you say, Eula Mae?" I asked.

"Me! While he was lying there snorin' last night, I got up and… Sister, I knows it ain't his money. He was lying to me all along him sayin' he won it in a poker game and then lying 'bout sendin' for me when he got all setup in San Francisco. So, I took all his money, ever' cent he had on 'im and hid it over there in that pot. Left 'im with nothin' but his train ticket… and that ticket didn't say he was goin' to no San Francisco. That man's headed to Atlanta, 'less they printed the wrong city on it! That happen? Then I rolled up some ol' newspaper, put it in his fat moneybag and kissed 'im good-bye. That man left here with nothin' else, like he left you and me, honey."

Sally lifted the plant out of that big pot. Out came bills floating to the floor. All my money was there at my feet. It was Eula Mae's blessed payback.

"There it be. Ever' cent," Eula Mae declared. "Eighteen years of cents, huh, Lelia?"

I was the only one cried out by then. There were so many tears I wondered if we might ruin the money we'd gathered.

"All right, ladies. The show's over for now. I best get breakfast ready if you're goin' to church," Sally said.

In one clean sweep, Eula Mae had paid back John Davis for all his lies and saved me from having to tell my daughter her education was not to be. Sister did it with love for Lelia and me as she handed a wad of shredded newsprint for the sleight-of-hand man to start his new life.

How do you thank someone for returning your stolen dreams?

PACKING FOR SOMEWHERE

54

T HE DAY THAT carried the dream we'd long awaited finally arrived. While Lelia readied her things, I wandered into the kitchen to have a cup of coffee. The women who'd been so much a part of our lives surrounded the big table like they'd been waiting for me. I wondered if they were having a meeting and if I might be the agenda. Lord, have mercy if they were gonna save me again! In concert, their eyes followed me as I went for my coffee.

"What's you all lookin' at? I leave the comb in my hair again?"

"Sit down, Sarah."

Sally nodded to my chair as Lucille, Becky and Eula Mae slurped their coffee anxiously awaiting Sally's speech.

"Fry 'er an egg, Sally," Becky said as I took my seat.

"No, she ain't eaten all week 'cause of her nerves," Eula Mae reminded me.

"She's gonna eat again when she knows Lelia is safe at school and she has a mind to eat," Sally quipped.

"I'll have her fried egg, Sally." Eula Mae announced. "Yeah, go fry Sarah's egg for me then."

"You know where the fry pan is, dearie."

Sally sat down next to me and dunked her toast in her coffee.

"What are you going to do with your time now Sarah?"

She asked as the meeting on Sister Sarah's salvation began.

"People ain't wearin' clean clothes now that Lelia's leaving for school?" I replied.

I wondered what these women were up to and figured I'd look them all in the eyes so they'd know I saw them doing it before they even done it!

"You know what I mean," Sally added. "All the time you spend worrying 'bout your girl. Got to fill that time with something else so the blues don't come knockin' again."

"Well, she gonna iron more shirts and send Lelia money so she can get herself things to look pretty when she meets boys," Lucille said.

Lucille could always come up with a workload for others even if getting her own done was problematic.

"Sarah, you iron a thousand shirts in a week— how much money that take in?"

I wondered if I could even count that high, a thousand shirts waiting for my iron. Lord, have mercy don't blind me from the agony of it.

"Guess 'bout five or six dollars," I replied.

It was true. Over the weeks before my daughter's departure to Knox College, I'd been thinking on what I'd do after she left and then for the rest of my days afterwards. Knew if I didn't fill my time up well, I'd be fretting over this and that, just as Sally suggested. I also knew I needed to get something going to earn a few cents on the side, what with Lelia's tuition and Louvenia's needs.

One day I thought about sewing aprons from scraps of fabrics cut from old blouses my ladies tossed at me for toting. As Eula Mae sat there smacking her lips after eating my fried egg, I asked what they thought about me sewing something I could sell at the farmer's market or at the church.

About then Ma Mere came in for her morning tea.

"You think Mrs. Washington sews her clothes?" I asked.

"She do, she sewed 'em too tight if you ask me!" Lucille injected.

"But ain't nobody asked you," said Ma Mere half asleep.

"I was thinkin' 'bout sewing aprons and selling 'em at the farmers' market after church. Think Mrs. Washington wears aprons?" I asked.

"Now why would she wear an apron if she don't cook?" Becky commented.

"Never thought of that," I replied.

"Of course, she cooks. You don't think that Booker does the cookin'?" Sally commented.

She knew 'bout Booker T. Washington because we left the weeklies on the big table till everybody had read them. Becky and Lucille always fought to get at the articles about the great lady so we could talk about her hair and clothes. Don't recall us ever having a chat about what Mrs. Washington did with herself when she wasn't all dressed, coiffed and on parade for our benefit of pride.

"But what about her hair?" It was something I'd thought about for some time. "Think she do it herself?"

"She got a hairdresser and she gots a dresser does all her washin' and ironin' and she don't wear no apron!" Ma Mere replied like she was Mrs. Washington's private secretary.

"How you know all that, Ma?" Lucille was always the skeptic.

"'Everybody knows," Ma said. "The woman's from New Orleans. They say she's a Creole princess and knows the King of France. They're real good friends, may even be drinkin' buddies. I tol' you, word gets 'round down there."

"Yeah? When did you ever go drinkin' down in the quarter with Mrs. Washington?" Eula Mae asked.

"Huh!" the dubious Miss Lucille responded like Ma had been tripped on her own tale.

"I only drink tea, you damned fool," Ma Mere huffed quickly lifting herself out of the trap.

"Ain't that what the King of France drinks?" Lucille countered. "Huh? Ain't it, if you knows so much, tea drinker!"

"I'd go have tea with the King of France," Eula Mae said, "Just 'cause maybe Mrs. Washington might be there and want to meet me. Then I'd ask her if she wore aprons, so's I could tell 'er Sarah here's gonna sew some out of rags just for her if she promise to buy one. 'Cept Sarah don't know how to sew none and hates doin' it when she does!" Eula Mae handily summed up my career as a seamstress. "But Mrs. Washington probably never goes to the farmers' market to buy aprons anyway."

In all my years at Sally's don't think I ever got much benefit from any of the meetings 'round the big table which I knew were lovingly aimed at sewing up the pulled-apart seams of my life. Still I frequently saw the advantage of adapting a course in the opposite direction these women figured was best for me knowing the odds were appreciatively less likely that I'd fall on my face if I did. Sill not being able to put anything in my nervous stomach that morning, I grabbed my letters to read down in the laundry while my irons heated.

The most amazing thing happened on the way down to the basement. Everywhere my thoughts propelled me all I saw were endless piles of shirts. Shirts over there, stacked on top of that, piled under this, all waiting for me to wash and iron. Thousands and thousands if there was a dozen. I couldn't count the number of things I'd ironed over the years. Tell me, Lord, is there something else for us tub women than being bent over a tub till we're destined to fall under it at the end of our days? Lordy! Did anybody ever have a dream headed somewhere besides a laundry house?

Strangely, I got to thinking what if the King of France invited me for tea when he was visiting New Orleans? Not something I'd ever thought on before. Didn't know if I'd go, but then why wouldn't I? Ain't I good enough? As I plunged my leathery hands into another tub I wondered what the King would think of me. What about Margaret Washington, wasn't she one of us? What if the wife of Booker T. Washington sent a buggy for me to join her at tea? I'd sure go 'cause she might be offended if I didn't show. Why wouldn't she have me over for tea? 'Cause she don't take to folks whose clothes are worn thin like mine? It's folks like me she's talking to up there on that stage with all them lights washing over her polished shoes. Are my hands too rough to hold a delicately painted teacup? Would Margaret be anxious I might chip one of her cups that probably the King of France or a Creole princess once sipped from? Can I someday learn to walk with grace and poise like this great woman? Where does dignity come from? Shop windows or the colored weeklies? Is it yet something the white folks bar us from like reading? But then again, is it something we deny ourselves and even each other at times?

Well, I could hear the women up there walking their plates over to the sink and appreciated what they got me thinking about. Yes, my thoughts were swimming until I finally gave up finishing my loads and headed up to my daughter's room to look over her packing.

Lelia came in while I was folding her blouses to get them just perfect.

"Momma, leave 'em be."

She gently placed them back into the drawer.

"Honey, what are you doing? You got to have your things ready for tomorrow. I was down at the tubs thinkin' on how long I'd looked for this very day. Since you were a baby and your daddy handed me a dented ol' tobacco tin with a few nickels rattling at the bottom, saying this here is for our girl; our very own. She's gonna go to school someday!"

Lelia puzzled as I rattled on.

"Whole lot of dirty clothes I done twisted the last drop of water out of to get to this day. Ain't it so, honey?"

Lelia looked as though she had some bad news to settle on me. And she did!

"Momma… I've got something to say. Something you're not gonna want to hear, too."

"Not about your Aunt Louvenia, is it?"

"No, Momma."

"Then fold your nightgown while you say what I don't want to hear. Go on then, I can listen while you fold your things again."

Well, I should have known something was going on 'cause I heard rustles outside the door. I couldn't hear what they were whispering; just the stir of hens scratching their big ears against Lelia's door.

But Lelia knew and found the courage to tell me. At that it was as if everything had gone up in flames!

"No! You can't mean it!"

"You've worked so hard for that money, Momma." Lelia said trying to calm me. "But I just can't take it from you. I've decided. I'm not goin' to college."

"What? But that was our dream. It's kept us goin' all these years." I reminded her. "What else was there?"

"Your own dream was there all along if you'd admit it, Momma. When are you gonna wake to it? That money in Daddy's tin could buy you your own dream today and not on some tomorrow. What I'm sayin' is; you got to use this money to rent a little house outside of town so you can get Aunt Louvenia back and Uncle Alex."

Her eyes grew large like her daddy's.

"Don't do this to me. You know I promised Minerva," I pleaded. "I tried for myself but I couldn't. I'm still a tub woman and that's how it's gonna be. Momma couldn't have a dream. I can help my own girl get free of the slavery of these tubs. Your schooling will free you to a world Minerva and Owen never knew; a life of dignity; of not havin' to work like a mule till you fall over dead. Please Lelia, when I go to the Lord, I can't tell your Grandma Minerva that you walked off from our dream when it was packed and ready to go."

"You put your life into this tin," Lelia said. "You filled it up so tightly maybe so there'd be no place for you to hold a dream for yourself."

"No, dear. My life is not in no tin can. You are my life. You are my dream."

Lelia knew this but we were both so very scared. Hardly any coloreds went to college back then but yet wasn't my daughter right? Hadn't I lived my own dreams through my hopes for my baby?

The thought would pester me for days but at the moment all I saw was my daughter's wavering. We sat on the bed holding hands. Finally, she smiled. At that moment I knew we were traveling on the same side of the road again. I wiped her tears and we went back to packing for never-ever dreams we'd been chasing from the day her daddy handed me that tin.

I opened the door to our room expecting the women to fall to the floor from eavesdropping.

"What is the matter with you women?" I asked as standing there with a pile of women at my feet. "Why are you putting nose prints on my door?"

"Lelia, she ain't goin' to Knox College then?" Ma Mere asked.

"Like hell she isn't!" I said. "What put that nonsense into your head? You all been down at my keyhole so long your thinking got cut off. You gonna go pack her lunch? Don't want her eatin' off no dirty train."

Lelia hugged them all. These sisters were with us through so many hard times and watched over her those long nights I was at school; I knew they felt nearly as bad as I did 'bout losing our little girl.

It was a sad and difficult day when we sent Lelia off but the women helped me stow my fears for the time being. Guess we got to the train station almost two hours early; no one said more than a word here and there. Lelia boarded and found a window to wave at us. I held back my tears as the train disappeared into the hazy distance. Didn't want my eyes to reveal what I feared: that when you lost sight of your loved ones heading into the unknown, you just may never see them again. It was the convention passed down by generations of colored mothers whose babies disappeared near the moment they left her body and long before she could give 'em a name. Will I see my child again, Lord? Or will the white shadows swallow her?

We headed back to Sally's with nothing much to say.

I did not feel Lelia's absence over the next few days as I labored hard over the tubs so's I wouldn't. Figured it was best that I didn't have a moment to fret. In a month I had to get the money together for the final payment on her boarding; that's all I concerned myself with for the moment.

Guess it was the following week when I was wringing out shirts that I'd washed twice because they were so filthy. I was holding my nose from the smell when the women started screaming in the kitchen and stomping hard on the floor up there to alert me.

"Sarah!," they screamed.

Then Sally hollered down to the basement.

"Get on up here quick!"

I ran up thinking Ma had done it for sure; she'd gone and put the kitchen on fire so she'd prove to Sally her cooking was no better than her ironing!

"Where's the fire? I yelled breathlessly as they stood there looking at me like I was the first fool they'd ever seen in person. But I couldn't see no fire. Not even Sally's toast was burning.

"Lelia! She done sent you a letter!"

Lucille hopped about like she needed to tinkle. So why was I standing there with my apron fanning the smoke that wasn't there? Lordy, is hysteria contagious? Knew it had to be at Sally's.

"Go on, open it," Eula Mae blurted. They all hovered about as if it was a telegram, the kind you know you never want to open; somebody dead.

"She's not gonna read that letter in front of us. She's gonna do it in private," Sally said and then slathered her toast with jam but motioned me to read it anyway. "Go ahead, Sarah. Read it so these hens can get back to doin' nothin' again."

Well, I owed it to my friends to share Lelia's letter. My hands were shaking as I tore the paper open and read.

"Dear Momma, I arrived on time and the college sent two students to fetch me at the station so I wouldn't get lost. My room is beautiful and looks out over the green. Everything you packed came out perfectly without the tiniest crinkle. Bye for now. Love Lelia."

"That's all?" Lucille asked.

"Who's she met there?" Ma asked. "She say?"

"Yeah, she got a boyfriend yet?" Eula Mae inquired.

Sally shrugged her shoulders and went on kneading her dough while my heart went sailing back to my baby's last smile at the train station. Yes, my daughter had made it all the way there and wouldn't be wearing no wrinkled blouses like she'd just come off a cotton field.

The never-ever dream that many said would never come our way was now ours for sure. Ours, Jeff.

GOT TO GO. GOT TO!

55

Hadn't Sally had been right all along? Some days the worries sank me deep. So deep that I wondered if I could climb out of the hole I was drowning in. Late summer after Lelia went to school, our laundry business got slow again. Had me worried. Seemed like folks could hardly spare money for tub women, yet I needed to send money to Lelia and Louvenia regularly or they might not eat. I couldn't stop worrying about Sister as I knew come winter Annie couldn't get out there over the rutted roads to see how she was doing. I thought and prayed on what I could do but there seemed few choices. Seemed as if the air between my row tubs was getting thin and I was starting to feel suffocated.

Early one morning I reluctantly headed down to the laundry but instead landed in the chair at my little table in the corner of the basement where I spent my breaks reading notes from Lelia and Sister as I waited for my irons to heat. This time I sat there with nothing heating but my scorched worries. No, couldn't seem to even budge to do much of anything. Then, somewhere in the quiet, I heard the steps to the basement creaking. It was Sally. She'd come to find me. How long had she been calling down them stairs? I suppose it had only been my thoughts I'd heard echoing off those dreary walls.

"What are you doin' down here sitting in all this blasted heat, dearie?"

Sally dropped a pile of clothes some customer had left off.

"Got to get a few piles in to soak," I told her, but couldn't budge an inch.

"You can't tell it's hotter than hell down here? Well, there ain't gonna be no tubs today, I can tell that. So, come up to the kitchen where Ma's making us some cold lemonade."

Sally turned to leave but stopped on the third step as I'd still not moved.

"The ice is sitting up there melting while you're sittin' down here melting," Sally announced. "How we gonna fix that 'less you lift yourself up and come get a glass of Ma's lemonade?"

From the steam my skirt stuck to that rickety old chair and then to my legs. I pulled myself up and followed Sally up thinking she knew in a minute what I'd been down there half the morning sorting in my mind: That I simply couldn't spend the day sorting piles of stinking rags.

Up in the kitchen, Sally handed me a cloth to mop my brow and Ma Mere handed me a tall jar of lemonade along with the sugar bowl.

"Go on, honey. Make it as sweet as you like it!" she said. "Then we gonna sit on the back porch where it's shady now."

"Ma drinks it sweet enough to near chew like some gritty cotton candy from the carnival, don't you Ma?" Sally commented. "There ain't a reason why you go down there to face what you don't want to face. You best come to terms with the fact you can't do it no more and when you do, you're gonna be ready to move on to something!"

"Why'd you say that, Sally? Ma asked. "Sarah ain't never gonna leave us. Are you honey?"

I knew Ma's word came from love, but the thought stuck just the same: the idea of never leaving that ol' dank basement. Just as I'd come to realize I couldn't face the tubs that day I also somehow couldn't see myself at Sally's for the rest of my days.

"Looks like it's time you go lookin' for a housekeepin' job," Sally said and nodded at Ma and me.

"That's right, Sarah!" Ma said. "Sally been a maid and knows a thing or two 'bout it. You get a housekeepin' job 'round here."

"You're still gonna do the laundry," Sally said, "but you'll be doing it for one family and not every stranger on the damned block and then some. Maybe they even have a machine to do it. Heard of that? Saw a picture in the papers. Can't image it really works."

"Who's the 'then some' on this damned block? That dirty ol' woman that lives with that damned ol' man Lucille say never takes a bath?" Ma asked. "That one?"

"Lordy, Ma! You're still listenin' to Lucille like she got 'er hands on the news the papers have yet printed."

It didn't much matter where Ma got her tales, she was right. If a machine could do tub work, there was no future for laundresses. Imagine hiding those filthy clothes inside a covered tub while some piece of machinery with no nose scrubbed the smell out. Lordy, show me the way to my salvation.

And yet the problem with Sally and Ma Mere's ideas was that there weren't any white folks who could afford a housekeeper. 'Round that part of town, they were mostly poor white folk like us, so poor they were living on the edge of where the coloreds were, which was already at the very edge of the poorest. Lord knows every day as I walked the ironing to our customers I seen in the windows of laundries so many young laundresses who would do anything to get her hands out of stinking lye water. That vision got me to think these women were spreading further and further out to find a piece of a dream, while I only sat in a basement waiting for steam to evaporate enough to see my own hands work that same ol' washboard I'd been staring at for years.

I knew what Sally was easing me into. Neither she nor Ma wanted me to move on, but Sally knew I had to. A few days later, I finally found peace with that realization and knew it was time to move on to a bigger city. I knew it was inevitable, but there were still days when only the thought of taking that first step to some new and nameless place jolted me right back into the day before. Yes, it yet dwelled somewhere in my deepest exhaustion that here was a warm bed at Sally's. I loved these women. They were family to me. I'd gone for years knowing there'd always be a tub of laundry to get to and therefore a meal somewhere at the end of a long day. Didn't I have it good? Yet I could not think about Minerva and not know she would have packed her bag for any journey at the first glance of freedom. The day when the gate was left open; she'd have grabbed her family and walked off without looking back. While that gate was never open for her, mine was unlatched and swinging and I owed it to daughter to walk through it.

The next day I went to buy a train ticket. I stood there at the station for nearly half an hour already feeling lost. I waited in the long line, but still didn't know where my destination was to be when the time came for me to put my money on the counter and answer the station man. Where to? Where did I want to go? That place any better? Or just a friendless destination at the very edge of somewhere I'd never be able to crawl back up from?

"Where?" he asked again.

The ticket man's impatient glare interrupted my mumbles and intruded on my thoughts. Would I find a place to live at…?

"Huh?" he asked. "Can you stand aside while you figure where you're wantin' to go?"

So, I told the man I sure liked Denver when I was there with John years before. Or was I only telling the man who moved ahead of me in line? What were folks like there? I asked the man's back but he only turned to look at me as though his back didn't hear my question either. I'd read it was better for coloreds there somehow. Where on earth could that be?

The only conclusion I arrived at was one I borrowed from Minerva. I recalled what Momma told me on Orchard Night: I didn't need to know all the answers to get by. Just had to have enough faith to match my train ticket to a tiny mustard seed-sized dot on the map posted above the ticket man's head. Things would unfold as the journey progressed. Or maybe they wouldn't, but wasn't that where I was already headed if I stayed at Sally's?

As I bought my ticket that day I'd then fixed the date I would walk out Sally's door and head off to somewhere in Denver. It was clearly printed on my ticket.

I told the women the next night at supper.

"Now, Becky, your sobbin' like a baby won't keep Sarah from leaving us," Sally announced.

She wasn't crying any more than me, but after our tears dried, the women all wanted to hear about my plans.

"She's a big crybaby lookin' for attention," Lucille said, her nose in the favored position.

"Now, who else we know likes to get in on the attention 'round here?" Ma Mere asked.

"Yeah, who then, Ma?" Lucille asked. "That's what I want to know. You mean Eula Mae, don't you? She's always actin' up to get attention, ain't she?"

Lucille could be as clueless as a preacher's wife conducting a Bible study in a whorehouse on a Saturday night.

"I don't know what I'm headed to; just know I need to go looking for something out there," I told them.

I didn't know what else to say. Just picking up and leaving didn't make sense so how could I explain it? I stood there looking at those sad eyes swimming circles around me.

"In my heart I'm searching for what's missing since Lelia left."

"There's plenty of rich white folks in Denver. She's gonna get herself housework. Maybe it's gonna have a rose garden, too! Huh, Sarah?" Becky declared. "'Cause I know your Louvenia loves flowers!"

"First Lelia goes off and now Sarah leaves us. Everyone is goin' somewhere, ain't it so?" Eula Mae said. "That scares me."

"Don't be scared, Eula Mae," Becky said. "'Cause ain't nobody gonna catch you gettin' far from this here supper table soon, honey."

"We'll have a big send-off breakfast for you in the morning."

Sally blotted tears and returned to her baking.

You know, I cried all night in Lelia's bed. Her Japanese things were still hanging where she and Ma had decorated. I knew I'd never see these women again and I didn't want to look into all those eyes that told me that they knew also because by then it wouldn't have taken much to toss my train ticket away.

That night I prayed for enough courage to walk out the front door. I held Jeff's tobacco tin, reminding myself that our dream for our daughter had come true. I folded Louvenia's envelope of dried flower seeds into my old cloth and put them in my tin. What else did I really have to pack? Well, I'd collected more than a few bits of hope, but for the time being they were safely packed away in my heart…waiting for another day.

More goodbyes wouldn't make anything easier, so the next morning before the sun invited the day to mark our calendars with a new number, I left. I was as terrified of what the days ahead might give or take. What were the odds I could even survive? The question echoed against my worn thoughts as I quietly slipped out the door.

Adrift In An Attic

56

O N THE TRAIN I watched the city where I'd lived remain fixed in my past as I tried to fix a vision of what might lay ahead. But like most days, my faith was as limited as my vision; I reckon 'bout as big as an attic in a birdhouse. So, I wondered how my dreams could be any greater?

The train arrived on time. There on the platform I noticed a woman waving a kerchief my way as if she'd been waiting for my arrival. In fact, she dashed right up to me.

"You new here in Denver?" she asked.

"How'd you know?"

"I'm good at picking 'em!" she responded.

"Pickin' what?"

"A good woman needing a room is what. See, I got me a place not far from here. Got a room with a clean bed. You come to my home and you're gonna be safe. Ain't no hotel near here gonna let a room to a colored."

"You got a boardin' house?" I asked.

"No. Just a room I let when my sister's not visiting. Helps me make ends meet. This all you got? One little case?"

"How much your room?"

"Don't matter. You leave what you can. We be fine with that. Come on now so I can to get our supper goin'."

Well, the word 'supper' clinched the deal!

I followed Nell remembering how hard it had been getting a room when I arrived in

St. Louis but how easy it had been finding a place on a park bench.

Nell had the warmest smile. On the way over to her place she explained that each day she headed down to the station waiting for the train to arrive so she could find herself a good woman. She said she could tell a good soul by the way they looked getting off the train. I was glad she read me as a good soul that day. The blessing of meeting Nell long endured in more ways than one.

Her place was real nice. Only three rooms as she slept on her sofa in the front. She kept the backroom nice and clean and had a jar of Louvenia's favorite sweet peas in the window.

"Here it be. I get you a pitcher of water and then when you're rested, I put supper on. The man next door gonna join us. He boards over there but they don't let 'im cook none so he buys our food and I cook it up over here. We get by."

Supper was good. My new friends were even better. The next morning when I was getting ready to go looking for work, Nell gave me a piece of paper.

"This is the address of my friend, Emily. She's got what you need."

"She got a boardin' house?"

"No, she's got a room up there. Used to be her attic but Hank made it over. Go see."

The next morning, before going to meet this Emily, I left Nell's and headed to hunt for work. Surely, I tell you that was a long walk from Nell's, but I could see Denver all the better.

The city was clean, and folks seemed nice. Walked so long I got to wondering what if my shoes weared out before I got a job? I stuffed a new piece of cardboard in the bottom to cover a hole. Finally found a grand street with fine houses. I knocked and knocked but nobody answered their doors. Shook me a bit as I wondered if I'd moved to a place where nobody lived! I stopped a colored woman carrying groceries. She told me that white folks never answer their front door 'less there's another whitey knocking 'cause they might think we're gonna get 'em if they do, or even worse, their white neighbors might figure they couldn't afford a colored maid to answer their door. How many ways can you add that up and it come to mean something? I wondered if I knocked on the rear service door, why they wouldn't be scared I'd still get 'em back there? Get 'em, they're thinking? Lordy, haven't we been trying for a hundred years to rid ourselves of them first? I swan, them white folks can't seem to get nothing right.

Late that day I knocked at the back door of one particularly sprawling place. I headed to the back figuring it had to be as back there as a back door could be.

About then the maid came out to hang her laundry.

"What's you doin' poundin' on the storage door like that?" she asked flipping the wrinkles out of her wet shirts. "You think somebody expectin' you? Maybe a broken clay pot?" she laughed. "Anyhows, that door only goes down in the basement!"

"I'm lookin' for house work. You know somebody needs help 'round here?"

I mopped my brow as the sun seemed pure determined to give me head throbs as souvenir for my efforts that day. She was nice, that woman.

"You know I can't bring you into the kitchen but wait here. My lady's gone now, so I'll bring out some sweet tea. You look like you need a sip of somethin'! Want some? And a piece of my coconut jellyroll cake? I made it this morning for Mister, but she done told me to throw it out 'fore I go home tonight 'cause it'a make her fat."

I wondered how her lady could be so stupid as to think that what her husband ate was gonna make her fat. Like I said about them white folks…

She paused before stepping back in for the tea and said quietly, "Now listen, if you see my lady comin' home early, like she do now and 'gain to see if I'm working, then you gots to run off down the back alley so's she won't see me out here talkin'. Hear?"

I nodded and eagerly anticipated some of her tea; I couldn't have been more parched if I'd just swallowed a tablespoon of sand.

She soon returned with cake and tea and we sat down on the back stoop where there was some shade spreading out.

"You best go down the street to the big white house where the roots on them two big magnolias cracked the walked," she said. "That's Bella Burke's. Bet you'll get a job there for sure."

I couldn't decide why my friend thought this bit of advice was so funny her cake near fell out 'a her mouth from her giggling. I could only smile back and nod while I ate mine.

"Then you gonna lose it the next week," she added.

"Lose what?" I asked. "What I gonna lose, I ain't even got yet?"

"Nobody works for that bitch more than a month. I'm tellin' you, just go down there and ask my friend Nona. She works for the woman next door now!"

Sure seemed strange that this woman was pleased to invite me to a party that she sure enough wasn't gonna show up at herself.

"But meanwhile you come over some mornings when you're out a' work again and we'll eat Mister's cakes! I bake one a week to throw out."

"You bake cakes to throw out, huh?"

"Sometimes pies. He nibbles on it a bit and then that night I tote 'em so my lady won't get fat. My kids love them cakes! Yes, Ma'am. That Bella up the street's a hateful bitch and nobody'll work for her long, can't stand 'er."

I thought surely I didn't leave Sally's just to come work for a hateful bitch. Then it wasn't as though I had any references for housework. Maybe this Bella and me best work something out 'cause nobody else will have either one of us. Nevertheless, she never been hateful to me, so I figured I wouldn't judge for now.

"How's it your coconut jellyroll cake comes out so good?" I asked my new friend.

"'Cause instead of milk I use a cup of heavy cream. But you see I tell my lady I use a cup of plain milk and then I cut it with water so she won't get fatter."

She leaned over to whisper something important.

"I ain't worried none 'bout her gettin' fatter, 'cause nobody even seen a fatter woman. There ain't that place left! She's already reached her destination, so why should I mind making her think I'm sellin' her a ticket to skinny she ain't never gonna stop off at 'gain! Ain't that right, Sister? She wants to go to skinny, let her find her own way and not out of my kids' mouths!"

"Well, I gots to think 'bout it. Don't know if I'd do different," I said.

"See, you already put the heavy cream it like me. And looky here, I use blueberry jam I make myself. It's better than that red jelly slop the grocer man sells for jellyroll cake that nobody knows what's in it. You ever hold up one of them jars wonderin' what could be so damned red in there and not be still alive?"

"No, I never."

"And always use fresh coconut. Don't let it set there uncovered gettin' dry on ya," she said giggling. "'Cause Mister don't like it dry and you're gonna have to tote it home late that night anyway, ain't ya?"

I hadn't eaten since I left Nell's so that cake tasted mighty good.

I just finishing when my friend suddenly jumped up with her tea sloshing down her front. Guess she didn't want nobody seeing her have it. What she'd seen was the long shadow of her lady coming wearing a big hat. Just as I raised my jar of tea to finish my friend grabbed it away and shoved another piece of the cake in my hand and told me to go hide in the bushes 'cause her lady would soon be looking out her kitchen window and be thinking we'd stolen her blind and were dividing the spoils on her back stoop while drinking her tea and eating her jellyroll cake she don't want none of anyway.

Lordy, these white folks stole us from our African shores to haul us over here in chains that they're still trying to swallow the keys to and damned if they're not yet blaming us for coming along with them in the first place. No, I was not so inclined to go hide in the bushes from some white woman. So, I swallowed the last bite of cake while my friend stood there like she was gonna pee her drawers. Then I thanked her and started down the side of the house where I paused to wave at the woman standing in her kitchen window drinking some of that sweet tea. I could hear her in there barking at Mister about where my new friend was and why the dishes weren't done yet. And that lady, Bella over there in the big white house with the two magnolias is the most awful bitch on this street? Lordy! All I could do was wonder if the train station man would give me my money back as I was already seeing myself heading back to Sally's.

But I didn't head back. I figured I'd best go see about a job at Bella's place the next day because walking down the streets with the sun and that sugary tea made my head throb. I was headed to the address Nell had given me on Becker Street for a room when I came upon a big white house with the cracked walk. Had to be Bella's, 'cause the rest of them houses up and down the street were mostly brick or had no magnolias out front.

I asked myself what if I just walked on? I'd sure be a coward and scared of some white woman who had a reputation of being a bitch. Like I'd never known a white woman bitch before? Me after doin' their laundry for so many years?

So, I decided to get it over with and headed down her cracked walk.

I rang and a woman swung the door open as if she thought I was there unscrewing the hinges probably to get at her silver. This woman, she couldn't be no Creole princess; she was whiter than a sheet and had blue eyes and mousy blond hair that she'd try to curl, at least one side of her head and that made her head look like it had one wing.

I told her I needed work. That immediately got 'er to fold her arms over her bosom like she was sure glad I showed up to collect her judgment. She glared down from her stoop like the Lord himself had ordered her to commence an inquisition on my soul. Then she looked about is if maybe somebody better might show up to work for the worst bitch on the street.

"No, Ma'am. I don't got kids," I replied as she moved down the list of white folks' questions.

"You drink?" Miss Burke demanded. "We're good Christians here."

Well, I think she wanted to know if I was a drunk like Jesse. But I had to figure on how to answer and not tell a lie. You see, I'd asked the Lord to help me get this job when I come up her cracked walk. Lord, Lord, make this woman give me a job, I prayed. I prefer not to lie 'bout having a sip now and again when I've just asked the Lord to listen in on how things are going for me.

"Don't drink nothin' Jesus didn't," I told her. I figured the Lord would find that acceptable.

"Good! I won't have it. You'll work for me six days a week from six in the morning till after you clean up from supper. I'll give you five whole dollars a week, if you last six months. Dollar-fifty a week till then. If you steal or break anything, I'll take it out of your pay. I mean it!"

I was indeed sure she did, too.

"Yes, Ma'am."

I answered but didn't tell her what I really meant. I dished her one of those docile grins white folks take to. Helps them think they're smarter than we. That's what Lucille told me a thousand times. I never did believe much of what Lucille said, but she was right as it gets on that one! A thousand times over.

"Now you can tote any leftovers my dog don't want. Ain't that nice? Be here next Monday early. Hear? Yeah, Monday. That what I said?"

At that she slammed the door in my face.

I walked off wondering what did this poor white woman think Jesus drank? Ginger ale? Did she just say I could tote all the scraps her dog don't want?

Well somebody helped me find the street Nell had directed me to where this Emily might have a room.

"Ma'am, I'm Sarah McWilliams. Nell sent me so I came to see…"

"I know why you're here if Nell sent you. You're already welcome 'cause nobody reads people like that woman! Let me show you the room I got for you. It's big and has two windows, one lookin' into the elms out front."

In her kitchen, Emily seated me at her table so we could get to know each other as she prepared supper.

"You like chops?" she asked. "That's what we're having tonight. You can stay?"

So, Emily was my new landlady and Hank her husband. She said I could go right up to my room through their kitchen. Over supper she told me they'd been married for thirty years and that she would live every one of them all over if she could. Well, she knocked off one or two years that it took get their recipe right. The whole time they lived in this same place on Becker Street where they raised their kids. Hank's ma lived down the street, or as Emily would say, on that too damned near street!

Hank was a barber; Emily took care of the house for him. He had his own shop down a few blocks, but it was for men only. White men that is. Even in barbershops, white men would not mix with coloreds although they expected their barber to be colored and fool with their hair with their colored hands. Lord, let me be the one to tell you; something went awfully wrong when you created white folks but then they say you started with them first so guess you had to work your way through it 'fore you got to us!

I was happy to find a place to live so quickly, but I worried about the summer heat and the winter cold up in that attic. When you're born in a sharecropper's shack on the river you know how deeply the cold can bite and how the heat and humidity of summer can suck the breath out of you. I'd barely been there a week when Emily told me I could do anything I wanted with my attic room, which was nearly half the size of her house.

I got to thinking I might someday paint the walls that pretty peach-color Louvenia loved and even worked up a dream that if I could save some extra money, Sister could come visit and maybe never want to go back. I was sure she'd like Emily.

A few days after I'd moved in there was a knock.

"Emily, honey. You already got some mail. Put it under your door?"

"No, come in, dear. My feet done quit on me and I got 'em soakin' here."

Emily came in with that big smile of hers. Made me feel good just being with her.

"That your dinner there? A potata?" she asked.

"I'm too tired to be hungry."

But she knew for real. It's what I ate most nights even if it took a while to cook on that little coal heater up there.

"I know you. You're watchin' your pennies for your girl's schoolin'." Emily yelled downstairs. "Hank! Get Jake to bring up some roast pork and carrots for Sarah here. Some of that spiced apple sauce I made this morning, too."

Then she pulled from her apron pocket a letter.

"A letter here, honey. I think it's from your girl."

"I sent her a telegram so she'd know I was doin' fine."

I slid Lelia's letter into my pocket for later as Jake, Emily's ten-year-old grandson, came in with a tray. The food smelled mighty good. Jake put the tray in front of Emily. The boy was too shy to look at me. I know he just wanted to get away from us women folk to go be with his granddaddy.

"It's not for me, Jake. You saw me eat, didn't you? It's for Sarah here. Put it in front of her nice-like, Grandson."

He pushed the tray across the table and went for the door.

"Now bring up some of that buttermilk cake I just frosted with caramel. Should be cool enough to eat by now. If you can bring that cake up without it splitting on top, you can have some, too," she said with a wink.

"Oh, Grandma…" He smiled sheepishly.

"Go on now before your granddaddy eats it up."

"Emily, I start my new job come Monday and, hallelujah, Lord, it ain't at the tubs!"

"Knew you'd settle in quick, you're a survivor," she said

"I got to survive. I know I got things I was meant to get done."

"Like what things, dear?"

"Funny, but I don't really know," I said. "Guess the things that keep brewing in my head. Like that."

Well, I was afraid to tell Emily about all the things that came crashing against my thoughts at times. Emily smiled.

"Every day the Lord lets us start the rest of our lives again!"

Chatting with my new friend I finished one of the best meals I'd had in weeks.

That night I slept feeling contented, thinking here I am, probably just where I was meant to be. Not unlike the day I landed on Sally's stoop with only a few cents to my name.

I had survived and the Lord had led the way.

Nona's Fried Cornmeal-Rolled Tongue

22

THE FOLLOWING MONDAY I took off early for Miss Burke's as I was eager to make a good impression. I left only seeing other maids crisscrossing the streets among the vendor carts making deliveries.

There was no answer when I knocked at the Burke's service door. I stood there for the longest before knocking again. Sure seemed as though nobody was home. I wondered if I should head back when the maid next door came out with her laundry basket and waved. I waved back and she came 'round her clothesline to look me over. Later I understood well enough that she couldn't imagine what kind of woman would come work for Bella Burke—because some time back she'd had the unfortunate job herself and knew a thing or two 'bout the maids who came and went back down the Burkes' cracked walk!

"You waitin' on Miss Burke over there?" she asked snapping her wet sheets.

I knew something 'bout lugging baskets of laundry, so I was amazed that this skinny woman with skinnier arms could snap them heavy wet sheets so hard no wrinkle could find a place to dry.

"I'm Nona," she said and then pointed a finger at me like a warning.

"You got here early but that don't mean you're gonna leave early! No, Ma'am! I'm tellin' you, she gonna watch you."

"Ain't nobody been watchin' me yet, that's for sure."

"'Cause she ain't there," Nona announced. "She gots her church-woman's meetin' breakfast first Monday every month. It's the only day she gets up 'fore noon! She goes early to bake her cookies ain't nobody gonna eat 'cause they's hard as a board and taste like sawdust. That woman left early. Yep. I knows 'cause my lady over here seen 'er through her kitchen winda while I was fixin' her breakfast and said to me, 'There goes that awful Bella!' Said Miss Burke done stuck her damned tongue out at 'er again! She tempts me, too, just like that."

"Tempts you by stickin' her tongue out?"

"Tempts me to chop that tongue of hers off, roll it in cornmeal and fry it up in chicken fat to serve my lady with 'er eggs. I fix 'er eggs near ever' mornin' you know."

"What?"

I wasn't certain I'd heard this all right and half expected this Nona to rearrange what she'd just said for clarification. She didn't.

"Then you're workin' for Miss Burke now?" she asked.

"Just got hired. She told me to come early and that's what I done, too."

I was about to tell her Miss Burke was expecting me at six and ask Nona what time she had but wasn't convinced if she even had her senses let alone the time.

She motioned me closer to the fence to hear more tales she'd surely rolled in cornmeal more than once before.

"You best be early and know she'll expect you to stay later and later every day," Nona said, "and then aim to pay you less and less every week! I knows! I used to work for Miss Burke over there. I tell you plain that woman is a holy terror! She hates my lady over here, 'cause when Miss Burke fired me, my lady over here hired me the same day. She sure enough did. They been feudin' ever since!"

At that point I wondered what they could be feuding over, Miss Burke and the neighbor woman across the fence, 'cause I'd not seen any reason they'd be fussing over Nona. But I hoped to find out before our chat was over and Nona seemed equally eager to fill me in but this time it wasn't no business 'bout fried tongues.

"You see, Miss Burke thinks everybody wants to get in her husband's breeches," Nona said giggling. "That's what my lady over here says every time she looks out the winda and sees that man comin' down the walk. Guess she says that 'cause he's so good lookin'. But I ain't never noticed," she quickly added.

Somehow I figured she had noticed 'cause I can read a glint in a woman's eye. Yes, living with Lucille, Becky and Eula Mae taught me much about what we claim not to see in the very men we hone our eyes on.

"My lady over here tells me every time she looks out 'er winda and Miss Burke puts her tongue out, that if I go lop that nasty ol' thing off, roll it in cornmeal and fry it up she gonna give me five whole dollars. Guess that would stop Miss Burke's nasty-mouthin' folks she thinks are lookin' at 'er man!"

"Yeah, well, guess nobody can stick out a tongue they don't got." I replied. "I ain't never met her husband. What he do?"

"Do? Nothin'. He dead," Nona declared.

"Miss Burke's husband's dead?"

"Of course not," Nona said. "How could he be dead but come walkin' past the window when my lady's watchin'? My lady's ol' man is dead. Least they thought him was when they buried 'im."

"Guess that leaves Miss Burke's husband then. What he do?" I asked.

"Do? I'll tell you what that man do. He ignore her. Pretend she ain't even 'round and that gets Miss Burke so worked up she goes hunting for skins," Nona said.

"She goes huntin' when she gets mad at 'im?" I asked. "Where at? The park down the street?"

"No! She goes huntin' for your skin. She's gonna be lookin' for a speck of dust you left in some room ain't nobody goes in so she can take out her meanness on your hide. And when she find that speck, and she

will even if it ain't there, that big ol' tongue of hers gonna come lookin'
for you. Then she gonna lash you good and hard with it."

"I been tongue-lashed by a white woman plenty of times before," I
admitted. "Gonna be again."

"Not like she gonna do to you!"

"I wanna know what kind of work he do?"

I thought the Burkes got to be rich given how big their place was.
Well, this Nona thought her words needed to hit the bottom of my ear,
so she got up good and close. Still I reckon I was the only one who hadn't
heard her big secret.

"He say he some kind of farmer. You ever hear of that? Yeah,
farm'acists, he say. You reckon that like some kind of city farmer? But
I bet that man never been near dirt in his life. Look at his pretty hands
and tell me different! No, it's that woman that does all the gardening,
her precious roses, you know. I seen her at it, too."

"You seen her at it?" I asked. "What's you mean?"

"I seen 'er out back in the garden and I know why she don't want
nobody watchin' her, too. She sneaks back there as soon as the sun come
up," Nona said like it was of utmost strangeness that a woman might
visit her garden before the heat of the day.

"Out there stripping the petals off all 'er roses," she continued while
jabbing my chest with her boney finger like maybe I hadn't grasped the
magnitude of these allegations.

"One by one, pulling rose petals off and laughin' like some damned
crazy when she doin' it!"

"She don't take to havin' flowers in her flower garden?" I asked.

"Ain't that strange? Even for a white woman. Then she goes and
carries 'em in 'er house singin' cradle songs all the way."

"What's she doing with all them rose petals?"

Nona made a motion like it was some sort of condition in Miss
Burke's head.

"I 'magine Miss Burke thinks if somebody sees her pullin' the rose
petals off it ain't never gonna happen! She rushes them rose petals in the

house and locks 'em up in jars and puts 'em in a secret dark place down in 'er basement."

"What ain't gonna happen?"

"She waitin' for 'em to hatch into babies! That's what!"

"She say that 'bout babies in jars down there?" I asked.

"She did and told me never to blab her secret. What's she gonna do to me 'cause I did?"

"Don't know, but I hope the laundry ain't down there with that business goin' on," I said.

"When I worked for Miss Burke, she told me never disturb her jars of pretty lil' babies."

With that I felt compelled to step back a good distance from this Nona.

"Cept they ain't never gonna turn into babies," she said as if she'd just read a notice posted in some paper. "'Cause I always seen her pullin' them petals off. Yes, Ma'am. Locks 'em in jars when nobody lookin'."

About then I got to thinking that Nona sure seemed to see Miss Burke doing a lot of things nobody else could have.

'Bout that time Mister came up the walk and Nona was right; he was one handsome man: Him with that raven-black hair and them blue eyes near as dark as wild blueberries.

"Hey Nona, when you gonna bring me one of your sweet little pies again?" he asked with an ornery smile. "Nona puts something real special in 'em," Mister said. "I love your little pies, don't I?"

Her eyes glistening like stars. Yes this woman giggled like a silly little girl.

"I'm Bill Burke."

"I'm Sarah McWilliams."

"My wife hire you then?"

"Yes, Sir. Last week and told me to be here today at six. I been here, too."

"Bella gets mixed up on some things," he said and winked at Nona.

"And some things she don't, huh?" Nona quipped under her breath.

"Come on in and wait back in my lab," he said. "My wife won't be home for a bit."

Nona rolled her eyes as thoughwqyu

he was leading me some place she might not mind going herself, or in fact had. What could I say? I followed him back as Nona watched our every step, as she apparently did everyone that headed up and down the Burkes' cracked walk.

On the rear of their big house was a glass door that entered a large work area with windows looking out over the garden where lots of pretty roses were in bloom and none looked as though they were missing a single petal. Inside there was boxes filled with brown bottles and the same brown bottles were also lined up on the long counter next to tins of something stacked high. Whatever this man did, I could see that he did a lot of it.

But I'd seen brown bottles like them at the carnival. The man selling them said they was filled with elixir and it would cure anything from gout to insanity if you were lucky enough to take some home 'fore the carnival headed out of town. Then the carnival barker brought out a crazy man tied up in a white jacket. He was talking nonsense to prove how much luck we best work up and then buy a bottle. After this poor man gulped a cap full of that tonic he smiled big, said his name and how he longed to go back to being a farmer now that his mind was thankfully cured. That same night Sally bought a bottle for her gout and said she also felt real good so she went and took another dose which nearly killed her. So now I wondered what good could come from all Mr. Burke's brewing and steaming pots that made the place smell something fierce.

"What kind of farmin' you do?"

I asked looking out at those beautiful roses that surely were tended by someone, if not him.

"You been listenin' to Nona over there? Ah, don't mind her. She don't even know what month it is. I'm a pharmacist. Sell remedies to cure folks."

"That mean crazies needin' a cure?" I asked. "Like the ones I seen at the carnival?"

"My tonic is for anybody who needs a cure for whatever ails 'em," he replied. "And I guarantee every bottle or your money back."

Nona made it sound as if Miss Burke took his tonic and, like Sally maybe went for a second swig. Then from meanness, maybe she passed a bottle or two over the fence to Nona who gulped some tonic before handing the rest over to her lady who apparently lived at her window looking for Mister to come along. But was it the tonic or Mister who made these women swoon?

"Mostly I sell to sane" he added. "You see crazies are crazy 'cause they don't know they are. That's how you tell 'em from the rest of us."

"You mean to say you sell tonic to folks who don't need it, but still aim to put down money for it anyway?"

"Well, yeah. They buy what's in my brown bottles so they don't never need it. It's called sales marketing," he said.

"Sales marketing is selling stuff nobody needs?"

"That's it in a cap full," he remarked.

"Where'd you learn all this?" I asked.

Couldn't figure what he could be brewing in all them copper pots that could be of any good what with the smell of cod liver oil and steaming sulfur.

"College. I studied chemistry," he said.

"My daughter's in college."

"You don't say? Not many colored girls go to college, I reckon."

"Your wife, she go to college?"

"Oh, yeah. You see that's where Southern women go to snare husbands so they can graduate to do nothin' the rest of their lives," he said but with a pretty smile. "Yes, Bella took advanced strategies in husband hunting, you know, husbandry. That and habitual moanin' exercises, the Southern gothic classics of self-pitying and many advanced classes related to the economics of shopping. Her final year was mostly taken up with senior courses in bankrupting a husband and writing papers blaming him for lettin' it happen. It's called the bills done come in, honey. You see, all Southern men know that a bill is a heart attack in an envelope you try your best to never open in hopes you can keep your heart beating till the following month's bills come due! Yep! She graduated with honors."

At that moment, Miss Burke flew in from her kitchen. Flew in like a tornado. It must 'a been near nine that morning, so I figured she'd apologize for not being home when I arrived for work. I would soon find that apologies came her way but not back out in the mail.

"I heard that, William," Miss Burke screeched. "You are belittling me in front of, what is your name? and anyway, why are you back here with my husband?"

"Sarah McWilliams, Ma'am."

I didn't know what to say. She was standing right there with her hands on her hips and could plainly see that we weren't getting much done. Then it dawned on me, what if she's one of those folks that don't know she needs Mister's tonic?

"She's been waitin' for you, honey," he said.

Bella snorted like a female bull and stared at him, then at me.

"Why?" she asked like a prosecutor yet waiting for that one alibi she'd yet heard.

"I 'magine you hired her, didn't you sweetie?"

"Of course, I hired her. Suppose to come tomorrow. You know this is the women's auxiliary breakfast, William. It comes on the same day every month."

"I did indeed forget which of the about same days it fell on. And so did Sarah here," he said.

"I'll say. You come back tomorrow like I told you. Hear?"

"Yes, Ma'am. I'll come back tomorrow like you said. 'Cept I guess you didn't tell me which tomorrow you meant last week. But I think I know now."

I was afraid of getting Miss Burke worked up in case Mister was out of tonic.

"Well, good then."

Miss Burke stomped back to her kitchen where I could hear her talking to herself as she banged her pots and pans on the stove like they'd been sassing her.

"She ever take your tonic?" I asked Mr. Burke.

"She's one of 'em that don't know she needs it," he whispered. "But I'm an optimistic man and I do believe good marketing will one day get 'em all."

On my way back home, I tried to sort things I'd heard and seen that day to put in a letter to Lelia and Louvenia. I knew they'd be delighted that I'd gotten away from the tubs and into housework, yet I still wondered what I had gotten myself into. Could I be working for a lunatic white woman, or was the crazy one really Nona? And if Nona's a bit crazy, was it 'cause she'd worked for Miss Burke who drove her near insane hunting for specks of dust ain't nobody gonna see? Or maybe they all been drinking too much of Mister's tonic!

Still as I saw it, Bella and I had to work something out 'cause I didn't have references to get a house job on a nice street. She, on the other hand, couldn't keep her help and what help she got had to contend with Nona looking to roll poor Miss Burke's lopped-off tongue in cornmeal. I just couldn't wait to get back to tell Emily 'bout the big top I was working at.

Yes, I'd surely left the carnival at Sally's and had joined up at the circus. I only hoped that meant I was doing better for myself.

In the Dust With Bella
and the Creole Princess

57

I STARTED UP FOR real at the Burkes' the next day. I got there early to
fix Mr. Burke's breakfast. Around that, I started peeling apples for
a pie 'cause earlier that morning Nona told me Miss Burke loved
pies. I figured if I was rolling a crust, she'd not wonder what Mister and
I were rolling in.

That day confirmed what Nona had told me: Miss Burke really did
stay in bed till mid-day. She was also right about the reason she woke up
late. It was because she didn't sleep well she went prowling for specks of
dust late at night. Still, the way I looked at it, her sleeping in was fine
with me; I could get my work done better without her looking over my
shoulder. But within the first few days at the Burkes', I realized that
when she wasn't looking over my shoulder, she was sure enough looking
over her husband's. When she wasn't doing that, she was looking Nona's
way or watching for the neighbor. Then when the neighbor lady caught
'er nosing 'round in folks' business, just like Nona said, out came that
tongue of hers. Yes, Miss Burke seemed to stick it out all the time like
when she was all dressed up and headed off passing her neighbor as the
woman grunted and sweated pulling weeds in her garden—out came
that tongue of hers! Happened a lot. There'd be Nona standing there

staring down as her Mistress weeding like them weeds were miraculous happenings that sprung up. Guess that was Miss Burke's revenge; making sure the neighbor woman knew she got the worse deal hiring Nona when Miss Burke fired her. And it got worse. You see this Nona had taken to carrying a box of cornmeal out to the clothesline which she set on the picket fence when she was hanging laundry. Then when Miss Burke walked by or peeked through her kitchen window to see what the neighbor woman was up to, Nona would shake that damned box like she was striking back at the devil. Forever Miss Burke asked me why silly Nona thought shaking a box of cornmeal was gonna get her clothes to dry faster. Lordy, somebody ask Mr. Burke to pass a round of his tonic to these women.

By the end of most days, Miss Burke was plum tuckered out having done absolutely nothing for hours on end. Yes, nothing made her days long and surely her head feel emptier, which must have caused her thoughts to clang up there in all that hollowness. That woman moaned about this and that and then she'd work her way to the top of her list of gripes and start all over again. At times I'd got to wondering if her moaning was contagious, because after even a bit of that woman's mouth it was all I could do to keep myself from moaning.

Well, I'd never told Bella I hadn't worked at a house job before. Sally's didn't count, as it wasn't exactly a fine big house like Bella's. But is sweeping one floor different from another? Sure, white folks' houses were different from ours; took more time to clean 'cause they had stuff in them. Houses for coloreds were not much more than a windbreak in most places I'd lived, with cracks in the door and packed dirt for a floor. Call it what you like, but I can tell you Minerva never worried about dust in her life. Unless she was wiping it off the little bit of food she had to cook up each night.

Well, just as Nona had predicted, it was about my third day at Miss Burke's that I started feeling her eyes following me while I did my chores. I didn't know what to do so figured I best do my experimenting in keeping her grand house when she wasn't home. So, when she went to watching me, I'd only dust. How can you get that wrong? I'd dust up one side of a room and then down the other and then turn and start all over again to impress her as to how thorough I was. All the while, I could feel her gray-blue eyes following me like drifting icebergs. Her looking at me like I was really the peculiar one. Didn't know what she was thinking, but figured she might be getting real suspicious and, sure enough, that suspicion seemed to ferment every day.

What was I to do? I had to think fast.

"Sarah, I been meaning to ask for your references," she asked. "Where did you work as a housemaid before?"

There was no time to work up a good story, something Emily would have helped me concoct, so feeling cornered, I blurted the first thing that came to mind. Ma Mere must surely have been on my mind that morning.

"Ah, I worked for a Creole princess, that's who."

Then I tried to escape my own tall tale by jumping back into my work. I headed through the drawing room for the dining room figuring the kitchen would be my sanctuary. I dusted in that direction like there was a plague of locust to beat off to the next farm. Still the dust I stirred up didn't shoo that woman off. No, she simply followed me.

"A Creole princess you say? I didn't know there were Creole princesses. That mean she's half royalty and half colored? How can that even be?"

I kept backing myself toward the door to escape. Survival is an instinct you don't have to think about first.

"Where are you going other than one big circle?" her big mouth asked.

Well, as the preacher said under the chestnut, open your mouth and the words will come. Guess that didn't mean they might not tumble out a bit scrambled.

"Sure, you know that Creole princess who came back from living in the palace of the King of France over there. Don't you know 'bout her? Somebody said she's the King's cousin or maybe even closer than that, huh?"

I never looked her straight in the eyes and hoped Jesus was too busy somewhere 'cross town to hear my story. Lying is a sin and you can read somebody's eyes and the way they squirm when their fib falls out to know when they are. I already knew that white folks thought lying was a particularly grievous sin but only when we were doing the fibbing. Guess Jesus did hear me and guided this poor woman to help me work my way out of the trap her demands for references had landed me!

"Oh, wait… I do think I've heard about her. Sure, I have. Everybody has. Haven't they? She has lots of jewels, don't she?"

Bella looked puzzled. Like it was a bit unnatural for her to team up with me to get our tales to match. But for whose benefit, I wondered. For the life of me, I'd never known of a white woman, except Sally, help me weave a story so I could get on with things.

"Why, yes Ma'am, she sure does," I replied. "And I had to keep them jewels polished up 'cause the princess never knew when some prince or princess was gonna drop by for tea."

She looked flummoxed, like she'd just been informed that an invitation from the King of France had just arrived by livery and she had no inkling as to what she might wear to the royal tea.

"Really?" she asked. "Distant Creole cousins of the King of France, here in our part of town. Yes, of course," Bella rambled. "Whereabouts does this royal princess from France live now? Round here I assume."

Did this woman buy into my story?

Later I found out that Bella sashayed right over to the church to tell her big-hat lady friends that she was now next to royalty, or at least used the same help as royalty, which in Bella's taxed mind was near to being the same.

Ma Mere's Creole princess had saved me, at least for the time being. But there were days when she had slipped back to France without a word and was nowhere to be found. On those days I'd be on my own again with this woman; Bella over here, Nona over on that side of the fence and me wading through the stew of tales that seemed to slosh over that little fence all week long!

Did I tell you 'bout the babies in jars?

A few weeks after I was settled in Emily's attic, I received a letter from Louvenia, except Annie hadn't written it this time. One of the church-women who came out to Sister's to visit had. The letter wrote that the Preacher had suddenly died that autumn leaving Annie and her kids with no father and no means of support.

Sister shared that the Preacher had simply worn himself out tending the souls of folks in the alleys 'round Jesse's place. His over-worked heart just went and took his life with it and nearly his family's. The things I'd seen living on Jesse's alley had probably broken his heart as there was so little one man could do. Could have been Louvenia or me falling down dead and nobody 'round to know. Dead at the age of forty-two. No one saw him lying there till hours after he'd passed—his flesh frozen by then. Those poor alley folks, not counted by anybody but him, the people he loved and loved him back, never got to bid farewell. Annie been standing there that night at her kitchen window watching for his return but never seen him at the mouth of that alley on the street leaving her dream, as Jeff left mine; broken by the very weight of those white shadows we lived under.

Where does a woman like Annie go with those kids and no hus-band? She ain't gonna find another man 'cause men knew the chances of staying afloat in those alleys were already slim so taking on a ready-made family lowered the odds appreciably. What did Annie do with her time when she didn't have a man to get supper for? Look over her calendar for the date the food would likely run out? Louvenia wrote that for days Annie walked circles in her head searching for that well to throw herself down to get the inevitable over. What were her options? The only thing that slowed the avalanche was she couldn't decide which was best: Leave her kids orphans or carry them with her to the Lord by her own hand. Well, she knew what Alex and I endured as orphans at Jesse's.

Thank the Lord, Sister came up with a solution for all. She told Annie that Jeff's chestnut tree awaited them. Sister was a good Christian woman and shared everything as the Lord commanded. Their desperation didn't frighten her. She'd been in that alley and yet still saw beyond its brick walls to an option none of them thought of; they'd all share survival. After the Preacher was buried, Sister got Annie and the kids to come out to her place and this time they'd never go back to that alley again. They would somehow manage by living off the kitchen garden and the peach trees in my orchard that were now producing well. They could sell some of the fruit they put up every year and deliver it in town along with Sister's mending and the laundry Annie could get done. It was good for the kids to get out of those dirty alleys. Louvenia wrote that they looked forward to summer again when they'd pick the flowers that grew every spring over Jeff's grave. Then all that was left for me to do was somehow get money back to Sister to pay the landlord.

Late each morning after I had cleaned up the dishes from Mr. Burke's breakfast, I'd go upstairs to Bella's room and pull the drapes open so she'd start to wake. Nearly an hour or so later after she'd finally pry her eyes open and so I'd go down to start her breakfast tray. The Burkes couldn't see to eating at the same time or even the same thing let alone in the same room. In fact, didn't do much together period. Well, I felt lucky to have anything to eat any ol' day but theirs was a different world than I'd ever witnessed up close. I could only laugh at the thought of telling my husband I wouldn't be getting up before lunch and expected the daily menu waiting for my approval. While Miss Burke picked at her breakfast that would largely go uneaten, I'd start picking up and dusting in her room to make sure she'd not go back to sleep as I didn't want her tongue-lashing for not getting her ready for her afternoon bridge game that I had to bake cookies for.

The objects on Bella's dressing table were so beautiful. Sometimes, as I picked up her room, I'd pause to gaze at the assortment of beautiful objects she'd collected. Seemed like they all reflected light like bouquets made of jewels. Couldn't even imagine where such fine things came from. She had bottles of perfume and atomizers made of sparkling rock crystal capped in silver along with beautiful silver-framed photographs of her folks and her favorite dogs over the years. But most were of Miss Burke herself showing off her big hats and holding to prominence her well-ringed fingers. I picked up one of those rock crystal perfume bottles and held it to the light and to see a rainbow of pastel colors reflected back. Who made them crystal bottles? Did they make them only for rich white women? Is it even possible that Mrs. Washington had a dressing table arranged like Bella's?

As I was moving her perfume bottles to dust, this woman jolted up from her bed and looked at me as though I was there to forced-fed her another day.

"You best not be touchin' my things," she barked.

I thought if the devil has a wife, bet she looks just like Bella over there with that silk thing hanging half over her puckered up scowling ol' face and that hair of hers standing straight up like a she-devil.

"I was just dustin', Miss Burke. Don't know how to dust and not touch nothin'."

"Liar! Those things you're fingering would be a waste on coloreds! And you best not take off with anything," she added. "'Cause I count everything over there every mornin' in case you're wondering!"

"No Ma'am, I ain't wonderin'. I'm sure you do. You got the time for it."

"Huh? Anyway coloreds breed like farm animals. You know you do! Don't need to go snatching my pretties to get a man, do you now?"

Oh, Lord, here was Bella's cud rolling out again, but I was the one expected to digest it whole.

"My husband," she whined, "doesn't notice me anymore. He has another woman; I can tell. Any woman can," she said in her Southern baby-girl voice that would have made even spun-sugar-bathed Melinda Burney nauseous.

"Well, just let it go. Let it be."

"Let it be? How?" she whined.

Letting something be was not something Bella Burke took to.

"'Cause you got no other choice. Let the pain go or it'll kill you like a thousand pinches of nightshade," I told her.

"Nightshade?"

"Poison, Ma'am."

"Well, it's easy for you to say. You're colored."

"Easy? Easy for me? If I carried every pain I seen in my life, every pain been put on me, I wouldn't be here now. But I got a daughter to think of. I 'member the Bible verse my momma taught me. Psalm 56… 'Lord, you know the troubles I seen for you have kept a record of my tears…'"

"Now how could that mean anything to me?" she snapped.

"Pardon?"

"How could you ever understand what it's like to be a white woman?" she blurted.

"You're right. I guess I need to walk a mile in your fine shoes before I can take the log out of my own eye. That sound 'bout right?"

How could I not wonder if Bella stuffed cardboard in the bottom of her patent leather shoes to cover the holes as I did?

THEM LITTLE JAR BABIES

58

I T WASN'T LONG before Emily and Hank seemed to have me down for supper most nights if I got back in time. If not, Emily would put a plate back on the warmer. Later, while I ate, she'd tell me what had gone on that day. It came that I ate with them so often that when I didn't have night school, I'd come home and start peeling tatas or whatever she had washed and waiting on the counter.

Many times, Hank brought his ma over for the evening. Grandma Ida lived down the street in the little house she wouldn't let Hank paint 'cause her husband had painted it to begin with and she was just as pleased with the color now as she was the day he painted it a quarter of a century before. That woman seen it all and didn't suffer fools. At least not fools like Emily and me.

Grandma Ida was near as old as God; in fact, she knew him when he was a nappy-headed child she said one evening slurping her coffee with whiskey. An awful lot of woman-history flowed from Grandma Ida after a few sips of Irish coffee!

"You're lookin' good this evening, Grandma Ida," I said, pouring her another so she wouldn't start mouthing off on Emily's cooking.

"You goin' blind, too? I 'bout dead!" she said. "And that's what I look like. Can't ya see nothin', you stupid girl?"

And that was Sunday best talk for Grandma Ida.

"Now, Grandma, you can't keep livin' alone down there."

According to Grandma, Emily was a stupid girl, too.

"Some folks think your place is deserted 'cause you won't let no paint touch it."

"They come knockin' at my door and they'll find out who's gonna be dead next. That's for sure!" Grandma said. "Anyway, I can't keep livin' nowheres. Tol' you I 'bout dead. Only gonna pack up to move one more time and that's to a box six feet under where rents is dirt cheap and your neighbors keep they mouths shut 'bout things ain't none of their business."

"Sounds like Ma will be needin' another sip of whiskey," Emily said as she reached for a new bottle. "I can tell by the speed her mouth is moving in. Twice as fast as the rest of her!"

"Yes, I do, too!" Grandma said. "And don't water it down this time!

About then Emily slammed her skillet on the stove like she meant for it to land upside Grandma Ida's head.

"It's a wonder I'm dyin' with the kind of things you do with a skillet?"

"Oh, Lordy! Here comes the cookin' conspiracy," Emily declared.

"I told my son he'd be sorry he married you!"

"Sure he's regretted marrying me." Emily quipped. "But who else would marry Hank with a mother like his as part of the deal? What's your answer to that Ma?"

"'Course I come along. Got to make sure my boy don't eat too much of your cookin'," Grandma Ida said. "Go over there and stir that slop 'fore it boils over."

I braced the stool so Emily could get the whiskey down from the top shelf. Don't know why she stowed it up there as Grandma Ida could barely stand on her own two feet let alone climb a stool to get to that bottle. While I was holding the stool, I noticed that lots of Grandma's hair had fallen out in patches.

"Why's your hair fallin' out?" I asked her.

"You two gots worse hearin' than me. Ever' thing's fallin' out or fallin' down on me! Give me that whiskey. Ain't you got it down yet? And that's with two of you doin' the climbin' for it! Gonna drink it on the way home where I hopes to have some peace from folks lookin' up my nose."

"You are not goin' home till after supper when your son can walk you back," Emily said as she worked butter and cream into the tatas. "You watch, Sarah, she'll be sleepin' on the sofa tonight and then wake at dawn barking for my biscuits."

⁓

I always enjoyed my morning walk to the Burkes'. It gave me time for my own thoughts before Miss Burke tortured me with her running drip of nonsense and then flooding my day with her made-up chores like hunting down dust ain't nobody on earth could see. One morning I got to thinking about Grandma Ida being near blind. I wondered what her eyes had seen and if the stories along our journeys were that different. She was born into slavery way before the war and lived through that carnage and survived Reconstruction when the South was handed back everything they'd lost. Folks called it sharecropping. Grandma Ida told me 'bout her kids living on nothing but wild collard greens and corn meal mush for months. Ever'day the same. Said she was weak; sick from hunger and sicker from eating that food. She married the barber who started Hank's place, but he died young. Grandma Ida bought herself some used washtubs and a washboard and somehow kept her family fed in the same little house they'd bought with every cent they could pull together.

I kept wondered about her hair falling out. 'Cause she was old? Or too many years of ill health? I wanted to somehow help Grandma Ida's condition but couldn't think how.

When I got to the Burkes' that morning, Mr. Burke asked me if I'd washed the bottles he was fixing to funnel fill with remedy. He filled a batch nearly every day depending on how many stores downtown had placed orders. I liked helping him but tried to do it when Miss Burke was away or asleep. She held to the notion that her maids were meant to serve her needs only. Seemed like her husband got in the way of that if he needed something too. He mostly let things be, always concerned that

Miss Burke would go to thinking him being up to something with other women, particularly her colored maids. That strange? To this woman, we were primitive and depraved. Just the same she worried her husband might just want to get in on some of it. Lordy, help me make sense of this white women before I end up catching her head throbs and go off having hizzy fits myself!

"Got your bottles all cleaned and dried, Mr. Burke."

"Bill. Just call me Bill is fine."

"What makes somebody's hair fall out?" I finally asked.

"Could be many reasons: fungus on the scalp can sure cause hair loss. Malnutrition, you know, not eatin' right. Even worryin' too much is known to be a cause for hair loss. You notice your hair fallin' out, Sarah?"

"No, not mine, but I know somebody's is."

"Well, try a little sulfur mixed with a little mineral oil. Tell your friend to eat good and not go to fret over things."

What Mr. Burke had said made me wonder how you go about telling folks to eat good when they're already fretting themselves sick wondering if they're gonna eat period?

Later that morning while I got the laundry soaking, I began peeling vegetables for the soup for their supper. Miss Burke had gone to a church tea that day, so I went up there late that morning to give myself a moment to sit at her dressing table and catch my breath. There I noticed her collection of fine toilet articles seemed to grow in number. What was her newest thing, I wondered? That silver box with the delicately incised monogram? Or a new tortoise-shell frame? Maybe the brush with the exotic wood handle; never seen wood like all striped light and dark like that. Sure always smelled pretty just sitting there.

I'd just opened the silver cap on one of the bottles to smell when Miss Burke barged in. Usually I could hear her stomping up the stairs. But not that afternoon. Guess I was too absorbed in those beautiful objects and wondering how a glass bottle could give me a feeling of utter delight just by looking at it. How does that happen?

"You best not be putting my alabaster combs in that hair of yours! Are you now?"

I could only wonder if any of her churchwomen ever heard such a tone coming out of that pouty little mouth of hers.

"No, Ma'am. Just picked it up to clean. That's all it is."

"I never seen a colored like you before. You are so very peculiar; over there lookin' at my things like they were somethin' special to you. How could that even be?"

"You're asking me, Ma'am? Or yourself?"

Bella always gave me lots to think about because to me she was the most peculiar white woman I'd ever met and yet she thought the same of me. I was a peculiar black woman, even if she'd never taken the time to know me beyond the shadow of my mop. But then I was her mop.

Bella looked at me suspiciously.

"What's goin' on here?

"Pardon."

"I do believe you got someone special 'round here you think you need to doll-up for. That right?"

"Just picked 'em up to clean."

"Did that Princess you worked for let you touch her things? That's what I want to know."

I could tell by the way she squinted her eyes that she never really bought the Creole princess tale; just used it to impress her church-woman. Still I figured it best not to take chances.

"Well, yes. Can't exactly polish up the jewels without touchin' 'em. And the princess, she always gave me lots of really fine things to tote. Don't she? Yes, I got a table at home covered with lots of pretty things from her. Sure, I do. You see, the princess is mighty generous."

"Yeah, well, don't princesses wear diamond necklaces most the time?" Bella asked.

"Oh, sure they do. The princess always said a person should look her best 'cause that means she's got pride in herself."

I picked up a crystal bottle and looked at it closely in case she wanted to be like the princess and give me something for toting. You see, I fig-ured her dog wouldn't want that little bottle first.

"Pride, you say? Well, of course a princess has pride; that's why she's next to royalty so to speak. But you're a colored woman. You think you're gonna wake up one day and somehow find yourself a princess? Only white folks have them kind'a dreams!"

Then Bella sat down next to me. Well, I tell you plain; I'd never sat that close to a white woman other than Sally.

"That one you were smelling is my favorite. From Paris, France. Smell it again. It's tuberose."

She picked up my hand and dabbed a bit on the back of my wrist and lifted it to my nose. I'd never smelled anything as pretty in my life.

"Now if you get the princess, who knows the king of France to invite me over for tea one day, even though she's only a Creole princess and that don't make her as good as a real one, I might someday let you have your pick of one of these here jars to keep. Like that little chipped one in the back there. Hear?"

"Well, yes, Ma'am, I sure enough heard it all now, ain't I? Sure have. But you see, folks been sayin' the princess is over visiting the King of France at his palace. Can't say when she's comin' home. Maybe she got herself lost in one of them big palaces and she's still over their wandering around. You think? No, don't know when she's giving teas again, but I put in a good word for you when she's in town again."

Bella picked up her brush of white boar's bristle. The back of the handle was silver; I'd polished her fingerprints off more times than I could count. She lifted that brush up and dropped it on that glass dressing table like she didn't care if it broke or not. The sight of that was jolting as I'd lived my first seven years in a dirt floor shack where there was no glass in the windows to keep the plagues of mosquitoes out.

"This here brush is not for your hair. It would break it right off if you pulled it through, don't you think? Well, I know it would."

How, I wondered did she know this?

"Somebody ought to be makin' nice combs for coloreds. Maybe with silver handles even."

Bella smirked as if I'd suggested horses should have silver caps on their brushes. But didn't they at the Burney place? With the Burney "B" monogram on every one. I know, I watched ol' Isaac brushing the horses and then Ella sitting on the veranda cleaning the bristles and polishing them while Jackson and I played.

"Smell this face powder here. This brand I get at the five-and-dime up town, but it would make you look like me. Well, it don't matter, you ain't allowed in stores to shop anyway 'cause you folks would probably break things with your rough hands!"

The way Miss Burke was talking to me, but also talking to herself like I wasn't really there, got me wondering if she'd skipped her remedy that day. I even worried she might start in on babies coming from jars that Nona was certain Bella kept hidden in her basement.

"Look like you? How do you mean, Miss Burke?"

"Pasty-white, like a dead woman rolled in cake flour," she said.

You know I'd just been thinking the same; that she looked all pasty. That got me feeling uneasy thinking maybe white folks really could read our minds.

"Don't know of any face powder for coloreds," she added as she looked in her mirror gazing at her own face. "Something for your mahogany skin. Oh, well, they'll come up with it. They're always inventin' things to spend money on. Ever try some oil on your hair? I mean, don't it look a bit dry to you?"

"No, Ma'am. Never tried scented hair oils." Of course, I had but wanted to see how different it was from what they made for white folks.

"Heat some up—then work a few drops into your hair and massage it into your scalp. Don't forget to brush each side a hundred times. I'll tell you my secret: don't tell Nona, she blabs everything to that neighbor woman over there. You know that woman's a Baptist? Well, no wonder about her is what I told William! I get my oil from him. Ask 'im for some. Take a jar of oil, then fill it with a pinch of dried lavender, a handful of dried jasmine flowers or whatever. Rose petals are still my favorite. You see I pick the petals early in the morning when they're dewy fresh. But cover 'em up so the sun don't wilt 'em. Then I fill a jar full of petals and pour some of William's imported oil over 'em and cover the top real tight. He has the funnels down there. Lots of them. Don't know why he needs so many. Then leave it in the dark basement till you're ready to use it and all you have to do is put that jar up in the window. The sun will release the fragrance like it does a rosebud's. Don't you think? Go over there and take down that jar in my dressing room window. I just brought it up from the basement yesterday."

I did as she said and brought it back to her but still worried what she might do if she found out that's truly not where babies came from. Mind you, she'd never had any children.

Miss Burke held the bottle up to the light. She looked transfixed which made me think she was coming down with a spell. She stared and stared at that jar almost like I wasn't there. Sure made me uneasy wondering if the rest of her mind was shutting down on her, too.

"See, look here. My tiny little babies floatin' around so peacefully in there. Maybe like the angels float up in the clouds. Yes, they are. Sure they are. See?"

She handed that bottle to me, but I didn't want no part of her jar babies even if she did throw in a few angels. No and I figured it wasn't my place to be telling no white woman that's not where babies come from. Anyway, she didn't like being told nothing she didn't want to hear in the first place.

Well, once and for all that other crazy woman, Nona, was right, at least in part. Miss Burke held captive little babies if only someplace in her mind.

"No, Ma'am. Don't see no babies in there. I think you got that all wrong. Where they come from, I mean."

"No, of course you can't see my babies, 'cause you're standing there like you're deciding which window to leap out. No, they don't bite," she said. "My sweet babies never bite."

She held up a bottle of her oil to the light of the window and pointed with the look of delight.

"Here, look close behind that rose petal is one. Tiny little baby rose buds. Right there. See it."

I took that jar and held it up to the light coming through the window.

"Now, buds from baby roses don't have fragrance, but they sure look pretty floating in that oil with all those big petals."

"That's what Nona's been meanin' 'bout them babies in jars," I mused.

"Nona? That woman again! You been spending too much time hangin' on that fence with that girl. If you're over there jabberin' with her, why haven't you told her that that box of cornmeal she puts on the fence won't make the neighbor woman's clothes dry faster. That girl thinks if she shakes a damned box of cornmeal till it catches in the wind her clothes are gonna dry faster. I swain! That's what Baptists do; think up silly things like that all day long. You see once I told that girl to put a pinch of cornmeal in her shoes to keep her feet dry but not the whole damned box! She got it all wrong, didn't she?"

"Yes, Ma'am. I tell 'er someday. Cornmeal ain't gonna get her clothes to dry faster."

Well it ain't the only thing Nona got wrong.

⁕

After being introduced to Miss Bella's brood of jar babies, I sneaked off early for the night. I needed to help Emily get dinner on so we could get ready to go see Mrs. Booker T. Washington who was speaking in town.

You see it had been a long time since I first saw Mrs. Washington and I wanted to see how she was holding up. I figured she probably didn't bother to wear that corset no more. I'd sure like to see how she mopped a floor in one if she did.

Emily and I scurried around getting supper on, gossiping about Bella Burke and ignoring Hank wanting to know what was for dessert that night. You see, Emily and I had decided the week before there'd be no dessert that night because we had to lose ten pounds before we went to see how much Mrs. Washington had let herself go, her being famous and all and probably living too close to the supper table.

A Tattered Hem

59

EMILY AND I often shared our great respect for Mrs. Washington as there were few women out there who'd earned such acclaim for their words and deeds. At times I wondered if this was because there were too many of us bent over tubs to hear the voice that might lead us along a different path? Or had folks simply given up listening for one? Surely there are many ways to express regard for someone you've never meet and unlikely to. For Emily and me, we couldn't leave off talking about the fine clothes Mrs. Washington wore and the dignity she exuded; her pride spilled over from the colored weeklies and we lapped it up like ice-cream.

We both wanted to look as nice as Mrs. Washington even if the toils of our daily lives hardly afforded any time for primping and certainly not the funds to be dressed like her. Still Emily and I dreamed and like Lucille and Becky, we also cut articles from the papers about the great lady to discuss her outfits and how we'd do things differently if we had the money to shop at fancy dressmakers and milliners or how we might have our hair arranged even if we were donning a milliner's dream on our heads.

When the night finally arrived to see Mrs. Washington, I was nervous thinking that there'd likely never been a colored woman who could draw a crowd unless you considered slave auctions. Again, I expected she'd be standing up there on a lighted platform in front of an audience of well-dressed folks. In eager anticipation, I'm sure I pressed my old dress a dozen times that week, yet it still didn't look like anything but one of Bella's castoffs. I know I wanted Mrs. Washington to see that she'd made an impression and that I embraced her pride.

We arrived at the hall only to find all the seats were filled; the only way to see her would be standing in the rear. Gaslights flickered above like a thousand candles as we bobbed to see the platform. Then, just as Mrs. Washington was being introduced, there was a rustle of excitement such that we could hardly hear her announced. As Mrs. Washington shook the hand of the woman who had introduced her, the entire place went silent till she smiled and nodded our reception. Then we burst into applause. There she stood, as straight and tall as the first time I came to hear her. With only a smile, she humbly accepted the applause that reverberated. Hungry eyes looked up at her with worshipful respect.

Well, I could still see she'd gained weight over the years. Oh, at least five pounds, although I'd convinced myself she'd mostly hidden it under that fancy suit that probably cost more than I made in a year. Emily had another opinion.

"That woman looks skinnier than she does in all the papers!" she whispered. "Don't she?"

The comment reminded me Emily had poor vision.

"She must not be a good cook," I responded sniffing out some imperfection in the woman that would make her a bit more like me. Still I hoped that Mrs. Washington and I had been on the same road somewhere struggling to reach the next day. Or perhaps down deep I'd always wondered what it would be like to be friends with such a great woman. Emily and I gazed up there at Mrs. Washington and then looked at the faces below aglow from the gaslights, heads juggling to find a view between us. My eyes worked that room trying to store up everything to write Lelia and Louvenia but couldn't think how I'd describe her in words put on mere paper. "Grace…." was all that came to mind.

"Who? Grace from church?" Emily bobbed to see.

"That woman up there has more grace than a queen."

Yes, the great woman commanded people's respect simply by the way she carried herself as though she was meant to occupy that very spot; even owned it for the moment she stood there along with a bit of us. Do folks respect her just because of the way she stands tall? My thoughts span in all directions.

"How could anybody talk down to one with so much dignity?"

My question garnered a jab from Emily's elbow as she was prone to doing when my notions floated off to those hazy fields we coloreds might find it dangerous to pitch a dream.

"Dignity rhymes with uppity," she said, "And uppity rhymes with gettin' lynched. That's what Grandma Ida said when I headed downtown wearing my new hat." Emily then added: "The one with the big feathers sticking up like the white women wear on Main Street."

I thought it unlikely that Grandma really said that, given the hats she wore but we'd all heard from white folks how uppity the coloreds were getting and the need to put us back in our places. But the one we should be knocked down to wasn't on any platform like the one that Mrs. Washington stood center of. Indeed, what you looked like, your very expression, a bit too much pride or not stepping aside as a white person passed could get us smacked down hard.

I looked down at my scuffed old shoes, the only pair I had, and my frayed hem and felt my leathery hands that had wrung a thousand tubs of enough brown water to overflow a sewer. Heaven knows my hair was a mess so I was glad we got there after the seats were filled as I'd hate to be right up there under her nose and her see me this way. The gas lights reflected off my best blouse shading it silvery along the cuffs where my iron had polished off the wrinkles.

Emily grabbed at my arm at the moment Mrs. Washington's last words and dragged me to the center aisle with her ample bosoms parting the sea.

"Where are you yankin' me to? Let go!"

Glaring eyes followed our rampage.

"Gotta meet Mrs. Washington," Emily announced.

Emily clutched my hand and raised it in the air as she dragged me up front like she'd caught a pickpocket and was displaying the hand that done the picking! Did she actually imagine Mrs. Washington was up there waiting to shake it?

"Oh, no, I got to get home now!" I squealed.

"You're always talkin' 'bout that woman," she said. "So now you got something to tell your grandkids; the time you met Mrs. Booker T Washington face to face."

Mrs. Washington was moving down the line shaking hands and saying a few words to those who wished to meet her.

Emily pushed me up there but the woman I dislodged shoved me back just as quick. Emily didn't feel the heat of that woman's piercing look that clearly suggested she wasn't gonna elbow me back but once.

Emily reached up and grabbed Mrs. Washington's hand first, which got me another elbow from the other side.

"Mrs. Washington, we're members, Sarah and me, of the Missionary Society," Emily said as she tussled with Mrs. Washington's hand. "Sarah is our president. Sarah McWilliams, I got here."

Emily held on to Mrs. Washington's hand like it was a souvenir from a county fair.

"I'm president……?" was all I could get out of my mouth.

"That's what I said, dear." Emily volleyed back.

Emily held Mrs. Washington's hand high so everybody could see she'd caught the prize and wasn't gonna pass it around. So, I offered the poor woman my own hand to shake so she could get hers back. Mrs. Washington looked right into my eyes like she was relieved and thankful of my gesture. My view of Mrs. Washington's nice smile was blocked when the woman next to me went to waving her hand between my face and Mrs. Washington like she'd waited long enough for her turn. Emily smacked it back down so I could continue my conversation with the great woman.

"Hello, Mrs. McWilliams. I'm certainly delighted you could attend," Mrs. Washington said.

"You heard of us? The Missionary Society?" Emily asked.

"I'm sure I have," Mrs. Washington replied.

"We'll invite you to one of our meetings," Emily said as she glanced around to see if anyone we knew saw us with our new best friend, Booker T Washington's wife.

"Thank you, ladies. That's very kind of you," she said.

Probably for safekeeping Mrs. Washington clasped her hands behind her back until she could distance herself from Emily and me. Yes, I'd just shared a few words with the foremost woman of color I'd ever heard of.

It would be weeks before Emily and I could stop talking about it. We headed home chattering over each other. I was hardly feeling important compared to the other fine folks even after being elevated in Mrs. Washington's view with Emily's quick election.

"What's the Missionary Society, huh?"

"Got no idea, but you been elected president," she said. "And I'm the one that voted you in. You see, I'm thinkin' you have more in common with Margaret Washington than you ever knew."

"Who? Me? What…?"

"Well, maybe she knows how to fix her hair up a bit better but I don't got it and you do. It's in you and Hank's said the same thing."

"Yeah, got what?" I asked.

"Honey, in the words of white folks, you just don't give a damn what the whiteys think.

Well, I knew there wasn't anything special that would ever put me up on a stage with Mrs. Washington, but I would always remember my friend's kind words. Yes, for a few moments she made me feel there was something unique about me that elevated me to Mrs. Washington's grace.

That night as I readied for bed, I asked myself what if one day Mrs. Washington ask me for tea? Living in Emily's attic things really started to change for me, at least in my thoughts. I think it was about then all the whys of my life stopped repeating themselves and became why the hell nots?

⟡

The next day I was running late for work, but that few minutes of extra sleep felt like a godsend even if it was gonna earn me a tongue lashing from Bella. Emily knew I was late and brought up some coffee shortly after she heard the kitchen ceiling creaking from me scurrying around in her attic. It was getting darker by the day that fall, so that Monday I knew I'd have to leave the Burkes' early to get across town for night school. My leaving early always got up Miss Burke's nose although me staying late got me nothing but another dustpan of her crumbs to count.

All the way to the Burkes' that morning, I felt annoyed and got to thinking that one way or another these white folks still believed they owned us. As I saw it, the only difference between my life and my folks' before the war is that white folks no longer bothered to house us, slop food or throw rock salt on the wounds they laid down over our backs. We have to take care of these ourselves out of the measly wages they tossed at our feet.

Scurrying all the way to the Burkes' that day, I thought about what I'd do about being late. Figured I'd dive into peeling a bowl of apples for a pie and when Miss Burke came down, she'd never know how long I been in the kitchen toiling away—or not. But that morning she'd already been down early. Nona briefed me as I came up the walk.

"Don't go out back to the laundry," Nona said. "That woman's already at it back in her garden. She's gonna see you through the winda!" Nona said. "She gots it bad. Oh, Lord, don't she now?"

Nona stood there shaking her box of cornmeal to ward off the evil white women's lingering spirit. By her reckoning, Miss Burke not only was getting babies from jars filled with petals; they were colored babies at that. According to Nona's latest rendition, Miss Burke was gonna keep them in the cellar till they growed up enough to work for her for nothing. Lordy! She didn't need to raise colored kids in the cellar for that; she already paid me near to nothing and didn't even provide me a place to sleep down there with her dog.

Well, anyway I already knew why Miss Burke was back in the garden. She had her church bazaar the following week and had gone to stripping rose petals while they were fresh and dewy to fill jars with her scented hair-oil treatment to sell.

"She'a tormentor!" Nona said. "She'a torment you in your sleep as good as the devil himself."

"Yeah? How's she do that now?"

I knew Nona's version of things typically had as many shades as Bella's rose petals. Still I couldn't resist.

"She took it up with the devil, my lady over here say so."

Well, I already knew Nona was a fool and I certainly didn't need to be asleep for Miss Burke to torture me, with or without the devil's prodding. No, she did it plenty while I was awake. "Scrub that better," she'd say. "Missed that spot. See that crumb on the other side of the room? How'd you miss that? You slackin' on me 'cause you think I'm not watchin' ?"

All the same I had to get my work done, despite Nona using me as a conduit over the fence for her hissy fits with Bella. Shake that cornmeal box and let's eat Bella's fried tongue for supper. It was all fine with me, so long as I don't got to cook it or clean up after!

The rest of the morning didn't get much better. Miss Burke walked in with her basket of rose petals just as I was filling my piecrust with sliced apples. Well, I give it to Nona, Bella sure enough had the look of the tormented.

"Aren't you late again this mornin'? Don't think I don't know even if I was in the garden!" she said like a Confederate spy waiting for a confession before the instruments of torture were unfurled. But I got to thinking, if she really knew, then why'd she ask? So, that was direction I went.

"No, Miss Burke, been near the kitchen all morning peelin' apples for a nice pie for your supper."

I just didn't tell her how far that "been near" really was. Maybe five or six blocks from her cracked front walk?

"I know for sure what you been doing. You were out there peelin' them apples on the porch so you could gossip with that Nona over there, weren't you? Now we're sure to have cornmeal in our pie because that silly girl is out there like a deranged maniac shaking boxes of meal all over the place."

Miss Burke put her basket on the table and went for an apron.

"I got to get twelve jars of my rose-scented hair treatment worked up for the church bazaar and I'm running late 'cause Nona was out early just to see what I was up to. Her and that box of cornmeal, huh! Truly I wonder if she don't sleep with a box of cornmeal!"

Lordy, how long had I heard the fussing between these women?

"Who but a complete fool would think a box of cornmeal was gonna help her sheets dry quicker?" Bella snarled. "But every time she hangs 'em, there's that box of cornmeal on the fence. And when I shake my head at her, so she knows that meal ain't gonna dry nothin' but the sweat between her toes, she grabs that box of cornmeal all over again and shakes it at me."

"Don't know, Ma'am. I sure as heaven don't know what to say."

And, Lordy, wasn't that the truth! I sure enough didn't know which one of those two women was worse as both acted like their minds had been dredged in cornmeal one too many times.

"The good ladies at church have agreed to buy a jar of my special rose-scented hair oil and give generously," she said. "That is, the good ones have. Did you get those jars of William's washed up and ready for me? Or were you too busy squawking with that fool over the fence turnin' the ground yellow under her clothesline with her damned cornmeal?"

While I chopped vegetables for their soup that night, Bella went to stuffing rose petals into the jars with the handle of a wooden spoon and slowly funneling oil in. All the while she was serving up ample helpings of her Bible lesson on Christian charity.

I decided to test whether the waters of Bella's Red Sea might part a bit for coloreds when it came to the charity she so loved to preach about. So, I tossed out my fishing net to see what goodies I might catch.

"Miss Burke, I'm thinkin' nobody makes pretty stuff for coloreds like your fine jars of scented hair oil, do they?"

Looking over her table of flower petals, oil and this and that, I was really thinking I could make some up myself and sell 'em to our the big-hat women at my own church. You see, I figured that if I sold just one jar to each of the big-hat women at church and they bought a jar for their ma and neighbors on either the good side of 'em, I'd be near rich— at least rich enough to buy a decent pair of shoes before the rains came.

"I don't know why nobody makes 'em for you coloreds. Guess folks figure you wouldn't take to 'em, they being true objects of beauty and all. But still there sure are plenty of folks makin' things nobody needs. Who knows? Perhaps one day some white person will make 'em and put 'em in stores you coloreds won't wreak havoc in. But then coloreds probably don't shop much 'cause they don't need nothin'. Well, I guess that's the way it was meant to be."

No, I couldn't make myself put the "amen" to Bella's sermon, but I decided to add a few words just the same.

"You're sure right, Miss Burke, coloreds don't seem to go shoppin' like white folks. Ain't too many shops for us, is there?"

I didn't tell her that colored shops tended to burn down from all the heat of their success along with a match or two tossed by envious white folks hiding under white sheets.

"Well, I suppose not," she said. "Guess the Lord intended it that way. Yet He might one day change His mind and forgive coloreds and let you have your own stores. But of course, not nice ones like ours. That wouldn't be natural; you all don't appreciate beauty enough for that or you'd not be livin' in such squalor 'cross the tracks over there."

Natural, huh? Bella's world was about as natural as the jasmine growing out of Melinda Burney's hair back at Grandview.

"White folks get their shops from the Lord, do they?" But then added: "Coloreds gots to make better wages to shop anywhere, don't you reckon, Miss Burke?"

I'd been hinting about a raise and figured this woman, who saw herself as a Biblical character from the Good Book, might see a heavenly vision of charity and give up another nickel a week.

"I really don't think the Lord's gonna forgive you folks that much. I mean look what a mess you all cause everywhere."

But I was thinking everywhere we was, we toiled the daylong cleaning up some white woman's mess. Guess it all started with they's babies' bottoms. 'Course, we caused that mess too, by doing their feeding.

"The Lord does make miracles."

I commented even as I figured the Lord had made a few messes of His own and I was standing there talking to one of His biggest.

"Miracles, as you rightly know, are accorded to white folks. That's plainly obvious," she said like I was the blasphemer. "It says in the Bible. Don't you read your Bible or go to church?"

"I want to go with you to your church to see what your Lord looks like," I replied.

That stopped Bella cold.

"Now, I don't know if you're bein' impertinent because I know you're not as smart as me."

Myself, I never once had a problem knowing when somebody was being impertinent, 'cause lip is all we got from these white folks so we knew their tune; it never varied much.

"I know you can't help yourselves," Bella continued. "But all good folks know what Jesus looks like. Of course, they do. He has blue eyes and blond hair. He looks just like His ma and that's what He favors. There are fine pictures of Jesus in the Bible. Anyway, why would you want to go to a white folks' church?" she asked hypothetically as I was sure no colored had ever been seen in her church 'cept to clean it.

I didn't tell her I already knew what Jesus looked like because Ella had told me many times. You see she saw Him one day at her back door needing His nappy hair cut so she trimmed it like she did Jackson's. Well, we all believed it in 'croppers' alley 'cause all sorts of magical things happened up in the big house that were mostly unimaginable to those of us living down at the shacks. Like the talk that there were fine tables up there laden with food that went uneaten while we were left to hope there might be some corn mush made with pork renderings to feed our fantasies on. Well, Ella got so much attention for cutting the Lord's hair that ol' Aunt Clara got jealous and went to telling folks she was the great-grand daughter, a hundred and one times over, of the Virgin Mary and she could cure all sorts of ailments if you had a nickel, which

according to her was half what the Virgin Mary pocketed for her services. Of course, nobody had a nickel to spare, so nobody ever proved
her wrong. But Aunt Clara must have been mistaken about being related
to the Virgin Mary, 'cause her eyes weren't even blue like Bella's and her
Lord's; no, ol' Sally's were pale green. Therefore, everybody knew she had
some kind of secret and sure wondered if the Virgin Mary had a hand in
it. Still weren't Ella's or Aunt Sally's notions as good as Bella's? Folks get
to seeing things differently. I couldn't get myself to think that the Lord
cares about somebody's hair. He's got enough problems getting a brush
through His own nappy mess after pulling on it from all the grief His
children get into. Nona alone has probably brought the Lord to near
baldness. Sure bet He's tired of seeing her box of cornmeal on the fence
there to ambush Bella!

Well, Bella Burke didn't like to think on anything that didn't fit
into her day just right. Her life was preordained to be bountiful by the
Lord Himself by virtue of her God-given skin color, or as we looked at
it, colorlessness.

"Wait, come back here!" she barked.

"Yes, Ma'am."

"You been spendin' too much time out back by William's lab. I seen
you back there, too!"

"But that's where your laundry tubs are, Ma'am. You aim to do the
wash yourself now, Miss Burke?"

I went to talking back at the woman because I figured no matter
what I wouldn't be getting no free jar of her scented hair oil let alone
better wages.

Freedom From a Shattered Goblet

60

I

T WAS ONLY a couple of weeks after Bella informed me that like herself, the Lord was certain to have blue eyes, that I once again found myself wondering why this woman couldn't get up in the morning when her husband did? Well, I'll give Nona this: Bella could surely torment as good as any, but then that was about all she had to do with her time.

Having these dark thoughts didn't help me get the morning off and it ended worse. Lord, I tell you plain; Miss Burke had for months been working me as if she had two Sarahs for the price of one. After doing three loads that covered all her clotheslines, I still had to carry her breakfast tray up those stairs. Mind you, it was never a single trip. No, it was daily up and down and up again because she didn't get that certain something that she really didn't want and couldn't stand the sight of the day before. Lordy, this woman was killing me a drop at a time.

"Didn't I say I wanted peach jam?"

"No, Ma'am, for sure you said strawberry and there it is spooned in your favorite cut-glass jam jar."

"Well, I don't think I could've said that 'cause I've got a hankerin' for peach. So, go fetch the peach like I told you.

"Yes, ma'am."

Still it always seemed that looking over her pretty things lifted my spirits even if that woman was over there moaning under her silk sheets. I enjoyed holding Bella's precious things up to the light which made it easy to contemplate a sweet life; one where you wake up to a table covered with beautiful objects that came from stores I couldn't even imagine being in. I wondered if it was even possible to have a beautiful table laid out like Bella's, her supper table or dressing table with all them sparkling trinkets but still have a life dark as Bella's moans suggested hers was. Somehow didn't seem possible. I wondered if these beautiful objects only came with lives bountifully served with dignity. And then, why don't all folks have a few beautiful things to deflect the ugliness of our days? I tell you, I could never figure out how this woman, who'd never worked a day in her life, was more deserving of finer things than the rest of us. Reminded me of Jackson's ma having an attic of beautiful dresses hidden away from her husband, which as a plantation-born child, put in my head that all beautiful things somehow derived from the attics of big white houses—fineries that drifted down from heaven through secret windows to those pale enough to deserve such beauty. Maybe even the same window Ella said white jasmine blossoms lilted in like snowflakes to scent Miss Burney's bath. Like Miss Burney's, Bella's world knew no want.

As Bella ate her breakfast that morning her slurping seemed to craze me more than other days. She slurped her big mouth on that tiny teacup worse than Grandma Ida who had only two or three teeth left up front. I knew Bella was sending the message she wanted her day's list of woes heard out and then repeated back to her in the correct order. That list seemed to grow with as many different-colored miseries as she had roses out back! Lil' ol' me is awake and ready to slap a pile of Bella woes on my help! I knew her good by then but her pouty face didn't win any sympathy from me even as it seemed to bring quick capitulation from her husband.

Bella finally finished sucking the last drop of tea out of that bitsy cup, not much larger than a big thimble and then near broke the damned thing slamming it down on the saucer to get my attention. Guess I'd been ignoring her while I did her room and she wasn't gonna stand for that one bit. When I went to pick up her tray, she knocked the water goblet off shattering it on that polished oak floor. As I reached down to pick up the pieces I began to wonder aloud.

"Bella, I been meanin' to ask you…."

I'd barely got the words out when the woman, who two seconds before was collapsed over her satin pillows—backhanded me so hard my vision blurred. Yes, that woman swung at my undefended face as hard as any man. I struggled to avoid falling backwards over her night table covered with her precious trinkets, but my head was swimming so badly I still fell to my knees.

"Don't you ever, in this house, address a white woman by her Christian name! You hear me good!"

There was a long pause before she resumed her lecture as I was holding my head to keep it from swimming away.

"Is that what they teach you at that night school?" she resumed. "That being the case, and I know it is, then you'd best never go back there if you know what's good for you. Who ever heard of a colored learnin' to read? What for? Now, get your mess here cleaned up and get down to the kitchen. I can't stand the sight of you today!"

I got myself back on my feet and could see in her looking mirror that my mahogany face was deeply reddened from her backhand. Well, I tossed her breakfast tray onto that stupid little table and walked out.

With tears streaming down my face, I passed Mr. Burke on the stairs.

"What's goin' on up there?" he asked.

But he could surely imagine what she'd done because that woman had worked the same deed on all her help.

William stomped up the stairs to Bella's room. I could hear her big mouth as I went for a rag with chipped ice to put to my face.

"I don't like Sarah's attitude," I heard her yelling. "She's been actin' like she's superior. I don't take to any colored thinkin' that. It ain't right or natural. No, I won't have it here. This is a Christian home!"

"Now let me tell you something, honey pie," I heard him reply,

"You have abused every house servant you could get to work here. If Sarah leaves, you'll be doin' your own cleanin' from now on in. Are you hearing? 'Cause I reckon folks at that church of yours will think that you doin' your own laundry is as unnatural as mules having offspring. No, Ma'am, I won't be payin' for any more help. Not ever again."

I can only imagine Miss Burke's terror at the thought of the big-hat ladies at her church finding out she was down to doing her own laundry and scrubbing her own floors. Lordy! When that news hit their big ears they'd surely be asking Bella to run along and join the coloreds' church across the tracks!

I had to work hard to keep my head up as I walked home as I was sure that folks noticed my swollen face and would know that I'd let some white woman backhand me to my knees. Then it hit me: I still had to find the courage to go back to the Burkes for my wages. You see, I'd sent my last pennies to Lelia and didn't know how I was gonna make it to the end of the month let alone beyond.

Up in my attic room all I could do was fall on my bed and sob. Emily tapped on my door, but I couldn't squeeze out from under the pillow I hid under to respond. She knew, didn't she? She brought in a tray of supper and put it on the table next to my bed. On the tray was a bowl of cold water that she dipped a cloth in and held to my brow. She never said a word as I lay there in our silence. But her caring presence alone brought calm to my raging heart. Yes, my thoughts were pounding as I knew I had to somehow get myself out of Bella's white magnolia-scented world or it would surely devour me. Lord, where is that underground railroad for a troubled heart hungering to flee? When Emily left, I reached for my Bible to mop my tears and dust away my anger.

I read 'the Lord is near to the brokenhearted and saves those who are crushed in spirit'.

The following Monday I got up early, slid new pieces of cardboard inside my shoes to cover the holes and set off for Bella's to humble myself for my pay. As I got close to Bella's I worked my chin up high just by thinking of what Mrs. Washington might have done? I knew she wouldn't cower to this white woman still the thought of swallowing one more piece of her crusty ignorance made me gag. I reminded myself that in all the time I'd worked for the Burkes, William had never once been unkind to me.

I was jittery as I walked up the side of their place. Mr Burke was standing there waiting. I hoped he was gonna pay me my money before chasing me off as Bella had probably demanded.

"Sarah, I been out here waiting for you. I'm really sorry about my wife's conduct the other day. It ain't right what she did. You've always been kind to Bella and patient with all her moods."

"There's never cause to slap nobody!" I replied.

"There is no cause at all. And I want you to know, Bella, she didn't used to be this way, so hard and all. Sarah, she's in there waiting to talk to you if you'd care to come in and hear 'er out."

There in the kitchen sat Bella at the table and it wasn't yet even seven in the morning. He'd eaten and there she sat with a plate of untouched eggs.

"Sarah, Bella here has something to say to you." William nodded to Bella. "Bella, what do you have to say to Sarah?"

Bella couldn't look at me but kept playing with the trim on her fancy lace collar.

"Well, Sarah, I didn't mean to say the things I did. No. You see, I had a real bad headache and you made it worse. But I know you didn't mean to, so I'm sorry for gettin' a tiny bit upset with you."

Said it to them cold fried eggs she was poking at with her fork so I knew there was little sincerity. I nodded to William, and figuring I wasn't fired after all, I went about my work without a word. I knew this woman had probably never asked forgiveness for the grief she'd caused a colored woman who'd served her like a slave. Well, that morning "something better" for me was no more than a limp apology from a pathetic spoiled white woman and keeping my job. Still, all in all, I'd gotten to the next day.

WELL, BELLA, NONA AND ME AGAIN

61

MY DAYS SEEMED to only grow longer after the morning of the broken goblet, but still we got by, Bella, Nona and me. Bella continued to fill her days with endless nothings and mine with ever-longer lists of things that I had to get done to keep her life properly polished up. I stayed mindful that someday I'd be needing this woman's reference to move on or there'd be no better job ahead. I'd only gotten the house job with Bella because no one else would work for her.

Nona seemed to like to remind me that I'd been with the Burkes for quite a spell; and to her that meant there had to be something going on more mysterious than Bella's jar babies in the basement. Going on?

One morning when I stepped out to hang laundry Nona yelled across the fence where she was taking hers down.

"Where's Miss Burke this mornin'?" Nona asked conspiratorially. "My lady say she was gone real early like she was sneakin' off or somethin'."

"Maybe your lady been sneakin' off a peek at somebody else's business is all."

"Then where she go?" Nona asked again.

"She's gone to church to work on setting up the bazaar and then to the market for things to make up a batch of her scented hair oil treatment. Tell that to your lady over there!"

I could see the neighbor woman up in the window waiting for Nona to return for the lowdown on Bella's whereabouts.

"Ah, huh. She gone, you here all by yourself, ain't you?" Nona remarked like she was practicing her spiel before she mouthed it back to her lady.

"What?"

"She gone, you here and so is Mr. Burke."

Nona looked back to see if the neighbor woman was still watching at the window.

"You doin' a count who's home and who ain't today?" I asked.

"I mean… you know what folks is gonna say 'bout that."

"'Bout what, Nona? You got something you're trying hard to not say real hard all the same?

"Huh? What I doin'?"

"I got my work to do. Got to get in there and get the table laid out to help Miss Burke with her special hair oil so she can sell jars at the bazaar."

"Yeah, you do the workin' and she do the keepin' of the money part of it! You gonna be there, too," Nona informed me.

"Me?"

"She gonna want her woman to do all the haulin' so she don't get 'er white gloves mussed. You be there standing behind her after you get it all set up on a big table. She sit there takin' folks' money and you standin' behind 'er all day smilin' to the whiteys. Watch how nice she gonna be to you in front of her woman friends. Lordy! She thinks she gonna go to heaven with wings the way she keeps that tongue of hers locked behind her big teeth smilin' to all them whities on church bizarre day!"

"Well, if I see that tongue of hers, I'll be sure to give it a good sprinkling of cornmeal just for you, Nona. Anyway, you sayin' you used to help Miss Burke at the bazaar?"

"Sure, I did. She don't want me to stay here alone with Mister is what I think. Huh?"

About then Miss Burke returned with her supplies.

"We got lots to do, Sarah. You best get your clothes pinned and come on in."

Then Miss Burke drew up so close to the fence that Nona near fell backwards. Guess she was expecting a good tongue lashing from Miss Burke.

"I got to get my babies tucked into their jars, don't I?" She said looking at Nona like she had a switch hidden behind her. "Your clothes dry fast enough today without shaking that damned box of cornmeal in the wind? Huh, did they?"

Nona could only gasp.

Miss Burke went on inside as I pinned the last of Mr. Burke's shirts to dry and Nona ran inside like she sure was gonna earn herself a nickle from her lady for some new tales on that Bella Burke and her maid.

Miss Burke truly loved to do her hair oil bottles and made them up real pretty with two colors of pastel ribbon twisted 'round the bottle and tied with a pretty bow after I dipped corks in hot wax and shoved in the bottle top. She was sure to have two or three tiny little rose buds floating in there which she said was her trademark.

Seemed as though Bella's bottles and the church bazaar were 'bout the only things that delighted her soul and that made both of our days lighter. How could I have known that these moments with Bella; her jars, scents, mixing oils and William's input on her project would make a mark on my life from then on?

"I still have two dozen bottles to fill," she said. "I'm goin' out to the garden and fetch more rose petals. Now I don't want you tellin' anybody at the bazaar this Sunday, but I put a few drops of my French perfume in each bottle."

"Why's that a secret, Miss Burke?"

"Everybody knows, well thinks, anyway, that Bella Burke has the most fragrant roses in town."

"I see. Well, I won't tell nobody your roses don't smell as good as the talk say. Nothin' much ever does."

Miss Burke grabbed her big garden hat so the sun wouldn't hit 'er face. Guess she didn't want to be going to the bazaar all red-faced like she'd been out picking cotton with the coloreds.

"You go see if Mr. Burke got those cork bottle stoppers in while I do."

"Yes, Ma'am.

I did always enjoy chatting with Mr. Burke. Never was he anything but real nice to me and over time we got to know each other. When Bella wasn't 'round we'd talk about this or that, mostly things he'd read in the papers, or I'd read in mine. I told 'im I'd been reading 'bout this colored woman named Annie Turnbo Malone who had her own hair product business. She started out mixing things herself and sold it in tins. I saw her ads in the paper where she claimed her product would keep your hair from falling out and make it grow so fast you could near watch it get longer. 'Course nobody had the time to sit in front of no mirror waiting for their hair to grow, so I guess nobody had the goods to disprove her. I wanted to order some of this hair product for Grandma Ida as I'd noticed her hair seemed to get worse. Emily said was 'cause Grandma used the same ol' soap she used to wash her clothes and over time it had burned her scalp in patches so badly they scarred over. Well, that certainly seemed possible; I'd been a laundress most of my life and knew what that lye soap can do.

"Mr. Burke, 'member when I told you 'bout my landlady's ma. Grandma Ida, who gots these patches on her head where no hair grows?"

"Can't say I do, Sarah. She still having problems?"

"I seen in the paper where you can buy a tin of special hair prepara-tion that will make your hair grow. You reckon it works?"

"Well, sure seems you and Bella are gonna both save us from bald-ness or at least make sure our hair smells real pretty."

I didn't tell Mr. Burke that my folks had lots of problems with our hair and suffered mightily from it. For us, a fine head of hair was a symbol of a having a better life where you didn't have to use lye soap because there was nothing else at hand.

"Sometimes when your scalp is damaged from combing it too hard, or from what you put on it, or even 'cause you don't wash your hair often enough a bit of fungus can get goin'."

"Fungus? What's that look like?"

I wondered if that was something that crawled over your head and all.

"It's too small to see, Sarah. But when you got a bad case of it might cause your scalp to itch or your hair to fall out. If that's the case, then a bit of sulfur in that hair oil of Bella's might do the job."

"You show me how? Sulfur in some hair oil? Maybe I can help Grandma Ida. She say her head itches something terrible all night and keeps her from sleeping."

"Yep, I can help you come up with something for Grandma. Our secret though. Bella wouldn't take to any competition at her church bazaar."

"No, I never tell Miss Burke nothin'."

Well, at least nothing she'd for sure really want to hear!

That evening I got home late while Emily was finishing up the supper dishes and Hank sat at the table cleaning his smoking pipes.

"Here she is!" Emily greeted. "And you are lucky today!"

"That's good news! I'll try to get the word to my achy tired feet!" I responded.

"You got two letters here from Lelia and one from Miss Louvenia."

I fetched my supper Emily had warming in the oven.

"Now, Hank, I know you have some nice men friends who are lookin' to meet a nice woman like Sarah. We talked about it, didn't we, honey?"

"What? No, I don't want to meet no nice men friends of Hank's or anyone else's," I declared.

"See, Emily, I told you. And all my real nice men friends are real nice 'cause they know to stay clear of wedding rings!"

"Married?" I said. "Lordy, I don't even want to hear the word."

"But you see, Hank knows lots of successful men. Some been comin' to his shop for years and they all talk about women."

"How do you know what we talk about?" Hank replied. "Truth is the men who come in only talk about gettin' away from some woman for a few blessed minutes of peace and that's why they come by to get their hair cut three times a week!"

"Sarah, don't listen to him," Emily advised. "Just look at that man. What would he be without a woman?"

"Lord, it's a question I gave up asking myself five days after you roped me in!" Hank quipped. "How do you know that Sarah doesn't have a man? She's a fine woman. Probably gots more than one."

"Right now the only thing I need is some sleep 'cause tomorrow I got to pack up Bella's bottles of scented hair oil and tote 'em all the way over to her church for the bazaar."

I put my plate on the counter, grabbed my letters, winked to Hank and headed upstairs. Needed to my rest to get through another day of Bella, Nona and me all over again.

SPINNING DREAMS FROM JARS

62

O NE MORNING I noticed Nona out the kitchen window as I washed dishes; her over there sweeping the stoop. I stepped out to ask her to snatch some of her lady's tuberoses. She'd cut me some to take home the year before. This year the bulbs had barely started blooming along the side of the neighbor's place. From afar the blossoms looked cream-colored but up close they had a soft powdery-pink color that I knew Bella favored. After her lady went off shopping, Nona cut a dozen stems and handed them over the fence and took my nickle. I never mentioned to Miss Burke where they came from as she'd not want anything from that Baptist woman as she called her.

I trimmed the stems and put them in Bella's favorite tiny cut glass vase and placed it on Miss Burke's bed tray. I wanted her to wake up to the fragrance of the flowers she always delighted in. However, Bella wasn't yet waking up that morning, so I didn't pull her drapes open. I left the vase next to her bed and carried her breakfast back down and tossed her toast in the garbage as I done the day before and so many days before that.

You see, Bella's mornings were getting harder and harder for her, no matter how fragrant the flowers were that I placed close to her pillow.

This year her delight in selling her scented hair oil at the church seemed to wane after only a few days. She even talked about not going to the bazaar all together. Mr. Burke gently coaxed her on; reminding her how much folks at the church looked forward to her rose-scented hair oil every year. Yet she seemed indifferent to things too far removed from those sparkling ornaments on her dressing table.

There came days she never really got up, never touched her breakfast tray and stayed all to herself in her room. Mr. Burke told me to leave her be, she'd be better the next day. Or so he hoped. Poor Bella, no matter how hard she tried, things in her life never seemed to come out as crisp as the blouses she insisted I starch and iron till they looked new so to impress her big-hat church-lady friends as to how crisp and orderly Bella's world surely was. To Bella, it made her only closer to the Lord. Yes, Bella's day-to- day life required everything perfect and in its place. Even perfectly tied with satin ribbons and smelling ever so pretty, like her days were all kept safely next to delicate sachets of lavender or rose petals meant to keep the stench of real life at bay.

Sometimes I wondered if she even realized I was getting tired of living on white folk's discarded cardboard stuffed in my shoes and being handed things to tote her dog had turned his nose to. No, I don't really think there was room in that woman's mind for such a notion; me wanting the things she took for granted was her due.

Guess there remained a brewing tension between us since the day of broken goblet. But then perhaps it was only me and my back getting sore bending over to pick up her daily life that was grinding me to the bone.

Mr. Burke was always good to me, wasn't he? When Bella was laid up or away visiting her sister, resting up from having done nothing for months, he'd talk to me out in his lab 'bout his work. That's where his life centered as life with Bella, even in her vast house, had little room for him. Alternately, he'd talk 'bout Miss Burke, a woman he'd lived with for years yet seemed hardly to know. I could see he was a lonely man and I wanted to help him, repay him for all he'd done for me. You see, unlike Mr. Burke, Bella only took from folks. She had nothing to give anyone and that seemed to include her husband. Don't recall me ever having a woman-to-woman conversation with Bella. No, she only talked at me requiring of me only a nod in response to her endless carping to let her know I was following her streams of thought which never went anywhere we hadn't already warn a path to. She moaned about this and that as I punctuated her sighs with all the nods she duly expected. As I sat there with her bottles, bows and stacks of moans colliding into my own thoughts, I started to hear a new voice and kept listening to myself just so I didn't hear Bella's aches.

I was past thirty-years-old and my knees had walked too many miles getting to the Burkes' to relish spending another day on this woman's hardwood floors. Yes, I'd spend any amount of time listening to a white woman's moans just to stay put in her kitchen chair for a spell. As a reprieve from scrubbing floors, I sat with Bella at her kitchen table as she pasted labels on her bottles stuffed with rose petals and her husband's concoction of lanolin, alcohol and what have you.

"Miss Bella, we got near fifty bottles of your hair dressing with your pale pink bow tied on here. You think you can sell that many at the church bazaar?"

"Of course," she replied. "You didn't come last year but the ladies all buy one and then one for their mothers, sisters and best friends. Sure they do."

"You must be a mighty help to your church with all your work here. I mean, are they gonna have enough to buy a row of pews and put Mr. and Mrs. Burke's name on?"

"Well, I don't know. I never think about the money," she responded.

I wondered what that would be like, not having a worry over money. Then to my gratification she pulled out a paper to show me how it works. She jotted some figures that in her mind added up at least good enough.

"I reckon William pays a nickel for the small bottles…" She paused again and then jotted more figures. "Guess the lanolin and rich oils he imports don't cost anything 'cause they're from his lab. Huh?"

"Right, Miss Burke. If he gots 'em back there, they sure must be free."

"So, the rose petals come from the garden and the bows, well, they're fine satin, so they must cost 'bout a nickel each as I know that shopkeeper overcharges for fineries. How much profit is that?"

"Don't know, Ma'am. Guess it depends on how much your church ladies pay you."

"Oh, well, they pay fifty cents a bottle. And it all goes to the church for the new pews."

I nearly swallowed my tongue! Fifty bottles means Bella took in near twenty-five dollars for a few hours of her time and lots of mine as free to her as William's imported oils. Twenty-five dollars was more than I made working for a three months from seven in the morning until I fell over at night!

Well, if Bella's ribbons and bows didn't get me thinking. What if I started mixing a few bottles on my own and Emily and I sold them at church? But would our folks buy one, then one for their ma and their sister along with who knows who? Even if I sold my bottles for twenty-five cents, I'd still be making good money.

Yes, Ma'am! I do think it was that afternoon that I was starting to see Nona's little pink babies floating in bottles of hair oil and that was just fine with me!

⁓

It was a day or two later that I came to Bella's extra early to see what Mr. Burke would teach me 'bout mixing things. I didn't think it was possible to get to their place any earlier than usual, but I was determined to help Grandma Ida with her itchy scalp. I figured it was the least I could do for all the nasty comments she'd made to Emily and me 'bout our sad cooking.

So, one morning I arrived extra early. I fixed Mr. Burke's coffee as usual and took it into the lab wondering if he would remember his offer to help me to work up a mixture of hair tonic to help Grandma's scalp.

"I been waitin' for you," he said as he took is coffee from the tray.

"Waitin' Mr. Burke?"

"You gonna be making products, got to start early. I'm down in the lab at five every morning."

"Yes, sir."

"So, let's get started. I've made up two mixtures here I want you to fill each of these bottles one at a time."

"All of them?"

"Yep."

I could hardly see what I would be learning from that. Still I always enjoyed chitchatting with Mr. Burke anyway. And we did. We chatted as I poured ingredients through a funnel. From there I went to filling bottles starting from the tall ones. It didn't take me more than a few minutes to get them all filled as I was sure quick.

"Done?" he asked, even as he could see for himself.

I nodded.

"That fourth bottle, end row there," he said.

"Yes, Sir?"

"You got so busy you filled the first ingredient twice. 'Cause you saw that bottle was full, you omitted the second ingredient. I sell that to a customer they're sure gonna want their money back 'cause a swallow or two burned a hole in their throat."

"Lord, no!"

"The Lord wasn't fillin' them brown bottles!" he said. "You got to know what goes in your products and measure carefully. Go on now, pull that one out and empty it."

"Yes, Sir."

Well, that was my lab lesson for the day. Don't think I could have learned anything more important.

Over the next few weeks, on mornings Mr. Burke had a few minutes to spare, he showed me all kinds of things, including the different oils he used to mix for Miss Burke's scented hairdressing. He pointed to a box of his bottles and told me to take as many home as I could tote. I guess it was then that I really realized all along he was helping me fill bottles of my own hair treatment.

If Bella could sell hers at her church, then so could I at mine. If the church folks bought a bottle or two from me, then why wouldn't the neighbors? And if mine was the best product, why wouldn't they tell their neighbors to buy some?

Well, the dreams started spinning from bottles and from that day forward they never stopped.

FEELING LIKE DROWNING A WHITE WOMAN

63

I DON'T KNOW IF Miss Burke got to wondering how much time I'd been helping Mr. Burke but she sure seemed to be getting herself out of bed earlier to head down stairs and see for herself. Sometimes she huffed and yammered about this or that only to end up handing me her breakfast menu before going upstairs where she was asleep again before I brought her tray up.

Sometimes she'd come down in the late afternoons. It was late one such afternoon after I'd just finished ironing her silk blouses, hung them to cool before I took them up to her closets when she caught me with no chore in one hand and sure enough guilty with a glass of sweet tea in the other. That woman snorted and grunted about like was aiming to give birth to some new meanness.

"I want you to take them bottles of my fine hair oil dressing down to the church on your way home tonight. Hear?"

She pointed to the bottles we'd prepared the night before.

"You're gonna tote all these jars so we don't got to mess with hauling 'em come Sunday when I'm dressed nice for church," Bella barked like I'd just soiled her new white church gloves.

"Miss Burke, your church is the other way from where I head home."

"And so?" she demanded.

"Gots to leave and go straight off tonight."

I didn't mention my reading class that night as she'd long demanded I stop attending.

"You can do as you're requested and tote some jars down to the church."

Bella huffed about like Nona had just emptied a box of cornmeal over her head and then asked her to stick her tongue out for the chopping block that waited!

"There's fifty bottles here and I'm thinkin' of doing another dozen or so. You'll be takin' a dozen filled bottles to the church every evening. So, you won't have time to go to no class and then be able to stay on top of the housekeeping. You know things are not lookin' as clean and shiny as I require. That's all there is to it."

"Yes, Ma'am. But tonight I can't stop by your church."

"You've got nothin' better to do!" she declared like it was me who slept in till noon.

"Like I said, not goin' by your church tonight."

With that, Bella's face turned beet red. Enraged, she marched over to the laundry door where her silk blouses were hanging.

"Look at these," she huffed.

"Yes, Miss Burke. I just finished ironin' them."

"You call this ironin'? Look at the crinkles! Not even a colored would wear 'em!"

"There ain't one crinkle, Ma'am! Not one!"

"You don't fool me," she snarled. "I know what you're doin'!" she exclaimed.

"Doin', Ma'am?"

"You're tryin' to humiliate me in front of my friends!"

"How, Miss Burke?"

"Here's how!"

At that, Miss Burke grabbed them blouses and tossed them into a tub of Mr. Burke's soaking overalls.

I dashed to grab 'em up but it was too late. I could only stand there watching those delicate ruffled blouses I'd spent all afternoon ironing melt into that murky blue water. I had to hold the side of the tub so I'd not grab that woman by the neck and shove her head into her own tub! There I knew I'd hold it under till she'd swallowed her every word!

"I will not go about with crinkles in my clothes lookin' like some colored!" She snorted.

It was good that woman stormed back up to her bedroom before I had the opportunity to put her out of her misery.

I dried my hands and tossed my apron into this woman's tub of bleeding indigo blue overalls and ruined silk blouses and left for the evening. Well, it wasn't the first time I'd had visions of drowning a white woman in her own washtub!

Late some evenings if Emily heard me pacing in my attic room, she'd come up to see what had me so worked up and would likely bring a whiskey to calm me. Emily was a friend I trusted; she knew not to take me too seriously when I got all hot and bothered. We'd sit at my little table near the window and catch up on things. Mostly I'd bad-mouth Bella and Emily would complain about Hank. By the time we'd mouthed off on ever'body we'd be laughing at our own stories.

But I was truly worked up the night Bella dumped a day of my ironing in her tub with Mr. Burke's overalls; I must admit the thoughts I had brewing came out a bit twisted because this time I'd been agitated enough to twist a certain neck down into a tub. Even had my Bible out looking for a verse that read drowning a white woman was no real sin, not if you really meant it.

"My, my, aren't you pacin' up here like a lioness?" Emily handed me a whiskey. "Why aren't you at the school reading the chapter you practiced on Grandma and me all week?"

"Bella is the reason! And I'll tell you, I fixed her good!"

"Bella? What's that woman up to now?" Emily asked knowing Bella and I butted heads regularly.

"Up to? She's up to her ears in filthy tub water and I shoved 'er ol' head down in it and stomped it!"

"My, my. That's what you've gone and done now is it?" Emily took a seat. "I see you got your Bible out. You gonna ask the Lord to help you be a better woman than that Bella?"

"I found the verse."

"Verse on what? Drowin' white women?" Emily asked.

"Psalm sixty-nine; verse fourteen. Just 'bout wore this page out 'cause of that woman."

I read like a traveling preacher. Even shook my fist to the heavens.

"'Lord, rescue me from the mire, do not let me drown. No! And deliver me from the white woman who torments me every day as sure as the sun comes up!"

"Praise the Lord He knows better than to answer half our prayers!" Emily said.

It seemed as if my reading made her squirm in her chair.

"That what the verses say, huh?"

"Emily, I do believe the Lord came to me while I was drowning that woman."

Emily eyed me skeptically.

"And the Lord, He never once said stop that business and bring that pathetic woman's head back up!"

"That so now?" Bella asked."

With that I continued my sermon.

"That's what Jesus was tellin' me. The Lord is my Shepherd. He leads me into the valley of the tubs where I drown that white woman!"

"So, sounds like she fired you again today!"

"I do believe that Jesus told me what to do. 'Sarah,' He asked, 'do you not think you're as good as any white woman? Who tol' you, you got to spend your life at the tubs?' Yes, Ma'am He sure did, too."

"Heard it all from the Lord's mouth right here in my attic. huh?" Emily asked.

"Me and the Lord figurin' how to get things fixed."

"What did Jesus say on that? Or did you fib and tell the Lord she'd only tripped on her loose tongue when she had that awful fall into her own tub? No, that don't seem likely given Bella's never been close to a washtub."

"You know what Bella asked me this morning? She said, 'Sarah, why do you take so much crap off me?'"

"Sure she did. Well, I can't help but imagine she meant to ask why you're so much trouble to 'er."

"That woman said, 'Do you actually think that I'll treat you with respect one of these days if you keep on taking my grief? No, Sarah that ain't never gonna happen 'round here 'cause I don't have respect for nobody on her knees scrubbin' my floors.' That's what Bella said."

"Honey, every white woman that ever lived in this city has said that and worse. But you've not only been listening to your white woman's big mouth, you went and memorized her jabber. Why is that, honey? No wonder your head's poundin' tonight. Even looks a bit swollen. Swollen with pride, that is. You fussin' about that silly woman again. Lord have mercy!"

"My head ain't swollen! It was Jesus who said to me, 'Why don't you get up from scrubbin' that woman's floor and start making your own job?' The Lord was gettin' worked up like you never seen!"

"That so? The Lord turned rivers red, leveled Babylon and you're up here thinkin' He could get Himself worked up over your little white woman mess?"

"Emily, I finally heard the voice I been waiting for."

"And that's what concerns me, dear. You best ask Mr. Burke if he's bottled a cure for hearing voices in the attic!"

"Damn it! The only voice I'm hearing up here is the Lord's."

"Just like Moses heard the Lord's voice? Like that? Or are you started hearin' Moses up here, too?"

"I been thinkin' on it for some time now and Bella got me to thinkin' all the harder today! I'm gonna start a little business. Gonna make hair tonic I can sell in pretty jars to all the women at church who can't go into whitey shops for nice things."

"What are you planning to do again?"

"I'm gonna mix up some hair and scalp treatments and sell 'em myself. Special hair products with good ingredients that won't cause our hair to fall out from lye burns. Emily, our people don't need permission from white folks to have dignity. I seen that when Mrs. Washington came to town."

"What's the matter now?" Emily asked.

"Is it too late for me to be talkin' 'bout having a little business? Not bein' a maid or tub woman no more? Is it only a bit of nonsense?"

"Sarah, you've always had dreams, haven't you honey? And you been talking 'bout mixtures and how to get your hands on jars and oils and this and that for weeks now. Bringin' Mr. Burke's catalogues home and adding up your figures down at the table while I cooked. You've already started something and I don't mean like what you started up with Bella today. Maybe you're the only one that hasn't come to terms things!"

"Guess I do know it, don't I? It's just sayin' it out loud that's hard."

"Why's that, honey?" Emily asked.

"You know, my momma told me up on Orchard Hill that my soul was a place to keep my dreams hidden from white folks. I'm not hiding my dreams no more."

"I hear you, dear."

About then we both heard a loud thumping noise.

"Listen to that!" I said. "I reckon that's Jesus callin' me to march on with these dreams I got brewin'…"

"Honey, I reckon it's only Hank pounding the ceiling down there with a broomstick to get me to march on with his supper. And by the way, we've got company tonight. Don't want you to embarrass yourself in front of C. J."

"C.J.? Who's she?"

I quickly sensed Emily had something brewing herself.

"Ain't she beautiful and with those broad shoulders."

Emily sure enough had a wicked glint in her eyes.

"Nice broad shoulders you say?"

"And big arms! Charles Joseph Walker is her name. Good-lookin' newspaper advertising man. This is the one that Hank's been meaning for you to meet and you been acting like you don't even hear 'im."

Emily headed to the door.

"A man? Now wait a minute here! You know I been down that road before with that fool, John Davis. Don't need a man for nothin'."

Emily winked like she'd just heard a different tune.

"Between Grandma goin' like a magpie down in the kitchen and you and the Lord Jesus at our table, it should be quite an evening. Should I bring my Bible to the supper table or is your sermon on drowin' white women over for the night?"

SATAN COMES TO SUPPER

64

I WASN'T AT ALL interested in meeting Hank's friend that night—hadn't even combed my hair and still had my uniform on. But when I got down stairs my mouth 'bout fell open. There in the dining room talking with Hank was this tall handsome man wearing a dark gray suit and vest.

"Sarah, this here is C. J. He's a newspaper man and I…"

But I didn't let Hank finish his introduction. All I could do was spin 'round fearing that if I opened my mouth more gibberish might tumble out. Guess about like Emily had just gotten an earful of. Why didn't she tell me she was having a man to supper? Here my hair looked a sight, and well, never mind. Heading for a comb, I jumped back into Emily's kitchen but nearly tripped on poor Emily.

"Are you that hungry, or what?" Emily asked. "Pushing me through the door like that."

Grandma Ida was sitting at the kitchen table snapping green beans for our supper.

"What's wrong with that woman, Emily?"

"Go on Sarah. Tell Grandma what your problem is so she don't start flappin' on hers."

"My troubles ain't no more than what your cookin' has done to my stomach, Emily!"

Emily knocked the pots around like she was hunting for one big enough to put Grandma's head.

"Anyway, I could use a new man in my life," Emily quipped. "How about you, Sarah? New man, I mean. One with big shoulders and all? I wonder if there's one nearby. Do you, honey?"

"I know what you mean," I replied.

"I could use a man more than both you's!" Grandma Ida added.

"Oh, Lord. For what, Grandma?" Emily asked. "For the past twenty years I been married to your son I've held in this hand a bunch of skillets. Some I sure could have used to beat some old women with. Which would you prefer I start with tonight?"

"It don't matter which damned skillet you start in on, it's all gonna end up in the garbage pail the minute you're finished bangin' on the stove with it. Huh, Sarah?"

I wasn't gonna get into it with Grandma Ida that night. Instead, I peeked out to look over Hank's friend. My, my, but he was certainly one good-looking man!

"It's Satan!" I said under my breath to myself. "Do not tell me that ain't the work of Satan sittin' out there."

Grandma Ida looked to Emily for assurance I wasn't off my rocker. But what could Emily say? She knew I'd been up in my room chatting with the Lord and here I was peeking through the door at what was surely the devil's angel man sent to tempt me.

"Never knowed of even one woman in a room worth listening to. I'm gonna go talk to the men. Come over here, Sarah and get me to my feet!" Grandma demanded.

"You're not going no place, Grandma!" I declared. "You'll go and tell 'em what I said. You best sit still till it passes from your mind."

"That'll be about two jiggers of whiskey from now," Emily announced. "Hand it to 'er and save us from more of her big mouth, Sarah."

I poured while Emily finished frying the chops and went to peek at C.J. again. But this time he caught me and winked.

"Oh, Lord, that's pure sin sitting out there," I said behind the kitchen door again.

"I'm beginning to think the only sin 'round here is in your head, Sarah," Emily said. "Go take this platter of chops out to the table!"

"Why's that woman hanging on the kitchen door? What's she gawking at out there?" Grandma Ida asked loud enough for C.J. to chuckle.

Emily could only roll her eyes at us.

"Now Sarah, while I take this bowl of black-eyed peas and plate of cornbread out to the table you march the old lady in."

"I'll march myself in!" Grandma replied.

For some reason I hoped to rely on Emily to help me regain a bit of dignity in front of C.J. However, that notion evaporated before I even folded my hands for grace!

"Sarah, I'll try introducing my friend, C.J. here…" Hank said before Emily cut him off.

"Satan!" Emily near shrieked like the ol' devil had just slid his horny ol' hand down her inner-thigh to feel how nice and soft it was!

"What's that you say?"

Hank shook his head at us.

"Satan! He comes in mysterious ways. Yes, he's in our midst according to Sarah 'cause she gots sin on her mind and I do think plenty of it," Emily announced. "You see Jesus been up in Sarah's room this evening to help her drown a white woman," Emily announced to C. J. "Yeah, that's her story. Sarah, here."

Emily's comment made Hank drop the chop he was forking over to C.J.'s plate.

"Woman, are you drunk?" Hank asked.

"Now didn't I tell you not to marry 'er," Grandma Ida reminded Hank. "She been crazy all along but you never noticed 'cause you were tryin' to keep her food down!"

"Shut up Grandma 'fore I take a skillet to your head when you're sleepin'," Emily said.

"Tell my son 'bout what that woman sittin' next to you was doin' to that white woman up in the attic! Yeah, I heard you up there in the attic."

"You tell 'im, Grandma," Emily responded.

"There's somebody up there?" Hank asked.

"No, she's up in Sarah's head." Grandma Ida replied for me.

"Say the Lord's blessin', Hank."

"Lord, bless Sarah for drowin' some white woman in 'er own tub," was Grandma's prayer. "Now if you can see your way to savin' us from Emily's cookin' tonight…

"Dear, Lord. Thank you for this bountiful meal but deliver us from the women that cooked it and then up and served their misery on C.J. and me this evening. Amen."

"C.J., earnestly, Sarah here's been talkin' to Jesus tonight. You see they're business partners." Emily said.

Grandma nodded in agreement, or was she merely gnawing up and down on that chop?

All the while this went on C.J. acted mannerly and paid no mind to all the crazy talk.

"What kind of business is that, Miss Sarah?" C.J. asked. "Gonna have your own laundry?"

I guess C.J. figured by the look I gave him that my business wouldn't be in no washtub.

"C.J. is the man who puts all them fancy ads in the weekly for things Emily spends her time fussin' to go shopping for," Hank announced.

"Well, she ain't never fussed over no meal she put on this here table!" Grandma added.

C.J. smiled and asked about this venture I'd only an hour before shared with Emily.

"So, Sarah. What about this business of yours; what kind is it for real?"

"You see, I work for a pharmacist and I've been working on my plans for making my own special shampoo to sell to our folks."

"Miss Burke had Sarah been filling bottles and jars with hair oil that she sold to her churchwomen," Emily said.

"That ain't no reason to drown a white woman!" Grandma announced. "No wonder Jesus come 'round to talk to 'er!"

I tried to ignore Grandma *and* Emily.

"I plan to start making hair oil products. Good products scented like rose petals."

I wondered what C.J. thought of a woman having her own business? It was something that many men, at least married ones, didn't take to as it might lead some folks to think the man couldn't provide.

"Rose petals, huh? Well, ain't that pretty? Sell 'em in stores downtown?" C.J. asked.

"I figure I need to sell 'em where folks can buy with no white woman standing in the shop door tellin' them they can't come in. So, I aim to sell to folks up and down the street and then get me some agents to help sell on their streets."

"Agents, huh?" Emily asked. "Jesus tell you bring the disciples in on this deal?"

"Every agent will sell to everyone she knows along with all her neighbors. Then she's gonna make enough money she won't be spending her days bent over no tub."

Hank smiled.

"Sounds like you're already rollin' on this venture!"

"But she sure don't know how to roll no biscuits!" Grandma added.

"Not me, Grandma, Sarah here is the businesswoman now!" Emily said. "'Member? I'm the bad cook."

"Ain't that the truth of it?" Grandma quipped.

"Hank's right. You got to be a bit of a gambler to be in business," C.J. added. "Take some risks, I always say."

"Listen to C.J., Sarah," Hank suggested. "He knows about these things."

"I'm gonna sell bottles at church and then from door to door," I informed everyone as though to make it official.

"That's a good idea," Emily said. "You can bring some to my door any day!"

"Well, I don't want none!" Grandma Ida said sucking in a green bean that sounded like it had to have been a yard long. "I see you comin' to my door, I'll fetch my skillet and put it to your head."

"Old woman, how long's it been since you could see anybody come to your door before they there were close enough to sit on your lap, huh?" Emily asked.

"Now, don't get Ma worked up," Hank said.

"Worked up? She's already been in that chair too long to get up period," Emily replied.

"Door to door? That's a lot of doors to be knockin' on," C.J. said. "I got an idea. Why don't you have the mailman knock on those doors for you?" C.J. asked.

I could see why this man was so successful at his paper because he took my notions seriously as if one day I just might be one of his customers.

"Why would the postman do that for me?" I asked.

"'Cause it's his job, that's why,' C.J. replied. "People order your fancy rose petal oil in the mail after they see ads in my weekly. You send it out to 'em in the mail. Let the mailman do the walkin'."

"He best not knock on my door and bother me to get up for it," Grandma said. "I'll throw a fry pan at his head to stop that clean!"

"Oh, shut up, Grandma. Who sends you mail anyway?" Emily said.

"The undertaker, that's who!" Grandma remarked. "Sends me reminders his part is past due!"

"Guess, I can't sell that way though," I commented.

"Why not? C.J. asked.

"The jars of hair oil will break in the mail."

"So, make your rose petal hair product solid in a tin, so it won't break. Like the pomade Hank overcharges to dab on my hair when he cuts it."

"But the mailman won't know 'bout the product; how to use it. Bella said you got to blot it with a towel a bit," I told C. J.

Emily decided to help me out.

"Bella's the white woman Sarah was baptizing up in her head somewhere."

Emily glared at Grandma like she was gonna get the same.

"Ask Sarah to wash your hair up there with her shampoo mixture,

Grandma. Your head stuck in a tub for an hour or so might bring some peace and quiet to my kitchen!"

"I wouldn't wash my damned feet in no tub of water been used by no white woman. Never know where she's been or what kind of crawlies she's got on 'er," Grandma announced.

Hank shook his head and spooned some mashed potatoes over to C.J.'s plate.

"You got to consider the advantages of advertising," C. J said. "Put an ad in there tellin' folks 'bout your hair oil, how to use it and then how to buy it."

"Ads in the newspaper?"

I could see it already; right next to pictures of fancy-dressed women like the kind we kept on the big table at Sally's.

"You start up your oil and rose petals stuff; I'll stop by sometime next week and show you how it's done for when you're ready to get serious about your business," C.J. said with a smile.

I lay in bed that night thinking that before dinner I dreamed of having a little business all my own. One I'd started in my attic room. Something to help me make a few extra pennies—just a little seed of a dream.

Yes, Momma, I do have a dream again, don't I?

END OF PART II

PART III

THE WEIGHT OF MY DREAMS

Ridding On A Door

65

WELL, THE YEARS went on. They came and went like the winds and yet I wondered if I still had it in me to conjure a dream of something else; that somewhere life no tub woman had ever arrived at.

So often it seemed to me that we tub women avoided the realities of our lives maybe as we avoided the brown sludge at the bottom of our old tubs. Truly, there were long days and lonely nights when the weight of my dreams seemed crushing. Still I kept the image of my daughter and her daddy close to my heart.

Still, there were so many of us who had less. I tried to keep this in mind and repeated it in my thoughts every day at the Burks. There at the big house with the cracked walk, I at least could earn enough to get to the next day. That had been my folks' only dream at Grandview; will my family see tomorrow? Will it only look like the day before? How can I get out if it does? Get out of wondering over the same question year after year?

Bless us who even hope for a better tomorrow 'cause don't that mean we still haven't given up?

I'd worked for the Burkes' for a long spell, and never once was Mr. Burke anything but good to me, unlike his wife, Bella Burke, who was nothing but nasty at every opportunity she could conjure. At times I wondered if Mr. Burke was especially kind to make up for Bella's meanness. Always helpful, here and there I'd ask him questions, or he'd show me how to mix formulas for my hair tonics in his lab; concoctions he was making to fill his bottles or things he knew about chemistry and all.

"You best bring me in a tin of one of these hair products you've been talking about."

"You mean Annie Turnbo's *Wonderful Hair Grower?*"

"Don't know what it's called," he said, "but if you can get your hands on one, I'll do a breakdown of what's in it. Then you can see about making it yourself."

"Wouldn't that be copying?" I wondered.

"Hell, no. Once you know what your competition is up to, you set out to make yours better. And then you own the market—at least till someone comes along and does one better on you.

"So, I got to be always improving my own shampoo?"

"And your customers will beat a path to your door, or so they say."

The following week I handed Mr. Burke him a tin of *Wonderful Hair Grower* and a few days later he told me what was in it.

"Nothin' too complicated here. Probably the same ingredients used in every hair product sold," he said. "How much you bet?"

"Tell me if I won. then I'll tell you how much I'll put down on your bet."

"Now, aren't you a shrewd business woman?" he said. "Well, you got yourself the usual base of petrolatum mixed with beeswax along with precipitated sulfur for psoriasis and oil. Probably the very same oil Bella markets at church with her floating baby rose buds that gets Nona so worked up."

"I've seen these ingredients in your catalogue you gave me to look over."

How long I'd wondered if there were a hundred secret ingredients in those tins of hairdressing that cost so much. In short order I'd used up all my meager savings to purchase everything on a list of ingredients that Mr. Burke helped me draw up and deliver to Emily's. Then one day we found out in the alley an old door tossed on a pile of boards. We dragged it home and put some wood crates under it to make a work counter for the blending of oils and scents.

After a few weeks of working hard on my scalp treatment I couldn't wait to try it on Grandma's bald spots. So, one Saturday night I called Emily to come up so I could try it on her thinking I'd be less likely to get a skillet upside my head—the kind Grandma Ida would likely wield if she didn't like my new hair tonic.

"What smells so strong up here?" Emily asked at my door. I'd not smelled anything as my nose had gone off duty at that point.

"I'm mixin' a bit more sulfur into my formula. It's good for the scalp, you know? Mr. Burke said so. Just been workin' some into my hair. Makes it feel silky, don't it? Sit down; I'll try some on you now."

Yes, Emily would be my first customer. Even back then I was thinking one day of having a fancy shop where folks could have their hair fixed nicely. That daydream went up in fumes when Emily took a closer look and all but jumped through the ceiling.

"Get away from me, woman!" she screeched.

She pointed to my shoulder aghast. Out of the corner of my eye I saw a dead bat laying there. But it wasn't. It was much worse, but just as dead. You see, a huge clump of my hair had melted off slid down to my shoulder. I grabbed a mirror and saw more clumps sliding off my head. Emily and I both screamed in horror.

Grandma went to stomping her cane on the floor down there.

"What the hell's goin' on up there? You back to drownin' white women? Stinks like she's already dead. Who's dead up there?"

Emily yelled back down to the kitchen. "Don't know for sure, Grandma. But it sure looks like Sarah's pride is badly wounded."

Well, I couldn't sleep all night as I could feel my scalp bleeding and I was getting worked up about what folks would say when they saw my head the next day.

The next morning my burning scalp woke up before the rest of me did. I yelled down the stairs to Emily in the kitchen to see if Hank had gone off to his shop. Didn't want him to see me for fear he'd never let me look in the window of his barbershop. Didn't know how I'd manage, but I had to face the day one way or another. About the time the sun peeked through Emily's kitchen window I'd worked up the courage to head downstairs for some coffee.

Grandma Ida was already sitting at the kitchen table slurping her coffee when I entered the room.

"Emily!" Grandma hollered. "Get a stick! Somebody done wandered into your kitchen from the alley."

Grandma could hardly see past her nose so I knew what I'd done to myself was sure enough bad. She went to waving her cane at my head to keep me at bay.

"That's Sarah, Grandma. She's gone bald like you from her hair oil treatment she made up to help you get your hair growin' back," Emily said grinning. "Ain't that right, Sarah?"

"I bet she caught scalp worms from using that white woman's brush!" Grandma announced.

"Sit down, Sarah. Go ahead now."

Emily grabbed Grandma's cane away to stop her from waving it at my head.

"I'll get some salve and one of my loose gardening hats for you. Sit down now and drink your coffee, dear. Everything's gonna be just fine… eventually… in due time. Sure it is."

Emily coaxed me into a chair. I sat there determined I'd not cry; not with Grandma squinting hard to see who was sitting across from her.

Emily dabbed salve on my throbbing bald spots.

"Well, looks here like you're gonna be wearing a big bandanna tied 'round your head for some time!"

I looked at myself in the mirror and that bandanna was truly the ugliest ol' cloth I'd ever seen. I'd seen it when Emily wore while doing her housework.

"Now, don't look so down," she said patting me on the back. "Nobody's gonna know what you have up under there or don't have…. much left of up there."

"Well, we sure know she ain't got no senses up there. That ugly rag on 'er head ain't gonna fool nobody different!" Grandma Ida announced, I'm sure to cheer me up.

I finally gave up hope that the Lord would come for me that morning—just strike me dead to ease the pain of it all; the pain of my yet burning scalp and the pain I'd feel as people gawked at me. So, after a few agonizingly sighs, I worked up the courage to head off for the Burkes'. As I walked, I guess I half expected everyone in town would be thronging the streets to see the bald woman hiding under the big ugly rag tied 'round her head like a mammy cotton picker.

I was already late, so I knew to expect Miss Burke to climb on my back. Sure enough, that was the morning she got up early for one of her church-lady meetings and she was down there waiting for me.

She started to speak as I walked in, but her mouth clamped down at the sight of the swirl of rag tied 'round my head like a bandage. It was a tiny blessing that she was so aghast at the sight of me that nothing would come out of her big mouth. She put her own hat on, looked at me like I was surely missing something, like maybe the better half of my head, and left for her church meeting without another word.

Well, my head was sore and itched all day and there were some nights back then when I couldn't sleep because the sulfur had eaten into my scalp bad. But, no I wasn't gonna give up. Every night I'd wash my bandanna so I could iron it dry in the morning before heading back to Bella's.

The following morning the woman didn't know what to say.

"That new? You must like it somethin' awful, 'cause you been wearin' it every day now," Bella announced, but sounded as though she was talking to herself again.

"I love this here bandanna. But I take it off when I get tired of it. I reckon in six months or so."

"Then you sleep in that scarf, too?" she asked.

How did that woman conjure the notion that I slept?

"No, Ma'am but I like to keep it close by."

"Here, pull that thing off your head. I got some real nice hats I was gonna take to the church bazaar this week. You might like one. Go ahead, take yours off. You can try one of these hats I don't like no more."

I fled as she got up to fetch her castoffs.

"Not now, Miss Burke, my cookies are burnin'."

Lord, if I then didn't have to cover my fib by baking a quick batch of sugar cookies 'cause for sure that woman would be looking for them come tea time.

In a few weeks my hair had grown in and was more beautiful than ever. Guess 'bout then I started to arrange it better, perhaps the way I'd remembered Mrs. Washington's. Mr. Burke thought so too and told me so.

Stinks Like Rose Petals

66

URING THE LONG weeks ahead, I continued to work on my scalp formula as my dreams expanded right alongside my long hours. I was no longer content to sell my special shampoo only to folks at the church; now I thought I could sell to the folks up and down the street on my way to church. It was easy to see sales everywhere as so many folks had brittle hair caused by the harsh home concoctions they made to use as shampoo. Potions that weren't much different from the lye soap they did their laundry with. I concluded that my only limitation was how much shampoo I could make on that ol' door up in Emily's attic and how many customers would take to it and put a quarter on my palm for a bottle.

That autumn Miss Burke drifted deeper into her dark moods. She told me she could hardly sleep most nights, which meant her getting up was harder than ever for Mr. Burke and me. Then one morning he gave her a bell, a servant's bell, to ring for me when she did wake up. She was truly delighted with the gesture and seemed to think he was indulging her all the more as she figured it ought to be. Mr. Burke whispered one morning that when that bell went to ringing it was really an alarm for both of us. Yes, we'd then know she was up and we'd soon be swerving from her rants on the evils of dust, Nona, the Baptist woman next door, him or me!

Now that Miss Burke was sleeping in later and sounding her alarm when she was finally up, Mr. Burke told me if I came early, I could use their laundry to make up batches of my shampoo to fill the bottles I was buying through him.

Eventually it came to be that Emily's grandson Jake would come by after school with his wagon hauling a box of sawdust to take all the filled bottles home for me. I'd give him some coins for the transport and if he sold a bottle or two on the way he'd get an extra dime. That got him busy stopping at the feet of every pretty woman he saw and then not letting them get by till they'd opened their pocketbooks. These women would buy a tin even though they didn't know what was in it because Jake's grin told them it really didn't matter much. He was a handsome young businessman making his rounds. It was another unexpected lesson for me; you could sell things more easily when there was a nice smile tendered with the transaction.

One morning I was working hard to bottle a new batch of scalp conditioner when Mr. Burke walked in the laundry holding his nose. I guess I'd smelled it so long I didn't know how badly it stunk in there.

"That's a mighty powerful odor there. Bella catch you mixing up hair products in her bowls?"

"Not yet. Didn't hear the bell, did you?"

"Nope. I think you're still using too much sulfur. It could burn your hair off at the scalp. That ever happen to you?" he asked with a bit of a glint in those midnight-blue eyes.

"Me? Why, no Sir. Makes my hair feel silky, don't it?"

Months before, Mr. Burke told me a bit of sulfur could cure scalp disease that was fungal. But I figured if a few drops would kill the bugs, a tablespoon or two would keep them from ever coming back. In my mind that recipe worked just fine. It sure did.

"Your new fancy jars came in yesterday while you were out marketing," he said. "Don't tell Bella. You know how suspicious she is."

"Don't worry. Miss Burke only sees and hears what she wants to."

"You noticed?" he added. "Well, she's sure been suspicious seeing her roses disappear. She thinks it's the snails strippin' the petals off."

"Oh, yes. Snails been bad lately. Got all Nona's lady's roses, too," I declared.

Late that same morning Miss Burke came down without ringing her bell. She carried a pile of old clothes and things she wanted me to haul over to her church 'cause she always liked making her grand entrance on Sundays wearing her big hat and sure didn't want anything in her delicate hands but her white gloves.

"My goodness, Sarah. That smell! What are you washing my clothes in?"

"Don't smell a thing."

Just the same I quickly opened the window.

"Well, it must be comin' from the lab. These here fine things I want you to take over to the church on your way to work tomorrow. It's only a few blocks out of your way. Of course, you don't mind, do you?"

Bella loaded down my arms with her last season's clothes and castoffs.

"You can carry 'em in this old satchel of William's," she said and dropped the rest of her pile at my feet.

"Yes, Ma'am."

It was then that I figured the time was as good as any, so I braced myself to give her some real bad news.

"Oh, Miss Burke, I need an extra day off."

She nearly gagged on the first sip of her coffee.

"Didn't you have two days off a week or two ago?" she asked.

"That was a month or two ago, Ma'am."

"I do declare; sometimes I think you don't like workin' here. Do you?"

Bella erected her posture.

"No, you most certainly may not have two days off." She huffed at my indulgent request. "I've never heard of such a thing in my life!"

❧

That evening when I got home, I didn't even go upstairs to put my things away; just went into Emily's kitchen to show them the clothes and things Bella sent with me. But you see, they never made it over to her church as there were those far needier on my side of the town and I knew a couple of them personally.

Emily, being one, was frying a chicken when I got in.

"You want me to slice the yams you got cooling over there?" I asked.

"I'm slicing them yams; bring 'em on over here with a good sharp knife," Grandma piped. And I want me some fried okra tonight so get down the corn meal for it."

"No, you don't need a sharp knife to slice those yams," Emily said. "You'd slice your fingers off. Then you'd come poke us with the knife for lettin' you have it with your bad eyes. No, I ain't in no mood to clean up after you tonight. What are all those clothes for, Sarah?"

"These here things are for the needy. Bella told me to take them over to her church but I got lost on the way."

"You sure did. Right here at this table are the neediest I know of! Ain't you needy for that white blouse with the embroidery I see there, Grandma?" Emily asked. "Ain't that pretty?"

"I'm workin' up a need for that little black hat I see over there, too. Hand it here so I can try it on," Grandma said then went bobbing in her seat at the moment Emily turned her chicken in the steaming fry pan.

"The house is on fire!"

"Old woman the house is not on fire and it wasn't the last time I made supper or the time before."

But Grandma wasn't too concerned the house was burning up 'cause she was already working her way into that fine black hat covered with all sorts of fancy things. I pulled out of the pile a nice black skirt.

"Ah, this is what I been lookin' for."

"That wool skirt?" Emily asked.

Emily pulled out a linen blouse that needed only a button or two.

"Grandma, Sarah's right not to do your beckoning since you keep sayin' you don't know who she is when she's standing right there."

"I tell you," Grandma said tugging that hat on her head every which way, "you don't have a bit of sense in that head of yours but you still done what I told. Don't that prove who still has her senses left?"

Emily poured us a cup of tea as I slipped on the black skirt and walked around to model.

"Ah, yes, Ma'am. She looks just like Mrs. Washington. She sure enough does," Emily announced.

I just smiled at the thought.

"Tomorrow is Bella's church luncheon."

"So, you gonna show up in her black skirt and stand there next to her to sell her some of your rose-scented oil with her own rose petals floating in them bottles you get from her man?" Emily asked.

While she's out in the afternoon, I'm goin' 'round our neighborhood to sell some of my shampoo," I reassured her. "Mr. Burke said he'd cover and tell her I'm doing the marketing."

I looked over the satchel I wanted to carry my samples.

"That Mr. Burke, he's a good man," she said. "Gonna start sellin' your hair oil to the neighbors?"

"Got to so I can repay him for all the jars he's ordered for me."

About then Grandma Ida threatened to get up out of her chair again.

"And you don't think that woman over there's crazy?" Grandma demanded. "I swain and you keep tellin' folks I can't see what's in front of me. She thinks somebody's going to buy something from 'er? Huh! That'a be the day! A bald woman selling hair pomade!"

Truly I needed every bit of encouragement I could get because I was frightened of going door to door to sell my shampoo. I already knew what Grandma would do if I came to her door: an iron skillet slung at my head!

Sharp Corners and
Sharper Elbows

67

I SPENT HOURS THE night before filling my tins till their sharp edges nearly made my fingers bleed but how was that worse than any lye soap-burn from having my hands in the tubs? I figured that come Saturday, the day I planned to take off from working for Bella, I'd get dressed in my black skirt, pack the jars of my excellent shampoo and tins of tetter salve and take off looking for new customers.

Having covered most of Emily's street, I planned to go around the corner and knock on doors till I'd sold every tin. So, I started knocking at doors around the corner and if the woman wasn't busy, I'd offer to shampoo her hair and give her my hair treatment. I figured if she was delighted, she'd surely buy a bottle and probably one for her ma. However, things didn't turn out the way I'd hoped. I'd gone to several doors with no response till knocking on one where a young woman with a baby opened her door.

"Yeah, what's you want?"

"I got something here for you," I told her.

Her eyes were shiny like she'd just won a prize at the fair.

"Huh? What's you got for me then?"

"My special shampoo made for folks like you. You let me show you how good it is and you're gonna want to buy a bottle.

"How you gonna show me?" she asked.

"You got a pitcher of water? I'll wash your hair right here on the porch. Yes, I will."

"Well, let me put my baby down for 'er nap. I be back with a basin. That do?"

"Yes, Ma'am.

It wasn't long before she'd returned. We chatted as I washed her hair. I made sure to use plenty of my shampoo so she could smell the nice rose fragrance.

"This is the first time I been off my feet since dawn." she said. "I got me another little one in there sleeping. You know, my husband, he always said I had pretty hair 'fore the babies come. Never thought so myself."

"This shampoo gonna make it beautiful again," I told her.

When I finished, I moved her chair closer to the edge of her porch so the sun would quickly dry her hair.

"Now, I'm going to work in a bit of my tetter salve into your scalp. Gonna keep it from goin' dry on you."

I rubbed her scalp good and hard and then combed it through. When I was finished, I pulled out a mirror so she could admire what I'd done.

"That tetter salve sure smells pretty. Smells like roses, don't it?"

"Yes, it does. A Creole princess who knows the King of France told me where to find the rose scent I put in it. Comes right from her garden. Yes, it sure enough does."

"It tingles a bit, that tetter stuff. It ain't gonna burn me, is it? My momma's lye soap burn my head good!"

"No, Ma'am. I use it all the time."

I held my mirror for her to admire her hair. About that moment her pretty smile turned upside down. You see, her hair had started to fall off in gooey clumps. I was sure it was because it was real brittle from just having the baby and all 'cause I knew I'd worked my formula to perfection. Hadn't I?

"Lordy! "What are these black lumps fallin' to my lap? These dead moths? No, Lord, they's got to be dead bats!"

She looked up to the porch overhang but what was falling to her shoulders wasn't coming from up there! She screeched like the bed bugs were at her

"What? This is my hair!" she howled. "It's burning off my head!"

Lordy, truly, I thought I'd fixed the problem, but the product was still too strong for her very fine hair. Just the same, my customer decided she'd fix me good. That is after she kicked over the table with the basin of water and hurled a tin of tetter salve in the direction of my head. I grabbed my things to make for the road when she went to yelling certain words the likes of which only the devil would delight in hearing.

"Look what you've gone and done! You made my hair fall out!" she said. "I catch you on my street again; you'll be eatin' that nasty poison!"

I was running as fast as I could but her words and her dog, along with a pack of his friends chased me 'round the corner even faster. I didn't know what to say.

"You can keep the rest of the jar of shampoo then... It will help your hair grow back in!"

❧

Yes, 'round every corner that day I hit sharp edges and sure didn't want to see Grandma give me that "I told you so" look. So, to get my mind off my troubles, I decided to head on over to the Burkes' and get something done for the day.

Miss Burke was still at her luncheon when I showed up. I put on a big apron so she wouldn't notice I was wearing her old black skirt that she intended for the needy at her church. Mr. Burke heard me knocking about with the pots and pans in the kitchen and came in to see what I was doing battle with this time.

"How'd it go? he asked.

"I'm losin' more customers than I'm gettin'. Lots more and I only had one today to begin with. My shampoo is real fine. But my tetter salve, it didn't make my customer happy. No, she's probably just around the corner with her rabid dog still looking for me!"

"Well, good for the scarf business, hey? Guess you better cut your sulfur again. Probably best think about adding some lanolin oil," he said. "It may counter the burn by slowing the sulfur working on the scalp."

"Lanolin oil? Miss Burke uses it on her face, don't she?"

"By the drum. I'm pretty sure they put it in soap and face cream, too."

"Face creams? How do you make that I wonder? Rose-petal-scented face cream. Yes, makes your face look and feel like rose petals. Sure it does, you think, Mr. Burke?"

"I think there's a marketing wizard standing here this kitchen and it sure ain't me!"

That all got me thinking big again. Big enough I was able to leave behind the failures of the morning and start thinking about formulating a new product. If I could sell one, then surely my customer would want to buy another, like my face cream. The only thing I had yet to figure out was how I was going to get that first customer and her not putting out a reward on my head.

Someday Like the Rockefellers

68

OW LONG CAN a day be? At times, when I find a moment or two to reflect on how endlessly long mine seemed back then I got to thinking about my folks working the cotton. My days started before dawn when I climbed out of bed to walk to the Burkes'. There my days were spent cleaning and cooking and tending to Bella's whims and then sweating to iron out her tantrums. I'd return home late with muscles aching too tired to sleep. So, I'd spend more time working on my formulas for my shampoo and hair treatment. Guess it was after midnight till the aches in my legs and feet eased enough to crawl into bed. All that left little time to think about men! Still, over the next few weeks I came to admire C.J.'s mind for business along with his charm, and, well, as Emily predicted, his broad shoulders.

It seemed that Hank had his friend over for supper more and more particularly on nights it was my turn to cook. While I peeled and stirred, Emily jabbered on about how handsome C.J. was and reminded me that he was just in the other room. Then she'd wink. Well, well, I thought.

I poured us a glass of whiskey and went upstairs to fix my hair a bit. Had been up there only a few moments when I heard a man's heavy steps and then a little tap at my door.

"That you, Emily?"

C.J. walked in with a mischievous grin.

"My, woman, it sure smells good up here. Yes, Ma'am."

"It's my special hair and scalp tonic. Smells like rose petals, don't it?"

"I do believe you have come up with something that could cause the downfall of all men. It smells just that good. Let me smell behind your ear to know for sure."

C. J. kissed my neck.

"And you don't need to climb on the bush to smell the roses! No, Sir. And you smell with your nose, not your lips."

"Oh, is that how it works? I best keep at it till I get it right then."

He turned my face to his and kissed my mouth for the first time.

"Lips taste like rose petals, too."

"You go 'round chewin' on rose petals to know what they taste like?"

"I've been known to do some nibbling and nibbling on rose buds is my favorite."

I handed him a jar of my hair tonic so he could get his big hand on something other than me.

Downstairs Emily banged on her ceiling to announce supper was waiting.

"You hungry?" C.J. pulled me to him.

"I mean for chops—and not one with a big bone in 'em like you got goin' down there."

"I'm starting to see real potential here. Big potential," C.J. said.

He pretended to look over things laid out on my work counter.

"What's your business plan?" he asked.

I pulled away and went to get the papers I'd been working on, cleared the table and gestured for C.J. to take a seat.

"So, is this your first board meeting?" he asked.

"This here board is just an old door Emily and me brung up to work on." I declared not knowing what a board meeting was. "This is what I figure it cost me to make a jar of my shampoo. A bit more for a tin of my tetter salve. Mr. Burke helps me order tins and jars at wholesale. This is how much a case costs." C.J. looked closely at my figures as I jabbed at my numbers. "Now, if I sell this amount here, this is how much I'll make from selling just a dozen of my special blend shampoos."

"Wow! You women spend that much on hair tonics?"

"And how much do you spend?" I asked.

"Guess not enough, huh?"

"And you're not using the right product, are you?"

"Nope. I'd wager not. Need to try a new one right here and now, don't I?"

"See, everyone out there has a head of hair. 'Cept Grandma Ida, I guess. Those folks are all gonna be my customers one day. You count 'em 'cause I can't count that high…"

"There's a whole lot of heads in this world, ain't they? Think how far you're gonna make the postman walk delivering all those tins of pomade."

"I've already hired agents; two tub women living up the street. If we can wash clothes, we can wash a customer's hair and apply my hair tonic. Then that customer will go to all her neighbors…."

"If they have a head of hair…," he said.

"And sell 'em a bottle or tin of my hair products. Of course, she'll want two for her ma, won't she? Then if I had ten agents a month selling to their neighbors and kin, that's how much I'd make after I pay for my jars and ingredients."

"Agents, you say?"

"That's here in Denver. Why not St. Louis? Or Indianapolis, Detroit and Natchez? Come to think of it, why not Pittsburgh and Washington, too?"

"You're gonna cover the world."

"Well, not the whole world but maybe every person of color who wants to look their best."

"Someday you just might end up livin' in a mansion like they say the Rockefellers do," he said with a grin at the absurdity of the notion.

"Don't know 'bout no mansion. Never been in a mansion, not even the Burneys'. This jar of hair tonic is my escape from living off white folks' scraps. Someday, Lord willing, maybe me and a few of my agents will say farewell to the tubs for good. Amen, to that!"

"It's a mighty big dream, too. Sure it is. Well, you sold me. I'll buy a bottle right now."

C. J. pulled out a big roll of bills.

"Two bottles and then you get one free."

"This woman is a natural born seller!" he said.

Thinking about how small my attic room had become since I started mixing up there, I wondered how many jars I'd have to sell to maybe one day own my own home. Nobody in my family ever owned their own place. It was a new dream for me.

Someday like the Rockefellers? Well, why not?

OVER OLD CRACKED WALKS

69

A T TIMES IT seemed as though things got so worked up in Bella's head that she went looking for someone to heap her misery on to release the pressure brewing in her mind and wasn't I always at hand? That morning she never rang her bell for breakfast, so I was sure she wanted to start something up with me.

I was pulling things out to bake biscuits when she hurled herself downstairs like a well powdered tornado. Bella surely reckoned she'd catch me stealing or knee deep in some sin we were ever so prone to. Keeping me in the corner of her eye, that woman snorted and paced about the kitchen. I kept rolling my biscuits even with her huffing at the back of my neck till she finally headed to the lab to get something worked up with Mr. Burke. She loved to catch him unarmed as well. I could hear 'em back there that morning. Her wanting more of something and him saying there ain't nothing left in any store that she didn't already have two of.

By suppertime Miss Burke had realized I'd been ignoring her as best I could, which always got up her nose. Then after I served up their meal and brought back the silver, service dishes, dessert plates, cheese dishes, breadbaskets and all the rest that I had to put out for her majesty every damned night, along with five courses of food I'd cooked up, I finally got to my cleaning up chores. Guess Mr. Burke was tired of this woman 'cause he soon took off for his favorite cigar shop.

I stood there at that sink washing dishes with my feet aching like I was standing on sun-baked rocks. Lordy, no sooner did I have things dried than Bella barged in to finish what she'd tried to start up with me that morning. First, she tossed her silly white-woman scrapbook on the breakfast table. She'd filled it with recipes for food ain't nobody ever heard of, let alone ever want to eat. Pasting scraps in books was what she did when she wanted to sit there watching if I was working and still be doing nothing worthwhile herself. There she hummed while she slathered her recipes with paste and complimented herself on her fine taste in food. Oh, Lord was this woman, who'd never lifted a pot, ever a fine cook! But I tell you plain, this woman never cooked up anything in her life but misery.

I think she sensed I was hoping to get out the door early that evening. The chilly fall nights were already getting dark early and there were no streetlights once I stepped past Bella's part of town unless you counted the matches struck by wandering drunks trying not to step on the toes of whores standing in the dark.

Well, it had been a long day, too long and I was tired to the bone and in no mood to stoop and pick up more of Bella's piles of self-pity. No, I got her dishes dried and decided I was going to head off no matter how loudly that woman moaned.

"Miss Burke, it's late; I'm headed off now," I said untying my wet apron.

"So early?" she said pretending to be dumb-founded.

For ages I halfway expected her to suggest I sleep on the back porch with the dog so I'd be in her kitchen even earlier and could stay even later.

"It's near eight now. Been dark for some time."

Then I held my breath before giving her the bad news that I expected would split one of our heads open, and Lord, I dreaded seeing what she might not have up in hers!

"And I be needin' an extra day off from now on, too."

Bad news out, I decided to get it all out but didn't look her in the face, just kept folding my tea towels to leave.

"Got to have Saturdays and Sundays off every week."

Lord, it did not sit any better than expected. I could tell by her heaving nostrils and the way her lips turned bluish that she was working up a mighty tantrum 'cause for Bella, no matter how many hours I put in, I still owed her more. Yes, I knew how she figured things; no matter what her numbers were they still computed less was best for me and more was hers for being white!

Her tone quickly became that of the confederate general who lurked just under her ruffled silk blouses. I tell you, that big mouth of hers spewed gravel in my face.

"Just what is goin' on here?"

She dropped her paste brush at her feet and looked to me to pick it up. Then she stood up in my face to signal she really meant business.

"Things been real strange 'round here lately!"

She glared at me like Melinda Burney did when she was aiming to backhand me out of her rose garden.

"Strange for you? Or for the rest of us?" I asked.

"What's that? Your job's in jeopardy. You best start feelin' lucky to get one day off."

"Oh, I do feel lucky for once in my life. Yes, Ma'am. Felt luck sneakin' up on me the moment I got out of bed this morning at five-thirty to make my way over here."

"Lucky, you say? Why, I have never heard of such a fool thing!" She screeched. "You don't even know what it is! You're a colored! What's lucky about that?"

"Like I said, I'm feeling lucky enough to be taking two days off a week from now on."

"Do you know who you're speakin' to?" she whined like a petulant child.

"Well, it sure ain't no Creole princess standin' in front of me!"

Miss Burke was livid. She started biting her lower lip like a pouty child working up a tantrum and fixing to pee a puddle on the kitchen floor.

"What would you do if you lost your job? What about references? Huh? Think you're gonna get any from me? No references and you won't get work 'round here, that's for sure!"

"Miss Burke, my folks were slaves with no references to white folks like you so I'm familiar with your form of bondage," I told her face. "As far as references: I might just pack up and go work for the Creole princess when she gets back from Paris!"

Her face turned scarlet because she knew the Creole princess story was all crap but also knew that I'd heard her tell all her big-hat lady friends her help once worked for royalty, so she couldn't admit she knew better.

I had this woman knotted in my apron string and was swiftly winding it 'round her neck. Yes, I'd decided to put her out of her misery once and for all.

"You're gonna be spending the rest of your days hangin' over a washtub. Yes, you will! And that's exactly what you deserve after being disrespectful to a white woman."

"Woman! You ain't deciding what I deserve no more! Since I was seven, I been makin' my way with a tub and washboard and it's about time you looked down one yourself. A tub! Down at the bottom of that stinkin' water where your soul goes swimming!"

"My what does what?" she screeched.

For a woman who bathed in rose water, putting her hands deep in dirty lye water was as frightening as it got. Only folks finding out she no longer had a maid could have shaken her worse!

"You know our delicate hands mustn't touch that awful lye soap. Anyway, what in hell are you good for but washin'? I'm tellin' you, nothing is what!"

It was all I could do not to backhand her. So, on the spot I made the decision to let Bella wallop herself. I stood there calmly, like Mrs. Washington would have, before landing the fatal blow!

"Nothin'?" I said as haughty as any white woman. "That so? Well, maybe it's 'bout time you started lookin' 'round 'cause you ain't been seein' a lot of the story that's sure been gettin' told 'round here!"

"What? What's been goin' on 'round here?"

Her voice modulated back to her Confederate general tone.

"Why, I sure as hell have! she barked.

Then she realized that she had no idea what she was talking about.

"What is going? I demand to know this instant!"

"Let me put it to you this way: You ain't never heard Bill say I'm good for nothing. In fact, you ain't never heard him say nothin' that wasn't real sweet to me, have you now?"

The woman's face froze. She could only sit there like she was watching Nona at the stove fryin' up her tongue and dancing a jig while shaking that box of cornmeal all over Bella's kitchen!

"You got no more to say, huh?" Then I jabbed it in deeper and twisted it as far as it would go. "Don't you just wonder what Bill has got to say 'bout things? Or haven't you been listenin' to him over the last few months? What else you ain't been doing all that time?"

"The… Huh?"

I got close to Bella's ear.

"Go ask 'im, Bella!"

"What? Ask who what?"

"You heard me woman!"

"I beg your pardon? This is no concern of my husband's."

She said with all the royal majesty she could muster. But her posturing didn't fool me as I knew I'd knocked the wind out of her. Her chin quivered something awful.

"Beggin' my pardon, are you? Now how does that feel to your pride?" I asked. "I don't know why I should pardon you, maybe just 'cause you're ignorant. The only lesson in life you ever learned was the delicate art of gettin' head throbs whenever you're needin' more attention. Or do you get 'em only when that man needs some attention, huh?"

"I get headaches all the time and you're the damned cause, too!" Bella screeched.

"Always talking 'bout colored folks like we're mules. That why white men start to throb someplace ain't near their heads when their wives get their head throbs?"

"White men do what? Who told you all that?"

"Who told me? Lord, have mercy, woman! Are you sleep-walkin' and can't see in front of youself?"

"I am not asleep and get out of my face!"

"Ain't you always thinkin' your husband's with some other woman. Huh? Been wondering who that woman is?"

The woman's big mouth shut down like she had a case of lockjaw.

"What in hell are you talkin' about? Nona has sure been mouthin' off again! If I talked to that neighbor woman, which I don't, I'd tell her everything you and Nona are up to."

"And you don't figure the neighbor woman's in on things too? Ain't she always watching for your comin' and goin'? At the backdoor of your itty-bitty mind, haven't you been askin' yourself, who's been takin' care of my husband while I was away? Bet you even noticed me fix up my hair real nice these days, too, 'cause Bill sure has!"

Bella's lower lip quivered something awful.

"Up at your sister's gettin' over your nervous condition with all those headaches you were juggling…"

"Damn it to hell, what in tarnation are you talking about?"

"And Nona and I were here all alone with your husband. Nobody lookin' over our shoulders watching us. Feedin' William. Takin' care of 'im. Takin' good care of 'im the way a man likes it!"

"You're a damned liar! And I always knew you were, too!" she exclaimed.

"That so? What have I ever lied about?"

Bella started wailing.

"Oh, Lord… nothing! My husband? When I was gone?"

"Yep. All the time you were gone. Bill and me and, well, Nona, too!"

"Nona?"

"Ain't she always just over the fence watching for you to come home? Yeah. Who's she watching out for?"

"No!"

Everybody on that block could have heard Bella's howls.

"But that's not all. That neighbor woman was lookin' in on what was goin' on here, too."

I barely had the words out before Bella screeched again.

"You've seen 'er snickering behind your back, haven't you?"

"That neighbor woman, too? I told you she's a Baptist and that means she's gone off and told the street! Maybe even both sides by now!"

Bella collapsed into that kitchen chair looking like she wanted to die. Poor woman, I could tell she'd be in bed for weeks. But this time I doubt if she'd be inviting her churchwoman friends to drop by to go over the details of her ailments. Them armed with tissue-wrapped gifts to speed her recovery. Not after there'd been talk of husband business heard up and down Bella's street. Lolling tongues just hang with that kind of talk that's seldom wrapped in delicate tissue.

"Not Nona, too?" she sobbed.

"Right over your kitchen table and with the curtains pulled open as wide as they'd go!"

I plopped into a chair next to Bella to hand her the details.

"Let me tell you all about it 'cause it went on for days."

"Oh, my God!" Bella howled.

"Like I said, for days we worried over you. Mr. Burke and me did. We worried and wondered if you were gettin' better and that's the truth of it. Your husband was so lonely without you."

"That's all you and William ever did together? Worry over me?"

"But how much is that, Miss Burke?"

"You have been real mean to me just now," she said. "Making me think Bill and you…."

"Doin' what, Miss Burke? Can't you see? All them ugly thoughts you keep piled up in your head 'bout your husband wantin' another woman and all them notions 'bout coloreds stealin', being lazy, can't do nothin' without a washtub, that's all in your heart. It was you spreadin' the meanness and as the Lord is my witness, you spread it on good and thick. All I done is send your meanness back to smack you."

Bella sobbed and laughed with relief that her husband had not being carrying on with another woman. At least not with Nona and me over the kitchen table. I handed Bella my apron to wipe her tears and she blew her nose in it like a trumpet.

"You ever been married?" she asked when she stopped her bawling.

"I worked for you almost four years and you've never once asked me if I was ever married. I bet you don't even recall I have a daughter. Yes, I was married but my husband's gone from me now."

"What happened to him?" she asked.

"Jeffrey McWilliams, my baby's daddy was lynched more than twenty years ago."

"What did he do wrong?"

With those words all I could do was hold on to my seat so I didn't situate my chair over her head. She handed me back the apron she'd snotted on.

"Did wrong? You think coloreds only get lynched for doin' something wrong? Why you poor woman. Even on a good day and that's all you've ever had in your life, you can't escape yourself! Here, you keep that apron to remember me by. I won't be comin' back tomorrow…or ever again."

I tossed that nasty apron in her lap.

"You can't leave here!" she said. "What will I do?"

For the only time in all the years I'd worked for Bella I departed through her front door and down the walk cracked by the roots of those old magnolias. There I paused to stoop over for the last time and picked up a fallen magnolia flower larger than my hand. Breathing in its sweet fragrance reminded me of Momma. I could feel her presence that moment.

DANCING ON ROSE WATER

70

THE NEXT DAY I got up before the sun rose to ready myself for the long walk to the Burkes'. There I sat on the edge of my bed half-asleep until it finally hit me; I had no work to walk to that day or the next. The sky was growing dark, like my mood, that fall morning. I pulled the blanket over me and heard that old familiar voice asking me 'what now'?

I lay there pondering the mess I'd made for myself. I brewed over how I'd keep up Lelia's education fees, send money to Louvenia and was there even a possibility of finding housework with no references? Lord knows I didn't want to go hunting for work at the laundry houses. I was well into my thirties and knew those places worked young women into old age quicker than a new girl could show up looking for a tub. Mercifully, I was too old for the tubs. In fact, I was too old for most any job a colored woman might find, and for a moment or two, felt as worn down as some old brush used to scrub overalls.

I lay there till the sun finally slipped up over the rooftops before heading downstairs where I knew Emily would be ironing Hank's barbering shirt and getting his breakfast.

"What are you doin' up this early?" Emily asked. "You still hearin' Miss Burke's bell?"

Emily had made her point well.

560

"I figured I needed to get up extra early to count all my money. You see, I have so much it might take me most of the day."

"Don't start worryin' 'bout Lelia or your sister."

"No? Then who's gonna worry 'bout?"

Emily handed me a cup of coffee as I sat down at the breakfast table.

"You know I once promised Sister I'd write the President a letter asking 'im to help our people. Looks like now's a good time to pull out the paper. But then I'd have to count my pennies to see if I have the postage to send a letter to the White House."

"Somebody tell you just because you're without work ain't nobody gonna say boo to you again?"

"Nobody needs to boo at me," I replied. "What I went and done to myself gots me frightened enough. I know what I have to do today. Got to go and ask Bella for my job back."

"No, you're not."

"You're right. She wouldn't have me and even if she did she'd work up a hundred conditions before she'd take me back."

"Hank and I talked last night. Yes, we did. We don't need your rent money for the next month while you get on your feet."

"Emily, you can't afford that. You got your bills and Grandma's to settle."

"We're all gonna be fine, thank the Lord."

"I got to go find a house job."

"First, you got to stop walkin' backwards," Emily said.

"Doesn't look like I'm walking nowheres today or tomorrow."

"You already got a job; you just need it to pay more is all."

"My hair products? I got only a couple dozen bottles of shampoo mixed and no more bottles to make more."

"Well, you're not gonna sell them bottles sitting here in my kitchen. The time you spend worryin' over things or looking for housework you could be sellin' what you got door to door. Take that money and go buy more bottles."

"Of course, I can. Then, come Sunday, I'm gonna to set up a table at church and sell even more," I added to Emily's drift.

"Which church?" She asked.

"Ours, of course."

"And then which church after that? There's one on the next block over. Hell, go over to Bella's and sell your shampoo to her friends for half what she charges. All whites want something for nothin'! Ain't that's why they brought us here from Africa, honey?"

"I'm goin' over to our church this mornin' and talk to the preacher 'bout setting up a demonstration come Sunday. Yes, Ma'am. That's what I'm going to do. For sure, I am."

"No, you best go to the preacher's wife first. Let 'er know you got a business goin'. Give her a bottle of your rose-scented shampoo and let her do the talkin' to the preacher when she figures it's the right time."

"I got to iron my black skirt right now so I can go talk to the preacher's wife, just like you say, Emily. Guess my letter to the President will have to wait."

"Well, hopefully the President won't wear himself out running out to the post box every morning looking for that letter you've not yet sent!" Email added.

The patterns of life are hard to change for those who toil like mules somewhere in that thin air between one wash tub filled and another still soaking. When I woke up most days, I still jumped out of bed fearful I'd be late to Bella's. I remember my daddy bolting out of bed thinking he was late for the fields. I feared the simple act of sleeping in meant the same thing to me it did for him: A calamity pounding on the door like some overseer. But for some reason it didn't. No, when I woke up, I felt truly like a freed woman for the first time in my life. I could understand now why my momma woke with her smile of joy on Preaching Day. It was only Momma's reassuring words that Daddy needed to settle back on the moss-stuffed bed for a few more moments of rest; a sweet reminder that at least on Sunday there'd be no Isaac pounding on his rickety door. I felt that same serenity as I rolled over cold mornings for a few extra moments of sleep. Yes, I had plenty to get to those days, but hallelujah Lord, I could do it when I got to it. The days of wearing out my worn-out shoes when Miss Burke pulled out her servant's bell were over for me.

Still I had yet to know it.

The first Saturday after I left the Burkes' was my birthday; turned thirty-nine. Don't know if anyone in my family had ever made it to that age other than Louvenia. As I recall, it was on that very day when a special gift showed up in the mail. In the envelope was the same amount of money I would have been paid for working at the Burke's for three whole months! Lord, there it was! No note inside, just bills folded up in plain paper. But I knew anyway. It was Mr. Burke who'd done it; it was the kind of gesture that enabled me to survive those years. Bless this man, Lord. But ask Jesus to put a curse on that wife of his!

❧

Back in those early days, C.J. and me seemed to draw closer as he visited at Emily and Hank's table. There we'd talked about the things he'd seen and learned working with businesses 'round town. He'd share tidbits about the shops and places that ran ads in the paper he worked for. He had stories of how these shops started small, then when people heard about them from ads and bought their merchandise they grew. Everything in business, according to C.J., was building one block on another, step by step, or perhaps one head of hair to the next as I put it. C.J. made up charts he sketched out to teach me something about sales. Still I was determined to keep things simple; what's more simple than knowing there were lots of colored folks out there and they all surely needed my product because mine would be the best? That was as plain and simple as it gets. Market to every head of hair and those very heads would be walking 'round selling my products and that was to be my business philosophy.

I knew it would. The day came when I awoke wondering who had soaked my room in lye water so damned hot it had shrunk to a doll's house size? Yes, them walls were surely closing in on me; boxes of this and that stacked up everywhere. Over the weeks it got so crowded and smelled so bad of product being mixed and funneled that Grandma Ida threatened to get the law down on Emily and me.

"That a dead dog up there?" Grandma howled. "That dead, it ain't never gonna get up and walk away by itself! So, get to it!"

Soon I had five or six tub women working for me as agents for few hours a week. Mostly women I knew from church. Every week they came by and we had our little meeting over tea at Emily's table just like Bella did with her church women. Grandma was made honorary secretary to keep her mouth shut. Didn't work.

"Who the hell are all them women hanging on your table, Emily? Don't they know how bad a cook you are to be them sittin' there waiting for a plate of your slop?"

"They're Sarah's sales agents and they want to have their tea and cookies without your big mouth steamin' up the room!" Emily replied.

After the meeting, I would divide the number of jars we'd filled and labeled and my women would take off with them. Most would sell them within a day or two just to the folks they knew.

Well, maybe they all saw it coming before I did. Yes, Charles Joseph Walker and I were married. It wasn't a church wedding, just a visit to the City Hall and a paper we both signed with Emily and Hank as witnesses. It was all we had time for what with moving and all. Guess you could say it was an arrangement of sorts, C.J. and me. Perhaps more like a business partnership than anything. But I was a mature woman and was at peace with the fact that I had had my one great love with Jeffrey and never really desired anything that might intrude on the memory of those precious moments we had.

C.J. worked at his paper long hours and contributed by managing my advertising in his office while he ate his lunch. They gave me credit to run my ads. As soon as I had extra money I purchased even larger ads thinking they would catch the eyes of more folks. Although I went knocking on doors most days with my satchel, I started getting orders through the mail as well. Every time the postman came, I'd run to the mailbox. For me, these sales coming in was a daily pat-on-the-back that my ideas were working.

Sometimes I stayed up till the wee hours working on my formula, filling tins and pasting labels. We sent out boxes of my product packed carefully in sawdust nearly every morning. The postman would deliver the orders to my agents and collect my money on delivery. Then he'd turn it over to me when he came for the mail the next day. I figured that the three cents it cost to mail the product saved me from bandaging three blisters and so, the more stamps I licked, the more my feet thanked me.

It wasn't long, a few months perhaps, before I needed even more room for my growing operation. Seemed like those days followed each other in a haze 'cause I had no time to be counting the hours I was putting in; had orders to get out. After long and sometimes heated talks with C.J. on the topic, I decided we best move to Pittsburgh. Why, he asked. Simple: because it was the center of operations for Mr. Carnegie and his business empire, therefore it had to have something to offer me as well. Pittsburgh was the rail center of that part of the country. Supplies arrived by track all day and didn't return empty. We were soon packing for Pittsburgh and new adventures.

We moved from Emily's attic to a nice place I found. It was two-story house with a veranda porch and a large work shed out back with room to store all my ingredients, tins and packing materials. I scraped together a nice down payment and was the first person of my family to own my own place and did it without twisting the water out of any rag a white woman had tossed at my feet.

'Bout then I started thinking about making short trips out to the countryside where folks never got to shop to see if I could sell my products. The thing is, it was dangerous for a colored woman to travel the open roads unless dressed as a cotton picker, maid, or tub woman. The abuse directed at us by white folks never abated. It became that country churches were the safest places to meet and demonstrate my wares. I knew these churches weren't coming to me so I traveled to them. I'd introduce myself to the preacher by letter and a few weeks later would receive an invitation to come visit. Beforehand I'd arranged to stay with my agents while on the road. And Lord, let me tell you, it was a long and dusty road at that.

Sales got to the point I could hire some extra help to mix my formula for hair treatment, leaving me more time to experiment with new formulas. Still, I never gave the entire formula to one employee. Each person knew only a part of it and I would add the last ingredients myself from the formula I kept in my head.

The new agents working for me were filled with pride over having a colored woman boss for the first time in their lives. They appreciated my endeavors so much that they always put in more effort than I ever reasonably thought was my due. And I gave them their due; respect, compassion and good wages to take home to their families.

About six or seven months after we'd settled in Pittsburgh, C.J. returned from his job at the paper for lunch and saw how things were bustling. Bottles and tins of my product were being boxed up all over the kitchen, back porch and the shed for James, my new man, to take down to the post office.

When C.J. walked in, I had large kettles heating in my kitchen filled not with chicken soup, but with lanolin warming to fold into the special ingredients along with my imported rose fragrance that my shampoo was made with.

"Look at all this. My, my! Ain't we busy beavers 'round here?" he said.

"Sometimes when I pause I'm overwhelmed. So, I decided I best not waste time pausing."

"Yes, Ma'am. This place is sure hoppin', ain't it?"

It was moments like these that I paused to reflect on where I was; a tub woman with a small but growing business that had nothing to do with the tubs. As time traveled, it came that I could no longer recognize my own life. What day was it that I stopped drowning in stinking brown tub water and started dancing on rose water? Well, the calendars had become blurred for me and maybe that was yet another blessing.

"Look at me: The daughter of slaves, a slave myself in most ways,"

I told C.J. "and now I'm building a business, tin by tin, box by box, customer by customer."

"And lots of money comin' in. I see good times ahead on this road," he remarked.

He looked dashing in his new suit the tailor had delivered that morning. As respectable as any piece of wool Mr. Carnegie ever wore.

"What I see is opportunity. Something I aim to follow wherever it takes me and Lord knows what direction's comin' next!"

"Opportunity, is it?" C.J. asked.

"Everywhere there's a head of hair, there's a customer standing at her door waiting for me. She just doesn't know I'm on my way!"

"The printer's here. Wants your decision on the product name for the labels you want printed along with a check for his work."

"I've prayed on that and have now decided. This business will be called the Madame. C.J. Walker Manufacturing Company."

"Not the Sarah Walker Company?"

"How many times did a white person demand I address them as Mister this or Missus and yet to them I had only one name? Maybe like their dog. Don't think Bella Burke even knew my last name. Now, everybody will know me only as Madame. MadameC. J. Walker. I'm not Sarah, Sally, or Jane no last name tub woman to nobody no more!"

"You know, at the rate you're growing this business, you'll be needing to hire more help soon," C.J. mused.

"Lelia will be returning to me in a few months. Can't even imagine what she's gonna think of her momma now. Will she recognize me?"

Yes, I am... Madame Walker

71

IT SEEMED AS though Lelia had been gone for ages even if it had been only a few long months. So much like her daddy, the day came when her restlessness overcame her and she wanted to leave college and work for her momma. I wondered what my daughter would think as the long hard days she was away had worn on me like decades. I now faced that strangeness of being known to folks I'd never met simply because they'd seen my image in the weeklies.

Over the months since moving to Pittsburgh, I'd come to know Harriet, the dressmaker, as a fond friend. She was the seamstress who lived in a boarding house around the corner from my place. Harriet had worked her fingers to the bone for a decade as head seamstress in the backroom of a white woman's fancy dress shop. Over the years she'd gone without and saved every penny she could so when she had had enough of the woman she worked for, she set about to open her own shop. But nobody would rent her a storefront; at least not in the white part of town. But the thing is, the silhouettes of Harriet dresses were complicated, and her fancy imported trims so dear no colored woman could afford them let alone have a place to wear them. So, it would be of little commercial benefit to open a shop on our side of town.

Nevertheless, Harriet's determination kept her going. Like me, nothing was going to stop her. Come a wall we couldn't march around, our determination dictated we'd chip at it till it crumbled low enough we could crawl over! In Harriet's case, she hired herself a white woman who couldn't sew worth a damn and had her upfront telling customers it was her place and that Harriet was merely doing hems and alterations in the backroom. This arrangement worked well enough even though my friend was denied the satisfaction of having her customers compliment her fine work.

Typically, I'd stop by Harriet's for fabric selection or fittings after closing so her white customers would not distract from our chats. One evening I arrived to look over trims she'd ordered for my outfits and get my second fitting on a new travel suit that I would wear on the train to Knoxville.

"Now, MadameWalker, I got a nice pork chop put back for you!" she announced.

I was perplexed by this statement as there was never a mention of us sharing a meal when she rang me on the telephone I'd recently installed.

"Honey, I just had my supper. But thank you just the same." "That's just fine. You can take one home. But be sure and eat it as soon as you get back!"

"Just what are you talking about, Harriet? You're doubting if I finished my supper or not?"

"What I'm certain of is that if you eat any better—I'll be letting out these seams again. Then I got to thinkin' that isn't a bad idea. I'm a business woman like you," Harriet said. "See?"

"No. I have no idea what you're seein' but I'm wondering if you need to put your spectacles on! Are you gettin' into the fried pork chop business or something?"

"Why, no, dear. I'm in the dress-making business so if I convince you to eat a few more pork chops every week, you're gonna put on a few more pounds."

"So, what if I do? C.J. sure likes my full figure."

"That's music to my ears! When can we start planning this new wardrobe for you? With lots more yardage to cover them pork chops you're carrying on those ample hips. Look how much you've spent in my shop the last few months. I hope for you to double my sales 'cause you're my richest customer. In fact, as business is slow this month, I'll send you home with two pork chops. You like buttered potatas, too? Want a little cream mixed in 'em?"

"Well, I swan. I am not carrying no pork chop on me!"

I laughed but then Harriet smacked my backside as she pulled the last straight pens out. That was the beginning of my slimming. C.J. and I had discussed the importance of me always being well dressed in public as such would draw attention to my name and business. Yes, my appearance was a method of promotion that traveled well everywhere I went without a single word.

"And then if I keep you fed real good—you like chicken gravy? I can tailor many more fine outfits for you, I'll soon become as rich as my friend, MadameC.J. Walker."

"Ain't that the truth? Charging me like I was a duchess and all."

We laughed till she opened a box of chocolate bonbons for nibbling. I declined her fancy chocolates and in so doing saved myself the price of further alterations.

"Well, dear. If I didn't charge like you're a rich woman, you might not feel like one and that would trouble us both. Isn't that right?" Harriet asked.

"Why not charge me as though I were still poor? I was entirely comfortable with those prices."

"I will, MadameWalker," Harriet was quick to reply, "when you go back to being a tub woman, I'll cut you a discount. A bitty one."

The day I longingly awaited finally arrived. I would take a train to Knoxville where my daughter would be waiting for me. I was so anxious about what Lelia would think of her momma that I could hardly sleep.

On the train I wore Harriet's traveling suit, which I knew was the latest in fashion as she'd copied the design from a Parisian magazine. She assured me I'd be dressed just like Mrs. Rockefeller. I had no idea, as I'd never met Mrs. Rockefeller, but I had met Mrs. Booker T. Washington and dressing like her would please me just fine.

My suit was light beige with a beige-peach colored satin trim on the collar and cuffs. To go with all the fancy trim, Harriet had her milliner make up a fine hat of the same color with elegant ostrich feathers tinted to match. I also purchased a small diamond brooch for my lapel that dangled large black pearls.

Even though I'd been traveling on business for months by then, I still harbored deep fears that being on a train would only convey me to a destination I had no desire to end up at. How strangely small my world was back then and how easy to imagine the fears my parents knew at the thought of Isaac putting them off the Burney place; the soil that as slaves they never departed from even in death. They could only have wondered and whispered their fears as they lay side by side on their moss-stuffed bed late in the night. What could be out there that wouldn't be worse than right there under their bare feet? They could not have known of the many worlds that lay beyond Grandview.

When my daughter departed for college, I'd emptied the education tin to get her to Knoxville. Now I was travelling there First Class; that is to the extent I was permitted. This scenario required I purchase two tickets, one for myself and one for my "white woman," the one I traveled with as attendant. However, this woman didn't exist past the second ticket I purchased. Yes, just as Harriet comparatively paid double with her white woman up front, I paid double fares in those days and then frequently paid an even higher price in so many other ways once onboard.

It was unusual for train companies to have white porters except up front as supervisors. Most train porters were colored which caused management issues as these operations sure as hell wouldn't promote a colored man. That would set a dangerous precedent where we might misbelieve that hard work might one day payoff. So, the train companies made sure porters had white bosses and these men typically worked the first-class coaches.

The train had barely taken off before I heard them; white stewards speaking annoyingly loud perhaps for my benefit should I have forgotten my place.

"Heard there was a Negra in First Class," one announced from the galley near my compartment.

"Somebody's maid. Sure she is," the other replied as he pulled trays out to set up for lunch service.

I was famished as I'd been too nervous to eat breakfast that morning so I pulled the service bell not knowing what might confront me.

"That's her compartment," the white steward snapped.

Perhaps by then they wondered where my white woman was allowing me to ring for service like I'd paid for those tickets myself. I could only wonder if Harriet's smart traveling suit had put these nigger dogs on my scent; the scent of rose water I'd bathed in earlier.

"Tea, please. I'll have tea service now."

I attempted to break his stony-faced glare with a smile knowing I'd just stirred his notions as to a colored woman being so presumptuous as to request service. Even in those few feet between us, there was too great a distance for him to value me as a paying customer. No, I was sure that all he saw was the undisguised bare fact that I was not dressed like humbled mammy or laundress. In fact, at first, he looked like my request needed translation as if I'd spoken in the heavy dialect of a slave or that of the simple minded. Perhaps this was unjust, and he was merely a stupid man that warranted more sympathy than scorn.

"You expect me to get it… for you?"

His words were tinged with hate.

At that a handsome young colored man appeared. I'd seen some shadow play outside my door but thought it was the white steward's reinforcements as I knew white folks were oriented to group intimidation—an inherent instinct toward mob mentality I always thought.

"I'll bring it!" this young man said confidently.

They were only three words from his young bold mouth but the way he delivered them and the gaze he put on the white steward changed the atmosphere. The white steward appeared discombobulated by this confrontation; he was much smaller than this handsome young man that had responded to the situation.

"This is my section, you!" The white steward proclaimed, but it was modulated in tone than he'd used in addressing me. "And I'll be countin' all the food money, too."

Perhaps this coda was to remind me that colored folks were held to be thieves by those who had stolen our lives for so many generations.

This steward paused outside my door for the young colored man to open the way for him in order to avoid brushing up against him. Their eyes sparred. The young colored porter stepped aside barely enough for the steward to angle sideways and slip past him.

I asked this determined young man what his name was.

"Freeman Briley Ransom, Ma'am," he replied.

His relaxed expression belied his youth.

"You been workin' here long?" I inquired.

"Just for the summer, Ma'am. I'm hoping to go to law school this fall," he said.

He spoke with pride thinned with hesitancy. I'd born these same unsure feelings often enough to sense them in others—those chipped and dashed hopes one is forced to put away for a maybe better day ahead.

The white steward reappeared with a tray of sorts for tea. I don't believe anything had been washed. Or perhaps he spilled on the way to my compartment. He sat the tray down so hard it spilled more but thankfully not on me. What did splatter on me was his message; servant or no, I was not welcome on that train—certainly not in a saloon car elegantly appointed for use by rich white folks. Indeed, I knew that other coloreds that had this message tossed at them could just as easily be tossed from a moving train. My palms went moist at the thought.

Mr. Ransom jumped in to clean up the tray.

"Law school? What will you do when you graduate?" I asked. "Have you decided?"

"Don't know yet. Most days just gettin' through school seems a stretch too far to see beyond."

"Indeed, I do understand. I'm ready for lunch now. Would you bring the menu?"

"Don't know if they'll allow it in this section. Might have to move to the other car to get some food. Here, they only serve whites."

I should have assumed coloreds ate in segregated areas and yet my stomach sang a different tune. I never could convince my empty belly it was different from any white person's. At that point it was growling louder than Grandma Ida's after eating one of her favorite butter-and-onion sandwiches. In third class compartments, we usually brought our own food, if we had any, because even if they served us, it was usually double the price for scraps that should have been tossed out; take it or leave it their glares dictated.

"I see," is all I could say not wishing to provoke an incident.

I knew this young man would be witnessing enough assaults to his dignity ahead so I was determined to accept the situation I had no control over and let it pass.

"Sorry, Ma'am. I'll bring a proper cup of tea though."

The young man took away the filthy tray the white man had nearly tossed at me. He no sooner stepped out than I heard another commotion in the galley.

"You spilled again!" I recognized Freeman's voice. "You keep drinkin' this way and you might spill over the side of this here train like you do your tea trays! Who'd ever know? Best not slop on my customers again, hear?"

I wondered if any white man had ever before slopped something on a colored woman and been threatened with ejection? Ejection was a journey white folks figured only coloreds traveled. Off a train sliding face down on the gravel slope to that final moment ending in eternal rest.

Minutes later Freeman brought a beautifully prepared luncheon tray. Yes, I would eat after all. There was plate of roast beef, potatas, carrots and a piece of hot apple pie.

"Aren't you risking your job with that tray?" I asked.

"I know what's right. That's all I'm doing. Long as we're doing right, we all got to answer to only one boss," Freeman said gazing to the heavens.

Unbeknownst to either of us those few words would bring us together for years to come.

"At the end of summer, I would like for you to contact me. I may be able to aid you with some work in the future."

I offered my business card.

"MadameC.J. Walker? You're MadameWalker?"

His eyes twinkling like a child's.

"I read about you in the weeklies."

"Yes. I am… MadameC.J. Walker."

DAYS OF LELIA

72

MY STOMACH FLUTTERED as it did the day I walked down the aisle to marry her daddy. I was determined to make our daughter proud. As the train arrived, I pulled out a large hatbox and put on the new hat. I cared little if I'd fooled them into thinking I was someone's maid. I wore it knowing that hat cost more than a month's wages for the men working on that train. I pinned on my brooch and pulled out the matching string of black pearls concealed down my blouse. Yes, I came from the cotton fields and would never deny it, but that was many miles ago. Now there were new rules and I'd made them for myself.

The porters' eyes darted back and forth in amazement as I stepped off. Perhaps they'd never seen a colored woman so attired. White folks stepping off the first class coaches also appeared confounded. I'd never felt as stared at as I did that first evening in Knoxville. I could hardly have known then, but it would be commonplace in the years ahead.

The platform was crowded. Those big liquid brown eyes, where were they?

"Momma! Over here!"

Lelia's voice rang through the din of train whistles and bustling people. Oh, Lord, I thought, she'd gotten even taller and looked so beautiful and graceful as she made her way through the crowd. As I waited for my daughter to fall into my arms, I easily forgot about all those hard glances shot my way from the white passengers. I opened my arms to her and wondered what her daddy would think of us. At that moment, my husband's dream of his child learning to read and write had been realized. It was a dream he'd started in that dimpled tobacco tin. Perhaps his last one and yet it lived beyond him and still fed us with hope.

As I held my daughter tightly, I happened to gaze over her shoulder and saw what was headed our way. My eyes were so full of tears I thought I was seeing an apparition. But no, it was Louvenia walking towards us. She was dressed to the nines.

"Oh, Lord. Look who I see comin'!"

Tears rolled down my face. Sister and I had been exchanging letters through Annie for months about her joining me. It took her a long time and much courage and prompting from her niece to make this journey alone.

"Sister, the years of our dreams getting cracked and broken over tubs are over."

"And a few cracked bones, too. But they're all healed now, ain't they?" Louvenia whispered as white folks paused to stare at us. "'Cause we's together finally. We is!"

"What would Grandma Minerva think of her daughters now?"

Lelia patted at our elegant attire.

"Look at you, Sister. You look so fine this evening. Like a duchess, I'm thinking."

"Like who?" she asked. "I saved up a bit of the money you been sending me, Sarah. When I got to Knoxville where Lelia was waiting, I walked right into a whitey dress shop. They said to me—like they was bein' nice—that I could buy me a dress but couldn't try none on in the store. I didn't care. No. Just picked out the prettiest one I could find and put it on the counter. My, weren't their mouths gaping like fly traps when I pulled out your money to pay 'em."

"You are fine ladies," Lelia said beaming.

Louvenia's coming had been fraught with apprehension. Things in our lives were moving so rapidly that Sister was unable to sit down with Annie and send off a letter letting me know she was coming. Louvenia later told me she'd signed over Jeff's little acreage to our friend. Said it holding my hand thinking I'd be hurt. I'd purchased the place for a meager amount as it was way out there where nobody wanted to live. It was only a couple of acres, the cabin that Louvenia and Annie lived in with her kids along with the few peach trees left in the little orchard. And my husband's chestnut tree. I was pleased with what Sister had done, giving it to Annie as our friend had helped us so much over the years.

On the return trip, the three of us chatted like magpies as soon as we were situated in our private compartment. Even as we jabbered, I convinced myself we'd never be separated again. Louvenia came fixed on living with C.J. and me so didn't bring much with her, but then she never had much. She'd saved nearly every penny I sent her thinking the bounty we enjoyed might run out like the cornmeal did before the end of the season back at the Burneys'. But things were going well for me and the trials we faced ahead were not to be empty cupboards. We had more than a bit of hope. We had seven-fold of the Lord's bounty to share and I felt in my heart that the thread momma wanted to bind her family together was almost, despite the odds, tied again. Yet it dwelled in my heart; where was our brother and what were the odds he'd faced heading to that somewhere?

It didn't take us long to get situated in our private compartment. I felt silly wearing the hat from Harriet's shop in the compartment, so I took it off. It barely landed on the seat next to me before Louvenia swooped it up. She tried it on and strutted about the compartment like any finely dressed big-hat lady. Sister could always wear a hat better than me. She knew how to cock it just right and lift her chin like a grand lady who'd suddenly escaped her shyness. Well, anyway, I had to display my hair when I was in public, so decided not to wear fine hats too often. I'd already accumulated a closet brimming of beautiful hats to give Sister one day. Yes, it was another dream of mine: to delight her soul with a cabinet of fine hats. Several helpings of joy like the joy that little feather bird had once brought her.

"You know I can't sit too long in once place," Sister commented. "No, I sure can't."

"Well, Louvenia, I reckon you best take a stroll to work the kinks out of your legs. Anyway, that hat you got on surely needs airing, don't it?" I said with a straight face.

Ignoring me, Sister worked her ankles in rotation like they were bothering her—the circulation being cut off down there, what with her fine new shoes still too tight. No, she didn't fool me none. I winked at Lelia and she grinned back. We both knew that Sister was working her way out of the conversation to go parade that hat to the other passengers.

"That's what I was thinkin'. A little walk to get my blood moving is what I best do."

"Sure don't want them feet to fall off," I said. "I'd have to call the porter to go lookin' for 'em and he'd sure expect a big tip."

Again, ignoring me, Sister adjusted her new hat and strutted off.

Well, I thought, wherever Jesse was, whatever part of hell he dwelled in by then, I would sure have liked for him to have gotten an eyeful of Sister walking down the aisle like Lady Astor herself.

Louvenia had made her way to third class where she got into a conversation with a young woman who'd stopped her to complement her fine attire. Louvenia invited her back to our compartment. Along the way Sister apparently shared the tallest tales imaginable about me. Yes, my dear sister had convinced Tildy that she was about to meet one of the wealthiest women of color ever. Well, never mind, I thought, as we were all having a fine time.

Tildy marched into my compartment ahead of Louvenia, glanced at Lelia and then at me. Looking puzzled she looked again at Sister like she was uncertain as to which of us was the rich woman she'd come to look over. Then she bent to look me over more closely as if I were a mannequin made of plaster and sawdust, or perhaps to see how closely I resembled my photos in the weeklies. Tildy held her hand to her mouth to keep the goshes from escaping. As time went by, I became accustomed to folks looking me over as if I could be hiding a secret. Guess just the same way Emily and I looked over Mrs. Washington as if she was so fine, she couldn't be for real and if we looked close enough, we'd find her hem frayed like ours and see reflections of ourselves in those very threads.

"Why, is that you? Huh?" Tildy asked, looking at Louvenia for confirmation. "You're the richest woman in the world, ain't ya?" Then she drew back as if she had fallen into a trap and looked to Sister for reassurance. "That her?" she asked. "That the rich woman you knows?"

Louvenia nodded and the biggest smile came over this young woman's face.

"Now dear, I am not a rich woman like some folks been sayin', including Miss Louvenia here." I knew Louvenia was spreading silliness. Sister's eyebrow arched like it was challenging me to prove her wrong. "No, I have a small company and I…."

Tildy's excitement got the best of her.

"It don't matter none, Ma'am. I ain't never heard of a colored woman being rich. Even a little bit rich and having her own somethin' or nother. Have you?" she asked as if I were an actress playing the part of a wealthy woman.

Sister smiled and adjusted her elegant hat like it was all the proof needed to back her tales.

"And you gots your own motor to go 'round town in, too? That right?"

"Now, who told you that, I wonder?"

I wasn't sure if the articles C.J. was getting into the papers to promote me were preceding me or if Sister's improved circulation had benefited her story telling.

"No, dear. I'm sure not rich. Just a hard workin' woman. What do you do to make your way?"

I knew what her answer would likely be and delighted in seeing this child's eyes light up from my interest.

"Well, Ma'am. I get up before the Lord does. Sure, it do seem. Then I get 'cross town as quick as I can 'cept in winter when nobody gets no place quick with all that snow. Sometimes I take the trolley to get over to Miss Martha's when I gots a dime. Folks say she gots the finest laundry house 'round. She been teachin' me to iron real good, too."

"How long you put in there each day?" Louvenia asked Tildy.

"From before the sun comes up till it disappears behind the bank on Main Street. That's when I know I gotta go home. My momma keeps a plate hot for me."

Tildy's eyes expressed pride and warmth. Louvenia grinned like she was showing off her first born.

"Tildy," I said.

"Yes, Ma'am."

"May I call you Matilda?"

"Ain't nobody calls me Matilda but the preacher," she replied.

I could tell Lelia liked this young woman as much as Louvenia.

"That's because the Preacher has respect for you," Lelia said.

"How many loads can you wash up in a day?" I asked.

"She can wash up a laundry house full. She's a strong girl, ain't you child?" Louvenia commented as any momma would have for her own.

"Why, sometimes I can get twenty loads when I'm up for it," Tildy said with pride and a bit of exaggeration. She didn't know I'd made enough trips to the tubs to know what happens to your back after a dozen or so loads.

"Do you work on Sundays?" I asked.

"That's the Lord's day. I go to church in the mornin' and then in the evening for prayer meetin'," she said.

Lelia poured her a cup of tea.

"But you can do maybe twenty loads the other six days?" I asked.

"I sure do try, don't I?"

"How many loads will you wash in thirty years?" I asked.

I noticed Louvenia glance at Tildy's hands; already worn and cracked like a much older woman's.

"Don't know if I can hold up that long. Don't know anybody that old, I guess. That's real old, ain't it?

Louvenia and I squirmed at Tildy's notion of old.

"Honey, where you gonna put them kids when you're at the tubs?" Sister asked.

Tildy sat up in her seat as if somebody had shaken the finger of judgment at her life.

"I gots to get a husband first," she said. "My momma told me about that."

"There's something special in you, Miss Matilda."

Lelia and Louvenia smiled in agreement.

"But how you know that?" Tildy asked.

She flinched as if I'd broken into one of her dreams. I reckon hidden in the same place she hid much of her pride. Somewhere white folks couldn't dash it.

"You got on this train this morning and ended up in first class chatting with the richest woman in the city like you're old friends," Lelia said.

"Why, ain't that so?" Tildy remarked. "I am special then, ain't I?"

Tildy put another three spoonful's of sugar in her tea as Louvenia offered her the plate of shortbread to help sweeten the taste more.

"Yes, dear. And I can see you sharing that very specialness with others. I want you to come to work for me as a Madame Walker agent. If you can sell five tins of my hair product every day for six days I bet you'll be making more money than working the tubs at Miss Martha's."

"And your hands don't got to touch that dirty ol' lye soap water to do it."

Louvenia smiled like she'd just helped to promote Tildy to a better life.

"Never thought this mornin' I'd end up working for the richest woman 'round," Matilda announced.

Matilda's life took a big detour that day and headed to an entirely different direction than she even knew existed. Her warmth and endearing charm enabled her to become one of my company's best agents.

Five years after the day we met Matilda she was able to buy a little house on the edge of the town where she was born. She was the first person in her family to own her own property free and clear and she did it with two young kids that came along that were never tied to the bed posts with no apron string like Minerva's little girl, Sarah.

DREAMS LEFT BEGGING

73

Long after Louvenia was settled in she continued looking about in disbelief whispering that she was glad to be back. But she wasn't really back as she'd never been to the new house except perhaps in her dreams that grew from our letters.

I looked forward to the Saturdays when Louvenia joined Lelia and me and dressed up to go shopping. My daughter took great pleasure in helping her aunt try on new hats or purchase a new pair of shoes. It always seemed to delight Sister's soul, her having had only one pair of shoes during our years at Jesse's. On the walk back from our shopping sprees, Louvenia always asked if we thought the shoes she'd selected would last a good long time. But then, often as not, she'd keep the shiny pair in a box only bringing them out to show one of her friends. Seemed like it was months before these new shoes would ever touch the ground. Yet I knew she kept things stored back sure that the good things would run out on us. Perhaps like a wonderful dream that weaves through your slumber but always breaks apart upon awakening. Always the old fears creep up on you when you're weary; the fear that once again you'll be back to staring into a bare cupboard and left wondering how many years to go before the end of the month?

One day Lelia and I were in the office eating Sister's leftover pot-roast sandwiches when I shared the story that Ma Mere had told me years before. It was about how much different her life had been from that of her sister, Marbella, by virtue of Ma's darkness. Ma's momma was Severine, a white woman. Her daddy was Albin, a black man. Yes, Ma was colored and she was as dark as rum with molasses folded in. Marbella, she had light eyes and that saved her from being put in the kind of slavery Ma knew even as a young woman. Marbella could pass as white, at least in French Creole society of New Orleans. Passing, however, was more than the paleness of skin. It was an art you were taught young; an act you'd best cultivate like nice table manners or you'd soon find yourself eating their scraps at the backdoor with the rest of the help. To save her daughter, Marbella, from a life bent over a tub, she took her to one of them Creole woman down in the Quarter where she would learn airs and how to talk and act like fancy folk.

That's what Ma explained one night as we had our cup of dark coffee with some of Sally's Irish whiskey. I asked Ma why she'd never talked about her sister before. She looked at me for the longest time before words would come. But the pain in her eyes told most of her story.

"They's called them girls *plaçees* 'cause *plaçage* means 'placed' in French."

I didn't understand at first as I'd never been to New Orleans yet knew from the other women at the boarding house that things were real different down there.

"See, if your momma's white and your girl comes out lookin' the same, them folks figured she best be placed with one of them white men down in the ol' French Quarter. They's business men who come over from France to get rich and wantin' a woman from the Quarter to take care of 'em. Them men knew they ain't gonna find some white mistress to clean up after 'em, cook, do laundry and still have it in 'em to do the dirty late at night after the kids been scrubbed and tucked in. No, a man's got to have more than one woman for all that. Or, mind you, one *plaçee*. Ain't that the truth, Sister?"

"A placed Creole woman?" I asked.

"Them fair girls they'd start trainin' by the time they was five or six. Ma's momma, Severine took Marbella to the Quarter to a Creole woman. Addie was that woman's name. She done been training these young woman for years. Well, they's still chil'ren. That's all they was, too, but they got reared different from then on. Yes, Ma'am. They ain't never gonna pick cotton or lean over no washtub. No, not the pretty ones and to show they ain't meant for that was taught special airs and manners they know them French men take to. These young girls gonna be sold dear. Back then they'd get a few hundred dollars for black slaves if they was healthy but for them fair girls they'd get maybe a thousand dollars if they's real sweet and pretty. Those old rich French men would sure pay *très chère* if they worked up an itch for one. Yes, Ma'am, they'd pay dear to be the first to get at 'er."

"Then what became of these girls?" I asked. "Them *plaçees*?"

"The fancy-girls, like my sister Marbella, got to be beautiful and pale, near to white so then them Creole women would dress 'em up in white like bridesmaids and trot 'em out at a cotillion like they's show dogs. You know, like the poodles them French folks take to. They put flowers in their fine braided hair and fit 'em in white satin gowns. White, white, white, that's all there was to it. What do you think a Creole princess is? Then on cotillion night them Creole hags would clap their hands like at a dance and tell them girls to sashay 'round the room in a big circle so the old French men could look 'em over. Them young Creole girls, they only 'bout twelve-year-old by then but they sure as hell knowed that if no French man came to fancy 'em they'd sure enough end up at the tubs or the cotton fields with the rest of us. Yes, ma'am, you know they would, too. Then their rewards for bein' pretty gonna be from some stinkin' overseer who ain't taken a bath, him comin' from behind to take his pleasure. I'm tellin' you, and they knew it even if they were too young to know 'bout them things yet. That'a be their life from then on; fightin' that stinkin' ol' man off their tail night and day."

Ma cleared her throat and took another gulp of coffee before going on.

"Then on cotillion night, if a white man took to one of them fancy-girls, he'd go put an offer on her. But them old Creoles, like Addie, made sure the men had plenty to drink first. They knew there'd be a better deal—more money in it for them, if they got them ol' men softened up early in the evening. From what I heard, the punch bowl never ran low on rum come cotillion night. No, Ma'am. Then if a man found the flesh he fancied he'd send a boy over with a purse of money to Addie's for her trouble. That's the way they did it. Marbella told me them ol' men licked their lips as them little girls strolled 'round in circles—them being stared at like French poodles in a mating pen—even had jars of flowers all about the hall to keep them girls from choking on the smell of them ol' men's cigars and their stinkin' lust. That's the way she remembered it. Marbella told me look like she could still smell 'em."

Ma Mere went silent as she rocked. But that was no rocker.

"Them pretty young *plaçees* might see to comin' along with the white man," Ma continued, "if he'd come to terms with Addie who done laid out the deal. He sure wouldn't pay good money if she not take to the situation. She knew she'd have to come give herself to his pleasure and no other man have 'er. After he spent her flower and she'd birthed his young'ens, Marbella had three girls, didn't she? he'd keep her good enough and maybe even give her a house and money to get along on. But still that Frenchman knew, knew that if he didn't keep to the deal he ain't gonna get himself another fancy-girl down the way. No, them ol' Creole women wouldn't have it. Addie new the rules. Folks said she got rich doing them girls that way. Yes, that's the way they worked it so's to keep it deep in their pockets. Got to keep the girl you bargained for or you ain't invited back to no more cotillions! Guess it made it better for them *plaçees*."

"How was it better?" I asked. "They ain't even women yet."

"Because, you fool, when she got sons from that man she could get 'em apprenticed in trade and hope to get 'er girl-childs set up like a *plaçee*, too." Ma said. "If her sons got into a good trade, when that *plaçee* get old, and thank the Lord her white husband finally dead—then she wouldn't die alone in no poor house on the edge of town 'cause she too old to work the tubs. No, come a day then she gonna go live with her son. Then she could eat and keep a fire going in winter. Like that, you see? But the thing is, Marbella had three girls. And she was scared all her days that Emeline, Amie and Camille would end up being near sold to some old rich man like what happened to her.

Ma filled her mug to the brim with whiskey but lost in her thoughts it ran over. She didn't notice even as she stared at her mug. I grabbed a dishrag and mopped it up.

"If that man got tired of his *plaçee*—or if she wouldn't lay down for him no more, or maybe he wanted to go back to France with all his gold—he'd cut her ties to his bedpost. If she'd been real careful all them years she been with him she might have enough money stolen back so that she could get herself a little dress shop or a hat place down near the French market where them Creoles shop. Or maybe get some rundown boardin' house goin'."

Ma pulled her chair up closer like she had a dark secret to whisper.

"Don't you know? That's how I ended up with this here boardin' house. Marbella bought it near the day after her ol' man put in the ground. Some say he got poisoned. No matter, he dead and she come looking for me. You see, Addie knew I was Severine's girl too. So when Momma died, she come for me and then took her place. Big house in the Quarter with a wall around it. From then on, till Marbella come for me, I was that Creole's slave-child. Can you see what I mean?. Yep, lived with the rats in the basement."

"You and Marbella worked this boarding house together?"

"But ain't nobody ever knowed we was sisters. Hell, no."

Ma's trembling chin punctuated the pain that came with these memories.

"Me and Marbella, we had to go on tellin' folks I was her kitchen woman 'cause she had to keep making like she was too white to have a colored for a sister even here on the edge of nigger town."

Ma sat there shaking her head in shame and dabbed at her tears with that old rag soaked with whiskey.

"Bein' white kept the chances for her baby girls better. She had to, don't you know? Can't you see?"

Ma glanced about the dark kitchen as though Marbella was still over in the corner nodding her head to Ma's thoughts as they poured out.

"So, what happened to Marbella?" I asked.

"One morning, 'bout ten year ago my sister told me she don't want no more and wasn't gonna get up."

"Didn't want no more?" I asked.

"Life, honey. Said she was done with it and wanted it over. Said she'd done all she could for her girls. Rest was up to the Lord but He'd sure be blessing her if He took her easy 'cause she was wantin' to go. But just the same if He wouldn't take her, she'd lie there till her life petered out. It don't matter none to her. You see, my sister, she never got over her Toby. It was only him she saw in 'er dreams. The ones she kept locked away in her heart."

"Who was Toby, Ma?"

"She never said nothin' to her kids 'bout Toby. I know she never 'cause she didn't want to burden them for not loving their real daddy. But I knows 'cause every day Marbella prayed to Jesus to be free of her chil'rens' pa. I heard her. Then when the Lord freed 'er from that ol' man, he dead, she tol' ever'body that she was never gonna live with no old man ever 'gain. See, when you ain't young no more, you got only girls and your pretty worn off from hard work, it's only them ugly old men who come courting. And sure enough near the day after Marbella's ol' man buried they come callin' with ol' geraniums in hand they'd done pulled up from some alley and rolled in an old newspaper. Them swaggering about with them weeds like they still had some real man left in 'em. Showin' off with airs they was with their damned copper pennies tinkling in they's patched pockets so's to impress her. Marbella said they ain't nothin' but old men with a pocket full of pennies and unpaid bills waitin' back at they's dirty ol' houses. Yeah, she knew what they was wantin' and she say she ain't gonna spend the rest of her days bringin' some ol' man the pot to pee in and wiping drool from his mouth after she fed him till he finally dead for real. She had enough of that. She said if she gonna have a man, he gonna be a real man like Toby."

"Why couldn't Marbella go be with Toby after her kids' pa died?"

"'Cause Toby was dark as pitch. You know he worked for Marbella's ol' man, Adolphe, even dug his grave. Did it singin' like it was Mardi

Gras. But folks in the quarter, they watchin' everything goes on down there and don't they still keep they's mouths wide open on what ain't goin' on, too? Sure, they do! They talk too much, them Creole hags. If Marbella gone off with a dark-skinned man she would have pissed on everything she done for her babies."

"What could she do then?" I asked.

"See, them Creoles, they think they's better than us. They' have no more to do with my sister if she didn't say white, white, white, between her every breath and then look down her nose at the niggers who jump aside when she passed them on the street. They'd tell her to her face— them Creoles hags would—that she best haul her tail over to niggers' town and be a nigger whore and not be seen at church no more with the good Creole folks if she ain't gonna act like one. White, white, white, is 'bout all they could talk 'bout, them Creoles. Then her girls' chances of passin' white all gone, too. What momma gonna hand her own a jail sentence like that? Like shovin' a washtub at your baby girl and tellin' 'er she ain't gonna be done with it till the day she turn it in for a pine box and put in the ground, so get to work!"

"She never took up with Toby then?"

"She saw him when she could. But it was real hard 'cause them Creoles always lookin' 'round for something to talk about. Then one day, before Marbella and Toby could see a way it was too late. Oh, Lord, I 'member that day like it was yesterday. It was the morning when Toby's brother come by our place. He ain't never been by before but I knew who he was 'cause he looked just like Toby but shorter. I was out back hangin' laundry and seen him comin'. I yelled up to Marbella's window from my clothesline. She come to the kitchen door and before a word come out of his mouth, she knew why he was there. Knew it had to be about her man. She put her hands over her mouth so she wouldn't scream. Guess it was the way his eyes looked right into hers before he could even tell 'er. Then he drew up close and whispered. Marbella near fell dead right on the back stoop 'cause her Toby, he got his arm caught in a motor gear that morning; chewed it off to his elbow. The boss man, he say he don't need no doctor bills. He gots plenty of cheap help with both arms. He tol' 'em take that Toby to the back and let him be.

"Don't know what's you mean, let him be?"

"Let Toby bleed to death like a gutted hog. Think the day when he gone was the day Marbella figured, Lord, I ain't gonna take no more of it! I know that was when her life was spent even if she had few short breaths to go she was still good as dead 'cause no more dream left for her; no more Toby waiting somewhere at the end of her days."

Ma swallowed hard and gazed at her feet like down there was the map to find her way out of them tangled thoughts. But there never is one. Down at the bottom of our dreams where our hopes once stirred as they waited for their day, the air is just too thin. Well, I ain't never heard no rich person say their air was too thin, have I?

"Sarah, I got to ask you. It troubles me. Got to know for sure. You think the Lord let Toby come for Marbella the day she passed on?"

"What's you mean, Ma?"

"'Well, one morning I went up to Marbella's room to see what she was wantin' for breakfast. Her face, I still 'member—looked soft and pretty laying there on that pillow like she already gone to Jesus. Scared me. I asked her how she feelin' and was she was gonna get up? 'I been beggin' for this day,' she said like she happy for it."

"Beggin' for what, honey?" I asked Ma.

"'Toby, he's comin' for me today. I can feel it. I gots no more wait to go,' she said. "I tol' her, 'No, Toby ain't comin' by, honey. You know he gone now. He gone, but you got to get up today. You know you do.' My sister smiled like she knew something I didn't. I went back down to get her tray. Fixed her some porridge and cream and went back up. But she was gone. Had only a smile left on her lips gone white. You think Toby really come for Marbella like she told me?"

"I know he did, Ma. I know Toby's spirit come to take her to the Lord. That's why she was so at peace. That's why she died with a smile, 'cause she was going to be with her Toby. She was headed to Jesus and that's a place where there ain't no machines chewin' off a man's life."

Ma sobbed till she choked. Then let the rest of it ease out.

"The week after Marbella buried, Sally and me was packin' her things up. Found this dress of hers all folded nice in a pretty box. That dress was all brown from the seam at the shoulder to the cuff with the broken lace. She always wore pretty things, you know."

"Why was it all brown, honey?" I asked.

"Toby's blood. You see, she'd gone to him that morning. Ran all the way there. Dead blood all dried on her sleeve where she been holdin' him back from death. Hanging on to him, she was. Guess the only thing he could give her to keep was the last of his blood. Boss man, he drained Toby of everything else. Marbella, she left me this boardin' house 'cause her kids was set up good enough and she knew I'd be living in somebody's cellar like a dog, working only for my food 'cause I ain't light. This place was all run down. That was when I took up with Sally. She had a bit of money put back 'cause she been a maid in Boston for near fifteen years. When her lady died she left Sally a few pennies. "Bout a penny for every time I wiped that ol' woman's stinkin' ass,' Sally said. Her and me, we went to fixin' this place up with her money; got a new roof and all. We aimed to do things our own way here. Sally and me, we figured on making it just fine without no man, too. Don't need one tellin' us what was what—pass me the gravy like I say! That's the way it was and that's the way we kept it."

With that, Ma patted my hand and went off to bed.

We never talked about Marbella, her three daughters or Toby again. But I recall that over the years Ma would have visitors once in a while that seemed to slip in the back door quietly. They were all pretty young white women. Three of them. Still I could tell they were special to her but she never introduced them. Just seemed to want to pretend they were like fancy folks from somewhere stopping for a meal. While she served them they chatted real quiet, almost in whispers like they didn't want nobody to hear. They were her nieces, Emeline, Amie and Camille. Sally told me and said don't tell the others. Marbella's girls gone off and married white men but still came back to visit Ma Mere on the sly. Nobody knew but Ma and Sally. When they left, Severine's girls, they'd leave money on the table for service. Ma, she'd sit there weeping with those coins tied in her aching hand. Sally'd say 'It don't matter none. They meant well or they'd never come by at all, dearie.'"

After I told my daughter the story of Marbella—one of those stories that will never be told in the papers about the lives that touched me along my journey—she understood why I wanted dark-skinned people working for me and featured in my advertisements.

Someday I aim to sit down and tell Bella how dark Jesus' sun-baked skin really was. But I suspect even if Jesus sat right there next to us nodding His head and pulling up his sleeve to show her she'd still not believe either one of us or her own blue eyes.

Down Along White Camellia Road

74

On New Year's Day, many of the colored weeklies announced the coming of a new age when we would be voting and have true freedom to learn to read. However, the day I read these editorials still felt like all the ones before. Truly, what had changed in the South since the Civil War? Some of the plantation aristocracy calling themselves Knights of the White Camellia still considered it their Christian duty to spread Klan doctrine to the farthest reaches of a lynching rope. During the months before this "new age", there'd been dozens more lynched in the south and even a few in the north. The terror of the white mob was spreading like fever from a swamp—the toxic swamp of hatred.

My image had been in the papers all over the South by then. So, what could have been more dangerous than for a colored woman to travel the back roads of southern states, let alone in a fine new touring motorcar? Such could so easily provoke the unbridled hatred of white folks. How could I have known the degree of risk as there'd never been a woman in my position? Back then every mile of my life was uncharted and without precedent. Despite the inherent dangers, there was no other way for me to reach my rural customers other than to go to them as most had never left the parishes and counties they were born to.

Many times, I traveled only with my driver, Otho. But there were times when Louvenia or one of my agents—such as Matilda joined me. But at home C.J. repeated that he simply had too much to do and failed to see the point of taking such risks anyway. He seemed to suggest that I was flaunting my wealth in Klan faces and such a provocation could be fatal. Therefore, I headed along those dark roads without him. Someone had to.

My office wrote ahead to churches that had invited me to demonstrate my products and give a talk that might inspire them. The churches I visited were along dusty roads which rutted ankle-deep in mud in winters. Still out there land was cheap because it was swampy or too rocky for a plow. That's where my people built houses of worship and found community tucked far enough away from the eyes of white folks. To reach my people along those roads, I'd have to travel through plantation lands where the white aristocracy still lived leisurely on those white verandas close enough to smell their white camellias that were yet tended by the hands of the coloreds they once owned.

On these trips, the preachers didn't announce the actual date of my arrival till just prior to the Sunday I'd arrive so the Klan wouldn't have eyes or guns cocked for a fine touring motorcar being driven for a woman of color.

We toured in my Cole Palace Motorcar which I'd purchased for that purpose as it was large enough to hold my luggage and samples. I think Otho enjoyed these travels despite the inherent risks. I recall him gripping the steering wheel like it was the reins of a big hay wagon, the kind he'd spent his youth driving. Perhaps he was determined this new kind of horsepower would outrun the good ol' boys who were oft fueled by whiskey, ropes and burning hot hatred. You see, Southern nights were seldom ever hot enough that the Klan wasn't out looking for a roof or cross to set ablaze. Or one of our men to burn alive. How many times did I pray that if my journey was to be over that night, please Lord, let it be by a sniper as I drove past and not by being dragged out of my car, brutalized, raped and then lynched.

I was scheduled to arrive at the next church before supper, but we found ourselves seemingly lost on one of those unsigned back roads that twisted and turned like lynching ropes. The autumn night was starless and so black it appeared as a vast emptiness that could easily swallow the lost traveler; nobody to help you out there but they might show up for other reasons, the Klan that is.

For long empty miles we sat silently as Otho stared in stony silence over the vast nothingness ahead. The lights on the Cole stared down on the endless dirt road leaving the overgrown roadside a black void where the shrieks and howls of night critters dared us to declare ourselves. I was certain I'd recognized our fears springing from the blackness but it was merely the shadow of an owl swooping over the road just ahead of us.

On the way we often pulled our scarves down to keep the dust out of our hair and faces. Otho broke the silence when he requested we pull our scarves down to conceal our blackness even on that black night. But I'd already seen him, that white farmer up the road there. Earlier we'd passed a couple of farmers returning from their fields in dilapidated wagons piled high with corn stalks or hay. From hate, their expressions turned poker red at the sight of me passing them. Those split-second flashes of rage sent shivers down my spine. Louvenia grabbed hold of my arm as if their hate-filled stares might knock 'er to the ground, a place she'd visited too many times by then. No, there wasn't one of us that hadn't been knocked to the dirt by a white man or woman.

"Don't worry, Sister." I admonished. "That ol' farmer, he can't bother us none."

So constricted was my throat I wondered if she heard my fear.

"Why not?" Matilda begged. "Why he can't?"

She looked back as we left him in the dust but not nearly fast enough.

"It's gonna take that man an hour 'fore he can get back to get his guns and come for us!" I answered.

"Then I be waitin' for 'im!"

At that Sister opened her purse and unwrapped a rag that held what looked to be the same ol' rusty knife she'd held to Jesse's throat the night his whore came calling. This soft-spoken woman was the bravest I knew.

Yes, I thanked the Lord they'd not be able to get that wagon back fast enough to alert Klansmen to put the nigger dogs on our trail. I suggested to Otho we'd be all right even without concealing our faces. That was my silent prayer as I reached for Louvenia and Matilda hands as we lumbered down that southern road where every screech from the wild jolted me like the screech of a death blow. But, no, I would not hide from anyone. Anyway, where is the sanctuary from evil?

Otho's eyes were not good at night. I was often his sight on these trips after the sun went down. I was watching the road ahead when suddenly I saw lights fluttering. It was all like the white that fluttered outside Jeff's cabin that night. Looked to be a frenzy of torches waving back and forth across the road ahead. They were waiting for us after all. Oh, Lord, God! It was the Klan!

"Otho…!"

"I see 'em, Ma'am!"

He braked to slow the Cole enough we would not turn over as he turned to speed us the way we'd come. Would the farmer back there have his wagon fixed across the road to block our escape? Even in the deepest fatigue the mind tumbles our thoughts for another chance at survival. Is it all just a roll of the dice? We colored rolled hard on the sides of country roads too many times to never win. But then the voices came.

"MadameWalker, ain't that you?" I heard yelled.

"Oh, Lord God…" Matilda screamed. "It's the Klan up there! They're gonna get us!"

But no, not this time. You see, them shouts in the smoky air that hovered over the road were my people. They'd come to light our way to the church. When my heart finally stopped pounding, I said a prayer of thanks. The folks waved but no one was more joyous than we. With their torches, they waved Otho through a small opening in the trees back to where the church was hidden. Even that late, the preacher and his wife came out to welcome us.

"We thought you might get lost this late," the preacher said. "Don't want to lose your way this far down White Camellia Road."

We climbed out stiff with fear and yet still shaking.

"Men, quick, put them torches out," the Preacher said. "Leave it dark 'fore anyone figures we have guests. Then you all best sleep on the pews. Don't want nobody headin' down that road alone tonight."

Just as in the days after the Resurrection when the faithful were harassed and driven into secret places to meet, folks in the country churches I visited practiced the tradition of Christian sisterhood. Here they welcomed us into their homes for safety from the road with hospitality and accommodations. Every time I crossed their thresholds, it was easy to remember the warm faces of Sisters Hannah and Rebecca and how they welcomed Lelia and me that cold night nearly two decades before. The little clapboard churches we visited throughout the South were unique by virtue of the folks that built them with their blood and sweat. Strangely, that made them alike. Didn't they all have an erected steeple pointing high? I wondered if this was to remind us that if we couldn't see the Lord anywhere in the South we might direct our hopes to the heavens above. Lord, how far from our daily lives is that? Most folks were dirt poor out there and not many could read scriptures, yet they kept faith that our struggles would lead us to God's promise of a better life if we could only endure this one long enough. But how long would that struggle be, Lord? How could I not ponder that most of my people's tribulations were struggles against white hatred, that strange kind of rabid nigger dog rage from the same folks that built their own sweet-smelling camellia life off our backs. I wanted to spread a bit of hope to my people that since I'd escaped the drudgery of the tubs, perhaps there were others who could somehow escape theirs. Yet it was never easy. Even after they met me at the church socials, I was uncertain if they believed I was that woman in the papers. I accepted this skepticism as well as their exaggerated notions of my wealth. These good people simply had never heard of a colored woman doing well. It didn't matter much how that was defined they still hungered to see it up close.

In these country parishes that I traveled folks were frequently victimized by traveling sleight-of-hand men. Dishonest hucksters who believed it was okay to turn a profit merely because they were able to swindle folks with their snake oils after which they'd get out of town fast. There was little honesty in commerce. That was the reason I needed to meet my customers face to face and discuss my products. Even apply them with my own hands—the hands of a tub woman. That way I could show them I had nothing to hide; there was no trickery. I faced them in person standing behind everything my company sold.

The next day we joined folks for the service. Afterwards was a special social that lasted most of the afternoon during which I demonstrated my products to mostly women. As I chatted with the womenfolk the men tended to drift off with Otho to look over the Cole he kept shiny no matter the road dust. He smiled at their notions on operating a motorcar and responded to questions about the great machine we'd arrived in.

"Nope. As big as it is still can't plow no field with that there motorcar," or, "Got to change them damned tires made of a rubber tree, too often, if you ask me!"

The man was flummoxed and declared he'd never seen a tree like my tires. I'd suggested to Otho he offer to take the men for a spin. Later he told me the old ones said they'd heard for sure that the speed of these motorcars could cause your thoughts to hurl right out of the county, a place they'd unlikely ever been.

These were the same simple folk Louvenia knew back along the roads that passed Jeff's cabin and among whom her shyness disappeared. We were eager to hear about their lives just as hungry as they were to know about the rich colored woman who'd swept into theirs for a few fleeting moments riding in a motor carriage as big as the president's. I hoped this curiosity would lead them to search for this dream in a tin of hair cream; the dream of feeding your kids every day. How could that even be, their eyes quizzed and then looked to me for the answers. How

I knew those expressions as they'd been inscribed on the pages of all our stories.

As I walked around shaking hands, I was bemused overhearing a young woman say to another, "She gots a palace! That's what my ma heard. And she keeps her white maids scrubbin' floors from mornin' till night else she takes a stick to 'em 'cause they's so lazy, them white maids is!"

"Well, of course she gots a palace," the other quipped back. "But she don't got no white maids 'cause who ever heard of a white woman knowin' how to scrub a floor?"

Matilda was often right there with her own rendition.

"That's for sure what you say! 'Cause Madameknows they'd steal her blind as soon as they gets their hands on her silver and jewels."

These were young hungry wide-eyed women who'd never left that county parish and probably had only one pair of shoes.

"But Madamestill lets them white folks in her fine home to see her phonograph player and gold harp so long as they give Otho a real nickel and then they gets to look at her piano, too. But can't touch nothin' with they's dirty filthy hands. No, Ma'am! Otho gonna take a stick to 'em if they do!"

Matilda was eager to promote my image even if prone to embellishments; mostly things she'd heard since childhood of the things we coloreds were accused of. Even so, over time Matilda became a well-dressed and impeccably groomed young woman. However quick she was to abandon her old ways of dressing she was not so quick to leave behind her old ways of thinking, particularly if she could draw an audience to hear her notions about my supposed gilded life. I didn't worry much as I figured it was no more fanciful than what most folks had read in the weeklies by then.

At times these gatherings became a kind of competition between Louvenia and her darling, Matilda. Louvenia stood on one side of the room delivering stories of my prosperity to a such a fevered pitch that it quickly exceeded even that of the Rockefellers, while Matilda was on the other side painting bigger tales for a bigger ears and then bigger sales commissions to flounce back at Sister. When one upstaged the other, I could expect the other to come tattling about her foil's excesses.

But this time it was Otho who filled my ears on what Matilda was saying.

"MadameWalker, guess I best be tellin' you now," Otho was more than agitated. "Or we'll be walkin' home. Miss Matilda over there done told folks the one that buys the most *Glossine* will win your motorcar! Yes, Ma'am! One of 'em done bought fourteen tins already and says she's goin' for money to buy more so to drive herself home in your motorcar! Told 'er don't know 'bout that! Didn't know what else to say."

Well, it wasn't the first time I had to salvage the wreckage from Louvenia and Matilda's exuberant tales. I went over to the woman who had probably spent a month's food money on buying all those tins and explained that what Matilda really meant was a successful job as a MadameC.J. Walker agent might enable one to one day own her own motorcar but that I would need the Cole to get home again. The woman took no offense as she was having a good time. Instead of asking for a refund she confided she knew better and only wanted a ride up and down the road to feel like a rich woman for once in her life. She pulled out a newspaper clipping of me in my smaller electric car that she said she had pinned next to the stand where she kept her Bible to remind her our folks got blessings, too. I told Otho he could relax. We wouldn't be hoofing it back home and suggested he offer the woman a spin as courtesy of the MadameC. J. Walker Manufacturing Company. Moments later the Cole was filled with passengers and sailing off. An hour later and two or three cups of tea for me, Otho returned all worked up again. Seems like the Cole was near out of petrol and he knew of no place to purchase more as no one in those parts had a motorcar. That was no problem, explained the woman who had purchased much my *Glossine*. Her husband would go fetch some from one of the farmers who'd surely have a few gallons on hand. Turns out the preacher had arranged for us to stay the night at this fine woman's and she was planning a great Sunday supper for us. As it was, she wanted to know how to sign up to be one of my agents.

We left the Cole at the church and joined Emmie and her fourteen tins of *Glossine* and headed off to her place in buggies. There, Emmie's daughters had already begun preparation for supper, which I know eased Matilda's mind; it had been almost an hour since she had that second piece of pie and she was wanting to know what we'd be having for supper. As skinny as that child was, she still ate like a field-hand!

Old Stories Along
New Roads

75

EMMIE AND HER husband, Jacob, had a nice place down the road from the church. Like most folks they'd worked as 'croppers and were among the few who'd managed to escape that slavery and get themselves a small farm, maybe only a few acres. Over time they'd worked hard and built the place up. With it eventually came a brood of kids, now grown.

That evening would be one of the most memorable of my tour that season. For Louvenia, Matilda, Otho and me, it was like spending time with extended family despite the fact we'd just met Emmie and her family. The laughter of that evening quickly eased the weariness of being on the road for us. Otho and Jacob were off talking about how Jacob got his small farm that his son now mostly worked. I could hear them laughing as they got the barbecue going out in the pit. Back in the kitchen, Louvenia helped Emmie make the sauce with Emmie stirring and Sister adding a pinch of this and that. The kitchen was sweltering from pies and bread coming out of the oven. I still think of this fine woman when I smell freshly baked bread.

I suppose Emmie noticed my weariness that evening and suggested I go out on the porch and keep her ma, Cecilia, company. With delight,

I escaped the clanking in the kitchen and went out to sit a spell. I smiled listening to the cackling of the women in the kitchen and the men howling over jokes in the shade where those jokes surely belonged. Still nothing delighted me more than my chat with Grandma Cecilia.

"You best go tell 'em I want me some hot biscuits with that barbecue pork," Ma Cecilia told me.

"I was just in there, Ma'am. They know you want biscuits and Louvenia was rolling a second pan just in case you're hungrier than you let on," I said. "And Louvenia is the best biscuit maker there is."

"Now that can't be."

"No? Why not?"

"'Cause ever'body knows I's the best cook in this here county," Ma Cecilia announced with pride. "Now what if they don't work the buttermilk in right? It's gotta be good and cold when you fold it in."

"It was, too. I seen that jar of buttermilk they brung up from the cellar sitting there so cold fog is comin' out of their nostrils," I said.

Ma Celia was only partially satisfied with my response.

"Now, tell me what else you seen 'cause I don't know you. Don't know your folks. They from 'round here? Emmie say you're a rich woman. How can that be? Ain't never been nobody rich 'round these parts. Sounds like pure foolishness what I heard them sayin'."

"You know how folks exaggerate when they're havin' a bit of fun. They don't mean nothin' by it. Anyway, I assure you, they're meanin' the riches I got stored in my heart and not in some bank."

"How many kids you got?" she asked.

"I got a grown daughter. Her name is Lelia. How many kids you got?"

"How many did I birth? Or how many growed up?"

Matilda came out with jars of sweet tea and sat down on a stool next to Cecilia's rocker.

"I birthed nine babies. Four of 'em still alive," she said. "Emmie's my youngest."

"Where you from?" I asked.

"I was born in South Carolina. That's what theys say. Close to the

Sea Islands where they growed the cane. Worked them fields near soon as I could walk and still slap squeeters off. They got 'em big as horse flies down by the water there. Don't 'member much more. Worked them fields ever' day right next to my mammy."

"How many kids your mammy have?" Matilda asked.

"Don't 'member that, neither."

Ma Cecilia looked off through the trees like she could count the lost ones somewhere in those hazy shadows of her long-gone childhood.

"How you don't 'member how many sisters 'n brothers you got, Ma'am?" Matilda was always persistent. "I got me two brothers and one sister."

"'Cause when they come off the teat, Mas'er come for 'em and take 'em away, chil'e. Never saw 'em no more," she added. "Lord, but don't I still hear ma howling when she hit the dirt like she wounded. Reckon Mas'er's fist shut her mouth. How many is that then, chil'e?"

Ma Cecelia went quiet and stared out into the nothingness her memories had provoked. Matilda, not knowing what to say or do, looked to me for prompting. We waited for Ma to rein her recollections into the moment.

"Got to go back, way back there past the cane and count ma's howling is the way I come to it—one on the ground near her bed screamin' bloody murder. I was little but sure still hear it, don't I? One out in them fields. One at the Mas'er's backdoor where I followed 'er to beg 'im to give Ma 'er baby back. You countin' fer me, chil'e?"

"Where'd that man take 'em?" Matilda asked.

She'd only heard stories of our slave days, seen a few backs criss-crossed with scars but never witnessed the horrors like Ma Cecilia and her momma, a slave like mine, had.

"He sol' 'em. That what he say he done but some folks, they say different. Say he kill 'em to get ma back to work quicker than a nursin' mammy ever gonna. Don't know. Maybe if they was good healthy babies he sol' 'em 'fore they got sick and died. Sol' 'em 'fore ma went to beggin' for 'em too much. Sol' 'em way far, he must 'a done. Don't want your nigger's kids just over on the other plantation. No, they's got to disappear far—far so's your field hands stop fussin' 'bout that baby and get to work."

Ma Cecilia's eyes belied yet another truth; there was no far *enough* distance to keep a mother from worrying about her child. The pain of losing a baby follows you like a shadow all the rest of your days. After nearly every sentence she shared, Ma Cecilia looked to the horizon as if waiting for them babies, her lost sisters and brothers, to come back to her, maybe like we still waited for one day to come with Alex. Was she trying to conjure the faces that she never really knew? Or even what they were called? Tom, Nellie, Ortella and maybe, James? Or names given to them that rhymed with the master's dogs? Got to put a new name on your slave's babies so her momma won't recognize you if you get loose and try to find your way back to her. Here I am, Ma. I's your… and then again the dream fades faster than water poured over that dry sun scorched earth you're hoeing.

That was the someday Cecilia still longed for even after eighty years of knowing it would never come. Her pleading eyes told me so.

I spoke to break the spell.

"Your momma and daddy worked them sugar fields cuttin' cane?"

"All them days. Overseer, he wouldn't let mammy stop workin' till she gonna have them babies. When granny knowed it was ready to come she'd put an ax under the straw laid in the shack waitin' for it."

"Granny gonna kill that baby so the Mas'er don't get 'er?" Matilda asked.

"Kill it?"

Ma Cecilia smirked as though murder was only second nature to the lost children born to plantations.

"Granny don't have to kill it, swamps do that. Overseer do it quicker. No, granny put that ax under the straw to cut the pain so mammy don't scream so loud her ear split when she come to catch that baby when it drop out of 'er. But one time that overseer come by when she on the straw waitin' fer the baby to drop. He say 'look at you! I know you ain't gonna have no damned baby today. I know you ain't for real! So, get yourself out to the cane and help get it hauled in.' But Mammy just lay there. Couldn't do no more. Can't he see she gonna have that baby she so swollen? No, he don't see nothin' but that cane he gots to get in. So that overseer, he tell a boy to go fetch his belt. Gonna cut Mammy's back open for being lazy, he tell 'er. I heard 'im! The men dug a hole in the dry dirt big enough for mammy's belly. Drug 'er out and pushed 'er belly down in that hole and then put his belt to back. She screamin' something awful. That night the baby come all right. But he gots belt marks across him's tiny back forever, don't he? Granny say just so the Lord knows what that overseer done to my mammy when he goes to beggin' to be with Jesus. No, Jesus don't know that overseer. He best stop bangin' at the Lord's door 'cause ain't nobody gonna come and give 'im peace."

Guess I needed to slow the weaving through of my own memories of Minerva and Celia's tribulations on a plantation. I got up, kissed Ma Cecilia's brow and went in to help in the kitchen. Matilda pulled her stool up to Ma Cecilia's rocker and stroked her hand, looking deep in her eyes as if they would reveal the part of the story she yet couldn't.

Those white shadows are ever there crisscrossing your worst dreams like the lash did our backs.

❧

After it cooled down that evening, we gathered around two tables pulled together on the porch for supper. Can't even remember what all Emmie, her daughters and Louvenia had cooked up as there were so many dishes.

We held hands as Jacob and Otho led us in prayer.

"This is the best barbecue I ever ate," Otho remarked. "Who made the sauce, I wonder?"

"I think Emmie did, Otho," I said.

"No, it was Miss Louvenia that added just the right amount of dark brown sugar—and a little something extra," Emmie replied with a smile.

"When did you learn to make barbecue, Aunt Louvenia?" Matilda asked. She'd sat next to Ma Cecilia to tend her needs at supper.

"In the city. We had the best barbecues. Oh, Lord didn't we though?" Louvenia said.

I was puzzled 'cause I'd never remembered even one at Jesse's.

"What did you barbecue, Aunt Louvenia?" Matilda asked. "Chicken or pork? What?"

Louvenia cocked her head and looked down her nose at Matilda and then at me.

"Ask Sarah, honey. She knows, don't you, Sister? Sure, you do! You done butchered it yourself."

"I don't recall," I said not wanting to challenge Sister about a barbecue I had no recollection of. But then I got to thinking with that smirk of hers she was surely aiming to jab me to a place I'd surely not wish to head; her doing it right in front of those fine folks at their own table. Everyone paused for their next bite as they waited for me to respond.

"Sure, you do, 'cause you ate up most of 'im," Sister added.

"Sounds good. What did you cook up, Sarah?" Jacob asked.

"My husband… is what she roasted!" Louvenia announced. "Didn't you, honey? Sarah got damned tired of his big mouth so one night she cut 'im up, salted him down and poured barbecue sauce over 'im and roasted him out in that alley like the ol' hog he sure enough was. That right, honey? Sure, it is. You 'member now, don't you?"

Holding her little finger out like a Creole princess, Louvenia forked to my plate another piece of meat dripping in sauce.

"Yes, my little sister Sarah, you know how sweet she is. Well, one night she up and cut up Jesse—was gonna put 'im in cannin' jars but I said don't bother, honey. Let's just have 'im for supper 'cause that man will go bad on you quick! And, Lord let me tell you he was as rotten as they come!"

Matilda's fork fell on her plate.

"That's what I did, too," Ma Cecilia announced. "Got tired of my man, him wantin' this or that as soon as I sat down to eat. So, I took a meat ax to his head one night."

"Ma, you did no such thing to Pa," Emmie said. "You just thought 'bout it a few times like any woman."

What could I say?

So, I said nothing and simply smiled back at Louvenia who looked right proud of herself for shutting my mouth up for once.

Nobody said a word for the longest time. Can't imagine what Emmie and Jacob thought about the folks they'd brought into their fine home that day. But I could tell Ma Cecilia had heard worse. She reminded me of Grandma Ida after a couple of whiskeys. After the story on Jesse every word she heard was funny as hell to her.

I'll never forget that evening or any of the old stories we shared that night like one big family.

Standing High Among Men

76

As time rushed to meet me my days seemed only to fold over ever faster. Or was it me simply running from the pages of calendars chasing after me? One can easily loose the direction of where the journey is headed or the seemingly endless miles ahead or those even longer distances to get back home. Yes, my days were only moments long.

I was informed that the National Baptist Convention was celebrating the Emancipation Proclamation that proclaimed our freedom and the end of slavery as we knew it then. Though I'd recently given speeches on Negro women in business in more than a dozen halls, I stopped on my way home to address this auspicious gathering. I thought of Louvenia's devotion to President Lincoln as I walked on stage to face what they told me might be as many as twenty-thousand people hungry for a word of hope. My sister had an engraved picture of President Lincoln which she kept in her Bible folded on the page with the picture of Jesus. Don't know how many folks were in that sea of faces. What folded into my thoughts was the growing number of lynchings reported in the weeklies. As I looked out over the crowd, I knew I was looking into the faces of those who would meet their deaths from violence before the end of the year. How could I not wonder if we as a nation would ever progress to a time when federal anti-lynching laws would finally be enforced?

Just that morning I'd read about the two men who were burned alive by a white mob in Statesboro, Georgia. The neighboring governor of Arkansas made the announcement, "you educate a nigger, you spoil a good field hand." This man went on to say social equality would only bring about "a lot of dead niggers." So what was it like for me traveling in a fine Cole to speak to my people? Along every mile I knew that I was all but signing my own death warrant. Yet all the same, before the ink had dried on one response, I'd accepted another invitation to speak in yet another town. Someone had to go!

What was that last stop, Otho? Where again are we headed? How far behind us is home? I could hear these words even in my sleep.

&

I was glancing over the orders my clerks were sorting when Lelia breezed into my office.

"Momma, Mr. George Knox is here to see you. He's out in the warehouse speaking to C.J. Shall I ask him in?"

"No, dear. I was on my way out there. Those boxes been shipped to Atlanta?"

"James took them down to the train station this morning. Agents should be getting the new products by the end of next week."

In the year nineteen-fourteen Knox was the country's most successful publisher of colored-owned illustrated weeklies. The advertising campaign C.J. placed in Knox's papers had done exceedingly well for my company. By then my ads were appearing in the mid-west and south and I was exploring markets beyond the south even as far north as New York City. As orders piled up it became more troublesome to get my hands on sufficient quantities of ingredients. All the same I still embraced my simple business plan that anywhere there was a colored head stood a customer needing my products.

I handed my daily instructions to my head clerk and stepped out to meet the celebrated Mr. Knox. C.J. was standing outside the warehouse smoking a cigar with my guest.

Mr. Knox kissed my hand when C.J. introduced us.

"Madame Walker," Mr. Knox began, "it's a pleasure. C.J.'s probably mentioned to you I wanted a chat about placing more of your ads in my weeklies. But honestly, I've looked forward to meeting the woman behind the fastest-growing colored-owned business in the country."

Mr. Knox's nod to C.J. made me wonder whether this man had the notion that the lightening-fast expansion of my enterprise was somehow derived through my husband? My image was on the tins in the hands of my people around the country. Did he imagine that was merely for marketing?

"I understand the fastest-growing business, but that's only on this side of the Mississippi. Thank you, Mr. Knox," I said and signaled my intent to expand further west.

As C.J. had noted to me, folks loved to hear about the business owned by a colored woman. It may have made good copy, but I was entirely skeptical that folks would be equally interested in reading about the thirty years I spent bent over a tub that got me to this day.

"Sales near doubling quarterly,' C.J. remarked. "Just need more agents to follow along your path to the rich Pacific, hey, Sarah?"

"Are you attending the National Business League convention?" Mr. Knox asked. Asked my husband, that is.

It didn't surprise me that men who came to my office to sell their services or products instinctively directed their comments and questions to C.J. even in my presence. I knew it was hard for them to accept that a woman could operate a business larger than a hat shop. But then a colored-owned business like mine had never existed before. Not with a woman at the helm. I knew that in most men's minds it simply wasn't natural for a woman to be in trade. Yet strangely so many of our men could easily envisage us raising a brood of kids, putting food on the table and still work the cotton fields or the tubs all day and well into the night. I'm still bemused at the habit I had of erecting my posture when speaking to male peers. Guess it goaded them that in my mind we were equals in all respects; except as far as opportunity. In that regard, we had an advantage over the men: easy access to a washboard when the ends simply would not meet!

"Isn't the convention headed up by Booker T. Washington himself?"
I asked.

I'd read something about it in the papers. I wedged myself between
Mr. Knox and C.J. so he would direct the conversation to me as well.

"Is Mrs. Washington participating?"

"Mr. Knox is organizing the event for Mr. Washington, aren't you
George? Yep, the great wizard himself." C. J. said.

Then with a frozen grin, he stepped aside, perhaps daring Mr. Knox
to feel the awkwardness of responding to woman directly.

"You see, Booker won't admit women to his yearly conventions. No,
he won't. Only men of business get invitations."

Mr. Knox's glance darted from C.J. to me. He looked as though
he was waiting for C.J. to remind me I had something burning on the
stove. My exit would enable the two of them to get down to the real
business at hand that being determining what my company ought to be
doing by their count.

"Not even his wife, Margaret. Ain't that so, George?" C.J. asked.

Did he really need confirmation from Mr. Knox that women should
stand down to a man's rules? Coming up on ten years of being in business for myself surely he understood it didn't matter to me whose rules
they were; they simply weren't mine. You see, I was well into writing my
own and I now had excellent penmanship.

"Why not?" I inquired. "Mrs. Washington commands so much
admiration and respect from our folks. Why would she not be invited
to speak?"

"Like Mr. Knox said, it's only for men," C.J. stated as if quoting
scripture. This comment galvanized me as I was no longer inclined to
hold my tongue when faced with a man's dismissive tone.

"Why wouldn't I attend that convention?" I asked, perhaps in part
thinking out loud. "I should think I've got as much to contribute as any
man standing there."

I quickly wondered what kind of situation I'd worked myself into?
Was I truly ready to take on a confrontation with Mr. Washington if he
publicly slighted me? Such would be costly to my image. Yet if I didn't

make an appearance, I might be perceived as being weak to the very women I was urging to stand up and away from the tubs!

Hypocrisy is something I loathe. I knew that if I didn't appear, I'd be tacitly bowing to the prejudices all women struggled against. That simply wouldn't do for a business owned and largely staffed by women who also sold to and profited from women. My image was what drew attention to my products. I knew I would have to do something about this convention and considered the situation as potentially one of my greatest challenges.

⁂

I had invited Mr. Knox for supper that night. By the time we'd completed our business talk and C.J. had shown our guest around my manufacturing facility, Louvenia was ready with her fine spread. She had a bit of a twinkle in her eye when Mr. Knox chatted with her. His gentlemanly politeness was something she'd never experienced during her years with Jesse. I recall hearing Sister assure Mr. Knox that he mustn't worry about thinking himself drinking out of vases because they were only fancy cut crystal table glasses. He thanked her and complimented her fine taste. Louvenia glowed.

"So, Miss Louvenia, what do you think about Madame Walker traveling around the country and becoming so well-known?" Mr. Knox asked.

"I only think about what some mean white folks might think," Sister responded. "Do you want some more of my roast, Mr. Knox?"

C.J., who chose not to accompany me on my trips, quickly changed the subject.

"You know, Mr. Knox is a good friend of Mr. Washington. Yes, he is, ain't that right, George?"

"Is it true George that Booker T. Washington dined with President Roosevelt in the White House, or is that just tall tale?" I asked.

"No, it's true, Sarah," Mr. Knox replied. "Only a few weeks after President McKinley was murdered, the new president, Teddy Roosevelt, invited Booker to the White House for supper."

I knew it had to have been the first time in this great nation's history that a colored man had been invited to the White House.

"You know I always wondered if that was true or not," C.J. commented. "That was more than a decade ago and no coloreds been invited to the White House since!"

"It was nineteen-hundred and one when Booker went to the White House, but you see white folks got so hot-and-bothered 'bout a colored being the guest of the President, ol' Teddy regretted it before Booker put a fork to his mouth. The following day Mr. Roosevelt claimed Mr. Washington only had a bit of lunch with the President and when that didn't appease the white folks' anger, Mr. Roosevelt simply pretended he never knew Mr. Washington had been to visit and certainly couldn't recall what they had for supper when he did."

We laughed, but how funny is that?

"Now we got President Wilson and the only door he wants us to walk through is the voting booth," C.J. said. "After we mark his name on a ballot, he's got no use for us."

"Mr. Knox, you know Sarah made a promise to me that one day she's gonna write the President a letter asking him to do something about all the lynching. Didn't you, Sarah?"

"Yes, Sister. Someday I will petition the president to help our people."

"You really think he's gonna read it?" C.J. asked. "I mean, he must know who Madame Walker is. They say he don't take to coloreds thinking they got any kind of rights."

"No, you're right, C.J.," Mr. Knox nodded. "President Wilson has directed all federal offices, including the post office, to rid their agencies of Negros and replace us with white folks. While Mr. Wilson doesn't see any use for colored postmen, he does think we're good enough to polish his silver and iron his bed sheets in the White House. How does that add up?"

"They got coloreds working in the White House?" Louvenia asked.

"Only as laundresses and butlers, Sister."

Later that evening while Mr. Knox and C.J. were talking over brandy and cigars, I excused myself and went upstairs to retire. Later,

I'd just put down a novel I was reading and sat down at my dressing table when C.J. came up with his newspaper. He seemed to be in a bit of a huff, so I wondered if he and Mr. Knox had gotten into it as far as their politics. But then C.J.'s moods always seemed hard and often that hardness landed on me. That night he didn't greet me when he entered, just plopped in an easy chair behind me as I sat at my dressing table. He opened his newspaper and huffed.

"After your next business trip we're takin' some time off to relax," he announced.

I knew he was provoking a quarrel. We'd had several heated discussions about C. J.'s disinclination to accompany me on my tours. These trips were indeed exhausting and fraught with unpredictable dangers, so I could not entirely fault him for avoiding them. And yet I felt most men would instinctively desire to escort their wives on such travels. C.J. seemed to always measure his manhood differently.

"C.J., you know I can't. How long have I had this Caribbean trip planned?"

"Don't tell me you're serious about this business of going to Haiti?"

"It's a nation of coloreds, governed by the same. How serious should that be for our people? For my business?" I stated.

"Well, I just may have Otho drive me in the Cole to New York for a few days while you're off again."

"That seems unlikely," I responded. "Otho will be with me."

"Now why would you take your damned driver?" C.J. pounced. "You'd be payin' for a ticket just for him to handle your trunks!"

"Otho will be joining me to drive the Cole. The motor will be shipped for my use later in Jamaica, Cuba and Costa Rica as well. Haven't decided if Otho and the Cole will accompany me to Panama, or I'll ship it back beforehand."

"Good God!" C.J. shouted as if my trip was a ploy to curb his delights in New York.

"I'm leaving on the *Oruba* for Kingston in less than two weeks," I reminded him. "God willing, as you put it."

He snapped his newspaper open and pretended to read again.

"Well, just the same, I've decided we're taking some time off! You can postpone your trip as easily as you planned it. Easier, in fact," he announced—as if he were dressing down his housekeeper.

"Postpone my trip to the Caribbean so your holiday will not be inconvenienced? You know, C.J., you don't decide things for me," I said calmly even as his tone bridled.

C.J. jolted up to confront me in no uncertain terms. Yet these terms were not unfamiliar as I'd faced them many times on the long roads that lead to that evening. He tossed his paper on the carpet and jumped to his feet posturing in a way that always got up my nose. I couldn't think of a way to deal with it other than to respond in kind. C. J. glared at me in my dressing table mirror.

"You're never satisfied, are you?" he snarled.

"Is it about satisfaction? Mine, yours or ours? C.J., your dream was to be rich but keep things the old ways: Your woman tied to your needs by an apron string. My dream is to be free of all harnesses. That means I'm not having no white woman, no white man or even a colored man including my own husband mouth off on what I best do with myself. So, let's not have this talk again!"

I didn't mean to slam my brush down so hard it broke the dressing table glass. But then it hardly felt bad at the moment as I'd paid for it and everything else in that room where C.J. slept in luxury and tossed his newspapers around like he did his finally honed disdain.

I wonder now if either of us could really hear the other. Don't know when we started traveling down different roads grasping at different dreams, but from the start of our marriage it had never been about love. No, it was only about deals. Perhaps even worse, it was mostly centered on cold hard cash and whose pockets it would ultimately land in.

"We'll see about that! And what we'll see is Booker puttin' you in your place at that convention. That is if you have the disrespect for this man to show at a place where you're clearly not wanted!"

"Where is my place then, C.J.?" I demanded. "Have you determined that again today?"

"You're a woman! You don't know where a woman's place is?"

His nostrils flared.

For several months I'd felt the heat of C.J.'s efforts to situate me in a place he'd outlined himself even as I was exploring ever bigger places to assert myself and my business interests. And wherever I stood in business, I knew that near me stood women reading my every move like they read everything that was printed about me in the weeklies.

"You know my momma told me, 'The somebodies gonna be the nobodies and the nobodies gonna stand up and be counted one day.' I plan to be counted among you men at Booker's convention and you won't find me down on my hands and knees there. Not even for the mighty Booker T. Washington.

"Look at you!" C.J. barked. "Who the hell do you think you are? This is Booker T. Washington! He knows the president of the United States! Even had lunch at the White House. That's more than you'll ever say!"

I didn't care who Mr. Washington knew. My identity was no longer an open question to me. I knew exactly who I was and where I was headed and didn't need no man's permission to go in the direction my dreams dictated.

C.J. stormed out and was gone all night. At least I assumed so as I'd locked the bedroom door after it slammed.

I Am the Daughter
of Slaves!

13

CERTAINLY MR. BOOKER T. Washington was fully aware of my
achievements in business. Not only did my name and that of
my company appear frequently in the colored-owned weeklies along with his but I'd sent substantial donations to the Tuskegee
Institute which he was founder. Nobody there had any problems with
my name on those bank drafts.

The convention for the colored business community was to be in
Wilberforce, Ohio, with many luminaries attending. I yet wondered
whether Mrs. Washington would be there or was even the wife of the
"great wizard" unwelcome? Increasingly, I noticed that my name was
mentioned alongside hers when the newspapers wrote about colored
folks of achievement.

The day of Mr. Washington's convention drew near. In anticipation, I'd
studied up on topics of concern to colored-owned enterprises and felt prepared for any discourse. I was determined to appear at Mr. Washington's
convention in full force. You see by nineteen-fourteen I had nearly
twenty thousand agents working for me. I figured if I accomplished

nothing more, I would at least make an appearance and do it in a fashion that would make as much of a splash in the weeklies as the great wizard's appearance in Wilberforce.

Hearing that I would probably be the only woman there, Lelia and Louvenia had developed a few strategies of their own for making my presence known in a large hall filled with powerful businessmen. It became a special cause for them to send me into battle well-armed or at least grandly attired for my likely downfall. One evening Lelia sauntered into my study on edge. I was certain by her sighing it had something with her Aunt Louvenia. Sigh, sigh, till finally I paused to hear her side of things.

"Yes, dear. What is it?"

"I didn't say there was anything wrong, did I?"

"Well then, I'll get back to my papers," I said, knowing better.

"You know what Aunt Louvenia's up to?" she asked. Then she went on without looking me in the eye, a signal it was a particularly grave Louvenia matter that would take some time to untangle. You see Louvenia and Lelia had strongly differing opinions about how I ought to make my entrance at Mr. Washington's convention. I knew I would eventually get an earful from both: Lelia's view would take the position of an educated woman who'd never been on a plantation and who had never met her grandparents who were born as slaves. Louvenia would speak from the degradation of having once been a slave herself. I'd seen their arguments played out before. I knew my daughter was apt to make a preemptive briefing intent on sabotaging her Aunt Louvenia's overture for my attention. Knowing this, Louvenia's tactic was to come late at night when she would confront me as to how troubled she was about something Lelia was not doing quite right and the certain disaster that would assuredly befall us. The argument would eventually devolve to a laundry list of complaints. As I recall, the most recent issue for Sister was that Lelia had paid full price for a roast without first dickering with the butcher. That conduct could put us in the poorhouse, Sister assured, even as I sent checks to numerous charities including the colored orphanage in St. Louis where Lelia had been cared for. Today's problem was as onerous for Lelia.

"You know Aunt Louvenia has selected one of her hats for you to wear to the convention?"

I took this briefing as seriously as I could.

"Momma, that hat is simply too large."

"Oh, dear. That does sound grave," I affirmed. "And right in front of Mr. Washington, too. I wonder what we must do to avert this calamity."

"There! You see! Aren't you glad we're discussing it?" Lelia asked.

"Yes, dear, I am. But don't you think my wearing a grand hat might get my name in the papers? Isn't that the very reason I put so much into my attire when in public? What more could I ask for than a photograph and comment in the weeklies where they'd certainly mention my business? Dear, Louvenia's ways may be different from yours, but she's not such a silly woman with her notions on hats. Have you seen President Wilson's wife without a large hat in public? Don't they make her appear to be standing as tall as the president?"

I pushed a newspaper across my desk for Lelia to note a picture of Mrs. Wilson on the steps of the White House with the president to greet an ambassador. What propitious timing on Mrs. Wilson's part to get her image on the front page just when I needed to reference large hats for Lelia's benefit. I considered sending a note of thanks to the First Lady.

"Right there, Mrs. Wilson standing among those powerful men and looking just as tall as the president of the United States."

"I didn't think of that," Lelia said.

"Sometimes we have to toot our horn good and loud because there are folks who don't want us entering their halls 'less we're bowing with cap in hand like 'croppers at the master's backdoor. Mr. Washington has determined that I will not be acknowledged even at his backdoor simply because I am a woman. Seems to me then my only recourse may be to storm the front doors because they surely will not be expecting me at the head of their parade."

I was about to retire that evening when Sister decided to add her thoughts as to how I should best Mr. Washington on his own ground.

"I have something I want to show you, Sarah," she said.

"Louvenia, I don't have time to try on any hats right now."

"Now how do you know I'm thinkin' about a hat? Lelia say? What if I was gonna show you a nice sweet-potato pie? Then what? You'd feel mighty foolish thinkin' you know what I'm thinkin' when you don't. Ha!"

"You know if you really had one of your sweet potato pies I'd already smelled it and probably had a piece, Sister."

"That so?" Louvenia huffed. "Then you're tellin' me you ain't gonna wear a fine hat to that meetin' with all them rich men looking you over like you know they're gonna do?" Louvenia asked arms akimbo.

"Yes, but I assure you that the rest of me will be appropriately attired," I said.

Louvenia always held that a substantial woman would never appear in public without a hat. Moreover, very substantial women wore very substantial hats. Mrs. Wilson would surely nod agreement to that.

"Well, I just hope you're not the only woman there who ain't got the sense to dress like you know you ought'a." Louvenia said in her best Minerva voice.

"Sister, very likely I'll be the only woman there period. Anyway, with all the new products out, don't you think it best that I show my hair? We want these men to be talking about the MadameC.J. Walker Manufacturing Company to their wives, don't we? If I wear one of your fancy hats, they'll be wondering if I'm hiding something."

"Well, I guess you're right. Sarah, no matter what you wear, you're still smarter than the lot of 'em!" Sister kissed my cheek. "Who knows? I bet they all drink sweet tea out of mason jars like 'croppers!"

We laughed and Louvenia looked to the heavens as if Minerva was surely up there smiling at her daughters.

"You know momma would be proud of you," she added.

⤬

Otho had spent two days polishing the Cole Palace Touring Motorcar that would deliver me to the grand entrance of the convention hall.

Well, I was certain of one thing, I would be the only attendee arriving in this manner.

Mr. Ransom and I left a few minutes late to ensure the convention-eers got a grandstand view of my arrival as they thronged the entrance to the hall.

"You think your motor is larger than President Wilson's?" Freeman asked.

"Should I pull up to the White House to see?" I asked.

"Don't know really," Freeman said, "but I reckon you're the only one who'd do just that!"

"You mean the only colored who would!"

"That's what they say. MadameC. J. Walker, richest colored woman in the country."

"You know, I don't think my folks ever crossed the river over to Vicksburg. They never had a cent to buy even a ferryboat ticket."

"And now you could buy 'em a riverboat. A real nice one, too!"

"What would they think, Freeman? What would they think of me, or even hearing of a colored woman going to a big convention like this to hear a colored man who's met the president of the United States? And that man is married to the most famous colored woman in the nation?"

"Don't know what your folks would have said, Ma'am, but then I'm still unsettled wondering what Mr. Washington will say when he gets wind you're aiming for his convention!"

This convention had been announced many times in the papers resulting in a rush of press waiting on the steps for arrivals. Otho slowly drove the Cole up to the convention hall entrance. Even with a bead of sweat on his brow from nerves, I sensed Freeman swelling with pride upon our grand arrival. But then he was dressed in a businessman's suit which gave him a free pass to the event. Nobody was expecting me to appear, so it certainly hadn't occurred to anyone to monitor the hall entrance. Even so, I felt somewhat like an escaped slave slipping through Confederate territory in a skirt. I had to make it through those doors somehow and over enemy lines to the middle of the hall without causing a ruckus that would get me summarily escorted out.

"Freeman, some of these folks are the most important men of our race. I recognize them from the weeklies."

"Kind'a wish you hadn't reminded me of that," he said smiling bravely and nodding to the different groups of men as we passed. Their startled glances were reminder that I was indeed not expected. Entering on Mr. Ransom's arm was comforting, but I did have second thoughts about not having worn one of Sister's hats as I suddenly felt a need to hide under something.

"Don't know why, but I think I'm trembling," I whispered to Freeman as we passed through the throng of men conversing in the lobby. "Here, in this hall, I am scared of my own people. Don't seem right."

"I'm used to being where no one wants me," he said tipping his hat to a man that looked of disbelief as I strolled past.

Across the lobby I spotted Mr. Knox surrounded by a group of men. His deep resonating voice felt like a good omen. Or perhaps I simply wanted it to be.

"MadameWalker. Over here!" he yelled. I was glad to have a friend there. That left only about five hundred or so to win over—not including the great wizard himself.

"Mr. Knox, so good to see you! You know Mr. Ransom? He's recently completed law school and has joined my company as counsel."

"Congratulations, Mr. Ransom. We best make our way into the hall before it gets too crowded. I think we should sit as near to the platform stage as possible."

Folks stepped aside as the well-known Mr. Knox walked to the center of the auditorium with Freeman and me.

Mr. Washington was known to be a stickler for punctuality and, unlike his gracious wife, never had a moment to waste on small talk or hand shaking. In fact, he walked on stage looking a bit surly; his unusually pale eyes quickly scanned the hall causing stragglers to scurry to their seats. Thankfully he didn't readily notice a woman seated only four rows in front of him. As the room went silent, I took a deep breath hoping to slow my palpitations and wondered if it would be best if I only sat there and listened. If nothing more, I would have at least achieved what no other woman had: a seat at the court of Booker T. Washington. "So, that's the legendary Mr. Washington?" I whispered to Ransom. "Looks like any other man to me."

I waved my fan to disguise my hand's trembling.

"Let's not draw any conclusions here, Madame," Freeman said. "Got to be a reason we're down here stuck to our seats and he's up there holdin' the pot of glue."

Mr. Washington looked out over the audience as though he was daring anyone who might think of interrupting him to stand and pray for forgiveness. However, no one stood; no one even muttered a word. I'd never felt such a loud silence. Surely all these grown men were not sitting on their hands merely to keep their mouths shut? I hoped nobody could hear my fan buzzing like a swarm of wasps. Whipping a bit of attention away from Booker? Then it dawned on me: Truly, why wasn't Mrs. Washington attending? Did she know something I didn't? Was I setting myself up for the biggest humiliation of my life? My moist palms stuck to my silk fan which suggested that this could be the case.

In the hall's stone-cold silence, Mr. Washington commenced his speech. At least thought he would. But on the man's first sentence, Mr. Knox rose from his seat in the face of the great wizard. The audience froze. One man, there at my side, stood alone in that great hall; a concert of scowls challenged him to be seated again. Who would dare stand with the Great Wizard up there? Someone was interrupting the mighty Booker T. Washington and every man there wanted to know who possessed such temerity?

Yes, it was obvious that no one had ever witnessed the great man interrupted in this manner. Heads span like tops for a glimpse of the culprit. I prayed that the drop of sweat running down the back of my neck was not visible. What would Mr. Washington do to me? Would there be bit of verbal lashing from the great one; or simply the ejection of Freeman, Mr. Knox and myself from the hall as the other conventioneers tittered over our obvious sins.

"Mr. Washington, before we get started here today," Mr. Knox's firm voice filled the auditorium, "I would like to take the opportunity of introducing to this convention…."

The words had not escaped before Washington hurled a searing glance our way. One that could have ignited a bonfire. He was not accustomed to this effrontery. No, he wasn't. And it got worse. I later discovered Mr. Knox had previously written to introduce me to Mr. Washington and recommended I be introduced formally at this convention. Unknown to me, Washington had his secretary send off a letter stating that under no circumstances would a woman address the convention. A letter that I was later informed Mr. Knox conveniently failed to open.

Washington appeared highly pestered.

"Mr. Knox, I do indeed see you down there still waving at me, Sir. There will be several speakers today; they are clearly noted on the program and you, Sir, are not one of them. Kindly take your seat so we can continue."

I wondered if the audience saw sparks because I could feel them!

"I call this convention to order and that means we will be hearing only the speakers I'm about to announce."

Washington shuffled his notes like Mr. Knox had cast his thoughts over the room where they would undoubtedly be collected by the rest of us.

The fog that blankets my thoughts when I'm frightened rolled my way again, but this time from Washington's podium. I don't think I even heard most of his opening statement. Washington's mouth was moving but all I heard was the preacher's words to me after I lost Jeffrey: 'You'll know when the time is right. Demonstrate your faith. Open your mouth and the Lord will give you the words you need. He will take you to the next step on the journey.'

I stood up. Determined as I'd ever been before, I would indeed be heard. Nearly forty-five years of this dismissive attitude had brought my determination to a finely chiseled razor-sharp point. Yes, standing there among men I would not be dismissed like a house servant.

I proclaimed loudly: "I am the daughter of slaves! I have a business that is a credit to the women of our race!"

Washington's glares jabbed at my words, but they came rolling all the same.

"I am a woman from the South. I was orphaned when I was seven! Surely you will not ignore my message."

The audience rustled in their seats, but I did not break the lock my eyes had on Booker's. I would leave there at least knowing that no man would silence me, not even in a moment of silence as my message, without words, made it very clear to every man there; I had arrived as their equal and would so stand.

But history will record that I was indeed acknowledged!

Mr. Washington ultimately recognized me that day and when I was finished speaking, the entire hall applauded.

The following year I received a personal invitation from Mr. Washington to address the next convention as guest of honor

The Two MadameWalkers

77

WELL, WEREN'T THEY right about me? Daddy said I was the antsiest of his kids, worse than any boy. Louvenia always claimed I could never keep quiet and that when I was too tired to move my thoughts still marched to destinations I could never have put a name to. Jeffrey once held me down in a chair and whispered something I didn't understand at the time... "Just let it be for now!" Don't recall if his whispers calmed the ruckus brewing in my head but I've never forgotten the kiss that followed.

So, it was no surprise to anyone that I quickly determined that living in Pittsburgh had proved entirely unsatisfactory. I'd gotten tired of the filthy air, the dirty streets and the even dirtier attitudes that were so easily slung at coloreds. It wasn't long before I felt it was time to move on in search of greater opportunity. Though I was already bringing in more each week than any colored woman in the country, I had come to believe that Indianapolis might offer better opportunities for manufacturing and a certainly a more hospitable climate, so once again I was packing for new destinations. Or rather C.J. and I were.

Well ahead of my move to Indianapolis, I'd written introductions to several of the most prominent of colored businessmen making my objectives known. I would commence the manufacture my hair products in this city of commerce and continue to grow my business based from

Indianapolis. C.J. placed ads in the *Indianapolis Recorder* announcing my arrival and worked something out with Dr. Joseph H. Ward, the most prominent physician in Indianapolis, who offered to make introductions on my behalf to our community. C.J. handled it so that the ads he placed announcing the opening of my business also informed my new customers that I would be staying at Dr. Ward's beautiful home on Indiana Avenue where I would give the first demonstration of my products at a lovely reception. Dr. Ward and I benefited from having our names linked in the papers and became the best of friends; a friendship that endured the stormy years ahead.

With Dr. Ward's generous help, we settled in quickly and became a part of the community. After only a few months I was able to purchase, in my own name, the very place Dr. Ward had helped us rent. It was a large yellow-brick house with twelve rooms on the best street that colored folks could live on. This made me the first of my family to own my home. Since I had little to move to the new place, I used the opportunity to purchase some of the fine things I'd long desired including a gold harp and fine organ. While I decorated the new home, C.J. started going on trips here and there in the fine touring motorcar he'd purchased for himself. Certainly, as a mature woman, I figured these were not entirely business trips, but I didn't ask any questions as he didn't interfere with my decorating schemes. The business of our marriage ran smoothly, at least smooth enough for the time.

It was all quite strange for many folks I encountered: a woman of color spending good money to decorate her home with expensive musical instruments, books, art, fine carpets, and works from Tiffany's. Where did the money come from they surely wondered? And talked. And that talk, as C.J. pointed out, helped spread the word about my products and got my name in the weeklies which included my picture departing Tiffany's in New York City. C.J. was astute. He taught me that folks remarking on the accoutrements of my personal life reflected on how successful I was to determine how legitimate my products surely were. Yes, success speaks for itself and I would learn, does so eloquently.

Soon after my purchase of the North West Street home, the young

Mr. Freeman Ransom became my border. He'd been working in Indianapolis for some time building his legal business and selling real estate on the side. He continued to demonstrate his loyalty by advising me on the properties I purchased which turned out to be excellent investments. In fact, having Freeman nearby proved to be another excellent investment. I wonder if it was sometime during these years that I began to see myself not only owning my own property, but also building on that land. Visions of an orchard rising from the rich soil I would own one day had remained in my soul from those fleeting days Jeff and I lived in the country. I think this dream stayed with me just as one never forgets the taste of a fresh peach just pulled off the branch, or the look in Jeff's eyes when I fed him peaches from a mason jar.

∽

It was only a few months after we moved to Indianapolis when Emily wrote that Hank had had a stroke and although partially recovered, he could no longer keep up the long hours on his feet at the barbershop. They were selling their place in St. Louis and, with my encouragement, decided to move near to us. Grandma Ida had passed away sometime before. I was delighted by the thought of renewing our friendship and Emily wanted to try her hand at being my agent. With her warm and large personality Emily was an immediate success. I'd never forgotten the treasure of Emily telling Mrs. Washington that I was president of some society she had elected me to which gave me a precious moment to feel I stood on equal ground with that great woman.

I loved Emily, but that didn't mean I'd make it easy for her when she arrived in Indianapolis. No, business is business. To make sure she pulled her weight I figured I'd put that woman under my thumb and then press her till she squealed.

Soon after Emily and Hank had settled into a place about a mile from us, she started coming to my office where we'd jabber over coffee. One morning I was shuffling through the new orders when she stepped in looking bedraggled.

"Did you come to help me catch up here, or just to mope?" I asked. "What's your problem?"

Emily plunked herself into a chair across from my desk to elongate her sighs.

"I have the right to mope," she announced soulfully.

"Honey, don't know if it's your right, but you sure have cause, now don't you?" I snapped but she didn't seem to hear me at first.

"Today's my birthday and Hank's completely forgotten. He's probably out with C.J. again."

"That's what I mean. Hopefully now you'll give up your ruckus over another birthday!"

Emily finally realized what had just tinkled her ears.

"What did you just say? Ruckus?"

She sat up stiffly.

"Got cause to mope? Is that what you said?"

"Hearing's not so good these days? Yes, dear, Hank's good to forget your birthday. If only you'd let the rest of us forget, too." I said. "Don't we all know it's for your own good?"

I said mimicking some sweet-mouthed southern white woman. The kind that made us both cringe.

Emily glowered like she'd sooner smack me than anything.

"What? What did you just say?" she huffed.

"Honey, you know we've noticed how many times we got to repeat ourselves 'round you? You hearin' me good now?"

Emily gasped and rose to her feet, both her fists on her ample hips and told me off!

"What did you say to me, woman?"

"Lordy, do I need to write it down? You're eyes holding up at least? Well, this might help you."

I scribbled on a scrap of paper and pushed it across the desk. She grabbed at my note, but I guess it didn't make for good reading because she'd barely read two words when her face turned beet purple.

"Hearing my foot! This here says I gotta fat ass!"

"Dear, there are two things a woman shouldn't be reminded of. Her age, when the numbers get that far gone, and how big your rump has gotten. I mean when the numbers get that far from side to side! Don't have a yardstick at home to know, or you just can't see good enough to read it?"

I grinned so wide Emily could see my wisdom teeth.

Emily looked stunned. She sure enough did.

"Why, Sarah! I'd never speak to you like that," she sighed. "You've changed since you got rich. You sure have!"

"No, you wouldn't dare, honey 'cause you know I wouldn't take your lip. Rich folks don't, you know. Well, I guess you don't!"

I stood there batting my eyes like a rich white woman who figured her grief had to be put up with.

About then I thought the blood was going to stream out of that woman's eyes. Emily reached for my ear, surely to hold it so she could spin my head and then smack my mouth as it came back around.

"I don't need no yard stick, I got a fist here to measure your mouth. Come over here and let's get to it!" she said tipping her chair as she dashed around the table to wallop me one. "Gonna pull your dammed hair out so good you'll never again sell another tin of that axle grease!"

Well, thank goodness I had a very large desk 'cause Emily had very long arms and they were sure determined to put a clamp on my big mouth.

"Now you sit that big butt back down and act like a lady!" I screeched.

I ran for my life barely out of reach of those long nails she was aiming to sink deep into my neck. And there, outside my office hearing everything was Hank, C.J., and Lelia, with Louvenia and Matilda and all my staff. While I was abusing Emily, they'd been quietly setting up a birthday table with a strawberry cream cake and presents. C.J. opened a bottle of champagne as we broke out in singing Happy Birthday. I kissed Emily's cheek and thanked her for all her years of friendship and wished her many more years of my abuse to come.

❧

One evening after I'd returned from a long tour, Louvenia and I wanted to see a moving picture show. We'd been to the Isis several times and enjoyed the pictures and the great organ music that accompanied them, so it was with delight that I found myself an evening with no engagements. Sister and I arrived at the Isis where we stood in line to purchase our tickets. The sign posted read "Tickets Ten Cents". I put two dimes on the counter and slid them toward the ticket woman.

This woman glared at me and rolled them right back like my money was soiled or certainly unacceptable.

"Can't you read none?" She proceeded to pull out a cardboard sign and stick it in the window. "We got a new policy here at the Isis. Coloreds got to pay a quarter for a seat in the back!" she exclaimed. "I guess that means you, don't it?"

I looked behind me and saw that most folks in line were coloreds, my color, that is.

"We aren't payin' no quarter!" I informed the startled woman who apparently was not accustomed to the new policy being challenged.

"Then step aside 'cause I won't even take your damned quarter for sassin' me like you done!" she replied.

"You will hear from my lawyer if you do not give me two tickets this instant!" I informed the woman.

"Huh! You're a colored. What do you think any lawyer's gonna do for you's? Now get on out'a here 'fore I call somebody out."

"Come, Sister." Louvenia tugged at my sleeve. "It's late and I'm too tired to sit through a moving picture show anyway."

We did leave but the next day I had a chat with Freeman. I instructed him to file a lawsuit in the Marion County Court against the Isis Moving Picture Palace. Low and behold the theater backed off their two ticket-price policy. It was perhaps less from my lawsuit than the word that'd spread fast after I filed. You see, once talk got out, coloreds lined up at the Isis by the dozens, asked the price of tickets and then shook their heads at the two price tiers before walking off. Lots of empty house seats make a different kind of noise than the jingle of coins in the cashbox! And Lord, if it isn't deafening to profits!

It was only a few months later when I was discussing the building of a large manufacturing facility, one that would be of fireproof brick, that I decided to add another major structure, a theater. Yes, the Majestic Walker would be next door and would honor all guest as equals. Isn't it amazing how some slights along the way can turn into majestic dreams?

❧

Later that year after I'd returned from a tour of the east I went into breakfast. C.J. was already seated at the table buried in his usual newspaper. Guess he knew I'd returned the night before. Lelia didn't think C.J. had been in the office but his whereabouts seemed a mystery. Well, I knew it was hard for a man to have a wife with her own business let alone the ever-growing attention the press tended to focus on me. These articles tended to exaggerate my wealth. I didn't know what to do about that, but then I also didn't know why I should have to do anything. Success is a free ad running around town by word of mouth!

"Good morning, C.J."

I expected him to put down his paper so we could start the day right.

"Looks like the orders piled up while I was away."

I was sorry I'd said that as there had to have been a better way for a wife to greet her husband. I guess by then it was only business interests that tied us. Strangely that would ultimately be what would unbind us as it seemed all that we ever discussed was the ever-climbing sales figures even if there was seldom a conversation as to the impact these sales had on my agents and their children.

"I took some time off," he remarked still failing to look up from his paper.

"You had to do that while I was on the road?"

I asked calmly. Just the same, C.J. became very angry. I sensed that he had much anger bottled up. Perhaps we both did. I knew he would argue about leaving him alone to tend things in the office and then I would retaliate with for not tending to business above his pleasures. The cycles of our conversations were ever more predictable.

"I'm not going to work this hard till they put me in the ground, Sarah."

It was the sincerest thing he'd said to me in ages. Still I'd always thought that working hard was the way to avoid being put in the ground before my time. There was never such a thing as a tub woman who put food on her table without being bent over a tub.

"We worked hard to reach this place in our lives," I conceded. "Guess you have the right to pursue your life as I intend to pursue my own the way I see fit."

Certainly, a wife telling her husband she would not simply follow him along his own journey was jarring for C.J. and his notions of manhood.

"You're never going to slow down, are you?" he challenged. "No matter what, no matter who?"

His eyes expressed his pain and confusion, but I was still not offering to follow his or any man's lead. Yet, women of our race didn't just pick up and move on in life as I'd done. If we did pick up to go, it was too frequently only to escape a man's fist or to go hunt for the scraps of white folks.

"I've moved forward, C.J. What matters to me now are those nameless folks who follow my success with their own. You know there ain't nobody in this country helpin' colored women, but me. Ain't nobody."

"And I don't matter?" he asked.

My answer to that was deep in my silence. Still he heard this silence and slammed his fist down on the breakfast table.

"I don't matter enough to answer?" he railed.

"And yet even now you still don't understand, C.J.? I don't answer to no man. Best leave it at that."

While I'd been gone, and C.J. was spending more and more time on the road, I'd learned that C.J. was not only back at home enjoying his motor but a few other delights that were keeping his wheels spinning. And she happened to be on my payroll!

C.J. had hired Dora Lorrie himself. I sensed early on how very determined he was that she work in my manufacturing facility and learn all she could. But it was Ransom who discovered what drove her: the hope of taking over both my husband and my business. You see Miss Dora claimed she was besotted with C.J. and he apparently loved to hear it. What man doesn't? Somehow, she'd convinced this otherwise smart man that they should go to town and manufacture hair products with my formulas and with money they would come to extract from me. This woman saw herself slipping into my shoes as the new MadameC.J. Walker. From then on there would be fine homes, travel, motorcars and large sums of money crossing her greasy, rose-scented palms. But I had different notions for this silly woman and Freeman would broadside her with them.

Freeman followed the C.J.-and-Dora escapades for a few weeks as he collected needed evidence. When I determined the time was right and would bring the least amount of ugly press, I instructed Freeman to quietly file a petition of divorce. By then Dora had falsely assumed she'd acquired all my product formulas and went to manufacturing in some kitchen across town. There she went to referring to herself as MadameC.J. Walker, at least at her kitchen sink she did. You see, this woman had been prodding my staff over the months for bits and pieces of my product formulas, and they, all loyal to me, fed her bits and pieces of concoctions sure to make Dora's hair fall out when she put them all together. Yes, this woman figured she'd soon marry C.J. and make her new title official as the new MadameC.J. Walker. But things didn't proceed as she planned. C. J. got cold feet and didn't appear at court for the divorce, which the judge granted. He received no settlement, but I did settle with Miss Lorrie. I sure enough did. I sent Otho over to her place with a big box to help her step out into her in new life in my shadow.

"Miss Dora, I gots a box here from MadameWalker. I mean the real MadameWalker."

"What's in that box? She payin' up for all the grief she caused me?" Miss Lorrie demanded—something she was amply proficient at.

"Yes, Ma'am. Here's a box of Madame's old shoes. She says you best wear these if you plan to keep followin' 'er 'round town."

"Old shoes? I want money!"

"But you see Miss Dora, they's good as money 'cause Madame Walker buys real nice things and pays dear for 'em! Don't she now?"

Otho dropped the box of old shoes at Lorrie's feet and headed back to my Cole as this woman clutched a pile of shoes and ran to hurl them at the motor like it was my head she was aiming for. Otho said when she'd thrown everyone at the back of the motor, she pulled off her own shoes and threw them, too.

Nobody heard from this new Madame Walker again, maybe walking along the paths I'd walked wasn't the easy street she'd expected.

With C.J. gone, an era of my life had concluded almost as quickly as it had commenced years before in Emily's attic. Now and forever, I would no longer fight no man for the direction my life would lead. There would be no one holding me down to a vision that was no greater than a dollar and no longer than the day he could spend it.

I moved ahead with my visions for my business and did it without a husband. By the time my legal affairs with C.J. and his woman were over, I was ready to move on again. Lelia had already settled herself in New York City where life so delighted her, she seldom wanted to leave. She loved the dynamic mood there and the interesting people who were less defined by race than by what they had to say or the song they sang. According to my daughter, Harlem was happenin'! Before long, I began to consider her request that I also move there. Soon we were having a townhouse built, a single location that would serve as both our home and my New York office while my manufacturing would continue in Indianapolis next to the Majestic Walker Theater under construction.

In the meantime, there were receptions to attend and give and many more roads to travel.

DREAMS WASHED AWAY

78

M Y LONG DAYS had left a weariness that followed me like a fever I could not shake. As the holidays of 1915 drew near, recollections of Christmastime with my folks easily drifted through my thoughts. At times these memories lingered and left me wondering how many holidays could be left for me as I was now nearly a decades older than Minerva and Owen when they passed on.

Despite the toll it had been another successful year for the MadameWalker Manufacturing Corporation. Much of it I'd spent traveling the roads visiting my agents, signing up new ones and demonstrating my products at churches and halls around the country where all too often I witnessed my people falling under the weight of their struggles and ultimately being crushed by them.

The day after Thanksgiving, Lelia, Louvenia and I went shopping for Christmas decorations. To make our holidays glimmer, we purchased dozens of tiny hand-blown and painted ornaments the salesman touted as having come from Bavaria. Sister so delighted in these delicate glass treasures and called out their multitude of shimmering colors as she held them at the end of her fingertip against the light. Like the bellies of fish, she exclaimed and delivered the delicate objects to our tree with hesitancy as though she could only reluctantly release their beauty from her fingertip. Hanging from the tip of an evergreen, she'd touch it ever so gently to see the colors shimmer again. As we decorated our tree that year I thought of Minerva and Owen and their endless struggles. The bounty that surrounded us on this holiday was beyond any dream they could have conjured during those Christmases back at the Burneys' where we fed on nothing more than the shimmering belly of a fish that daddy had caught down at the river with Alex and Samuel.

In anticipation of the holidays, Lelia had been busy organizing recipes we'd collected over the years. Many had come to us by word of mouth and consisted of little more than ways to turn ground corn into a meal by tossing in this or that. Hadn't we eaten it every way imaginable over winters so cold that decades later a body could still become ill at the thought? Lelia, Louvenia and I sat around the table sipping tea and eating cinnamon cookies as we laughed at the hundred odd ways to cook the hog-intended ground corn our keepers had doled out in hard times as though it was some kind of manna from heaven. There were moments when I was troubled by the thought that my warm kitchen and bounty-filled larder mocked those memories. Yes, truly somehow we'd triumphed but there was a bitter taste to it.

Still I enjoyed these special moments that we spent together in the kitchen going over recipes, baking, or simply visiting our pasts. That year, Emily and Hank were joining us for Christmas and Louvenia declared she was determined to cook up the finest Christmas supper ever. All I wanted was to nibble over these sweet days and savor our moments together as I recalled the ones I'd had with Owen, Minerva, my brother and Jeffrey. Perhaps it was the smell of cinnamon, cloves and cocoa that brought bittersweet "what ifs" during these moments. Like, what if during Christmas supper, I gazed across to my husband at the head of the table as he listened to his daughter describe some special moment that had amused her that day. What if my folks could warm themselves by my Christmas fire for hours on end? Even let one burn an entire cold night and still have enough wood to make a meal the next day? The what ifs can be jagged when laid against one's heart.

"Will Hank want some black-eyed peas, Emily?" Lelia asked.

"You know he will. He thinks he can't eat ham without 'em."

As Emily scooped dough for the hush puppies, Louvenia stepped to the parlor door to taunt Hank eagerly waiting his supper.

"Now, Hank, I had us a nice tenderloin of pork smoking over hickory chips out back. Wrapped it in bacon just like Emily said you liked," Louvenia announced.

"Why, that sounds just fine," Hank announced.

"It sure did to me!" my sister carried on as I peeled the yams. "But then you know what happened?"

Sister sounded so glum everyone hushed to hear.

"That ol' dog I feed at the kitchen door is what. Smelled my roast out on the barbecue pit. Yes, he did, too. That ol' dog reckoned that roast was meant to be his Christmas supper and done dragged it down the alley. I seen 'im, too! Don't you reckon you best go after him? See if you can't get a bit of our roast back?"

I stepped to the parlor doors to witness more of this exchange.

"Go chase a dog down the alley you say?"

"Oh, Hank! You know I got us some black-eyed peas to go with your smoked roast that's back there sitting on the stove that ain't no dog been near," Sister announced with a wicked smile.

"What about the turkey?" Hank clamored.

"It's gonna have your favorite fresh oyster stuffin," Sister confirmed.

Everyone had a chuckle at Louvenia's tall tale.

Sister and Emily returned to the kitchen just as I was putting together the baked sweet potatoes. I put a nice bourbon cane syrup-glaze over the top with a sprinkle of pecans and slid it into the oven as we waited for the turkey to cool. Emily folded the linen napkins, monogrammed with large "W"s while Lelia pulled out the silver we'd all helped polish the day before.

"Aunt Louvenia, what did Minerva and Owen fix for Christmas dinner? Momma never talks about those days much."

"Well Lelia, that's because there ain't much to talk on, is there Sarah? As far as what we had to eat on Christmas or any day. Nope, there wasn't much on any table on that plantation, 'cept up at the big house. When I was little, I was sure I could smell what the Burneys were eating just by listening to Ella tell Momma what she'd been cooking up there. I guess sometimes Ella, she'd sneak us down some sweet potatoes when Miss Burney was in her bathing tub."

"Maybe a turkey neck or a ham bone to flavor some soup on Christmas day," I added. "After the Burneys were off to church to celebrate the bounty we put on their table."

Emily served cups of spiced tea and sat down. Sister needed something more to help her wrestle the memories and sloshed some bourbon in her cup.

"You know that your ma was born just a couple of days before Christmas so she don't 'member her first. But I was born before the war with the North," Louvenia reminded Lelia.

"Your Aunt Louvenia was born a slave." Emily added. "Like your grand-folks."

"Lord, wasn't I just that?" Louvenia said. "Our Christmases weren't much different over the years, before or after the war. No, they weren't. Cold and empty is what I 'member. Turned gray in winter like everything else along that ol' river. Empty bellies and nothin' but tall gray shadows up and down the 'croppers' shacks for months. Guess that's why beautiful colors delight my soul now. You think that's why I love flowers so? They called it Grandview, the Burney place. Grandview 'cause Burney lands stuck out like a finger pointing at that ol' river. Sounds like a grand view, now don't it?" Sister said. "Well, let me tell you."

"On summer nights folks gathered along the water to gaze at the lights over the river in Vicksburg," I added. "Hardly no one ever been there."

Louvenia's eyes darted around the kitchen as her thoughts jolted her deeper into those dark times.

"Yes, sometimes all you can do is stomp them memories back down."

I patted Sister's hand. She smiled and drifted back to our conversation.

"I was seven or eight when Momma tol' me to run up and get Ella," she said. "Baby comin', she say. Ella helped deliver Sarah, she did. But ain't a good time to birth a baby. Not when there's hardly no wood for a fire. No, but I guess birthin' ain't never easy for a 'cropper ma. I heard

Daddy sayin' to nobody in particular that year was real bad for folks livin' by the river. Owen, he'd used up ever' bit of credit to borrow seed from Burney the spring before. When Momma could walk the fields 'gain, she helped us work. No matter how sick and tired you are, you got to sow your seed early so the first rains would get it growin' good. I worked so damned hard. You can't know what it's like, Lelia. Ain't no words for it 'cause it's a lot worse than even that. Ain't it Sarah?"

"Yes, Sister."

"Then the rains, didn't they come again and again?" Louvenia continued. "All day it rained and then pounded our shack roof all night. You know we laid there in all that damp darkness with the sound of drips pattering on that ol' table like a clock ticking away. Holes in the roof Burney never would fix. No fire, no candles and sure as the hell we lived in, no food. Well, you don't 'member that first Christmas in eighty-six, Sarah, but you seen the same since."

I could add nothing to her recollections but knew she was right; even years later when I was a child at Grandview nothing seemed much different.

"Water rose all the way up the banks to the 'cropper's shacks," Sister continued. "Rose higher than anybody ever 'membered then stood right at our stoop stinkin' like a chamber pot and waitin' for someone to curse it on back down to the riverbanks. Your granddaddy Owen did, too. Cursed that Mississippi till he spit, but that river paid 'im no mind. 'Cause one morning when I woke up, I knew for sure that somebody come in the night and done shoved our shack right down to the river's edge like it was a boathouse. I thought maybe Daddy did it so he could get them catfish without walkin' down the slope. But it wouldn't take much to push that shack down any hill; lappin' at the steps to our door that cold gray water was. What's you gonna do 'bout it, that water wanted to know. I kicked it away as hard as I could. Lick, lick, lick at my toes, it did. Got so bad Daddy lifted us up on the table, Sarah, Alex and me, then went waddin' through muddy water to see what the other 'croppers was doin'. They all gone? They get out in time? Him thinkin' maybe that river carried off folks nearest the banks. But I guess that river finally got tired of lappin' at our doors, 'cause days later it went back down again but only as slow as the sun finally sets on a blistering day in July. And, Lord, I'm telling you, it took all the seed we done sowed with it. Yes, two or three weeks after we worked them fields there was nothin' left for us but weeds sproutin' in rows that looked to go beyond forever. Them standing tall like a choir in green robes rejoicing to the sun for deliverance. Yes, Ma'am, them weeds taller than me."

Sister sloshed more bourbon in her tea and took a deep breath like she was relieved to get it out, these things that follow you no matter where you go. Maybe like a shadow.

"What did Burney say?" Lelia asked.

"Burney? Why, he ain't 'round!" Louvenia replied.

"Where was he, Louvenia?" Emily asked.

"He gone. You know he hate to get his boots soiled. Wouldn't do if plantation folks thought he looked to be workin' his own fields. The ferry from Vicksburg come to Delta for the Burneys to get out in time. They headed off to her folks' guess over there on the hills above Vicksburg where the rich folks live. 'Fore she left, Miss Burney tol' Ella she best not let that muddy water get so high it come over her white veranda and stain it clay-color and pour into her parlor doors to soil her fancy rug. If it did, Miss Burney say she gonna cut the blood out of Ella."

"What did Ella say back to Miss Burney?" I asked.

"She sassed Miss Burney good. Ella tol' that woman she was gonna piddle on her damned ol' rug ever' morning!"

We laughed at the notion of a house servant telling her white mistress that she'd be using her imported carpet for a toilet just to spite her.

"But I tell you one thing, Ella, she cleaned out the Burney larder, brung everything down to the shacks. Never seen so many jars of peaches, jam and peas in all my days. Ella say she don't care if Miss Burney never come back 'cause if she didn't, Ella was gonna fill 'er big bathing tub and soak herself in some of Miss Burney's white jasmine scented suds ever'day from then on."

As I recall Sister's words that holiday it seems so strange that Ella had predicted what was to be her destiny.

"Oh, Lord, Lelia. I can't imagine Ella filling Miss Burney's tub for herself," I said. "She was probably only allowed pan baths back in the shed. Sister, tell them what the river brought us after it carried away Daddy's spring seeds."

Louvenia poured a splash of bourbon in Emily's cup.

"Fever! That's all that comes with the high-waters, just fever," Sister replied. "When them stinkin' waters rose to violate our shack, that's what they brought. That and waves of squeeters that come through our window ever' night. Then that mud rotting 'round the 'croppers' shacks smelled like piss-pot dumpings. But like ol' Clara said, no matter nothin' 'cause folks livin' on the river still got but two choices, huh, Sarah? You can starve or let the fever take you that is if the flood don't carry you away first. Guess if you was lucky, you'd go by fever so you don't got to watch your kids die. They's bellies so empty they look to 'a been stomped on by a mule."

All these years, I wondered what Louvenia's thoughts were about our folks dying of the fever so young as we never talked about it. To shake these memories away, I went to fiddle with something cooking on the stove.

"You want me to crack some more pecans to top them sweet potatoes, Sister?"

"No, I reckon there's enough. Keep some back for another day."

Sister's eyes locked on the clock above the door like it would chime a warning when our prosperity was near to running out and those pecans she was holding back might be all that was left to us. A thing we could grab up when we fled the high waters of life. Lord, how many cold winter nights at the cabin had Sister's supper been only roasted chestnuts off Jeff's tree?

How did Minerva and Owen survive?" Lelia asked with amazement. "What did they do with Momma when she was so little?"

"Well, as far as I was concerned, your Grandma Minerva best go feed Sarah here to the dogs," Louvenia said with a straight face. "'Cause they was out there hungrier than me and always on the prowl. I reckon like that nigger dog, Isaac."

Emily jumped in, "Don't listen to your Aunt Louvenia, Lelia. You know your granny would never let no wild dog get at her kids."

"No? Who got at me then?"

Sister eyes turned black like she was face-to-face with Isaac again. Lelia knew about that man abusing Sister and the curse that momma put on him for it.

"Sarah was safe up on the table to keep 'er out of the mud in our shack. The 'croppers, they stayed in their places waitin' for that brown water to go back down; ate moldy cornbread till even it run out on us. Then daddy stomped in that mud up to the big house to talk to Burney 'bout more credit for seed. Heard daddy tell momma he wasn't gonna be taken down by no river. Said he was yet strong and could feed his family as good as any man."

Then Louvenia went silent once more.

"Don't know how a big man like Owen could even get up after days of eatin' nothing but scraps of cornbread dipped in hog lard."

Lelia was so lost in Louvenia's story she didn't notice her gravy bubbling on the stove. I got up to stir it as it thickened.

"What else, honey? We sowed more seed borrowed from Burney on more credit. He had to give it, don't you know, or he'd end up having no crop to take into Vicksburg that year. Yes, momma and daddy, Alex and me out wading in that mud, stickin' seeds in holes our fingers made. From sun up till dark, we was. All day daddy kept mumbling that all the mud was really a blessin' and we's gonna have the biggest crop ever. One or two of them seeds in a poke in the mud, as I 'member and sure as heaven I do. I still wake in the night wondering if my fingertip is bleeding like it did when I was little after pokin' in that rocky soil for longer than I thought a day could be. Still hear his voice. Hear Daddy sayin' to Momma that he already owed Burney most all the crops he could ever harvest and then only if there ain't no more floods. 'Can't get ahead,' she mumbled back. But Daddy, he say she wrong 'cause then one day that sun finally come out good. We felt like the Lord had blessed us. Hallelujah! We's saved. Yes, ma'am, that sun come back and made the mud dry in front of our eyes but then it blazed on turning that clay soil to stone. That's how hard it got. Bit hotter ever' day folks said up and down the shacks. Stayed till the dirt cracked and then them seeds we'd planted withered as soon as they sprouted. Yes, them fields cracked open pleading for water again; maybe the worst drought ever on that river. Don't know. Sure knew how many buckets of water I carried up from the river to keep Ma's cabbages goin'. We was just little ones, Alex and me. Miss Burke, she don't like the dust that blew up off them fields so she headed to Vicksburg. Went on a riverboat all dressed in white linen lookin' like she ain't never been close enough to dirt to touch it."

"Minerva told me that what the drought didn't get, the army worms did," I told Lelia.

Louvenia nodded and went on with her story.

"So, then we prayed the drought would let up on us and there'd be a sprinkle again. Oh, Lord, just spit on us, we prayed. And so they came. The rains came and filled up the cracks in the dusty soil and rose again till it broke off the banks. When Burney showed his face down at the shacks, I heard him tellin' the 'croppers a good bit of Grandview done been carried away the night before. He said it was his land that river stole and the 'croppers best head to New Orleans to get it back for 'im, or just the same, come up with the money to pay 'im back for the seed that went down river! Don't know why I thought he was pointing at our empty bellies when he pointed which way to go lookin' for his seed done got washed away."

"Go looking for what?" Lelia asked.

"Oh, it never mattered; we always owed the man everything he could put his hands on starting with our throats right on down to our mud-caked toes."

"What did Minerva and Owen do then?" Lelia asked.

"We lived in that shack with standin' water on the ground all over again. But you don't never get used to it. No, you don't. I 'member that stinkin' slimy mud just like my feet still in it," Sister said. "You know, I still wash my feet 'fore putting on my shoes. It's 'cause I'm just sure I's feel some of that mud oozing between my toes that ain't really there. Ain't that strange?"

That was all she could say on it, so I continued where my part of our story mostly began: My last year at Grandview.

"They died, honey," I told my daughter. "A few years after the Christmas I was born. Owen and Minerva just had no place else to go beggin' for one more day for their family. So, they died. It was but a few weeks after the waters went back down when fever come up. Steamed up from hell like ol' Clara said it would. We buried 'em one night up on Orchard Hill. Ella and Jackson were there. ol' Clara, Samuel and Jane, too."

I griped Sister's hand.

"You know I always figured their prayers were answered 'cause they wouldn't have to work one more day in that mud or another summer with the blistering sun lashing their backs. That's what I told myself when I was little. Owen and Minerva, they freed of workin' like farm animals for hog food and scraps from the big house. Ain't that right, Sister? You think that was their dream; to follow Jesus to his Orchard?"

Louvenia had no answer. Who can choose between an agonizing death by the fever or slow one from starvation and still call it a dream come true?

"I'd do anything to serve our folks a supper like this one we's makin' today," Louvenia said.

"And for them to sit down with us at the table and know they'd still have something to eat the next day, too." I added.

❧

Almost from the day Louvenia came to live with us, we regularly wrote letters to Annie and asked if there was word on Alex. Had she even heard from his wife, Mary? But Annie's response was always the same; seemed like nobody had heard from them in ages.

One Friday I was leaving for my office when the postman delivered a pile of letters. I noticed one was from our friend and took it upstairs to Sister.

"Looks like a letter here from Annie, dear. Let's sit down after supper and share it."

I knew she always looked forward to hearing from our friend and about those kids she so loved. Louvenia reached for Annie's letter but I sadly failed to notice her hesitancy.

"You got a notion what you may want for supper tonight, Sarah?" She mumbled but still never took her eyes off that letter.

"No. Whatever you come up with, Sister."

Even now I still remember the look on Louvenia's like that envelope was double stamped with pain and sadness.

Looking back, I recall that day was very long for me. While my staff opened the day's mail and sorted it into piles of orders, notes from my agents and customers, I spent time in my laboratory looking over new products. On many days, it seemed that no sooner had I arrived than it was already near suppertime. I always looked forward to returning home in the evenings where I knew Sister would have the kitchen warm with her baking and pots of soup or sauces simmering on the stove. She always had a hearty supper prepared. On this evening, I left Lelia finishing her work and headed home on my own. Getting home I found there was nothing on the stove, not even a pot waiting to be filed. It was an eerily cold and silent kitchen that greeted me.

"Sister?" I yelled out. "Louvenia…?"

I went to the foot of the stairs and yelled up.

"Louvenia…"

I tell you now I expected the worst. I went up thinking that my sister was no longer with us; she'd passed away all alone on that cold day.

Her door was ajar. It was dark in there. I pushed it open to see her lying across the bed. She always looked so much like Daddy. But on that day, she was even stone-like. She stared up at the ceiling like our daddy did before he passed on.

"Sister…?"

"What?" she finally replied

"Why are you up here in the dark? Didn't you hear me callin'?"

"No. Must 'a been asleep," she replied.

"Are you feeling alright?"

Without a word Louvenia handed me the letter from Annie. She'd not opened it. Even though she couldn't read, she typically opened these letters for the tiny pieces ribbon or cloth Annie's girl, Nettie, sent to show the colors of her sewing.

"I should have taken the time to read Annie's letter this morning. Guess I'm always in too much of a rush. I'm sorry for that, Sister."

"It don't matter. I already know what it says. Lord, have mercy, I 'magine I knowed 'fore Annie even wrote it."

"Knew what?" I asked. "It's cold in this room. Come on downstairs. I'll get the stove lit and make us some eggs for supper. Then we'll read Annie's letter together."

"Don't want no supper."

She motioned to the letter she didn't seem to want to touch.

"You go on and read it 'fore I get up from here. It gots to be read sometime."

I lit the lamp and sat on the bed. As I tore the paper open Sister's eyes continued to chase the shadows from our movements over the ceiling.

"Dear Sisters, it's taken me a long time to write… You know how I need the preacher to put things into words that will help bring peace to things. Lord, rest his soul.'"

"Alex gone! He dead, ain't he?"

Sister's words stumbled as she reached to dab a tear. She didn't have to repeat them. I resumed reading as tears streamed down her stone-like face.

"Annie writes, '…week ago I was in town. Folks who knew Alex' wife Mary say they got word on your brother. He'd been traveling with a carnival roadshow for a long spell. But then they never heard no more. One of Mary's folks headed over to the next town when the carnival was camped there to find out what they could. They say, the carnival folks did, that Alex had taken off some time before. Said he needed to find better work closer to his family and couldn't be traveling from parish to parish. He went looking for work just outside of Vicksburg, but none was to be had. Some folks, the Klan, they thought, stopped Alex when he was on foot just outside of town. Him looking for farm work. Word got back these men told him he was for sure a vagrant and he gotta be put on roadwork or he'd sure work himself into trouble. Folks been saying maybe he was aiming to interfere with the white women who lived along them roads. Brother Alex, he say he ain't no vagrant and they ain't taking him in to work the ditches for no wages. So, he ran off. Took off across the fields. They say, the Klan put it out, that this colored boy gots to be guilty or he'd never run off like he done. So, they shot your brother. They shot Alex in the back. He's dead!'"

I couldn't go on as Sister and I were sobbing so.

Sister's throat finally released a few more words.

"I tol' you, didn't I?" Louvenia sobbed. "I tol' you he gone! Where they bury 'im? Annie say? We gots to go pay our respects."

I skipped over portions of the letter to find the end. But, truly there's never an end to something so unknown as to what were those last moments of a dying loved one.

"No, Sister. We can't go where they buried Brother. Annie writes she thinks they put Alex in a place gots no markers."

"I know what them white folks did. They buried 'im with criminals and poor folks got no name, didn't they? That what Annie mean?" Louvenia asked.

"Yes, Sister. That's probably what she means. He's buried where nobody but Jesus can find 'im now."

"Like our folks is buried up under them weeds in the Burney orchard?" Sister asked. "That kind of place?"

"And like Jeff rests under his flowers."

"You know they gonna bury us all in time." Louvenia wept. "The white folks is gonna bury us and then they gonna say they never knew us to know where we rested; rest where there ain't no white shadows crushing our backs no more!"

LITTLE ALICE

79

A FTER MY DAUGHTER'S long persuasion, I made the decision to live part of the time in New York City. It took her a while to convince me, but she was ever so right. It was good for business to live in this creative, cultural hub. I hired the architect Vertner Woodson Tandy to build a townhouse on Lennox in Harlem. No sooner were we situated than I opened another hair salon. It would be a place I could offer my products and my people could enjoy a few moments of luxury they'd witnessed only when cleaning up after white folks' whose moments of luxury were always stacked on our backs.

One bright morning I had a notion of walking to my salon and told Otho I wouldn't need him; that he should take the day off. I set out about ten o'clock looking forward to enjoying the warm sun and window-shopping along the way. This was the day I came upon Alice. I recall her as being so tiny that I couldn't decide at first if she was a woman or merely a child. She was pitifully thin, and her worn dress hung on her like a veil. All too well I know the silvery shine fabric takes on when it's been pounded on a washtub till you can nearly see through it. I'd worn that drab gray color for decades.

While her hair was badly mussed it hardly detracted from her soulful eyes. It was these eyes that captured me. I knew that lost gaze into nothingness; one devoured by hopelessness. I'd seen such empty stares in my own mirror and in the eyes of those I'd met along my years on the road. This child was standing there gazing into that shop window. She looked longingly at a certain dress with small bows and tiny pink buttons running down the front placket. Her eyes reached longingly to touch it. I decided that somehow this would not be the day this young woman surrendered to her despair. I tried to strike up a conversation.

"Good mornin'."

"What's you want? Huh? I ain't botherin' you none!"

She snarled and pulled back as though I might harm her.

"My, my, child. You don't have to step back from me. Do you have work?"

She pulled back further. It was the kind of reflex found in one who knew the staggering weight of being accused of vagrancy.

"Huh? Ain't none of your business," she snapped. "The kind of work you got, I got no need for! So scat!" she said.

"What kind of work do I have?"

She looked me over with disdain.

"Dressed up like that, you 'a whore. I seen it. It ain't no better than being dirt poor even if you dress like you're somebody special," she said. "You still ain't no better than me!"

"What's your name, child?" I asked.

"I ain't a child. I gots two kids."

"My name is Sarah. I got a daughter named Lelia."

"So what? We all got daughters to feed."

"I'm no whore, dear. Rest assured. I know you do what you must to keep your kids. You got a stubborn spirit; I can see it in you just standing here. Ain't there times when you feel like it needs to fly or it's gonna kill you? I know you do, 'cause I had it, too. You're a survivor. I can show you another way to get to the next day. I know I can."

"Where'd you get them clothes if you ain't no whore?" she demanded. "Your lady give 'em to you so she don't gots to pay ya?"

"I'm no maid and I don't work for no white woman. Work for myself now," I told her.

"If you really ain't no whore then how'd you get them things you got on? That's what I wanna know."

"Fine, then come with me. I'll show you something I believe you've never seen before."

"What's you wantin' from me anyhow?"

She looked shaken probably wondering what sleight-of-hand might put her deeper under the heels of the desperation that was already trampling her life.

"I know you don't need me, but I just might have a need for you."

"You needin' me, huh?"

She looked up the walk like I might have accomplices closing in.

"Well, you comin'? Or you afraid to walk down the street with another woman?" I asked.

"I ain't 'fraid of nothin'! Where's you headed then?"

"I got something going. Want to share it with you. If it's not to your liking, you can move on and keep your bad attitude and sad-lookin' hair all to yourself like you been doing to keep yourself safe. Ain't that right? You got nobody, do you?"

"Well, ain't you high 'n mighty with all that talk of yours?" she hissed.

"I'm no higher 'n mightier than you, dear. Are you comin' or you got your afternoon filled with engagements?"

"Filled with what you say?"

I sensed young Alice was a bit intrigued, so I motioned her to follow. I had to see how much courage was hidden behind her mask of toughness because I always believed certain strength was required in the struggle for a better life. Alice couldn't bring herself to walk alongside me. Perhaps she wasn't altogether sure I wasn't leading her into an ambush, so she followed behind a few paces. When I paused to gaze into a shop window, this young woman also did but kept me in the corner of her eye.

I knew this woman-child had seen many colored women coming and going from my place by the time we arrived; some nodding their heads or waving as I approached.

"This is my place. I welcome you as my guest."

"This here ain't no fancy whore house?" she asked.

"No whores or pimps in there."

I went up the steps and waited with the door open till Alice worked up enough courage to step forward; a first step to something new for her that was probably beyond any dream she'd ever permitted herself.

"What's your name, dear?" I asked.

"Alice, they calls me. I ain't never been a guest. What's you got in there?"

Dottie, my salon manager, must have heard as she greeted us. She was a big woman with a soft voice; the kind you would think would only come from a tiny delicate woman.

"Dottie, this is Alice. Can you fetch 'er a dressing gown?"

Alice looked about for something to jump out at her. Don't think any of the other customers noticed; they were enjoying having their hair done and chattering back and forth. I wondered if Alice had ever been in such a place filled with mirrors reflecting the light from my fancy gas-lit fixtures from Tiffany's.

"Yes, MadameWalker."

With Dottie's smile I could tell she'd read the situation. She never let her eyes leave Alice's to drift below and so capture a glance of her shabby dress.

"I ain't never been in a place like this here. Sort 'a like what heaven gotta be like, ain't it? All pretty and colored like flower petals is. This a place for coloreds?"

Alice's hard expression quickly withered to an innocent's stupefied wonderment. Like one that had gone to bed hungry but then had awakened to a magnificent banquet. Not one we the poor served at, but one where the poor were the honored guests.

"From what I've seen, everybody on God's earth is colored. Just a whole lot of different shades which sure gets some folks riled up, don't it? We're building hair salons like this around the country. For customers like you. Places where folks are treated with dignity. I want to show you how well we treat our guests."

I guided Alice into one of the chairs. Again, she pulled back.

"Oh, no! Not me. I gots no money," she declared ever so convincingly.

"I know dear. Go along with Dottie. You'll be fine with her."

But Alice's skepticism waxed high.

"What? You wantin' me to clean-up for you back there?"

"No. Miss Alice. I'm gonna show you how MadameWalker treats her guests," Dottie said as she assisted Alice into a guest smock.

"Dottie, some tea would be nice for MadameAlice and some cookies if we have some back there."

"You got sugar?" Alice asked.

"Yes, Miss," Dottie replied. "There's a silver bowl full of sugar cubes just waiting for you."

"Madame," I responded. "MadameAlice has two kids"

"MadameAlice, we got some warm shortbread back there. I'll send some out for you dear," Dottie said.

Alice's gentile smile is forever etched in my memories of that day.

I had to return to my office for a meeting with my architect but knew Dottie would provide one of the most memorable experiences of Alice's young life. One she could never have imagined she was destined for when she stood in front of that shop window.

As I walked back to my office, I recalled years earlier when my own sister paused to look in the window of a milliner's shop and gazed longingly at the hat with the beautiful feather bird. How that bird stirred her hidden dream of someday having something special like the big-hat women at church wore and how it lifted her spirits for weeks. I decided to do the same for Alice. I stepped into the dress shop where young Alice had stood gazing earlier that morning. It was where I'd purchased many fine things for Lelia and lovely blouses for Louvenia and me.

"That dress in the window. Need the smallest size, I 'magine. Send it over to my shop this afternoon wrapped in tissue. Put the name 'For MadameAlice, From MadameWalker' on the enclosure."

"Yes, MadameWalker. Put it on your account?" the saleslady asked.

"That'll be fine."

After lunch I decided to return to my shop with hopes that little Alice would still be there. There she stood appearing all but speechless. Dottie had arranged her hair becomingly and the dress I'd purchased fit fine. This child didn't seem to know what to do with herself; she tied her hands behind her back as shyness overtook her.

"Alice, honey, turn and show Madameyour fine hair and new dress," Dottie directed.

Alice turned a slow pirouette for us.

"See, I told you, dear." I said.

"It's not me, is it?" Alice whispered.

Where was the poor child who expected an altercation from me earlier? Never underestimate what an ounce of dignity can do to lighten the burdens of a weary traveler along her journey. Truly, I knew as I sold that ounce in tins all over the country.

"Sure, it's you. All we changed was the outside, but you can feel it all the way inside, can't you?"

I lifted her chin as another smile erupted on her sweet face.

"You made the outside look like my heart feels inside."

Her voice was gentle now like I'd not have believed could have come from this young woman.

"You see? Now you're ready to train to be a MadameC.J. Walker agent," I told her as I departed. She responded with only the biggest smile I'd seen that day.

I was only up the street a bit when I heard the pattering of feet. It was Alice but this time running towards me.

"Ma'am, you really want me to work for you?" she asked. "I been a whore. Nobody wants a whore."

"You believe in Jesus, child?"

"He ain't been 'round much from what I seen."

Her chin lowered by the shames of her past. A past she'd probably never had an invitation to step away from till that morning.

"More than you think. Open your eyes, child. Why else would He tell me to come walking your way and then pause to say good morning?"

"Don't know." she said.

"Every day and everyone is new again when we believe the Lord can bring salvation and peace to our lost souls. You're a child of God, the fruit of his blessed Orchard. Live like you believe it and bring others to his bounty when you come to sit at his table."

I don't remember any MadameC.J. Walker agent going through training faster than lovely Alice. She was so hungry for a new life that she couldn't learn fast enough. With just a mustard seed of faith, little Alice built herself a dream of a different life as an agent for my company.

Arriving At Lewaro

80

THERE WERE DAYS when I tried to step out of myself if only to
see where I was headed along this road that no other woman
of color had traveled. Yes, the very paths I'd charted for myself.
Still daily I felt their hate like the hot breath of the nigger dogs on my
back.

By now I'd been MadameC. J. Walker for over a decade yet many
mornings still woke up thinking I'd best jump to get the water heated for
the tubs. These things shadow us, you know; those never-ending tubs of
stinking laundry will always be piled up somewhere in the corners of my
thoughts and then, it seemed, even in the recesses of my dreams.

What they'd long been printing in the weeklies had become true;
when it was all added up, I'd become a wealthy woman. I'm told that
before me there'd never been a rich woman in this country who had not
inherited her wealth. I made my own way from the tubs to an attic and
a tin of something I mixed up that might offer an ounce of pride to my
people. Now my name and image were on thousands of such tins sold
around the country.

I think what drove me along this journey were the stories of those
I met. The folks who came to my demonstrations hungry to see, that
is, to see in me some glimmer of hope that might lift them over to the
next day. I was the one they'd heard about who had somehow found a

dream that didn't disappear at the end of that stone sleep for those who labor under the weight of their white shadows. For such a long time I wondered what I could leave behind that would be a lasting symbol of hope? Something to remind my people, as momma had once told me on Orchard Hill that we didn't have to hide our dreams from white folks deep in the threadbare pockets of our souls. This symbol for me was to be Lewaro.

I'd worked so hard and traveled to so many destinations that I hungered to slow down. The dream I'd once shared with Jeffrey of having an orchard to grow old near never wore thin over the miles I'd dragged it. From our days at the cabin, I still longed for that orchard of fruit trees where we would sit in the shade watching our grandchildren play as the fruit ripened into peach jam and cobblers. To his memory, I held on to this dream even if Jeff would never share in it. No, my anger for being deprived of the touch of his eyes has never quelled not even with the accumulation of wealth and acclaim that came my way. Don't 'magine it ever is for the women of those men broken in two by a noose. It was because of these passions that I'd determined that I would create an orchard for my husband's memory. A place to put to rest the unfulfilled dreams of two lives now mortgaged to no one.

Vertner Woodson Tandy was a young architect who had demonstrated enormous talent in a profession that seldom countenanced coloreds. My New York townhouse on One Hundred Thirty-Sixth Street he'd design became the envy of Harlem. Therefore, I again retained Mr. Tandy to design a new home for us, this time out of the city, a place to end my days. From those precious memories of my folks, I instructed him to locate a secluded property that overlooked a river. One that would have acreage enough for an orchard. Yes, I guess these were the seeds of my dream of Lewaro. It would be a mansion as no other colored in this nation had built—at least not for herself.

I expressed to Mr. Tandy specific ideas about the home. Like the New York townhouse, it simply had to be the finest. Mr. Tandy's scouting for suitable properties in upstate New York concluded in Westchester County, near the Vanderbilt country seat and close and yet ever so far in more than distance from the Tiffany and Rockefeller mansions. Only about twenty miles from New York City, the site was about four acres at Irvington-on-Hudson. I knew at first glance this property was ideal as it would provide me with the pleasure of gazing out my bedroom windows over the Hudson River to the hazy violet sky over the palisades beyond. This was very horizon beyond which I knew Jeffrey waited for me. There just on the other side of my final breath.

The day came when Mr. Tandy arrived at my office with a final set of drawings. Lelia was working with me when my secretary escorted him in. I'd not shared with my daughter my intentions for building at Irvington as I desired it to be a surprise.

"Mr. Tandy, I've waited longer than you could possibly imagine for this day."

That comment piqued Lelia's attention.

Tandy followed me into my inner office where he unrolled the drawings over a large table. Even at first glance, I knew it would be the most beautiful mansion I'd ever seen. Never in our deepest imaginings could Jeff and I have thought such a place would have been in the reach of any colored person, let alone ours. Living in a stable was not nearly as far behind me that I could not smell it. My thoughts threaded through Mr. Tandy's comments as he went over the floor plans and described what the views would be from the more than thirty rooms.

I could only wonder as he flipped through the drawings: how did I get to this day? How did I survive? Whoever once paused to calculate the odds for this American daughter of slaves?

Lelia embraced me.

"This is your greatest dream, isn't it?"

"Thirty rooms to hold thirty dreams," I agreed.

"A room for every year you worked the tubs." Lelia remarked.

I said no more on the drawings as I wanted to wait till it was all completed to share the actual experience with my daughter. It had to be on a special late-night visit to the orchard—just as Minerva and I shared our special moments on Orchard Hill. Then would be the time I'd recite the verses Momma gave me and pray Lelia's daddy would be ever close in spirit. Within four months of the day Mr. Tandy submitted his designs my home was well under construction and I was shopping at Tiffany's for interior appointments.

❧

Months of traveling dusty roads can suspend time but nonetheless it can't be held back entirely. While my home was being completed, I was back travelling through the south and east. These miles in the back of the Cole had left me depleted and weary; so many hours shaking hands and all so often facing long lines of those who'd given up on their dreams; was never offered a reason not to. Often on the road I wondered if I'd gazed up similarly at Margaret Washington when she was up on that stage as folks do me now. Weren't we all hungry for a chance at a dream? When our dreams are stolen they yet still leave marks on our souls, Jeffrey once told me, and every time we fall back to our hopelessness the scars are only etched deeper. I know those lingering glances at me along the journey were heavily marked by years of disappointment my people endured: forty acres, a mule and then absolutely nothing in hand. Truly, what is more absolute than nothing?

Our last trip back to New York City was particularly tiring and lonely for me.

"You gettin' weary, Madame?"

How many times over the years had Otho expressed his kind concern?

"I can pull over under them trees up ahead for a rest if you got a notion."

I was probably fine, but it was Otho who was really working to keep his eyes open.

"Yes, pull over Otho. Let's close our eyes a few moments," I suggested despite my eagerness to be home again.

There was much work to catch up on when we arrived back in New York: piles of sales reports to review, letters and notes from agents and customers to read and new products to dream up. The Indianapolis manufacturing facility was working two shifts to keep my army of agents supplied. Guess they numbered nearly twenty-thousand across the country, and as always, the calendar was heavily marked with the dates I would appear before different groups around the country. Even sitting at my desk looking at the stacks of mail tired me.

At long last the day; Otho would drive me up to Westchester County to see Lewaro. It had been nearly completed the week before, but I'd been too busy to make the trip. Or perhaps I was simply too afraid.

Lelia came into my room on the morning I'd planned on going to Irvington. She had a lovely breakfast tray to get my day started just right.

"Otho's already down there waiting for you," she announced. "I told him you wouldn't be coming down for an hour or so. Think he's as excited as you to be headed up to the new place."

"There's been so many crates shipped there."

"Have you determined a date for the housewarming?" she asked. "I read Mrs. Washington's note saying she was looking forward to it."

"No, not yet. Seems like there's always so much to do."

"Aunt Louvenia keeps saying you work too hard because you worry you may wake up to find it's all gone. That true, Momma?"

"Maybe that's really one of Sister's black dreams. You think?"

"You know, Momma, Aunt Louvenia's right. You've been looking tired lately."

"When we have everything settled, I'm going to take a nice rest," I told my daughter. "You know I will, too."

Even at that moment I wondered if that was likely to be true?

Lelia had offered to accompany me to Villa Lewaro later that morning but I needed to go alone the first time if only to calm the spirits that I knew were waiting.

Otho was patiently waiting at the Cole by the time I got downstairs.

It was a delightful sunny drive up to Irvington. Made me think of the day I married Jeffrey. I motioned for Otho to pause as he entered the drive. I wanted to gaze at the villa's majestic dignity perched on that knoll. Truly, Mr. Tandy had created a stunning place. When we had originally discussed the commission, he'd submitted several preliminary concepts with stately columns aligned along the front façade. However, I didn't want a home that evoked plantation houses seen along those White Camellia Roads of the South. Accordingly, he altered the design and created a semi-circle classical-style portico. There was never a southern mansion like mine. Mr. Tandy shared with me that only the Rockefeller and Vanderbilt mansions nearby were as magnificent. That was likely to have been an exaggeration, but I appreciated the intent all the same.

I decided on the drive up that I would enter for the first time through one of the side entrances as I wanted to delay using the front door till Lelia and Louvenia joined me. I directed Otho to drive me around to the *port-a-cochere* side entrance. He jumped out to escort me in.

"That's alright, Otho. You take a rest while I inspect the finished rooms."

"You don't think I best come with you, Ma'am? My hearin's not so good. May not hear you if you need me."

"I won't need a thing, Otho."

As Otho situated himself with his newspaper in the Cole, I pulled out the key I'd tenderly wrapped that morning in the old cloth I'd kept ever so long in Jeff's tobacco tin. The moment felt like a sacred rite.

Inside, the new parquet floors were polished to such a gleam that I saw myself staring back up. Who is she? That tub woman? Don't know why, but I couldn't help but look at my reflection off those floors as I progressed from room to room, all many times larger than my folks' shack. The face reflected back kept asking: You sure you belong here? Who are *you* to have a mansion? Ain't never been no colored woman ever had a fine place like this! No colored man, either. Nobody told you that? Is it really yours? Or are you just flying on a dream like you been known to do? These voices weighed heavily on my heart. Still I had no answer so I gazed up at the high ceilings to jar away the thoughts.

I walked into my grand foyer where the spirits waited in silence, yet

I could feel them all the same. I told myself it was only the rustle of a breeze working up, but I knew they'd be waiting; the spirits of my folks and their folks before them. Weren't we all waiting for a dream to come true for one of us; those nobodies gonna be the somebodies come one day as Momma promised?

"Sarah, you best go find some kindlin' for your ma to get a fire goin'!"

Daddy whispered so's not to disturb momma draped over their bed from exhaustion. But there was no flame for me to tend that day. Only a thousand sparkles scattered across the room from the chandelier high above. Doubt if my daddy had ever seen a crystal chandelier. Don't know where he would have. My folks, born in the same shack they died in never once put a foot inside the big house they labored for. How does one describe majestic to slaves that lived in a dirt floor shack? Crystal prisms cut like diamonds to scatter broken bits of light wherever your eyes take you. I turned in circles as I reached to grab a fistful of the glitter my chandelier scattered before me.

"Sarah, Ella's got 'bout a tin of sugar hidden away in the big house." Momma whispered through the din of my memories. "Come Sunday, we's gonna have us some peach jam from the fruit them pickers left behind!"

I ascended the stairs but paused to hold the handrail and count the many doors to the many rooms before me. These mahogany doors waited to be opened and would never be shut and barred to my people. With both hands I held on to the rail wondering what would happen if I turned to look down the stairs? Would every step that I'd climbed to get to this day drag me backwards? Would this country ever countenance a colored woman living in the sacred domain of its wealthiest white families? What would happen to us now that I'd dared to break their rules again?

In the beginning I'd kept the purchase of my property a secret. To avoid suspicion, Freeman retained a white woman to file the deed on my behalf. How could I not wonder if my duplicity would inspire white folks to burn us out on some starless night? Would they drag us out and lynch us? How many of my people saw their successes burned to ash?

And would the flame throwers be the same white folks who lined up to accuse us of being good-for-nothings? The Bella Burkes of the world that called us shiftless and lazy? So, what will this house say to these folks? But isn't that why I built it? A mansion for a Negro designed by a Negro and built with Negro money all to challenge the notions they lived by; that was always the path I trod along the journey to Lewaro even when I didn't know it.

I walked down the long hall to my room. I'd instructed Mr. Tandy to situate my bedchamber facing the palisades and have doors open to a sun-filled sleeping porch that I planned to spend hours watching the sunsets looking for Jeff's smile.

After long minutes staring over the river, I descended the stairs but did not hold tightly to the railing. Perhaps to remind myself that I did not have to hold anything down to keep what was truly mine. It would all be there waiting even after I stepped outside to see the gardens. I slipped off my beige satin pumps and dropped them with my purse at the edge of the stone terrace. I needed to feel the cool, moist soil clinging to my toes.

I guess that's when I heard him. He could always break through the darkness he dragged.

"Minerva!" the familiar voice screeched.

Yes, it was ol' Isaac seeping up from hell.

"You in my orchard 'gain?"

It's my orchard now, I told Burney's overseer. Mine and my family's. The sweat of our brows for a century has finally returned the bounty! Get on out there and clean up them weeds so you know what it feels like to be stooped over all day! Move along 'fore I run you off this place! I told this nigger dog. Momma, how long had I held those words? Now I don't hold my tongue!

I walked deeper into the shadows where just as you told me, Momma, the tree branches arch over me like angels' wings. Gonna hide and protect us in the Lord's orchard. That's when I noticed him standing over there as if he'd been waiting all along—his smile could still find me even in all my darkness. I shivered in fear. Oh, Lord, Lord! I shouted.

Was it fair of you to leave me all alone only to keep coming back in my dreams? Didn't I promise you, Jeffrey McWilliams that I'd never leave you? I still dream of you after all these years… every twist and turn of the road… your tender lips smile back.

The wind blew leaves over my bare feet as I walked deeper into our orchard as he walked away backwards; always out of reach, even in my swollen dreams. But my rage followed into the depths of the very darkness of those moments. There was a stick, only a broken branch, and I grabbed it. As they stood there glaring at me, a poor and defenseless woman with a child, I took it and beat them, beat them as hard as I could. I'll kill you! I will kill you for murdering my baby's father! With all my might, I thrashed the trunk of that tree. But they were all gone before the first swing, those men who lynched my husband. Even the memory of their faces was now buried under recollections of those thousands of faces along the journey that were filled with white hatred.

I pulled out my old cloth and wiped my clouded eyes.

"You lookin' for me? Heard your voice callin'."

"You're here?" I asked.

"Of course, I's here. Here waitin'…"

But where was he? Back hiding in my dreams?

"What do you want from me?" I asked.

"I's over here waitin' to take ya home."

"Where?"

"Over this way, Ma'am. Got your shoes here. Don't look like you're seein' good today?"

"It's dark."

"Just under them trees where you's standin' is all. Come on out. I think I best get you home now," Otho said.

"This yours, Ma'am? This here piece of cloth. Got a big blue 'B' stitched right in the middle there pretty as you please. What's that 'B' for? How long you had it? Sure looks old."

"Ever since the day I became a motherless child."

I took the cloth that I'd brought my key in and placed it on a lowest branch of the nearest fruit tree.

"Why'd you do that, Ma'am? Can I ask?"

"That cloth with the Burney monogram, Jeff will know that I'd arrived. Arrived at his orchard where I will wait."

"Yes, Ma'am. That cloth's gonna remind 'im?"

"Remind us of what my momma told me," I answered.

"What's that, Ma'am?"

"'The nobodies gonna be the somebodies come one day. Otho…'"

"Yes, Ma'am. I's right here."

"I can't see you."

"No, guess 'cause that sun blindin' ya, ain't it? We best head for home. Take my arm now. We'll be on our way back. Your Cole is waitin'."

"I know……. he's always waiting…"

The Great Woman
Who Became Me

81

M Y SUMMER TOUR of 1916 had been very long and hot—a sticky heat like only the South delivers. Every day I faced the kind of humidity that sucks the air out of you even as you're running for the shade that always seems to be out of reach like everything else.

I'd noticed Sister had grown increasingly quiet. Over our days on the road we'd passed through frightening lands—lands where our brother had disappeared somewhere and then again in those pitiful scenarios our minds so easily conjured.

But how vulnerable could we be? Let me tell you, we had already committed the offense of traveling in a grand touring motor through parishes where plantation mansions were still painted white by the coloreds who had never truly escaped simply because there was no place to escape to. We were guilty when we crossed these county borders and could never have known where they hid under their white sheets. It only took one lynching rope to shatter an entire family and down there ropes were never in short supply even as everything else was for us. Therefore, I reckoned it would be best to send Louvenia back home on the train as I knew it would make her less vulnerable to her ghosts. It wasn't easy persuading her that the long drive back would be too exhausting. She asked repeatedly how long till Otho and I would be headed home again?

I touched her cheek. "Sister, we'll make it back home soon, I promise."

There was never a time when our parting wasn't hard. I wanted to reassure Louvenia that the lands that I would soon journey through would never reclaim me; bring me to my knees again. Still I could not say it. At the train station Sister sat in the motor as if she simply couldn't get out to face one more mile. Otho fiddled with her luggage, wiping the dust off to give her time to linger but those moments evaporated like the sweat on my forehead. Sister clung to me as we walked toward the train. Her eyes were as sorrowful as the day my baby and I left her behind at Jeff's cabin. Matilda cried and pulled Louvenia from my embrace, tugging her to the train as the whistle screeched a shrill warning as if announcing that Satan had just escaped from hell. Sister kept tight hold of my hand taking me with her to the edge of the platform. It was as though she was determined to convey me safely home as well. How many times had we saved each other by then? Again, I promised Louvenia I would return soon, real soon! However, she knew these kinds of promises were only air passing over our lips. This farewell had a different meaning because I knew if I didn't make it back home, I would have proved Sister's ultimate fears were dead right. We'd never really crossed over to a better life; it was all just a black dream. I bit my quivering lip as the train steamed off. Matilda waved sorrowfully out the window. My sister didn't wave. She gazed back at me motionless as I disappeared from her sight.

As I watched the train fade from view I heard the white folk's chit-chat turn to snarls. Their comments were littered with broken slurs that splattered against my back; the back that I'd turned to them. I wondered if Louvenia sensed the tension stirring on that platform as she stepped onboard. Surely, she noticed the gawking white folks out her window as I waved them off. Why, you wonder, were these folks so bothered by me? Simply because I'd committed the offense of daring to dress as fine as any white woman and not cowering to the sidelines, head bowed, like a well-humbled maid or tub woman. No, they expected me to step aside to their static glances and keep my eyes on the ground as they passed so's not to offend their notion of my place.

I walked back to my motor ignoring their glares as they nipped at my heels like packs of nigger dogs that I knew they were meant to move me along to that place they referred to as our side of town. Their rage was palpable but no worse than the time before or the ones I'd face ahead.

Otho's hands fidgeted nervously on the steering wheel as I situated myself on the rear seat to hold mine steady. This day had started like so many others; like so many in our lives period. That night I wrestled with my dreams to steal some sleep but never won. No, they were always trailing us—those dreams of having seen your loved ones for the last time.

How far behind us could the nigger dogs be? How fast can I run this time? Lord, how I knew there would come a time when there'd simply be no run left in me.

On the drive down that dusty country road, I pondered my journey, this long road I've traveled that began in a shack on the Mississippi River. For decades I wondered if I'd ever escape the tubs; now there were days when it was my very success that seemed to trip me.

Lelia and Freeman had been sending telegrams reporting daily affairs in my office. They knew my route and sent coded reports ahead to the churches awaiting my visits. Everything was fine, orders multiplying every quarter. The number of sales agents—and customers—had been growing in virtually every state, particularly in the Midwest and the East. There was no reason for me not to be at peace, yet I was not. There would always struggles ahead and alas, the unfinished ones that yet followed me.

The first thing I noticed as Otho pulled up to the tiny clapboard church were the stacked brick piers that served as its foundation had sunk unevenly in that swampy soil. I figured the congregation had probably built on land that nobody wanted; far enough out of town where white folks wouldn't harass them. Like so many of the churches that had invited me for a visit, this parish was so small it couldn't afford a full-time preacher.

It was a preacher from another church along with his young wife who came late in the morning. His wife taught reading after services. Even at that, this poor man still had to work a few acres farming to feed his family. The Sunday of my visit, the preacher brought a bushel of freshly picked corn and his wife greeted me with a bag of green beans for the journey home. City folks, she said, never have enough food fresh off the farm. Didn't know if it'd keep till we got back but knew I could give it to somebody along the way; there was never a shortage of empty stomachs in those parts. Everywhere I went I witnessed hunger leaving many sinking unevenly under the weight of their days.

After the services, I set up my products on a table at the rear of the church. There was no big barbecue on this stop as folks were so poor there was nothing to roast but the preacher's gift of corn. As the old women husked the corn young girls twisted and knotted the husks into dolls. Then the rain started coming down in sheets. I could hear it pounding on the tin roof above my table. Despite the downpour, the men managed to get a smoky fire going out back under the over-hang where they roasted the corn. An old granny heated tins of freshly churned butter she'd brought to bathe it in as little ones rustled under my display table hiding from their mothers. Not seeming to mind the rain, I saw the old men chatting with Otho out by my motor. They held old newspapers over their heads. Those weeklies folks brought to church to pass along any news to those too far out there to get any. As soon as I'd finished my demonstration big plates of buttered corn-on-the-cob were passed around. My visit was a special thing, one elderly woman told me with a look of pride. I was to them a great woman, she said. But, Lord, how can I say it? To myself I was yet a tub woman that had merely survived. All the same I knew what the odds were.

I was chatting with folks when a woman worked her way over to me. During my demonstration, I'd noticed her gazing at me from the back. She looked at me as if the world I came from was as remote to her as the moon. Perhaps it was my fine traveling suit. Yes, there was some dignity in my life and no colored woman had ever heard of this before. Folks wanted to see my different life and so looked me over closer than my products. They knew I was sincere, but they'd undoubtedly waded through too many layers of lies and false promises that they knew could cut away the dreams. I wondered whether I would sign up any agents that day as I could feel their skepticism—their doubts that in working for my company their lives could somehow be better. Perhaps, the next visit, I kept thinking, I will win more over. The woman worked up enough courage to step forward to chat.

"How's it feel bein' back here where you come from, Madame Walker?"

She wrung her hands as if she was shamed I'd see how crusty and calloused they were. Or perhaps like Louvenia did when she was scared. I seen calluses like hers. Right here on my own hands. I grasped her hand to shake—held it in both of mine so she'd know we belonged. I easily felt that she longed to know if I recognized her struggle somewhere in the depths of my own. At the moment our hands clasped there was no distance separating our humanity. This poor woman embraced by me, the first colored woman she'd ever met who was not poor. Yes, I was to these women and so many thousands more that great woman who visited. I answered her question.

"Scares me being here. I still see the exhaustion pullin' my folks down—down till finally they couldn't get up no more."

Her eyes widened like she'd just heard the voice of an old friend who'd heard her story before and wanted to again. Yes, those eyes softened like I'd succored her soul by knowing I'd not forgotten her world simply because I'd crawled on to another.

"No, I never stop hearin' the stiff moans of my folks from somewhere in their stone sleep," I said. "The smell of that life livin' like farm animals, it's still in my nostrils."

"You's the only colored woman ever got away, I reckon. That's what folks say; you the only one who got herself out of the tubs and cotton fields. But you know, our men, they hang 'em from the trees 'round here. At night, when I goes home past the swamps," she said, "I know I can hear a man cryin' out there somewhere. I know I can! Cryin' for mercy.

Even he done been cut down and put in the earth I still hear 'im. Maybe it's gonna be my man I hears one day. That's what I dream. Then sometimes when I's walk through the shacks late, I hear womens with hungry chil'ren gots no man, no hope and no place to go lookin' for none," she said as her glance collapsed to her feet. She reached to touch me putting her hand on my arm. "And I don't know if my chil'ren gonna hear their ma wailing someday, too. Lordy, tell me they ain't!"

What could I say?

"Not a day goes by I don't pay my loneliness a tear or two, Sister," I replied. How could mere words salve her fears? She had to know I had a full stomach and money for food to put on tomorrow's table. Alas, even my table may have been larger than her shack.

I put my arm around this woman who could have easily been me standing there, and Lord, why wasn't it? I felt her pull back at my touch; that reflex to avoid someone from feeling how worn and thin your dress is, or from knowing how long it's been since you had soap for a good bath and the shame you feel for it. If only I could, I prayed, ease her fear and shame even if only to provide a moment's reprieve. Like a few moments when she didn't worry about feeding her kids perhaps 'cause their stomachs just couldn't hold no more. Fear is so much more stringent when there's no place to hide it and it's only the surrender you still face. Your mantra becomes, ain't nothin' left for me. Ain't nothin' to go on for. Lord, I prayed, give this poor woman a reason not to surrender.

Otho startled me when he approached. I knew by his expression that something was wrong and thought it had to be Sister and Matilda not getting back safely. I was sure of it as I'd awakened the night before dreaming of that man that got thrown off a moving train because he dared to walk through the white section. Otho handed me a telegram. I felt my stomach gulp as if I'd swallowed it.

"It's a telegram. Don't open it!" the woman urged. "Maybe somebody's dead!"

Folks closed in to hear the bad news.

"They'll still be dead if I open it, dear."

My heart stumbled a few beats as I read on and then slipped it into my pocket.

"Otho, bring the Cole 'round."

"See, I tol' ya. Somebody's up and died on ya! Happens all the time, don't it?"

Her words were meant to return my sisterly understanding. I knew she figured everything in her life had to be preordained and that she was as defenseless from these forces that imposed boundaries on our lives as the nigger dogs that dragged us back under their fences where they would never let us leave. I can understand that to the marrow. How many decades was I bent over a tub stinking of the same notions? Happens all the time? Her words looped my thoughts like the tune of an organ grinder. I can still hear them in my dreams. I breathed deeply to settle my jarred composure.

Otho had the motor waiting by the time I'd packed the products. I offered this kind woman my samples as a small gesture that, I at least, had faith in her. Never knew her name, though I'd seen her face reflected off a thousand similar stories along my journey; stories of midnight walks through frightening swamps and the wailing cries for mercy from the soon to be lynched. I suggested she sell the Madame Walker products I'd brought and use the money for her family. Then if she took to all that selling, she should get a letter to me about being one of my agents. She grabbed my hand and kissed it as if I were a prince. Her tear-filled eyes were the last thing I saw as Otho drove off. In her hand, waving farewell was a tin of my product. I prayed that small tin might feed her hopes and get her to the next day. You see, that was my journey by then; scattering bits and pieces of hope from tiny tins.

As I drove off that day it was what faced me around the next bend that I now feared the most.

Returning Views

82

S OME THINGS—PERHAPS MOST things—never really change in the South. Life simply moves along like pebbles skipping over a dark pond; circles of water spread in concentric circles really aiming to go nowhere. Here the saltry Southern days follow one another, only undulating off the calendars like all the yesterdays. Still I wondered how it could possibly be the same? I held that telegram bracing for what I might find as we headed down that drive sheltered by oaks. These moments were as bittersweet as any along my journey.

He was waiting for me between those old columns that guarded his door. Standing there alone where I'd left him more than forty years before. His dark blond hair was the same honey-color as his ma's. Jackson grew to be taller than his daddy. Strangely, in my dreams he'd remained the child with summer white hair whom I played with for a few summers. It was under the Burney veranda to escape the heat; the heat of his ma's glare.

"You got my telegram."

Jackson Burney descended the steps of his mansion to greet me.

"You came back. Couldn't imagine why you ever would but glad of it none-the-less."

Strangely, as I once again put my foot down on Burney lands my first thoughts were that his great mansion was no longer white. Not the remembered white as the clouds I knew floated up there to keep the big house cleansed and cool. Now everything looked to be touched by the gray shades of gloom.

"Never thought I'd return and see your face again, Jackson Burney."

He kissed my hand. Don't 'member if a white man ever had before. Guess not. I found myself still easily drawn to his warm smile.

I 'member it was so strangely quiet that afternoon—like that floating silence before a storm. Grandview was not the bustling place it once had been. But then the help was all gone—worked to death; their ashes scattered to the winds. No, there was no longer anything grand about the place. Perhaps there never really was except to a 'cropper's child who'd never seen anything as magnificent as those now crumbling columns.

Jackson offered his arm to lead me into his home; that big white house where we 'croppers shared our imaginings of the happenings inside.

Jackson sensed my apprehension as we walked through his foyer. Didn't he even as a child? The drawing room seemed strangely dark for that time of day and left me wondering why the heavy maroon-colored drapes were still drawn.

Perhaps only to hide those few secrets the camellia class still owned.

"I was never once inside your home, was I?"

I found myself looking about, perhaps half expecting petals of gardenias to lilt from the chandeliers or wherever Ella imagined they came from. Born from the sparkles of crystals she once whispered.

"Sparkles… See 'em in your mind, chil'e, dancin' over the walls when the candles are lit. Magic makes all them different colors and if you catch a sparkle dancin' on the wall then all your dreams gonna come true one day. See if it ain't so!"

And I did and it was.

"I guess we were mostly under the veranda hidin' from Ella," Jackson reminded me. "Now you're rich enough to buy the whole damned plantation! I read the papers to Ella. Even read you live right near the Rockefellers' in the biggest mansion in New York. That true?"

"Don't know, Jackson. Never been in a mansion but my own."

He offered his arm to escort me.

"Come; let's step out of this musty old place and into the garden."

The smell of magnolia blossoms followed the breeze and reminded me of Ella cutting a big white flower for Minerva to keep in a jar on our table. I remembered momma grabbing eyefuls of that bloom as she went about our supper. It was the only thing of beauty in our shack. It was the only thing even close to white.

On the veranda I realized I'd never known the view from on high but only that of looking up from the dirt. Never thought how we must have looked down there, dirty, as we waited to attend or were we simply waiting for their scrap?. Behind me I could see all the way down the path to the 'croppers quarters close to the river's edge. Those shacks were nearer to the big house than I'd remembered as a child. Perhaps because there was no longer a freshly sheared lawn marking the boundaries of my world. A lawn we knew to never cross without an invitation. At that moment it was easy to wonder if the boundaries that defined our lives had truly fallen off as easily as the toss of a pebble. Yet how many of my people had drowned in those very ripples over the century the Burneys owned Grandview? Then why, I wondered, had it all turned out so differently for me?

"Nothing's the same now, is it?"

Jackson's pastel brown eyes darkened as he looked out over his lands like the view was as startling to him as it was now to me. His lost boy look was jarring. A pallor had set in on my friend's world.

"Looks different but inside feels all the same," I replied.

Some feelings don't fade away like white paint on a veranda or the green of what was once a mansion's fine lawn now gone to weedy pasture.

"Guess you're right. It's all 'bout the same. Sure it is! You know the South; we don't take to change readily. I 'magine 'cause we don't figure it's takin' us to a place we'd wanna go. Makes it easier to slow the days. Don't we like our lives frozen thick with tradition?" he commented. "Predictable, like a good julep. But things a lot different for you. Ain't it so?"

What could I say?

But I tried anyway.

"I had further to go and no place to go back to."

As I went down the splintered steps towards Miss Burney's garden I caught my foot on a vine of dead jasmine intertwining the lattice where Ella had once twisted off pieces for Miss Burney's hair. Made me think that this place would forever try to trip me to my face even without Jackson's ma's backhanding me there first.

We ambled down to the shacks.

"Guess I don't go down these paths no more. Got no friends down there, do I?"

His smile reminded me that the ultimate distances in our stories hadn't diluted our friendship.

"No, these paths through momma's rose garden most assuredly will lead me back to where I don't care to know again. How 'bout you? Does the past offend your senses?"

There could be no answer that wouldn't twist the moment between us.

Our voices fell silent as we sauntered through the 'croppers' shacks, but my thoughts still yammered along asking why I'd returned. Because of Jackson's telegram, or to see if my view of the past was better from the distance of time? Yet my recollections were getting mired in the whispers working their way up between the shadows of those shacks. These tortured memories of Owen, Minerva, Alex and Louvenia Breedlove, ol' Clare, Jane and Samuel.

I looked up to Orchard Hill as we walked. It was eerily silent up there except for the rustle of dry leaves blowing over parched earth and the screeches of the squawky grackles. Or were those the shrieks of ol' Isaac? Him growling his hatred from that hell his sins had relinquished him to? Maybe the only thing not faded from the years was that ol' man's blistering hatred.

"Minerva! You up in my orchard 'gain?" Isaac bellowed from hell.

I looked at Jackson to reassure myself that mean ol' man was not around. Jackson nodded and we walked on.

"Put your mind to rest."

I still could rely on him to vanquish that devil.

"The ghosts, they've all gone now," he said.

Surely, he was right but how real could they be? The splintered shacks we approached quickly pulled on my thoughts.

"They're not called slave quarters any longer?" I asked.

His tendered smile was pained. I began to understand that Jackson too was haunted by these lands. Hadn't he made himself a slave to them and his southern traditions? But who was left to tell this man that unlike the rest of us he'd always had the keys to the gilded gates of his own prison?

"The whole damned place is a slave quarter. Now I'm the only slave left; slave to my dilapidated house sinkin' in this clay soil from the weight of all my daddy's sins. You can see for yourself, can't you? Everything you escaped still holds on to me."

He winked and a cautious smile appeared on his lips where it froze. Jackson was always at ease with our differences even as they'd shifted as nobody could have predicted. Nobody but my momma who reminded her children that the somebodies gonna be the nobodies and the nobodies gonna be the somebodies come one day. Here, I, a child of slaves, stood there by invitation of this prince of the camellia class as he described my mansion.

Who could have told this story?

With thoughts of Minerva echoing between them shacks, I began reciting the verses she'd taught me on this profane soil.

"Days are comin' when all that is in your house and that which your ancestors have stored up till this day shall be carried to Babylon and nothin' shall be left, says the Lord."

"Still keepin' the verses?" he asked.

"They helped me through some dark days."

Strangely, it then hit me for the first time.

"Jackson, my momma taught me the verses but she never knew how to read. Who taught them to her?"

"Why, Ella, of course."

His mischievous grin took me back to our childhood.

"Ella, I think of her often."

From somewhere in the recesses came my momma's voice again.

"Sarah, get on in now. Yer daddy's waitin' on us."

I looked about to see shack doors hanging on their hinges. Where had all the souls disappeared to? Were these doors swinging open because their return was expected? A return to the misery of sharecropping because what the white folks had warned was real; there truly was nothing waiting for us beyond Burney lands? So, if you know what's best for you, tuck in your dreams and swallow another day of misery.

"There's no one waiting here, is there?"

Suddenly I realized I was standing in front of my folks' place. Unlike the other shacks the old splintered door was closed. I was never expected to return. No, I was expected to perish in a breath of air lost between two tubs.

"I know that door! This is where I was born, isn't it? Where Jesus came for my folks."

Jackson nodded and stood back so the spirits could look me over.

Yes, I had returned, and the view was so very different, wasn't it?

"I got to be alone here for a few moments, my friend."

"Take your time. It's the only thing we got plenty of 'round here."

Jackson drifted on up the path alone.

It seemed to take many moments to collect my thoughts and decide if I could even pass through that threshold again. That door had never belonged to me yet was suddenly the door to my very soul. Why was I frightened? Scared that ol' Isaac would come pounding on it again? What moans and sighs had those walls heard before? Would they ask where I'd been all this time? Had I really escaped the shadows of Grandview? If I had, then why was I standing again in the very dust their whispers had stirred?

Oh, leave me be, I pleaded against my recollections.

I pushed the door open and like a blast from a furnace came the cries, whispers and then the moans of the souls awaiting word on my escape from these lands. Out of the corner of my eye, lying there on that table, I could still see my folks all shrouded in Burney sheets. But, no, they aren't really here for me, are they? They've disappeared under the soil somewhere hidden beyond the weeds up on Orchard Hill where no overseer could harass, and the shadows of drudgery had been finally severed from their worn heels.

The floor in the shack was covered in dirt still my vision floated back forty years to see the swatches of cutout clothes lying there like snow-white magnolia petals chopped from the Burney sheets. The arrogance of the dark blue silk Burney monogram hissed of the white camellia class that indulged in the finery they squeezed from our misery.

I bent over to grab one of the cloths but only caught a pinch of dirt in my fingers.

They were still long gone. Nothing but pinch of memory mixed with the dirt had remained for me. Yet their voices still reached to claim me.

"Owen dead! Don't separate my kids!"

Momma's moans echoed from the dirt of the floor where she'd laid at Burney's feet begging for her children with her last breath.

The window was still curtained with Momma's tattered apron. Don't know why, but I was compelled to pull it down for the final time. It crumbled like a dry leaf as I tried to fit the strings around my wrist where Momma had tied it to the bedpost while she worked the fields to feed the big house first.

I reached into my bag, pulled out a cloth and dabbed at my tears. To honor my folks, I would hide my fears. I left to join my friend.

Jackson was waiting for me up there eating a peach. He leaned against a railed fence that no longer separated anything and handed me one. I took a small bite so I didn't have to speak for a few moments. We walked in silence back to the big house. How could Minerva have envisaged the son of her oppressors offering me, his invited guest, a peach from the orchard she so loved?

I wrapped the pit in my cloth and tucked it in my purse with thoughts of Jeffrey and his gift of peach pits from which he'd served his dream of our own orchard.

Again, we entered through the front door of the mansion. In a hundred years, no colored person had passed that threshold as guest. As I entered the drawing room a cold gust of air swept the room and tinkled the crystal chandeliers.

It left me frozen as if I was once again in the presence of Jackson's ma.

"I can feel your momma's presence. She knows I'm here."

"She comes to see if everything's the same at Grandview. But I pay her no mind."

"You never did…"

"Look out there. I see somebody comin' down my drive with my excellent tatas. If it pleases you, go on upstairs, room at the end of the hall. There's gonna be somebody up there wantin' to see you."

It was the sound of Jackson's riding boots crossing the polished pecan floors that made me wonder if he'd endeavored anything beyond the slowing of time in his familiar world where he'd stopped all the clocks anyway. Perhaps nothing more than whipping up the gleam on his English riding boots so like his daddy's.

I went up the stairs for the first time trying to imagine white clouds wafting through the rooms to cleanse them of field dust we worked up to assure their white camellia lives were always well stocked and bounti-ful. Those rooms were cool and shaded, just like that veranda. But what was still crisp and white anymore? Glimmers of light revealed dusty old portraits of Jackson's family. Robert Burney and Melinda were up there, alongside a painting of his grandma with her maid at her feet; a colored woman gazing up in bewilderment at that woman's haughty face like a jester humbles herself at the feet of her sovereign. These works were now all fuscous and veiled in dust; their once gilded frames gone rusty brown.

When I reached the end of the hall, I opened the door.

There she lay in bed patting at the comforter to get it all arranged nicely for a visitor. Her drapes where pulled open. Enough cloudy light filtered through to reveal her face.

"Ella? It's me, Sarah."

"Come closer. Knowed ya come back someday. Jackson knew, too. Yes, we knowed ya be a great lady. Sure! You got Minerva's guts."

Ella motioned me to draw near.

"No, Ella; same ol' Sarah. You been here your whole life. Are you happy?"

"Ain't no reason not to be at my age. Not worth the time bein' unhappy. It's all near done now, chil'e."

Ella reached to pat my hand like I was still a child.

"Jackson takes good care of me. Just like I took care of him when he'a baby." Her smile revealed her deep affection for Jackson. "'Course I still gotta take care of him. He can't help being a Southern boy, now can he?"

"Miss Ella, you taught Momma the Bible verses, but who taught you, Ma'am?"

"Why, Jackson did. If'en ol' Miss Burney ever caught that chi'le teachin' a nigger woman to read, oh, Lord she'd whopped his hinny!"

"Now, Miss Ella! When did Jackson ever get whopped?"

"Whenever I thought he needed it and I tell you plain, he needed it plenty! Jackson's more my kid than Miss Burney's. You know she never had a feelin' for her own. Never 'member that woman lookin' that boy in the eye even when she was talkin' at 'im. She thought motherin' was keepin' him dressed up like a doll. Just like her, not meant for nothin' real. Just a decoration for this here plantation."

Ella reached over to whisper.

"ol' Miss Burney's in hell now and didn't I pack her bags for the trip? Hallelujah for answerin' my prayers, Lord. Yes, ma'am. Had enough of her big mouth chasin' after me all day. Came in this room one mornin', her layin' here on this bed ringin' that damned bell of hers and I's pulled the sheet up over her sour face. Oh, I did, too! She went to hollering at me somethin' fierce like she done got the bed bugs on her. Twitchin' and jabbin' her boney ol' finger at my face again.

"'You nigger, I ain't dead yet!' she hollered. But I tol' her, 'Yes'um, but you gonna be by the time I finish with my supper. So, get on with it 'cause I's movin' my things in come mornin'! Done waited long enough!'

I sat here on 'er bed and went to bouncin' the mattress and tol' her, 'Got to put me a board under this here bed 'cause it's too damned soft for me af'er sleepin' on yer floor so many years. Did I ever tell ya, Miss Burney, how many year I been sleepin' on yer floor? Guess not, I been too busy scrubbing 'em to complain much the last seventy summers, ain't I? You still there, Miss Burney? Don't want to keep ya!'"

That woman, she grunted and twisted to get at me one last time.

'Nigger! Get off my bed or Isaac gonna cut yer back open with a whip I give 'im!' That's what that Christian woman said 'fore she went to hell. But I asked her 'fore she did if she could hear 'im. 'Hear that?' I asked. 'Isaac's callin' ya, Ma'am.'

"'Huh? Where's he?' she clamored with the sheet still half up on her face and all."

"'Oh, I reckon he's waitin' in hell for ya.' I said real nice, too. 'I'll rip the skin off ya,' she said back."

"I tol' her I ain't got none left fer you to scratch at. 'Cause you been peelin' the skin off my back since the day Mas'er Burney sold off my mammy. I 'member that day! I sure do! Even 'member my lil' sister getting ripped away from mammy. I ain't never seen 'er 'gain. Anyway, you'd have to get up outta this here bed and you ain't never liked gettin' out of bed even when ya could. Now, Miss Burney, any of that stuff on yer dressin' table you plannin' to take with ya?'

"That ol' woman went to slappin' at me till she croaked. Yep, doctor say she had herself a heart attack. But how can that be? She aint got no heart. Yes'um, she got worked up real good. Ain't nothin' new 'bout that. But, Lordy, wasn't it just her big mouth the only thing that worked on 'er the last twenty years I toted her bed pan? Can't even count how many bedpans she weared out. Well, now's she's in hell where she belongs! Ain't it so? But since I's a Christian woman, I's hope it's no worse than the hell that woman put on me. But 'cause I ain't a good Christian, I's sure hope it ain't no better, too."

"Oh, that would surely delight Miss Burney, you takin' over her room and puttin' your things out on her dressin' table and all," I said.

Ella smiled wickedly as if her rebuke of Miss Burney brought her pleasure. Well, there are different kinds of justice.

About then Jackson returned but Ella was already fatigued. I wondered if down deep she still struggled against Miss Burney's misdeeds. How could she not? Them things follow you like a shadow all your days.

"Are you up here talkin' 'bout Momma?" he asked Ella.

"I been tellin' Sarah 'bout Samuel down there who brung your tatas 'cause you can't grow nothin' yourself, ain't that right, Sarah? 'Fore Sarah leaves for good…"

"Now you know I ain't forgotten, Ella."

He winked. They still talked between the words. I wondered what their secret was.

"Come here close, chil'e." Ella motioned me for a hug and then whispered loudly in my ear. "You know how proud we's of you. You're an angel of hope for us."

She grabbed my hand like she wanted to hold me from leaving.

"Guess you best go for now. I needs my rest."

Ella averted her teary eyes and released my hand and fell back on her pillows.

"Come, Sarah. Ella, I'll bring your supper up later."

She could share no more and waved us on. I left Ella's room thinking what a good friend momma had in her and what tales they could have pawned off on each other in their old age.

Jackson escorted me downstairs. The winds had kicked up and were knocking at the loosened shutters used to keep the scorching sun out of the rooms, or maybe to keep the spirits that haunted the place from escaping with their own stories.

But then was it really me who needed to escape?

"'There'll be a good rain for sure tonight," he said.

Otho had the Cole pulled up to the entrance but Jackson led me in another direction.

"Where're you leading me?" I asked.

"Promised Ella I'd show you her special place."

His voice dropped to a whisper as though we were sitting on a pew at church.

"She never thought she'd still be 'round for you to see it. It's a blessin' to her that you returned to Grandview." And then he added, "And to me as well, Sarah Breedlove."

"You're taking me up to Orchard Hill, aren't you?"

"Don't be afraid. ol' Isaac's long gone. But I bet he's still workin' for Momma down in hell. You suppose?"

I never doubted Miss Burney and ol' Isaac were in league.

"They did have an understanding."

"Yeah, Ella reminded you of that just as I thought," he said. "Yes, Ma'am, Ella sure has herself a pile of secrets on Isaac. Maybe she's gonna tell Jesus the whole story on that ol' man one day! You think?"

"Tell the Lord 'bout Isaac?" I asked.

"She just might tell it all…one day, God help 'em!"

We walked the path to the clearing at the top of the Orchard Hill. Tiny droplets of rain, the size of tears, ran down my face. My vision was completely blurred by the time Jackson paused on the hill high enough that no fog shrouded our ankles. His strange expression looked to me as if he had something to confess, but no words followed. None were needed as I could then see for myself. There at my feet were two simple black stone markers chiseled with my folks' names.

"Ella did this? She marked my parents' graves?"

"She counted Minerva as her truest friend. Did it with her own money after Momma died. Earned it all selling peach jam to the plantation folks and me."

Then Jackson pointed a few feet beyond. There were two more headstones. One had Jackson's daddy's name, the other his ma's.

"You buried your kin next to colored folk?

Jackson smiled as I bent over and put my hands on my parents' headstones.

Finally, I think I understood why my life's journey had detoured me to these Burney lands. There was a feeling of peace that came over me. I now understood this was the view I was meant to return to.

There was nothing else to say so we returned to the big house in silence.

Otho had the motor running. The rain was falling hard when he jumped out with the umbrella. Jackson and I bid farewell. Otho had probably never seen a colored woman and a white man embracing as equals. Such could never happen in the South. I looked about for the last time.

"It all looks different, doesn't it?"

"Don't ever let your dream go. Hold on no matter what folks say," he admonished.

Jackson's eyes were sad as though he too had a secret, one that had stalked him from the depths of his own shadows all these years. With that, I wondered if his own dreams had rippled across the surface of his life, spread to nowhere and then disappeared forgotten under the gray watery-like surface of recollections and marred memories of his past days.

"Farewell, Jackson Burney…"

As Jackson reached to kiss my cheek, I saw Ella peeking through the window tearfully waving farewell with an old hanky. Probably one she'd washed and pressed for Miss Burney a thousand times.

I wondered if that cloth had a dark blue monogram like the sheets Miss Burney had left behind.

Jackson looked down at his boots. I knew we'd said it all. I entered my motor and Otho drove off slowly. At the gate, I turned to gaze back down that long drive shaded over by those ancient oaks. Jackson stood there at the steps of his mansion. Rain was coming down so hard I couldn't tell if he was crying. But I knew he'd never leave Grandview, though.

How strangely it had all turned out.

JACKSON

83

THOSE LONG SUMMER days at Lewaro were jasmine sweet and yet still tugged my heart back to Grandview and those brief days of my childhood with Jackson Burney. Fleeting thoughts entwined as the times I wondered if Jackson's ma wore Jasmine in her hair to smell its sweet fragrance or were those delicate flowers hanging down her honey blond hair to make it prettier? Why do we hold on to these things? The memories we fold between the pages of our thoughts like dried flowers pressed between the pages of a book of stories we keep hidden; the stories that anchor us to our past and the friends that dwell there yet.

There were few white folks along the journey that recognized our troubles, yet I always knew Jackson could smell jasmine and still taste the life we 'croppers ate. How many times did he save me from his ma, or ol' Isaac? Wasn't it this white child that carried down to us burlap bags filled with Ella's plunder of his ma's larder?

Far from Miss Burney's veranda and in the cotton fields Momma's words were always at war with the dust on her tongue to get out.

"The nobodies gonna be the somebodies. Gonna be!"

But truly where did that leave these somebodies in the end?

I still recall those rare times at Grandview when Ella, if she thought there'd be a few moments grace from attending Melinda's needs, would come down to the shacks to chat with Minerva and the other women. Time had to be stolen from their labors for 'cropper women to sit and talk a spell. Moments when their words weaved back and forth only punctuated with their chorusing groans of weariness. Late at night these women lingered in the stale shadows between the shacks where they wondered if ol' Isaac might report to his mistress their words. Everybody knew Melinda Burney plied Isaac with tips like scraps to a stray dog. Lord, you paid your price; all of us did, to serve the big house.

Yes, these women seen it all, hadn't they? Like when Ella flinched as Momma lifted her swollen arm so the moonlight could reveal a new smattering of bruises. Ella always had them.

"Why she never let you sleep?"

Momma's anger sliced her words like the preacher's spittle did his when talking 'bout the white folks and their mean ways.

"How that woman figures you gonna get your work done with no sleep?"

"That woman," Ella replied, "when she wake up, she come in, sneak in, she do, just to catch me sleepin' so's she can kick me awake. Then she bend over to grin in my face for jumpin' from 'er foot like a frog! She always goin' on 'bout me bein' her froggy nigger."

As a child standing with the women talking about things that happened up in the big house, it's the grief on Ella's face I remember most. Ella's pain not just from being kicked, we all got kicked but because the very woman that done it was the one she'd served. Did it for nothing but leftovers from the kitchen and the privilege of sleeping on a rag rug at the foot of Jackson's bed, rather than down in a 'cropper's drafty shack that only pretended to keep the dust out but made no such pretense when the rains came.

But over the long years of hard labor things never got any better for Ella. That's the way things in the South were ordered and didn't we all think it so read in the Bible. Wasn't that the tale they beat us with?

❦

I so remember that day. There was a cold feeling that came over me on that very sunny morning now long ago. A kind of feeling that brings fear so bad you're chilled. In so many ways, I wonder if I didn't feel this premonition coming like something bad was on the hunt for me. These thoughts seemed to hide somewhere between my memories of the folks I'd come to know along the journey. Who? Who sends prayers my way and lingers to hear the 'amen'? Who pleads for me to hear them yet says nothing when I reply?

That sunny dark morning Louvenia had cut a basket of flowers we'd grown from Jeff's seeds. Together we were arranging them in a large Chinese jar on the parcel gilt hall table for Lelia's return from New York when that strange feeling seemed to swallow me once again.

"You ain't chilled here on this cold marble floor, are you, Sarah?"

Louvenia put her hand to my brow as though I might have a fever.

"You been workin' too hard. You always get chilled when you're tired. I know you do."

"I'm fine, Sister. Fine."

Most times when these feelings stirred, I reckoned it was Jeff whispering through the shadows; nudging me to stay on some path or avoid the ones where danger lurked. Down deep, I felt this special premonition. My hands trembled and went cold. Sister watched closely as we poked our fragrant gem-blue daphnes into the Chinese jar.

Finally, I laid down the long-steamed flowers and decided to be alone. But from whom or what? I abruptly went upstairs to disappear under my comforter.

"Want me to finish here, Sarah?" Louvenia asked.

"Yes. You always arrange the flowers so well, Sister."

"I tol' you. You're still weary from that last trip." Sister added from the bottom of the stairs. "You best take a rest."

In my bedchamber, I pushed open the windows to look out over the river and saw a dark gray cloud roll over the palisades beyond. The day had turned on us and aimed to deliver a late spring rain.

Then, as I stood at the window it thundered—thundered so loudly I cupped my icy hands over my ears. Sister entered as the rain came down in sheets and pounded the side of the mansion.

"I've never heard such loud sharp thunder."

"Didn't hear no thunder," Louvenia said.

"The thunder nearly broke my eardrums."

Sister wrapped my shoulders with a shawl.

"You didn't hear that? I reckon like a faraway cannon?"

"Thunder you say? No, honey. Didn't hear nothin', but that sky sure looks like it means business, don't it? See that rain? No, guess not like what's comin' in on this here floor!"

As I think back to that day, it didn't really sound so much like thunder as it did a gunshot, the sound of a rifle even.

Sister pulled the windows closed and shook her head like she'd caught me sleepwalking from a bad dream. Still the anxious feelings I'd had that morning lingered.

That night I tossed in bed. I couldn't help but feel there was something I'd forgotten, or some forgotten thing I needed to do. I didn't fall asleep till late and so guess I woke up the following morning late. It was already a sunny day when my maid pulled the drapes open. While I waited for my breakfast tray, I wondered why the day before I'd been so strangely anxious. A few days later the answer arrived.

It was in the morning mail. There on my breakfast tray was an old brown envelope. I put it aside without opening as it brought back the chill I'd been running from. Just a piece of paper, I kept telling myself. Perhaps it was those large scrawled letters over the face of the envelope as if written with a dull pencil with a whittled tip. Or those much smaller mark-throughs likely made by someone correcting the address with a different lead. The kind of marks the postman might make if you ran out to catch him when he came by. What I put down on this here envelope, you'd ask if you couldn't write well. This right, what I wrote? Gonna get there? You gonna take it? Who then?

The envelope was postmarked from Delta. I read my scrawled address several times before finally opening it. Madame Walker, General Delivery, the Villa Lewaro, Irvington-on-Hudson. Inside on the roughly folded foolscap and folded over some yellowed news clipping were a few scrawled words. Before I deciphered the message, I noticed the signature. Ella had sent it, but I already knew this. Just did. Certainly, knew that Jackson had taught her to write some. Many times, as a child, Ella had showed me with pride her name painstakingly printed out. Before I attempted her letter, I unfolded the clipping which declared it all. The heading read that Jackson Burney was gone. Dead. He'd taken his own life with his daddy's favorite hunting rifle and did it there on that fancy imported carpet the paper emphasized along with the purported price. The very same carpet he loved to soil with mud from his ma's rose garden, a ritual he performed to bring her attention down on him.

Lord, Lord, was that the day I heard the thunder?

The Burney's were all gone then. Nothing left but that old house with the long drive of oaks planted by Robert Burney's granddaddy nearly a century before. Jackson had shared with me on my visit that he'd been selling off parcels of land from time to time to make ends meet. But they never did, nor did he even care. His life couldn't come together either as Jackson could never reconcile his daddy's life in the white camellia class supported by 'croppers; those unfortunate children of the old slavery. I wondered if that's why he seemed to take pleasure in the gradual evisceration of Burney lands. Jackson, ever dominant over his world even as a child, would assure that the old south would never rise from the sins of the Burney dynasty.

Lordy, Momma. The somebodies gonna fall on their own knives?

I went back to the letter. Reading deep, I could make out enough of Ella's message even if the words failed to convey it entirely. Truly she'd written that Jackson was gone and that she was heartbroken from it. She didn't have to say more. I understood. Who else could she share her grief with?

The next day I sent Freeman to Delta, via Vicksburg. He'd always sorted my legal affairs with utmost caution and discretion, so I knew he could look into Ella's well being during this hard time for her.

Took Freeman four days to get to Vicksburg. I waited anxiously for his telegram. I worried about what might befall Ella not having Jackson.

What do you do when you're crippled with rheumatism, can hardly walk and the reason for your life comes crashing down on you, bleeding over the Persian carpet you beat the dust out of a thousand times?

Had Ella been rolled down the gravel road off the Burneys' in a manure cart? Bustled off like Sister and then Alex and I were?

Louvenia eased my concerns when she cautioned that no Klansman was going to profane the Burney place. If Ella were still there, she'd be all right till Freeman arrived to help sort things or spirit her away if need be.

I received the first telegram from Freeman a few days afterwards. As I read, tears slid across my visions of Ella up in Miss Burney's room. She was so proud that for the first time in her life she had her own room and even her very own bed, Miss Burney's and nobody was kicking her awake on cold mornings. Her sitting upright with her faded comforter and those dozen or so magical little whatnots she'd lined up on Miss Burney's old dressing table. Probably trinkets that Jackson had given her. They's all mine, she reminded me and undoubtedly herself. Precious objects; gifts from her boy thoughtfully displayed on a faded gilded chest that belonged to Jackson's natural ma. Yes, Ella could finally claim things all her own to treasure.

Freeman telegramed that it took half a day to get from Vicksburg to over the river to Delta. He said that the Burneys' front door was wide open when he arrived late that evening. Likely only blown open, he later added, as there were no caretakers left to bolt down the place from the storm the night before. The sounds of wind howling through that big ol' house had frightened Ella. She surely thought it was an intruder, he said. Probably the Klan had come at last as it did for most of us. At least someplace and time in our thoughts and nightmares.

Miss Ella? You in here, Ma'am?" Freeman called from the foyer. "Ma'am, this is Freeman Ransom, MadameWalker's attorney here. Come to help you."

Freeman said he then heard Ella's faint moan up the stairs. Not wanting to frighten her, he went up slowly, speaking as he did.

"Miss Ella. This is Freeman. No need to be afraid now. Madame sent me to see about you."

Later Freeman shared with me that as he approached her door he heard fearful moans grow louder. He tapped on her door before opening it. Ella had positioned an old chair up against it for protection. Freeman easily pushed it back over the old pecan floor. She must have thought she could still hold the outside away as Jackson was no longer there to keep the real world at bay.

"Ma'am. This is Freeman here. MadameWalker sent me. She got your letter. You send MadameWalker a note? I know you did."

Ella, yet half-hidden under her comforter nodded through the dark musty room that swarmed with flying bugs being near the river and all.

"You're alright now. Nobody's going to hurt you none, Ma'am."

With that Ella lessened her grip on the comforter.

"There's no light up here. You got some candles or a lamp?" he asked.

"Don't 'member."

Ella looked to be coming out of a daze and only just aware there was a man who had walked through her fog and stood just on the other side of her severed dream.

"How long you been up here, Ma'am?"

"Long spell. Don't know," she replied.

"When did you eat last?"

Ella couldn't recall.

"Got something down there in the kitchen to feed you? I'm going to fix you something. I'm hungry too."

Ella nodded yes and no and then some.

"Well, I'll go to work on that and find a lamp or some candles. You'll be alright now."

Freeman said he went downstairs, lit some candles, and found his way to the kitchen but there was nothing to eat.

Wondering what he would do so late, he walked out onto the Burney veranda to collect his thoughts and get out of those musty rooms. There was no table laden with crystal and silver dividing platters of sliced ham with scrambled eggs waiting as in the days of the Burneys when they returned late from a plantation ball. Freeman said there was nothing but broken latticework and chipped paint that blew over the veranda like brittle snowflakes. His every step creaked over the old boards. Across from where Miss Burney's rose garden had once been, Freeman saw Ella's makeshift chicken coop where he found a few eggs.

Back inside there was no butter to fry them, so he boiled them and brought up a bowl of salted chopped eggs for Ella.

"No, don't eat them eggs. They's for Jackson! He always have 'em in the mornin'."

"Yes, Ma'am. There's plenty of eggs down there for Jackson," Freeman assured Ella as she spooned the eggs down ravenously. "Can you tell me what has happened the last few days? For as many days as you can 'member?"

It took a long while for Ella to get her story out. Her thoughts were twisted between those realities she could not take on. While they ate, broken thoughts came from Ella that Freeman struggled to pieced together. All the while Ella exclaimed that Jackson might need her. Did Freeman hear his call? She did and best go to him in the nursery. But she was too weary to crawl out of bed. Jackson, she said, he'd called her when thunder was pounding the sky. Ella's memories swept her back to the nursery where she slept at the foot of his bed and was the only one that protected him from the thunder. The thunder of his ma's indifference.

ROAD TO MY LYNCHING

84

Despite Freeman being weary from the trip to Delta he remained up with Ella late of nights sorting the brittle pieces of her anguish as they fell from her dangling thoughts.

"They come for me," Ella said after another long pause.

"Who, Ma'am?"

"Them men. That night they did."

"You 'member men comin' here to Grandview?"

"One come up to the door, he say, 'Who in there with you?' I tol' 'im Jackson! He say, 'No, nigger, Jackson Burney ain't in there.' I say to that man he in here! That man, he tell the other one I's crazy-like. He say all niggers gone crazy they old."

"What did you say back?" Freeman asked.

"I tol' 'im I gonna tell my boy he been sassed by two white men gonna get they's mouth fixed good with my tub brush when Jackson hears of it!"

"Yes, Ma'am," Freeman replied. "What else did the man say?"

"He say he gonna take me into town! He say somethin' 'bout Jackson, he buried now so I gots to go all the way over to Vicksburg with 'em and keep my nigger mouth shut."

"He took you into town?" Freeman asked.

"Gonna be a lyncin'."

"That man say?"

Ella got quiet again. Just as Freeman was about to go downstairs and let her sleep, she jolted up like she'd heard something and then struggled to get out of bed.

"Ma'am, you best stay put," Freeman admonished. "It's real late now."

"Jackson, he don't come when I call 'im. I know he down in his ma's roses. He gonna get dirty and Miss Burney, she gonna take a switch to me 'less I get the child cleaned up 'for supper."

"No, Jackson is alright. He is Ma'am."

Settled down in bed again in, Ella continued about her late-night callers.

"Took me into town, them men did. Had a wagon out there. Said get in. Gonna be a lynchin'."

"Lynchin' he say?"

"Don't say it when they come. They just come."

"Who came?"

"Klan, they come for us all, don't they? Gonna be a lynchin' for sure."

"They said they were the Klan?"

Ella paused for a long moment and then yelled towards her window like he might hear her from the rose garden.

"Jackson! You know it's near dark. Get in here 'fore I fetch my flyswatter!"

"I'll go tell Jackson you been callin' him," Freeman said. "You think you can sleep now?"

She asleep when his last words fell off.

Freeman drew the shutters closed as the rain was coming down hard and then lit a candle next to her bed. He went downstairs to find a place to sleep aiming for the sofa in the drawing room. By candlelight he maneuvered through the large room, looking at the Burneys' riches scattered about. A grand piano on one end, large paintings of this and that relation covered the walls, brocade covered chairs situated for plantation folks to chat about life on the river and Melinda Burney's huge imported carpet under his feet. There in its center was a large brown spot; the spot where Jackson's life drained from him after that thundering gunshot.

Bled all over his ma's carpet like the paper printed. Above on the ceiling, near her chandelier, was a huge hole that went all the way through the upper floor. Big enough to stick a head through. Or perhaps let the soul of a prince escape from his family's sins.

Yes, that was the place where Jackson took his life and did what he'd been orchestrating since a little boy; bring his daddy's world down.

❧

Freeman telegraphed that he didn't know what was going on there at Grandview. Wrote that Ella was frequently unable to do much but iron a shirt for Jackson, cut a jam jar full of flowers for his room, or fix him the egg that would never be eaten. I replied to Freeman that it would be appreciated if he stayed on till he could sort things. Obviously, there'd come a day when somebody would be packing her off Burney lands. Heaven only knew where that would be. There were many ditches beyond Burney lands. Most back-filled with the souls of those who came before and had worked the cotton.

The following morning Ella was down in the kitchen early making bread and while not recalling having met Freeman the night before she went on like they'd known each other for ages. She fixed him some eggs and he tried to figure out what had transpired since Jackson's passing.

"Ma'am, you got relatives 'round here you planning to go to?

"I got no folks. No. They's all gone. Burney, he say way back my sister dead."

"Burney did?" Freeman asked. "When did he say that?"

"But ol' Clara say she knows better. She say Burney, he sold my sister she a baby. Then he say she dead. Throwed into the river to feed the catfish! I ain't never had the time to count up all his lies. Guess I can't count up that far, can I?"

"You got any other folks?"

"'Course I do."

"Well, that's good news. What's their name?" Freeman asked.

"Jackson Burney, he say I ain't never gonna leave, even if ol' Isaac come for me like he did Sarah and Alex."

Now and again Freeman was able to work the pieces together. Seems these men came late at night soon after Jackson's burial next to his folks on Orchard Hill.

"Some men came and took you all the way over there, you said. You think you went all the way to Vicksburg?"

After seventy years and some, Ella sure enough knew that when anything went wrong at Grandview a colored would be found to bend under a whip to make things right again. She told Freeman that she trembled something awful that night as she sat on the damp straw in the back of a wagon headed down the road into the vast unknown. Those men said nothing to her, or at least nothing she remembered or understood. As she told Freeman about that night, he said she trembled, her spoon rattled on that old crock bowl she ate her boiled egg from. All she knew was she was going to be lynched. That was why they came for her. Her own time for the rope had arrived. That's how Freeman understood Ella's broken phrases between the long pauses and comments about tending Jackson. Her boy was gone. She was prepared to go to Jesus, too.

Freeman finally figured out why she was taken to town. Ella was taken to the county clerk's office, which everybody knew had a jail in the basement and there told to sit down. There were two other white men in there that Ella described as the kind that visited Jackson's daddy from time to time to talk business. They looked her over before asking her if she was moron. Or perhaps they only told her she was 'bout the same, Ella couldn't remember more. She didn't know exactly what a moron was so didn't reply.

His voice was loud and sharp with anger.

"This nigger woman ain't no moron. That is, she ain't all the way gone. She been at the Burney place all 'er life. Was too stupid to leave when the rest of 'em run off, so Mr. Jackson Burney, he let her stay on. That's what river folks been sayin'."

"That right?" The man behind the big desk asked. "You got some of your senses, nigger?"

Then he mumbled some words to Ella he read off a paper twisted up in one hand before handing it to the other man. Well, lots of unrecorded business was finished off in the basements of county court houses all over the South. All these words the man was rattling off apparently put images in Ella's head that the matter had to do with the Burneys. There was a dead Burney. Ever'body knew who the Burneys were. Been 'round that county parish for more than a hundred years.

Ella figured these officials were reading her an official death sentence. She told Freeman that her throat constricted as they spat their words at her. Said it was 'cause the Lord was preparing her for the rope. This was the lynching business she'd told Freeman about. There was a dead Burney, she kept hearing over and over.

Then the man behind the desk asked: "Do you understand what I've been tellin' you?"

Ella shook her head no. His yelling didn't help her to understand.

"Jackson Burney has named you in his will. He has bequeathed Grandview to you and all the Burney lands. Well, guess it was his right to do so, although I can't imagine what was in his head. Looks like it's all yours for the rest of your natural life. Do you understand what I just told you?"

"Yes, Sir. I reckon."

"Now there's money left too, what Mr. Robert Burney put in trust for Jackson, guess that goes to you as well," he said. "That's what it reads here in the will of Jackson Burney. Not much left, but you probably don't need much if you're simple-minded and all," he said, his voice tinged in anger.

The notion of a colored inheriting even the tattered remains of one of Delta's proudest plantations must have stuck in his craw something awful. A mansion that Ella's ancestors had whitewashed a thousand times, but never allowed in, she was now the mistress of.

"You got anything to say, nigger woman?"

"Got to get back."

"You goin' go back to Grandview? Live there by yourself?" the man asked. "That what you're aiming to do?"

"Ain't never been away from there till now. Ain't never," Ella said.

"Ain't it something? This here is the richest nigger woman in the county! Maybe even the state. I mean how many hundreds of acres left at Grandview?"

"You know that ain't right! A nigger doin' this to the plantation folks," the other man said in Ella's presence. "But ain't nothin' can be done about it. Jackson Burney had this legal will drawn up by lawyers in New York City and notarized right proper. I know why he did it up there, too. Ain't no local judge gonna buy it ain't for real and set it aside if some Burney cousin show up one day and say it ain't right what Jackson gone and done!"

Ella told Freeman she'd never even been to Vicksburg on a Saturday even to buy a pair of shoes. But then she never bought a pair of shoes for herself in her long life.

Yes, the woman that had spent her life at Grandview, kicked in the head more times than she could count, was now mistress of Melinda Burney's chambers and the rest of her once jasmine-scented gardens and mansion where white clouds swept the rooms free of dust.

Maybe you were right Momma. The nobodies do become the somebodies and not just in Summerland.

ELLA TOLD ME

85

AFTER HE'D GONE into Vicksburg to look over the legal documents it took Freeman several days to work matters out for Ella. Actually, that's not completely what happened. I retained a white lawyer who would not be denied access to the filed will of Jackson Burney to make a certified copy for Freeman to pore over.

Not known in Vicksburg, Freeman had drawn stares—him being a fine colored man in a suit. Word spreads fast. Seemed like everywhere Freeman went in the white part of town there was thick talk. What's that I hear about a nigger woman getting the Burney place? Now that can't be, was the common drift; the Burney mansion, too? Or they mean one of them shacks down by the river? Surely, that's what they mean, ain't it? When asked if he was in town on business and if that business had to do with the estate of Jackson Burney, Freeman knew that for Ella's interests he best neutralize all this talk and so he responded that he'd heard said that there was one woman staying on to keep up the place till things could be worked out. He didn't want any nighttime visitors dragging their rage veiled under white sheets to Ella's mansion door. Folks Freeman spoke to appeared to be suspicious, but still nothing untoward happened out at Grandview.

In town, Freeman went to discuss the matter with the Preacher at the church Louvenia and I attended in Vicksburg. The Preacher's eyes got big and he clasped both of Freeman's hands with joy.

"You came to answer my prayer," the Preacher told Freeman.

"Don't understand, Preacher."

"Well, this church has been praying for Will and Dabney. You see, they was 'croppers on the Frederick Hudson place outside of Macon, Noxubee County. Oh, it's 'bout two hundred miles east of here. They got put off the Hudson place and made their way back here to Vicksburg where Dabney has a sister. I'm told somewhere across the river near Delta. That's gotta be down the road from Mr. Jackson's place. I mean now Miss Ella's place."

According to the preacher, it seems Will and Dabney were 'croppers having been sold as slaves to one Frederick Hudson. Certainly, the south made out well in the war they'd lost. Southern breezes carried their concerns about not having slaves all the way to the White House and President Johnson's southern sensitive ears. Now that Lincoln was gone, no need to continue all this nasty business about who was to bear the burden of supporting the camellia class. Reconstruction meant exactly that. Rebuild things off some folks' backs but we won't call them slaves no more. They'll be sharecroppers and have the privilege of living on the plantation, working the fields and rebuilding the camellia class from what the north did to it; what Lincoln told them to do to those fine river folks who were born to love the sweet fragrance of magnolias blossoms. The only thing that changed was a bit of paperwork for the 'croppers. They could borrow to buy seed at a thousand times markup and then borrow to buy hoes to plant it, all written down in account ledgers no colored could ever look at again. Interests piling up, doubling and tripling till the 'croppers finally came to their senses and realized they'd never be going nowhere in this new slavery.

Will and Dabney were such folks. Worked the Hudson place for scraps of promises that this here acre gonna be yours soon, kind of talk. Yes, this acre and that shack gonna all be yours. You just got to keep on and on and on working for it and get us paid up even. Then it's yours, that is, when it ain't worth nothing no more. However, there weren't enough years in enough centuries to pay off the accounts the white man spoke of. Then one day Will and Dabney, past seventy, couldn't put in no twelve-hour days in those fields. Well, accounts come due just the same and they come fast. Pay off your bills, like a good Christian would 'a done, or be off with you. There ain't nothing else to talk over.

Seems like Dabney had always told Will she had folks, an older sister, she seemed to think, living outside of Vicksburg. Maybe 'croppers she thought, so they headed that way and somehow made it to Vicksburg where they ended up at the mercy of the church. Women in the church found them a place to sleep, somebody's sleeping porch. But the thing is, these same bills for past accounts for old 'croppers were coming due all over the south, so these folks were mostly sent packing. Stray dogs, ol' Isaac called them if his 'croppers had kin that showed up at Burney gates for a piece of stale cornbread. Lord, didn't he know 'bout stray dogs! Folks could hardly feed their families most years so how's a church going to care for all these old 'cropper folks can't do much but rock on the porch? But Will and Dabney were a fiery couple. They couldn't work no fields, but they still needed work to feel useful. Preacher saw what needed to be. He proposed to Freeman that Will and Dabney head on over to Delta and work something out with Ella. Will could keep the garden planted and Dabney could help Ella care for Jackson's memory if it eased Ella's mind.

Later that night Freeman returned to Grandview with supplies aiming to talk this out with Ella. Things were still cloudy in her head with some days better than others. On the good ones she went out and gathered her eggs and even worked her way up to the lower orchard in hopes those peach trees would give up peaches from their old brittle branches for a pie. Then she prepared them a good supper, which they had that night on Ella's veranda. Freeman met with a farmer who'd long been bringing things 'round for Jackson from farmers' markets near the docs. He'd stopped when the shutters on the old place were closed due to mourning for Jackson, but resumed bringing milk, vegetables, freshly caught fish, along with flowers and even special things he picked up along the docs for peddling to his customers, this time pineapples.

Freeman sliced the pineapple and mixed in the sweet juice some rum he found locked up somewhere. Ella had never had pineapple and, claimed at least, that she'd never had rum. Freeman was dubious on the second account. They sat chatting as they enjoyed their fried fish, summer vegetables and rum in pineapple juice.

That rum got Ella freely talking 'bout things she'd never told anybody about, 'cept maybe Sam's ma, ol' Clara.

"You tell lil' Sarah I know what!"

"Know what, Ella?" Freeman asked.

"What happened to that ol' man, Isaac!" she said. "I tell you plain, it was the night we buried Owen and Minerva up there on Orchard Hill. She tell you 'bout that?"

"No, Ma'am. MadameWalker doesn't speak of those times to me."

"The 'croppers, all of 'em and ol' Clara, Sarah and Alex and Jackson and me, it was. That's what I 'member."

"What, Ma'am?"

"Black nightshade is what!"

"What's nightshade?"

"I never done nothin'! No, I never," Ella asserted, then worked up a crazy-like laugh that got even the serious Mr. Ransom howling alongside her. "Minerva, she sure did come after ol' Isaac just like she say she gonna. That's what happened. Got that man good for what he done to 'er kids. Oh, Lord, don't mess with a nigger ma and her kids!"

"Yeah, what got 'im good, Ma'am?"

"Berry pie!"

"Berry pie got 'im good, huh?" he asked. "Like you done made yesterday with the berries the boy brought 'round for you?"

"Just like that! Ain't it so? I made a good berry cobbler that morning and lef' it on the veranda to cool. Isaac, he come 'round when his nose smell it. I say, you come up on the veranda here. Mistress is upstairs and won't know. You have yourself a big bowl of my cobbler, I tol' 'im. He come up maybe thinkin' I was doin' evil on 'im 'cause ol' Clara, she done tol' 'im he gonna die from what he done all them times to Minerva and her kin. That ol' man looked at me real close, like I hidin' something. He say, ol' Isaac say, 'I ain't 'fraid of no nigger house slave!' I know you. You done put a pinch of nightshade in that there cobbler! You're wicked as the devil's bitch". I tol' 'im, look over there at my boy. What's he eatin'?' Jackson was at the kitchen table with cobbler all over him face. Ain't no nightshade in my cobbler I tol' Isaac and smiled good in his face. So, he gobbled up a bowl of my cobbler but no sooner he put that wood spoon down than ol' Isaac's belly give 'im grief. Yeah, something in that there cobbler, he started thinkin'. So, that big ol' man went howlin' for Burney. He thinkin' he gonna die for sure. Ella done slipped nightshade in his cobbler! She gots to pay!"

"You killed Isaac"? Freeman asked.

"No, I ain't killed nobody. Burney, he seen Isaac run up hollerin' he been poisoned. Gonna die when the nightshade gets down to the bottom of his belly. He gone! No, I not kill nobody! Burney did!"

"Old Mr. Burney poisoned Isaac?"

"Nah, he don't never bother with Isaac. But Isaac, since the first days when Miss Burney come to Grandview to marry the Mas'er, he been makin' trouble. Heard Burney say it was like that."

"What kind of trouble could Isaac cause between the Burneys?" Freeman asked.

"I tell you later. But when Isaac went to hollowerin' he gonna die, Burney he already waitin' for it to be, ain't he? Waitin' for the right time till Miss Burney finally say she sick of that ol' man so he best head on down the road for good. Isaac howled for Burney to come save 'im. Burney say, sure, I do that for you. Go down to your hog's house and stay quiet while I go get a doctor. Isaac begged Burney to hurry and get that doctor 'cause he gonna die from Ella's nightshade cobbler if he don't!"

"Burney go after the doctor?"

"Him? No, he come in and finished Jackson's bowl of cobbler, told me to put more cream on it first. Then had himself another bowl from that second cobbler just come out of my oven. Burney, he got more cobbler on his face than Jackson! Can't go into town with a face covered in berry jam."

"So, what he'd do?" Freeman asked.

"Burney, he tol' me to go down and fetch Samuel and bring 'im up to the big house. Burney gots something to tell 'im but he tol' me not to fuss with it till I got Jackson bathed for bed else Miss Burney get worked up. I done what Burney say. I put my boy in the bath. Then got 'im clean and shiny. Then put 'im in bed. Then went to tend Miss Burney, I always brushed her hair ever' night. Then I was so hungry, went down to have some of that second cobbler, I did. Then I hurried off real quick to fetch Samuel just like Burney say."

"Who's Samuel, Ma'am?"

"Samuel? He ol' Clara's boy. He Owen's friend. They go fishin' every Sunday, don't they?"

"You know what Burney said to Samuel?"

"Sure I do. I listenin' when I scrubbin' the kitchen floor. Door over there open to Miss Burney's veranda. Burney, he standing right 'bout where your chair is. He say to Samuel, 'Isaac, he got stomach cancer. Guess he gonna die now,' he told Samuel."

"How'd he know Isaac had cancer?"

"Burney? He don't know nothin'. I reckon Minerva told Jesus to tell Burney when he prayed. No, that can't be, 'cause Burney, he never pray. Got no time what with countin' all his money and all."

"What happened then?"

"Burney, he tell Samuel it ain't right to let nobody suffer none. Samuel nodded 'cause he knew that be right. He tol' Burney Isaac shouldn't suffer like he made all them 'croppers suffer. Burney said he was pleased Samuel was a good Christian man and understood 'bout things. Then said, Isaac be down in at hog's house suffering bad anyway! Yes, that Isaac is for sure sick like rabid dog!"

"What did he do? Mr. Burney, he shoot Isaac? Shoot 'im like a rabid dog you're sayin'?"

"White man can't shoot no white man. No. Just 'cause Isaac gonna die, still be murder. Then Burney look long and hard at Samuel so that man knows he mean what he say. Burney say to Samuel, 'you best go up tomorrow and backfill that old well near the shacks down there. Hear?

Don't want my boy fallin' in no shaft. You understand, Sam?' Burney said. Samuel tipped his hat and walked off 'cause he knew what."

"What did he know?" Freeman asked.

"Samuel knew it was time, time meant for Minerva's promise to get Isaac. Isaac, he just never knowned when it would be, did he? But he sure knew just the same didn't he? Knew someday Minerva was gonna come for 'im! That man must 'a got to thinkin' I done it for Minerva. Givin' 'im some dried nightshade flowers ground up in his cobbler. No, I never. Didn't have to."

"Did ol' Clara, or her son, Samuel do it? Put poison in Isaac's berry cobbler?"

"No, nobody gonna go to hell for Isaac. Nobody did nothin'!"

"Nothing don't ever kill nobody, Ma'am."

"Oh, yes it do when it's meant to be! See, Isaac, he long been 'scared of what Minerva tol' 'im 'fore she died. She gonna come back and get 'im! Isaac, he think he got some nightshade put in his cobbler and I put it in there 'cause Minerva got me to! Isaac gonna die real hard, ain't he? He knowed that his belly gonna be like mules stompin' it good! Damend good, too! Blood comin' up through his nose and all. That's what nightshade do. Devil's weed, we call it. Isaac, he figured Burney ain't never gonna go after no doctor, so he got himself drunk to ease the pain. Pain knowin' he not goin' to Jesus! No, he goin' to hell quick and ugly! Then Isaac took a walk in the night, moaning like a beaten dog and stumbled down by that ol' well. Some folks say he done throwed himself in to get it over with."

"Ma'am, folks don't just walk over to a dry well shaft and throw themselves in 'cause they got a real bad belly ache!"

"No? Guess nobody tol' ol' Isaac that. Anyway, he knowed Minerva was tellin' the truth. She gonna get 'im. And, Lord, she sure enough did!"

"How'd Burney know he had cancer then?"

"Burney, he don't know nothin'! See, Isaac always got heartburn, don't he? Him whinin' all the time 'bout this or that ache so he don't got to go to the fields and watch over the 'croppers. Oh, he too sick, he say to Burney. Gotta be in bed all day. And all the time he in bed with his bottle he was looking up at the winda to see if Minerva was there watchin' and waitin'. That last night, when he seen a woman looking down at him, it blinded 'im! That what ol' Clara say. He was blind with fear and couldn't take no more of keepin' awake watchin' for Minerva to come at him with her rusty scissors again! Ain't nobody got to face the Lord Jesus Christ and tell Him they done it to ol' Isaac. No, Sir! Shadows done ate 'im up! Shadows followin' Isaac's since Minerva and Owen passed. Yeah, them white shadows is where Minerva waited all that time till that man walked himself over to that well and it must'a swallowed 'im like the whale swallowed Jonah."

"Well, Ma'am, the Lord made the whale puke up Jonah, didn't He?"

"And ol' Clara's boy Samuel say he waited to see if the Lord was gonna make that well puke up Isaac. Waited till it stunk so bad down in the black hole he done what Burney tol' 'im to. Filled it up! Don't that mean the Lord, He ain't never gonna puke up Isaac? That's what ol' Clara sure tol' us! You ever hear ol' Clara preach down by the river?"

"No, Ma'am. I ain't never heard her preach."

Freeman later said he never could figure out the entire story about Isaac being chased around the well till he flung himself in. He just let it be. Well, anyway, that tends to be the way things are settled in the south: quietly and without fuss.

TILL A BAG OF TATAS
COMES TRUE

86

I RECEIVED REGULAR TELEGRAMS from Freeman whenever he could get into Delta and responded by urging him to stay on as long as he could. Perhaps this was due to the guilt I felt for not being able to come to Ella's aid. My years on so many roads had taken their toll and I found myself not able to recoup my strength easily. I'd finally accepted this and knew I simply could not go back to Grandview, particularly as my friend would never again be there.

As Louvenia predicted, the Klan never profaned the Burney place looking to harass any coloreds that hung on after Jackson's passing. Grandview was as quiet as any monument to the plantation class. For the longest time folks were still leaving large wreathes of laurel woven with wide black velvet ribbon on the Burney gates in memory of Jackson Burney's passing. At times I thought about Freeman and Jackson, their lives were so different yet at their cores similar as both men sought justice in their own remarkable ways. In Jackson's small world, coloreds, particularly me, benefited from the power of his personality over that of his ma's and also that of ol' Isaac and the stick he welded. Even Robert Burney never crossed that child. Jackson knew how to play his folks off on each other to get what he wanted or needed and what he needed was frequently meant for others. He knew how to leave the big white house a howling mess perpetually under repair while he was already razing it from the other side all over again. We all heard their hollering up at the big house, the Burneys on the veranda hurling recriminations. Their broken dreams slowly dying like sweet jasmine in a southern draught; one steam at a time till only Jackson was left. Ella's life, like Minerva, Owen's and their children would have been sorely different had it not been for Jackson. Still he couldn't save himself. Jackson couldn't leave Grandview and move on in the new century. All he could do was soil his ma's fine carpet with his blood in retribution as he'd done so many times on so many paths he'd muddied for that very purpose. Yet, at times I wonder if I'd survived because of this one man? Then I wondered how many others were asking that themselves?

Yes, and for one man it was simply the dream of tatas that came true.

I recall on my final visit to Grandview, while up visiting with Ella when Jackson seemed to be expecting someone at the veranda door. Ella said to receive a bag of tatas Samuel delivered every week and to say a word 'bout growing them although it wouldn't take much more than a word as there ain't much to it. Yet I still remember how strange it seemed, potatoes and all, Jackson not being much of a farmer. I recall Ella saying the only thing he ever grew was daffodil bulbs he planted after he had his Ma's rose garden turned under. Perhaps this was one of his last tantrums. The final, I reckon, being with his daddy's shotgun on his ma's carpet.

"I know about all that," Ella said that last visit as the sound of Jackson's boots disappeared down the corridor. She told me that one summer Samuel, ol' Clara's boy, returned to Grandview after being gone for years. He'd given up sharecropping and had moved closer to Vicksburg where there was less risk of crops flooding. But things didn't go well. Years later he showed up at the Burneys' where he'd been born and reminded Jackson he'd tended his daddy years before. He was hungry. Samuel offered to work for a bag of tatas. And he'd be available if Jackson needed some help from then on. So, Jackson, he told Ella to bring Samuel on into the kitchen and feed him good. There after

Samuel never really left Burney lands again. Ella told me that Jackson and Samuel went down to the river plenty of times and talked while Samuel fished. She said Jackson, he always come back to the big house looking real tired and then disappeared into his room for hours. I wondered when Ella told me this, what a white man, and a colored man could have talked about that long?

Some weeks after Samuel's return to Grandview, Jackson told Ella that a certain mister would be arriving by riverboat from Vicksburg the following day. She was to wait for him on the veranda till he showed, then bring the man on in through the kitchen. Bringing folks in through the service door was Jackson's way of making it clear what their place was. Ella told me she recognized the man when he arrived by a fancy hired buggy. She brought him in and told the man to sit at the kitchen table till Jackson appeared. Ella said she remembered the man by his fancy suit; the kind Jackson had upstairs in mahogany wardrobes but never wore. She said the man, he'd been coming 'round in Robert Burney's days when he would spend hours going over papers in the Master's study. Ella would be beckoned to yank Jackson out from under his daddy's desk so they could finish the work at hand. To leave, Jackson found it easy to negotiate a bribe of a handful of hard candy if he'd only quit his daddy's study peacefully. Ella giggled when she told me this.

Ella said Jackson was too busy with nothing to do to be spending time with that man that brung them papers as he did every week for ol' Burney and wasn't happy about the meeting.

The man jumped to his feet when Jackson entered the room.

"Young Master Burney, I have everything prepared as you directed, Sir."

"Seems it 'a been a long journey out of your way if you hadn't."

Jackson informed him without motioning the man to resume his seat.

"Where do I sign these important lookin' papers of yours?"

"Now are you perfectly clear this is what you want to do, Young Master Burney?"

"You have yourself convinced I'm lackin' in clarity of the mind?"

Jackson perused the document with no more diffidence than if it was a shopping list.

"No Sir! Mr. Jackson."

Ella said that man flinched when he found himself leaning heavily towards the wrong side of Jackson Burney.

"It's just I ain't never heard of our folks, good plantation people I mean, givin' away land. Burney lands no less and to a nigger and not in exchange for a bag of potatoes every week as you have so directed."

"Now, surely you did not come all the way to Grandview to inform me what you heard over in Vicksburg where I am more than delighted never to see again!"

"No, Sir! What?"

The man looked flummoxed.

"I got near a thousand acres of daddy's land left. I don't think any-body's ever gonna know what happened to five acres if I give 'em over to Samuel as I have so directed in these papers you marked up with important sounding words that probably cost me a bundle. How much are you charging me for all these highfaluting commas? Well, I wouldn't be able to go out there and find the other nine hundred and ninety-five acres if they was screamin' that my Daddy's watchin' me sign away my legacy. Anyway, Samuel is the best potato grower in the south. Don't you just agree?"

"A what? Huh? Potato grower?"

The man was only getting more confused 'cause Jackson was doing to him what he loved to do to his momma. He'd trip 'er with a stick and then ask 'er whatever did she trip over!

"But your man, Samuel, he's a nigger!"

"Now don't it just seem that you think I'm lackin' in the mind and now can't see well? But I see all too well, don't I? Sure, I do. I see that you, sir, don't see the value of the god-damned best tatas in the South! Now ain't that a troublesome thought?"

"Huh? Why, yes, Sir! Mr. Jackson. "I mean, no, Sir!" the man replied. "What is it that troubles us again, Sir?"

"Your apparent lack of vision is what we were talkin' 'bout here!" Jackson reiterated.

"I do see now and certainly understand," the man quickly responded and nodded in the affirmative. "What you have here is an excellent investment. World's best tatas. Sure, they are 'cause your daddy was good at his investments just the same. Yes, Sir, he sure was and built the state's biggest fortune from what folks say."

"Well, let 'em say all they want, them fine folks over in Vicksburg," Jackson added. "Daddy was good in piling up his money and then begrudgingly had to leave it all to me just so Momma wouldn't get her sweet smellin' hands on any more than what she'd gone through when Daddy was still 'round. Guess he figured Momma's spendin' habits might cause him to turn in his grave. More than once, I reckon. Now I got to do something with it, all that money, I mean. In my opinion, folks ain't never gonna stop eatin' tatas, so how could the tata market go south on me?"

"Why, Mr. Jackson, Sir. It surely will not! I mean not like cotton did some years back."

"You see? That's exactly what I mean. So, then why don't you invest in Samuel's tata farmin'?"

"Huh?" The man's mouth did not close yet nothing came out for a spell. "Invest in a nigger farm?"

"Now, I've had time to glance over these papers you brought by despite the aggravation of all these commas comin' and goin' all over these damned pages. Well, guess it looks fine all the same."

"Thank you, Sir. I will count the commas and make an appropriate deduction in your bill for the aggravation," the man stated.

"Two hundred and fifty-seven commas. Here's my signature so now you may go."

"Yes, Sir. Mr. Jackson."

Well, Jackson may have looked at things differently than his daddy, or for that matter, most of the plantation folks, but he never swayed from the notion that his folks taught him good; that being, he was *the* prince of Grandview and always would be even as it crumbled at his feet.

No, while his daddy never tolerated sassing from any coloreds, Jackson never countenanced the same from white folks who served him and could leave them dizzy just wondering if they'd annoyed him.

Ella told me that Samuel got himself set up on his acreage and when in season, he brung around a bag of washed potatoes every week or so. Jackson met him on his ma's veranda and would hold up one of them potatoes to the sun and talk about how it was the finest in all the South and that they were both gonna get rich off bags of tatas!

This went on for ages, the two of them like that.

One day when Jackson was over in Delta, where he seldom went, as he didn't like being away from his home and Samuel came by the big house. He knocked at the kitchen door but with no bag of potatoes.

"Samuel, you come to fetch some of my eggs for Jane?"

"No, Ella," Samuel replied. "She got 'er chickens goin' now."

"Then what's you want?"

"Got to say somethin'."

"Well, Jackson, he ain't here. He gone off to Delta."

"I knows. Passed 'im comin' up the road. Want to tell you, 'cause then you can tell Jackson for me."

"Tell 'im what, Samuel?"

"I want'a say somethin'. ol' man Burney, he never done good by me. He not the kind," Samuel said.

"No, he no good. Miss Burney, she worse."

"Yeah… I knows," Sam said. "Wanna give my thanks and respect to Jackson. None of my people ever had their own land. He give me five acres and when my boy come back home to live with us, he give 'im five too. Jackson did. He say don't tell nobody, but he give me money to build a shack. Got it built. Got's tin on the roof. Don't leak none. Got's me a glass in the window. ol' man Burney, he never give us nothin'."

"You tell Jackson you're right happy then." Ella suggested.

"No, you gotta, 'cause you and Jackson gots the same voice between you, is what my Jane say. He know you, you know 'im. He understand when you tell 'im what I come to say, what the weight of it is. Then he know the way I means it.

"I'm gonna tell Jackson you come by, Samuel," Ella replied. "I knows who you is. You ol' Clara's boy and Owen's friend. I tol' Jackson that when you come by long ago for food. Jackson, he knows. Yes, he knows about it all, don't he?"

"He do. And tell 'im, my woman, she gets up early and sits on a chair near the glass winda waitin' for the sun to come up over the trees beyond our place. Right there, every mornin' she pray for Jackson. Pray for his soul to find peace."

Ella said Samuel said no more. Only turned and walked back down the path he came back to his own place about a mile down the road from the gates of Grandview.

✧

For several days Freeman divided his time between Ella's affairs, which he and the preacher worked to sort and some simple repairs around Grandview in preparation for Will and Dabney's anticipated arrival. He wrote that Ella was doing well, even if her thoughts were sliced mighty thin some days. Said she seemed to like rocking on her veranda while Freeman hammered down the old dried planks that humidity had curled up so she could walk over them and get to her carrots and squash from what was once ol' Miss Burney's rose garden. Then other days weren't so good and Ella seemed to drift back into the old days where she'd be sitting in Jackson's nursery.

One day, when Freeman made it back from a meeting with the preacher in Vicksburg, she was sitting there at the end of a not so good day still rocking on that veranda.

"Ella, you haven't been out here all day, have you? Just sittin' here in all this sticky heat?"

"Been waiting," she mumbled looking over where Melinda's rose garden had once been.

"You waitin' for me, Ma'am?"

"Tol' you I gots to go down and tell 'er."

Ella struggled to pull herself out of that old rocker.

"Let me help you. I got something here for us to eat. Bought some tins in town."

"Go down to the shacks," Ella said, still not fully aware of Freeman's presence as if she was only conversing with her own thoughts.

"Go where now?"

"Get down to Minerva's door. We got to talk. Jackson, he's got the croup. She gonna know what to do. I been thinkin' on it all day, just can't 'member what Minerva say. Jackson, he gots the croup again."

"No, Ma'am. It's too late to traipse down to the river's edge. There's nobody down at the shacks no more. Don't you know?"

"Minerva, she never gone. No, she never leave 'er kids, you know." Ella said as Freeman led her back in the kitchen. "I got talk to her now and 'gain."

"Sure, you can talk to her in the morning after you've had some rest," Freeman said.

Inside Freeman got Ella into a chair while he fried their beefsteaks. He chopped hers into tiny pieces and mixed it into the mashed carrots she insisted were still waiting down there in her garden to be harvested.

While they ate supper, Freeman tried to talk to Ella about Will and Dabney, them coming over from Vicksburg and caring for her and all.

"Dabney? No, my sister, she gone. She dead," she told Freeman.

"How'd you know about Dabney? She and her husband, they're the folks gonna come to help us here."

"Dabney? She dead. That what they said."

"Who said?" Freeman asked.

"Burney say. Say my sister dead and I ain't never gonna see her 'gain 'cause she gone far and I ain't seen 'er. No, ain't no more."

"When did Burney say that?

"When I a chil'e."

"Don't know 'bout all that, Ma'am," Freeman responded. "Don't know these folks, but the preacher says they're good people and they want to come put some time in here helpin' you. That's all we got to worry 'bout for now."

Then one day Freeman wrote that Ella was sitting there staring out and raised her hand towards the garden and patted at that direction. Like she was patting the head of a child or perhaps admonishing one.

"I tol' you not to get dirty, chil'e. Your ma's gonna have my hide if you get chicken shit on ya 'gain."

But Jackson had long escaped his ma's clutches. He was past getting dirty in his ma's rose garden and Ella would soon be too.

Near his final days at Grandview, Ella asked Freeman to walk her down that long drive from the mansion. It was as if she was finally walking away from things herself; leaving Grandview and heading for the Lord's Orchard.

With her hand in Freeman's, she smiled and asked him to make sure she rested next to her boy up on Orchard Hill between Jackson and her friend, Minerva Breedlove.

A few weeks after Will and Dabney's arrival, she was back with her boy again up on Orchard Hill. But then she'd never truly left him.

LEFT UNTOLD

87

IT WAS SOME time before I found myself ready to sit down with Freeman and hear the entire story of his trip to Grandview to sort for myself all that had happened after Jackson's passing. With Freeman in Indianapolis and me spending more time at Villa Lewaro, or with Lelia in New York City, it never seemed to be the right time. Finally, I was at peace with Jackson's passing and ready to hear the rest of the story about my friends Ella, Jackson, ol' Clara and her son, Samuel and his Jane as well as about Isaac's mysterious end near to the time of my folks' passing.

The week before Mrs. Washington's visit, I requested Freeman train from Indianapolis to New York City and then on up to Irvington-on-Hudson. He arrived late at Lewaro, so I met him the following day after he'd rested. For most of that morning we talked; Freeman telling me about Ella's last days, the Burney place as he'd left it and also about Samuel, the last of the Burney 'croppers.

That morning I greeted Freeman on the terrace above my garden pool.

"Shall I have cook prepare you a breakfast?" I asked.

"Nope. She already did."

"And you can only eat one after that long trip from Indianapolis?"

We descended to the lower garden where my man had placed some garden chairs for us to sit and chat.

"Ella, she knew I was leaving and fretted till the day I packed for the return," Freeman said.

"Surely she didn't want to see you go. You were so kind to her."

"She had this and that she wanted me to take to Samuel's on my way back to Delta to catch the riverboat over to Vicksburg."

"Like what?"

"Oh, she'd gathered some eggs for Jane, some carrots from her garden, and…"

"And?" I asked interrupting Freeman's hesitancy.

"Well, she wanted me to cut 'er some large flowers that last morning…"

"Magnolia blossoms?"

"Yes, Ma'am. Got a ladder; cut 'er three or four large buds off an old tree had to be a hundred years old."

"Were they for Samuel?" I asked, even as I anticipated a different response.

"No, Ma'am. For Minerva… and…"

"What?"

"Ella handed me a canning jar and told me to take 'em down to the shacks, told me which one and to put them in water on the old table down there."

"My folks place…?"

"I reckon, Ma'am."

"Why do you think Ella was so insistent that you stop by Samuel's? Did you ever meet him?"

"Not till that last morning on my way out. Ella had many good words on Samuel and Jane," Freeman replied, "so I looked forward to it. Samuel's is no more than a mile or two from the gate of the Burney place along the old road back to Delta, so I hardly minded accommodating her wishes."

"Was Samuel surprised at your visit?"

"Don't know, Ma'am, but strangely, I had a feeling his wife was expecting me. She was standing there on her porch as I came up as though she'd been standing there for ages waiting for the time the three of us faced that morning. She waved for me as though I was an old friend even though she'd never seen my face before."

"Tell me everything, Ransom."

"Samuel was there and said his wife knew I was coming. Said Jane could feel it. Ella must have told them about me when I was in Vicksburg. Samuel walked back in and Jane motioned for me to follow. Inside she went to make us coffee, but Samuel, he headed over to the far corner of the cabin and sat in the shadows with his arms crossed over his chest like he was needing to protect himself from something. That got me to wondering if Sam and Jane had argued that morning. Jane motioned me to take a seat there at the table close to her little wood stove where she heated water."

"I remember Jane when I was a child. She and ol' Clara spent much time helping the 'croppers during fever season with herbs and poultices and kettles of fish stew they passed between the shacks."

"Jane seemed annoyed with Samuel. 'Come on over here!' she told him pointing to a stool at the table. 'He gots to bleed it out 'for it seeps to the bottom of his soul!' she said to me."

"'What Sam?'" I asked. "'You got something you need to get out? Something 'bout Jackson's passing troubling you.'"?

"This man is here now," Jane said. "You gotta tell 'im, Sam."

"Ella, you know she told me that Jackson, he was a boy, but she seems to think he may have lured ol' Isaac down to that dry well hole he fell in. That right?" I asked Samuel. 'No, it ain't right what Ella say. She old and don't 'member' good', he said."

"'Tell 'im, Samuel. Tell this man what you been keepin' inside you,' Jane demanded.

'Quiet, woman!'

Sam looked mighty troubled. His mouth turned down like there was a rage worked up in 'im that he could hardly hold back no more."

"'ol' Clara, she tol' me!' Jane said as if the words weren't forthcoming from Sam then they'd come from her just the same."

"'Who knows what happened to the Burney overseer?'" I asked. "'They're all gone, Sam. All them folks; ol' Clara, Jackson and his folks, so who can hurt you now?'"

"'Things been followin' Sam all these years since he 'a boy,' Jane said. 'Like a shada, ain't it, Sam?'"

"'About Jackson?'" I asked.

"'It ain't the way Ella think.'"

"At that moment Samuel seemed to jolt from his chair. He came up nose to nose to me. 'Now you can see for yourself what I got to say!' Samuel said and then took the stool Jane motioned to. And I could see what was hard for him to put into words."

"His eyes?" I asked.

"Yes, Ma'am. His blue eyes. I'd not noticed when he was sitting in the dark. He said, 'When Miss Burney come to Grandview to marry Burney, he a lot older than her… She sent Ella down to the shacks for a boy to come turn her garden for roses that had come from Vicksburg. They's a gift from her ma. Had 'er 'bout three dozen to plant. Ella say the mistress might give me a quarter if I turned the soil good in her garden. I come up to her veranda. She stopped cold and looked at me real mean like. She young but had a real hard look on 'er by then. 'Who's your daddy with them pale eyes?' she asked pointin' her finger at my eyes. I knows what to tell 'er.'"

"What?" I asked.

"'Tell the man, Sam!'" Jane demanded.

"Isaac your daddy?" I asked.

Ella had told me Isaac was a cold man with pale eyes she thought matched the color of his hair she called ice-silver. She said his eyes were like ice on a pond that reflects the winter sky's blue color and no warmer.

'You kill ol' Isaac, Sam?'"

"'Tell 'im!'" Jane commanded. "'Let the words free your soul.' Finally, Sam told me. 'No, Sir. Isaac, he not my daddy.'"

"'Burney was!' Jane announced. She pounded her tiny fist on that old table. 'He got at Clara, Sam's ma when she a girl-child, he 'a boy of sixteen, that Burney did. Clara, she only twelve or so when he got to 'er.'"

"Just 'fore Miss Burney come to Grandview to live, Samuel added to Jane's announcement, "Burney brought me up to the big house when I still a boy and told me if I ever open my mouth 'bout him and ma to his new wife he'd come to the shacks and gut ma with a butcherin' knife and ain't nobody ever gonna do nothin' 'bout it'. Then Burney, he tells me to say from then on that my daddy is ol' Isaac. But I never could say it. No, I hates Isaac too much to say I'm his blood. Isaac, he gots the same blue eyes like Burney, don't he?'"

"Go on Sam, tell 'im the rest." Jane insisted.

"One night, Isaac, he come 'round ma's shack, he say he's wantin' to sniff down there at what Burney blame him for. Blame 'im to keep peace with his Missus. Them just got married.'"

"Blamed for?" I asked. "Stay good with young Miss Burney, he mean?"

"'Burney tellin' Isaac he best say he's my daddy. So, Isaac started comin' round regular to my shack. Him sayin' he wantin' a sniff at what he already 'pose to 'a got to.

"'Got to…?'" I asked Samuel.

"'My ma, is what. He come to mount 'er.'"

"'Isaac like an animal.'

With those words Jane covered Samuel's hand with hers.

"'She say, Clara say, you come on up to my door 'gain, I put a sharp stick in your eyeball what my boy done whittled for!'" Jane declared. 'But he come anyway. He come and come again for Clara. Used 'er like Burney did.'"

"'Isaac say nobody gonna do nothin' to 'im for it, too! Not never. He say "cause I gots Burney's balls in my fist here and I bust 'em like two walnuts if he ever tells me I gotta go from Grandview!' Samuel said."

"Samuel, he got Burney's blue eyes. Ain't nobody 'round Grandview with them blue eyes when Samuel born but Burney. But Miss Burney, she never knowned that, did she?"

"What did Clara do 'bout Isaac's nocturnal visits?"

"'Clara tol' Isaac that Burney ain't afraid of no overseer, didn't she Samuel?' Jane told me."

"'He said it. Said it all the time he come 'round. Isaac say, That right? Then I go tell the Mistress her new husband been down at the shacks with them niggers and made himself one of his own named Samuel who gots the Burney blue eyes.' Samuel, that's Burney's daddy's name. Clara named me after ol' Burney's daddy so he ain't never gonna forget I his son. Ma always said, Burney my daddy, he treat me decent if she named him after him. But, no he never.'"

"'Ella tol' me when she lookin' in the mirror brushin' Miss Burney's hair every night, Mistress would say she ain't never gonna have no Burney baby if she finds out he done it with the niggers,'" Jane added. "Folks say they heard Miss Burney yellin' at 'im that she never loved Burney enough to have no kid by 'im."

"'So Burney and me, we worked somthin' out', Isaac told ma. 'I stay 'round here as overseer by keepin' my mouth shut 'bout Clara and her blue-eyed nigger-boy down at the shacks and Miss Burney keep thinkin' her man is clean. Huh! Ain't that what we're all gonna say?'"

"'Sam, then you had a reason to kill Isaac,'" I said to him."

"No, he ain't killed Isaac!" Jane stated. "I know, he ain't."

"'After Jackson born, nobody said a word 'bout it no more. But Burney, he tol' Ella to come down to the shacks and tell Clara to never let me come near the big house, and not come near Miss Burney if she out in her roses. Not never, Ella said. So, I never come 'round. But Isaac, he think he's a real big man, don't he? He bigger than Burney, and act like he the real master of Grandview when Burney not 'round. Isaac sayin' if Burney messed with 'im he gonna be real sorry! Only Jackson knowed how to deal with Isaac! Isaac 'fraid of that boy!"

"Burney, he got tired of Isaac disrepectin' him all them years, didn't he Sam?" Jane stated.

"Did Burney cause Isaac's death down that well?" I asked.

"One night," Samuel continued, "Jackson come down to the shacks. Burney told 'im to come 'round. He give me a jug of his daddy's rum for fillin' in that dry well hole. Haulin' barrows of dirt down there took me days. That well deep, I tell you."

"Go on, Sam," Jane demanded.

"You murder Isaac then?" I asked.

"'No, sir!'"

"'ol' Clara did! Tol' me she was meanin' to for years', Jane announced."

"Clara? Yeah? Then how'd she do it?" I asked.

"I'll tell you. It was me and her," Jane confessed. "I'm telling you, we dragged an ol' plank down there to the well hole and flipped it over the top like a footbridge over that mushy clay soil. Then real slow and careful, Clara crawled over that plank and set that jug of rum on that old splintered board. She did. Could hardly see no jug, all them tall grasses. Then while I watched if anybody comin', she went up to Isaac's hog's house, stood in his window like Minerva always done till Isaac seen 'er. All the time he been told by Ella what Minerva said, 'Wherever you go, Isaac, I gonna be there spittin' in the wind blowin' your way!' Clara, she looked Isaac in the eyes, him real sick layin' there in bed half-drunk and tol' him just the same like she promised Minerva the day she died. Minerva gonna spit in his face one day like she done on his back that time. Isaac, he squealed like a gutted hog thinkin' Clara turned into Minerva and come back like she promised. His time finally come. Issac headed for hell like she say. He went runnin' from hog's house chasing af'er her in the dark. He gonna kill Minerva for good this time or he ain't never gonna get no peace! Clara, she seen me down in the dark,' Jane continued, 'I standin' next to the hole so she knew where to run but not fall in. Isaac, he drunk. He come runnin' down the slope to wring Minerva's neck. He near on 'er, but then she stopped by the well and pointed. 'There be your jug of Mas'er's rum, Isaac. 'Huh?' Isaac said. He cut off his chase and went for that jug of Burney's fine rum but didn't see no black hole there waitin' to swallow 'im. Him half blind from seein' Minerva' again, huh? That jug of good rum, it followed Isaac to the bottom of that well Sam say was near thirty feet deep filled with nailed up broken boards and sharp bones from the butcherin' scraps.

"So, Clara killed ol Isaac?"

"Did she? Or did they just all get what they most wanted? Clara, for what Isaac done to her—over and over again he come for. Minerva for what that man done to 'er family and Isaac got him's jug of fine rum… and peace from Minerva finally? But peace was all he got. You know why?'"

"'Why?'" I asked.

"''Cause Samuel done drunk all that rum Jackson brought by the evening before. Isaac, he chased a dead woman for an empty rum jug! Ain't it the truth?' Jane waited for Sam to say something."

"'Ma said next day she went to look down the well,'" Samuel added. 'She said she could hear 'im down there. Isaac beggin' 'cause he got 'a broken neck. He wantin' Burney to come haul 'im up with a mule and ropes so he can die in peace. Ma looked down that hole and said to Isaac, 'Minerva with Jesus. Maybe you best pray to Jesus that Minerva might come help you. But he laughed and laughed 'cause he don't know how to pray. Only to hate and abuse women. Two more days and ma told me to go do what Burney say. I filled in that old well. Isaac, him still laughing down there when I shoveled the dirt in. But now he gone just like Minerva promised. Three weeks and a day after Minerva and Owen went to Jesus, Isaac in hell!

"'What else you need to say, Sam?'" Jane asked.

"Jackson, he my younger brother and that's how I loved him, no matter what our daddy did to us. Jackson and me are blood and he put it right for what old Burney did to me. He give me this here land."

So, from the grave Momma kept her promise to ol' Isaac. She sure, as Issac in hell, did!

FAR CALLINGS

88

Yes, how many of us come to answer the call? Yet many of us are left waiting for the doors to unlock. I'd come to see this country as a place where my people were drawn to closed doors only to hear the clanking of locks from the other side. The keys to these locks the white folks kept hidden in every bone of our bodies.

The Negro weeklies were constantly announcing yet another lynching alongside editorials about some imminent war in Europe. My people couldn't figure the true reason for this conflict, nor why young Negro men should go marching off to foreign lands even as white papers declared a call to arms and touted war as the answer to Europe's aristocratic tyranny. What about the tyranny of white hatred here at home? I pondered these contradictions when Louvenia stopped in my dressing room to chat.

"You getting all dressed up now, ain't you?"

Louvenia ran her eyes over my new Parisian-style frock hanging on a satin covered hanger. It was sewn from one of the bolts of fine *peau de soie* I'd shipped from Paris on my last visit.

"Are you sure you don't want to come down and join us for tea?" I asked.

"No, I got things to do."

"Like what do you have to do that can't wait till later?"

I knew how shy Louvenia could be when special guests visited Lewaro.

"She's comin' to talk to you 'bout all these things goin' on, ain't she?"

"What things, Sister?"

"It's about Booker T. Washington. Folks say he likes to take things easy-like and not stir up a fuss that might get white folks worked up. But Mr. Dubois, he don't see things that way. No, folks say he aims to stir as big a dust as he can so when it all settles things gonna be better for us."

"What else have your heard?" I asked.

Sister whispered like the great wizard, Mr. Washington was just outside my door.

"Well, folks sayin' the fine Mr. W. E. B. Dubois been talking to the papers. Him sayin' that Booker T. Washington ain't no better than some ol' Uncle Tom butler who knows to keep his mouth shut when white folks tell 'im where his place is! That's what!"

"That is not what," I replied. "Where did you hear such talk?"

"Well, I must have been talkin' with your new cook." Louvenia said. "She reads to me the weeklies while we have our coffee in the morning."

"They are both fine men that serve their people in different ways. You see, they both have different notions on how the government in Washington should press southern states stop the lynching."

"Yeah, and every day in the south our men still die by ropes while folks is talkin' about how to say the word lynchin' just right! Don't we all know 'bout that? Who come to punish them white men that lynched Jeff? The President? Mr. Booker? Who come to say prayers over Jeff's grave or plant his flower seeds every spring? Ain't nobody but us!"

"Then you know about our petition we aim to present to President Wilson at the White House asking him to enforce federal laws against lynching?" I asked.

"Lelia done told me last week. But I was waitin' to hear more from you." Louvenia said. "Lelia say her momma is on the committee, ain't it so? She say you're aimin' to go to the White House in your fine motor with some important Negro folks and Mrs. Washington just might think you're insulting Booker by not keeping to the place he says coloreds best keep to and that's good and quiet in the back! You know she might think that, too."

"What else did cook claim was in the weeklies this week?"

I knew the new cook could barely read a recipe let alone one of the weeklies. Her notions were based primarily on the pictures she'd "read".

"Said there's gonna be a big war over there and some coloreds sayin' they won't go fight for no democracy on the other side of the ocean when they ain't seen enough over here to be sure of what they'd be fightin' for. Ain't that so?" Louvenia asked. "What's that democracy they been talkin' about look like for real? Our folks must be thinkin' that, huh?"

"You're right, Sister. It is the issue at hand; whether our men should show white folks we worked to build this nation and we're gonna go fight for democracy for folks over there."

"And you, Sarah. How do you see it? If Lelia were a boy, would you be packing her things for France or lock 'er in the larder till it's all over? I think colored momma's best be tellin' their sons not to go off fighting for no more white folks' deals ain't gonna put nothin' on their plates."

"What would I do? I've been doing it, Sister. On my tours I've stopped to speak to colored soldiers and have found them brave and ready to fight for what's right. I want to read this to you."

I pulled out of my dressing table drawer the note that had arrived the week before.

"This is from a young solder that I read aloud. 'We all remember you and have often spoken 'round the chow table of the words of comfort you gave us at your visit to Camp Sherman on the eve of our departure. Those words stayed with the men longer than any spoken by anyone that I have known or heard of.'"

"You see it best to encourage our men go over there then?" Louvenia asked.

"I can see how our men must support this nation to be thought of as part of it, even if it's not an equal part they often hand us. I can't see the federal government do anything to make these southern states stop lynching if we don't march right alongside white folks."

"Then sounds like you're marching alongside Mr. Dubois to Paris, France."

"Perhaps after we meet with the President and that unfortunately puts me at odds with Booker, which is a very unpleasant feeling."

"Well, it ain't the first time you been headed down the wrong side of the road with that man!"

We laughed at the notion I might soon find myself up Booker's crawl again but then he wouldn't have recognized me any other place.

"Sister, you ever thought about goin' to France one day?" I asked. "I mean after the war and all."

By then Lelia and I had made two voyages to France to introduce my products in Paris and were moved by the reception folks over there had given us. Seemed like the French saw more in me than the mere shades of color on a woman's face.

"You ain't won that war yet, so I guess I hold off on buying any tickets to cross the ocean. Anyway, Lelia say it takes days 'fore you see land again. That so?"

"It is. But the Cunard liners are like floating hotels. First we may have to obtain passports."

"What's a passport? Sister asked.

"Nowadays when folks go abroad, they need a special document stamped by the State Department so they can come back home. They're calling it a passport."

"Just coloreds need a passport?" She asked.

"I'm not sure yet. Lelia has asked Ransom to look into it before she leaves for her trip to Panama."

"That passport, it's sure gonna keep us here, or not let us come back if we do get away! Ain't that our history in these lands?"

Louvenia looked troubled. She stared at me in the mirror for the longest time.

"What Sister?"

"You don't 'member your promise?" she whispered.

"I've never forgotten a word of it. I promised you the day I left Jeff's cabin…"

"That one day you'd learn to read and write so's to write a letter to the President of the United States askin' him to see his way to stop the lynchin'. But you ain't writing no letter, are you? No, Ma'am, you're gonna call on the President himself at the White House. You know there ain't no colored woman that ever done that before. Ain't never, Sarah."

Louvenia's eyes filled with tears.

"You called to do this thing. I know it. You called to go to the White House, Sarah, and ask the President to stop the lynchin'."

I smiled, dried my tears and left to see how the kitchen was doing preparing for my guest. Sister was right. I never expected to meet the President one day but then it never crossed my mind that I'd ever be expecting Mrs. Booker T. Washington at my home for tea either. However, I had a thought on Bella Burke and the Creole princess I'd helped her conjure as a guest for tea at her own place—a day that never came. On this morning, I truly felt like a princess living in a world that was surely unimaginable to most woman of color.

At the bottom of the stairs, Otho had taken his position in the foyer to wait for Mrs. Washington's arrival.

"I can hear a big car comin' over the gravel drive, Madame Walker."

"Thank you, Otho. I'll greet Mrs. Washington myself."

"Yes, Ma'am."

Still Otho lingered.

"Oh, Otho. You know I'd forgotten. You've never seen Mrs. Booker T. Washington. So, then you be ready to open her door, won't you?"

"Yes, Ma'am. Here she comes. I go on out."

Standing there at Lewaro's grand entrance I glanced at the hem of my dress I'd worn for the very first time to see if it had somehow frayed in those last moments before I met my guest. Frayed like the one I wore to hear Margaret speak in St. Louis so many winters before. We were two women that had since covered so many miles along our journeys and yet had arrived at the same open door that morning.

"MadameWalker, your guest is here, Ma'am," Otho announced with great dignity like I'd imagine the head usher at the White House might.

"Margaret, so good of you to drive all the way up to Irvington."

Mrs. Washington gave Otho a big smile and her hand.

"It's been too long, Sarah. I think I get more word on you from reading the papers than your all too short notes."

"Then you've probably read what the *New York Times* printed. Lelia sent it to me. 'A wonderful house', the reporter characterized Villa Lewaro. 'A degree of elegance and extravagance that a princess might envy…'"

"I did read that, Sarah. And wondered when the *Times* has ever written about any Negro woman living like a princess before you. How can there be a doubt that you're the first?"

I guided Mrs. Washington to the drawing room where tea was set on a starched white linen table topper. There, in a cut crystal bowl floated large gardenias. Nobody but Louvenia knew this was the way Ella set Melinda Jackson's tea table. It was sweet of her to tell the kitchen help to do it up as fine as Sister could have imagined was the finest—that being like at Grandview.

"I've never been in so magnificent a home as this, Sarah."

Margaret gazed about smiling with appreciation.

"We still laugh about *The Defender* saying my home would 'create a furor for one of the Race was invading the sacred domains of New York's aristocracy.' So then it seems I create a furor wherever I go."

"Look at these beautiful painted ceilings!"

Margaret pointed to the clouds painted in the three insets above us in my drawing room.

"They're painted to look like they're open to the sky with bits of gold twinkling like stars."

"At the Burneys', when I waited for my folks to return from the cotton fields, I was sure the Lord showered the sky over the big house with stars. I never looked over my folks' shack to see if it was just the same up there. Strange how life on a plantation can so easily distort you vision? Like the dust out in them fields where we spent our lives."

"Yes, the Lord looks down at us all the same," she said. "Now if only we could learn to see each other the same light!"

"Only Negro money bought this house, Margaret. And a Negro was the architect and a Negro woman sleeps upstairs in a room that is not much further from the Hudson River than my folks' place was from the Mississippi."

"Where did you get name of Villa Lewaro?" Margaret asked.

"I didn't. Enrico Caruso visited and mentioned that such a fine place should have a fine name. So, he and Lelia came up with one on the spot."

"I heard Caruso at Carnegie Hall last season. This is as fine a mansion as any in Westchester County and made only more special because it was named by your lovely daughter and one of the world's greatest opera stars."

After a long and delightful tea and all too many sandwiches and tea cakes, Margaret and I chatted about the seemingly ever-growing number of lynchings. If there weren't a few lynchings on any week there sure seemed to be a few fires set. Yes, things sure got fired up when times were bad for white folks and then their anger so easily sparked on any colored that happened to be doing well.

"I've heard about the petition you plan to submit to President Wilson."

Margaret seemed to ease the conversation into matters where I did not entirely support her husband.

"Not only me, of course, but also the Reverend Adam Clayton Powell, Sr. of Harlem's Abyssinian Baptist Church, James Weldon Johnson, Fred Moore…"

"The publisher of the *New York Age*."

"You know him?" I asked.

"No. But I've read in his weeklies articles on your fund raising for the NAACP. And, of course Mr. Dubois, I presume."

"Yes. Mr. Dubois is part of the committee. We will call at the White House sometime at the beginning of August. It's been arranged by Mr. Joseph Tumulty, the President's secretary."

Margaret and I avoided the controversy brewing between Booker and Mr. Dubois' position as to whether our men should support the war effort in Europe, or how aggressively we should deal with the issue of lynching. She already knew I'd been active in selling war bonds for several weeks. I thought it best to leave things as is. Therefore, I figured it might be a good time to ease out of the conversation by showing my guest the gardens and orchard just beyond.

"You know, once you made your way in life as a tub woman," I commented as we passed through the dining room towards the terrace overlooking the garden. "You still go to bed early and get up early only to heat water for the tubs you're not gonna be hovering over all day. I still get up like that every morning."

We walked through the fruit trees that had been picked only a few days earlier.

"Every morning I'm out here pulling weeds and gathering berries that Otho planted along the edge of my orchard. You should see me, Margaret, a sight in my overalls… I'm a full-fledged 'farmerette'. We're putting up fruit and vegetables by the wholesale."

"Your orchard and garden are as lovely as your home although I can't imagine you out here in overalls."

We laughed.

As we strolled around my home towards the *porte-a-cochere* where Margaret's driver waited out of the sun, I decided to tell her something I'd kept from everyone, including Louvenia. Only Lelia and I had discussed this.

"Margaret, so long I've wanted to share something with you in confidence."

"Don't worry. I only tell Booker a small part of what folks share with me on my travels."

"Lelia and I have been discussing something for months now. We're considering moving."

"Moving from this fine home?"

"Home?" I replied. "Will this country ever say this is our home, too?"

"Where then?"

"I'm thinking of quitting this country all together and going to a place where the color of your skin isn't a burden one must struggle under every day. We're thinking of moving to Paris. In fact, I plan to apply for this passport the State Department is issuing."

Margaret was obviously jarred by this announcement but told me she understood my feelings. Things were not getting better in this country. How many of us still wondered if it ever would?

❧

The summer came and went too quickly. On my last day at Lewaro before I returned to my townhouse in Harlem, Sister and I spent a few sweet moments looking over the jars of jam, spring vegetables and summer fruits we'd put up. The pantry was soon filled with the bounty of our garden. Bright colored jars of strawberry jam, pickles, canned peaches and peas lined the shelves. Louvenia, however, knew I was attempting to divert attention from my departure. For days she'd been urging me to remain at Lewaro and continue to rest. I knew she didn't want to be in New York City but I had to show support for our men headed to war.

"You take lots of jars of my strawberry jam to Lelia," Sister admonished.

"Of course, I will," I replied. "I saw Otho put the box of your jams in the motor this morning. Were you up packing those before I got up?"

"You know you should be getting your rest here where you love it most and not going out on the road so much. Look how tired your eyes been lately."

I kissed my sister and got in the Cole for the trip to New York. It seemed as though all the way there Otho was peeking in his mirror at me.

"I'm fine, Otho."

"You sure, Madame?" He asked. "Maybe you're too tired to be travelin' today."

"We're only going twenty miles. What's twenty miles given the long distances we've traveled so far?"

"Yes, Ma'am."

I was eager to see Lelia. She had created a life in Harlem that so delighted her she seldom wanted to visit the Villa Lewaro. I was very tired when I arrived back in New York and went to bed before she returned from a party, so did not greet her till the following morning.

"Momma, I haven't seen you for nearly a month!" she exclaimed as she brought my breakfast tray in that morning.

"And I thought of that every day, my daughter!"

The following weeks were blinding. I continued to help sell war bonds to my people and urge them to support the nation's war efforts. Soon after I was appointed to the advisory board of the Motor Corps of American and Lelia became an ambulance driver for wounded Negro returnees. It had been Otho that taught Lelia to drive in part prompted by her momma's promise of a Cadillac motorcar if she did.

Lelia and I rejoiced with the nation when the war finally ended and yet wondered if the contribution of our men would be recognized. There is never enough courage in any of us to be able to read the daily list of war causalities without grieving over endless death and more suffering than we could have imagined. In December, I accepted an invitation from New York Mayor John F. Hylan to join him on a ship to welcome our men home in New York harbor. Onboard, drifting towards the great horizon, we toasted Champaign as ships returned our men. Behind me stood the Statue of Liberty to which I offered a silent prayer that our men would finally be liberated in their own country just as they'd fought to liberate a people across the ocean.

My war efforts had left me depleted, therefore, as my daughter had planned to be away to meet our agents in Panama for an extended stay, it was easy for me to escape back to Lewaro. I knew, could feel it, that the number of my days were dwindling no matter how hard I tried to hold them down for another taste.

THE LONG WHITE ROPE

89

I T MATTERED LITTLE where my tours took me as even without a single one in sight there were always ropes dangling in our faces. It was just before Thanksgiving when it happened. We were on the road having covered Montgomery and Meridian and made what was to be a quick stop in Greenwood. Matilda and I with Otho had been traveling from church to church in those outer parishes and staying at folks' homes at night where talk after supper frequently veered to the lynchings and the ugly acts by white folks 'round them parts.

There'd been abuses along the trip; there always are. In town a white woman who spat on me ranting epithets about her poverty and something about my rich nigger face. She put her own face against mine so I'd not only feel the heat of her hatred, but her spittle dripping down my face and onto my blouse. I gleaned from her shrill words that to her my wealth was somehow unnatural. We stepped around this woman headed to my Cole just as a white man threatened Otho for driving a 'stolen' car and shouldered him aside.

I sat down in the rear seat and picked up the paper Otho had been reading earlier. As he couldn't read well, he left them back there so I could explain things he'd noticed in the printed images. There'd been another lynching in the next county, the second that week. It was the usual scenario: A white woman, some imagined disrespect, a rope and another life all too easily extinguished. I was long past eager to leave that parish county and get back home. I knew my exhaustion made me vulnerable to clenching my fists. We washerwomen have strong arms. A thousand times over those weeks I felt like backhanding the next white woman who even looked at me wrong. I figured it best to move my thoughts ahead as I knew it would be a long drive home. Finally, the café handed sandwiches out the door to Otho. Naturally they would not serve us inside and we happily left the sneers and slights of that town.

By the time we were on the open road the sun was sinking as fast as my mood. The sky was a fireball red, which did little to ease my tension as it was the color of a roof set aflame by Klansmen. At times I wondered if the sky went flame-red every time an innocent man was lynched. Does it Lord? It was chilly; we couldn't eat at first, so Matilda and I bundled up and Otho pulled his collar high around his neck. The thought of rope burn on your neck always puts a chill on you, even in the worst summer heat. Matilda gazed out the motor looking like a lost child but then in our own country, weren't those of us dark-skinned all lost or were we merely stepped over and forgotten? But then why measure that difference?

I was silent over that bumpy road. Guess I was getting tired of changing the subject to diminish our fears by putting our thoughts over to a happier place. We finally ate our sandwiches in stiff silence. We'd barely finished, and I was about to ask Otho to slow for a place to stop for water when we approached those train tracks. He slowed with caution, looking up and down the tracks in the hazy night; he was always unsure of his sight and complained about what the sharp gravel could do to his tires. I never heard a thing. Otho surely didn't either as his hearing was poor. No train, no whistle, yet just as we approached the tracks it seemingly came from nowhere plainly determined to cross the road ahead of us, or even through us. It was a train headed our way.

Matilda let out a harrowing scream. My heart all but burst from my chest. I truly did not believe we'd make it across those bumpy tracks and only barely did. If Otho had frozen from fear for even the dash of a moment we'd been crushed to death. Perhaps thinking that train was on our tail, Otho sped ahead to the county line. Don't we all develop the instinct to run—head off fast in any direction from the many kinds of ropes that drop in our faces? Happily, only the howl of the train's whistle pursued us over to the county line and yet followed ringing in my ears most of the night. The nigger dogs are howling again, I thought. Even when you don't see them on your tail, you know they're closing in. You can always feel the chill of their drool dripping down your back they want to climb.I breathed deeply and finally got the words out.

"Otho… are you alright?"

But nothing came from his mouth; just a half-nod of his head in front of me. His eyes were still frozen on the blank horizon ahead. Don't know if the train's failure to whistle warn us was deliberate, but these were the times that we daily fought our way through and too often lost.

My heart palpitations were searing, like being jabbed over and over again with a pen knife. I grabbed my chest for fear it might crush against my ribs.

"Otho, Madame Walker, she's havin' a heart attack! Otho…!"

Matilda's screams pierced my ears.

"I get you there…" he yelled.

But where was there? We were in the middle of nowhere and it was all pitch black beyond our motor lamps. Once again, like so many times on the road, there could be no turning back.

I thought I would die of chest pains and wondered if we'd run out of petrol on some dirt road in Klan country. But we made it to the next town where Otho, on foot, found a doctor for coloreds. The man was thoughtful and quickly gave me something to calm my nerves and ease my chest pains. Then he recommended, in the strongest terms, that I cancel the rest of my engagements and return home for treatment from Doctor Ward. Reluctantly, I asked Matilda to telegraph Freeman and inform him accordingly. She also sent word to Louvenia. What I didn't instruct Matilda to do was forward to them the Doctor's prognosis. His notion that I was about to have a nervous breakdown and that my blood pressure was life threatening.

∽

It was only days after we'd gotten home again that the weeklies started putting out reports of the East St. Louis riots. However, word had spread much faster as we'd already heard pieces of the stories. The week the rioting started, I received a note from my friend Jessie Robinson who lived in East St. Louis. I'd known Jessie from my days at Sally's. She wrote of the riots and how she'd organized help for the desperately poor colored women who had fled fires and brutalities by running with their kids over to the Missouri side of the river. If not by name, I still knew these women, most of whom surely survived as tub women. I'd worked so hard to bury my long-ago struggles even as reports of these riots brought it all back. You see, it all started right there on the same bridge that I'd walked a thousand times to take my ironed-up laundry to my customers. Who couldn't see that the strife wouldn't eventually turn to violence? Yet the authorities did nothing but watch and smirk as folks fled for their lives over that old bridge.

Times were hard and when the big meat packing companies needed more workers, they'd send agents down to the south where there were seemingly countless men who'd stopped believing sharecropping would ever feed their family. The agents offered ten men the same job and cut the wages in half if twenty showed up for it. But frequently there were forty or fifty desperate men showing up for one job if not hundreds. So miserable was the pay at these packing places that empty-pocketed Irish immigrants wouldn't take the jobs. But for colored men it was still better than starving in the south as a 'cropper. Hundreds of men lured north to East St. Louis with only the promise of food on the table if they worked hard enough. Offer to fill a man's kids' mouths and you got yourself someone begging to be your slave. The cycles of exploitation are as predictable as the seasons. Come spring, a whole new branch of greed blossoms and the rich get richer as we are harnessed to gather in their bounty and pray for the scraps they might toss back in our faces.

It didn't take long before that old fever crept back out of the shadows and headed over to the east side of the river. The palpable fever of white hatred stirred up by coloreds showing up at the lines for work. The weeklies printed that the unions been telling poor white folks there was an invasion of coloreds headed to St. Louis and would keep coming in waves. Wages gonna be depressed even more. Did that mean ever'body gonna live like coloreds? Then to start a real blaze, one smoky night a motorcar full of white men drove around our side of the tracks shooting at the homes of coloreds asleep in their beds. Talk was that this was only the beginning of what was to come. Folks were saying that there's got to be blood spilled to quench white rage. Who's gonna die? Your kid sleeping and a bullet finds her? The next night colored men were organized and waiting for the next assault. There came a motorcar driving 'round colored streets. Where's the trouble gonna be tonight? My place this time? Who's gonna die? Your kid? Sure as hell ain't gonna be mine! The coloreds came out to defend their families. Shot the motorcar so full of holes it could have made a good sieve. Killed everyone, but they turned out to be cops looking for trouble; them driving 'round with no motor lamps. Lord, God, they was all shot in the head. Papers wrote that nobody could untangle the pieces of what happened nor the corpses after the motors, with their headless drivers collided. The newspapers pounded the white folks that they were righteous to have started it all in the first place and only more blood could put out the rage burning all over the city.

And the next day also went up in flames. It all happened before most coloreds even heard 'bout the cops being killed the night before. They's out doing their business, going to work and getting on the trains when a white mob came looking for revenge; gonna feed the fever's thirst for blood. One momma holding her baby turned 'round to see a club comin' to smash her face open. Her baby on the dirt left at her side screaming while the clubber went to let more blood. One old colored man, couldn't hardly see, was shoved off the train platform in front of an oncoming train by three nicely dressed white women who then wiped their hands on their dresses which were undoubtedly laundered by one of us. He was dead before what was left of him rolled to the gravel.

Nothing to bury. Colored porters were told to clean the mess off the tracks so no white woman would be unsettled by the splattered gore.

Next day the white papers wrote that President Wilson was accusing the Republicans of starting the whole damned thing. According to Wilson, it was because they were bringing in thousands of coloreds to destroy East St. Louis and make it uninhabitable for good hard-working white folks. Even unwound, the ropes are long and so easily twist around the necks of the innocent. When it was over, dozens more folks were dead and colored businesses were burned to ashes all over town. Yes, the sky glowed red again. Another innocent man dead and another widow searching for her man down along some past dream they'd shared. Lord, help us. In all the ashes, it would have been the only place she'd know to go looking.

✍

The week after I'd returned, Sister was nagging me to see Dr. Ward; I knew it was due to all Freeman's talk about my near nervous breakdown that got her worked up. I blamed Matilda for that, silly child. She had no problem getting Sister's ear on anything, so I was certain she'd filled her Auntie Louvenia's ears with the details of our return home.

I asked Otho to take me for the appointment I did not wish to face. Dr. Ward was expecting me and I the lecture I knew awaited.

"Well, young lady…" Dr. Ward repeated.

Could tell he was flummoxed for the right words. He'd checked this and that and asked me into his private office and invited me to take a chair across from him. The sun streaming through his tall window blurred my vision and made the room turn black. Lord only knows it could have been only the heat of that morning that put me on edge.

"Please don't condescend to me like a child. It reminds me of the way white folks speak to us, Joseph."

"All I'm sayin' is, you look weary, very weary," he commented. "How's your sleep?"

"Fine… How's yours?"

Well I didn't have to tell him how little I'd been getting over the last few weeks. Surely, he could tell by my sour tone.

"Little on edge?" he asked. "You sleepin' at all?"

"In the end what difference does my sleep make?"

Dr. Ward adjusted the drapes behind his desk so I wouldn't be squinting from the glare.

"Makes a big difference to your health," he said.

"How many of our people sleep well? I reckon not many in St. Louis. Guess it has something to do with wondering if the Klan's comin' to string up your man or riddle your door with bullets. Maybe put the roof on fire when your kids are saying their prayers."

Dr. Ward could say nothing yet his calmness was soothing.I went on.

"You know, I dream a lot."

"Having those nightmares again, Sarah? About that last night with Jeff?"

"And even before that. I dream of those days when I'm in my daddy's shack and the cold wind is hunting me down; blowing through the cracks in the door near my bed. That cold, it tortures me till I ache. Ache all over and even beyond that. Strangely, in my dream I awaken and look out the little window and see the Burney place up on the hill. So close and warm up there isn't it? Yet so cold and far away from us who live in the long cold shadows of them big white houses."

"It's been a year since you last saw me. Even back then I told you you're in need of rest." he said. "I've heard from the doctor that treated you down there after that near train accident."

I avoided looking at Dr. Ward and continued the telling of my dream.

"When I wake in my own bedroom, rested or not, I feel my warm silk bedcovers and see a room with flowers. Before dawn, my maid enters and lights the morning fire. No cold fights its way through my mahogany door."

"And then the bad dream's gone?"

"But not that bitter cold. It lingers like a nightmare. I know it's the same fear all our people sleep under. Even in summer, you sleep cold when your belly's empty. Ain't it the truth?"

Dr. Ward was grave. I thought of how different his expression was since the day we met back in Pittsburgh. He'd lost his smiling face, or had I lost my ability to see joy? But had we both lost our hopes as well? Well, guess the weariness had crept up on me more than I'd even realized.

Joseph knew I was a stubborn woman.

"Joseph, in the deepest part of my heart I truly believe the Lord raised me up from the tubs, not just to make me a rich woman or to prove someone of the race could do it, but to stop the lynching and that's what I aim to do!"

"Sarah, I implore you once again, like I've done many times for these last many months."

"Yes, I know. I got to slow down."

"Good friend, we're now well past that," he said. "Now you've got to stop traveling altogether. You have to turn your business over to those you trust and then enjoy that fine place you built at Irvington. Even consider spending half your days in bed from now on. Do you understand me?"

His eyes pleaded.

"Yes, Joseph, I do know. I known you're telling me I'm dying. But I've known this for a long time; could feel death creeping up on me like that chill I've ran from so very long. I'm not afraid. But I truly believe the Lord won't come for me till I've stopped the lynching. I know He won't take me till we convince President Wilson to stop that long white rope once and for all. Don't I owe it to Jeff's memory?"

"You can stay home and write letters. Even that might aggravate your condition. You your name's in the weeklies like no other woman of color before. Use your pen to get your word out and not the road."

"Joseph, tell me plain. How will I know when the end is near?"

Dr. Ward was uneasy with this question.

"As your blood pressure goes up, your kidneys will fail. You've indicated that may be the case now with those pains you been having in your sides. You'll be in a great deal of pain from then on until the end. You'll lose your eyesight. But that's just at the very end. But then if you can be persuaded to slow down, well, who knows?"

I did not tell Dr. Ward I was already losing my vision.

"Who knows? A few months at best?" I asked.

"At best," he responded.

I knew with those words that I had to work even harder to untangle my husband's memory from those long white ropes that had dragged it behind me for so many dreamless nights.

DANCING ON THE PRESIDENT'S SHADOW AND NOT FALLING OFF

90

OW DOES ONE come to terms with the fact that President Wilson, who so assiduously courted our votes, could betray us so easily? But hadn't every president since Lincoln kept silent as our men were cut down from trees?

I was the widow of a lynched man and knew I had to do whatever I could for my people no matter what the personal cost. On my journeys across these lands I met many widows, most of whom were tub women, who couldn't feed their kids. These women had no time to fret over what went on yesterday and had little enough hope to invest in the morrow. Who would fight for them, I wondered? Hope is a rope that can pull mothers out of that bottomless well of desperation but what happens when faith runs out like the cornmeal always does? Some of us planned a march in New York that summer to see.

July in New York City is so swelteringly hot that folks clank out-doors to escape the humidity of their apartments. On these days the noise of the city is incredible. But this day was different. The Negro Silent Protest Parade was planned shortly after the riots in St. Louis.

Many of my agents would march down Fifth Avenue along with thousands of other coloreds. The papers wrote that there were more than ten thousand of us and twice as many lookers lining the avenue—we would walk in absolute silence. Hundreds of marchers all dressed in Easter baptismal white, some carrying signs, walked a slow *pavane* as there was nothing to celebrate or bang a gong for. No there was no real victory for us waiting ahead. Still it was the quietest day I'd ever listened to in New York City even as there were quaking sounds heard by my people all over the nation.

We'd never marched in a protest of this magnitude before. It was heavy on my thoughts that a sniper might be on a roof and fire at the backs of women who marched with their children, after all, it was easy enough for the Klan to burn families out of their homes throughout the south. When my own husband was lynched, at the moment I landed at Jeffrey's jerking legs I heard that white man say "…in a year or two the niggers'ill be ours again!" I so feared we were losing the fight against the Klan. Moreover, President Wilson's duplicity put him on the side of the perpetrators yet I still would dance on his shadow even as white supremacy was being reestablished.

A few weeks after the march in New York, after hearing nothing from President Wilson suggesting he would move to enforce existing laws against lynching, those of us on the Negro Silent Protest Parade Committee had finally obtained the confirmation of the actual date of our appointment with President Wilson at the White House. We left New York by train to meet in Washington D.C.

I knew Dr. Ward would have been lecturing me the entire journey had he known of my plans. What could have been the words to have told my folks that their child was going to the White House to petition a sitting President and then share with them the long history of his racism? They would never have understood as the only President they were aware of, the man that lived in the White House so far away from their life in the fields, was President Lincoln—the man that freed them. Own and

Minerva had long held that injustice was not Christian and if only the President came to know of our long suffering he would help us or so was the myth the 'croppers passed around like a sacred tray of communion bread. Lord, what would President Lincoln say resting face to face with Jesus in Sister's Bible?

Mr. Tumulty's invitation to meet President Wilson was at noon on that sweltering first day in August. Our car arrived at the White House gate half-hour prior. With me on the appointment was W. E. B Dubois, the Reverend Adam Clayton Powell, Sr. James Weldon Johnson and the newspaper publisher whose weeklies had run my ads for years, Fred Moore. We sat silently on the way over to the White House like it was a wake we were attending. But like any wake, there is only one outcome. The dead still remain silent; their anguish unheard. Yet, all the same, I could still hear Jeff's voice like his head was lying next to mine on our pillow again.

The petition we would submit to the President, penned by Mr. Johnson, was withering in my sweaty palms but I'd already memorized it word for word. I said it aloud at the moment the Cole drove through the White House gates: "We believe that the spirit of lawlessness is doing untold injury to our country. We petition that lynching and acts of mob violence be deemed a crime punishable by Federal laws in all states…"

By then thousands of colored men and even some women had been lynched, but the count of those punished for these crimes still hovered at none or less.

We arrived early. A White House page escorted us into an executive waiting room where we were seated. My heart was pounding with thoughts of Louvenia's words reminding me that I was the first woman of color to meet a sitting president. The men soon were pacing the room. My thoughts jumped wondering where the President would receive us? Would he enter to greet us alone or with his secretaries? Or did he meet people, even coloreds, in fancy staterooms? But then a President had never invited any of my people to the White House except Booker T. Washington nearly two decades before us.

After about a half-hour a man entered and introduced himself as Mr. Tumulty. Without a word from his lips his eyes easily belied the fact we'd once again been lied to as this man could only gaze at the beautiful carpet hiding under his feet. He did so longer than I had when I entered the room as if he knew at one glance that we, too, knew he was the bearer of bad news.

He proceeded to inform us the President was detained on important matters and would not receive us after all. He did not declare the man was therefore hiding in the shadows of his white house, a place of cowardice that never knew Lincoln.

Mr. Tumulty mumbled something and then commented about the president being too busy that morning with the Farm Animal Feed Bill.

"Did you say farm animals, Mr. Tumulty?" I asked. "When was the President ever worried about colored people eating? Even the ones that voted for him?"

Mr. Tumulty did not appreciate my candidness and walked out without a further word. Shortly thereafter two White House ushers appeared to show us the door. It would not have surprised me if it had been the rear service door. The wake concluded; we walked back to the waiting Cole in stony silence.

✦

There wasn't much to say on the return to the hotel; only a few words on the feasibility of bypassing Wilson to bring our petition directly to Congress. But, alas, this was a Congress entirely controlled by white southerners.

"Why would we even think he'd see us after all?" I posed to my fellow petitioners. "It was Wilson that said 'Segregation is not humiliating, but a benefit and ought to be so regarded.' Said it and then segregated us out of all Federal jobs. That is except kitchen and laundry work at the White House.

Whatever else we chatted about is all a blur to me now.

I was eager to return to my room and rest. My vision was as blurred that day as my thoughts. I couldn't help but think that we'd not only failed our people, but also deeply concerned that Wilson's refusal to see us would be interpreted by lynching mobs as tacit approval of their crimes by virtue of the government's continued failure to prosecute the existing laws against the perpetrators.

At the hotel, I entered the lift for my floor and sensed the white woman flinch and move in the other direction from me. What should I have said to this poor startled woman? I am MadameC.J. Walker, the one you've read about in the papers. The richest Negro woman in America and I've just been to see the President of the United States but he was hiding under his lies and would not receive me? No, he had no new lies to convey today because he was distracted on working out the menu for farm animals. Was your husband lynched by a white mob, Ma'am? Should we go downstairs to the tearoom and share how we've somehow raised our children off the tubs and endured the loneliness of our widowhoods?

Yet I said nothing to this white woman who probably had never spent a day bent over a laundry tub. My heart kept pounding the same message. Let it be… Let it be… But the responding echo in my head throbbed louder; how many times must I let it be before it all goes toxic?

I exited the lift to that pathetic woman's apparent relief. Would she have been pleased if I'd jumped from the roof? I turned to see her peek out the lift gate as I passed a well-dressed elderly white couple. They easily reminded me of Robert Burney and his wife. My heart had more to say and pounded hard on my chest to get it out. Why are those people staring at me so? I stumbled on my hem walking over the thick carpet and received that white woman's blessing for it.

"That colored woman's a drunk!" this fine Christian woman screeched to her husband as I leaned against the corridor wall holding my chest. "Just a drunk!"

The chambermaids up and down the corridor seemed to confirm this woman's notions with their disdainful glances cast at my discomfort.

"I knew that would happen," her husband said, "once they let those Negras in! What did they expect?"

As I struggled to get my room key out, they brushed by looking as if the worst calamity that could befall them would be my agony collapsing at their feet for them to have to walk on a path they felt justified in not sharing.

"They should be kept on their side of the tracks!"

The woman averted her eyes at the disgraceful sight of me struggling to get my door unlocked before I collapsed. I could only think that President Wilson should have met these people as they would have had so much to chat about after the farm animals were properly fed. Yes, surely, they could have feasted on a fine supper the colored help had cooked up in the White House basement kitchen.

I entered my dark room and pulled at my hat to get it off. But my knees would not wait any longer and I fell to the carpet, my head bleeding from hatpin punctures. Was I there to pray? Or plan revenge against the white shadows that had swallowed another black dream? My wails were strangled by sobs as I struggled to climb onto the bed and bury my face in the coverings. Jeff, I tried! Lord, how I tried! What could I do? Forgive me. Please forgive me. I wiped my eyes on the pillowcase and prayed that the Lord would help Jeffrey understand why I was unable to convince the President to stop the lynching because I simply could not understand.

The next day I returned by train to New York and in Natchez a man was lynched. I wondered what his last words were to his children that morning when he left to struggle for their table and ended that struggle at the end of a rope? Got to go ask the president to help my people one day soon?

THEN IT WAS PARIS

91

Lelia said I appeared weary and worried about me leaving Harlem so soon. So, she soon followed me back to Lewaro to spend time savoring the quiet with me. Again, our days were filled with sweet laughter over long suppers with the terrace doors open to the view of the river. I never thought my daughter knew why I'd opened them every warm evening till once she winked as I did. She'd realized I was thinking of her daddy, the River Man, dwelling on the other side of that violet haze across the river.

While at Villa Lewaro, Freeman provided me reports on the operations at my manufacturing center in Indianapolis. Construction of the Majestic Walker Theater progressed slowly as it is entirely of brick. I read his daily reports or spoke to him on the telephone when we could make a connection over the wires. Sales were rising and my products could be found in many countries. He reminded me, I think, to keep me cheery as the gloom of the lynching issue grew darker as the days passed. While I'd come to accept that my health was unlikely to improve, I disobeyed Dr. Ward's instruction and was organizing another trip back to St. Louis to visit my old friend, Jessie Robinson, whom I'd not seen since the riots blistered that city. Along that journey I planned various appearances to address the issue lynching still happening weekly. I hoped that whatever county parish that I spoke in I might save a life from a rope or open the door for a mother to leave the tubs and join thousands of my agents. And again, as I sat across the supper table from his daughter, I wondered how my life would have been different if someone could have saved Jeffrey from the thugs under those fluttering white sheets.

Most days I could see my way to contribute to this or that organization. I wrote many checks to advance the anti-lynching cause and supported charities that benefited my people. Then other days I seemed to be unable to do much of anything, even sign checks. Crawling out of bed late mornings to enter my solarium to gaze out over the Hudson River was the most I could manage. I knew I had no choice but to end my days on the road soon. Yet I struggled to postpone that day to some other calendar that was just out of my reach.

Freeman was always on me to slow down and Louvenia was ever more demanding that I rest. Neither said a word to Lelia that I was unwell, or that my vision was getting markedly worse by the week. Sometimes my daughter would look into my eyes puzzled that there was something different about me, perhaps something wrong, but didn't quite know what. I was filled with horror at the thought there would soon come a day when I would return her look but no longer see her or her daddy's eyes gazing back.

There were always many guests coming to the Villa Lewaro. In 1919, I offered my home as a place for a meeting of the International League of Darker Peoples at which time we'd discuss plans to unify people of the races around the world and appeal for the kind of democracy that President Wilson extolled for post war Europe. Then I returned to New York City to attend the League's conference. There was talk of a group going to Paris at the very time when Wilson would be there for the peace talks at Versailles. Mr. Dubois had organized a conference he called the Pan-African Conference, which was also to be in Paris at this time. Although we'd exchanged a few notes, I'd not seen him since the day we called on President Wilson. Mr. William Monroe Trotter, who had had a similar experience at his visit to the White House years before had organized his own conference to be held in Paris, which he called the National Equal Rights League. He requested, and I accepted, along with my friend Ida Wells-Barnett, to be representatives of Mr. Trotter's conference. Never in my life had I witnessed so much effort to bring attention to the plight of the American Negro as was brewing at the end of the war. It left us all unsettled. Ransom was ever concerned about the impact my association might generate with these organizations deemed subversive and expressed his thoughts candidly in a letter I received at the Villa Lewaro.

"You must always bear in mind that you have a large business, whereas the others who are going have nothing," Ransom wrote. "There are many ways in which your business can be circumscribed and hampered so as to be practically put you out of business."

Yes, the air between our tubs was suffocating many of us but we were tired of breathing under water. No, I would not put my head back into a tub of brown water again.

How could I not wonder if Ransom's comments enjoined me to the many colored-owned enterprises that had been burnt to the ground over the same decade that I had been building mine? Nevertheless, what Ransom lost sight of, even as I was losing mine in the material, was that my drive to build my business was to help my people. Having wealth and not being able to contribute would bear on my soul more than anything next to the death of my husband.

It was shortly after I received Ransom's letter at the Villa Lewaro, that another letter arrived with a cautionary warning from Colonel William Jay Schieffelin. Although Mr. Schieffelin was a white man, he'd been made treasurer of the Welfare League of an all-Negro infantry unit and had read articles in the papers about my stance on Negro soldiers returning from war to find a better situation. I presumed he'd read my remarks to New York Mayor Hylan taken down by reporters standing around us shipboard as we went into New York harbor to greet the returning men. Mr. Schieffelin was as candid as Ransom in expressing his concerns. He urged me to be strident and take a cautious approach to the entire issue of rights for Negros suggesting that my public remarks could cause more harm to my people than good. I anticipated that there would be many minefields ahead that I would have to step over or around. Hadn't that been the case for me since I left Grandview? I sent off a letter the next day to Mr. Schieffelin reminding him that Negro soldiers were called by their country to defend its honor in Europe and have bravely, fearlessly bled and died that their honor might be maintained. Now what are they returning to, I wrote. Does any reasonable person imagine to the old order of things as they were for my people; to submit to being strung up, riddled with bullets or tossed on a hate-stoked bonfire? No! I wrote. A thousand times no! They will come back to face this terrorism like men whatever is in store for them and like men defend themselves, their families and homes. I concluded my letter to Mr. Schieffelin by adding that I did not wish for there to be conflict between the two races. My message to my people is this: Go, live and conduct yourself so that you will be above the reproach of anyone—but should even one prejudiced or irrational person infringe upon your rights as men, resent the insult like a man!

That fall I was invited to join the executive committee of the International League of Darker Peoples at the next meeting to be held at the Waldorf Hotel. As the public chatter about President Wilson's diplomatic objectives grew louder and louder, I fixed the dates for my own departure. We planned that I would arrive in Paris soon after Wilson's celebratory arrival had quieted down at which time I would maneuver to take center stage on the outskirts of the palace of the French kings at Versailles. My secretary and select members of Mr. Trotter's National Equal Rights League began plans for my trip to Paris. So many times, I pondered the paradox of President Wilson's refusal to meet me in his White House, yet wouldn't we again come as close as he stood in the Hall of Mirrors at the Palace of Versailles? There are different kinds of justice in life. I was reasonably certain that the French and then world presses that followed Wilson's state visit to Paris would also keep an eye cocked for any controversy that might follow him. I was determined to draw attention to Wilson's failures to secure true democracy for his people of African descent as he battled our lives for white European's rights and democracy. I knew there would be no weekly postings of lynching of white Europeans in the presses over there, as there were none. But the colored weeklies in American would keep running the numbers of those lynched and many were those that surely wondered who would be next. My husband or yours?

After my trip to Paris was organized and as I waited for my passport to depart, I decided to undertake the journey to Indianapolis to see my new product line, have meetings with Ransom and spend some quiet time with friends. It was just before I left that I received a telegram that Mr. Trotter would be unable to attend his own National Equal Rights League convention in Paris as the State Department had refused to grant him a passport. The telegram went on to emphasize the importance of me attending on his behalf. President Wilson had recently departed from New York City on a flotilla as large as an armada to demonstrate American might to those who already knew what devastation the war machines could inflict.

≪

I'd not seen the Robinsons for some time and longed to be back there in St. Louis where Lelia grew up. I accepted Jessie Robinson's invitation to give a speech on the lynching cause at the Coliseum. I headed to St. Louis after a brief stay in Indianapolis to look over my new line of products. It was a bitter cold season and I'd felt deeply weary tired for days yet still looked forward to some quiet moments discussing current happenings at my dear friends' home.

My friendship with Jessie had survived by occasional letters since I met her while living with Sally and Ma Mere. We were both members of St. Paul's A.M.E. in St. Louis. Jesse is a striking woman, every bit as tasteful as Mrs. Washington and a teacher as well. We met as volunteers at the St. Paul's Missionary Society. Few had ever encouraged me to push myself beyond the imposed rules put on tub women more than Jessie and Christopher whom she later married. She saw me through the long period of facing up to the fact that John Davis was not a good man and never would be. Then later Christopher introduced C.J. and me to

Dr. Joseph Ward in Indianapolis. It had been so long since I'd seen my friend Jessie and longed to have one of those all-night conversations where we sorted through every problem we could, from husbands to how we might end the terror of lynching.

I always brought on my trips a pile of mail to read while on the train. The first thing I opened was a letter from the State Department. To my utter astonishment I was informed that my passport had been denied. Yes, denied! Freeman was ever so astute in these matters and had told me before my trip that Booker's secretary had warned him that it was likely my name, along with those of other prominent members of the race, had been listed in the Military Intelligence Division file as subversives and potential enemies of our own country. Wilson apparently had wind of our desire to confront the lynching issue in Paris while he was there. The President had instructed his administration to block the travel of any American whose agenda might challenge his administration's policy or expose his racism at home. In fact, they stopped all people of color from going to France for the duration of his state visit.

This was devastating news to me. Even at that, how could I not wonder how much I could have accomplished in Paris given my deep fatigue?

It was Easter time when I arrived at Jessie and Christopher's lovely home but I felt no rebirth as this holy day is for. Perhaps it was a blessing that my passport to travel had been denied. I know I looked forward to some quiet time with friends and no longer had the stamina to worry about Paris.

My friends had a fine supper when I arrived. While we dined, we seemed to move to every possible current event; inevitably, the topic of my passport denial came up.

"What have I done to warrant this?" I was very angry. "I've supported war bonds and our men defending this country at every opportunity. I've never supported violence, even against those perpetrating the never-ending violence against our people."

"Why?" Jessie asked. "Need we remind you, you are the woman that went to the White House and faced down Wilson, the most powerful man in the world? And you did it with no army standing behind you, Sarah. What could Wilson's defense be? To hide in a closet from a woman of color to avoid the truths of his race hatred?"

"Wilson wants votes and to the white folks, demanding enforcement of the anti-lynching laws is a serious threat to their supremacy over the laws… and over us!" Christopher added.

"There's no difference. Wilson hides in a white house like the Klan hides under white sheets,' I added. "The laws are still trampled and I achieved nothing for all the roads I've traveled to reach the final end of my husband's rope."

"Justice will not be found in this life, but it awaits in the next!" Jessie reminded me.

"We won't need the Bill of Rights in the next life." I responded. "Our folks need the nooses cut down from the trees now."

I guess it was near the end of our supper when I suddenly started feeling very cold, that kind of penetrating cold I'd told Dr. Ward about. I figured it was a bad cold coming on. Shortly after supper I excused myself and went to my guestroom and crawled into bed. However, there were not enough covers to warm me. I soon knew I was very ill. Several times that evening Jessie peeked in and asked if there was anything she could do. But there wasn't. Darkness seemed to be washing over me in waves.

The next morning, I could not get up. Jessie stayed at my bedside but I could barely move as I was in such pain. I asked her to inform Freeman by wire. He would know what to do, as we'd planned everything should my health suddenly deteriorate. Soon Jessie's doctor arrived. Dr. Curtis wanted me moved to a hospital immediately. But I said no. You see, I knew that there was only one last journey left in me and I wanted it to be back to Lewaro.

SEEDS FOR HIS ORCHARD

92

J EFF, BEFORE THE final moments slip away I need to tell you this last train journey back to Lewaro was hard on me; the pain got so bad at times. My friend Jessie Robinson sent Dr. Curtis and a nurse to help me. He gave me morphine to ease the worst of it.

"Did you say something, Sarah?" Louvenia asked.

"It's near finished…?"

"Dear…?"

"Finished telling Jeff everything I seen along the journey…"

"You been chatting with Jeff up here for hours and hours," Louvenia said. "You went all the way back to the Burneys'. Even 'bout your return there that summer in nineteen-sixteen. Don't know if you seen all these flowers they keep bringin' every day. More out there in your solarium."

"Jeff, I could hear 'im again. Said he's gonna plant me a real nice flowerbed come Spring, didn't he?"

"He sure did, Sarah. I know he did. Gonna plant that garden from the very seeds you been saving so long."

"Told Jeff 'bout the day momma and daddy passed on. Jeff and me, we walked down the aisle at church with me wearing jasmine in my hair… Sister, you hear Jeff callin'?"

"I think I do. Sure, it's him! I know it is. Just over the river, high above those violet palisades you can see out your windows."

"Why do you weep so?"

"No, I ain't cryin'. I be right here next to you."

"You've always been next to me… And Dr. Ward…?"

"Dr. Ward is right outside the door. He's been caring of you since you got back from St. Louis."

"Lelia?"

"Lelia wired she's comin' back to her momma as fast as she can."

"I don't want her to see me this way…"

"You know she don't mind nothing 'bout her momma. Ransom sent a telegraph the day you got back to Lewaro tellin 'er she best come now."

"Sister, before I go to sleep, send Ransom in for me…"

"Ransom's downstairs. I'll send him up with the doctor."

"No, don't send Joseph. Don't want no more morphine… I got to be awake as long as I can.

"Yes, dear. Ransom be right up then."

"Jeff, I can't see no more. But I know it's still true. There's nothing beyond my window but the orchard and you waiting. No more roads to cross over to get there…no more boundaries to fight against…

"Madame Walker, it's Freeman here next to your bed. Got some of your mail here that your secretary opened for you. Just thought you'd want to know that Governor Smith has invited you to join him welcoming the troops back."

"Why are you crying Ransom…?

"No, not cryin', Madame. Just wanted Lelia…"

"No… It's the way it is meant to be. I knew when Lelia went off to Panama, that I'd be gone when she returned. I didn't want her to see me this way. You know my eyes won't let me see nobody now. They're closing my vision of this life as it should be and opening my eyes for the next life with Jeff in the Lord's Orchard."

"Last week at Carnegie Hall the NAACP celebrated your contribution."

"That's what Louvenia told me… Said there were a thousand of my people there. Said they all rose to their feet and wished me quick recovery… Yes, that's nice. Ransom. You best tell Sister I need to talk to her now…"

"You want Louvenia and me?"

"This time just Sister and Jeff… I got to ready something to show him and want Louvenia to help with it…"

"I get Louvenia back, Madame."

"Jeff, there's so much I meant to tell you about my days along the journey to Lewaro but then don't really know why I need to struggle with it so. You been there next to me all along, just like you promised, in every thought, in every breath, in every dream… you been there waiting."

"Sister, it's me. You need the Doctor?"

"No, want you to go over and pull the drapes open wide for me…"

"They is. All the drapes are still open from when you said to this morning."

"Is it sunny out there?"

"It's the sunniest day we've ever had in May."

"Pull open the drawer at the bottom…"

"The one here next to your bed?"

"Down under my Bible. Get it out for me, Sister…"

"Jeff's tobacco tin?"

"Open it…"

"This old cloth with the Burney monogram is what's you're wantin'?"

"Untie the cloth for me Sister. Real careful like. Don't let one spill…"

"These seeds? Seeds and a peach pit. These the seeds I sent you at Sally's boarding house that time?"

"You got to promise me when Lelia gets home—you take 'er out to the Orchard and plant her daddy's flower seeds for us. Then you plant that peach pit from Momma's orchard at Grandview. Tell Lelia not to worry none about her momma, I'll be with her forever. Just like Minerva was with us. I be waiting in the Orchard with her daddy and her granddaddy and the rest of the folks we love. We be waiting for you. You say the verse again… for me…"

"'Though I walk through the shadow of death… I will fear no evil…'"

"Louvenia, you don't need to cry. I'm goin' where I wanted to go for so very long. Jeff, he's been waitin'…"

"No, I ain't cryin' no more, Sarah. I ain't…"

"Sister, you and me, we've never been afraid of death. We done faced it eye-to-eye too many times. Now you got to let me go to Jeff."

"You can go to him when you're ready, Sarah. I'm kneeling here by your bed to hold your hand like I did the day when you left Jeff's orchard. You tell Jeff 'bout that day, too?"

"What…..?

"What do you see? Tell me what's out there over the palisades…"

"It's Jeff I see. He's there comin' for me. I know I do. Like he's comin' home from workin' the fields."

"I'm gonna hold your hand tight till he reaches to touch your lips again."

"He come alone?"

"What? No, dear. I see the rest of 'em comin' right behind 'im. They're all comin'. Sure, they are! There's Momma and Daddy and I can see Ella back there with ol' Clare. Yes, and Jackson's with 'em, too. They's all followin' Jeff to take you home. They's waiting for you honey. I'm gonna keep holdin' your hand here 'til you go on over to 'em. I will. Keep holdin' on to you."

"You always held my hand. Every step, Sister. Now I gotta leave you 'gain…"

"I know. It's alright. "Dr. Ward is here, Sarah."

"How is the pain, Madame Walker?"

"I want to help my people……………"

"It's over, Miss Louvenia… Madame Walker has passed on."

When you gift this book, you share the
extraordinary legacy of Sarah Breedlove
who became

Madame C.J. Walker.

For more on Justin Swingle's writings, join us at

LEWARO ROAD com

Book ISBN 978-1-7374087-4-1

Ebook ISBN 978-1-7374087-5-8

9 781737 408741